Boarding Pass

Standard

CHAPTER 1:
FAREWELL

Date
02 JUN

ROMÂNIA

PAŞAPORT

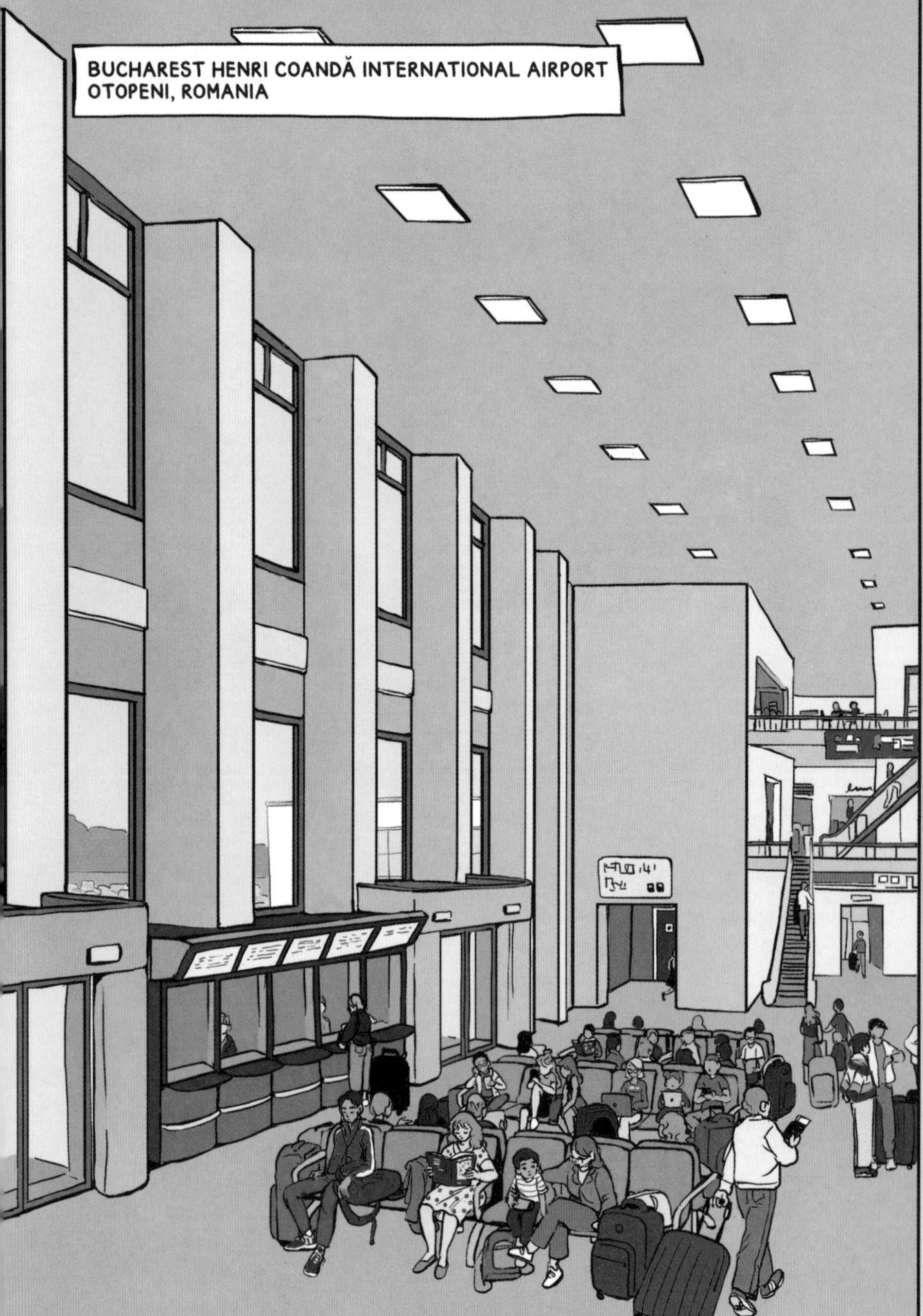
BUCHAREST HENRI COANDĂ INTERNATIONAL AIRPORT
OTOPENI, ROMANIA

THE
NEW
GIRL

CASSANDRA CALIN

An Imprint of
SCHOLASTIC

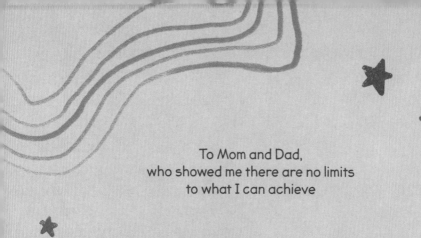

To Mom and Dad,
who showed me there are no limits
to what I can achieve

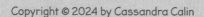

Library of Congress Control Number: 2023941485

ISBN 978-1-338-76246-4 (hardcover)
ISBN 978-1-338-76245-7 (paperback)

10 9 8 7 6 5 4 3   24 25 26 27 28

Printed in China 62
First edition, June 2024

Edited by Megan Peace
Book design by Carina Taylor
Creative Director: Phil Falco
Publisher: David Saylor

CONTENTS

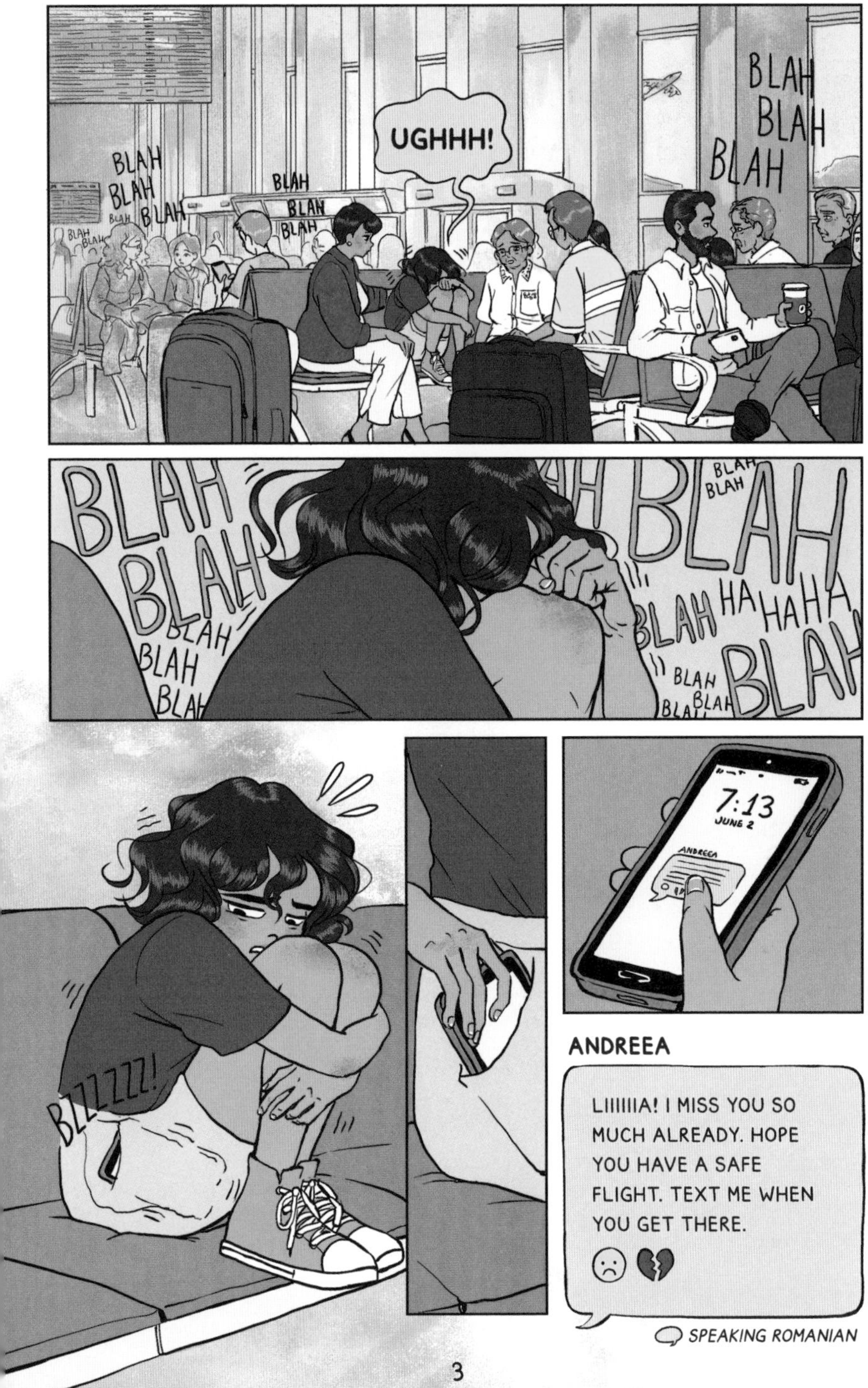
BLAH
BLAH
BLAH BLAH
BLAH
BLAH
BLAH
UGHHH!
BLAH
BLAH
BLAH
BLAH
BLAH
BLAH
BLAH
BLAH
BLAH
BLAH
BLAH
BLAH
BLAH
BLAH
HA
HAHA
BLAH
BLAH
BLAH
BLAH
BZZZZZZ!
7:13
JUNE 2
ANDREEA
ANDREEA
LIIIIIIA! I MISS YOU SO MUCH ALREADY. HOPE YOU HAVE A SAFE FLIGHT. TEXT ME WHEN YOU GET THERE.
SPEAKING ROMANIAN

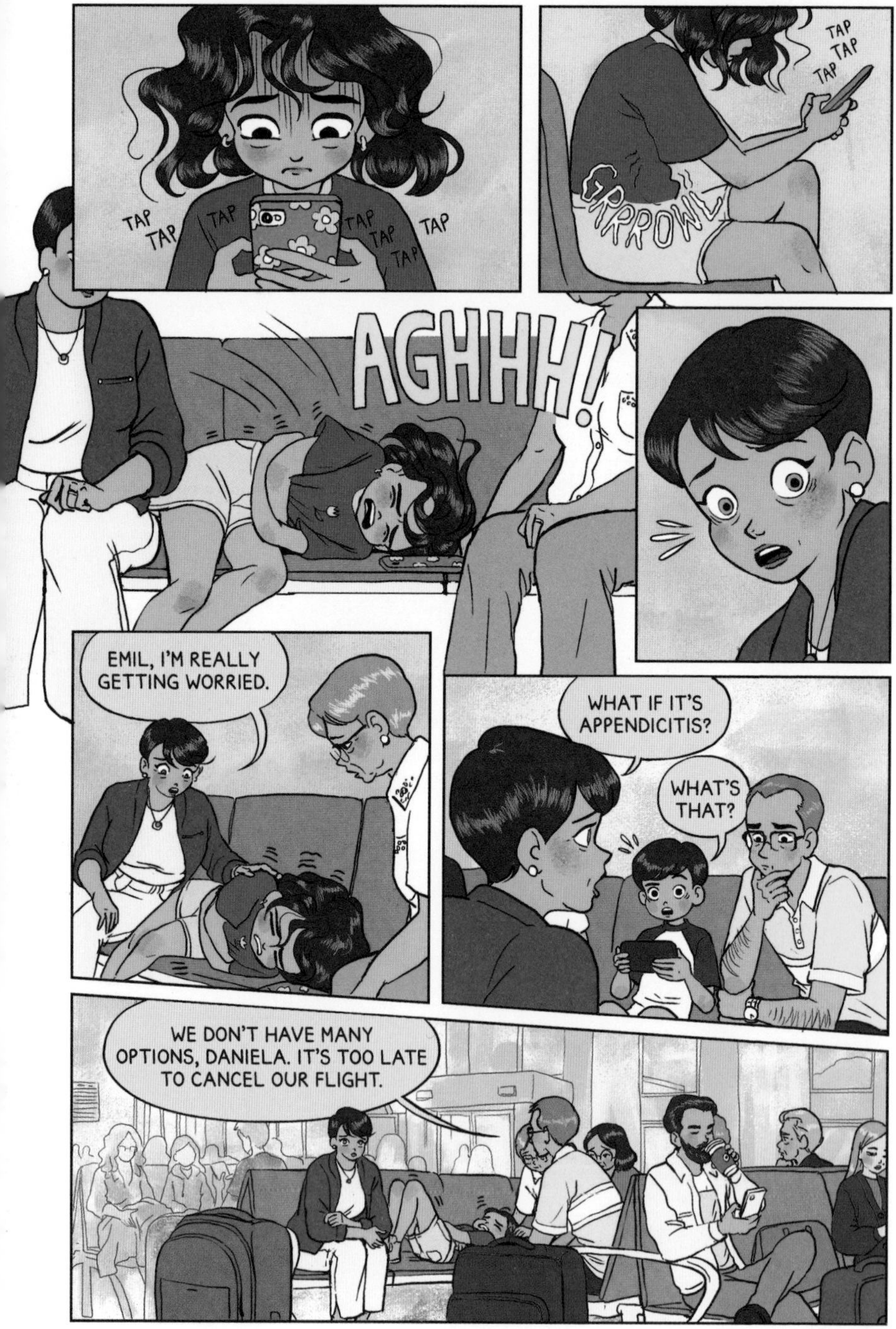
TAP
TAP
TAP
TAP
TAP
TAP
TAP
TAP
TAP
GRRROWL
AGHHH!
EMIL, I'M REALLY GETTING WORRIED.
WHAT IF IT'S APPENDICITIS?
WHAT'S THAT?
WE DON'T HAVE MANY OPTIONS, DANIELA. IT'S TOO LATE TO CANCEL OUR FLIGHT.

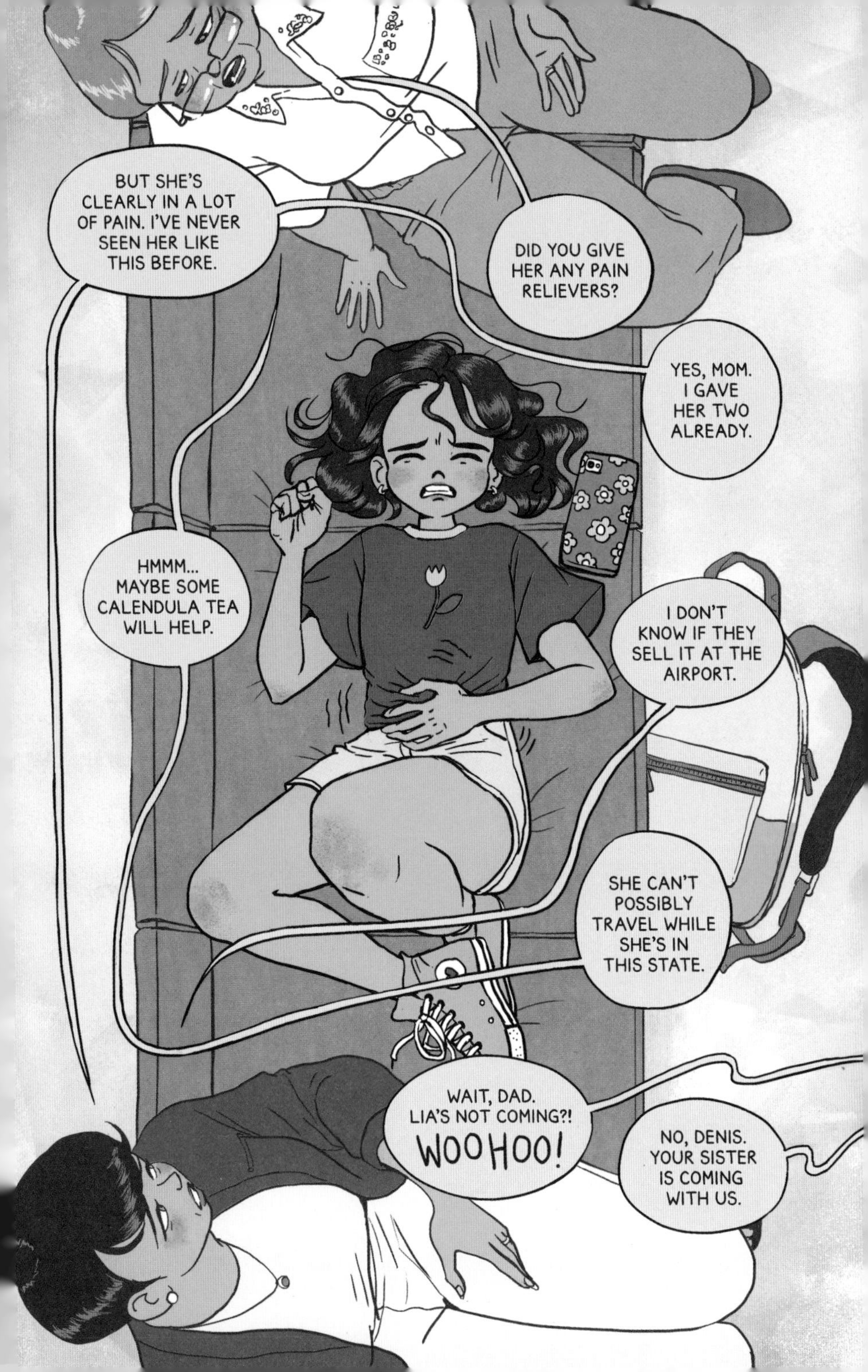
DID YOU GIVE HER ANY PAIN RELIEVERS?
YES, MOM. I GAVE HER TWO ALREADY.
BUT SHE'S CLEARLY IN A LOT OF PAIN. I'VE NEVER SEEN HER LIKE THIS BEFORE.
HMMM... MAYBE SOME CALENDULA TEA WILL HELP.
I DON'T KNOW IF THEY SELL IT AT THE AIRPORT.
SHE CAN'T POSSIBLY TRAVEL WHILE SHE'S IN THIS STATE.
WAIT, DAD. LIA'S NOT COMING?! WOOHOO!
NO, DENIS. YOUR SISTER IS COMING WITH US.

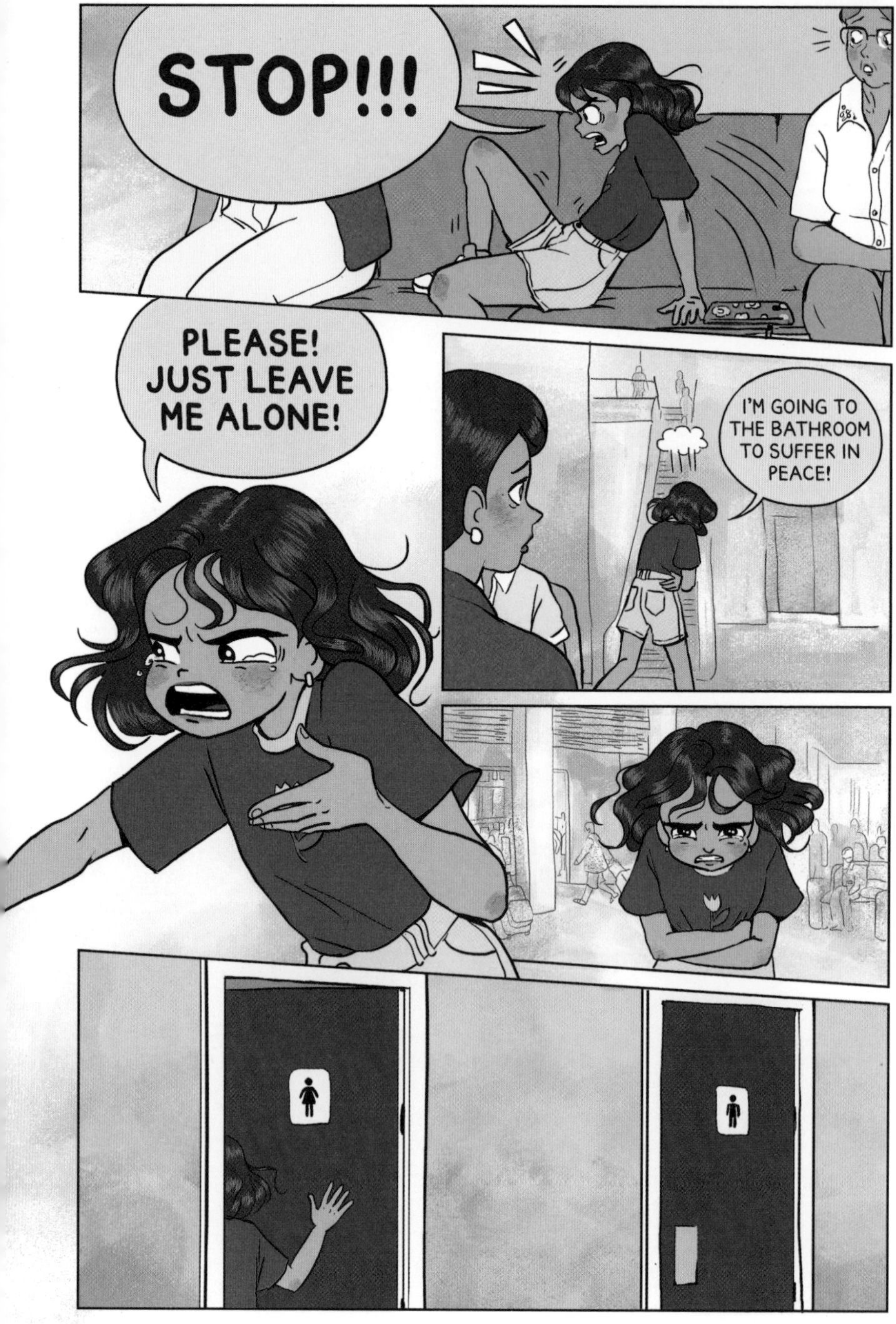
STOP!!!
PLEASE! JUST LEAVE ME ALONE!
I'M GOING TO THE BATHROOM TO SUFFER IN PEACE!

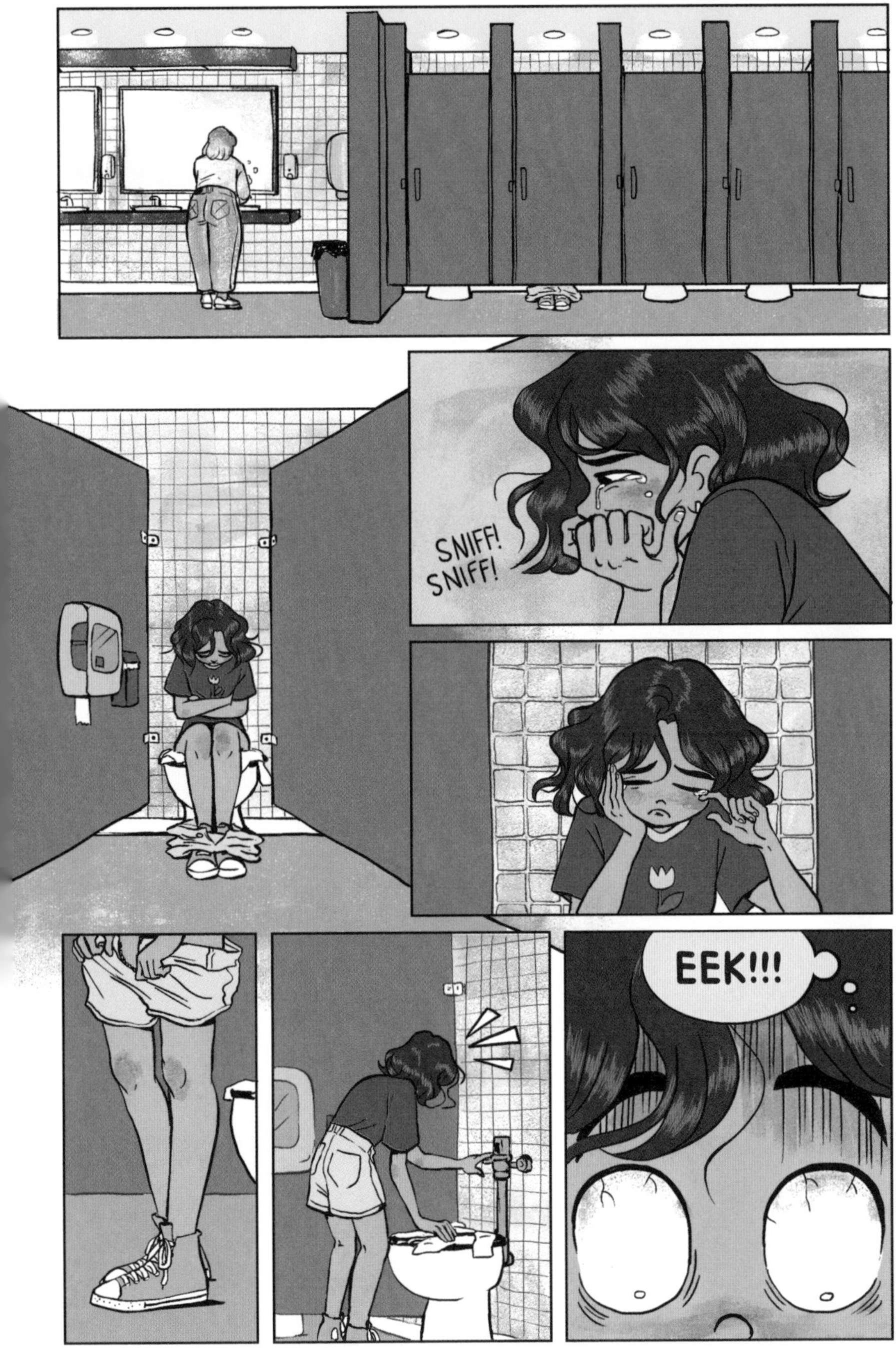
SNIFF!
SNIFF!
EEK!!!

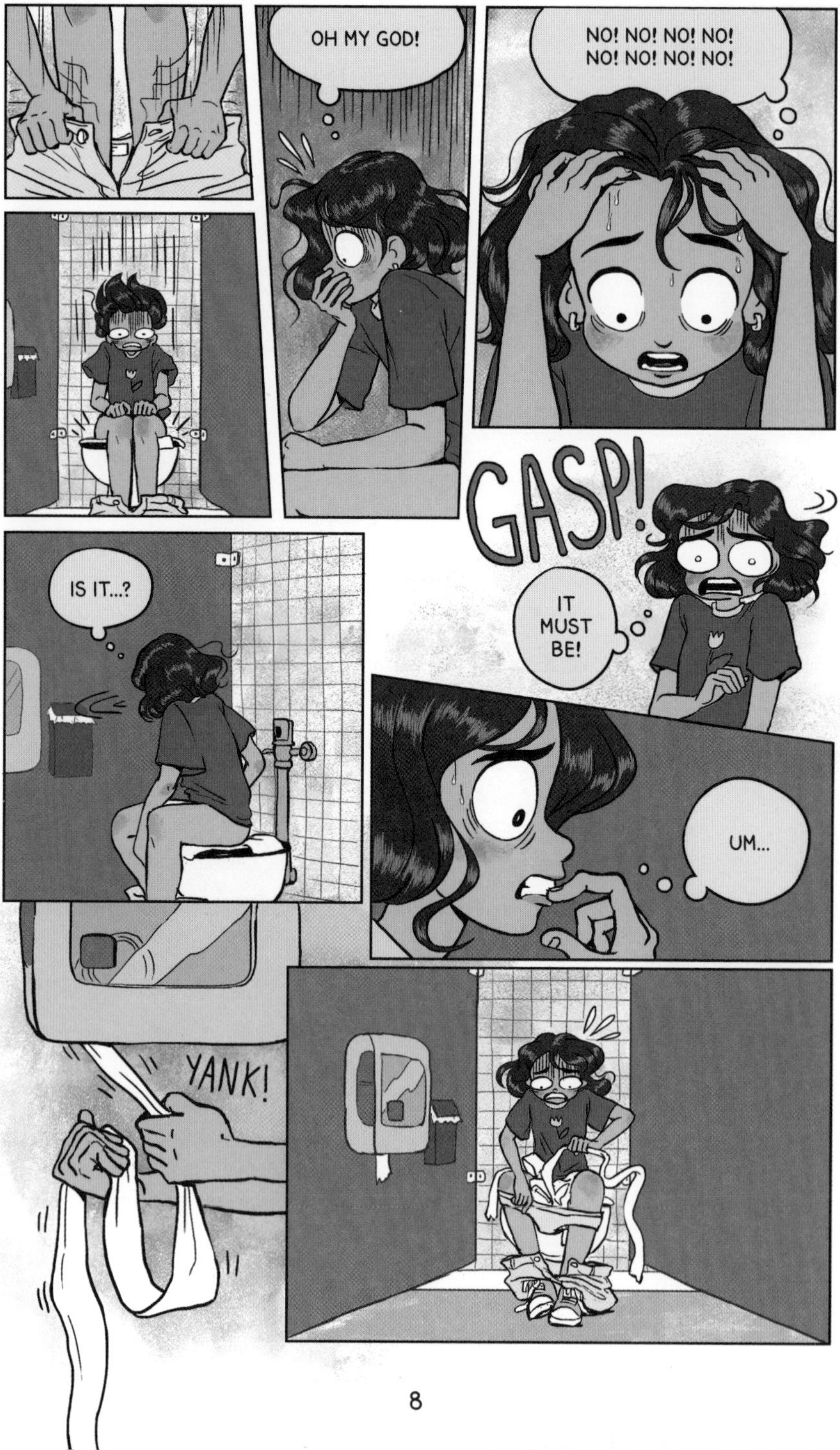
OH MY GOD!
NO! NO! NO! NO!
NO! NO! NO! NO!
GASP!
IS IT...?
IT MUST BE!
UM...
YANK!

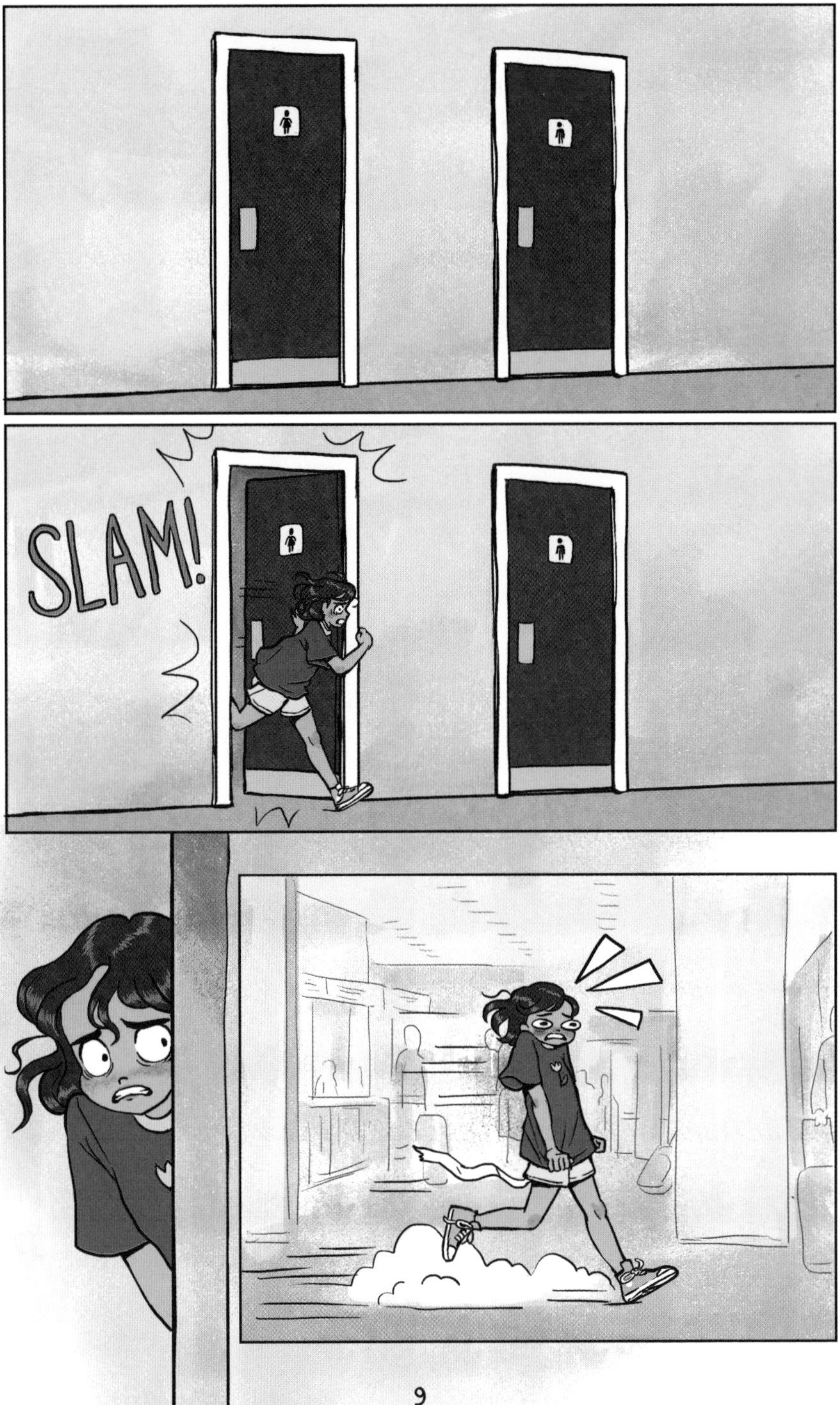
SLAM!

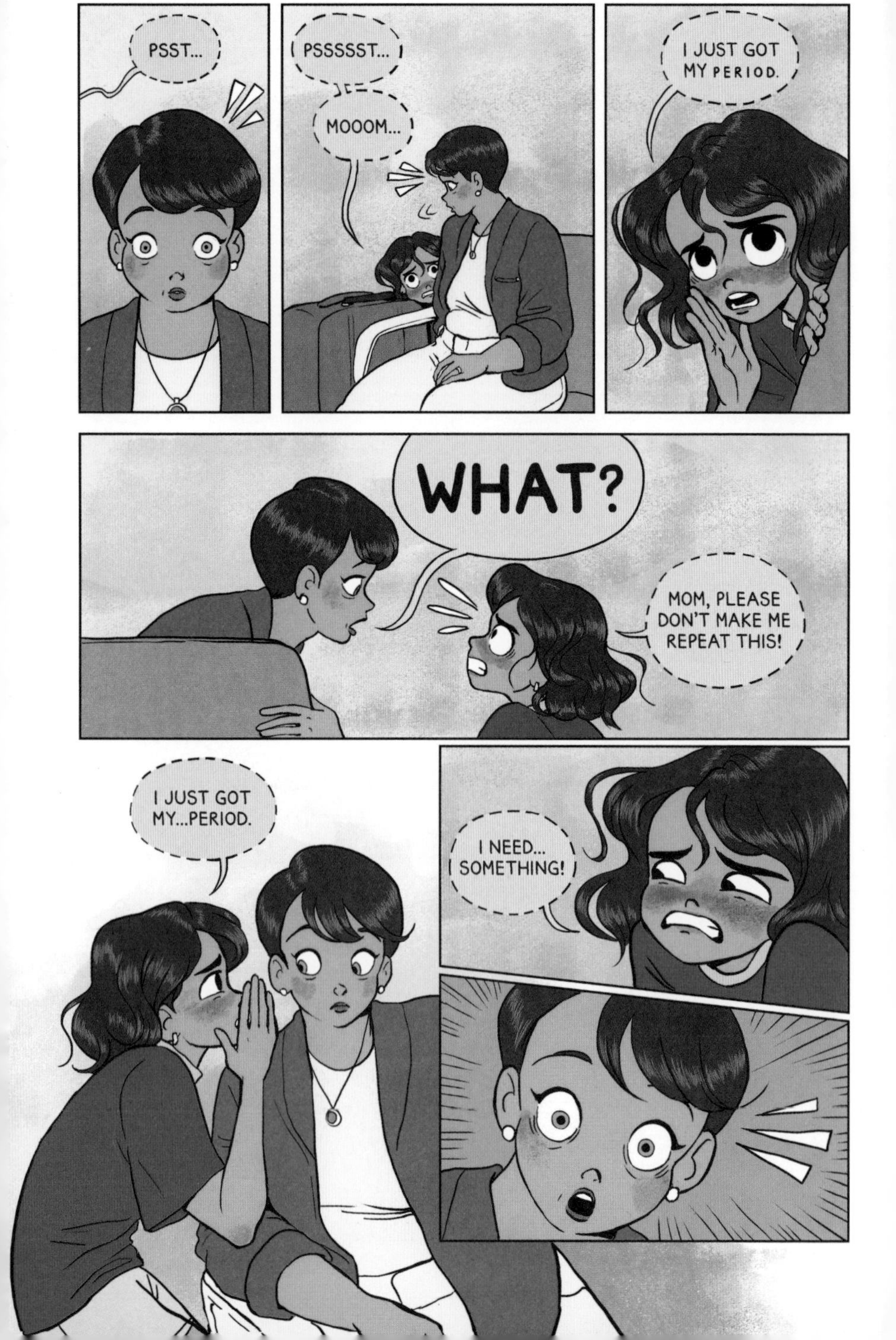
PSST...
PSSSSST...
MOOOM...
I JUST GOT MY PERIOD.
WHAT?
MOM, PLEASE DON'T MAKE ME REPEAT THIS!
I JUST GOT MY...PERIOD.
I NEED... SOMETHING!

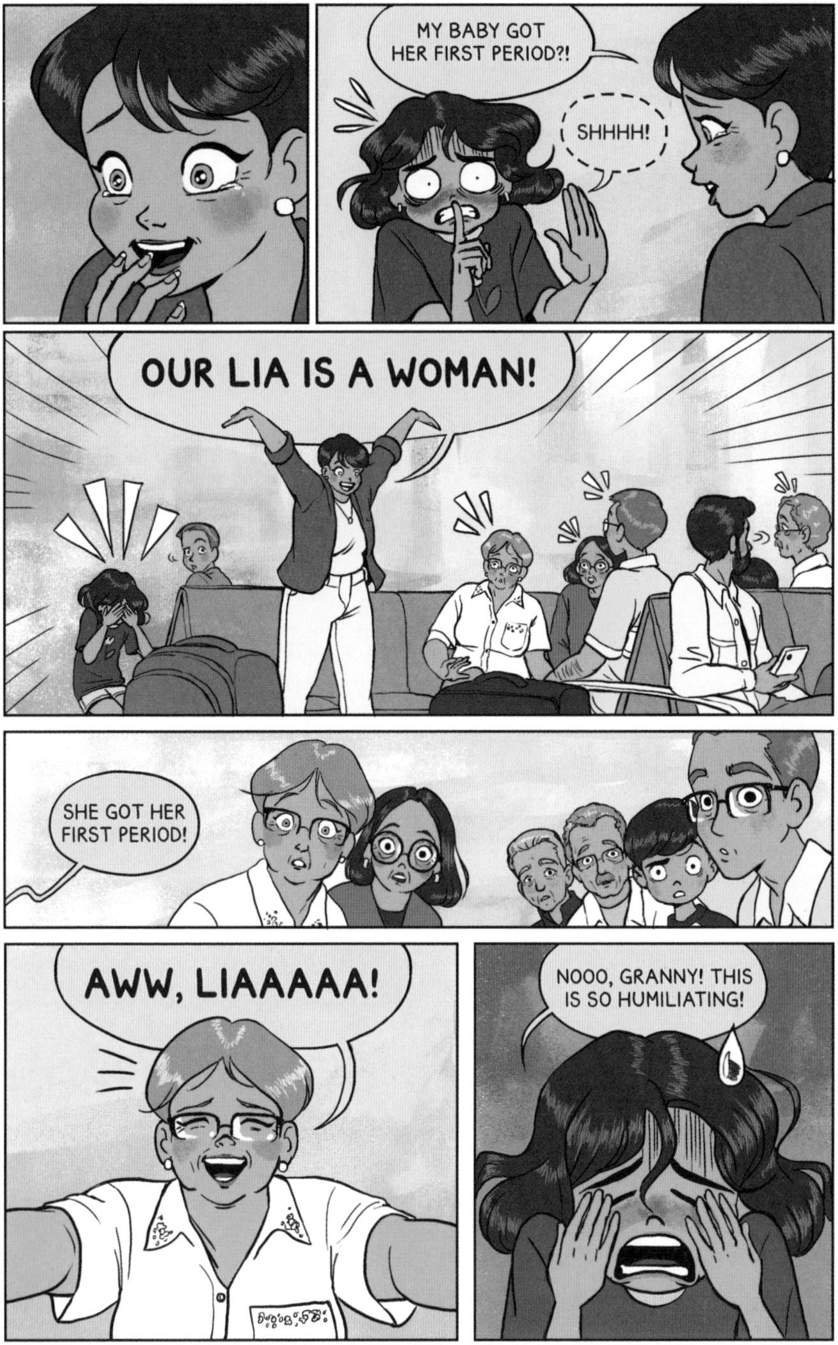
MY BABY GOT HER FIRST PERIOD?!
SHHHH!
OUR LIA IS A WOMAN!
SHE GOT HER FIRST PERIOD!
AWW, LIAAAAA!
NOOO, GRANNY! THIS IS SO HUMILIATING!

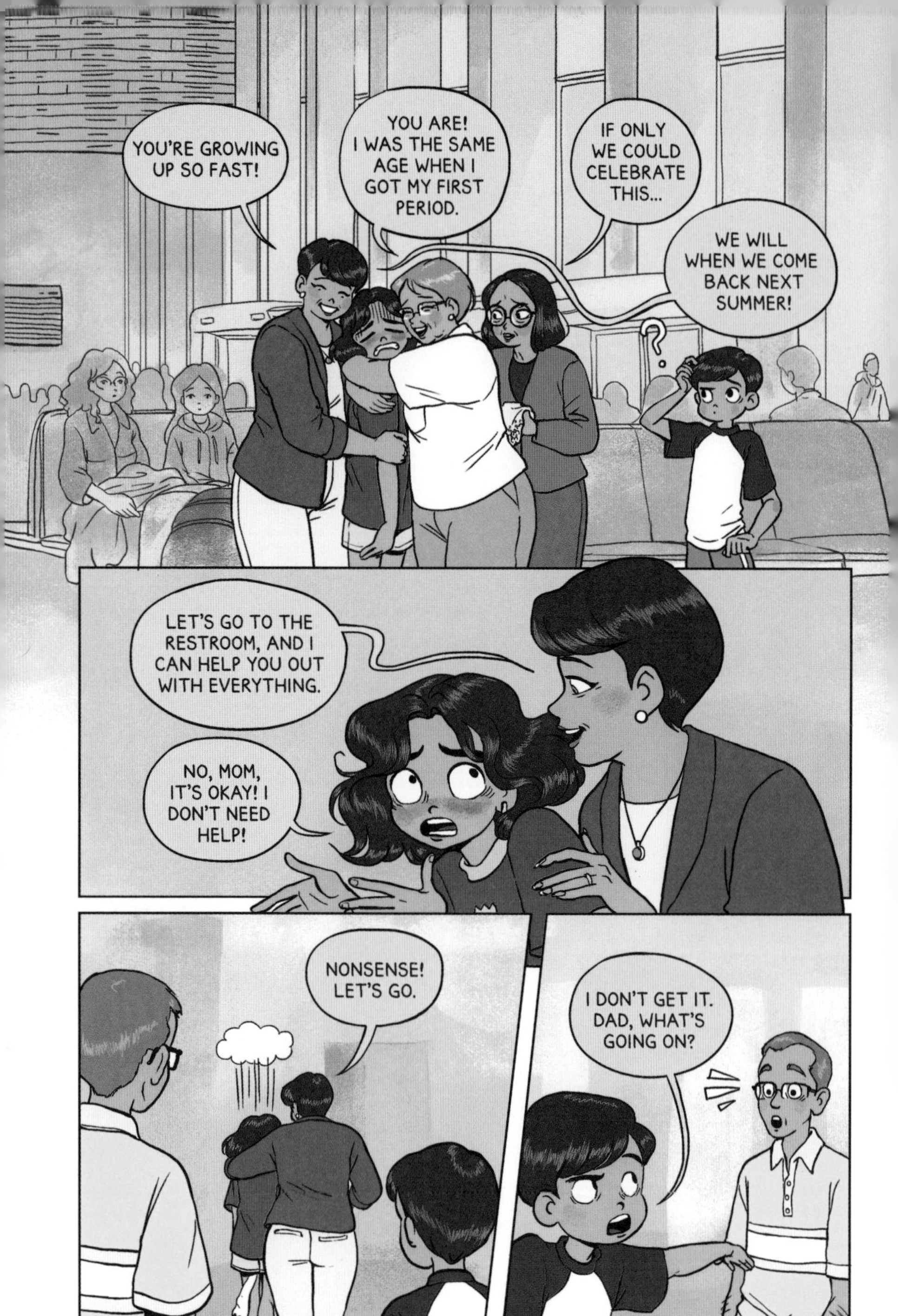
YOU'RE GROWING UP SO FAST!
YOU ARE! I WAS THE SAME AGE WHEN I GOT MY FIRST PERIOD.
IF ONLY WE COULD CELEBRATE THIS...
WE WILL WHEN WE COME BACK NEXT SUMMER!
LET'S GO TO THE RESTROOM, AND I CAN HELP YOU OUT WITH EVERYTHING.
NO, MOM, IT'S OKAY! I DON'T NEED HELP!
NONSENSE! LET'S GO.
I DON'T GET IT. DAD, WHAT'S GOING ON?

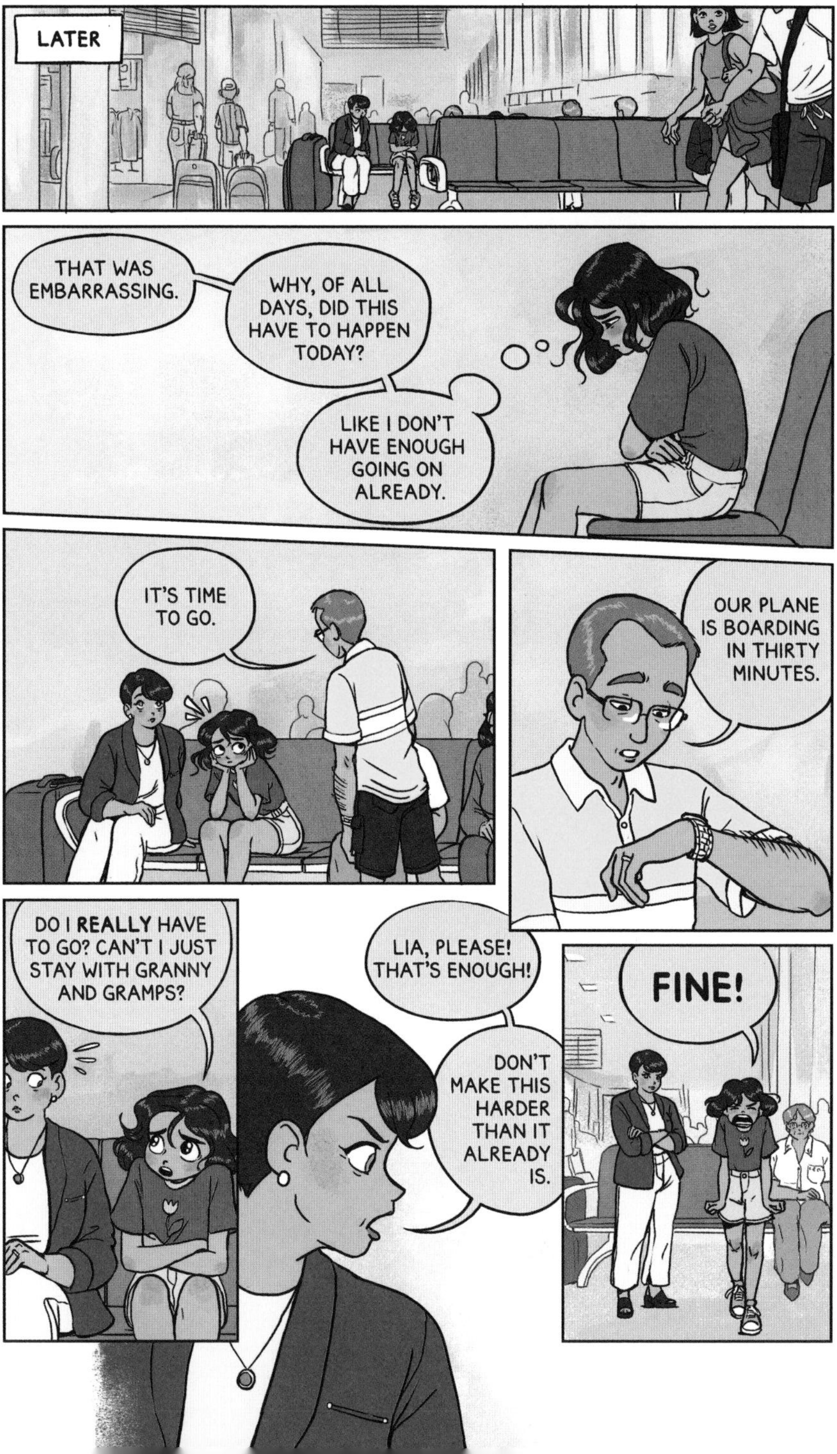
LATER
THAT WAS EMBARRASSING.
WHY, OF ALL DAYS, DID THIS HAVE TO HAPPEN TODAY?
LIKE I DON'T HAVE ENOUGH GOING ON ALREADY.
IT'S TIME TO GO.
OUR PLANE IS BOARDING IN THIRTY MINUTES.
DO I **REALLY** HAVE TO GO? CAN'T I JUST STAY WITH GRANNY AND GRAMPS?
LIA, PLEASE! THAT'S ENOUGH!
DON'T MAKE THIS HARDER THAN IT ALREADY IS.
FINE!

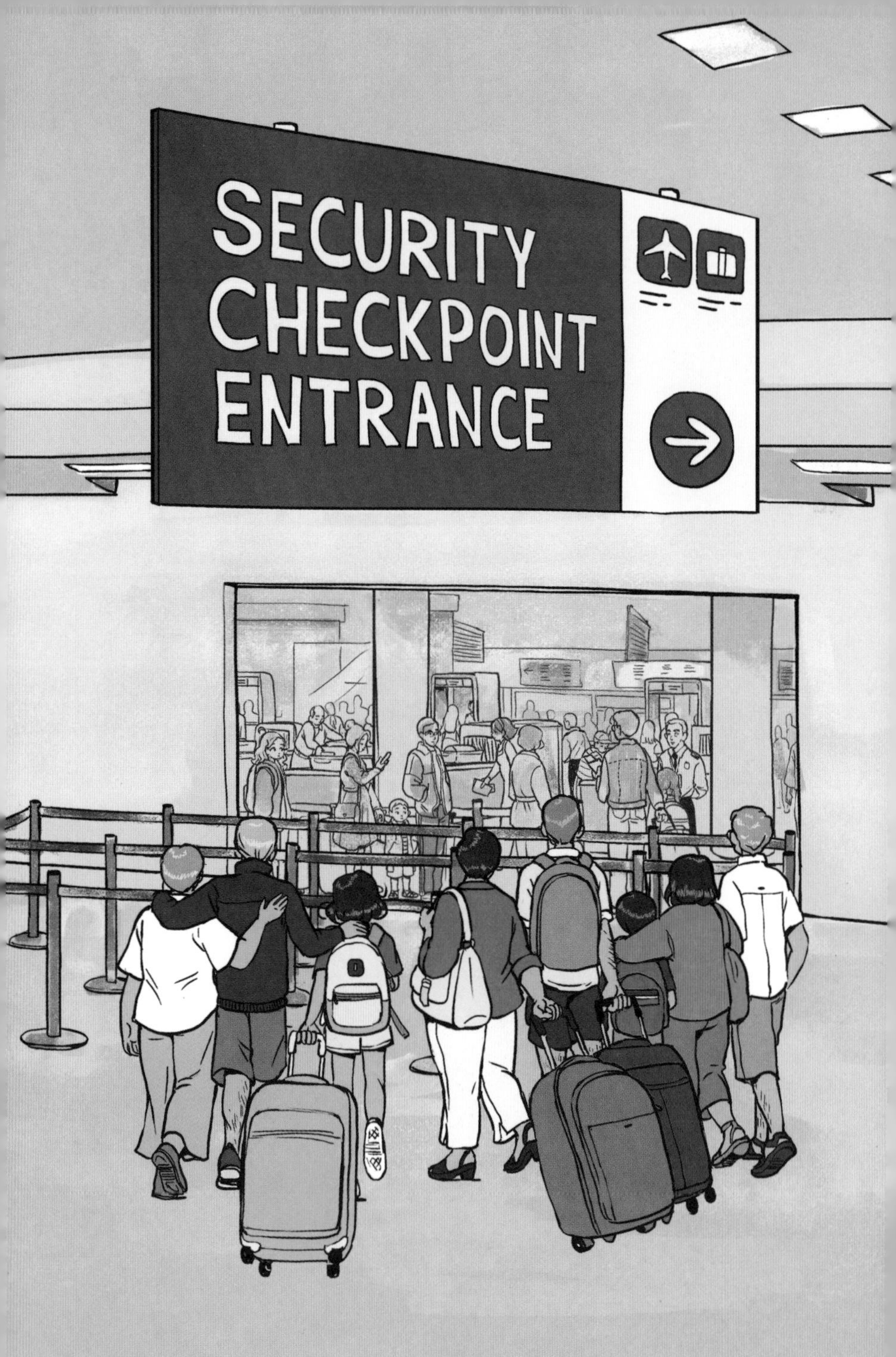
SECURITY
CHECKPOINT
ENTRANCE

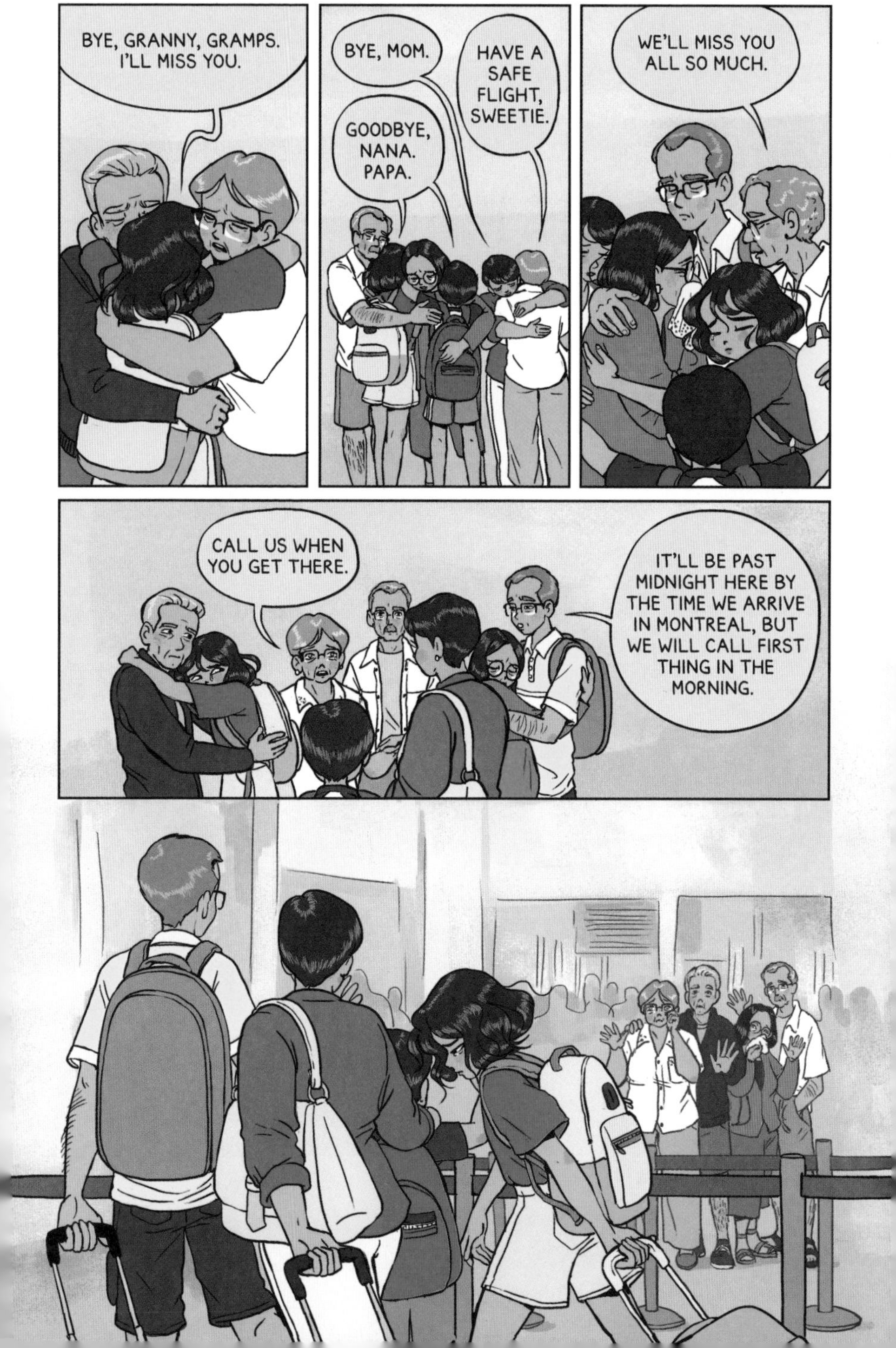
BYE, GRANNY, GRAMPS. I'LL MISS YOU.
BYE, MOM.
HAVE A SAFE FLIGHT, SWEETIE.
GOODBYE, NANA. PAPA.
WE'LL MISS YOU ALL SO MUCH.
CALL US WHEN YOU GET THERE.
IT'LL BE PAST MIDNIGHT HERE BY THE TIME WE ARRIVE IN MONTREAL, BUT WE WILL CALL FIRST THING IN THE MORNING.

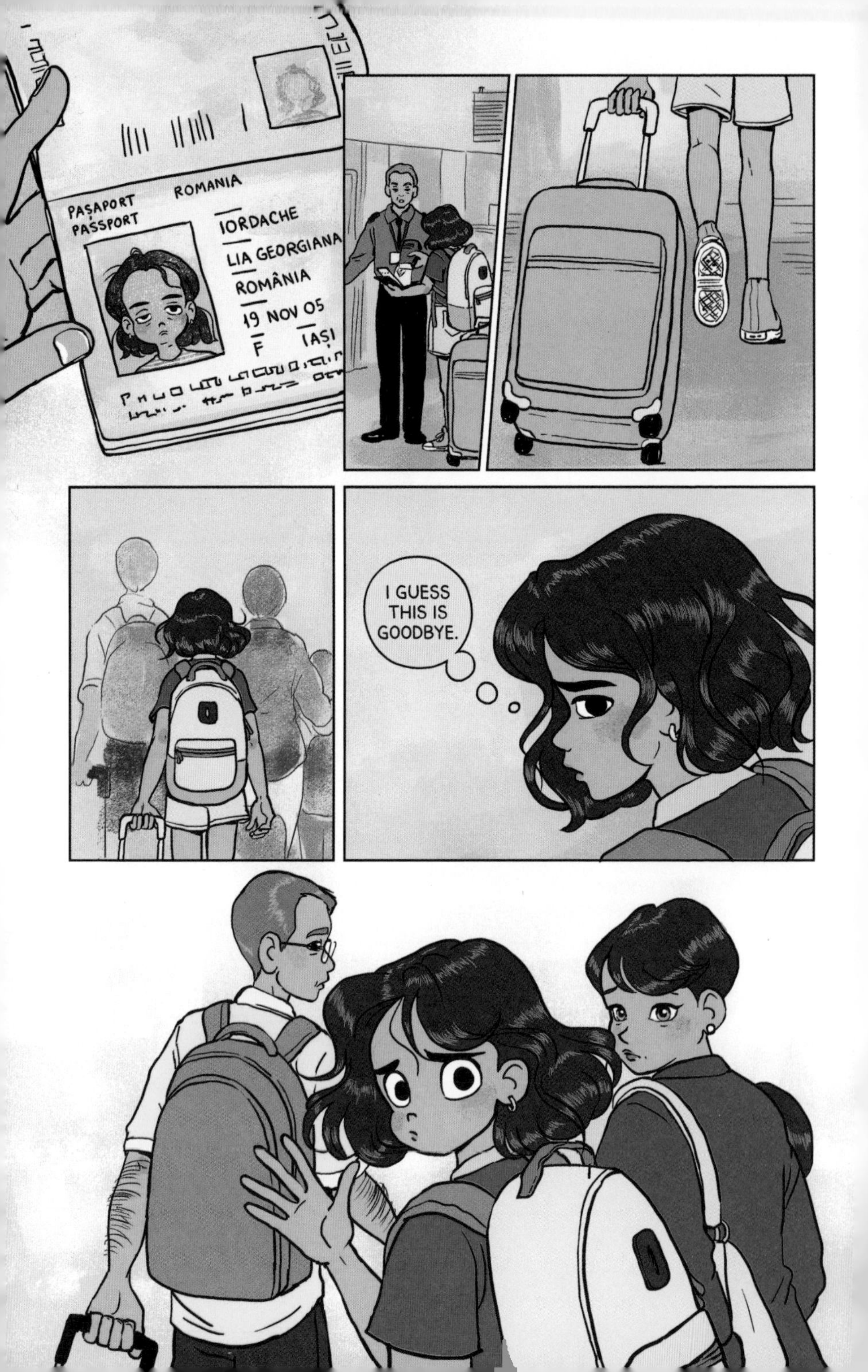
PAȘAPORT
PASSPORT
ROMANIA
IORDACHE
LIA GEORGIANA
ROMÂNIA
19 NOV 05
F
IAȘI
I GUESS THIS IS GOODBYE.

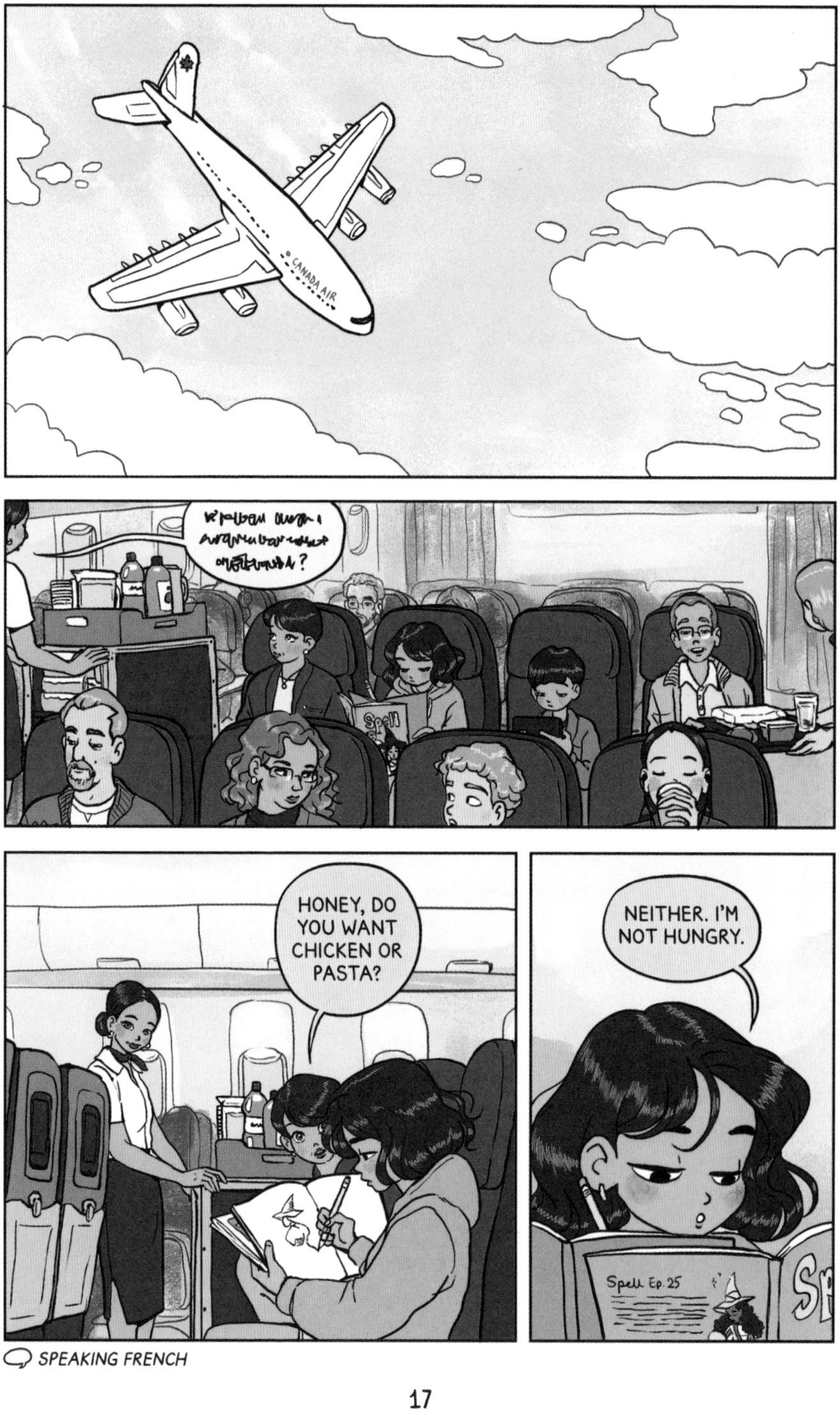
CANADA AIR
HONEY, DO YOU WANT CHICKEN OR PASTA?
NEITHER. I'M NOT HUNGRY.
Spell Ep. 25

SPEAKING FRENCH

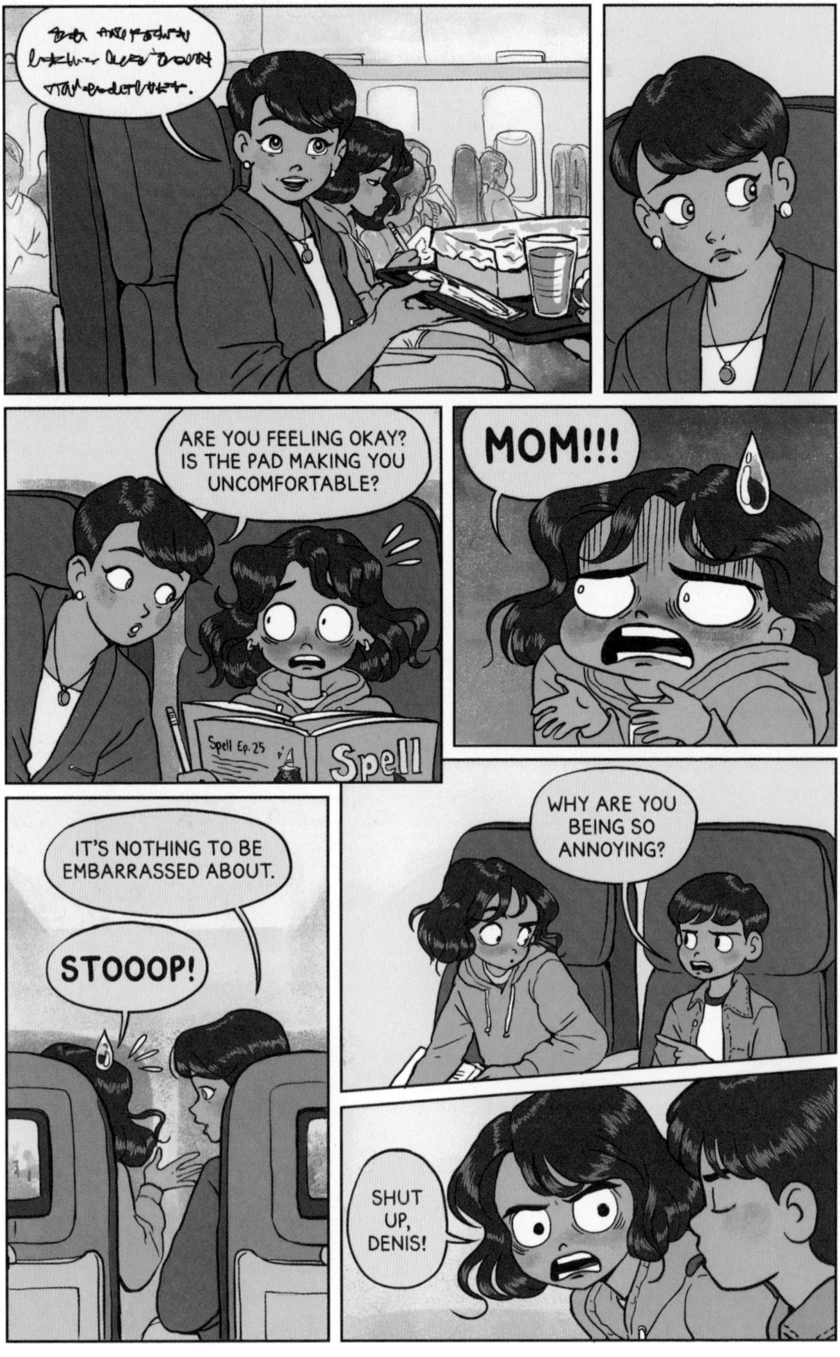
ARE YOU FEELING OKAY? IS THE PAD MAKING YOU UNCOMFORTABLE?
MOM!!!
Spell Ep. 25
Spell
IT'S NOTHING TO BE EMBARRASSED ABOUT.
STOOOP!
WHY ARE YOU BEING SO ANNOYING?
SHUT UP, DENIS!

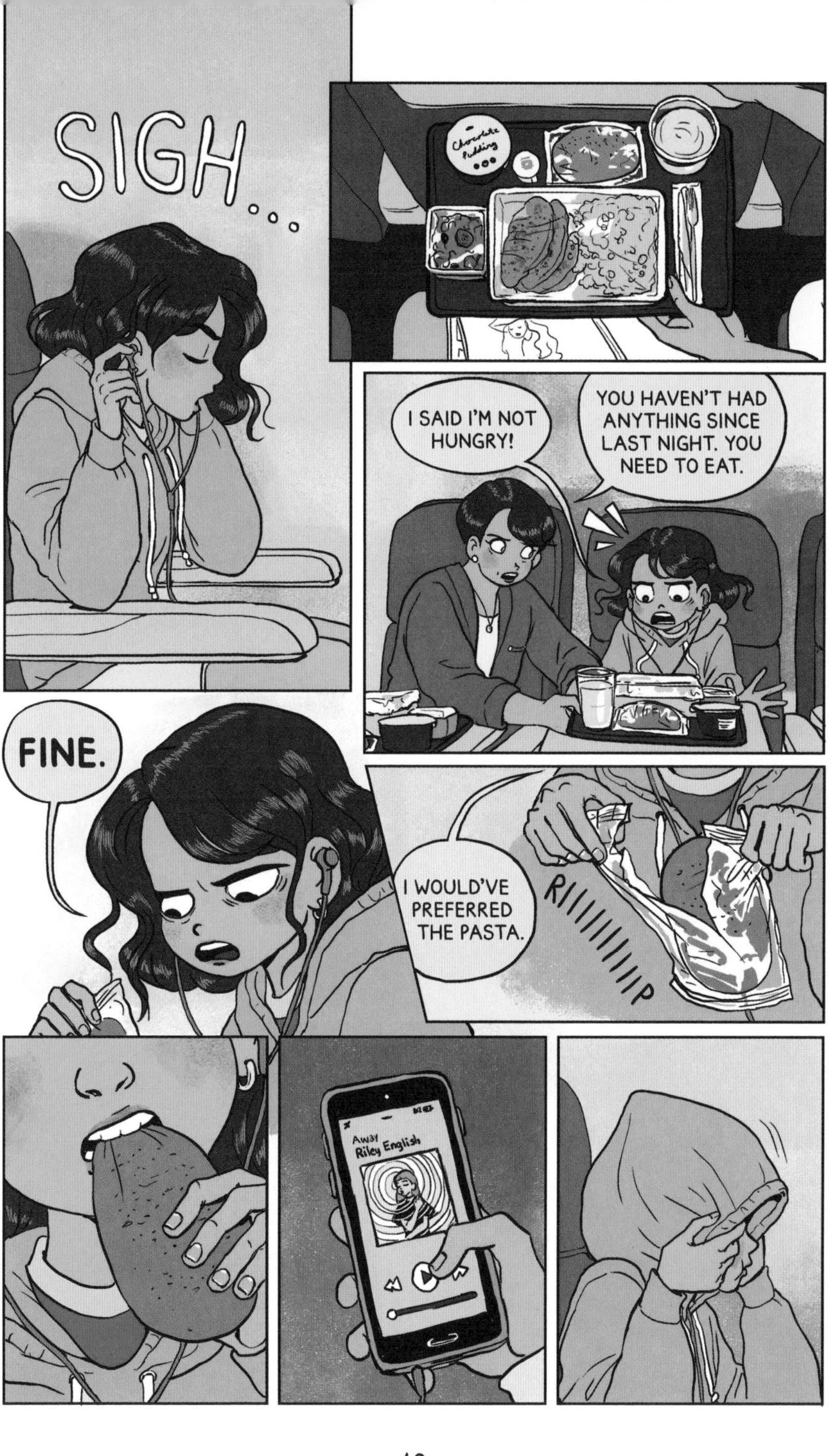
SIGH...
Chocolate Pudding
I SAID I'M NOT HUNGRY!
YOU HAVEN'T HAD ANYTHING SINCE LAST NIGHT. YOU NEED TO EAT.
FINE.
I WOULD'VE PREFERRED THE PASTA.
RIIIIIIIIIIIP
Away
Riley English

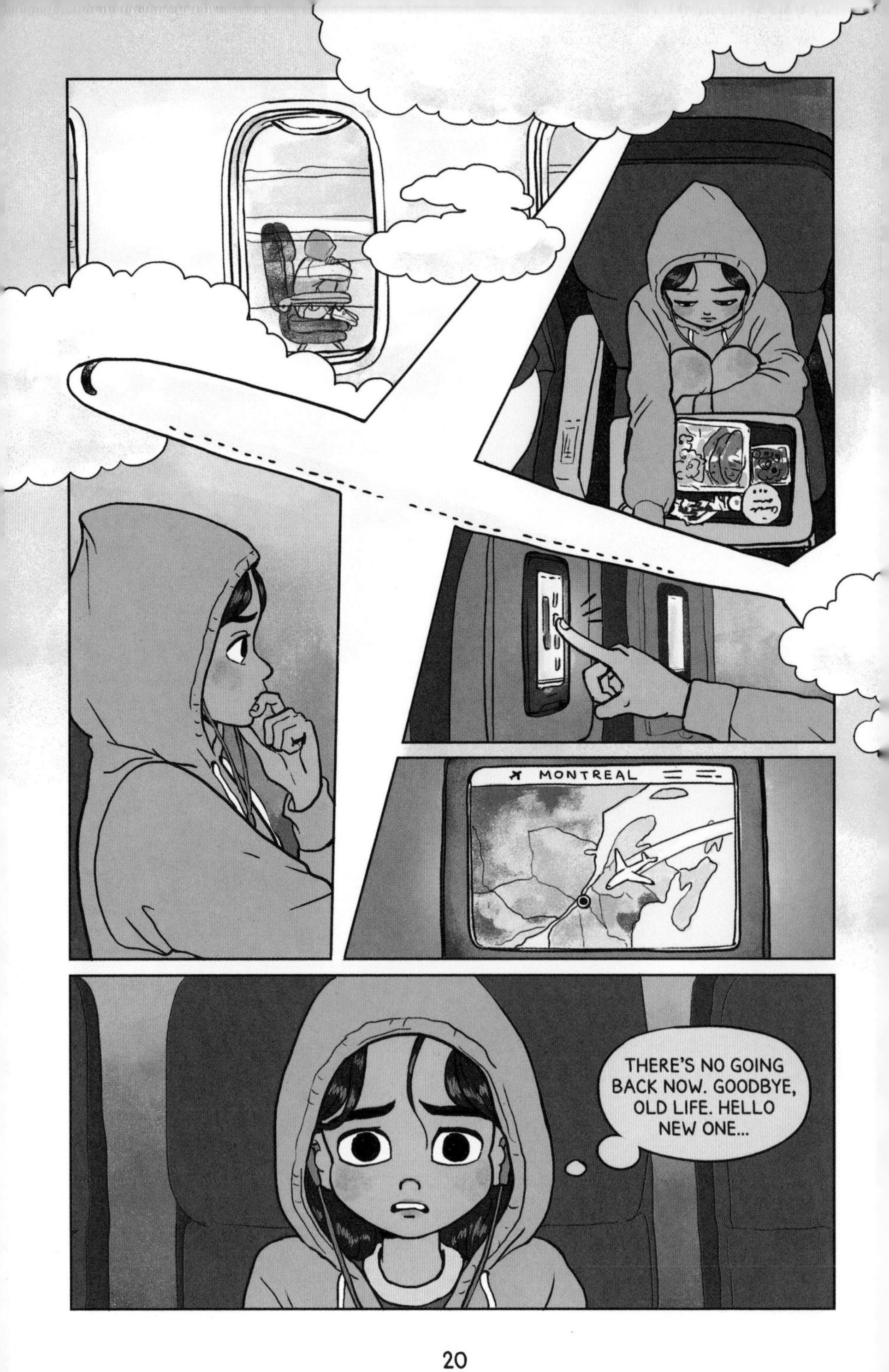
MONTREAL
THERE'S NO GOING BACK NOW. GOODBYE, OLD LIFE. HELLO NEW ONE...

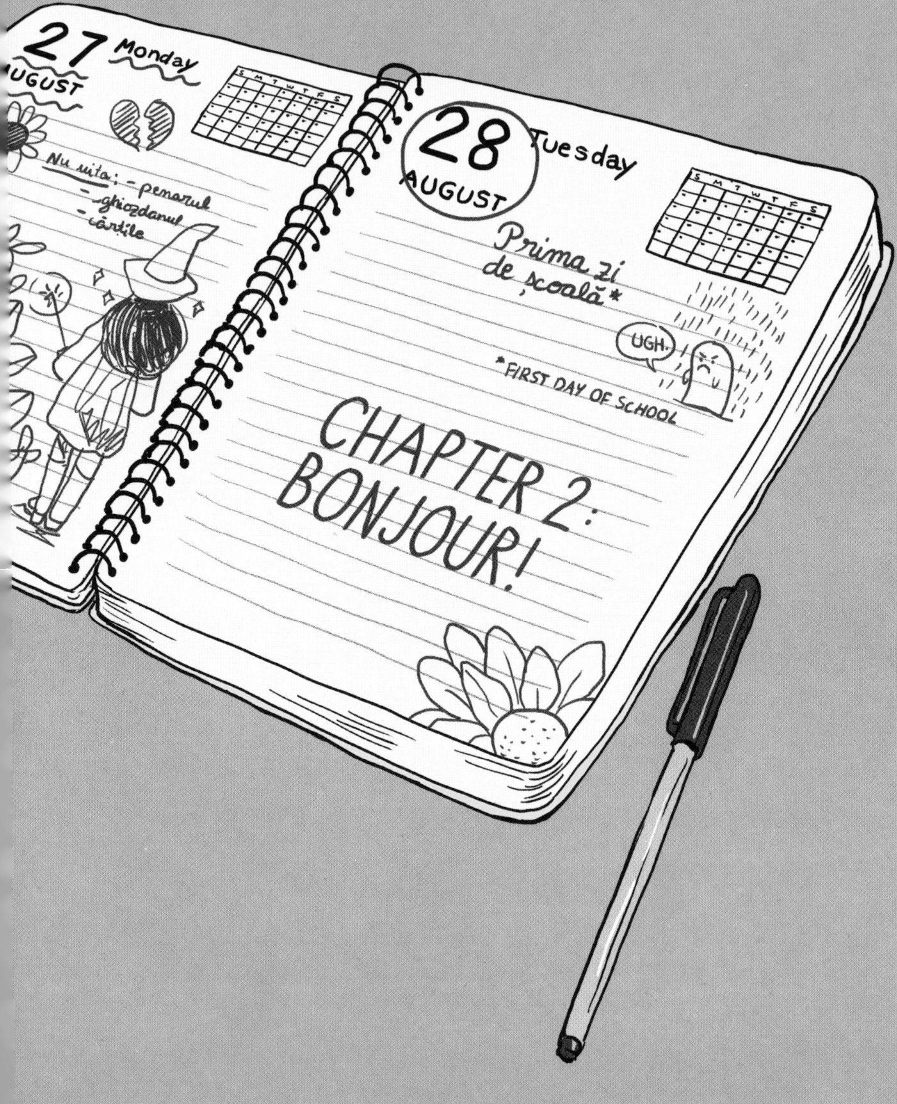
27 Monday
AUGUST
Nu uita: - penarul
- ghiozdanul
- cărțile
28 Tuesday
AUGUST
Prima zi de școală*
UGH.
*FIRST DAY OF SCHOOL
CHAPTER 2:
BONJOUR!

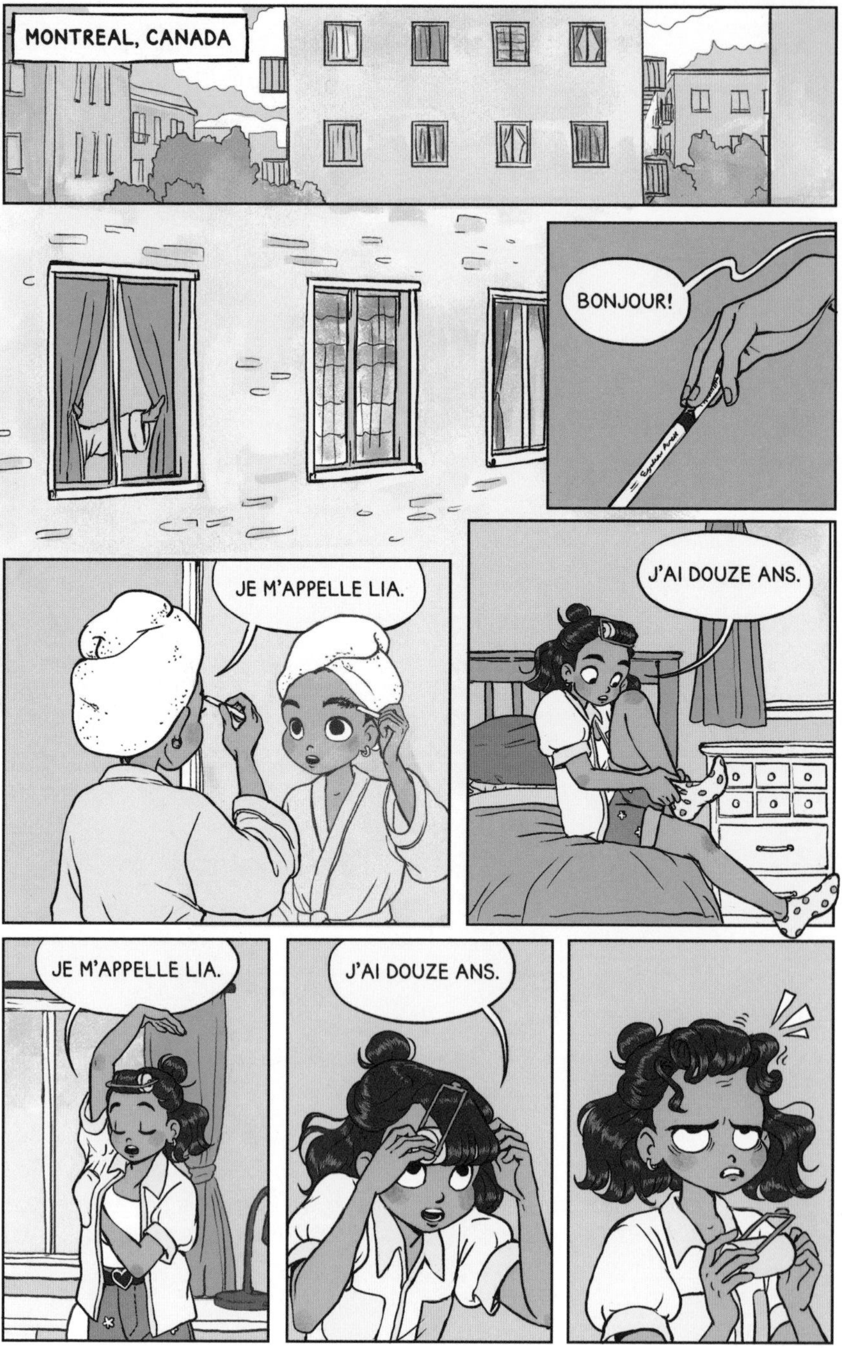
MONTREAL, CANADA
BONJOUR!
JE M'APPELLE LIA.
J'AI DOUZE ANS.
JE M'APPELLE LIA.
J'AI DOUZE ANS.

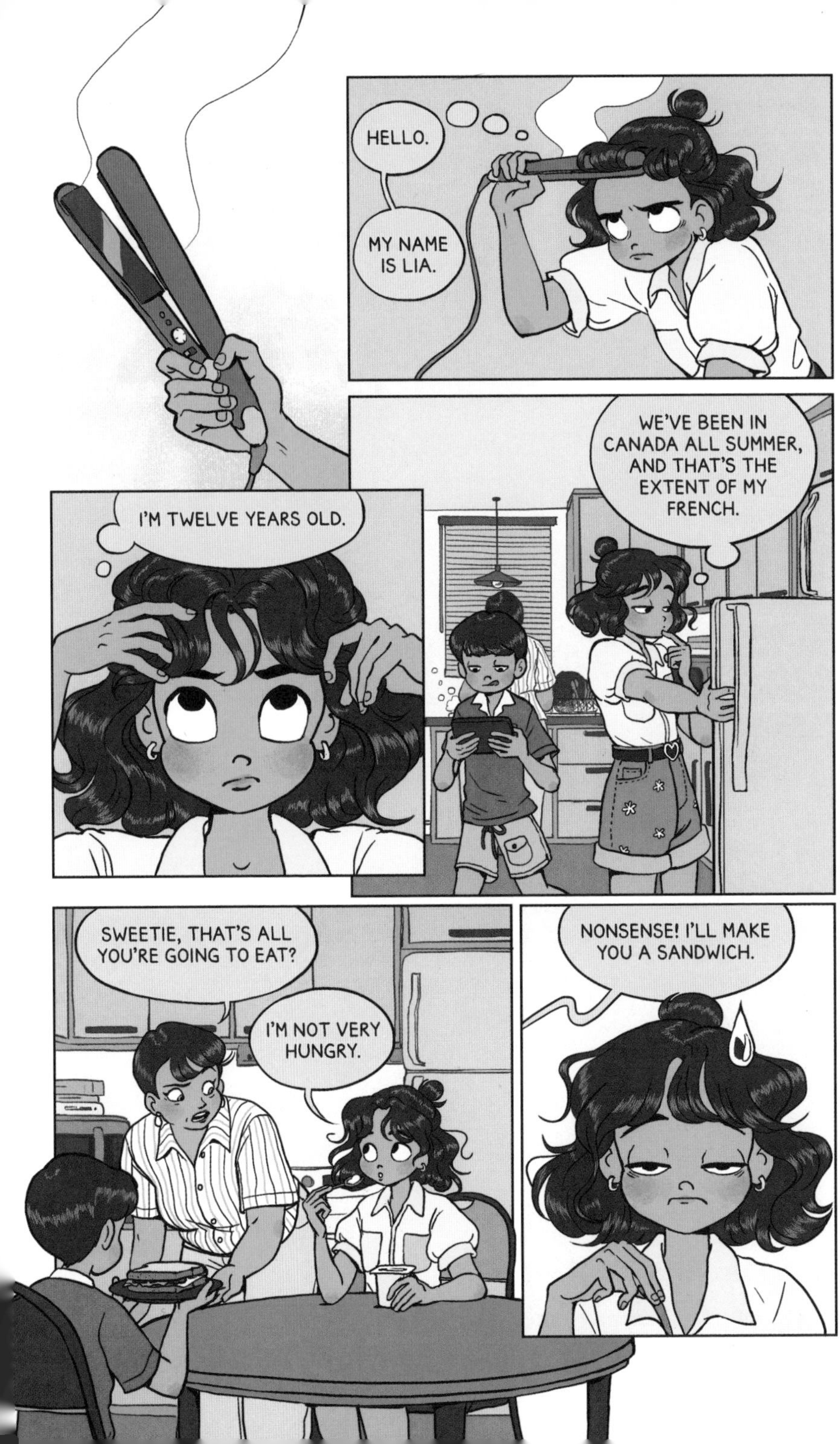
HELLO.
MY NAME IS LIA.
I'M TWELVE YEARS OLD.
WE'VE BEEN IN CANADA ALL SUMMER, AND THAT'S THE EXTENT OF MY FRENCH.
SWEETIE, THAT'S ALL YOU'RE GOING TO EAT?
I'M NOT VERY HUNGRY.
NONSENSE! I'LL MAKE YOU A SANDWICH.

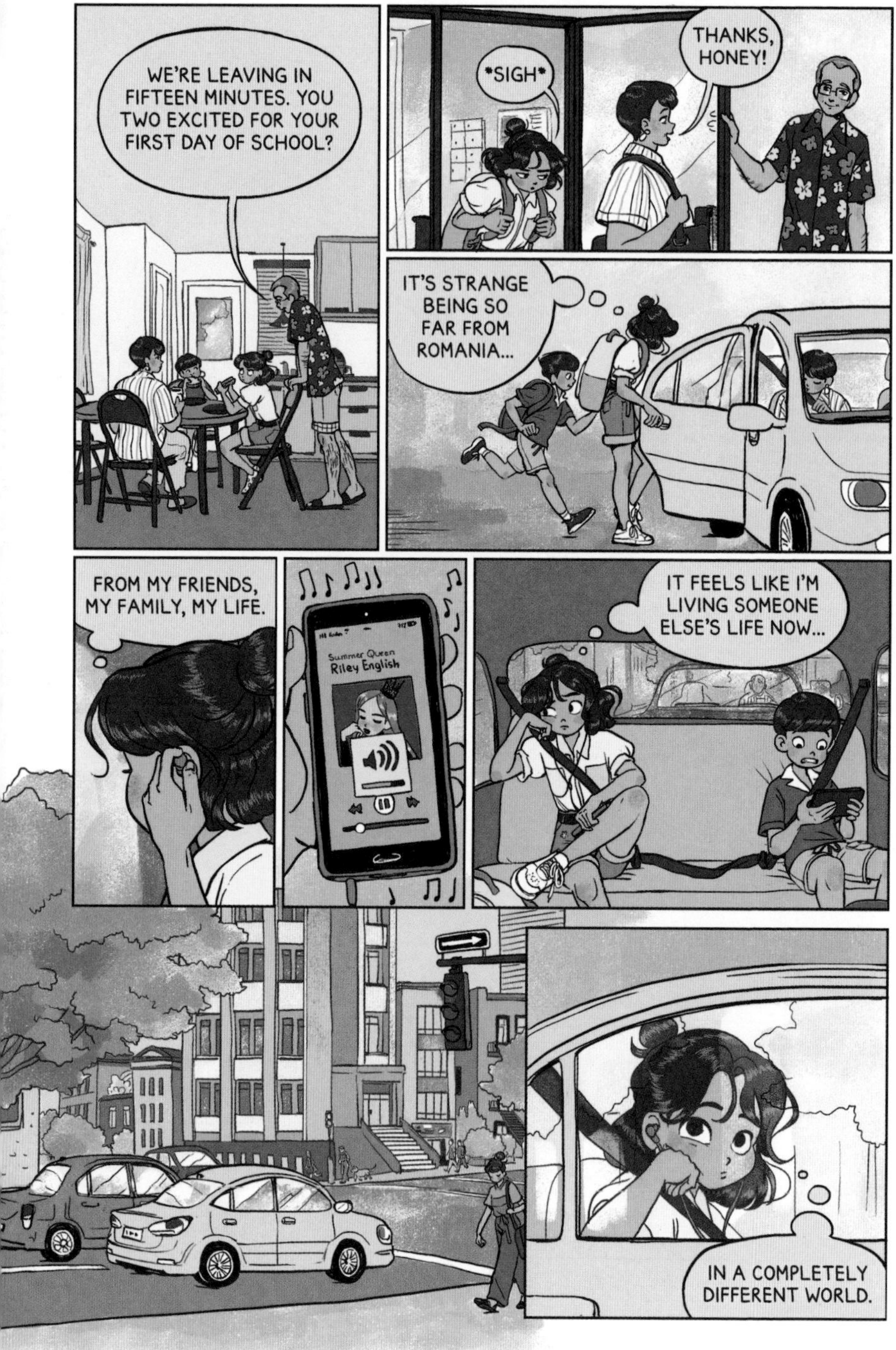
WE'RE LEAVING IN FIFTEEN MINUTES. YOU TWO EXCITED FOR YOUR FIRST DAY OF SCHOOL?
SIGH
THANKS, HONEY!
IT'S STRANGE BEING SO FAR FROM ROMANIA...
FROM MY FRIENDS, MY FAMILY, MY LIFE.
Summer Queen
Riley English
IT FEELS LIKE I'M LIVING SOMEONE ELSE'S LIFE NOW...
IN A COMPLETELY DIFFERENT WORLD.

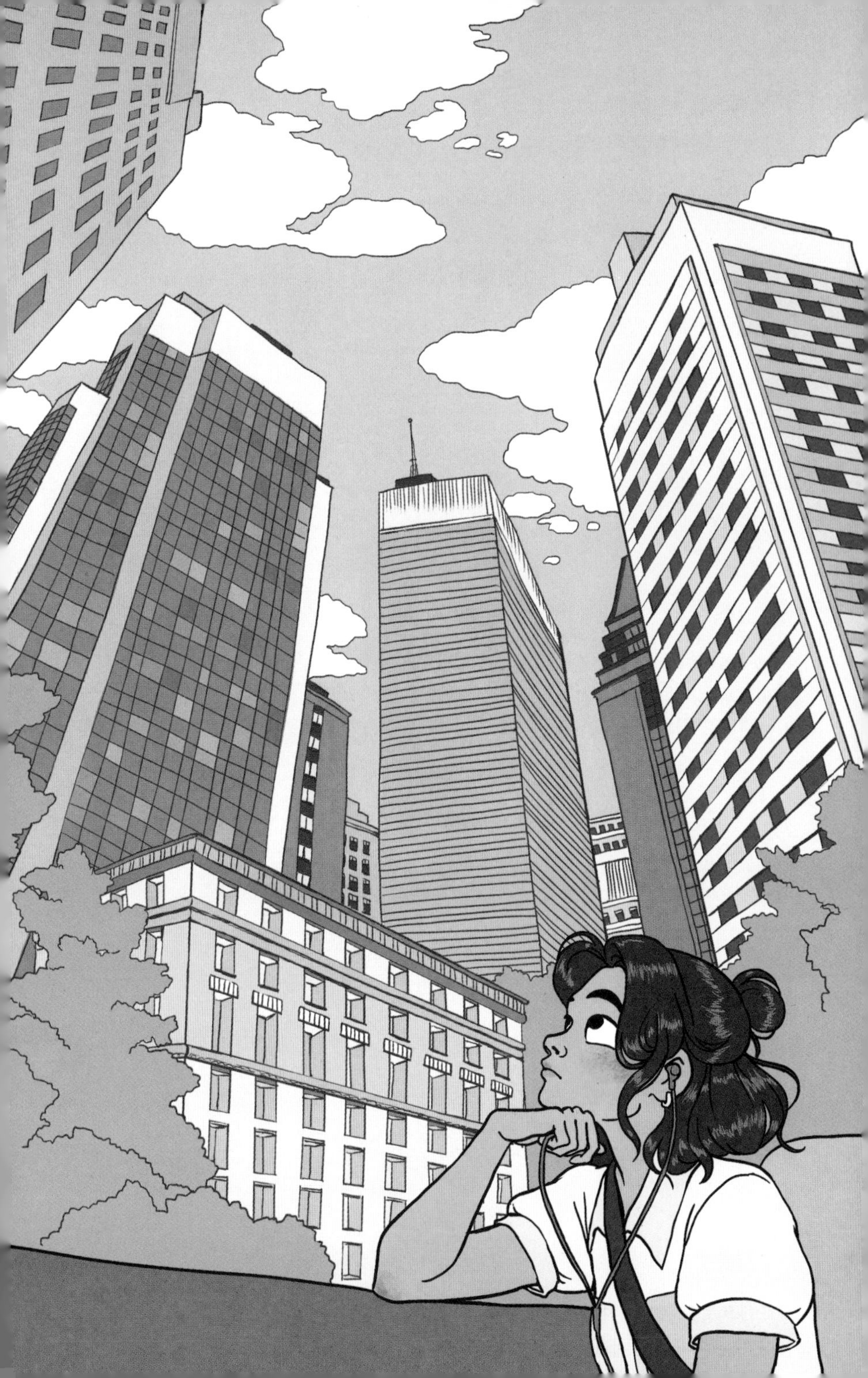

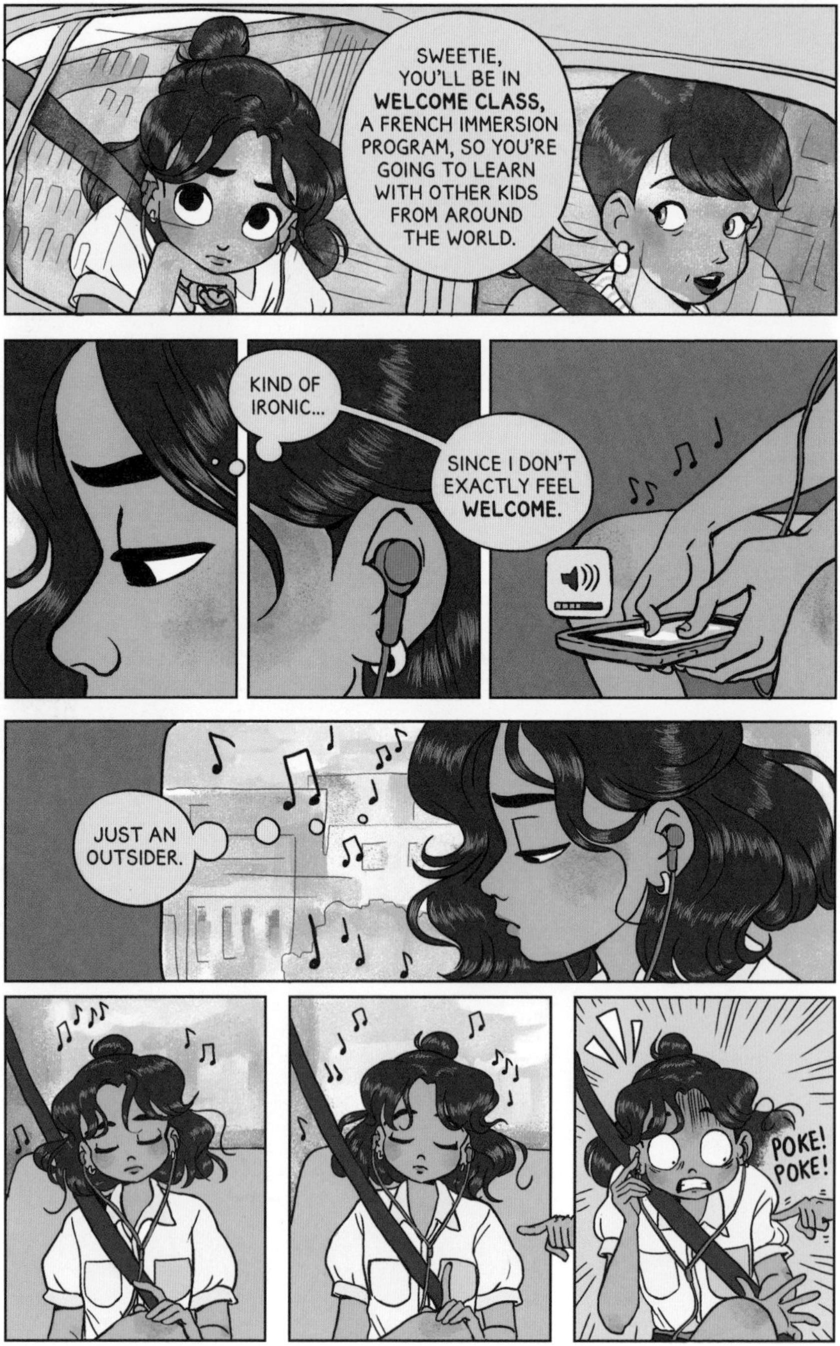
SWEETIE, YOU'LL BE IN **WELCOME CLASS,** A FRENCH IMMERSION PROGRAM, SO YOU'RE GOING TO LEARN WITH OTHER KIDS FROM AROUND THE WORLD.
KIND OF IRONIC...
SINCE I DON'T EXACTLY FEEL **WELCOME.**
JUST AN OUTSIDER.
POKE! POKE!

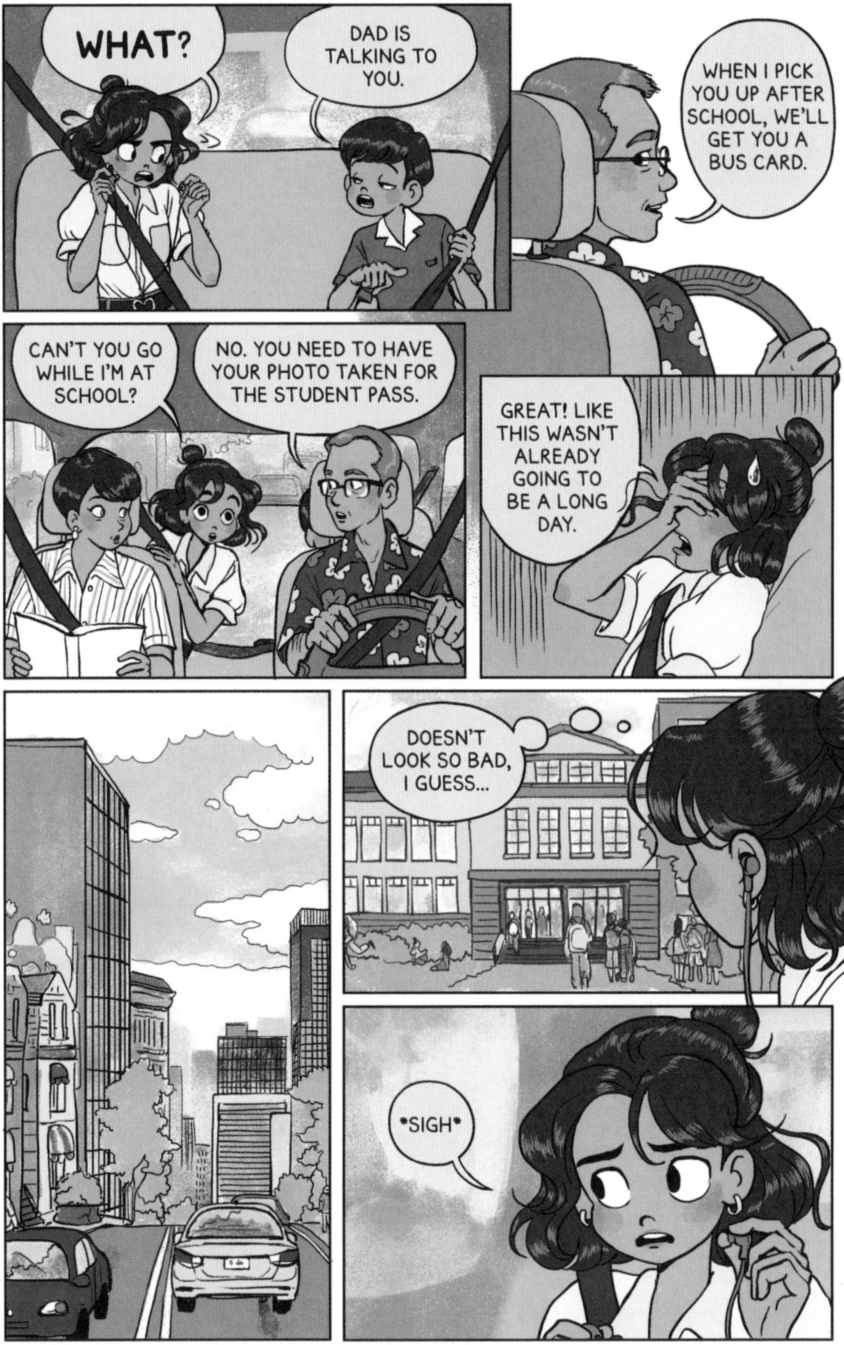
WHAT?
DAD IS TALKING TO YOU.
WHEN I PICK YOU UP AFTER SCHOOL, WE'LL GET YOU A BUS CARD.
CAN'T YOU GO WHILE I'M AT SCHOOL?
NO. YOU NEED TO HAVE YOUR PHOTO TAKEN FOR THE STUDENT PASS.
GREAT! LIKE THIS WASN'T ALREADY GOING TO BE A LONG DAY.
DOESN'T LOOK SO BAD, I GUESS...
SIGH

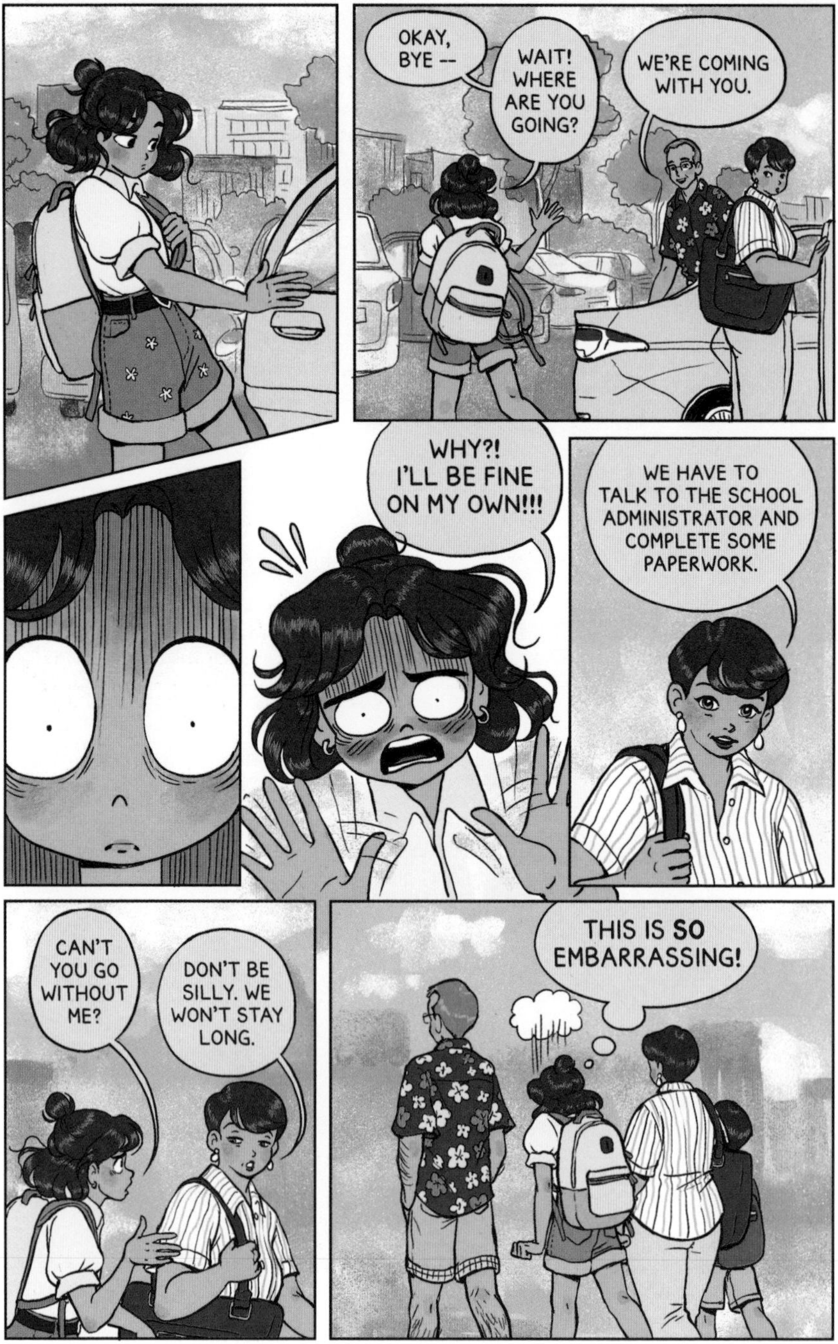
OKAY, BYE --
WAIT! WHERE ARE YOU GOING?
WE'RE COMING WITH YOU.
WHY?! I'LL BE FINE ON MY OWN!!!
WE HAVE TO TALK TO THE SCHOOL ADMINISTRATOR AND COMPLETE SOME PAPERWORK.
CAN'T YOU GO WITHOUT ME?
DON'T BE SILLY. WE WON'T STAY LONG.
THIS IS **SO** EMBARRASSING!

EVERYONE IS STARING AT ME...

AND MY PARENTS!

THIS MUST BE MY CLASS.

B 211

Classe d'accueil

B-211

DIM	LUN	MAR	MER

OKAY... BYE!

BYE-BYE, SWEETIE!

HAVE A GREAT DAY, SWEETIE!

LATER, DORK!

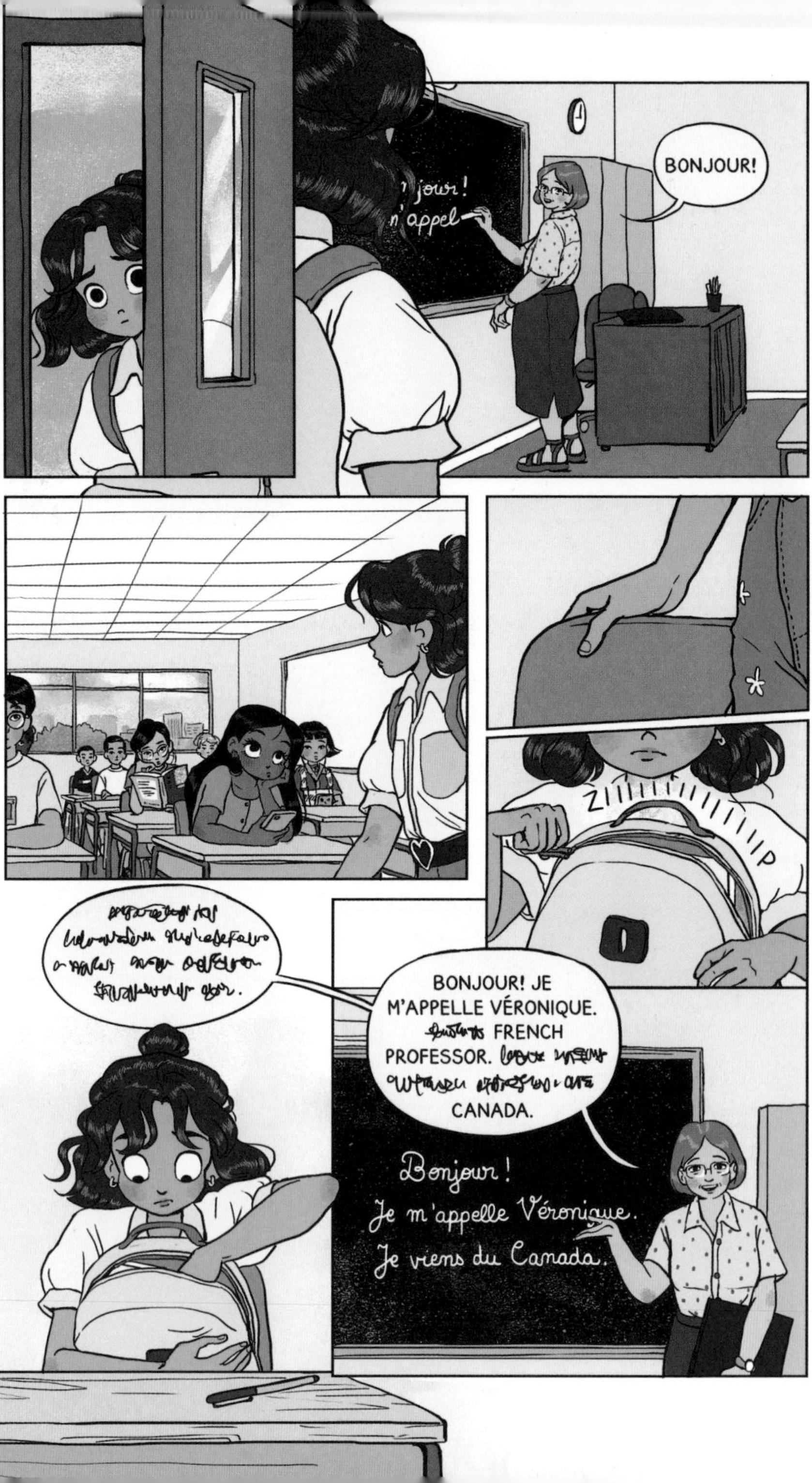

BONJOUR!
ZIIIIIIIIIIP
BONJOUR! JE M'APPELLE VÉRONIQUE.
FRENCH PROFESSOR.
CANADA.
Bonjour!
Je m'appelle Véronique.
Je viens du Canada.

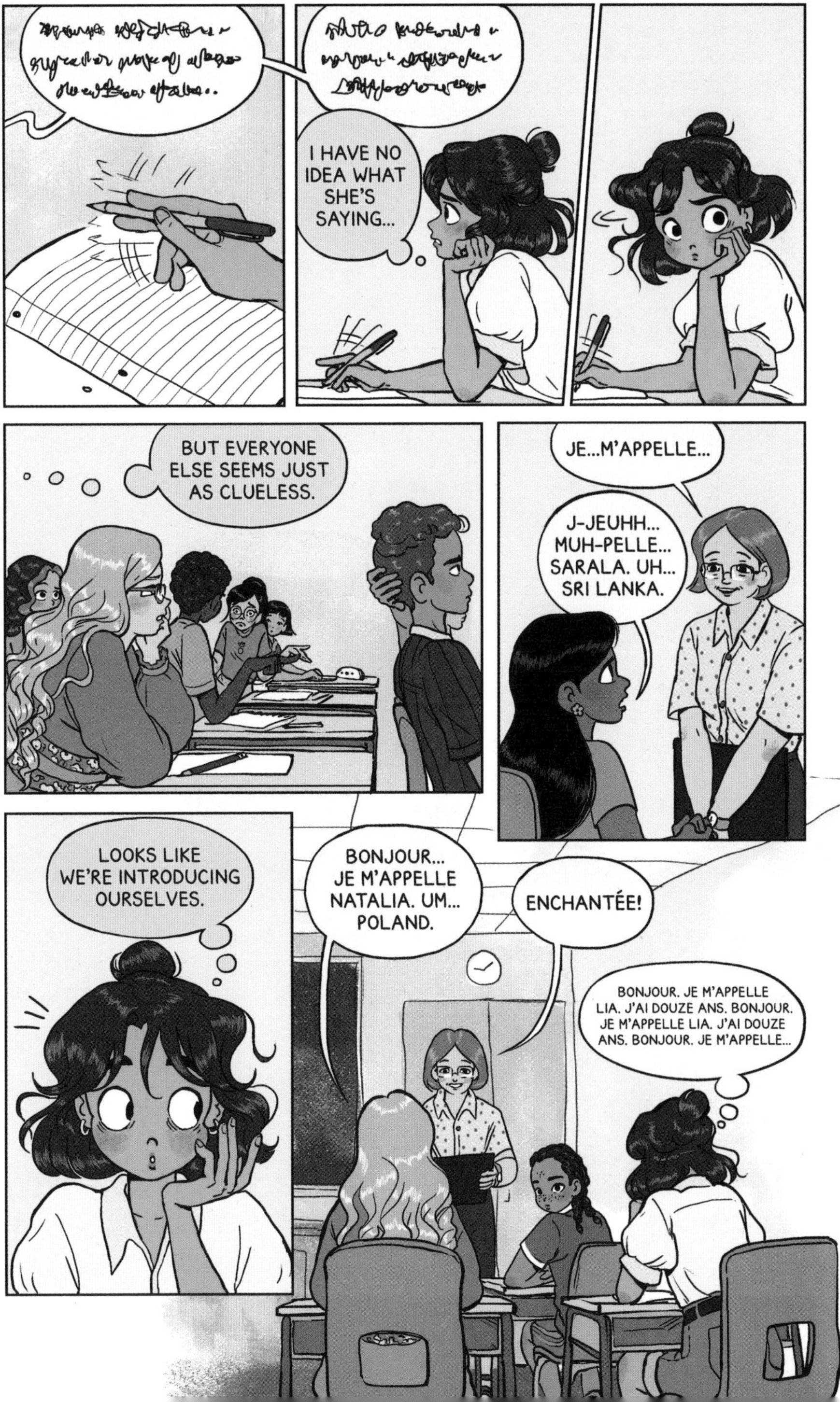
I HAVE NO IDEA WHAT SHE'S SAYING...
BUT EVERYONE ELSE SEEMS JUST AS CLUELESS.
JE...M'APPELLE...
J-JEUHH... MUH-PELLE... SARALA. UH... SRI LANKA.
LOOKS LIKE WE'RE INTRODUCING OURSELVES.
BONJOUR... JE M'APPELLE NATALIA. UM... POLAND.
ENCHANTÉE!
BONJOUR. JE M'APPELLE LIA. J'AI DOUZE ANS. BONJOUR. JE M'APPELLE LIA. J'AI DOUZE ANS. BONJOUR. JE M'APPELLE...

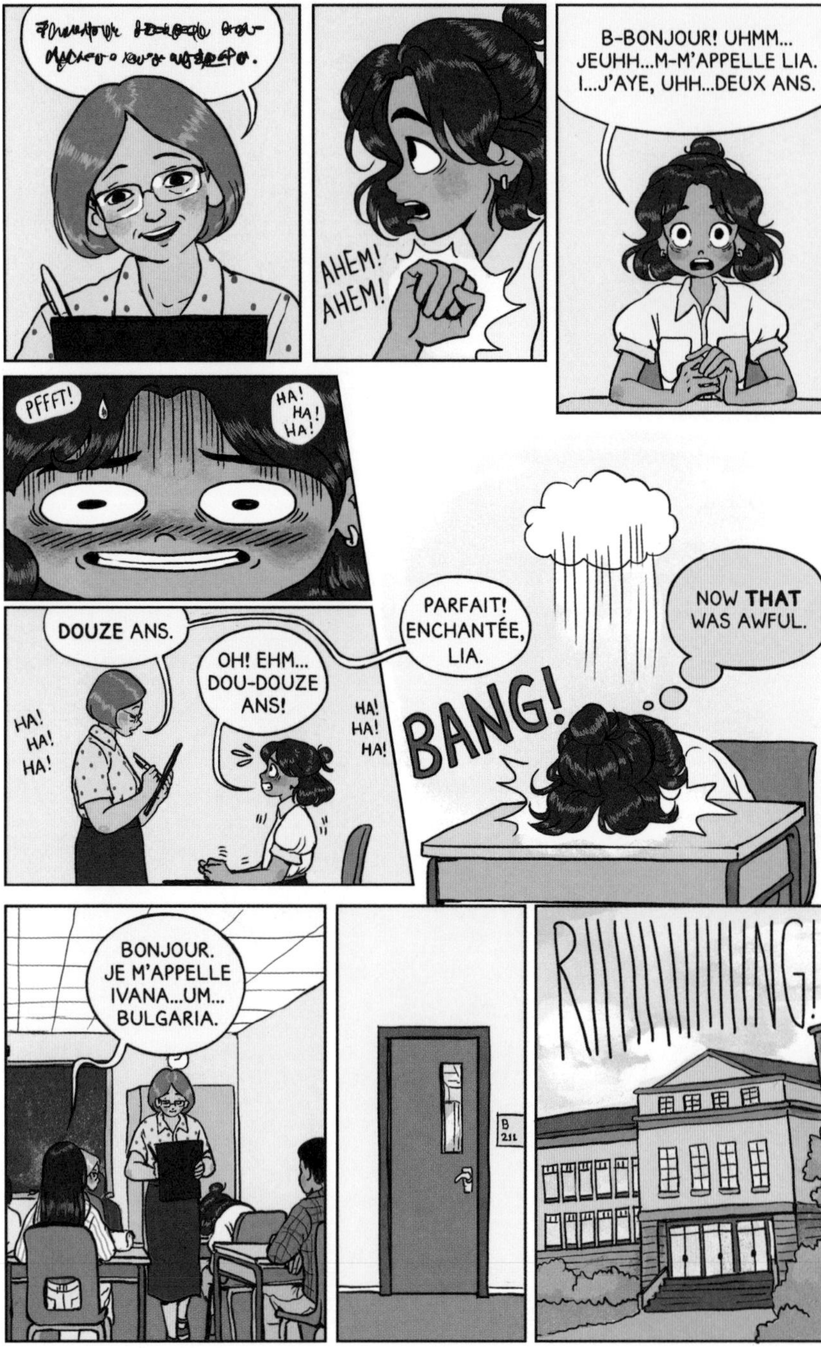

AHEM! AHEM!
B-BONJOUR! UHMM... JEUHH...M-M'APPELLE LIA. I...J'AYE, UHH...DEUX ANS.
PFFFT!
HA! HA! HA!
DOUZE ANS.
HA! HA! HA!
OH! EHM... DOU-DOUZE ANS!
HA! HA! HA!
PARFAIT! ENCHANTÉE, LIA.
BANG!
NOW THAT WAS AWFUL.
BONJOUR. JE M'APPELLE IVANA...UM... BULGARIA.
B 211
RIIIIIIIIIING!

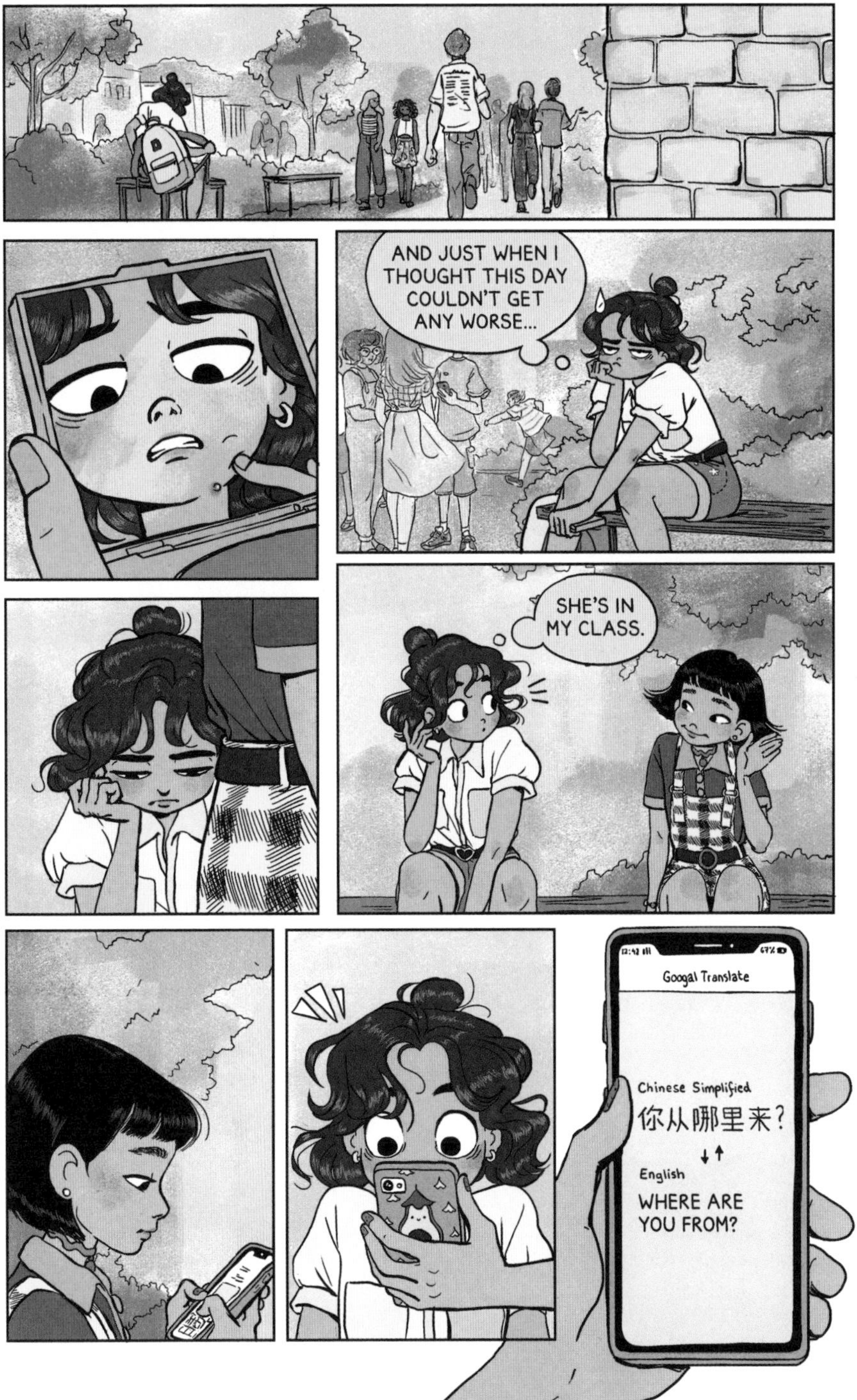
AND JUST WHEN I THOUGHT THIS DAY COULDN'T GET ANY WORSE...
SHE'S IN MY CLASS.
Googal Translate
Chinese Simplified
你从哪里来?
English
WHERE ARE YOU FROM?

RI||||||||||||||||NG!

ZI MEI.

LIA.

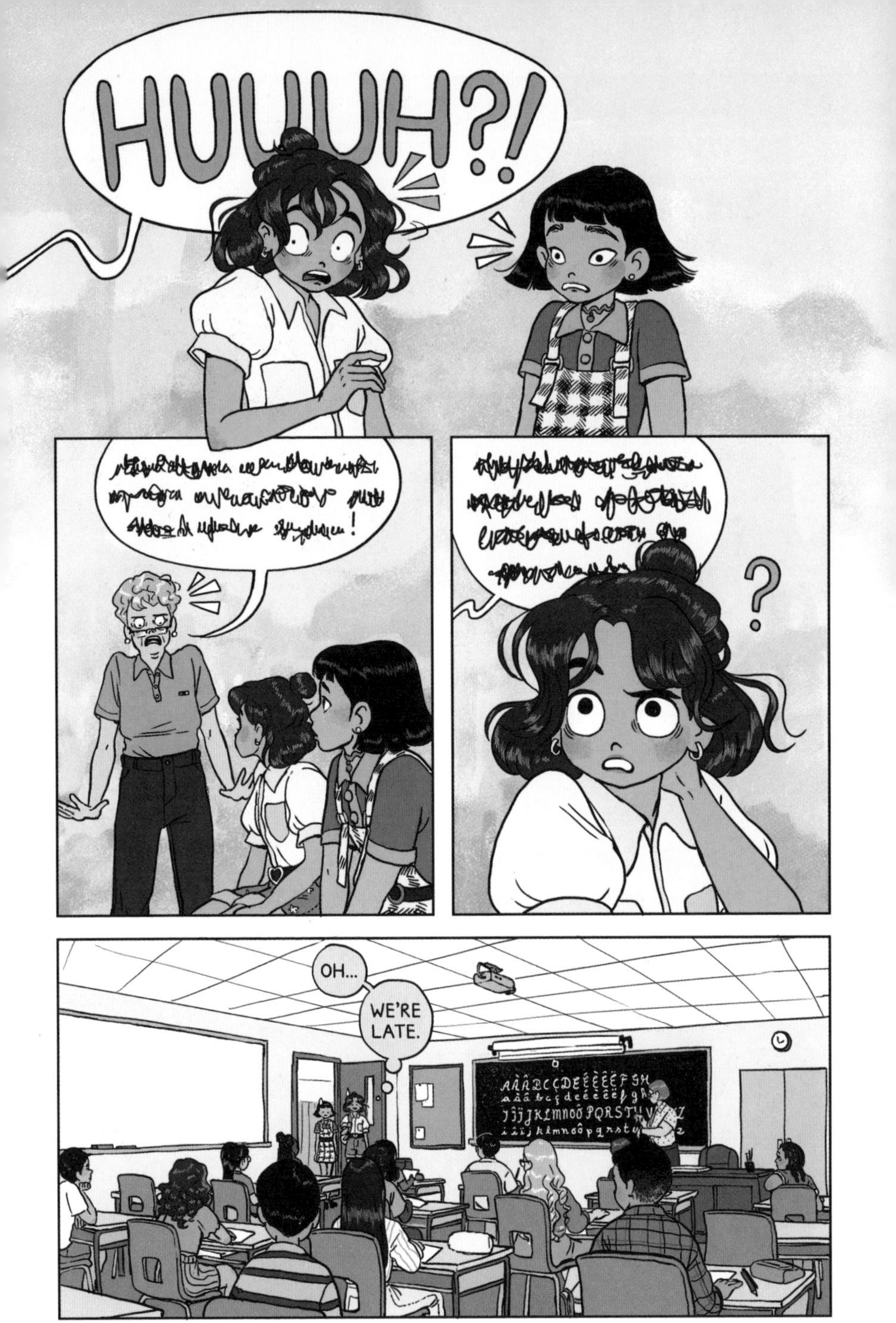
HUUUH?!
?
OH...
WE'RE LATE.

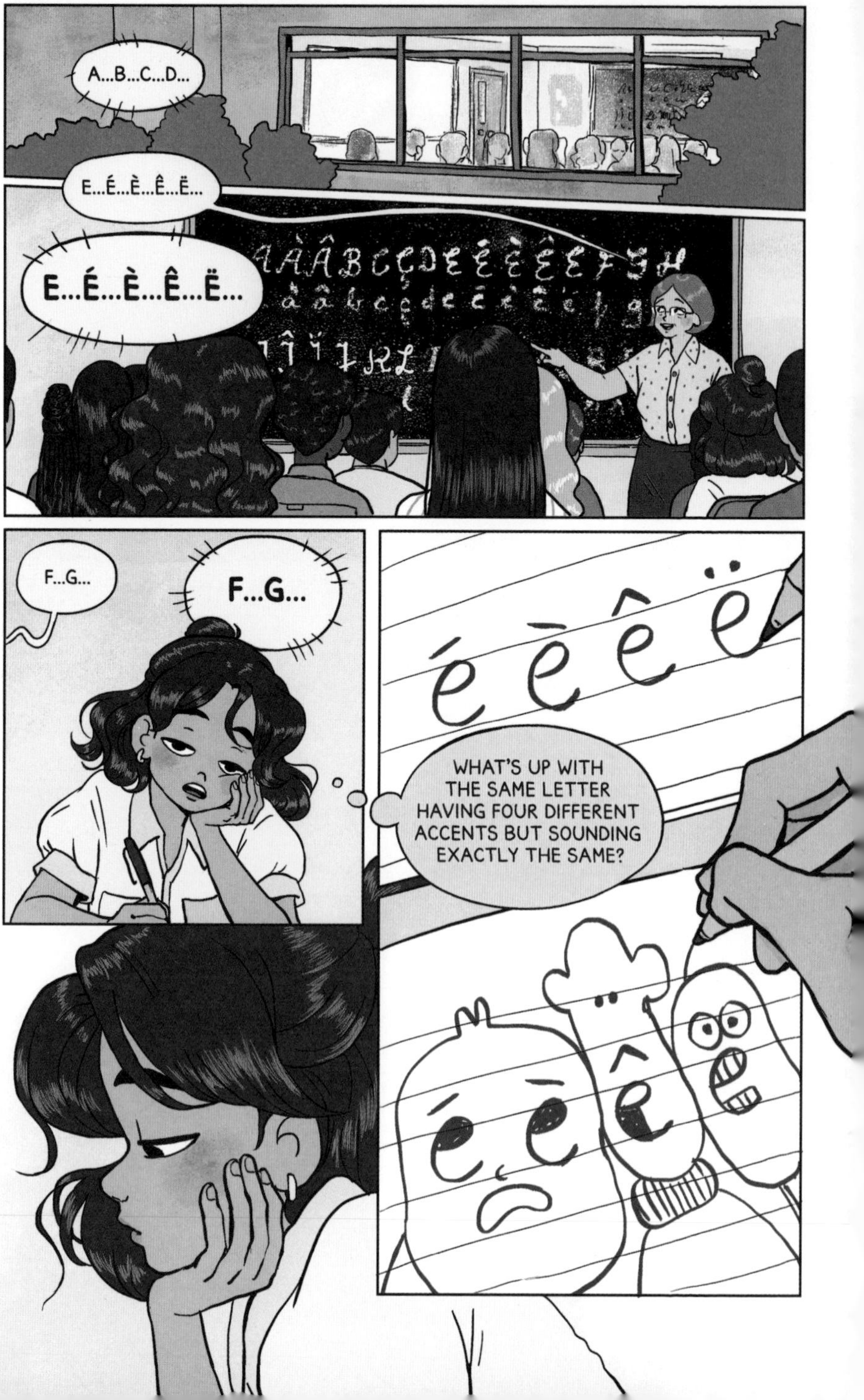
A...B...C...D...
E...É...È...Ê...Ë...
E...É...È...Ê...Ë...
F...G...
F...G...
WHAT'S UP WITH THE SAME LETTER HAVING FOUR DIFFERENT ACCENTS BUT SOUNDING EXACTLY THE SAME?

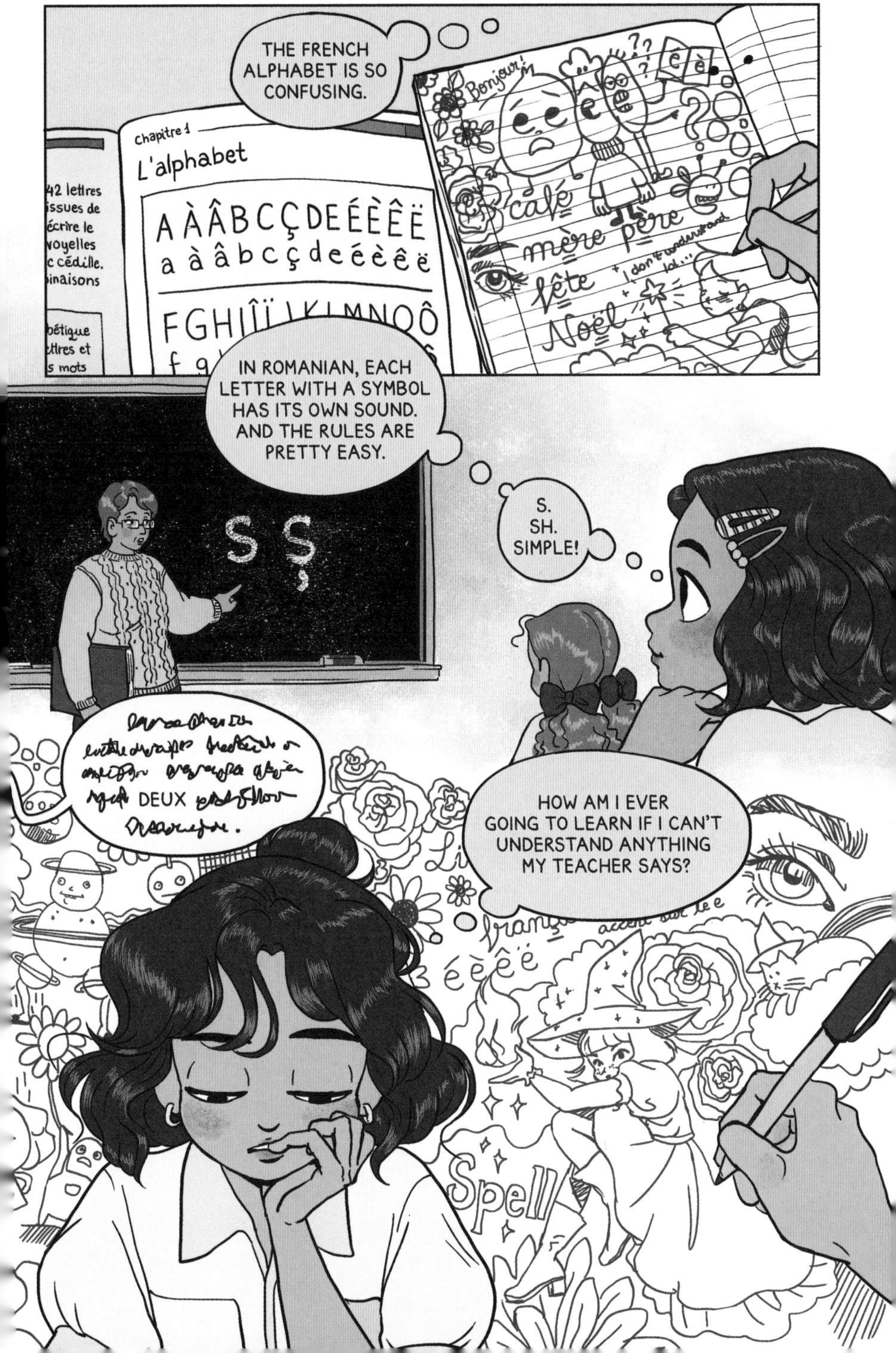
THE FRENCH ALPHABET IS SO CONFUSING.
Chapitre 1
L'alphabet
42 lettres
issues de
écrire le
voyelles
c cédille.
binaisons
bétique
ettres et
s mots
A À Â B C Ç D E É È Ê Ë
a à â b c ç d e é è ê ë
Bonjour!
café
mère père
fête
Noël
I don't understand lol...
IN ROMANIAN, EACH LETTER WITH A SYMBOL HAS ITS OWN SOUND. AND THE RULES ARE PRETTY EASY.
S Ș
S. SH. SIMPLE!
DEUX
HOW AM I EVER GOING TO LEARN IF I CAN'T UNDERSTAND ANYTHING MY TEACHER SAYS?
é è ê ë
Spell

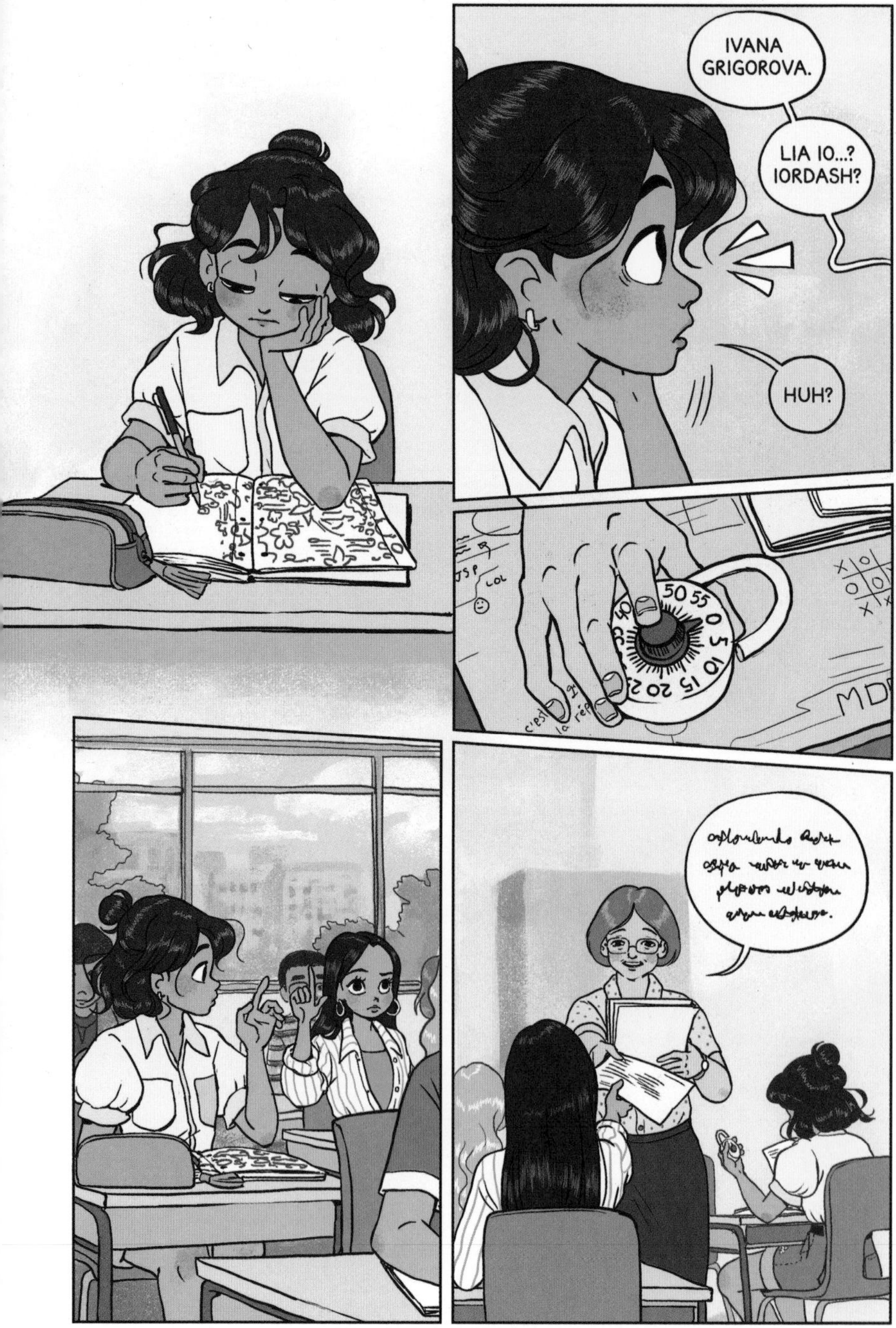
IVANA GRIGOROVA.
LIA IO...? IORDASH?
HUH?

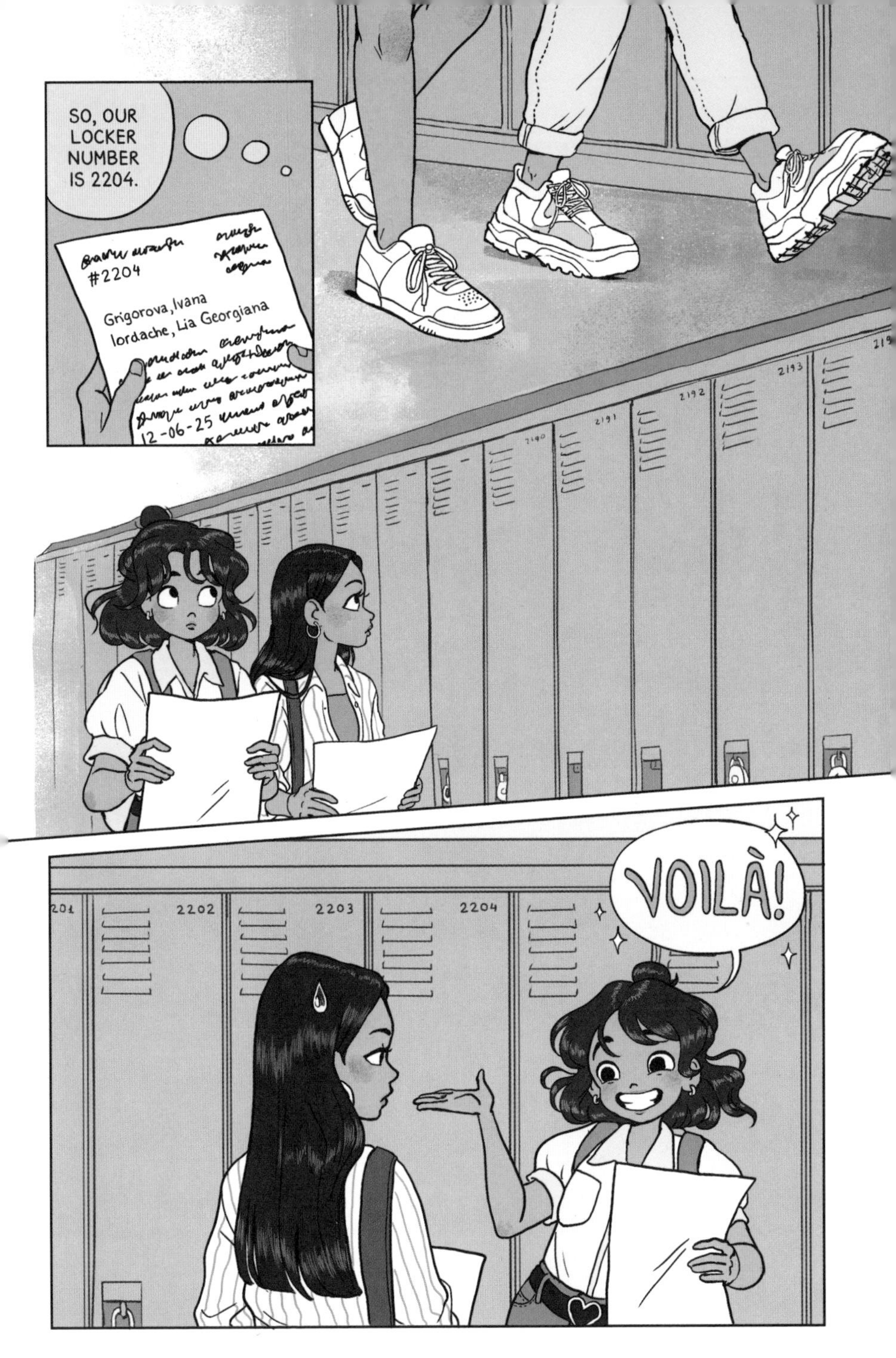
SO, OUR LOCKER NUMBER IS 2204.
#2204
Grigorova, Ivana
Iordache, Lia Georgiana
12-06-25
2190
2191
2192
2193
2201
2202
2203
2204
VOILÀ!

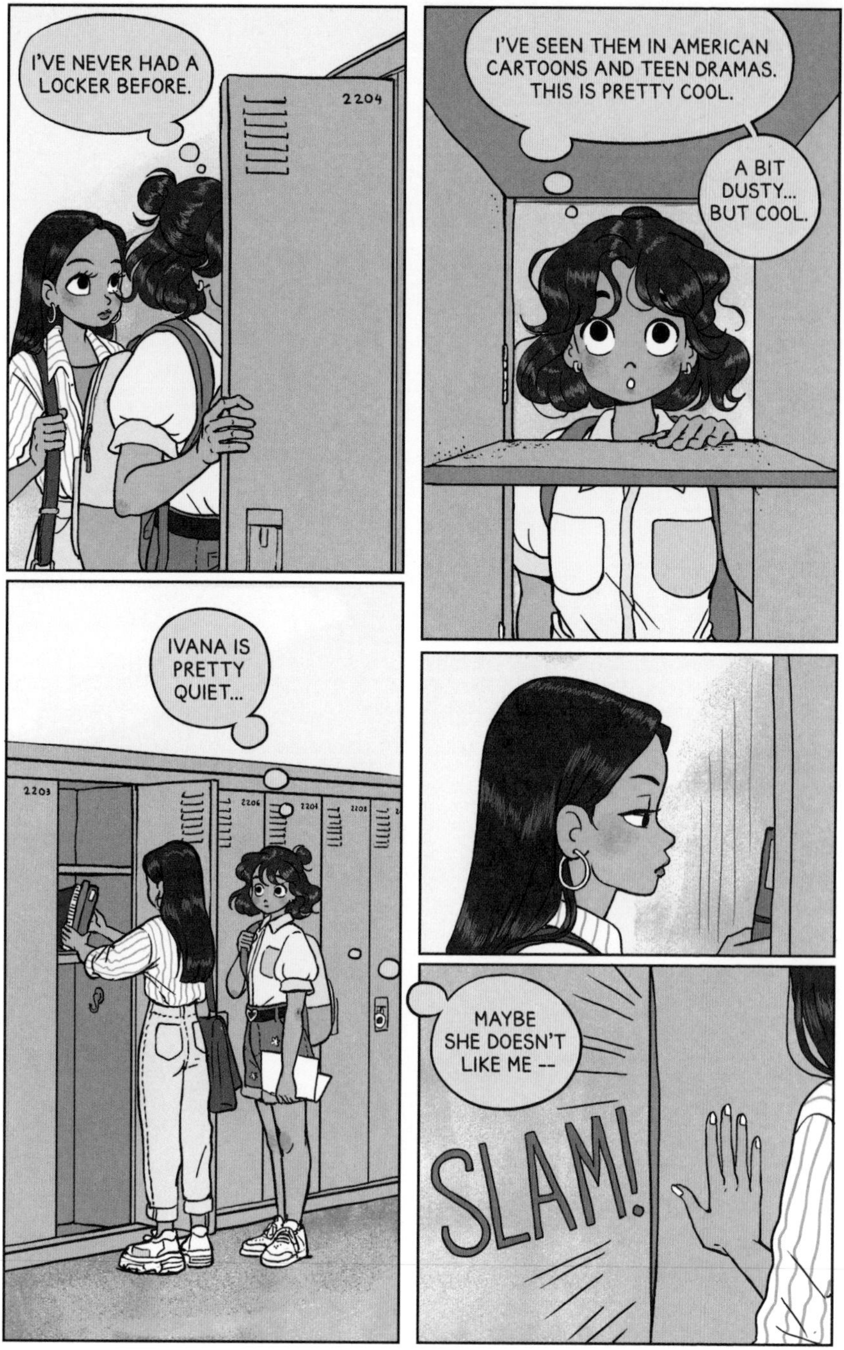
I'VE NEVER HAD A LOCKER BEFORE.
2204
I'VE SEEN THEM IN AMERICAN CARTOONS AND TEEN DRAMAS. THIS IS PRETTY COOL.
A BIT DUSTY... BUT COOL.
IVANA IS PRETTY QUIET...
2203
2206
2204
2208
MAYBE SHE DOESN'T LIKE ME --
SLAM!

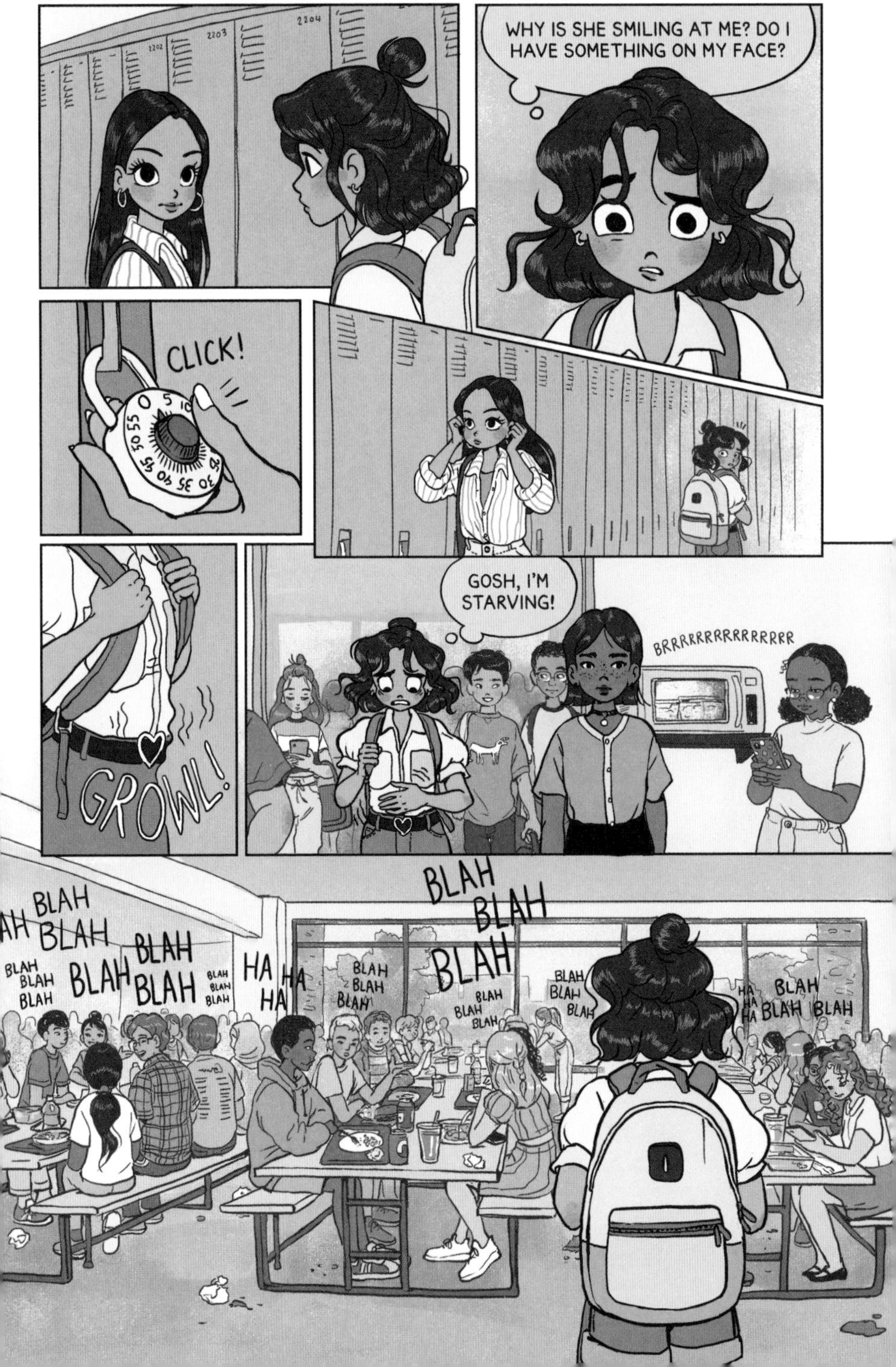
2202
2203
2204
WHY IS SHE SMILING AT ME? DO I HAVE SOMETHING ON MY FACE?
CLICK!
GROWL!
GOSH, I'M STARVING!
BRRRRRRRRRRRRRRRR
BLAH BLAH BLAH
BLAH BLAH
BLAH BLAH BLAH
BLAH
BLAH BLAH
BLAH BLAH BLAH
HA HA HA
BLAH BLAH BLAH
BLAH BLAH BLAH
BLAH BLAH BLAH
HA HA HA
BLAH BLAH BLAH

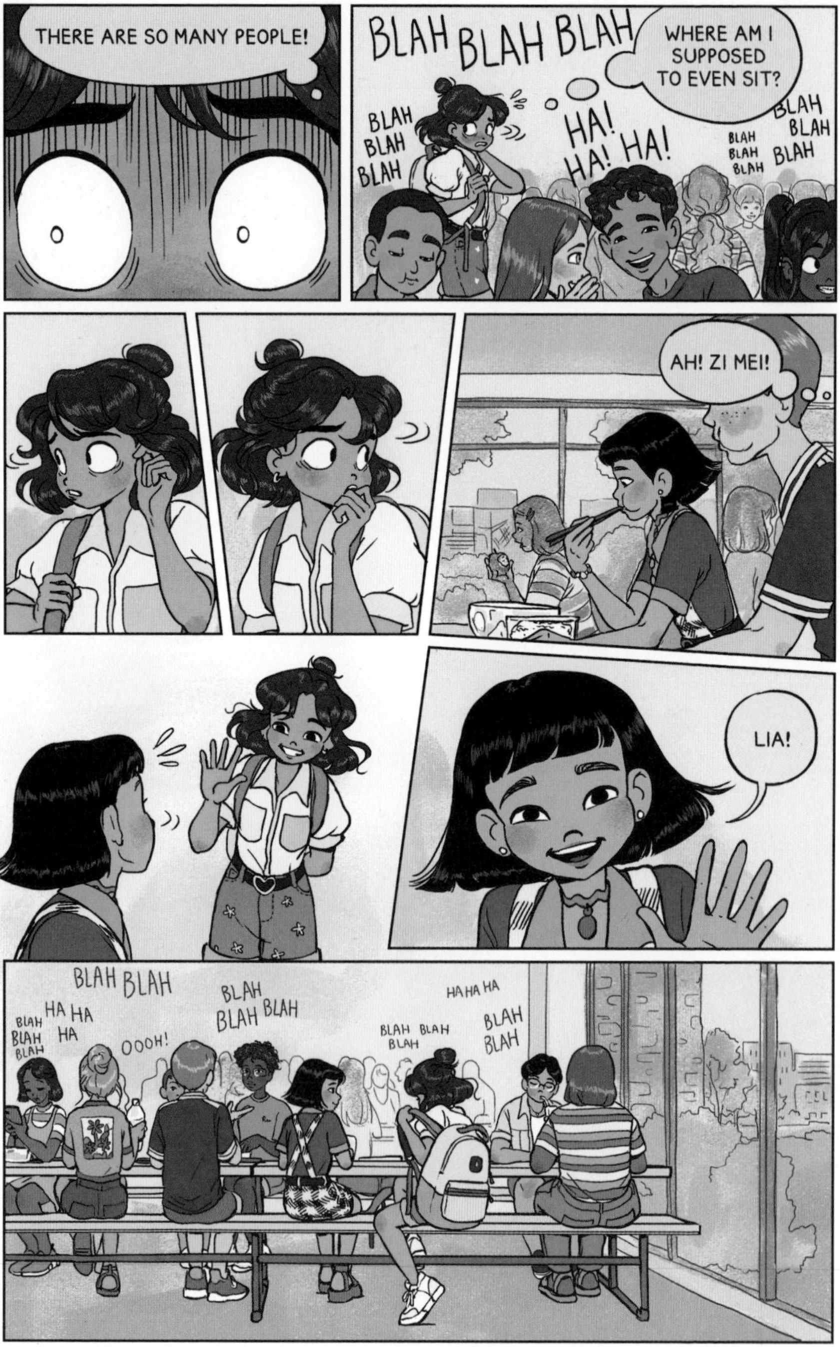
THERE ARE SO MANY PEOPLE!
BLAH BLAH BLAH
BLAH BLAH BLAH
WHERE AM I SUPPOSED TO EVEN SIT?
HA! HA! HA!
BLAH BLAH BLAH
BLAH BLAH BLAH
AH! ZI MEI!
LIA!
BLAH BLAH
BLAH BLAH BLAH
HA HA HA
OOOH!
BLAH BLAH BLAH
BLAH BLAH BLAH
HA HA HA
BLAH BLAH

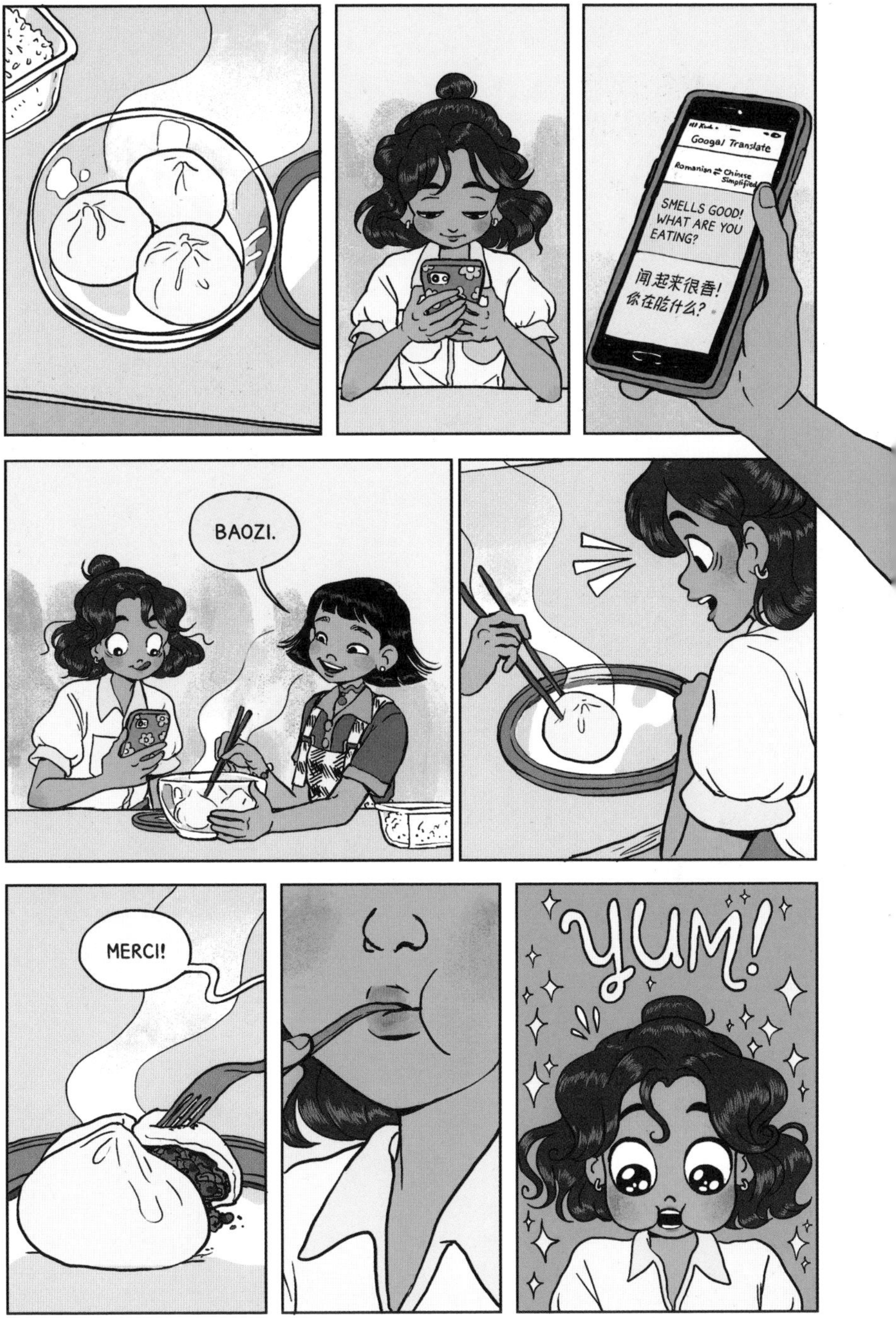
Googal Translate
Romanian ⇄ Chinese Simplified
SMELLS GOOD! WHAT ARE YOU EATING?
闻起来很香!
你在吃什么?
BAOZI.
MERCI!
YUM!

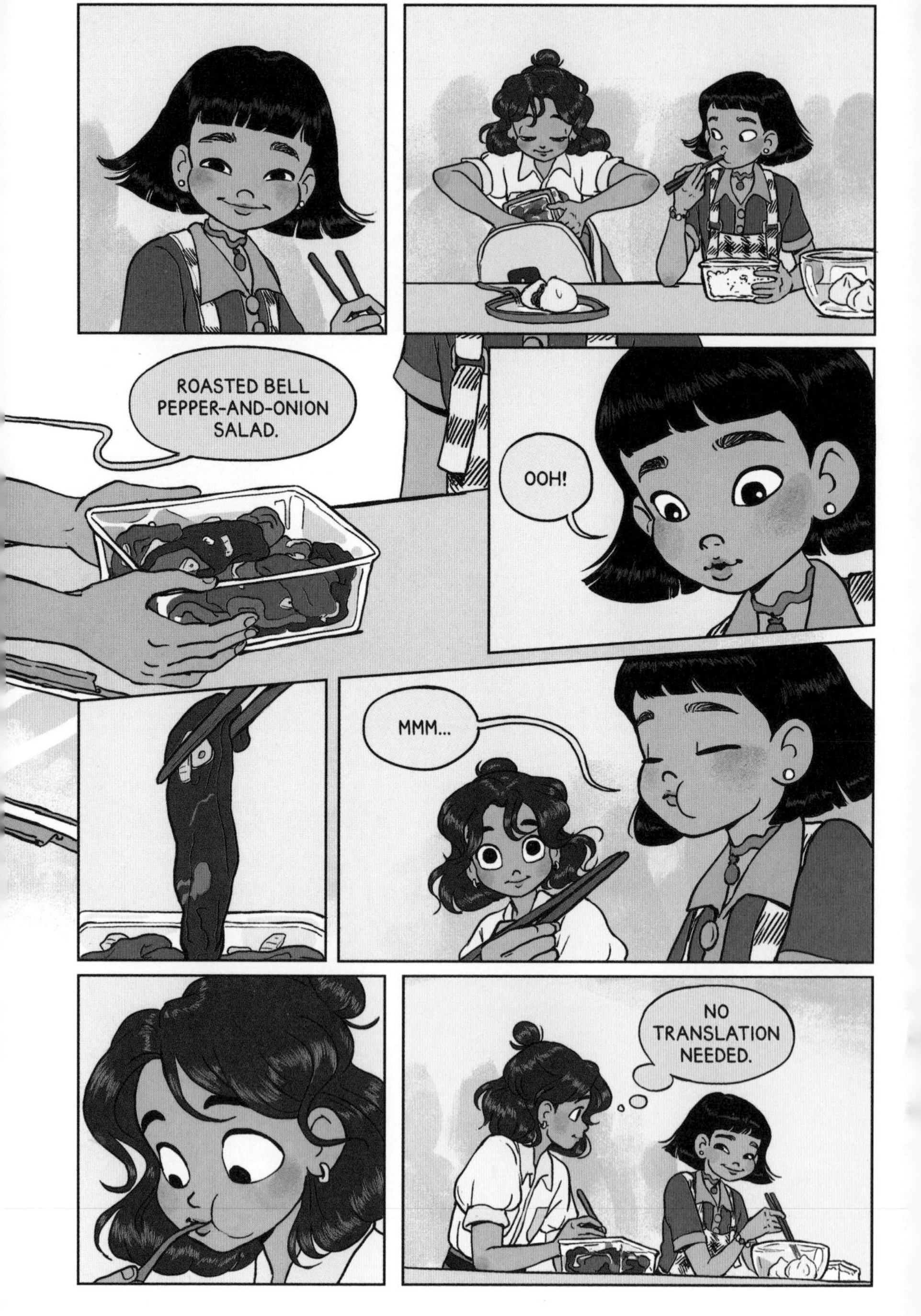
ROASTED BELL PEPPER-AND-ONION SALAD.
OOH!
MMM...
NO TRANSLATION NEEDED.

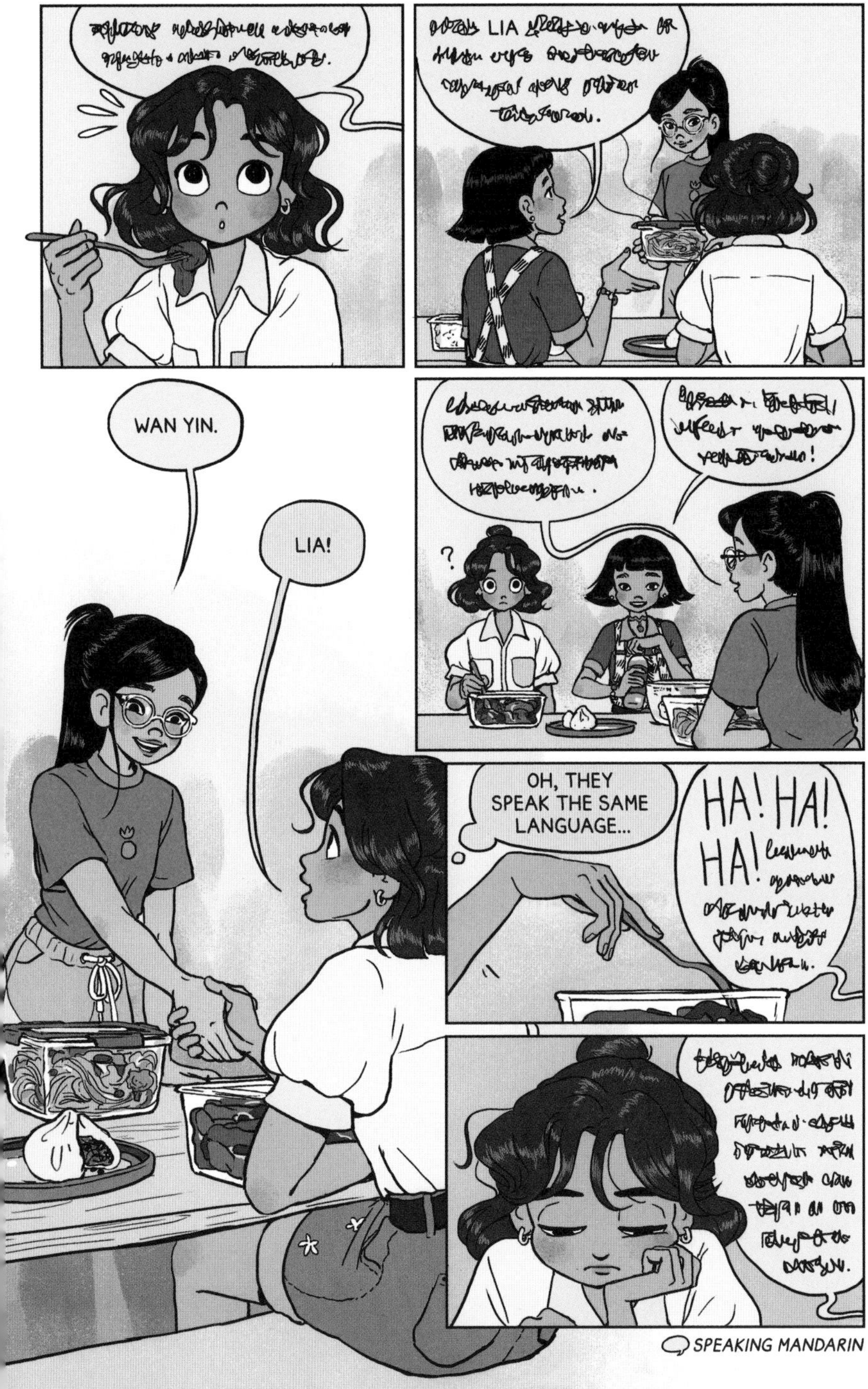
LIA
WAN YIN.
LIA!
OH, THEY SPEAK THE SAME LANGUAGE...
HA! HA! HA!
SPEAKING MANDARIN

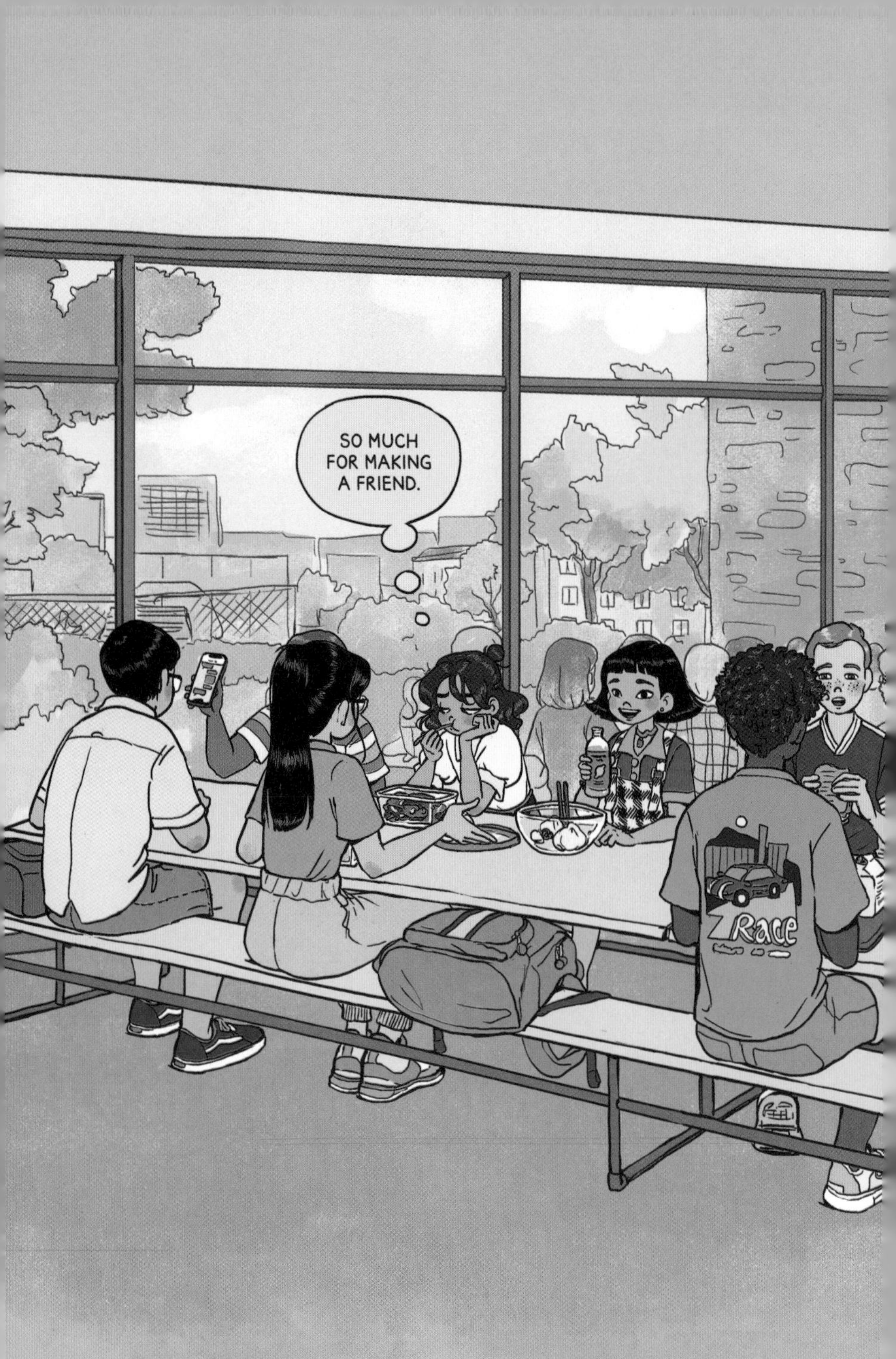
SO MUCH FOR MAKING A FRIEND.
Race

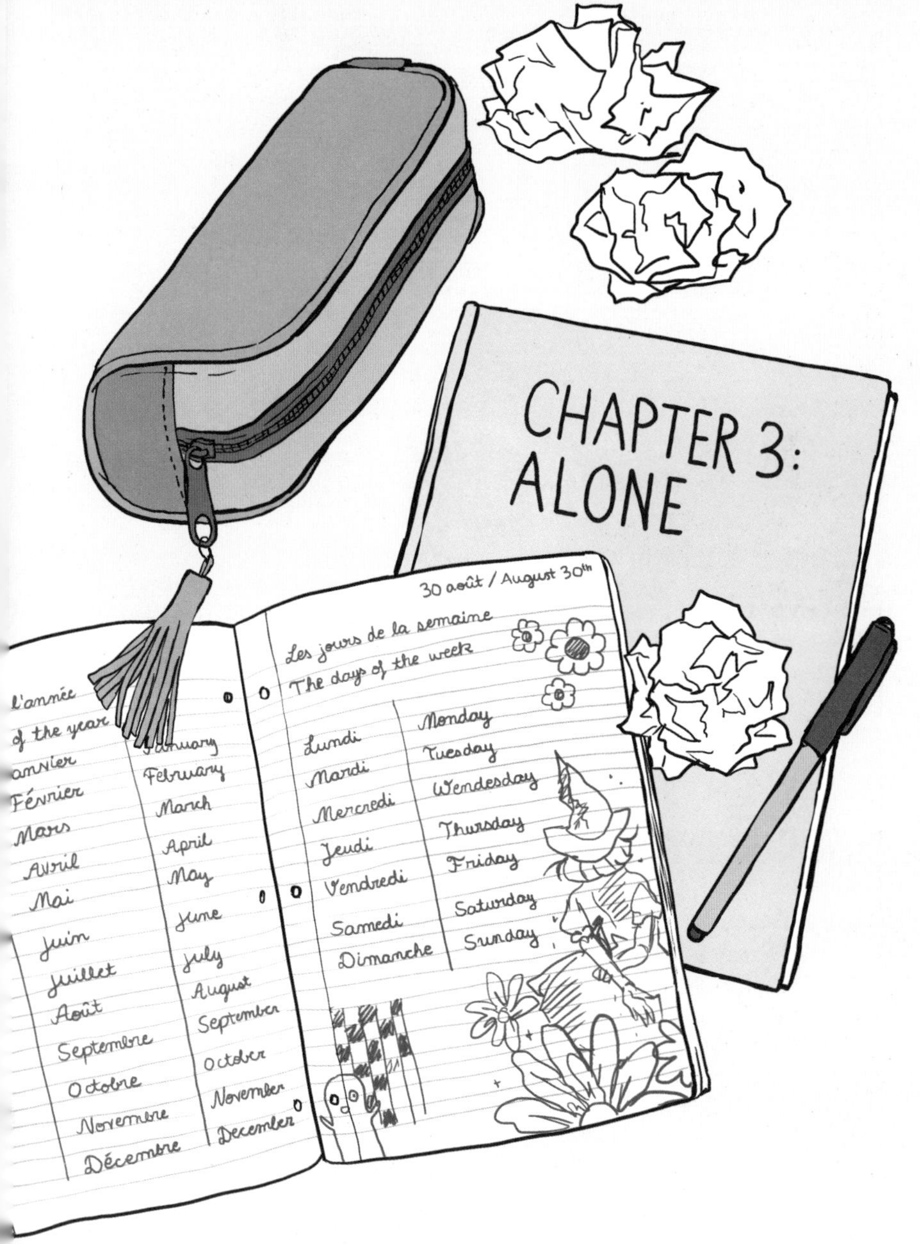
CHAPTER 3:
ALONE
30 août / August 30th
Les jours de la semaine
The days of the week
Lundi Monday
Mardi Tuesday
Mercredi Wendesday
Jeudi Thursday
Vendredi Friday
Samedi Saturday
Dimanche Sunday
l'année
of the year
February
Février March
Mars April
Avril May
Mai June
Juin July
Juillet August
Août September
Septembre October
Octobre November
Novembre December
Décembre

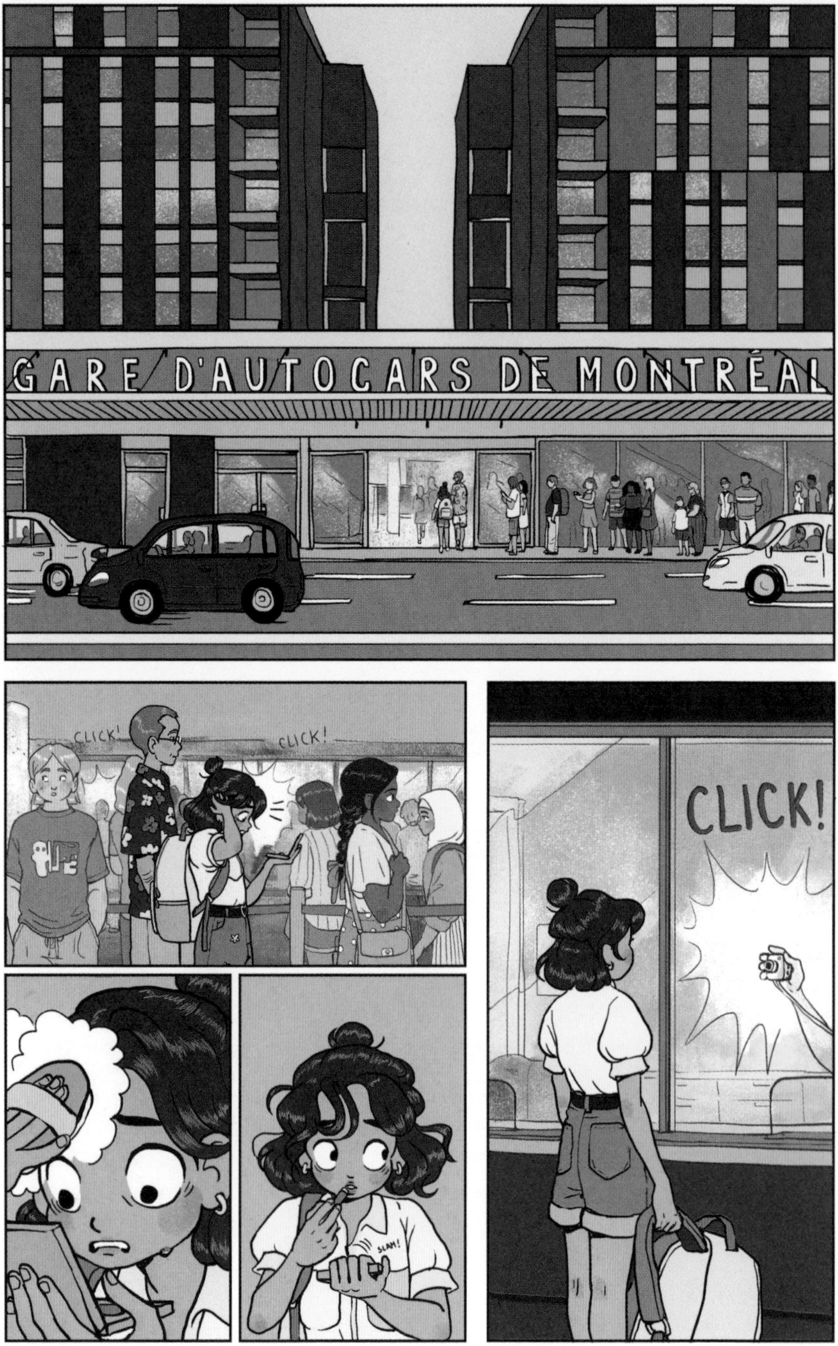
GARE D'AUTOCARS DE MONTRÉAL
CLICK!
CLICK!
CLICK!
SLAM!

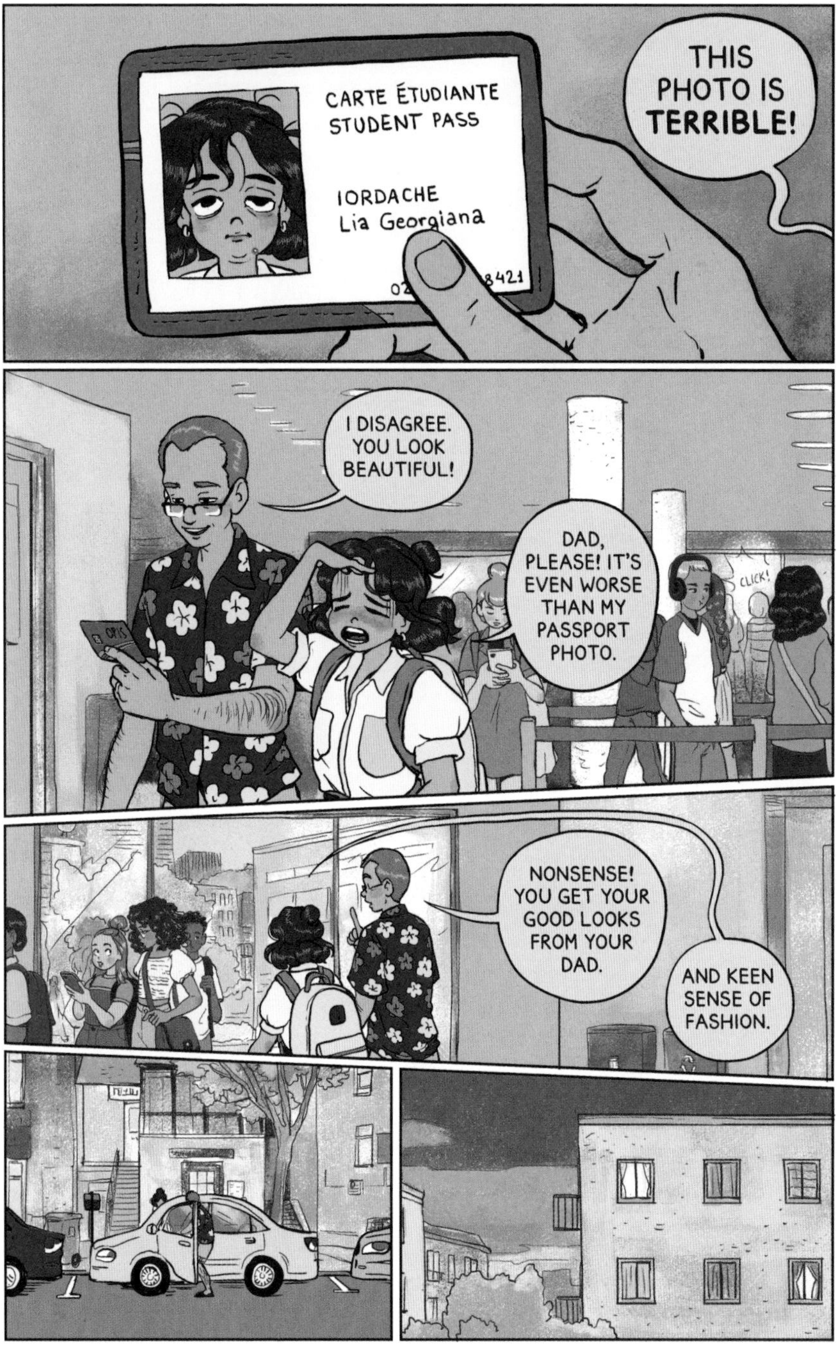
CARTE ÉTUDIANTE
STUDENT PASS
IORDACHE
Lia Georgiana
THIS PHOTO IS TERRIBLE!
I DISAGREE. YOU LOOK BEAUTIFUL!
DAD, PLEASE! IT'S EVEN WORSE THAN MY PASSPORT PHOTO.
CLICK!
NONSENSE! YOU GET YOUR GOOD LOOKS FROM YOUR DAD.
AND KEEN SENSE OF FASHION.

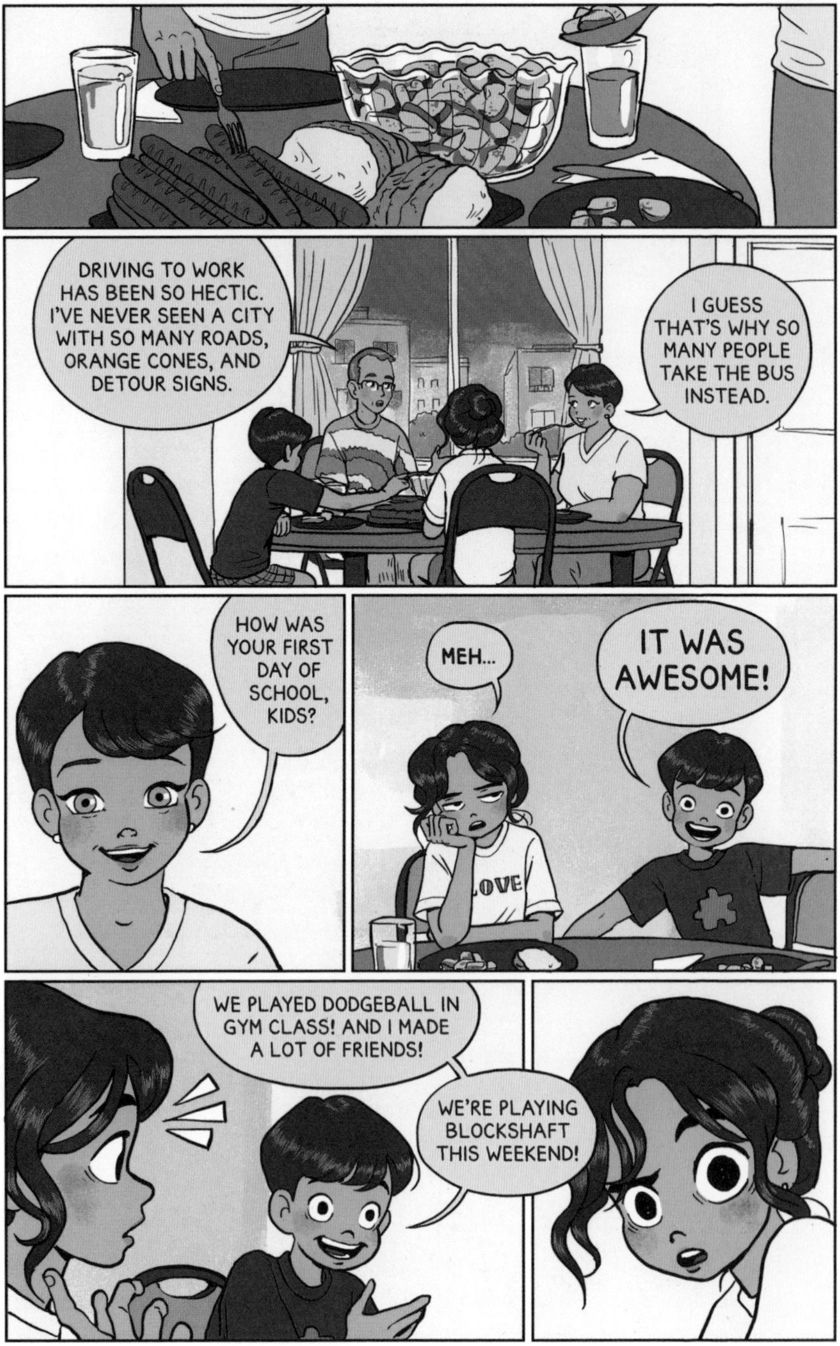
DRIVING TO WORK HAS BEEN SO HECTIC. I'VE NEVER SEEN A CITY WITH SO MANY ROADS, ORANGE CONES, AND DETOUR SIGNS.
I GUESS THAT'S WHY SO MANY PEOPLE TAKE THE BUS INSTEAD.
HOW WAS YOUR FIRST DAY OF SCHOOL, KIDS?
MEH...
IT WAS AWESOME!
LOVE
WE PLAYED DODGEBALL IN GYM CLASS! AND I MADE A LOT OF FRIENDS!
WE'RE PLAYING BLOCKSHAFT THIS WEEKEND!

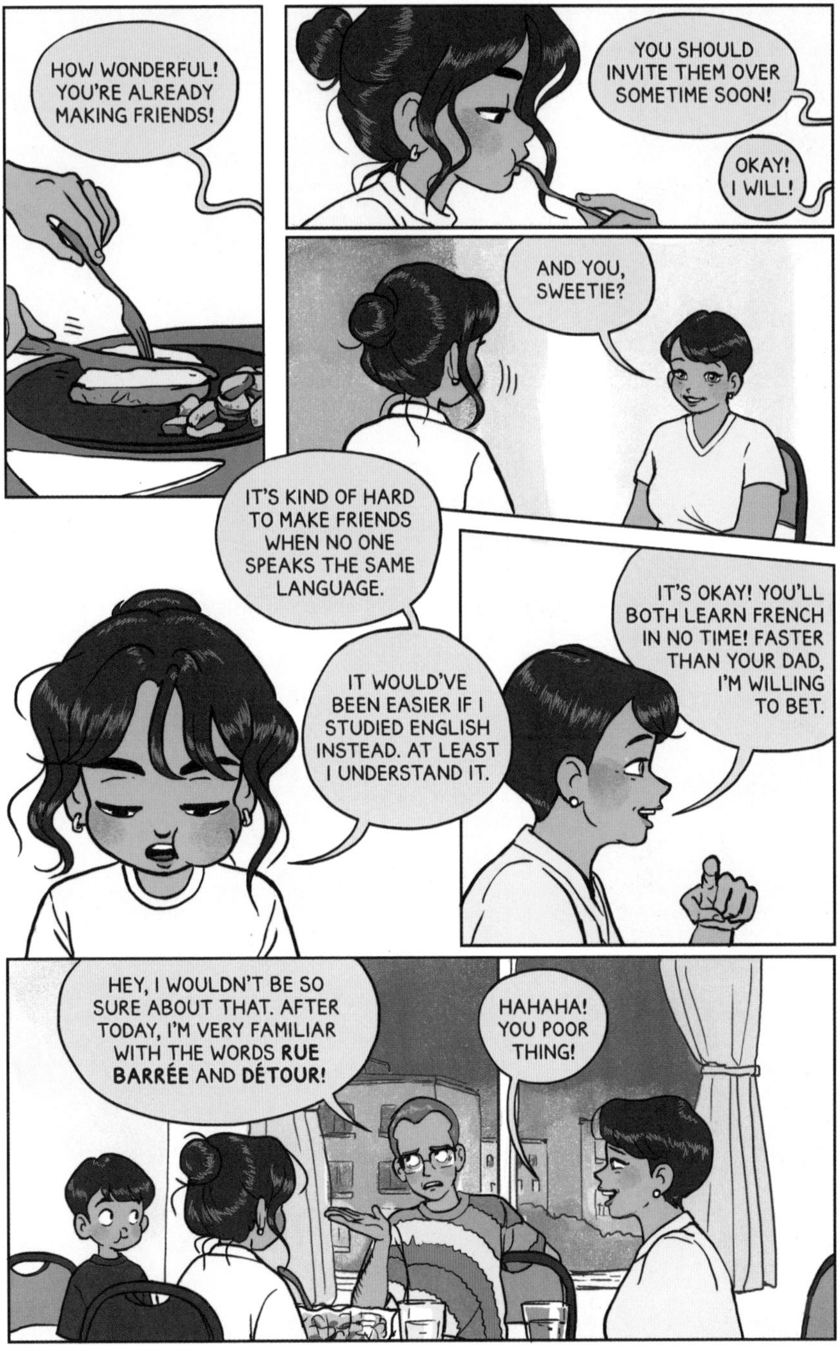
HOW WONDERFUL! YOU'RE ALREADY MAKING FRIENDS!
YOU SHOULD INVITE THEM OVER SOMETIME SOON!
OKAY! I WILL!
AND YOU, SWEETIE?
IT'S KIND OF HARD TO MAKE FRIENDS WHEN NO ONE SPEAKS THE SAME LANGUAGE.
IT WOULD'VE BEEN EASIER IF I STUDIED ENGLISH INSTEAD. AT LEAST I UNDERSTAND IT.
IT'S OKAY! YOU'LL BOTH LEARN FRENCH IN NO TIME! FASTER THAN YOUR DAD, I'M WILLING TO BET.
HEY, I WOULDN'T BE SO SURE ABOUT THAT. AFTER TODAY, I'M VERY FAMILIAR WITH THE WORDS **RUE BARRÉE** AND **DÉTOUR**!
HAHAHA! YOU POOR THING!

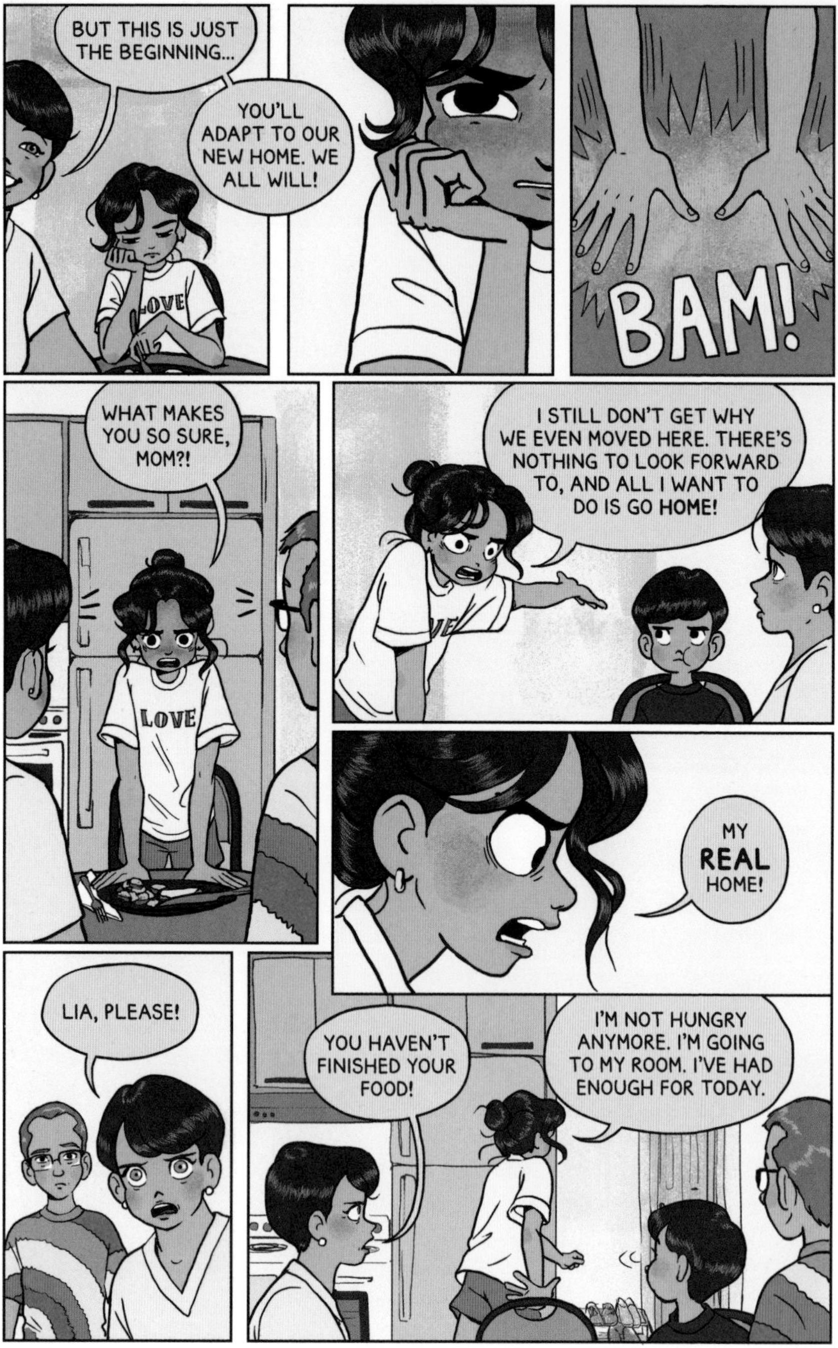

BUT THIS IS JUST THE BEGINNING...
YOU'LL ADAPT TO OUR NEW HOME. WE ALL WILL!
LOVE
BAM!
WHAT MAKES YOU SO SURE, MOM?!
LOVE
I STILL DON'T GET WHY WE EVEN MOVED HERE. THERE'S NOTHING TO LOOK FORWARD TO, AND ALL I WANT TO DO IS GO HOME!
MY REAL HOME!
LIA, PLEASE!
YOU HAVEN'T FINISHED YOUR FOOD!
I'M NOT HUNGRY ANYMORE. I'M GOING TO MY ROOM. I'VE HAD ENOUGH FOR TODAY.

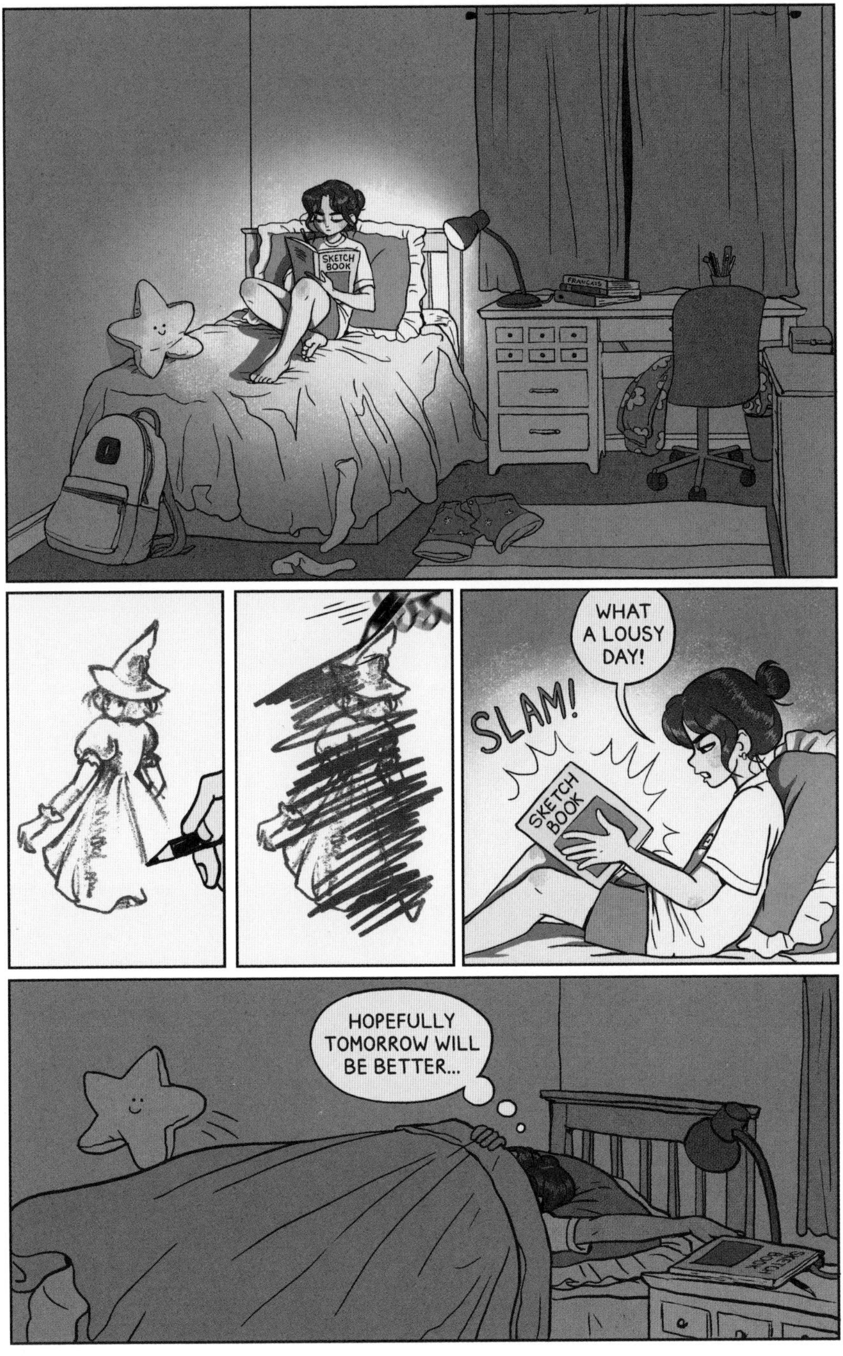
SKETCH BOOK
FRANÇAIS
SLAM!
WHAT A LOUSY DAY!
SKETCH BOOK
HOPEFULLY TOMORROW WILL BE BETTER...

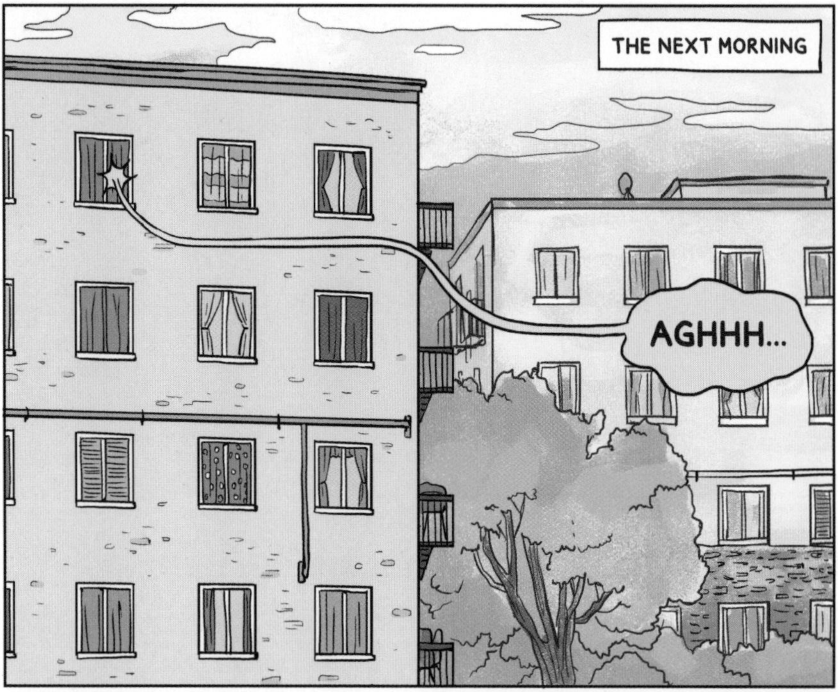
THE NEXT MORNING
AGHHH...

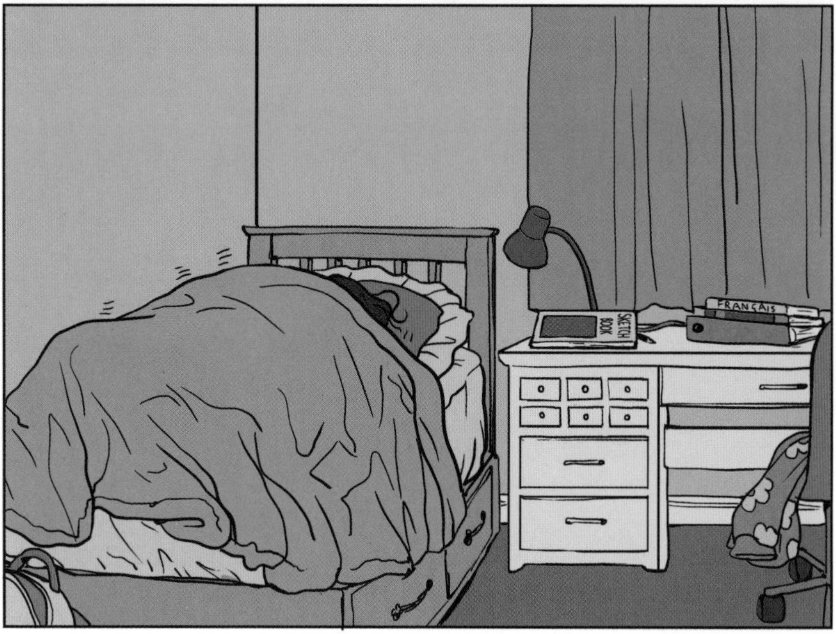
SKETCH BOOK
FRANÇAIS

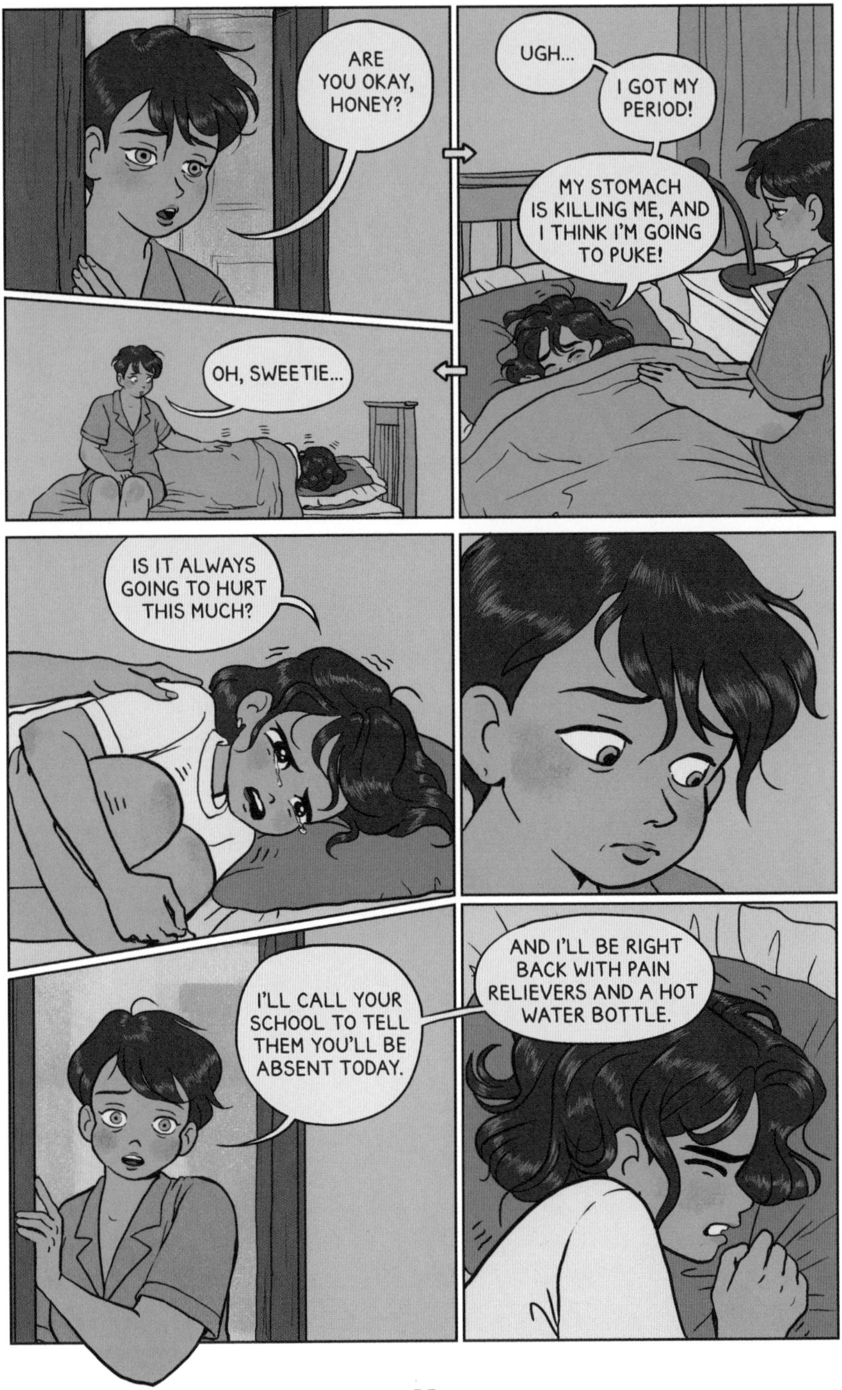
ARE YOU OKAY, HONEY?
UGH...
I GOT MY PERIOD!
MY STOMACH IS KILLING ME, AND I THINK I'M GOING TO PUKE!
OH, SWEETIE...
IS IT ALWAYS GOING TO HURT THIS MUCH?
I'LL CALL YOUR SCHOOL TO TELL THEM YOU'LL BE ABSENT TODAY.
AND I'LL BE RIGHT BACK WITH PAIN RELIEVERS AND A HOT WATER BOTTLE.

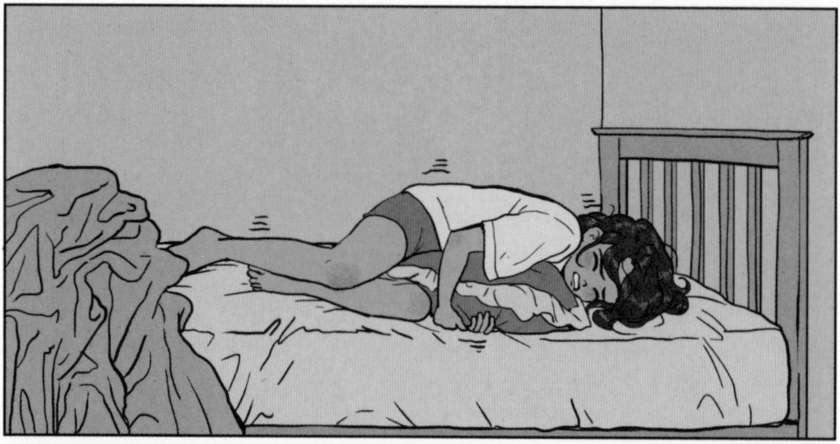

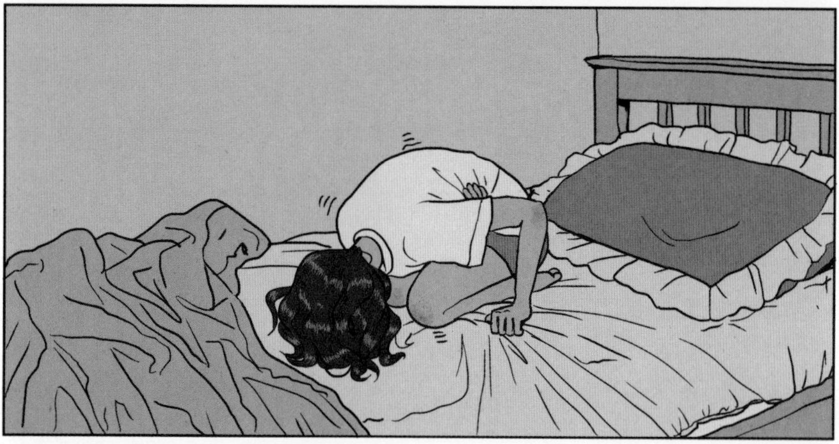

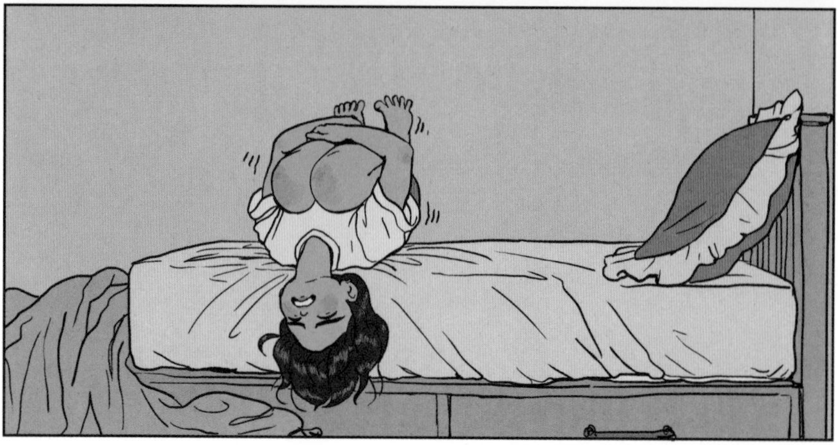

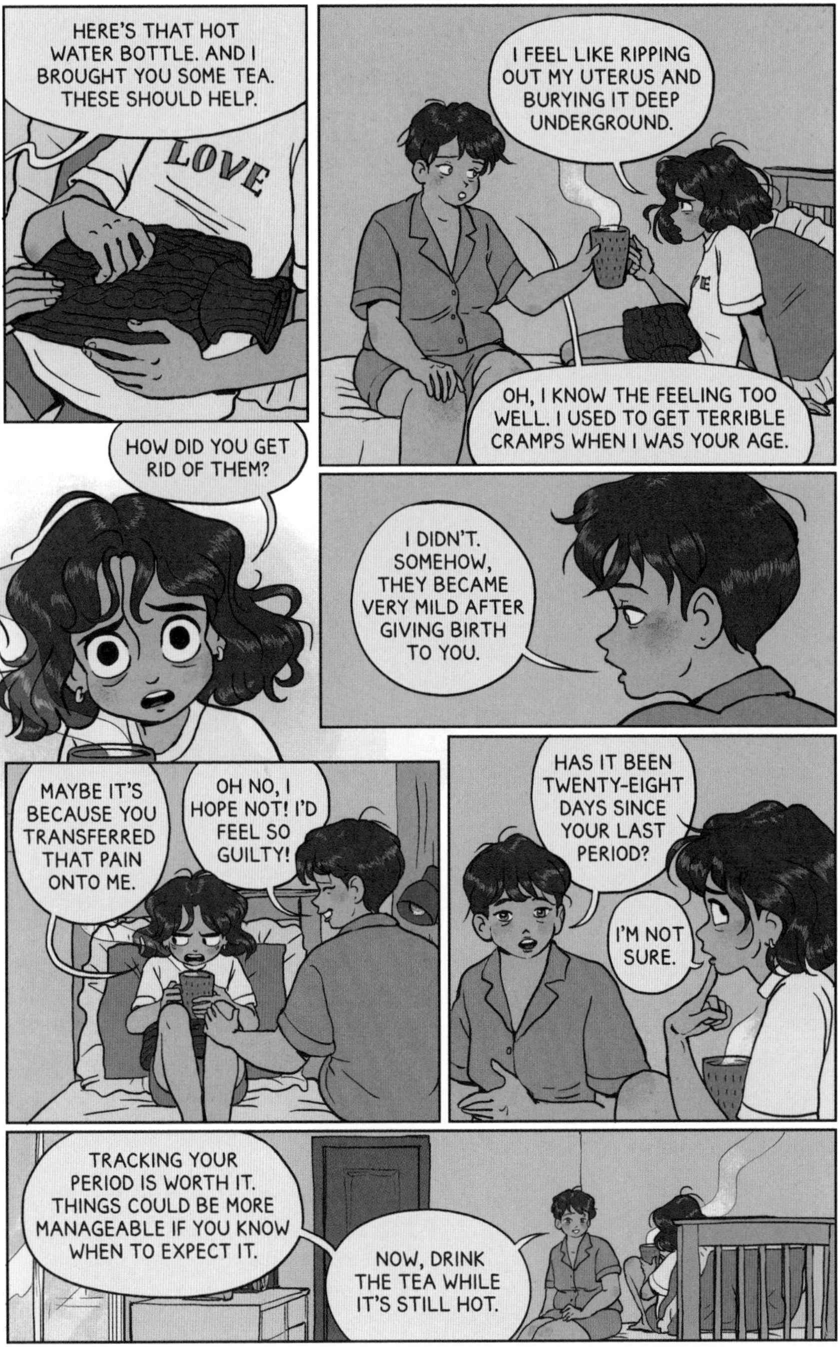
HERE'S THAT HOT WATER BOTTLE. AND I BROUGHT YOU SOME TEA. THESE SHOULD HELP.
LOVE
I FEEL LIKE RIPPING OUT MY UTERUS AND BURYING IT DEEP UNDERGROUND.
OH, I KNOW THE FEELING TOO WELL. I USED TO GET TERRIBLE CRAMPS WHEN I WAS YOUR AGE.
HOW DID YOU GET RID OF THEM?
I DIDN'T. SOMEHOW, THEY BECAME VERY MILD AFTER GIVING BIRTH TO YOU.
MAYBE IT'S BECAUSE YOU TRANSFERRED THAT PAIN ONTO ME.
OH NO, I HOPE NOT! I'D FEEL SO GUILTY!
HAS IT BEEN TWENTY-EIGHT DAYS SINCE YOUR LAST PERIOD?
I'M NOT SURE.
TRACKING YOUR PERIOD IS WORTH IT. THINGS COULD BE MORE MANAGEABLE IF YOU KNOW WHEN TO EXPECT IT.
NOW, DRINK THE TEA WHILE IT'S STILL HOT.

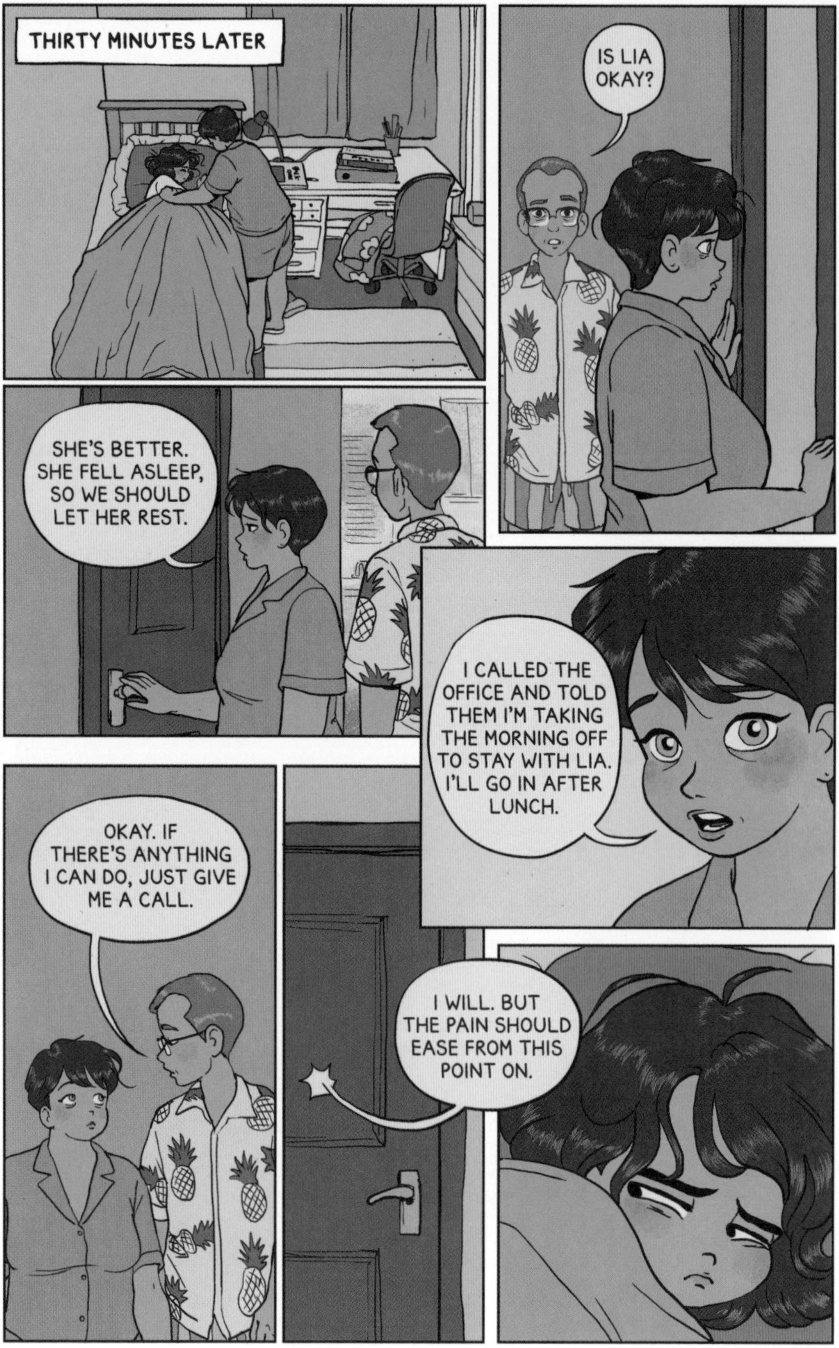
THIRTY MINUTES LATER
IS LIA OKAY?
SHE'S BETTER. SHE FELL ASLEEP, SO WE SHOULD LET HER REST.
I CALLED THE OFFICE AND TOLD THEM I'M TAKING THE MORNING OFF TO STAY WITH LIA. I'LL GO IN AFTER LUNCH.
OKAY. IF THERE'S ANYTHING I CAN DO, JUST GIVE ME A CALL.
I WILL. BUT THE PAIN SHOULD EASE FROM THIS POINT ON.

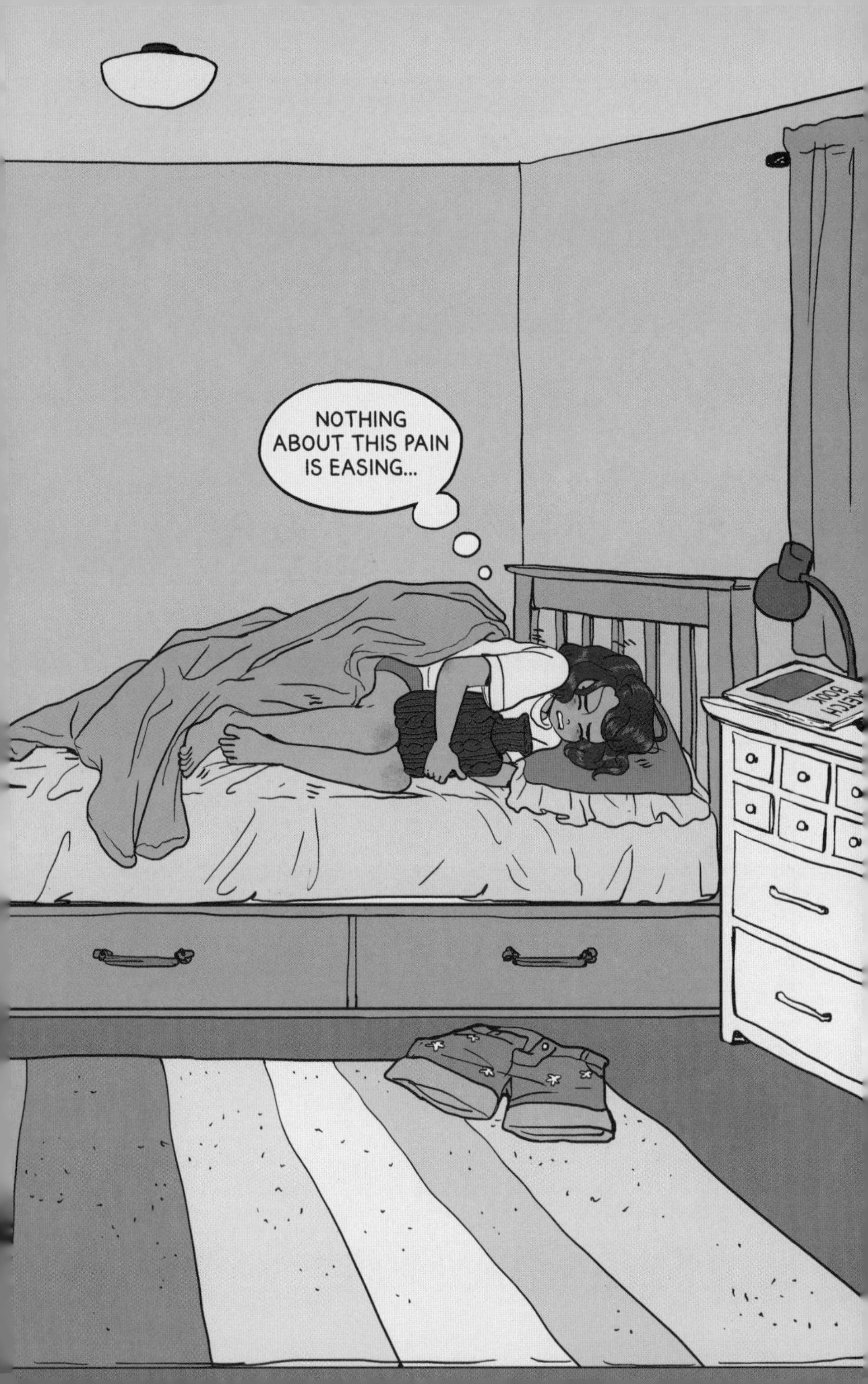
NOTHING ABOUT THIS PAIN IS EASING...

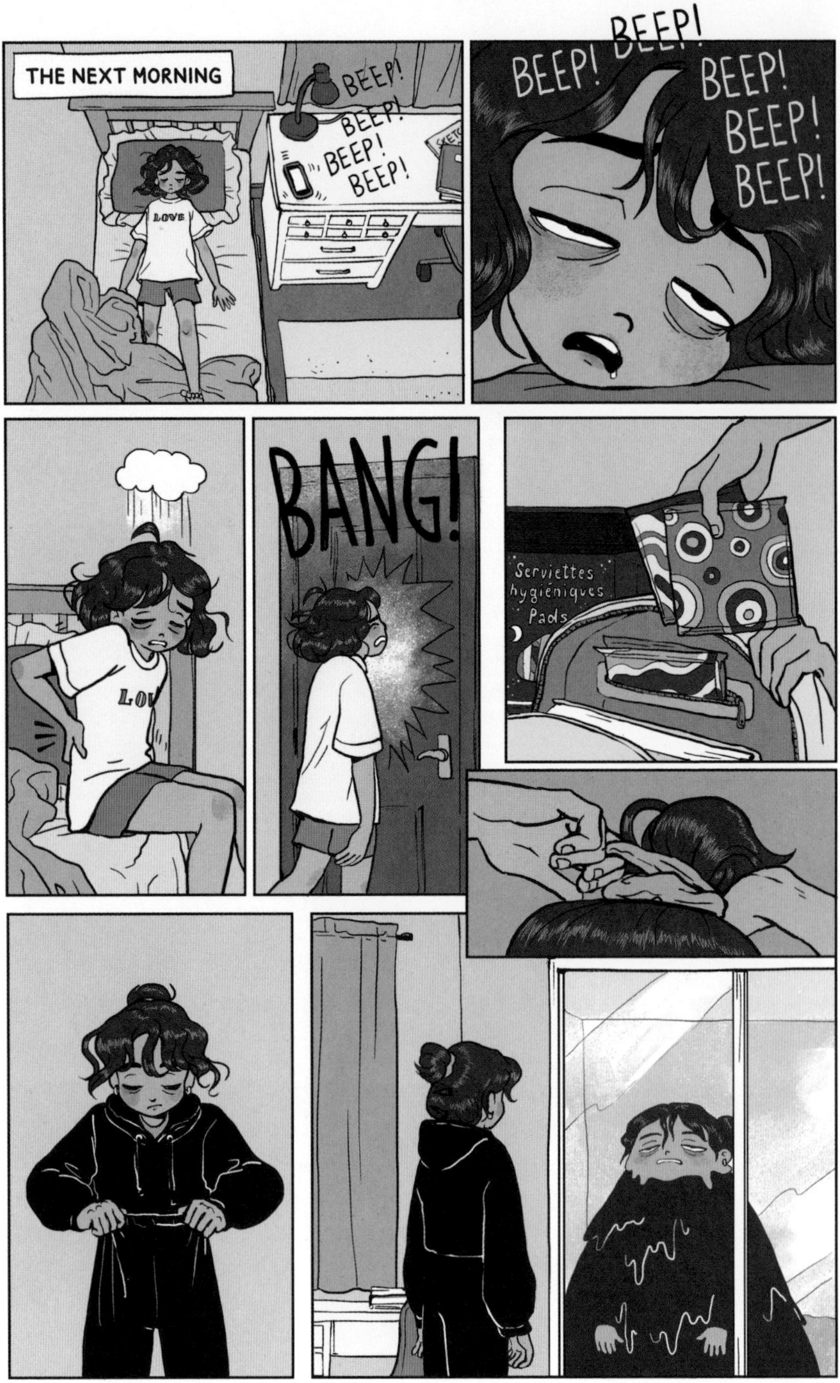
THE NEXT MORNING
BEEP!
BEEP!
BEEP!
BEEP!
BEEP!
BEEP!
BEEP!
BEEP!
BEEP!
BANG!
Serviettes hygiéniques
Pads

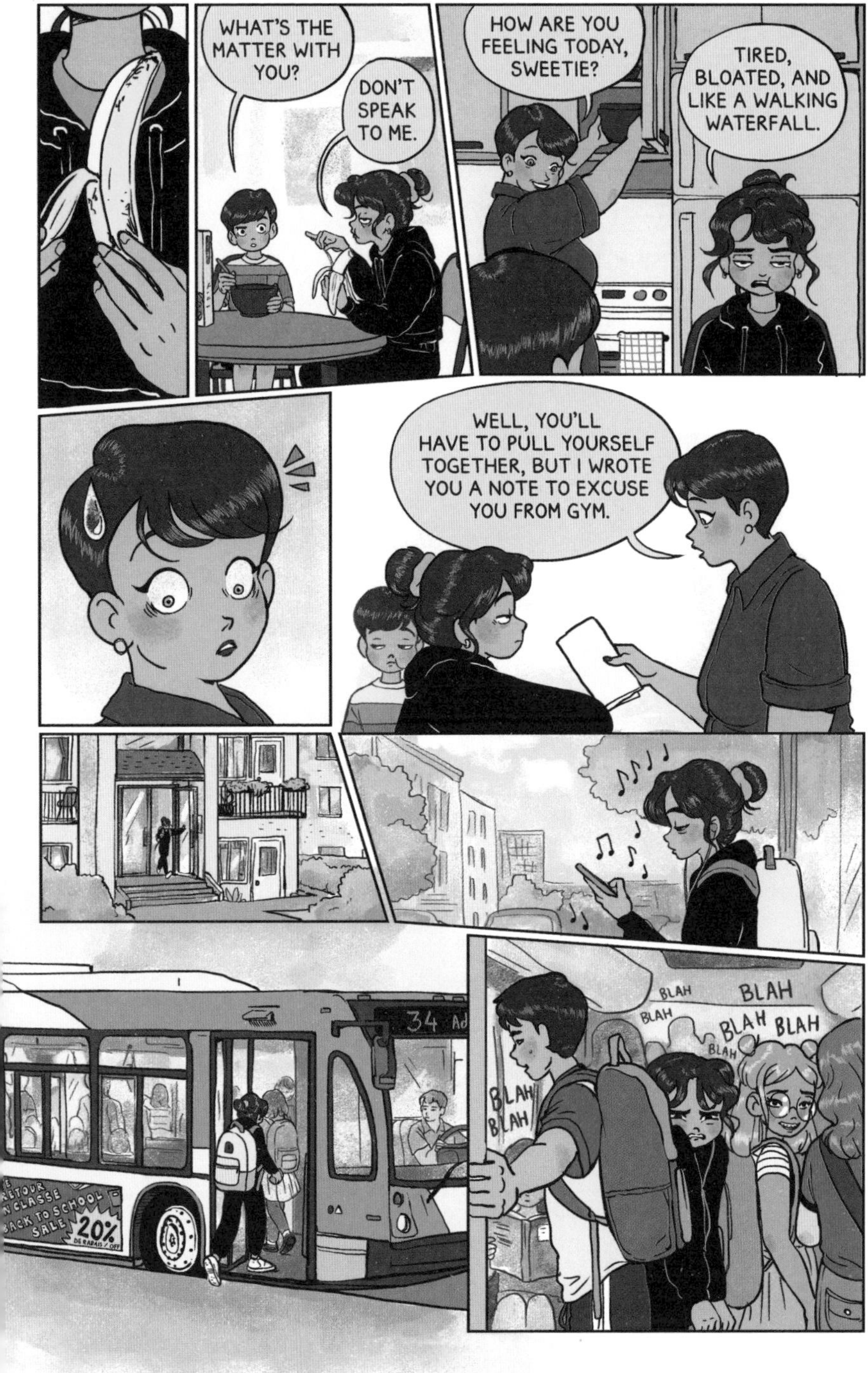
WHAT'S THE MATTER WITH YOU?
DON'T SPEAK TO ME.
HOW ARE YOU FEELING TODAY, SWEETIE?
TIRED, BLOATED, AND LIKE A WALKING WATERFALL.
WELL, YOU'LL HAVE TO PULL YOURSELF TOGETHER, BUT I WROTE YOU A NOTE TO EXCUSE YOU FROM GYM.
34
BACK TO SCHOOL SALE
20%
BLAH
BLAH
BLAH
BLAH BLAH
BLAH
BLAH
BLAH

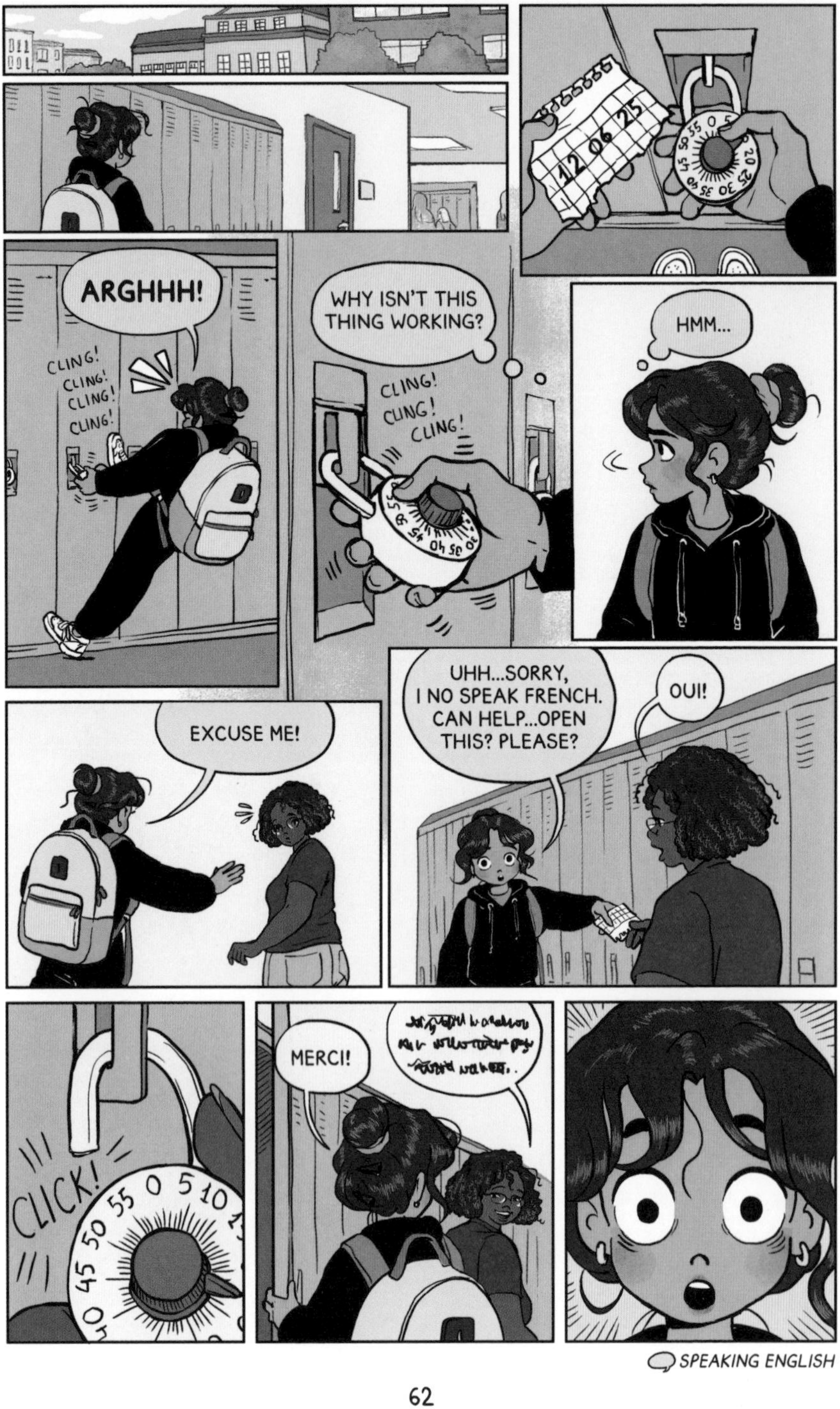
ARGHHH!
CLING! CLING! CLING! CLING!
WHY ISN'T THIS THING WORKING?
CLING! CLING! CLING!
HMM...
EXCUSE ME!
UHH...SORRY, I NO SPEAK FRENCH. CAN HELP...OPEN THIS? PLEASE?
OUI!
CLICK!
MERCI!
SPEAKING ENGLISH

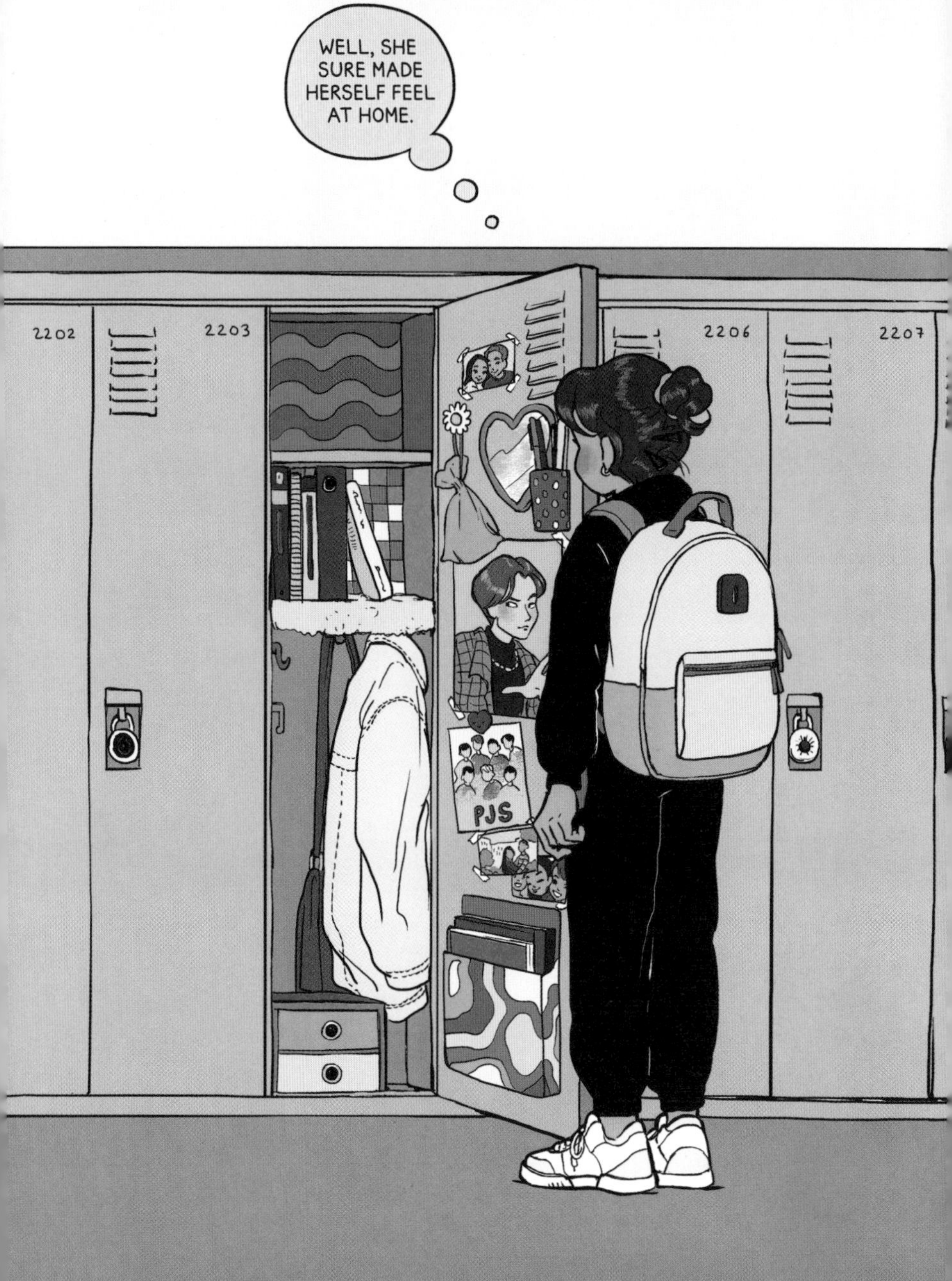
WELL, SHE SURE MADE HERSELF FEEL AT HOME.
2202
2203
2206
2207
PJS

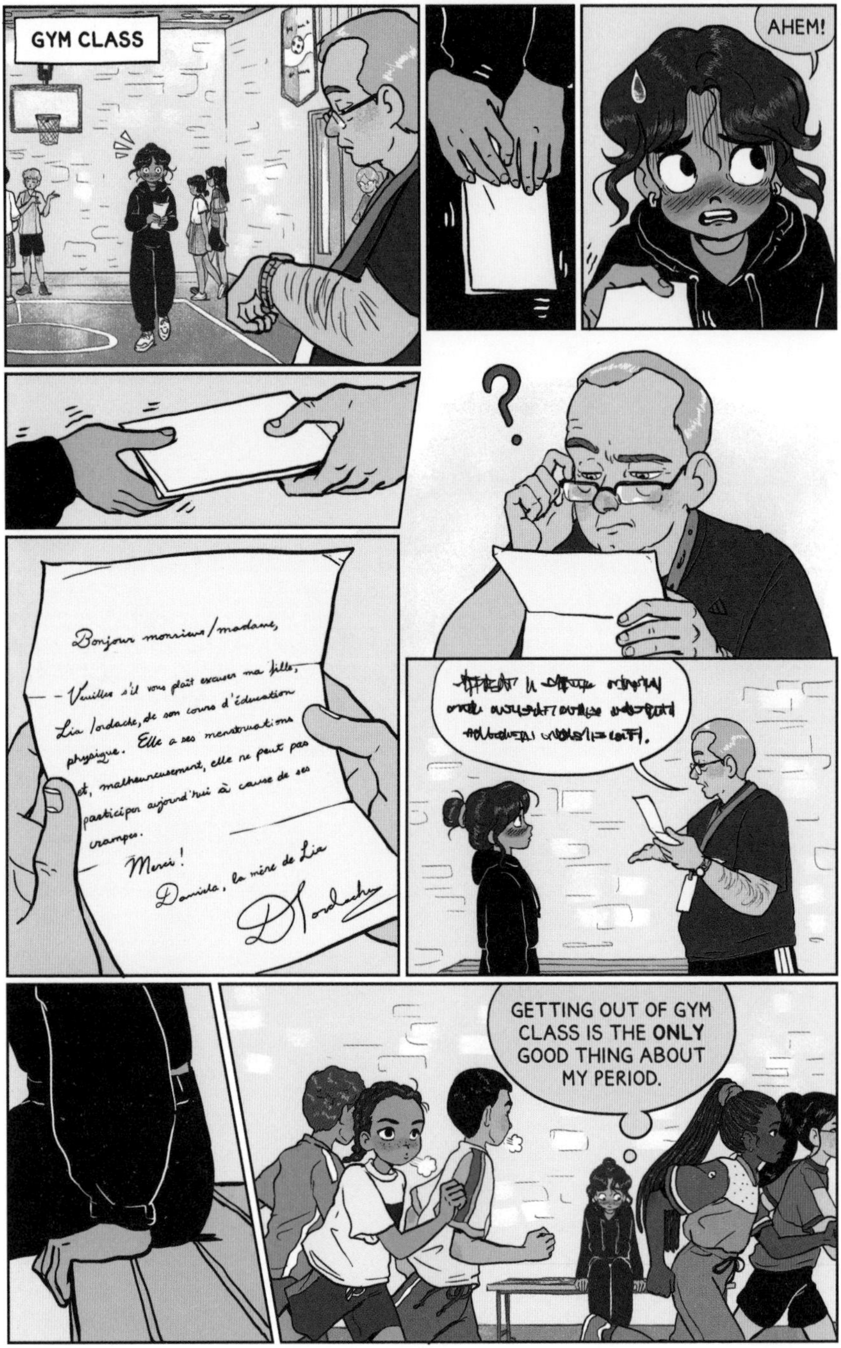
GYM CLASS
AHEM!
Bonjour monsieur/madame,
Veuillez s'il vous plaît excuser ma fille, Lia Iordache, de son cours d'éducation physique. Elle a ses menstruations et, malheureusement, elle ne peut pas participer aujourd'hui à cause de ses crampes.
Merci!
Daniela, la mère de Lia
D Iordache
GETTING OUT OF GYM CLASS IS THE **ONLY** GOOD THING ABOUT MY PERIOD.

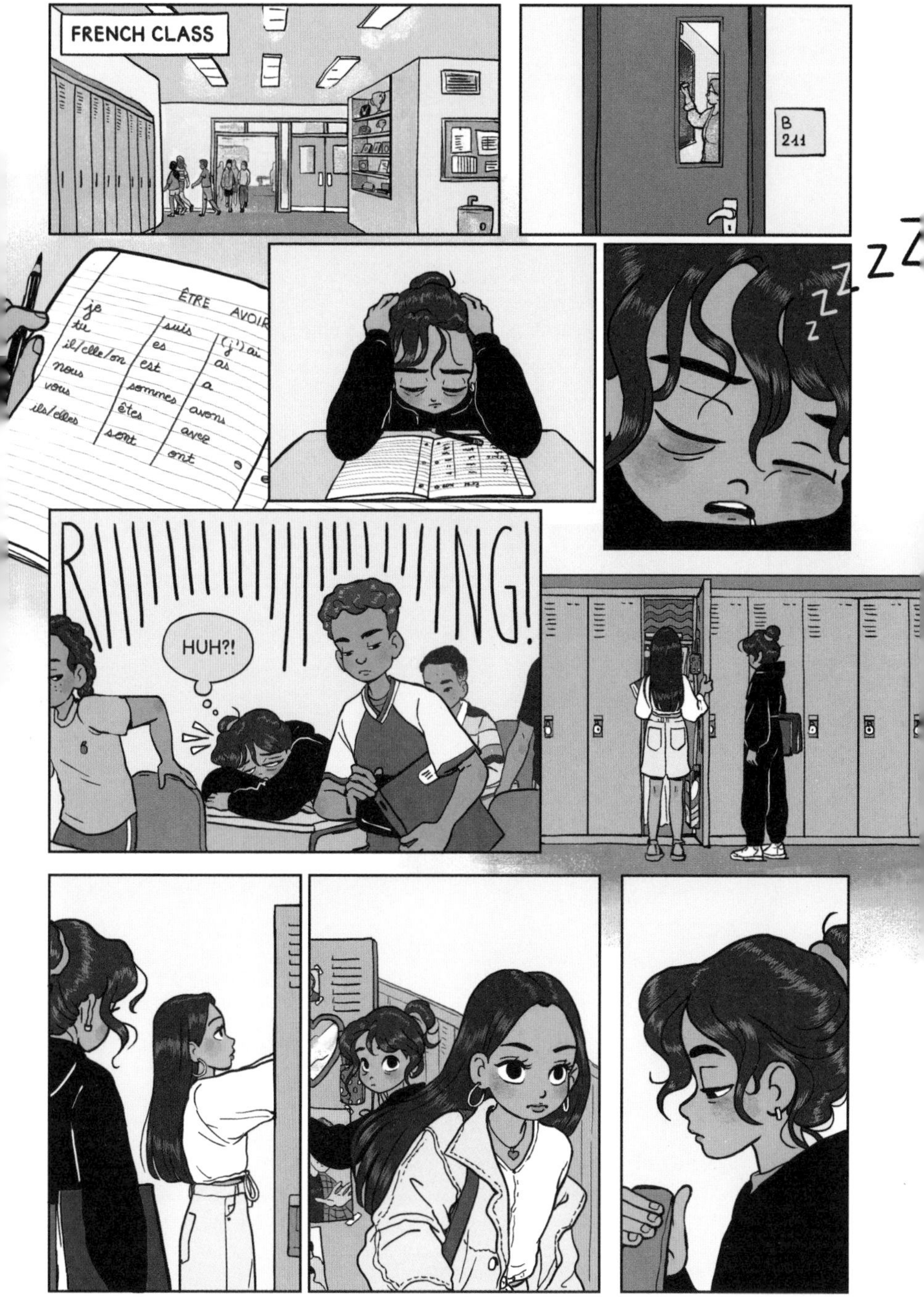

FRENCH CLASS
B 211
ÊTRE AVOIR
je suis (j') ai
tu es as
il/elle/on est a
nous sommes avons
vous êtes avez
ils/elles sont ont
ZZZZZ
RIIIIIIIIIIIIIIIIING!
HUH?!

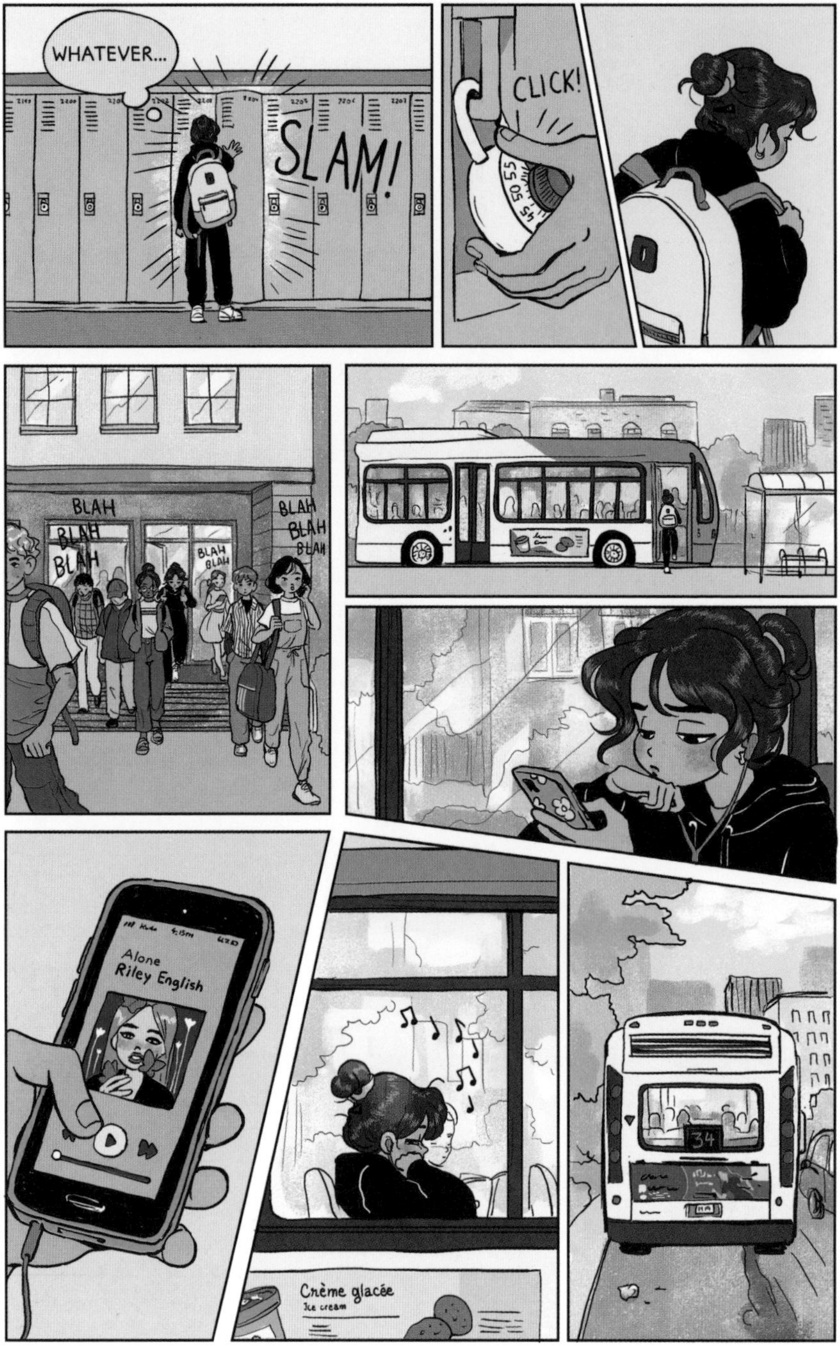
WHATEVER...
SLAM!
CLICK!
BLAH
BLAH
BLAH
BLAH
BLAH
BLAH
BLAH
BLAH
Alone
Riley English
Crème glacée
Ice cream
34

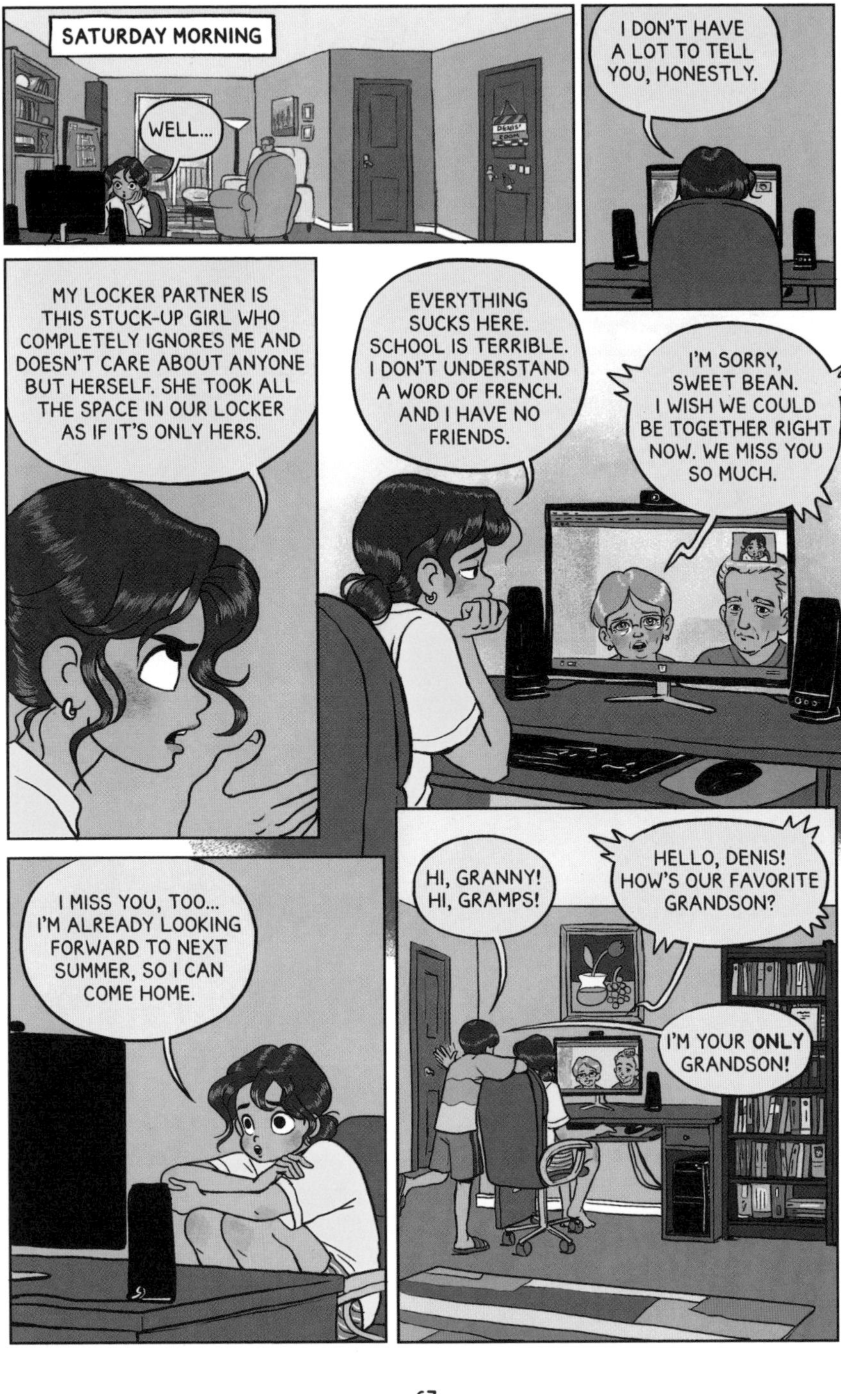
SATURDAY MORNING
WELL...
I DON'T HAVE A LOT TO TELL YOU, HONESTLY.
MY LOCKER PARTNER IS THIS STUCK-UP GIRL WHO COMPLETELY IGNORES ME AND DOESN'T CARE ABOUT ANYONE BUT HERSELF. SHE TOOK ALL THE SPACE IN OUR LOCKER AS IF IT'S ONLY HERS.
EVERYTHING SUCKS HERE. SCHOOL IS TERRIBLE. I DON'T UNDERSTAND A WORD OF FRENCH. AND I HAVE NO FRIENDS.
I'M SORRY, SWEET BEAN. I WISH WE COULD BE TOGETHER RIGHT NOW. WE MISS YOU SO MUCH.
I MISS YOU, TOO... I'M ALREADY LOOKING FORWARD TO NEXT SUMMER, SO I CAN COME HOME.
HI, GRANNY! HI, GRAMPS!
HELLO, DENIS! HOW'S OUR FAVORITE GRANDSON?
I'M YOUR **ONLY** GRANDSON!

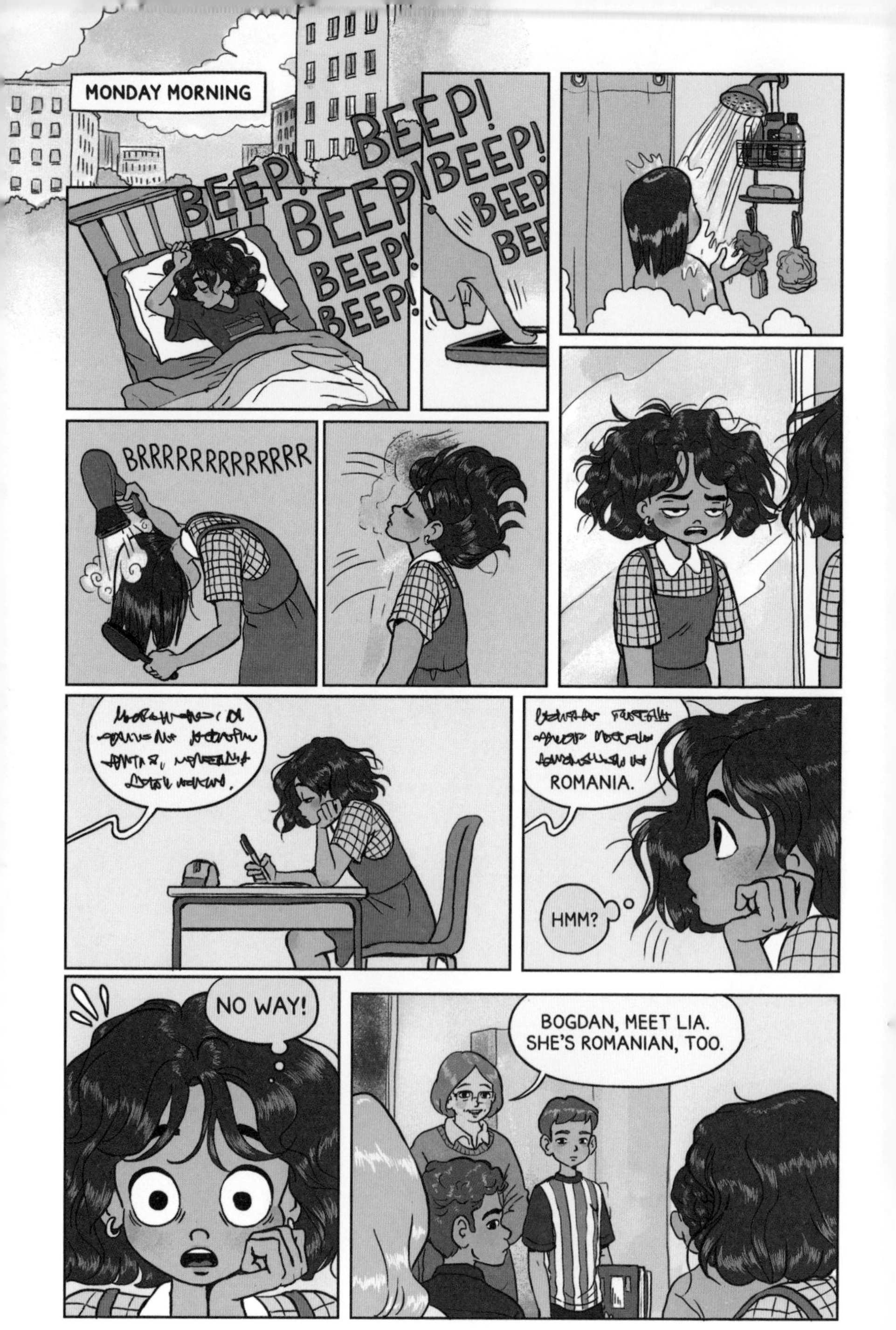
MONDAY MORNING
BEEP! BEEP! BEEP! BEEP! BEEP!
BEEP!
BEEP! BEEP!
BRRRRRRRRRRRR
ROMANIA.
HMM?
NO WAY!
BOGDAN, MEET LIA. SHE'S ROMANIAN, TOO.

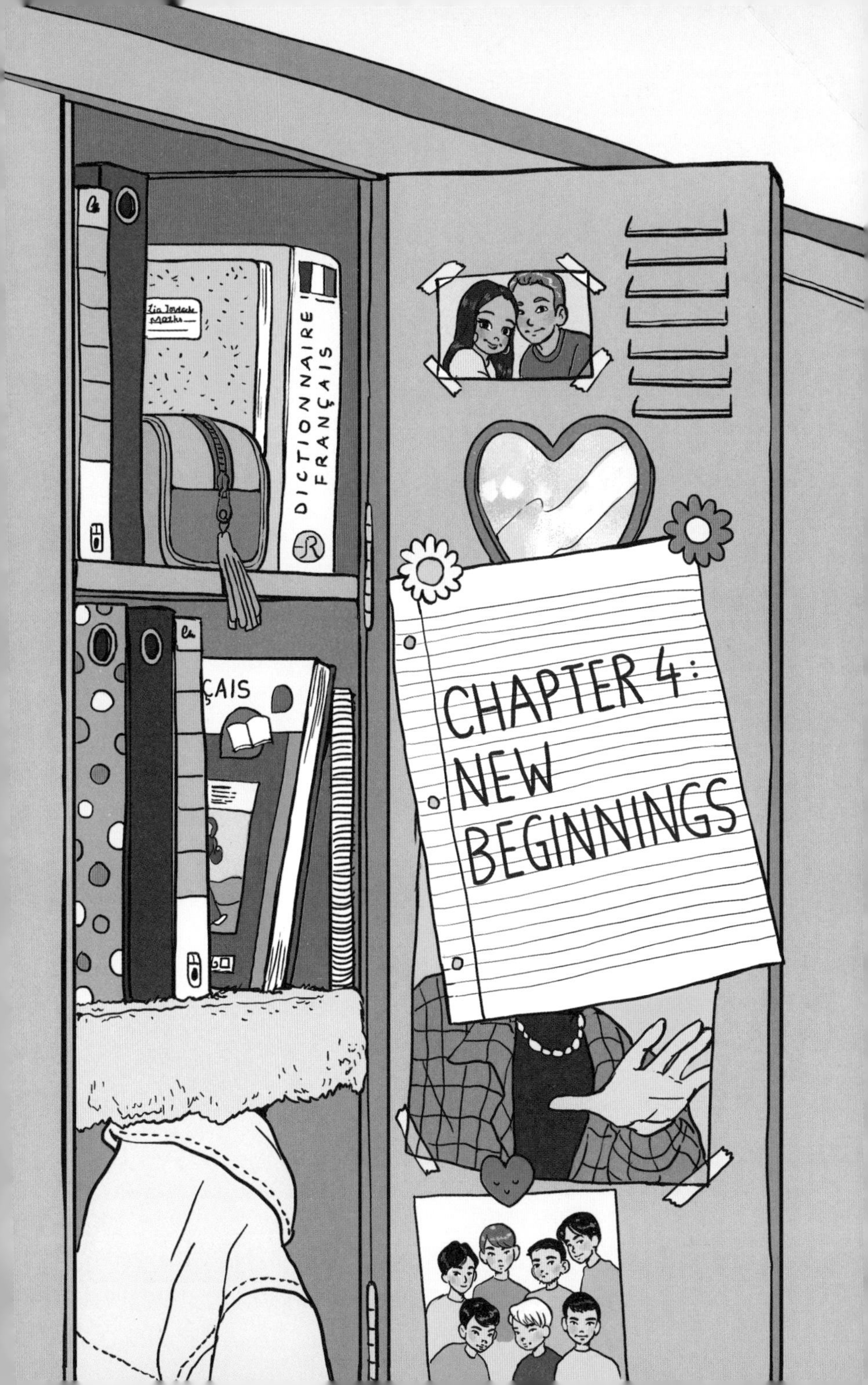
CHAPTER 4:
NEW
BEGINNINGS
DICTIONNAIRE
FRANÇAIS
ÇAIS

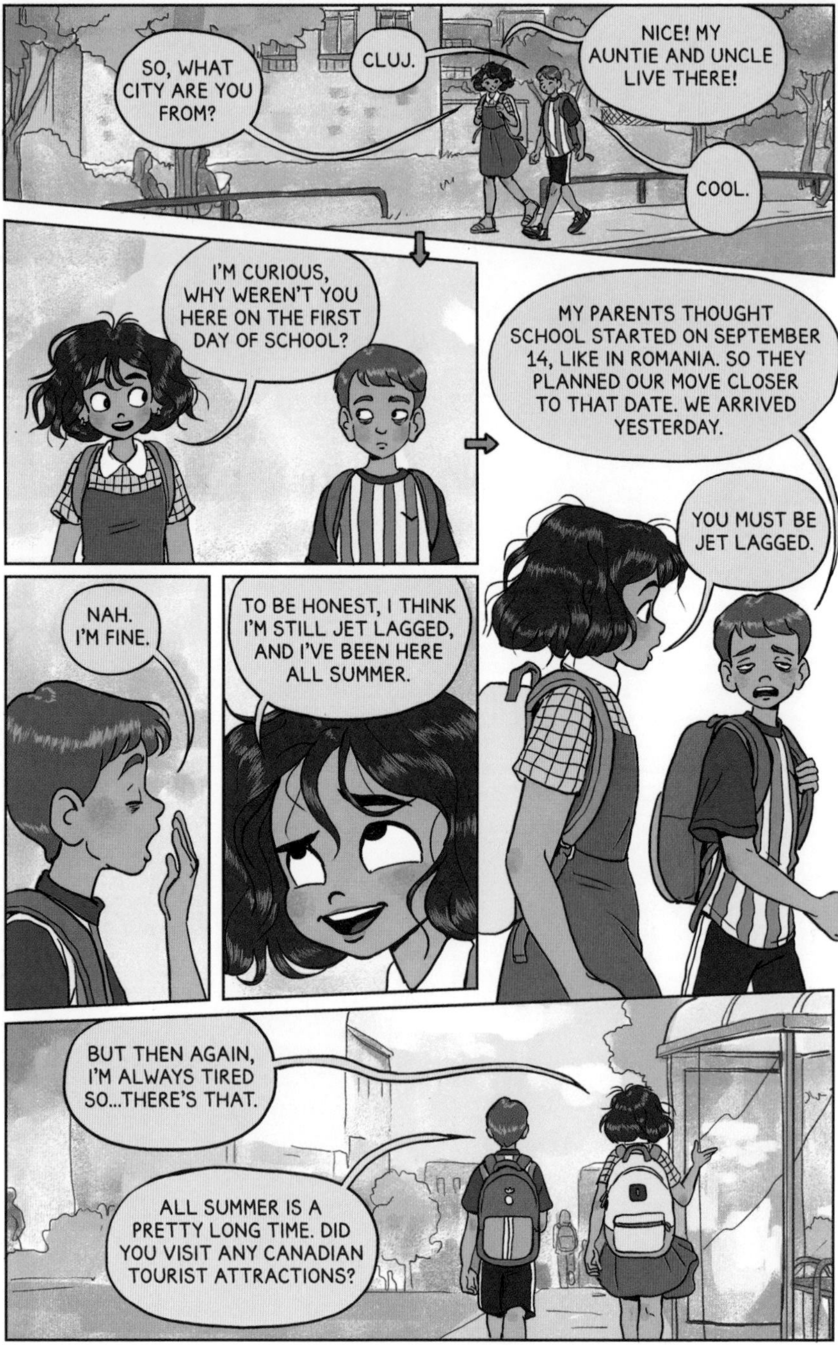
SO, WHAT CITY ARE YOU FROM?
CLUJ.
NICE! MY AUNTIE AND UNCLE LIVE THERE!
COOL.
I'M CURIOUS, WHY WEREN'T YOU HERE ON THE FIRST DAY OF SCHOOL?
MY PARENTS THOUGHT SCHOOL STARTED ON SEPTEMBER 14, LIKE IN ROMANIA. SO THEY PLANNED OUR MOVE CLOSER TO THAT DATE. WE ARRIVED YESTERDAY.
YOU MUST BE JET LAGGED.
NAH. I'M FINE.
TO BE HONEST, I THINK I'M STILL JET LAGGED, AND I'VE BEEN HERE ALL SUMMER.
BUT THEN AGAIN, I'M ALWAYS TIRED SO...THERE'S THAT.
ALL SUMMER IS A PRETTY LONG TIME. DID YOU VISIT ANY CANADIAN TOURIST ATTRACTIONS?

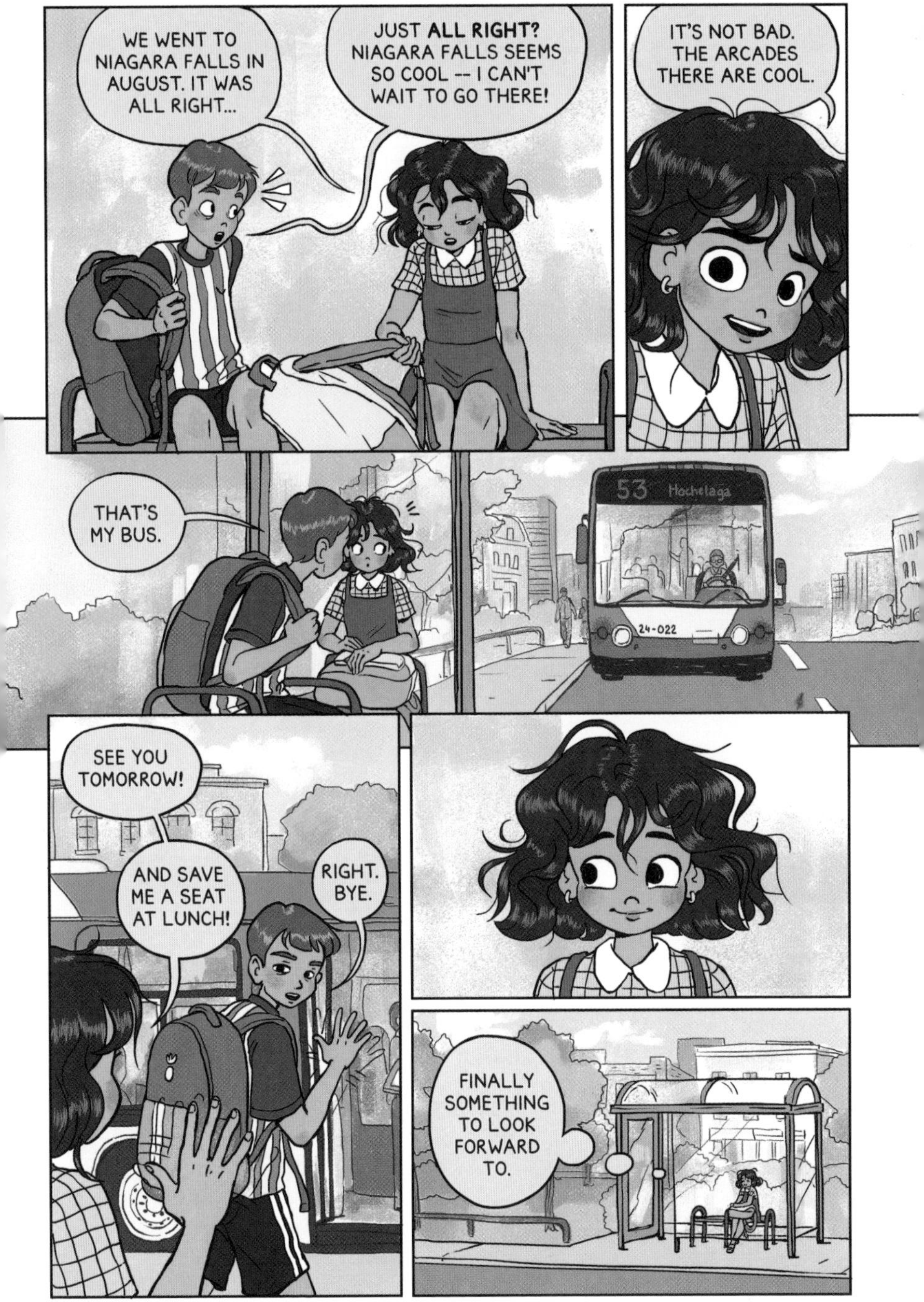
WE WENT TO NIAGARA FALLS IN AUGUST. IT WAS ALL RIGHT...
JUST **ALL RIGHT?** NIAGARA FALLS SEEMS SO COOL -- I CAN'T WAIT TO GO THERE!
IT'S NOT BAD. THE ARCADES THERE ARE COOL.
THAT'S MY BUS.
53 Hochelaga
24-022
SEE YOU TOMORROW!
AND SAVE ME A SEAT AT LUNCH!
RIGHT. BYE.
FINALLY SOMETHING TO LOOK FORWARD TO.

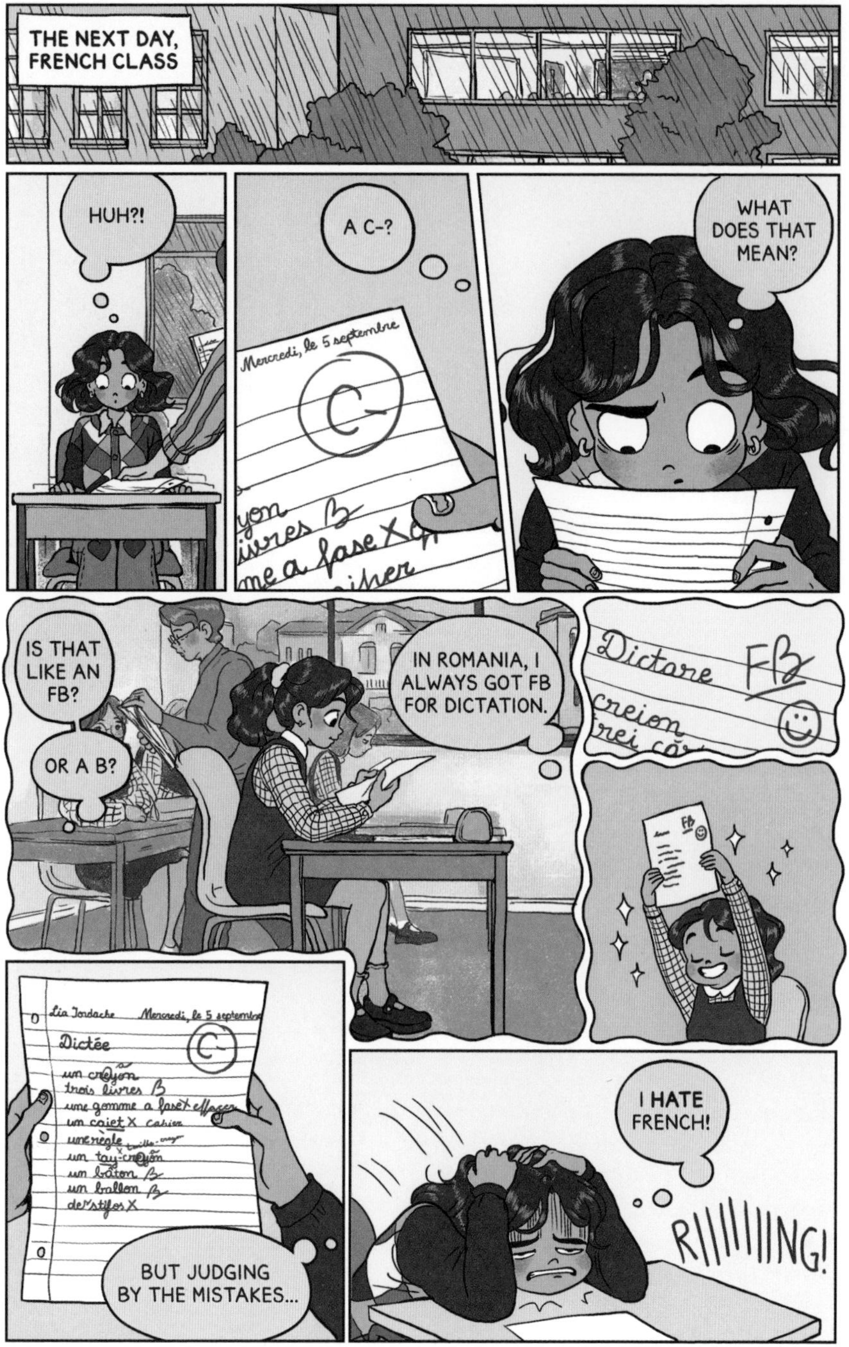
THE NEXT DAY, FRENCH CLASS
HUH?!
A C-?
Mercredi, le 5 septembre
WHAT DOES THAT MEAN?
IS THAT LIKE AN FB?
OR A B?
IN ROMANIA, I ALWAYS GOT FB FOR DICTATION.
Dictare FB
creion
Lia Iordache Mercredi, le 5 septembre
Dictée
un crayon
trois livres B
une gomme a fase X effacer
un caiet X cahier
une règle
un tay-creyon X taille-crayon
un bâton B
un ballon B
des stifos X
BUT JUDGING BY THE MISTAKES...
I HATE FRENCH!
RIIIIIING!

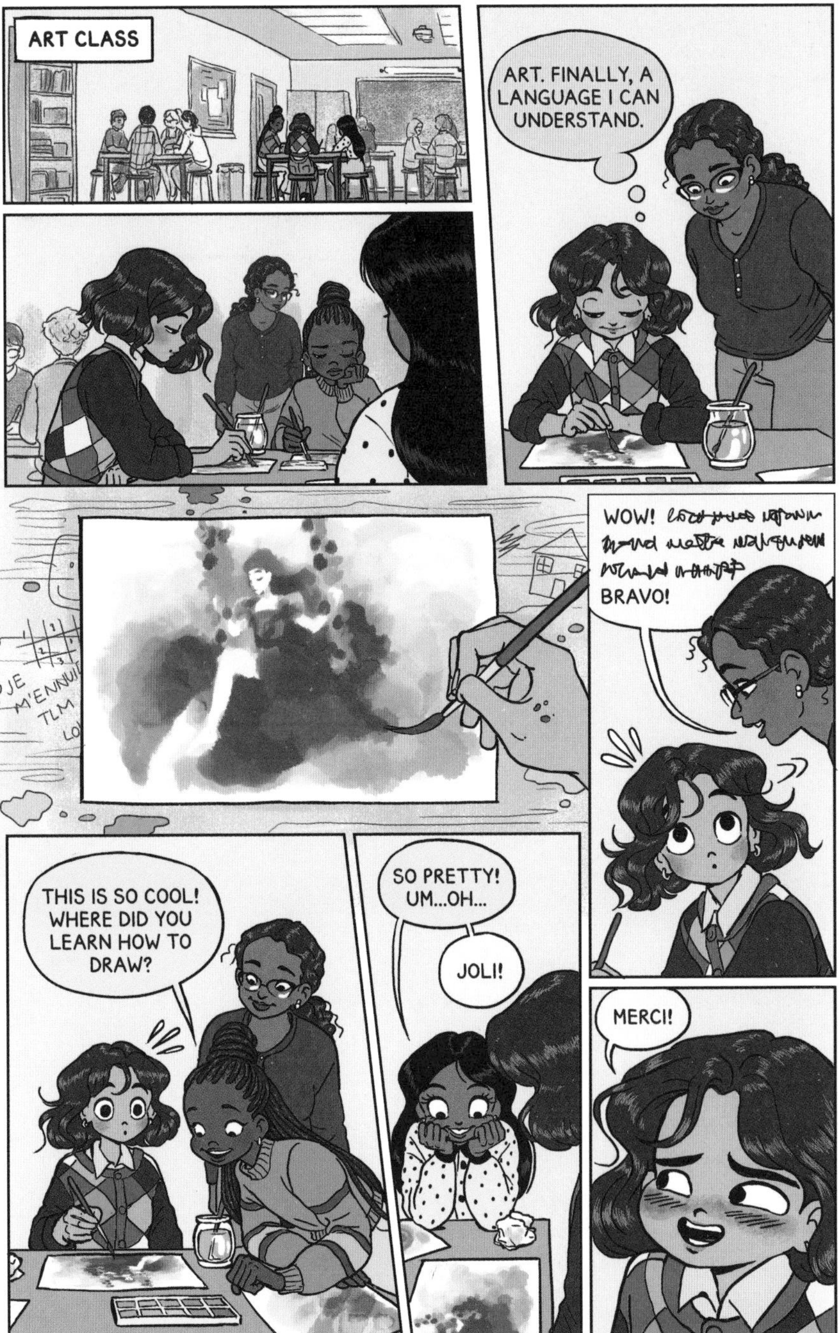
ART CLASS
ART. FINALLY, A LANGUAGE I CAN UNDERSTAND.
WOW!
BRAVO!
THIS IS SO COOL! WHERE DID YOU LEARN HOW TO DRAW?
SO PRETTY! UM...OH...
JOLI!
MERCI!

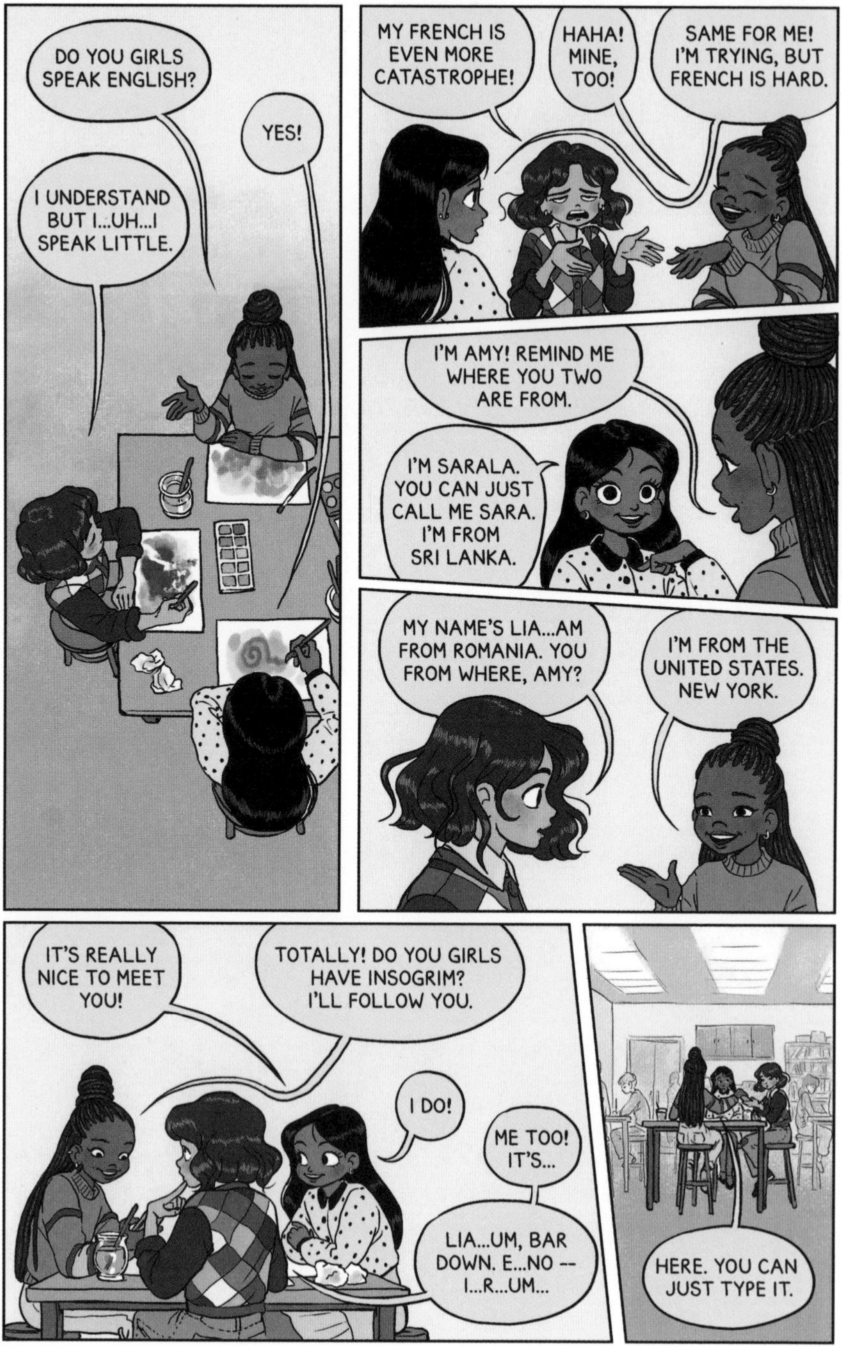
DO YOU GIRLS SPEAK ENGLISH?
YES!
I UNDERSTAND BUT I...UH...I SPEAK LITTLE.
MY FRENCH IS EVEN MORE CATASTROPHE!
HAHA! MINE, TOO!
SAME FOR ME! I'M TRYING, BUT FRENCH IS HARD.
I'M AMY! REMIND ME WHERE YOU TWO ARE FROM.
I'M SARALA. YOU CAN JUST CALL ME SARA. I'M FROM SRI LANKA.
MY NAME'S LIA...AM FROM ROMANIA. YOU FROM WHERE, AMY?
I'M FROM THE UNITED STATES. NEW YORK.
IT'S REALLY NICE TO MEET YOU!
TOTALLY! DO YOU GIRLS HAVE INSOGRIM? I'LL FOLLOW YOU.
I DO!
ME TOO! IT'S...
LIA...UM, BAR DOWN. E...NO -- I...R...UM...
HERE. YOU CAN JUST TYPE IT.

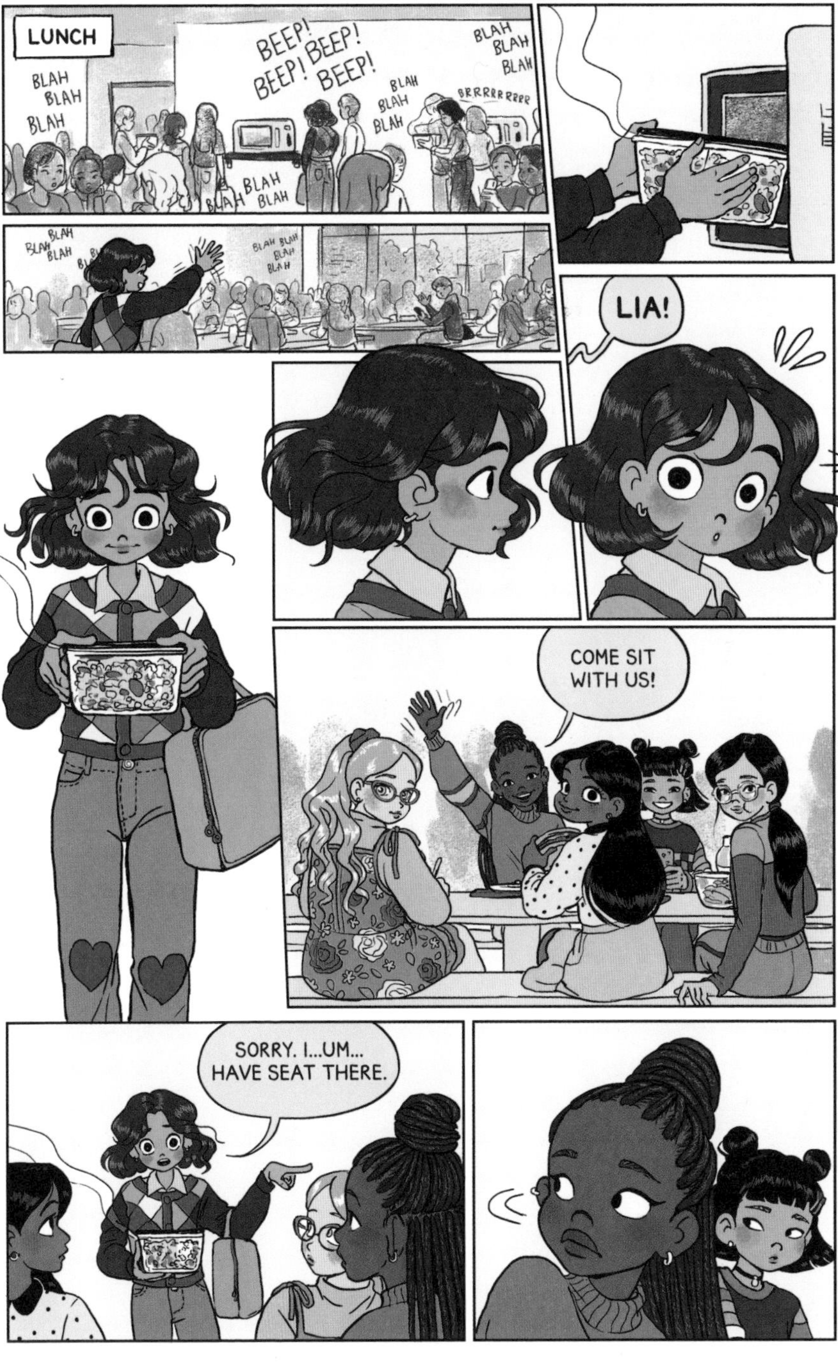
LUNCH
BLAH BLAH BLAH
BEEP! BEEP! BEEP! BEEP!
BLAH BLAH BLAH
BLAH BLAH BLAH
BRRRRRRRRR
BLAH BLAH BLAH
BLAH BLAH
BLAH BLAH BLAH
BLAH BLAH BLAH
LIA!
COME SIT WITH US!
SORRY. I...UM... HAVE SEAT THERE.

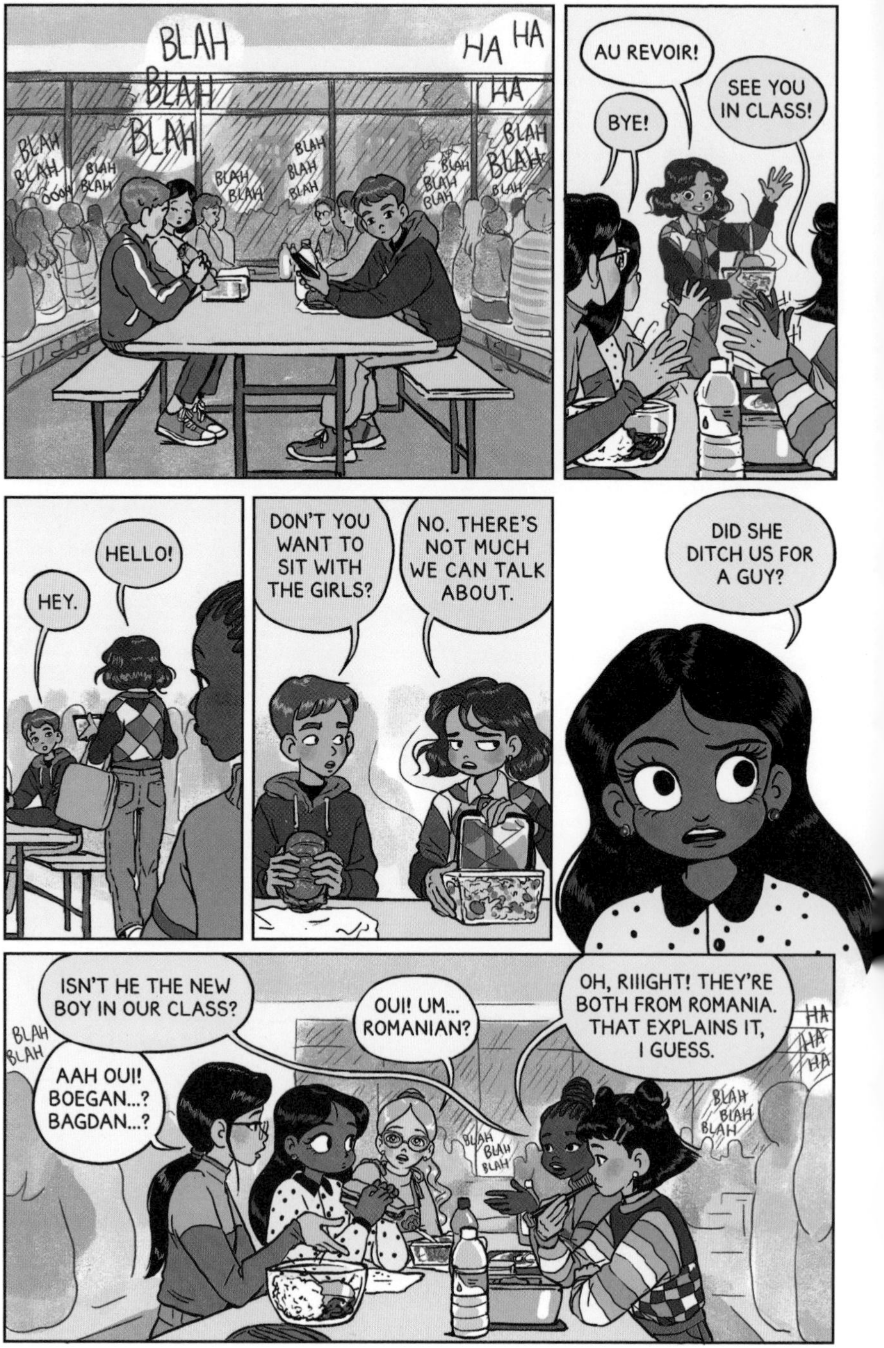
BLAH BLAH BLAH
HA HA HA
BLAH BLAH
BLAH BLAH
BLAH BLAH
BLAH BLAH BLAH
BLAH BLAH BLAH
AU REVOIR!
BYE!
SEE YOU IN CLASS!
HEY.
HELLO!
DON'T YOU WANT TO SIT WITH THE GIRLS?
NO. THERE'S NOT MUCH WE CAN TALK ABOUT.
DID SHE DITCH US FOR A GUY?
BLAH BLAH
ISN'T HE THE NEW BOY IN OUR CLASS?
AAH OUI! BOEGAN...? BAGDAN...?
OUI! UM... ROMANIAN?
OH, RIIIGHT! THEY'RE BOTH FROM ROMANIA. THAT EXPLAINS IT, I GUESS.
BLAH BLAH BLAH
BLAH BLAH BLAH
HA HA HA

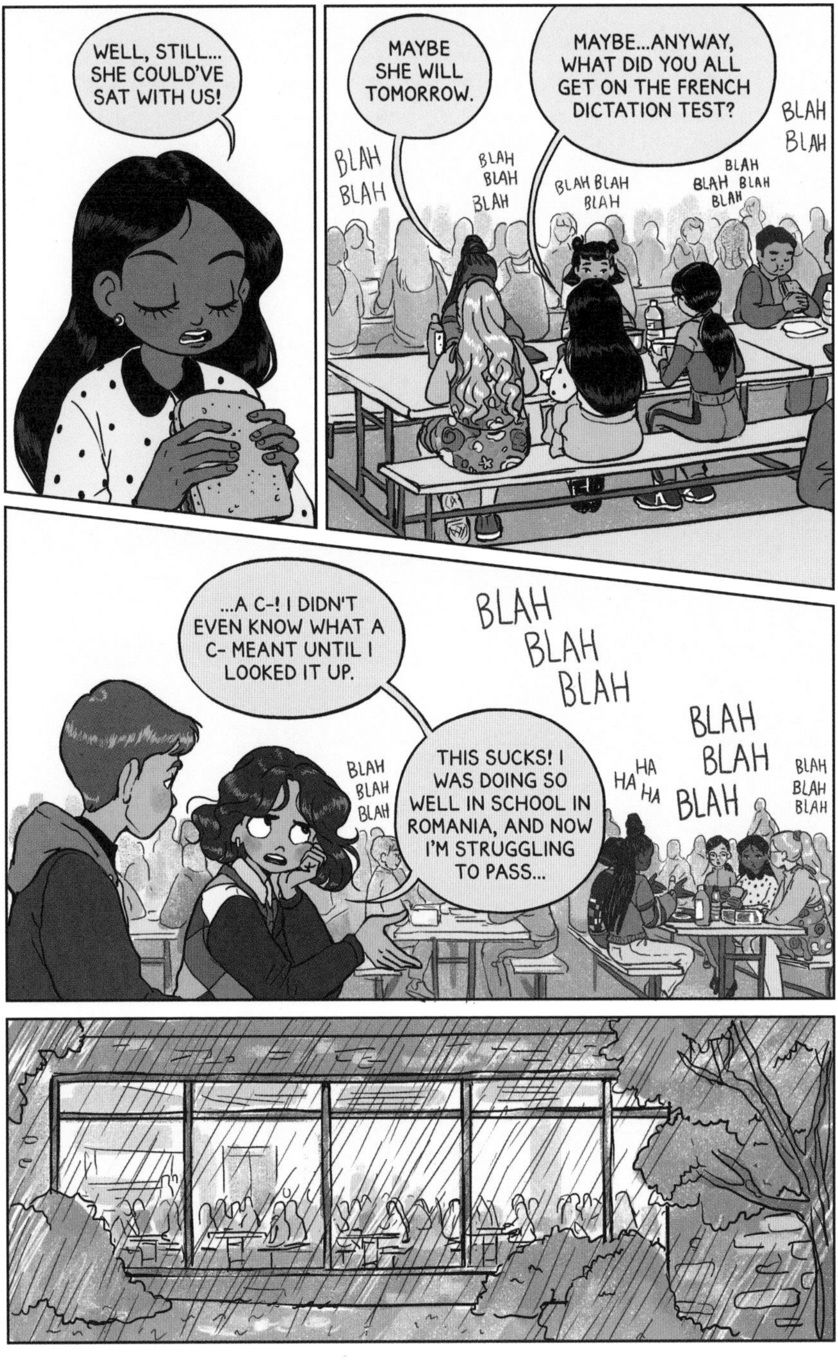
WELL, STILL... SHE COULD'VE SAT WITH US!
MAYBE SHE WILL TOMORROW.
MAYBE...ANYWAY, WHAT DID YOU ALL GET ON THE FRENCH DICTATION TEST?
BLAH BLAH
BLAH BLAH
BLAH BLAH BLAH
BLAH BLAH BLAH
BLAH BLAH BLAH BLAH
...A C-! I DIDN'T EVEN KNOW WHAT A C- MEANT UNTIL I LOOKED IT UP.
BLAH BLAH BLAH
THIS SUCKS! I WAS DOING SO WELL IN SCHOOL IN ROMANIA, AND NOW I'M STRUGGLING TO PASS...
BLAH BLAH BLAH
HA HA HA HA
BLAH BLAH BLAH
BLAH BLAH BLAH

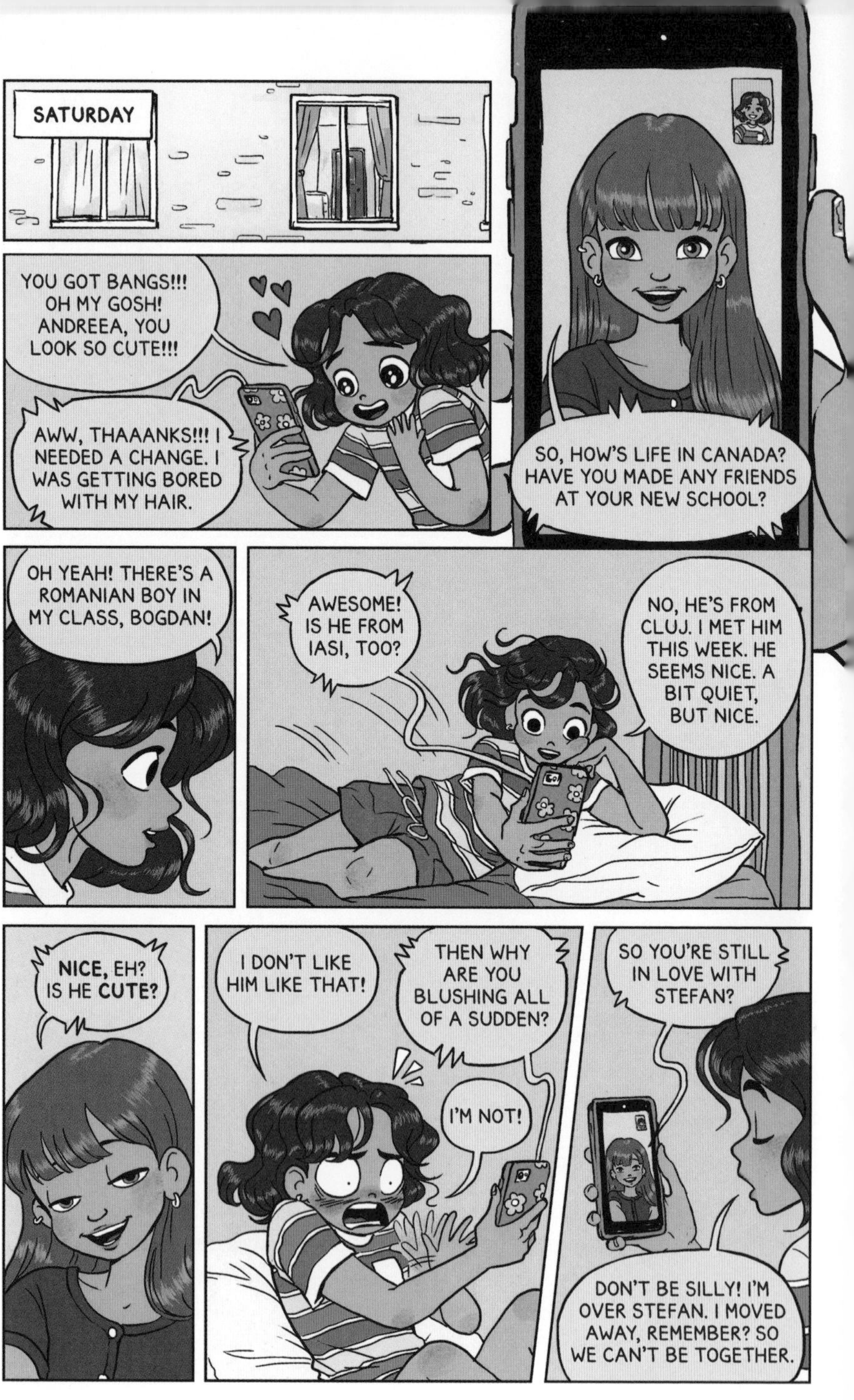
SATURDAY
YOU GOT BANGS!!! OH MY GOSH! ANDREEA, YOU LOOK SO CUTE!!!
AWW, THAAANKS!!! I NEEDED A CHANGE. I WAS GETTING BORED WITH MY HAIR.
SO, HOW'S LIFE IN CANADA? HAVE YOU MADE ANY FRIENDS AT YOUR NEW SCHOOL?
OH YEAH! THERE'S A ROMANIAN BOY IN MY CLASS, BOGDAN!
AWESOME! IS HE FROM IASI, TOO?
NO, HE'S FROM CLUJ. I MET HIM THIS WEEK. HE SEEMS NICE. A BIT QUIET, BUT NICE.
NICE, EH? IS HE **CUTE**?
I DON'T LIKE HIM LIKE THAT!
THEN WHY ARE YOU BLUSHING ALL OF A SUDDEN?
I'M NOT!
SO YOU'RE STILL IN LOVE WITH STEFAN?
DON'T BE SILLY! I'M OVER STEFAN. I MOVED AWAY, REMEMBER? SO WE CAN'T BE TOGETHER.

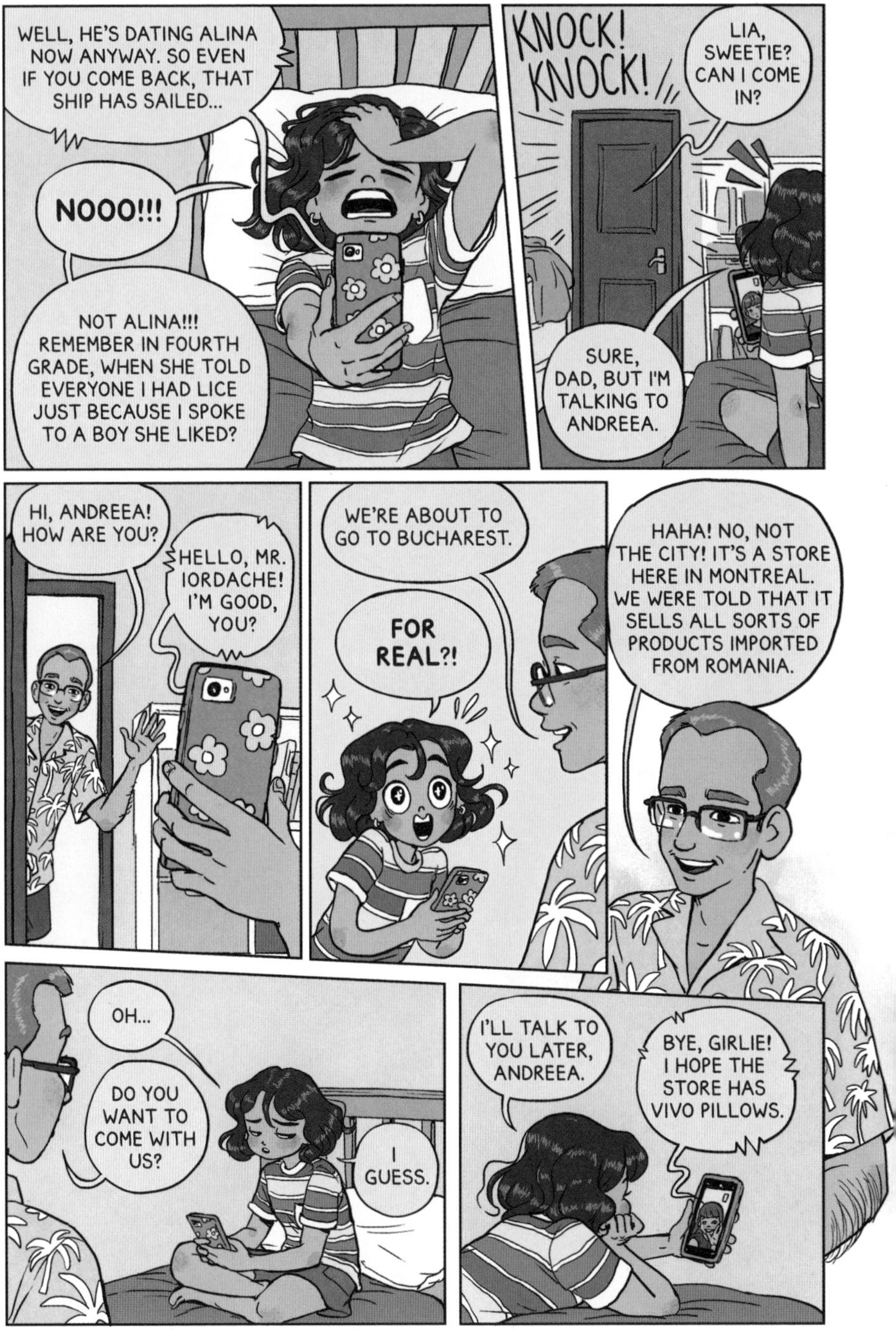
WELL, HE'S DATING ALINA NOW ANYWAY. SO EVEN IF YOU COME BACK, THAT SHIP HAS SAILED...
NOOO!!!
NOT ALINA!!! REMEMBER IN FOURTH GRADE, WHEN SHE TOLD EVERYONE I HAD LICE JUST BECAUSE I SPOKE TO A BOY SHE LIKED?
KNOCK! KNOCK!
LIA, SWEETIE? CAN I COME IN?
SURE, DAD, BUT I'M TALKING TO ANDREEA.
HI, ANDREEA! HOW ARE YOU?
HELLO, MR. IORDACHE! I'M GOOD, YOU?
WE'RE ABOUT TO GO TO BUCHAREST.
FOR REAL?!
HAHA! NO, NOT THE CITY! IT'S A STORE HERE IN MONTREAL. WE WERE TOLD THAT IT SELLS ALL SORTS OF PRODUCTS IMPORTED FROM ROMANIA.
OH...
DO YOU WANT TO COME WITH US?
I GUESS.
I'LL TALK TO YOU LATER, ANDREEA.
BYE, GIRLIE! I HOPE THE STORE HAS VIVO PILLOWS.

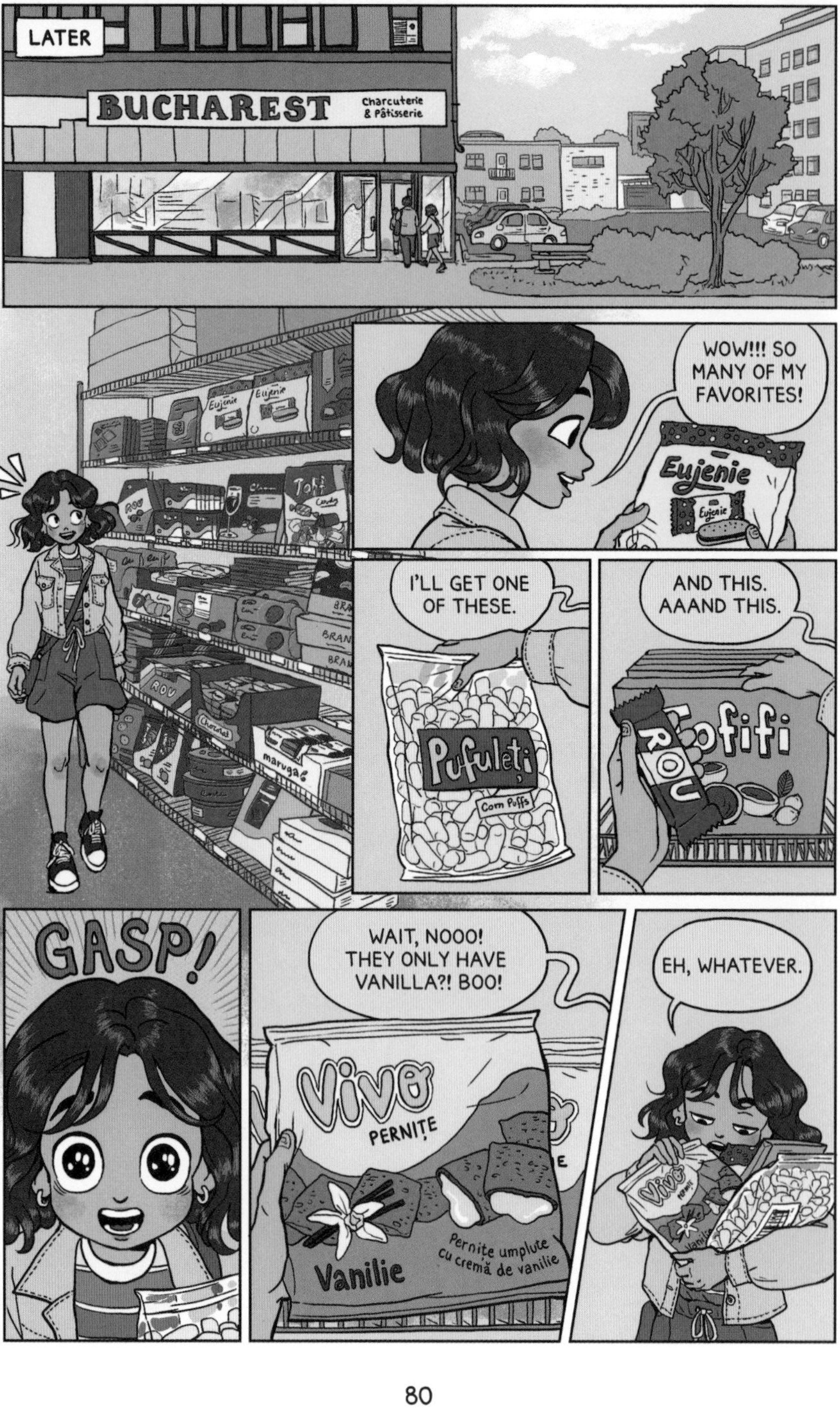
LATER
BUCHAREST
Charcuterie & Pâtisserie
WOW!!! SO MANY OF MY FAVORITES!
Eujenie
I'LL GET ONE OF THESE.
Pufuleți
Corn Puffs
AND THIS. AAAND THIS.
ROU
Tofifi
GASP!
WAIT, NOOO! THEY ONLY HAVE VANILLA?! BOO!
Vivo
PERNIȚE
Vanilie
Pernițe umplute cu cremă de vanilie
EH, WHATEVER.

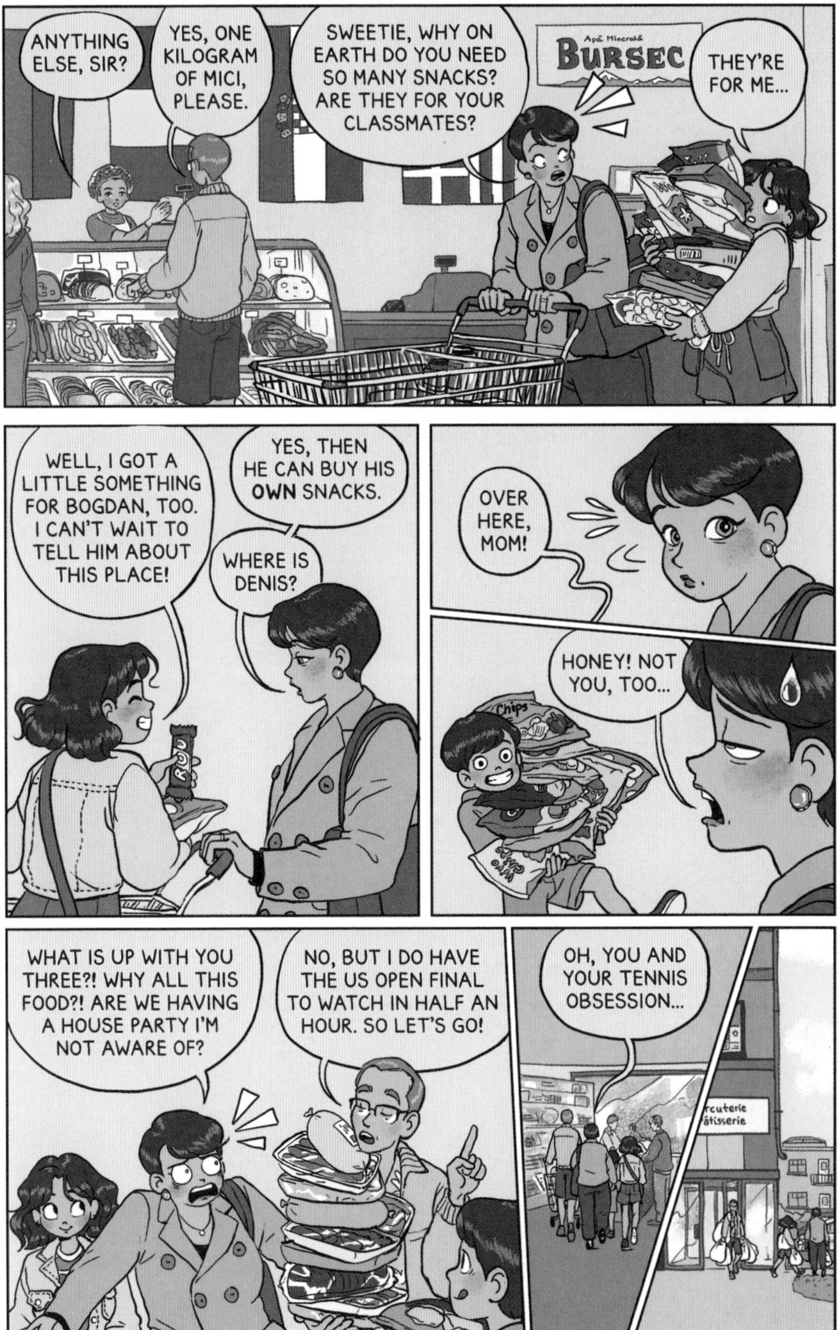
ANYTHING ELSE, SIR?
YES, ONE KILOGRAM OF MICI, PLEASE.
SWEETIE, WHY ON EARTH DO YOU NEED SO MANY SNACKS? ARE THEY FOR YOUR CLASSMATES?
BURSEC
THEY'RE FOR ME...
WELL, I GOT A LITTLE SOMETHING FOR BOGDAN, TOO. I CAN'T WAIT TO TELL HIM ABOUT THIS PLACE!
YES, THEN HE CAN BUY HIS **OWN** SNACKS.
WHERE IS DENIS?
OVER HERE, MOM!
HONEY! NOT YOU, TOO...
Chips
WHAT IS UP WITH YOU THREE?! WHY ALL THIS FOOD?! ARE WE HAVING A HOUSE PARTY I'M NOT AWARE OF?
NO, BUT I DO HAVE THE US OPEN FINAL TO WATCH IN HALF AN HOUR. SO LET'S GO!
OH, YOU AND YOUR TENNIS OBSESSION...

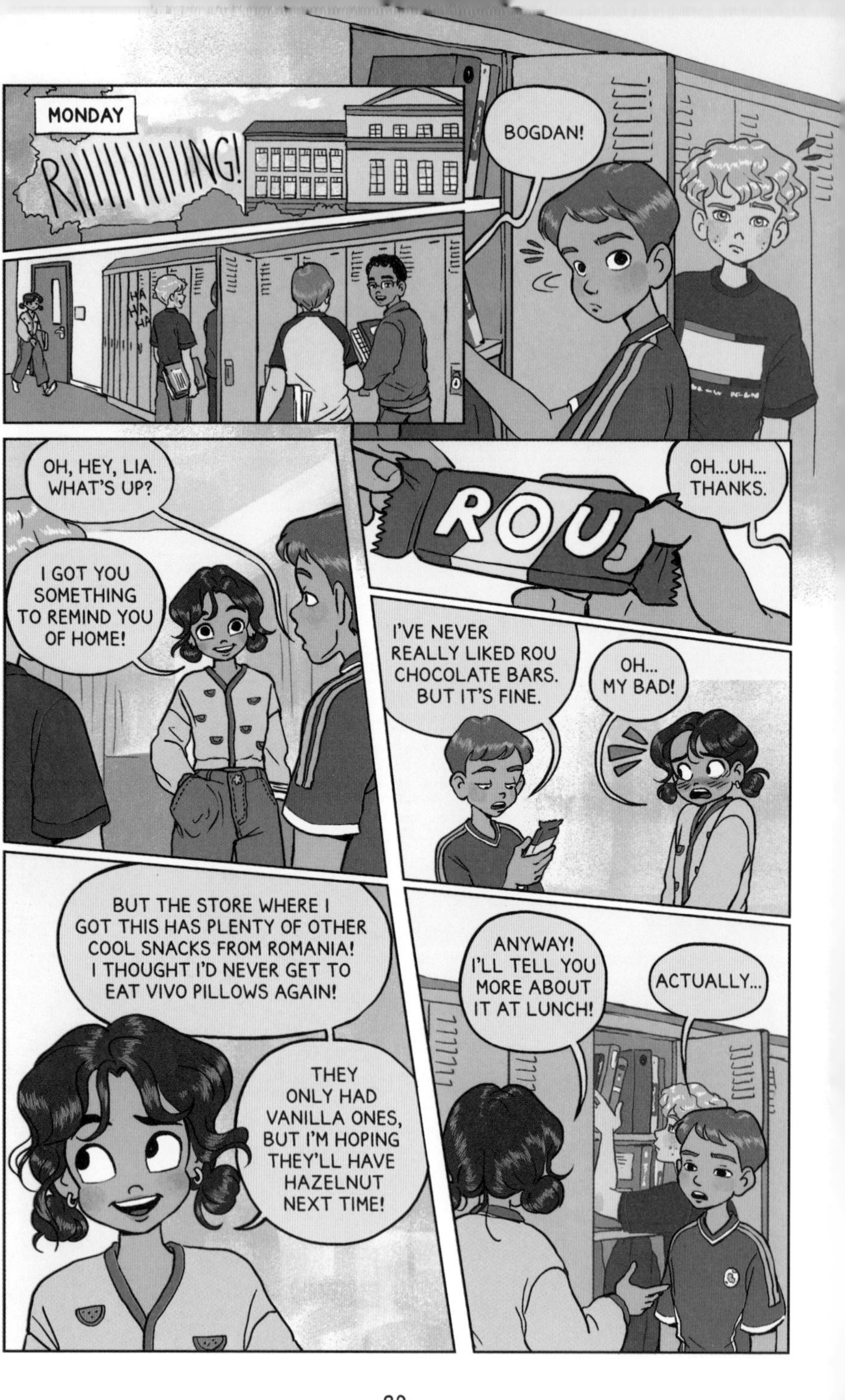
MONDAY
RIIIIIIIIIING!
BOGDAN!
OH, HEY, LIA. WHAT'S UP?
I GOT YOU SOMETHING TO REMIND YOU OF HOME!
ROU
OH...UH... THANKS.
I'VE NEVER REALLY LIKED ROU CHOCOLATE BARS. BUT IT'S FINE.
OH... MY BAD!
BUT THE STORE WHERE I GOT THIS HAS PLENTY OF OTHER COOL SNACKS FROM ROMANIA! I THOUGHT I'D NEVER GET TO EAT VIVO PILLOWS AGAIN!
THEY ONLY HAD VANILLA ONES, BUT I'M HOPING THEY'LL HAVE HAZELNUT NEXT TIME!
ANYWAY! I'LL TELL YOU MORE ABOUT IT AT LUNCH!
ACTUALLY...

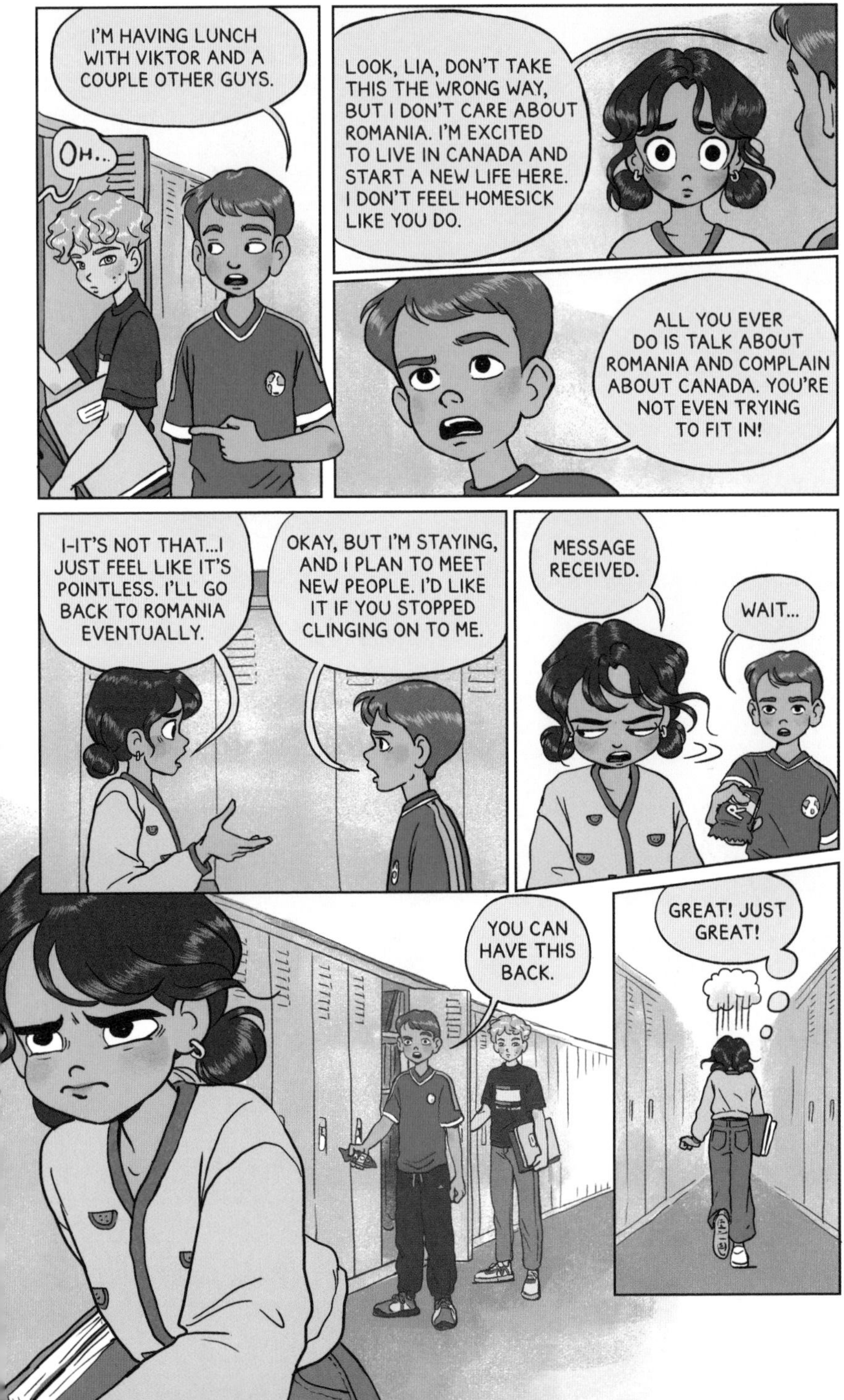
I'M HAVING LUNCH WITH VIKTOR AND A COUPLE OTHER GUYS.
OH...
LOOK, LIA, DON'T TAKE THIS THE WRONG WAY, BUT I DON'T CARE ABOUT ROMANIA. I'M EXCITED TO LIVE IN CANADA AND START A NEW LIFE HERE. I DON'T FEEL HOMESICK LIKE YOU DO.
ALL YOU EVER DO IS TALK ABOUT ROMANIA AND COMPLAIN ABOUT CANADA. YOU'RE NOT EVEN TRYING TO FIT IN!
I-IT'S NOT THAT...I JUST FEEL LIKE IT'S POINTLESS. I'LL GO BACK TO ROMANIA EVENTUALLY.
OKAY, BUT I'M STAYING, AND I PLAN TO MEET NEW PEOPLE. I'D LIKE IT IF YOU STOPPED CLINGING ON TO ME.
MESSAGE RECEIVED.
WAIT...
YOU CAN HAVE THIS BACK.
GREAT! JUST GREAT!

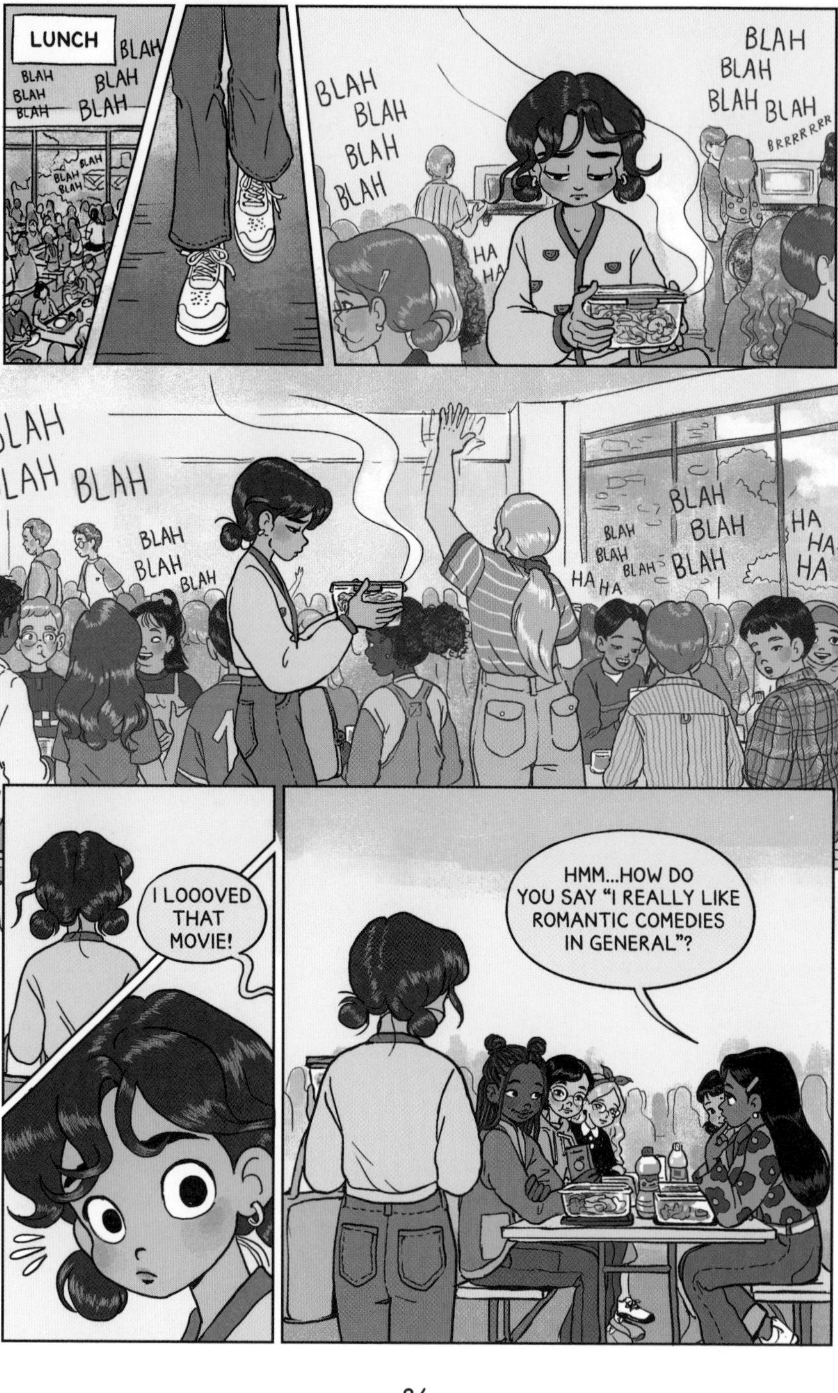
LUNCH
BLAH
BLAH
BLAH
BLAH
BLAH
BLAH
BLAH
BLAH
BLAH
BLAH
BLAH
BLAH
BLAH
BLAH
BRRRRRRR
HA
HA
BLAH
BLAH BLAH
BLAH
BLAH
BLAH
BLAH
BLAH
BLAH
BLAH
BLAH
BLAH
HA HA
HA
HA
HA
I LOOOVED THAT MOVIE!
HMM...HOW DO YOU SAY "I REALLY LIKE ROMANTIC COMEDIES IN GENERAL"?

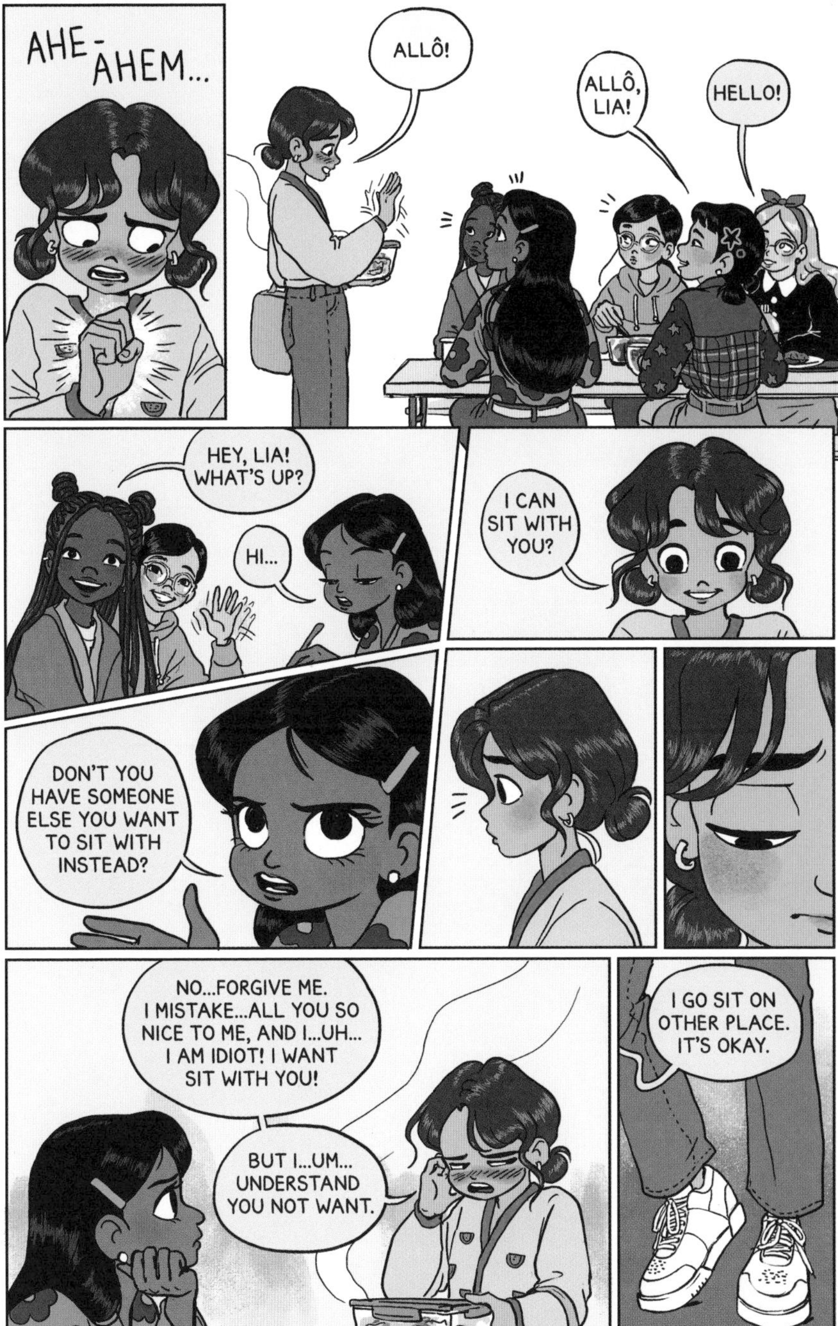
AHE-AHEM...
ALLÔ!
ALLÔ, LIA!
HELLO!
HEY, LIA! WHAT'S UP?
HI...
I CAN SIT WITH YOU?
DON'T YOU HAVE SOMEONE ELSE YOU WANT TO SIT WITH INSTEAD?
NO...FORGIVE ME. I MISTAKE...ALL YOU SO NICE TO ME, AND I...UH... I AM IDIOT! I WANT SIT WITH YOU!
BUT I...UM... UNDERSTAND YOU NOT WANT.
I GO SIT ON OTHER PLACE. IT'S OKAY.

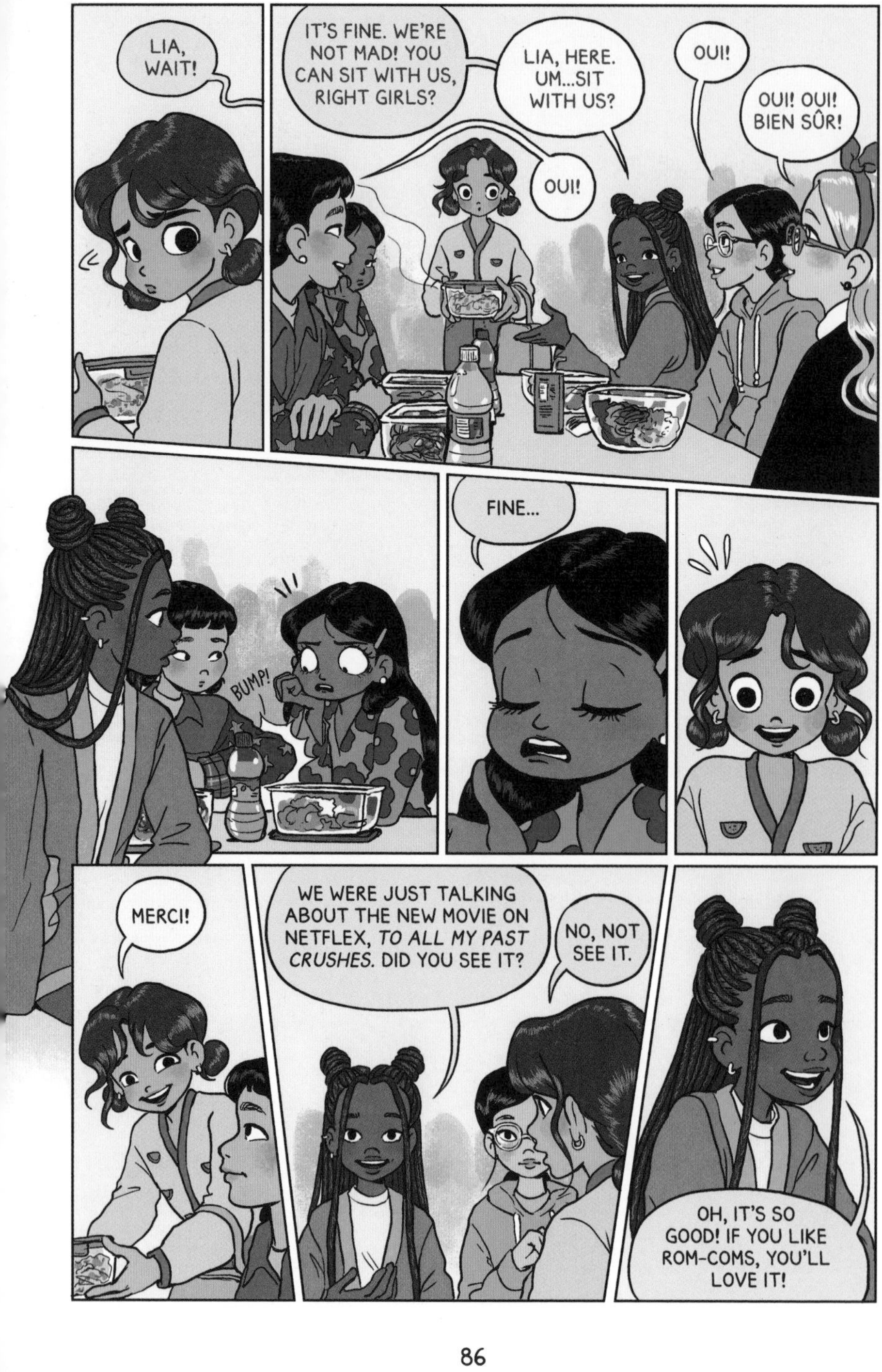
LIA, WAIT!
IT'S FINE. WE'RE NOT MAD! YOU CAN SIT WITH US, RIGHT GIRLS?
LIA, HERE. UM...SIT WITH US?
OUI!
OUI!
OUI! OUI! BIEN SÛR!
BUMP!
FINE...
MERCI!
WE WERE JUST TALKING ABOUT THE NEW MOVIE ON NETFLEX, *TO ALL MY PAST CRUSHES.* DID YOU SEE IT?
NO, NOT SEE IT.
OH, IT'S SO GOOD! IF YOU LIKE ROM-COMS, YOU'LL LOVE IT!

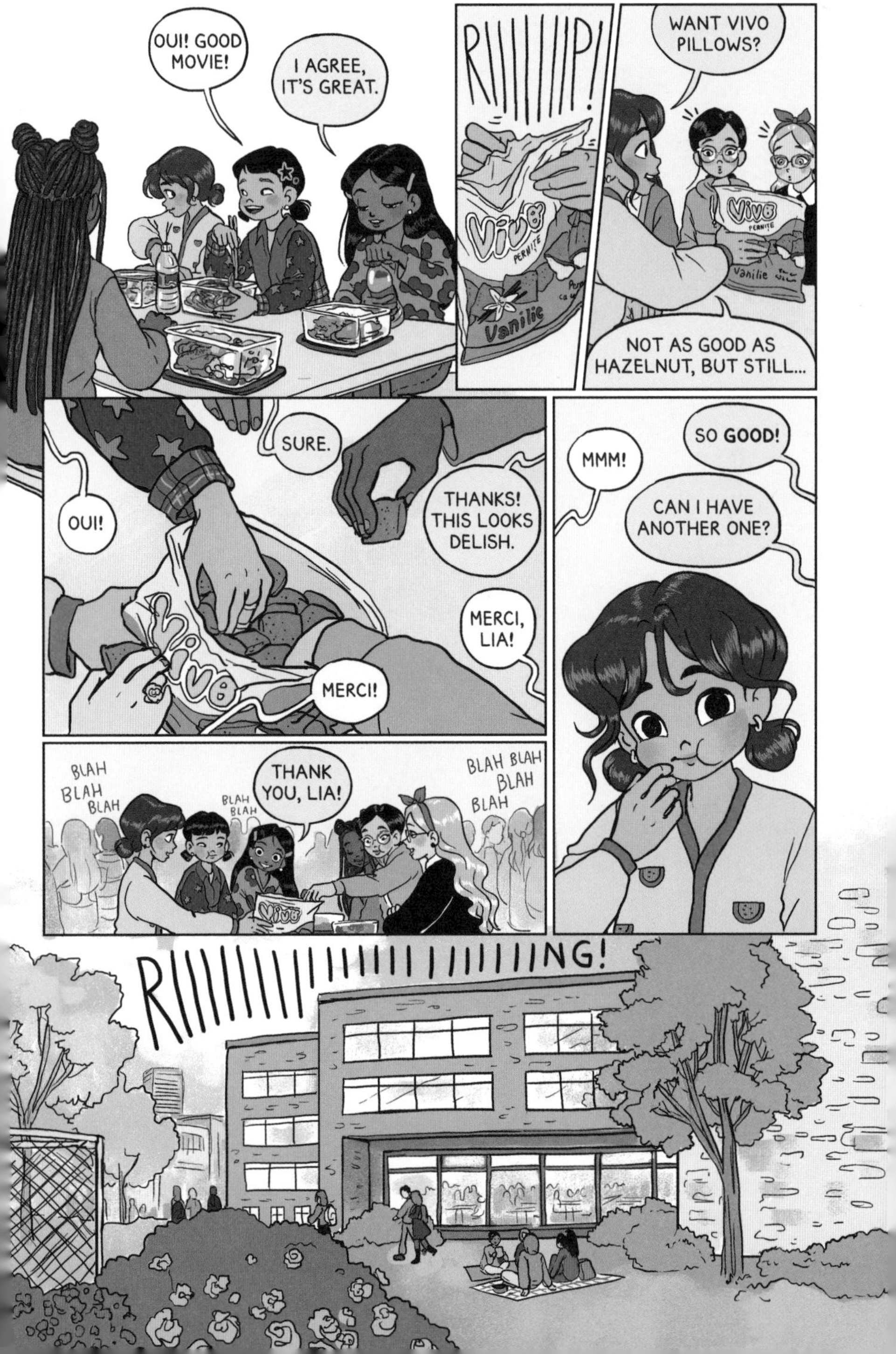

OUI! GOOD MOVIE!
I AGREE, IT'S GREAT.
RIIIIIP!
Vivo
PERNIȚE
Vanilie
WANT VIVO PILLOWS?
Vivo
PERNIȚE
Vanilie
NOT AS GOOD AS HAZELNUT, BUT STILL...
OUI!
SURE.
THANKS! THIS LOOKS DELISH.
MERCI, LIA!
MERCI!
Vivo
MMM!
SO **GOOD**!
CAN I HAVE ANOTHER ONE?
BLAH BLAH BLAH
BLAH BLAH
THANK YOU, LIA!
BLAH BLAH BLAH BLAH
Vivo
RIIIIIIIIIIIIIIIIIIIIING!

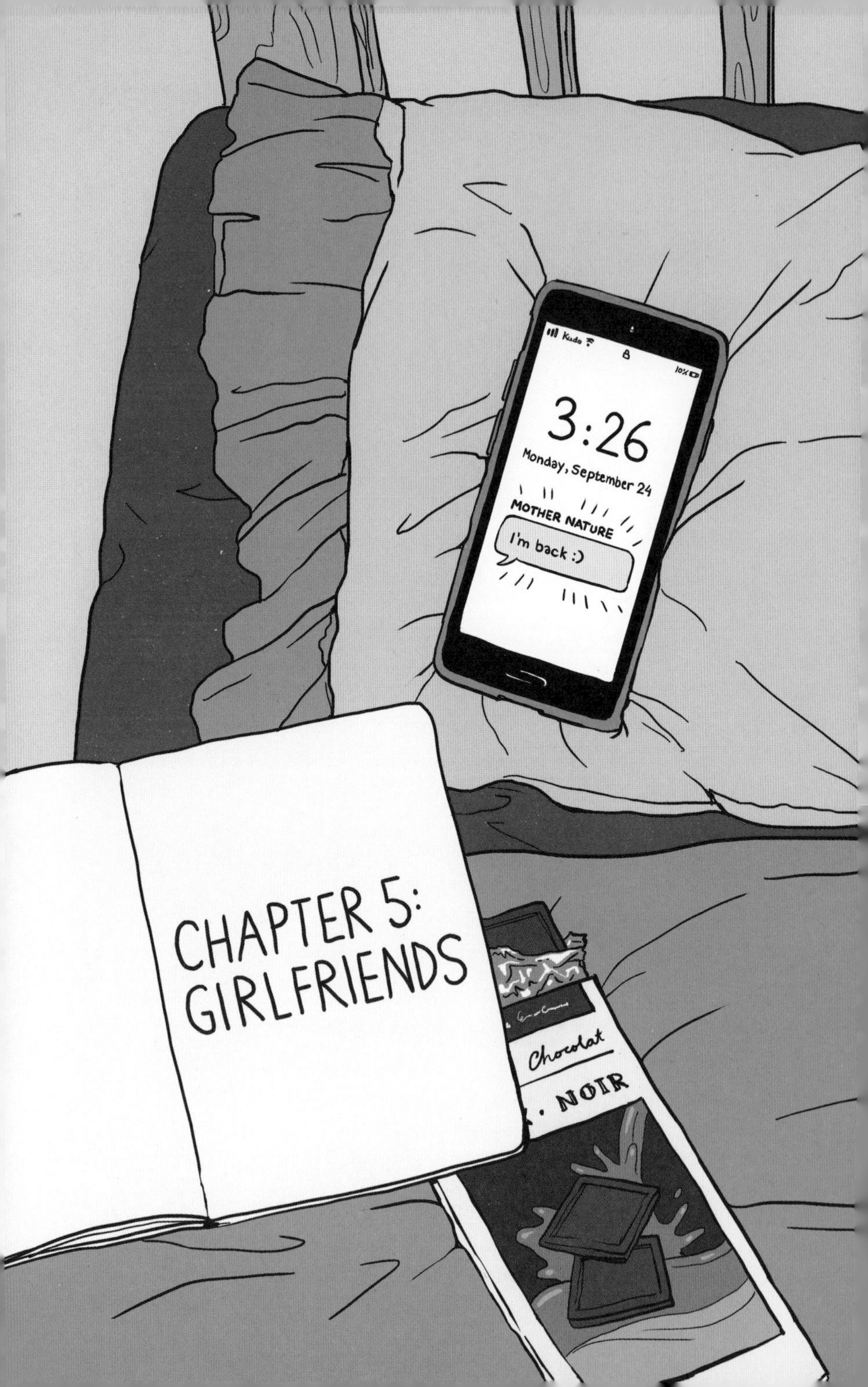
3:26
Monday, September 24
MOTHER NATURE
I'm back :)
CHAPTER 5:
GIRLFRIENDS
Chocolat
NOIR

LA CARTE DU QUÉBEC

NOT NOW... PLEASE...

GROWL!

YOU ALL RIGHT?

LEAVE ME ALONE...

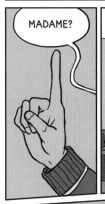

MADAME?

OUI, BOGDAN?

I THINK LIA IS SICK.

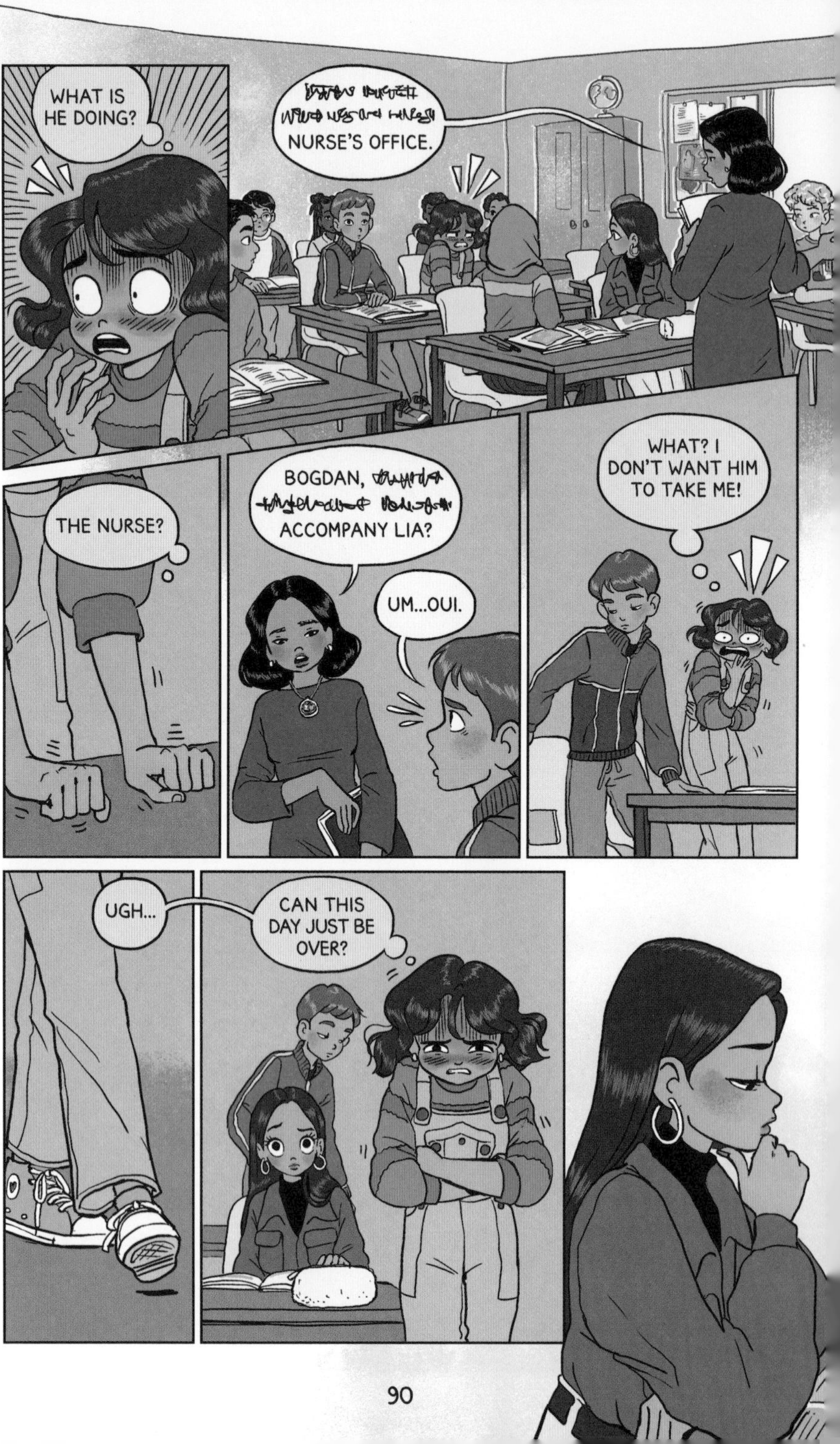
WHAT IS HE DOING?
NURSE'S OFFICE.
THE NURSE?
BOGDAN,
ACCOMPANY LIA?
UM...OUI.
WHAT? I DON'T WANT HIM TO TAKE ME!
UGH...
CAN THIS DAY JUST BE OVER?

GO BACK TO CLASS. I'LL BE FINE ON MY OWN.
YOU DON'T LOOK FINE. YOUR FACE IS SO PALE.
WHY DO YOU CARE?
I DON'T. I'M JUST DOING WHAT THE TEACHER ASKED: WALKING YOU TO THE NURSE.
YOU'RE **SO** RUDE!
LOOK, LIA, I KNOW YOU DON'T LIKE ME. BUT TRUST ME, IT'S BETTER THAT WE HAVE OUR OWN SEPARATE FRIEND GROUPS.
YOU'RE RIGHT. YOU'D MAKE A LOUSY FRIEND, ANYWAY.
WHATEVER.
THE NURSE'S OFFICE IS OVER HERE, I THINK.
GROWL!
KNOCK! KNOCK! KNOCK!

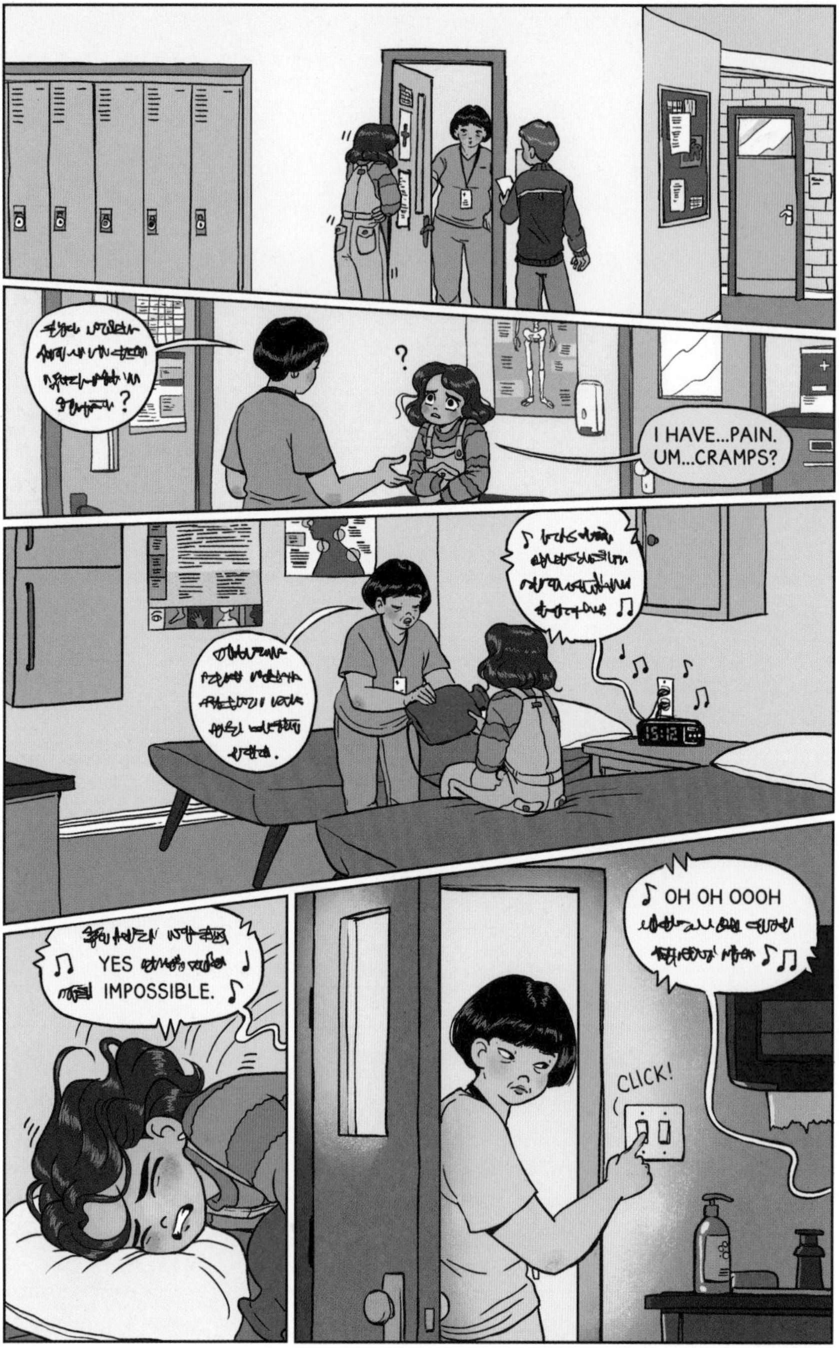

I HAVE...PAIN. UM...CRAMPS?
YES
IMPOSSIBLE.
OH OH OOOH
CLICK!

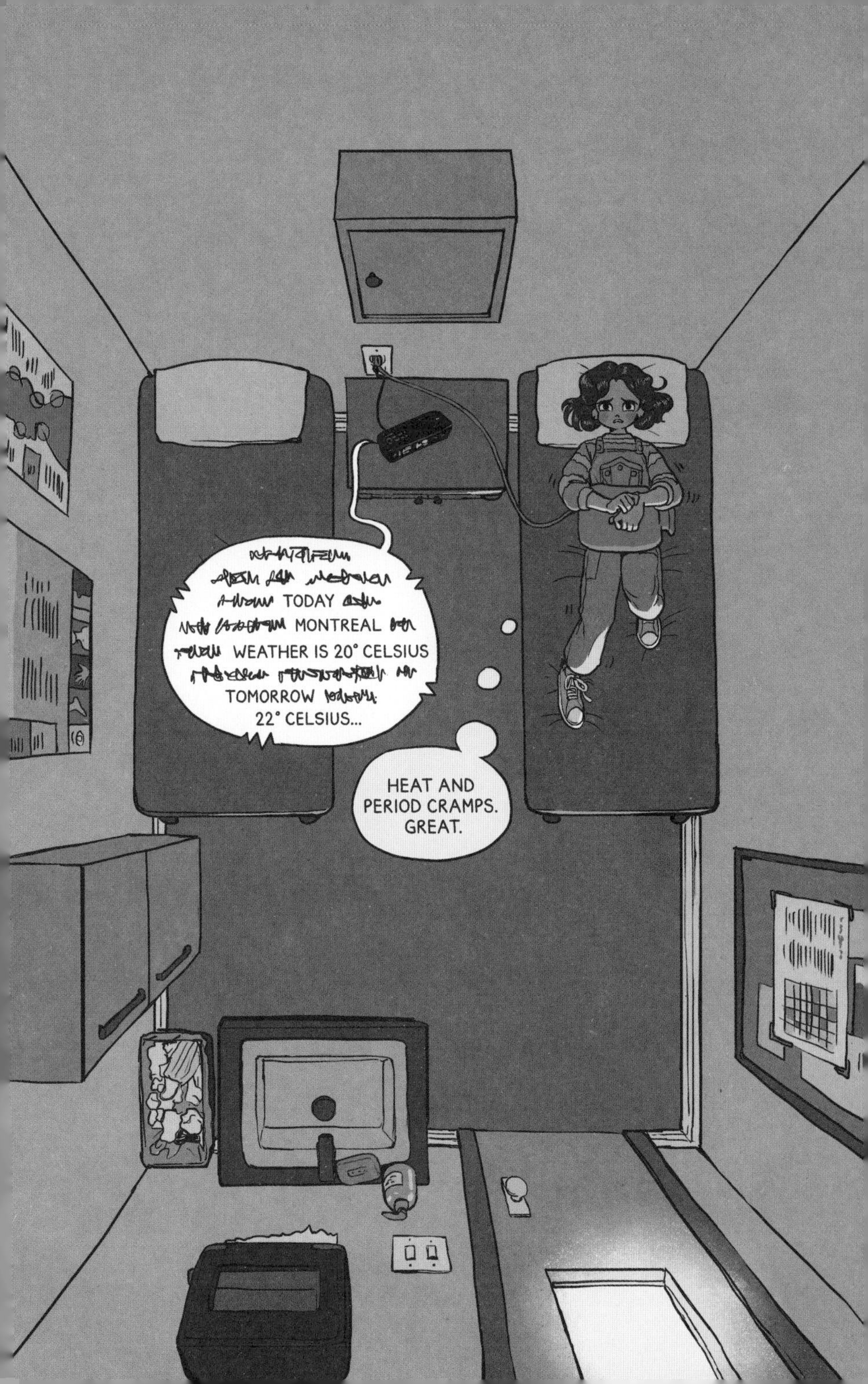
TODAY MONTREAL WEATHER IS 20° CELSIUS TOMORROW 22° CELSIUS...
HEAT AND PERIOD CRAMPS. GREAT.

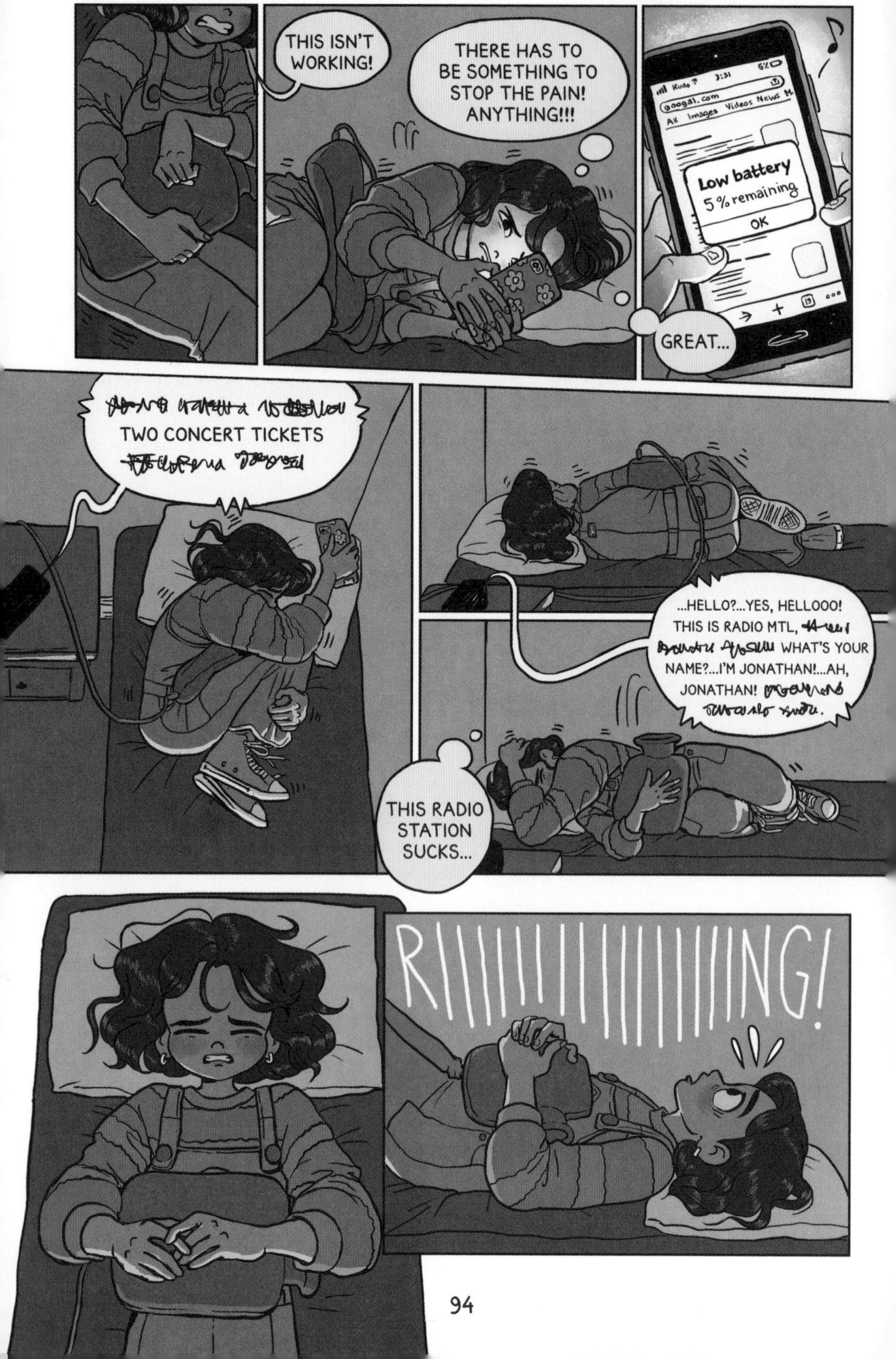
THIS ISN'T WORKING!
THERE HAS TO BE SOMETHING TO STOP THE PAIN! ANYTHING!!!
3:31
googal.com
All Images Videos News
Low battery
5% remaining
OK
GREAT...
TWO CONCERT TICKETS
...HELLO?...YES, HELLOOO! THIS IS RADIO MTL, WHAT'S YOUR NAME?...I'M JONATHAN!...AH, JONATHAN!
THIS RADIO STATION SUCKS...
RIIIIIIIIIIIIIING!

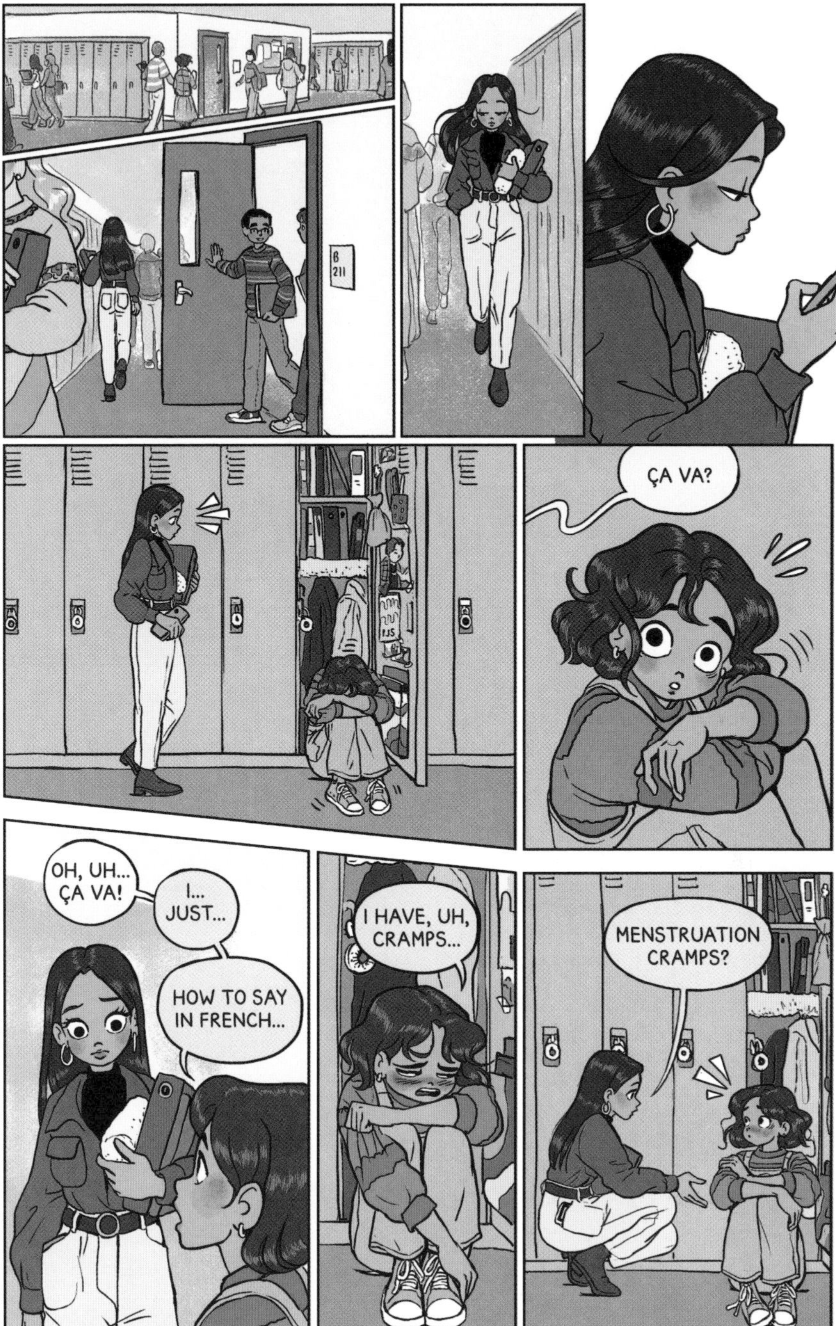
B
211
ÇA VA?
OH, UH... ÇA VA!
I... JUST...
HOW TO SAY IN FRENCH...
I HAVE, UH, CRAMPS...
MENSTRUATION CRAMPS?

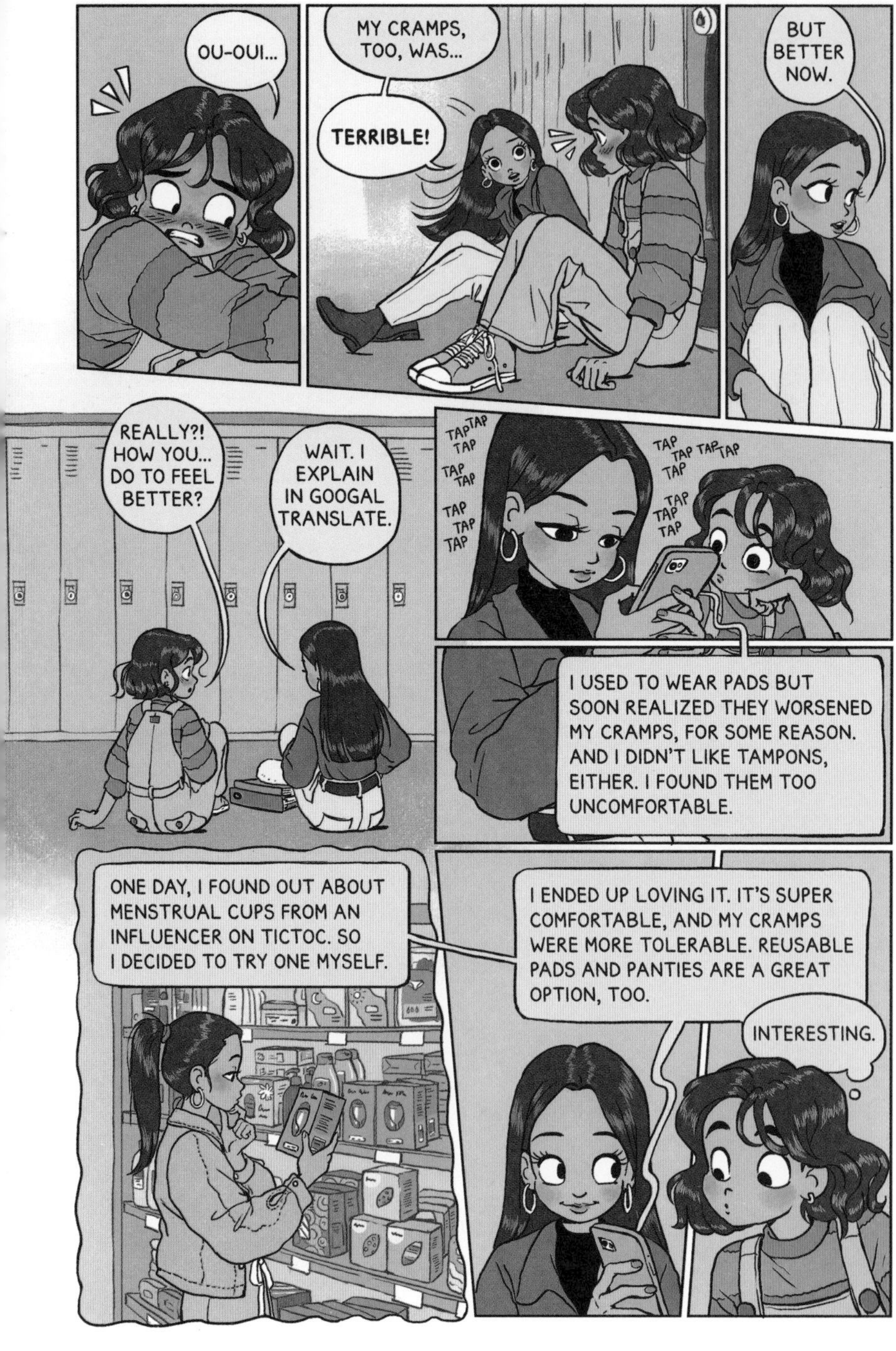

OU-OUI...
MY CRAMPS, TOO, WAS...
TERRIBLE!
BUT BETTER NOW.
REALLY?! HOW YOU... DO TO FEEL BETTER?
WAIT. I EXPLAIN IN GOOGAL TRANSLATE.
TAP TAP TAP
TAP TAP
TAP TAP TAP
TAP TAP TAP TAP TAP
TAP TAP TAP
I USED TO WEAR PADS BUT SOON REALIZED THEY WORSENED MY CRAMPS, FOR SOME REASON. AND I DIDN'T LIKE TAMPONS, EITHER. I FOUND THEM TOO UNCOMFORTABLE.
ONE DAY, I FOUND OUT ABOUT MENSTRUAL CUPS FROM AN INFLUENCER ON TICTOC. SO I DECIDED TO TRY ONE MYSELF.
I ENDED UP LOVING IT. IT'S SUPER COMFORTABLE, AND MY CRAMPS WERE MORE TOLERABLE. REUSABLE PADS AND PANTIES ARE A GREAT OPTION, TOO.
INTERESTING.

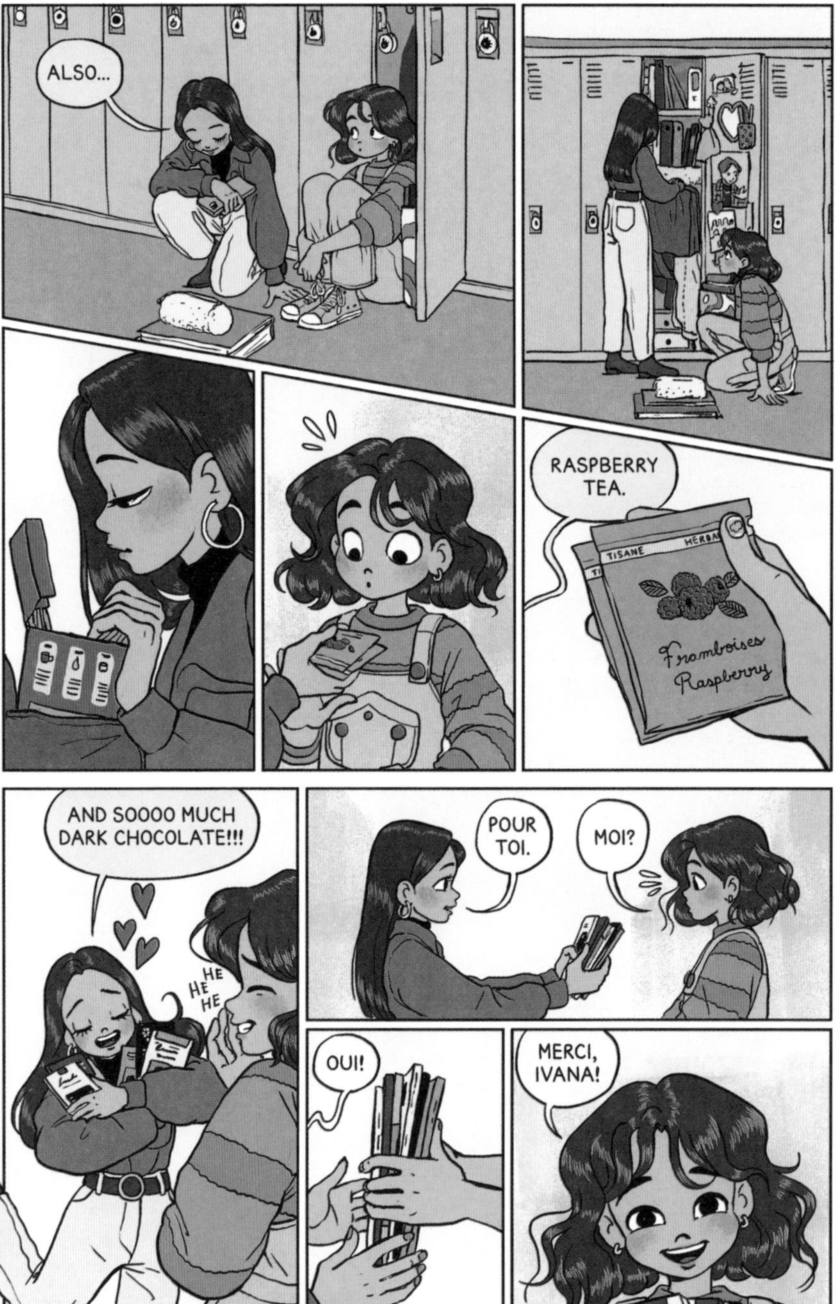
ALSO...
RASPBERRY TEA.
TISANE
HERBA
Framboises
Raspberry
AND SOOOO MUCH DARK CHOCOLATE!!!
HE HE HE
POUR TOI.
MOI?
OUI!
MERCI, IVANA!

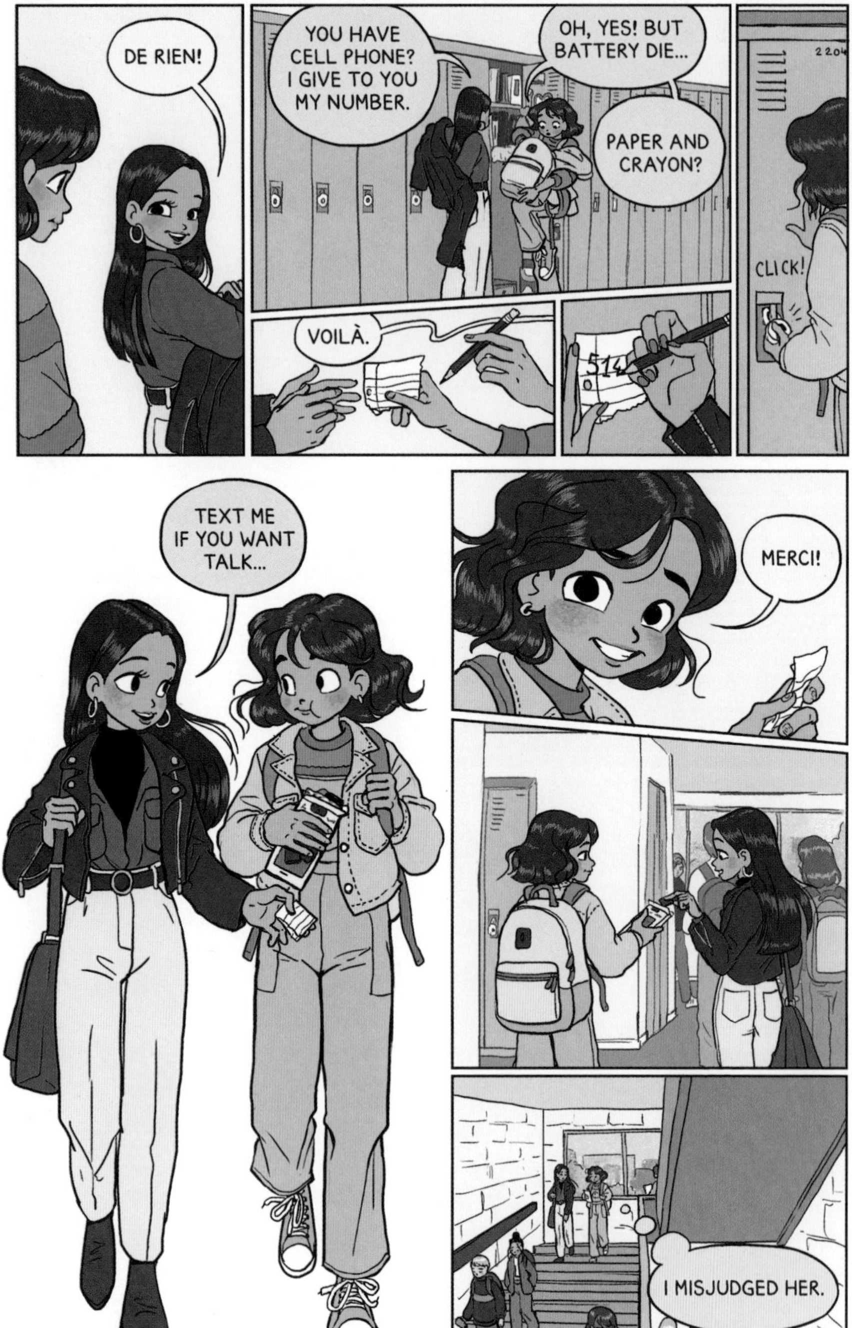
DE RIEN!
YOU HAVE CELL PHONE? I GIVE TO YOU MY NUMBER.
OH, YES! BUT BATTERY DIE...
PAPER AND CRAYON?
2204
CLICK!
VOILÀ.
514
TEXT ME IF YOU WANT TALK...
MERCI!
I MISJUDGED HER.

A FEW DAYS LATER

⟨▨▨▨▨⟩ WE'RE DONE! ⟨▨▨▨▨⟩ ⟨▨▨⟩ HERE IS THE HOMEWORK ⟨▨▨▨⟩.

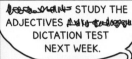

⟨▨▨▨▨⟩ STUDY THE ADJECTIVES ⟨▨▨▨▨⟩ DICTATION TEST NEXT WEEK.

⟨▨▨▨▨⟩ BOOKS IN FRENCH TO READ ⟨▨▨▨▨⟩*

⟨▨▨▨▨⟩ ⟨▨▨▨⟩ ⟨▨▨▨⟩.

Devoir

1. Lire le livre que vous avec choisi.

2. Écrire:
   - un court résumé
   - votre opinion

SOMETHING ABOUT READING A BOOK AND WRITING A SUMMARY... TERRIFIC. TONS OF HOMEWORK. AGAIN.

I GUESS I'LL SEE WHAT KIND OF BOOKS ARE IN THAT DUSTY OLD BOX.

Le LION et le RAT
JEAN DE LA FONTAINE

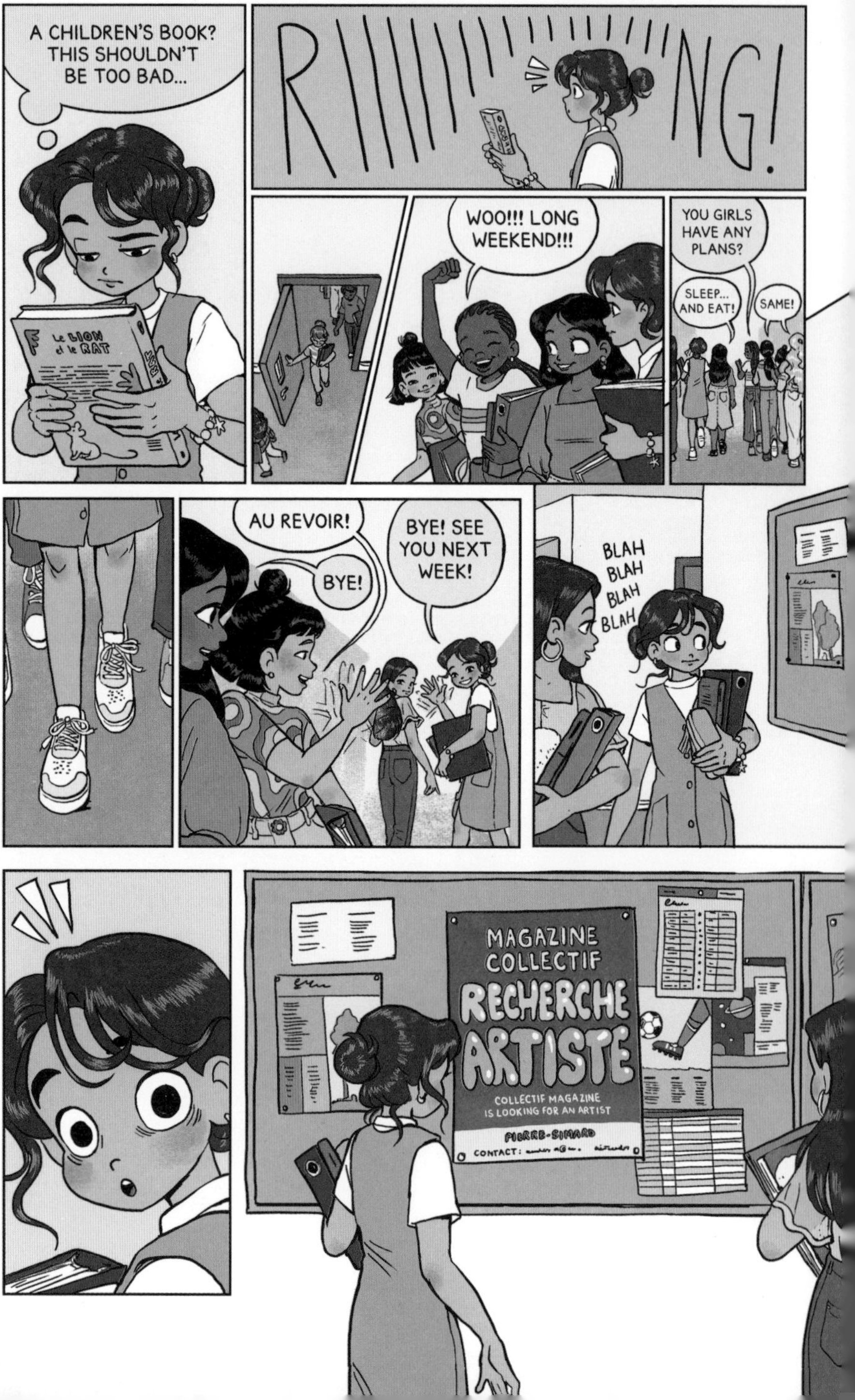
A CHILDREN'S BOOK? THIS SHOULDN'T BE TOO BAD...
Le LION et le RAT
RIIIIIIIIIIIIIIIING!
WOO!!! LONG WEEKEND!!!
YOU GIRLS HAVE ANY PLANS?
SLEEP... AND EAT!
SAME!
AU REVOIR!
BYE!
BYE! SEE YOU NEXT WEEK!
BLAH BLAH BLAH BLAH
MAGAZINE COLLECTIF
RECHERCHE ARTISTE
COLLECTIF MAGAZINE IS LOOKING FOR AN ARTIST
PIERRE-SIMARD
CONTACT:

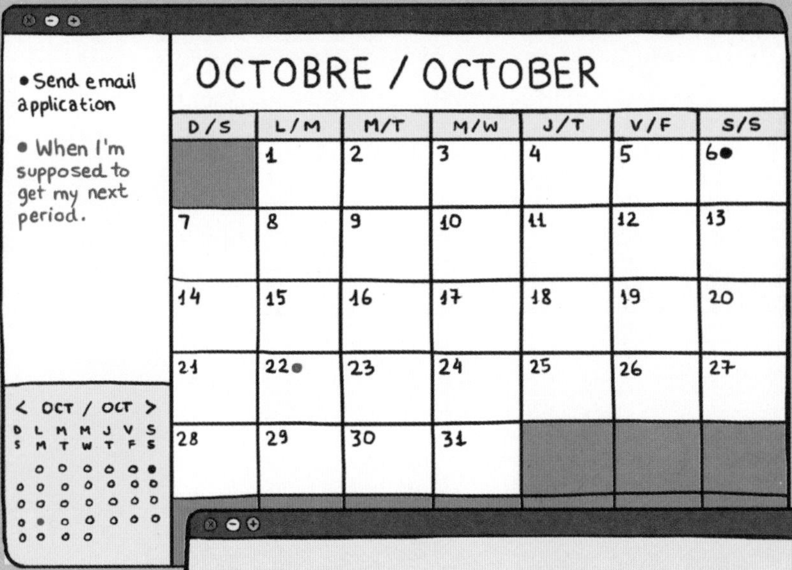

- Send email application

- When I'm supposed to get my next period.

OCTOBRE / OCTOBER

D/S	L/M	M/T	M/W	J/T	V/F	S/S
	1	2	3	4	5	6●
7	8	9	10	11	12	13
14	15	16	17	18	19	20
21	22●	23	24	25	26	27
28	29	30	31			

< OCT / OCT >

D L M M J V S
S M T W T F S

CHAPTER 6:
AN EXCITING CHAPTER

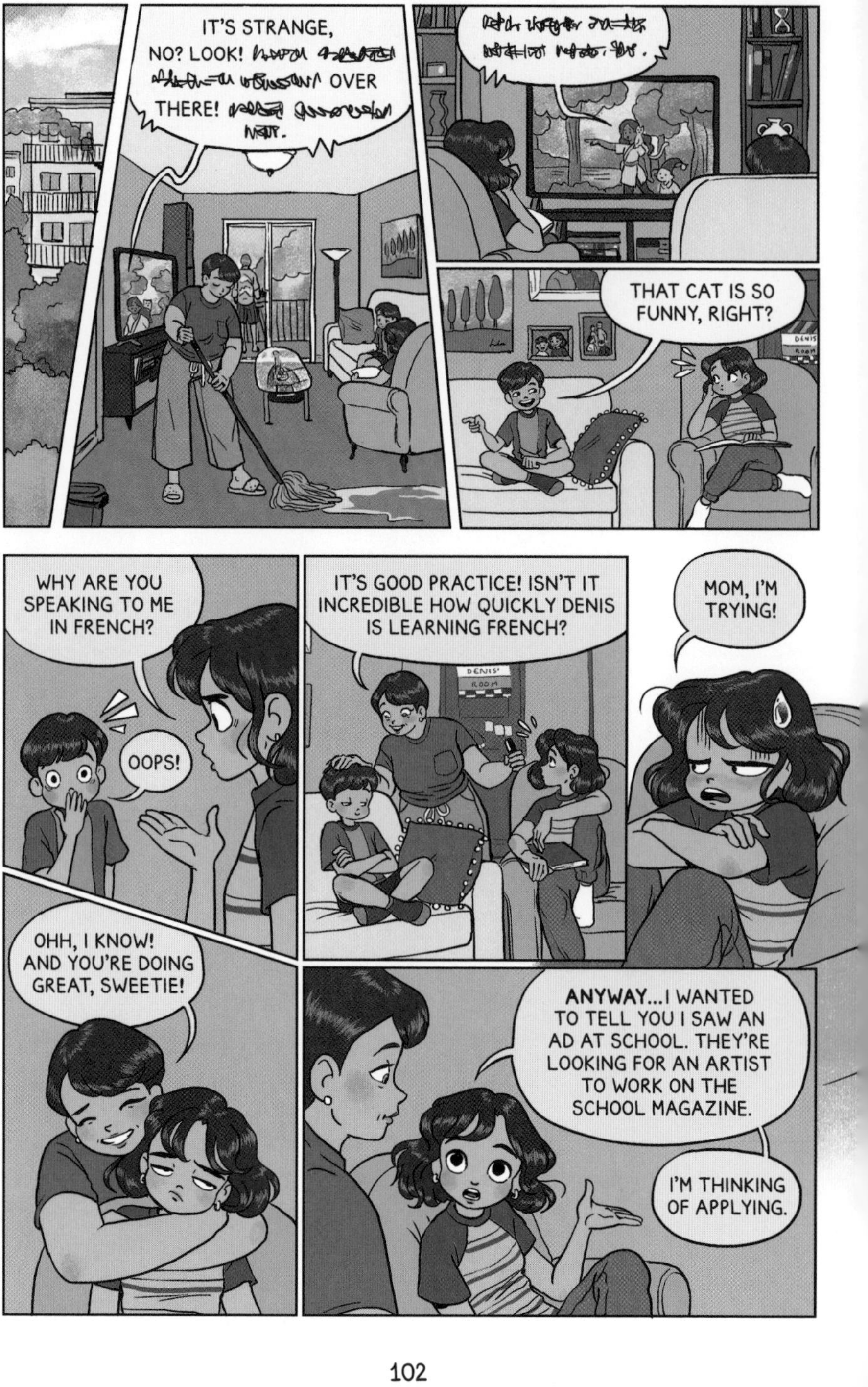
IT'S STRANGE, NO? LOOK! OVER THERE!
THAT CAT IS SO FUNNY, RIGHT?
DENIS' ROOM
WHY ARE YOU SPEAKING TO ME IN FRENCH?
OOPS!
IT'S GOOD PRACTICE! ISN'T IT INCREDIBLE HOW QUICKLY DENIS IS LEARNING FRENCH?
DENIS' ROOM
MOM, I'M TRYING!
OHH, I KNOW! AND YOU'RE DOING GREAT, SWEETIE!
ANYWAY... I WANTED TO TELL YOU I SAW AN AD AT SCHOOL. THEY'RE LOOKING FOR AN ARTIST TO WORK ON THE SCHOOL MAGAZINE.
I'M THINKING OF APPLYING.

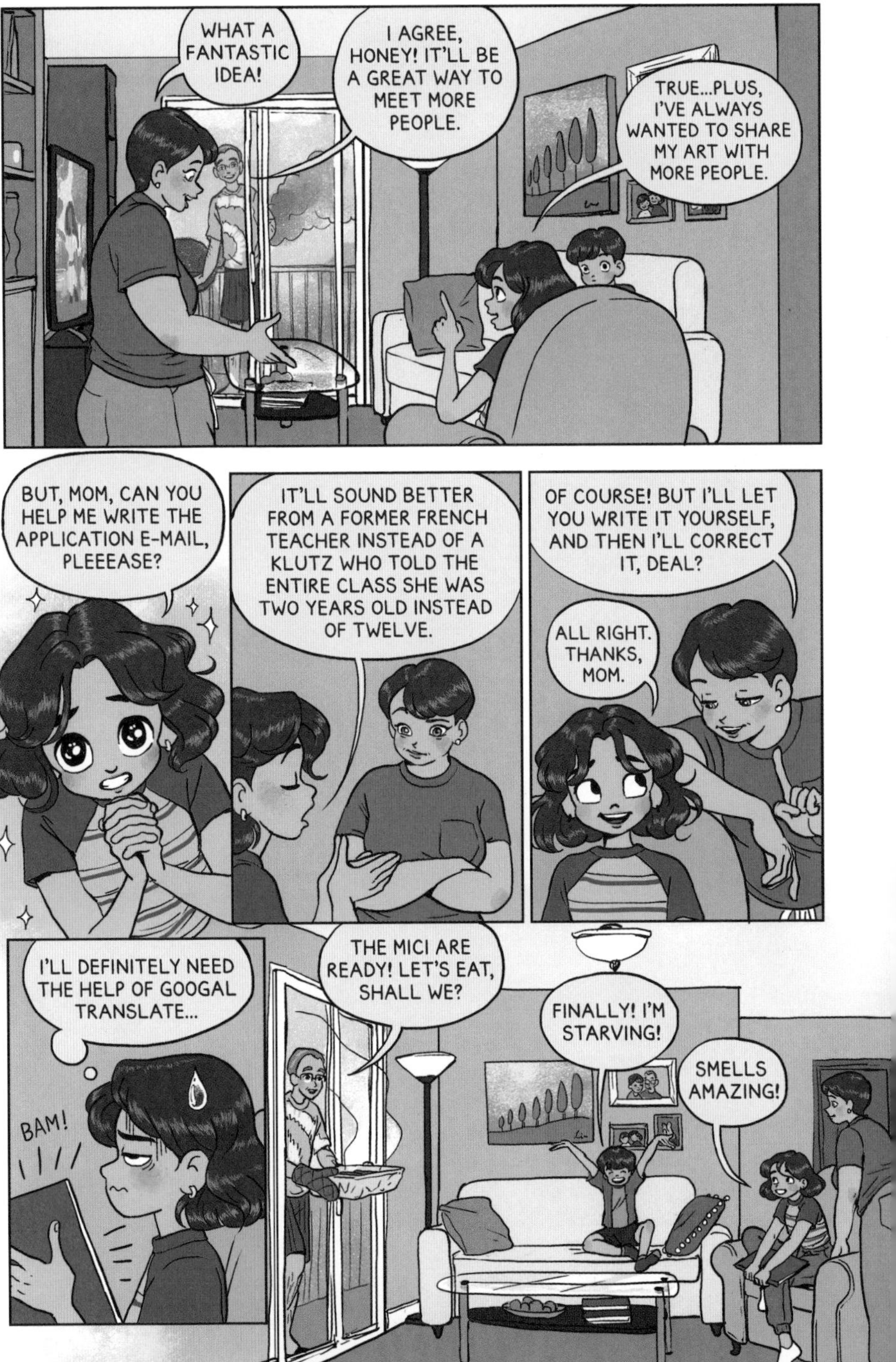
WHAT A FANTASTIC IDEA!
I AGREE, HONEY! IT'LL BE A GREAT WAY TO MEET MORE PEOPLE.
TRUE...PLUS, I'VE ALWAYS WANTED TO SHARE MY ART WITH MORE PEOPLE.
BUT, MOM, CAN YOU HELP ME WRITE THE APPLICATION E-MAIL, PLEEEASE?
IT'LL SOUND BETTER FROM A FORMER FRENCH TEACHER INSTEAD OF A KLUTZ WHO TOLD THE ENTIRE CLASS SHE WAS TWO YEARS OLD INSTEAD OF TWELVE.
OF COURSE! BUT I'LL LET YOU WRITE IT YOURSELF, AND THEN I'LL CORRECT IT, DEAL?
ALL RIGHT. THANKS, MOM.
I'LL DEFINITELY NEED THE HELP OF GOOGAL TRANSLATE...
BAM!
THE MICI ARE READY! LET'S EAT, SHALL WE?
FINALLY! I'M STARVING!
SMELLS AMAZING!

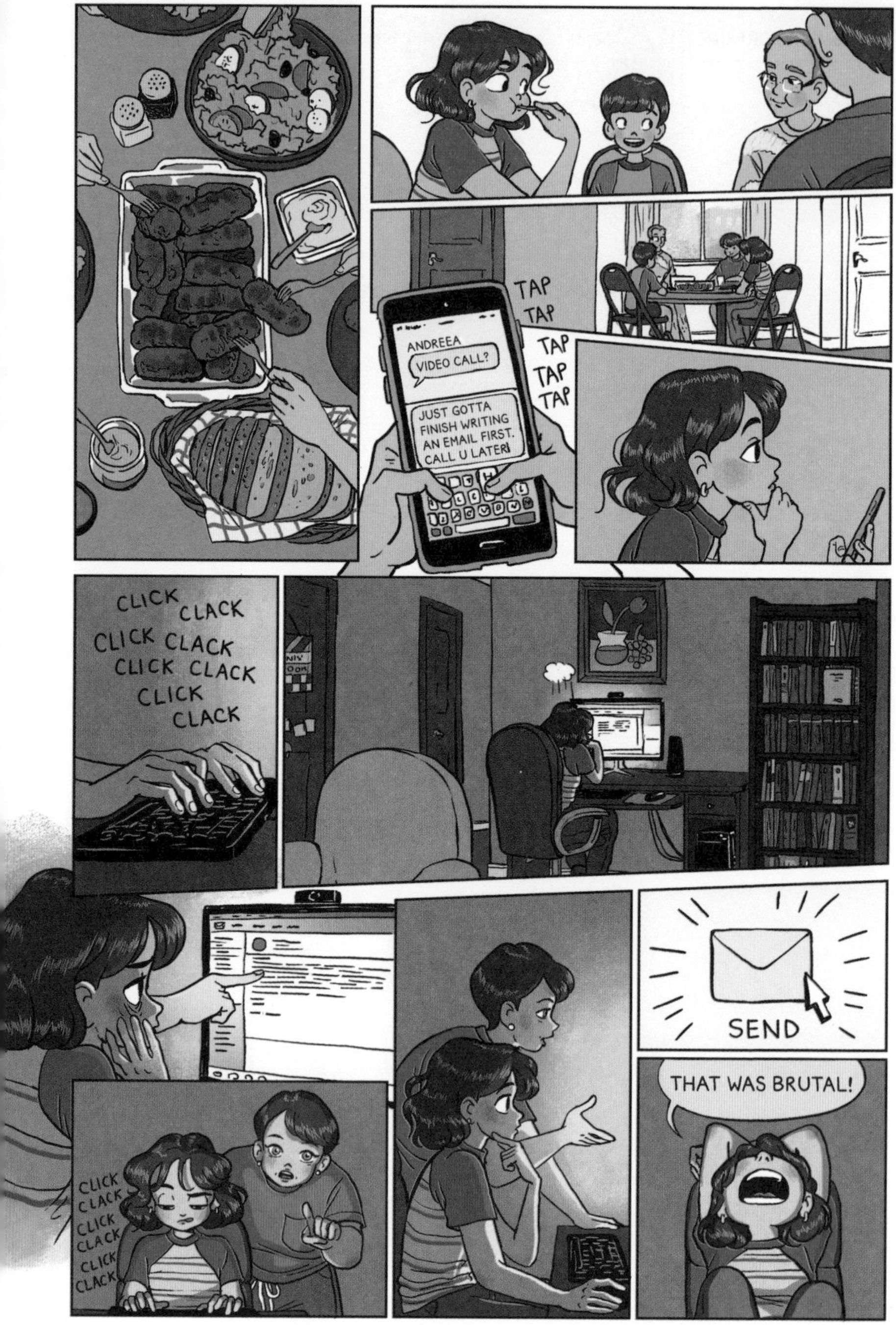
ANDREEA
VIDEO CALL?
JUST GOTTA FINISH WRITING AN EMAIL FIRST. CALL U LATER!
TAP TAP
TAP TAP TAP
CLICK CLACK CLICK CLACK CLICK CLACK CLICK CLACK
CLICK CLACK CLICK CLACK CLICK CLACK
SEND
THAT WAS BRUTAL!

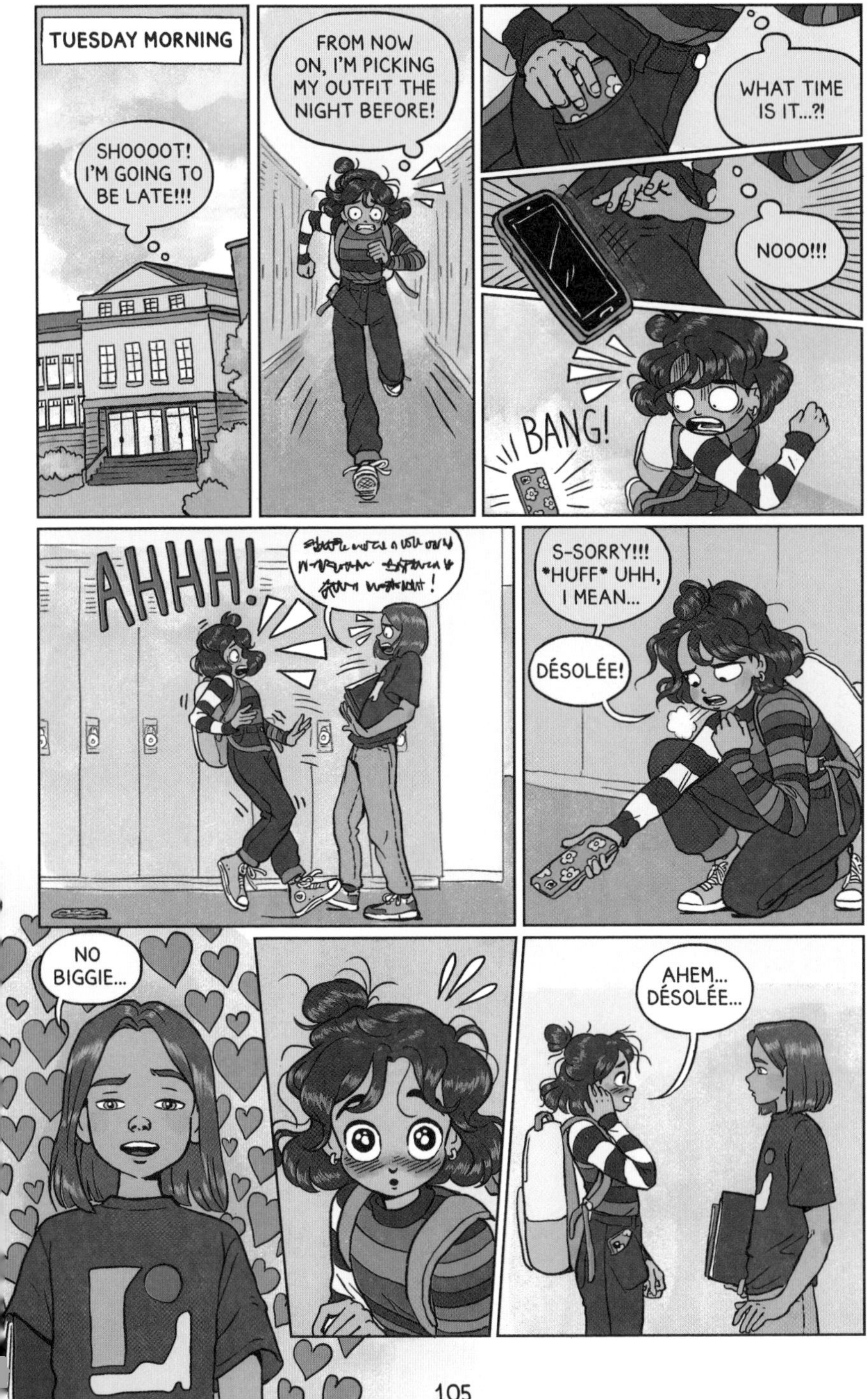
TUESDAY MORNING
SHOOOOT! I'M GOING TO BE LATE!!!
FROM NOW ON, I'M PICKING MY OUTFIT THE NIGHT BEFORE!
WHAT TIME IS IT...?!
NOOO!!!
BANG!
AHHH!
S-SORRY!!! *HUFF* UHH, I MEAN...
DÉSOLÉE!
NO BIGGIE...
AHEM... DÉSOLÉE...

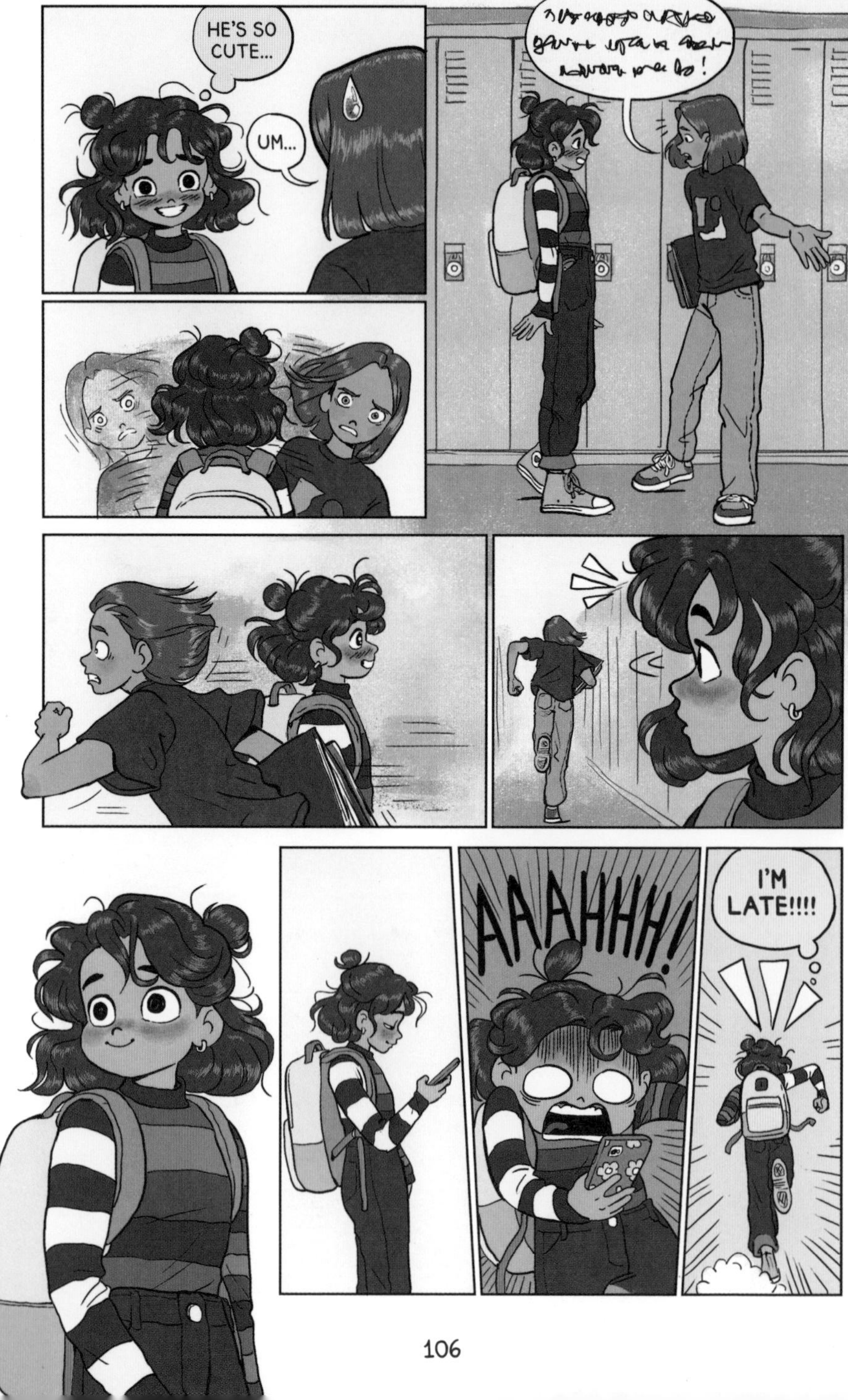
HE'S SO CUTE...
UM...
AAAHHH!
I'M LATE!!!!

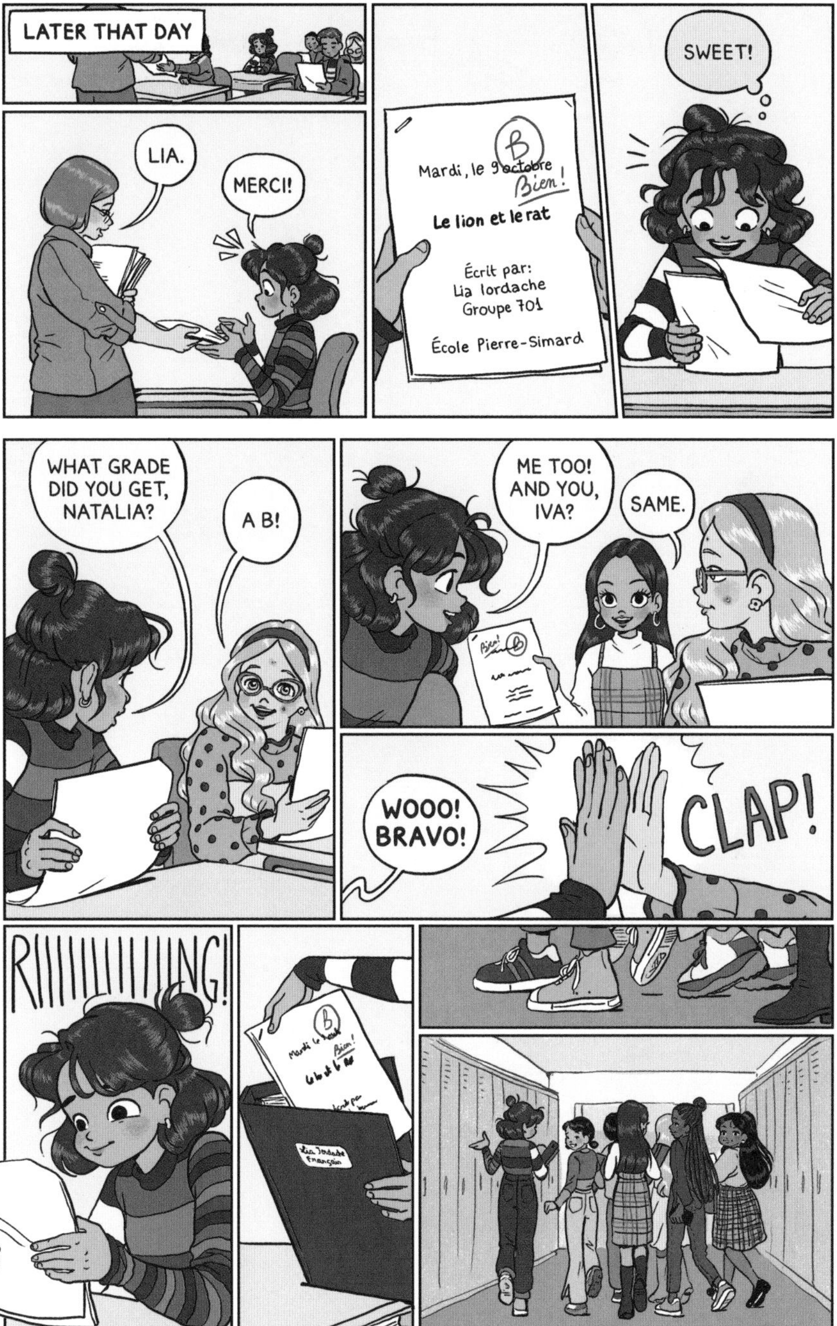

LATER THAT DAY
LIA.
MERCI!
B
Mardi, le 9 octobre
Bien!
Le lion et le rat
Écrit par:
Lia Iordache
Groupe 701
École Pierre-Simard
SWEET!
WHAT GRADE DID YOU GET, NATALIA?
A B!
ME TOO! AND YOU, IVA?
SAME.
WOOO! BRAVO!
CLAP!
RIIIIIIIIIIING!

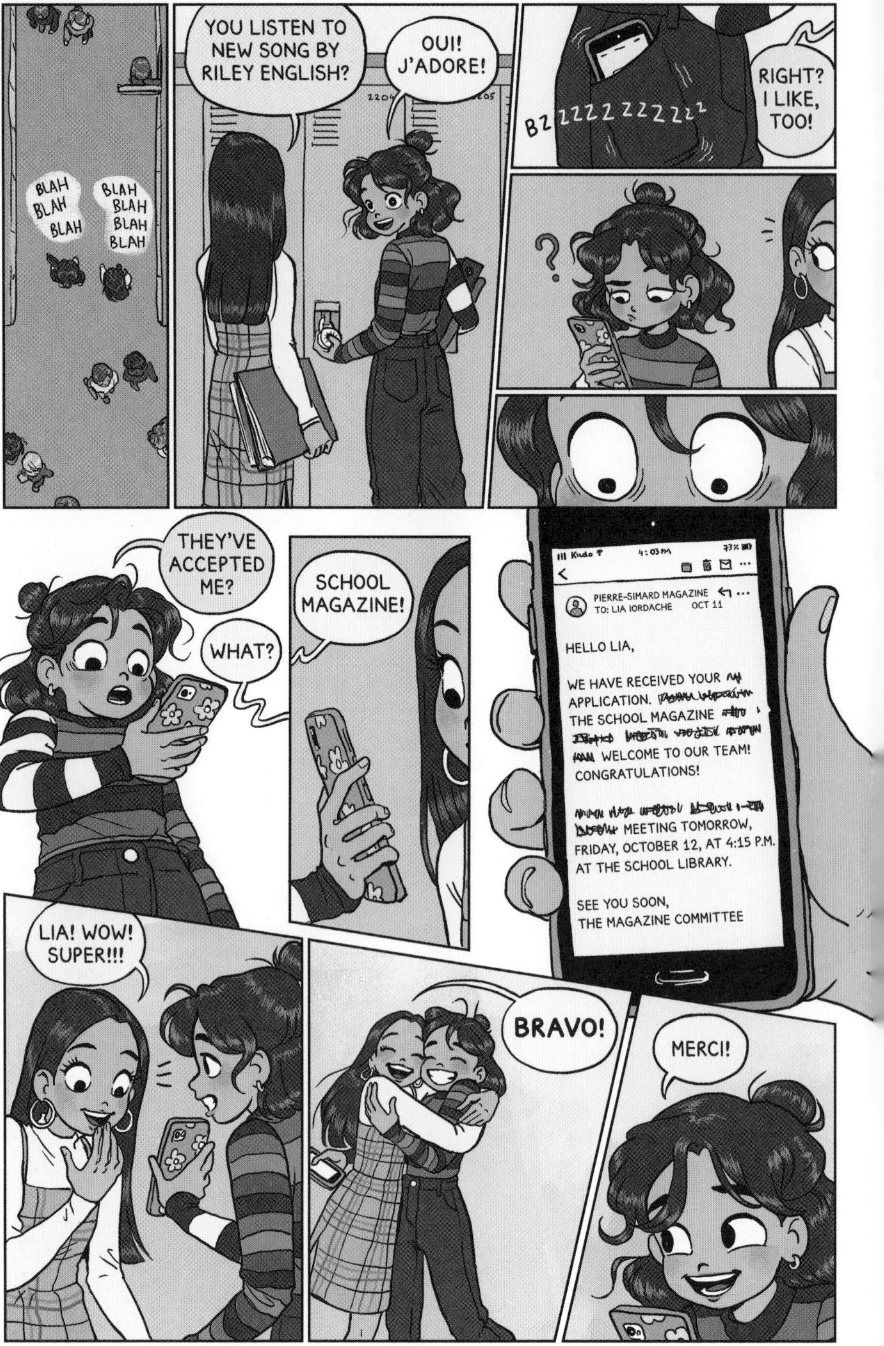
BLAH BLAH BLAH
BLAH BLAH BLAH BLAH
YOU LISTEN TO NEW SONG BY RILEY ENGLISH?
OUI! J'ADORE!
BZZZZZZZZZZZ
RIGHT? I LIKE, TOO!
?
THEY'VE ACCEPTED ME?
WHAT?
SCHOOL MAGAZINE!
Kudo 4:03 PM 73%
PIERRE-SIMARD MAGAZINE
TO: LIA IORDACHE OCT 11
HELLO LIA,
WE HAVE RECEIVED YOUR APPLICATION. THE SCHOOL MAGAZINE
WELCOME TO OUR TEAM! CONGRATULATIONS!
MEETING TOMORROW, FRIDAY, OCTOBER 12, AT 4:15 P.M. AT THE SCHOOL LIBRARY.
SEE YOU SOON,
THE MAGAZINE COMMITTEE
LIA! WOW! SUPER!!!
BRAVO!
MERCI!

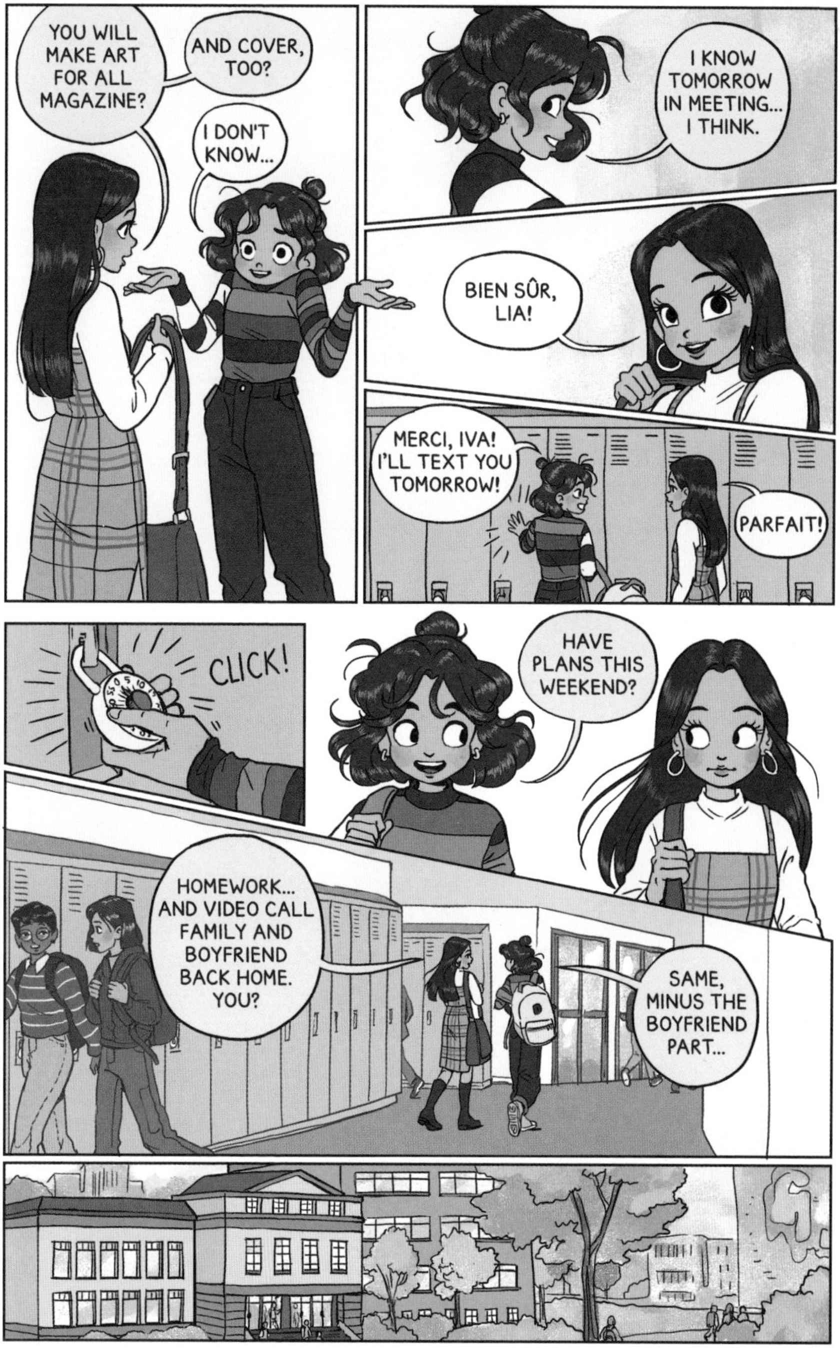
YOU WILL MAKE ART FOR ALL MAGAZINE?
AND COVER, TOO?
I DON'T KNOW...
I KNOW TOMORROW IN MEETING... I THINK.
BIEN SÛR, LIA!
MERCI, IVA! I'LL TEXT YOU TOMORROW!
PARFAIT!
CLICK!
HAVE PLANS THIS WEEKEND?
HOMEWORK... AND VIDEO CALL FAMILY AND BOYFRIEND BACK HOME. YOU?
SAME, MINUS THE BOYFRIEND PART...

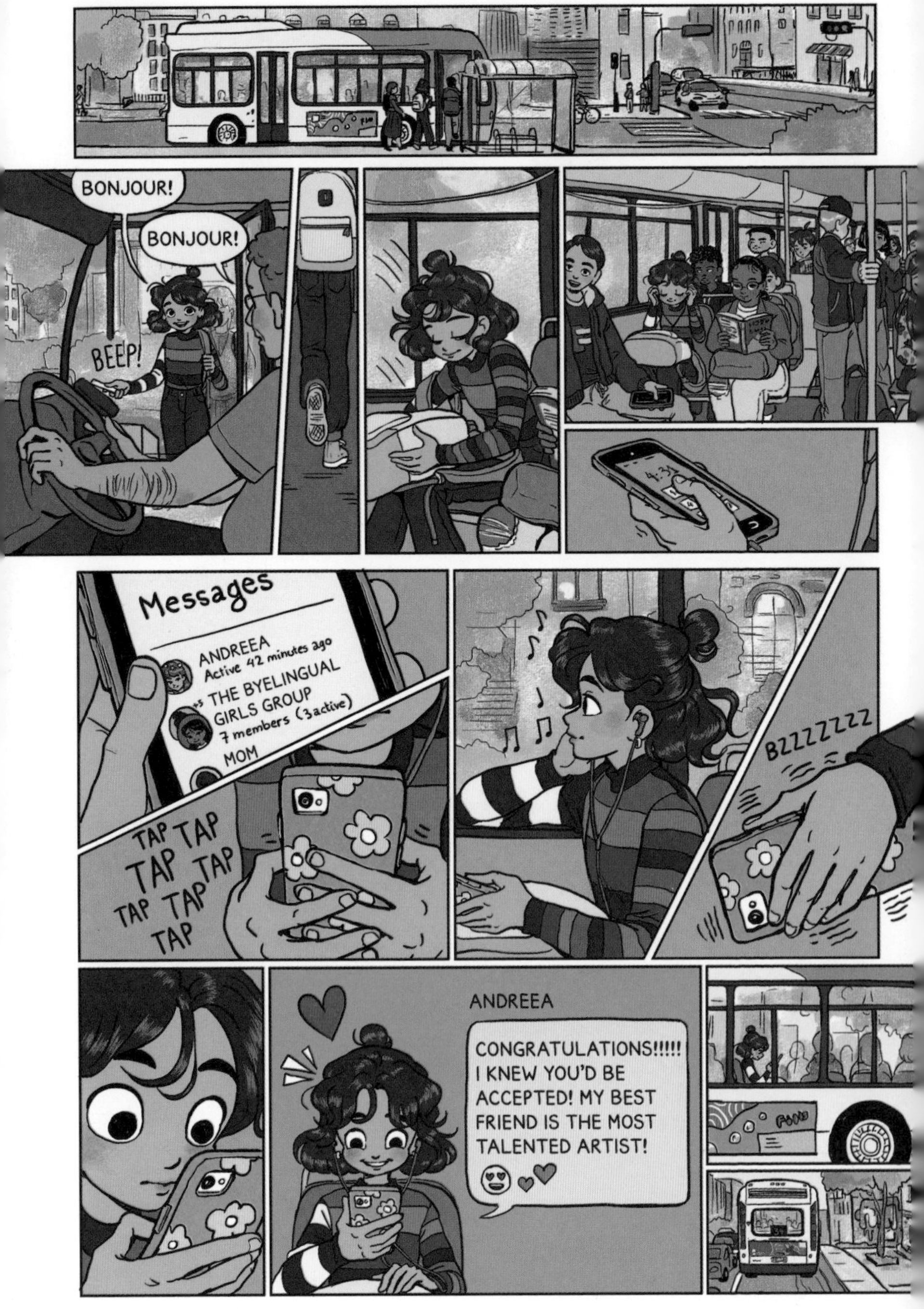
BONJOUR!
BONJOUR!
BEEP!
Messages
ANDREEA
Active 42 minutes ago
THE BYELINGUAL GIRLS GROUP
7 members (3 active)
MOM
TAP TAP TAP TAP TAP TAP TAP
BZZZZZZZ
ANDREEA
CONGRATULATIONS!!!!! I KNEW YOU'D BE ACCEPTED! MY BEST FRIEND IS THE MOST TALENTED ARTIST!

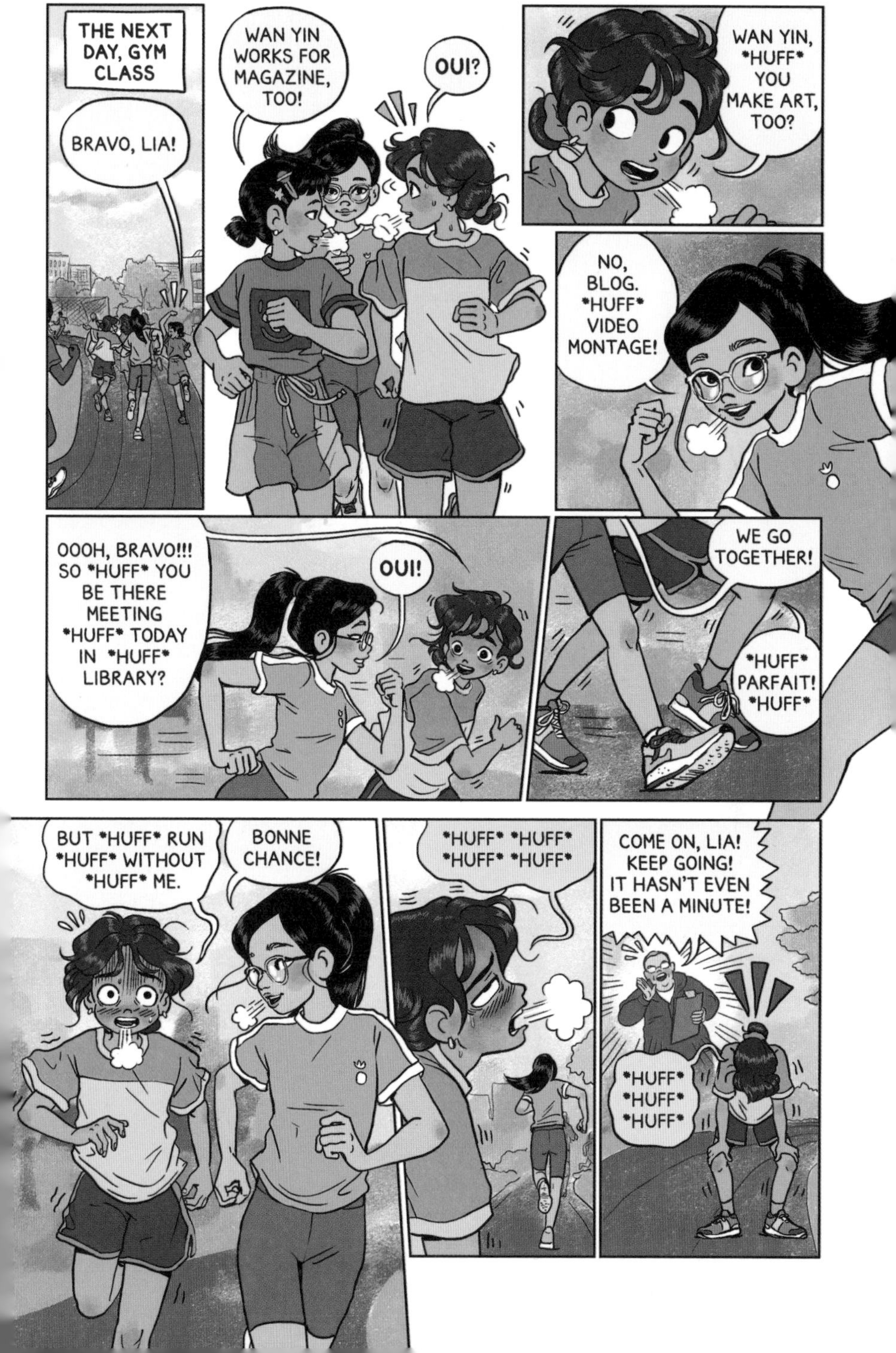
THE NEXT DAY, GYM CLASS
BRAVO, LIA!
WAN YIN WORKS FOR MAGAZINE, TOO!
OUI?
WAN YIN, *HUFF* YOU MAKE ART, TOO?
NO, BLOG. *HUFF* VIDEO MONTAGE!
OOOH, BRAVO!!! SO *HUFF* YOU BE THERE MEETING *HUFF* TODAY IN *HUFF* LIBRARY?
OUI!
WE GO TOGETHER!
HUFF PARFAIT! *HUFF*
BUT *HUFF* RUN *HUFF* WITHOUT *HUFF* ME.
BONNE CHANCE!
HUFF *HUFF* *HUFF* *HUFF*
COME ON, LIA! KEEP GOING! IT HASN'T EVEN BEEN A MINUTE!
HUFF *HUFF* *HUFF*

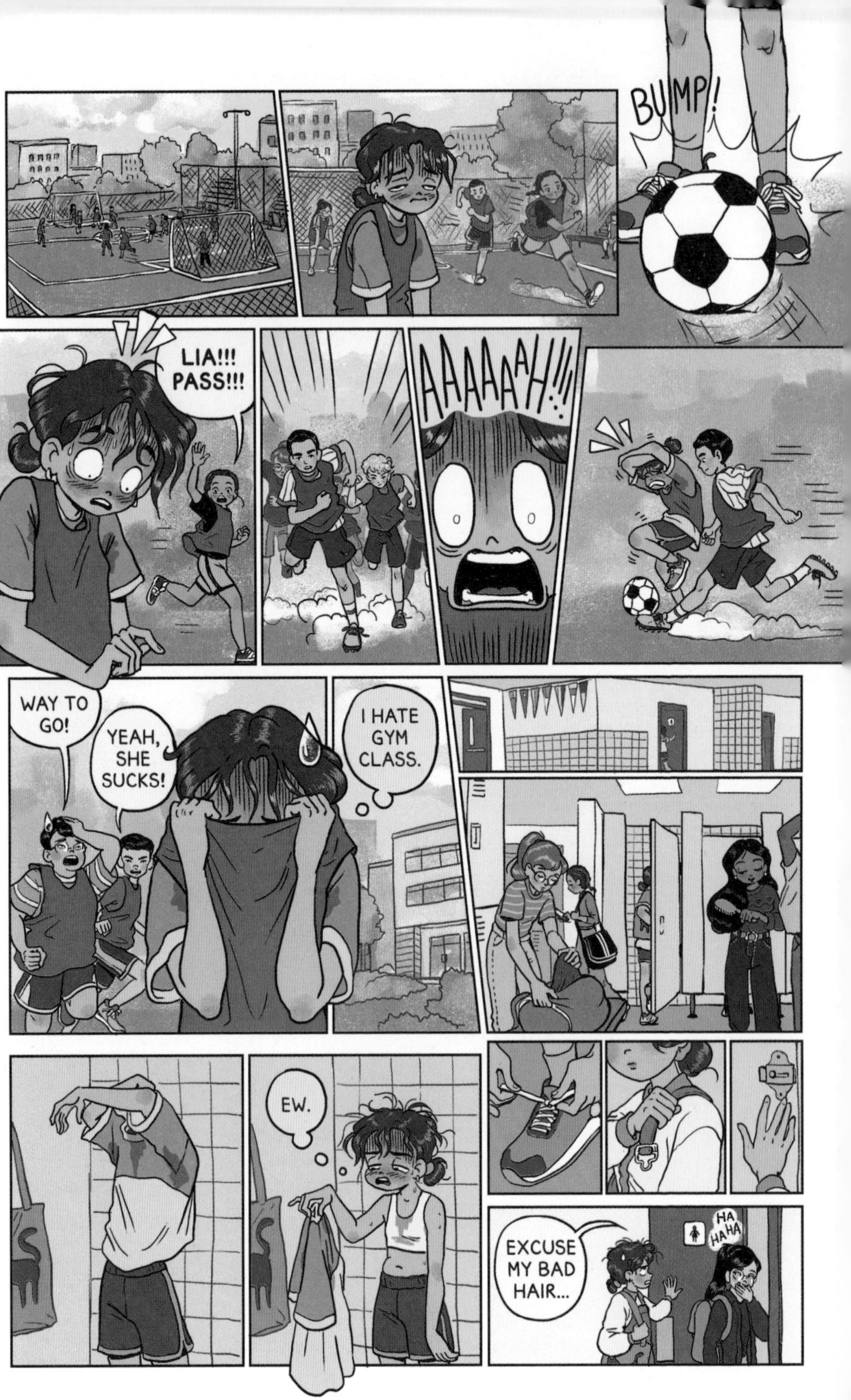
BUMP!
LIA!!! PASS!!!
AAAAAAH!!!
WAY TO GO!
YEAH, SHE SUCKS!
I HATE GYM CLASS.
EW.
EXCUSE MY BAD HAIR...
HA HA HA

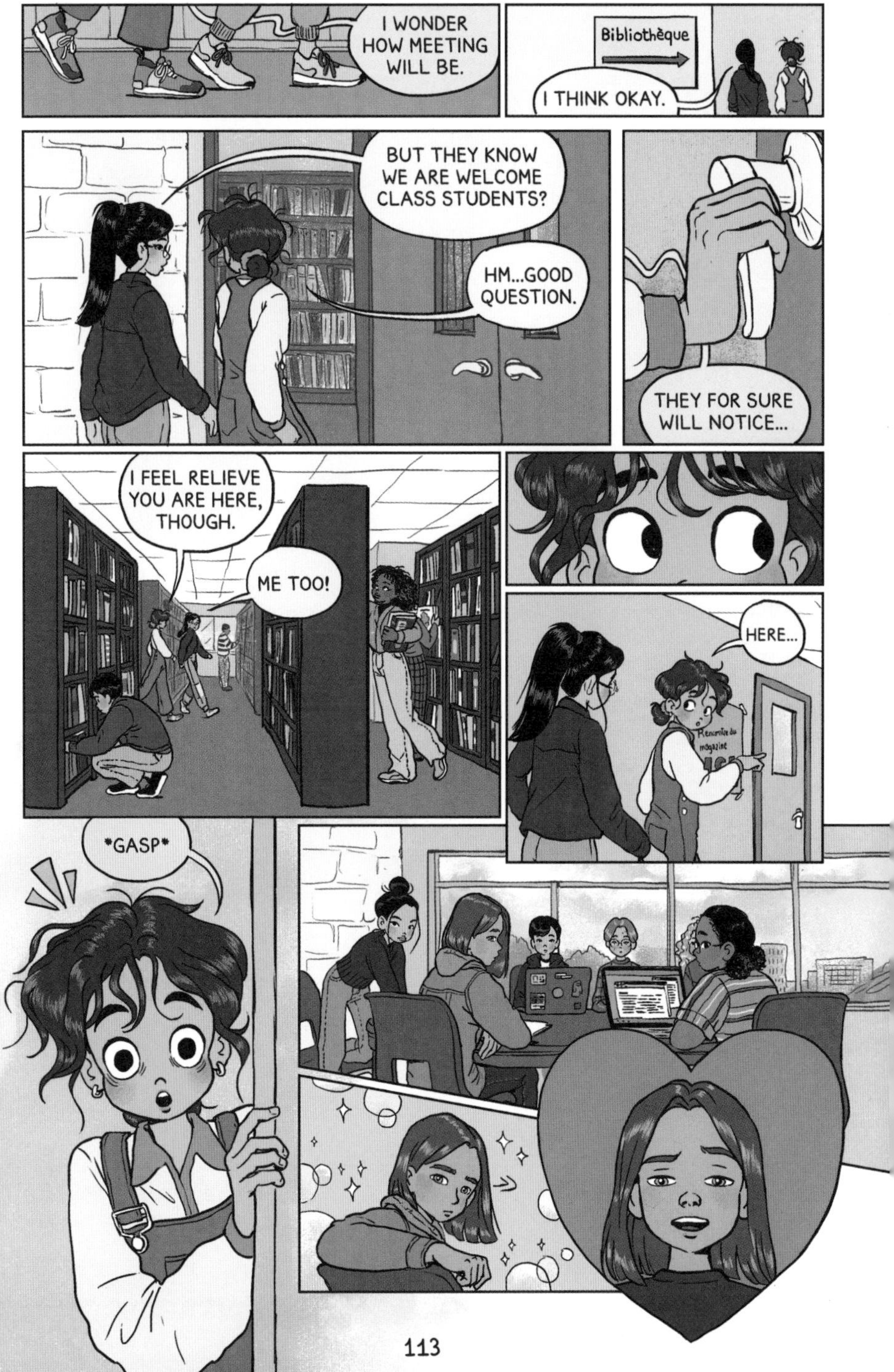
I WONDER HOW MEETING WILL BE.
Bibliothèque
I THINK OKAY.
BUT THEY KNOW WE ARE WELCOME CLASS STUDENTS?
HM...GOOD QUESTION.
THEY FOR SURE WILL NOTICE...
I FEEL RELIEVE YOU ARE HERE, THOUGH.
ME TOO!
HERE...
GASP

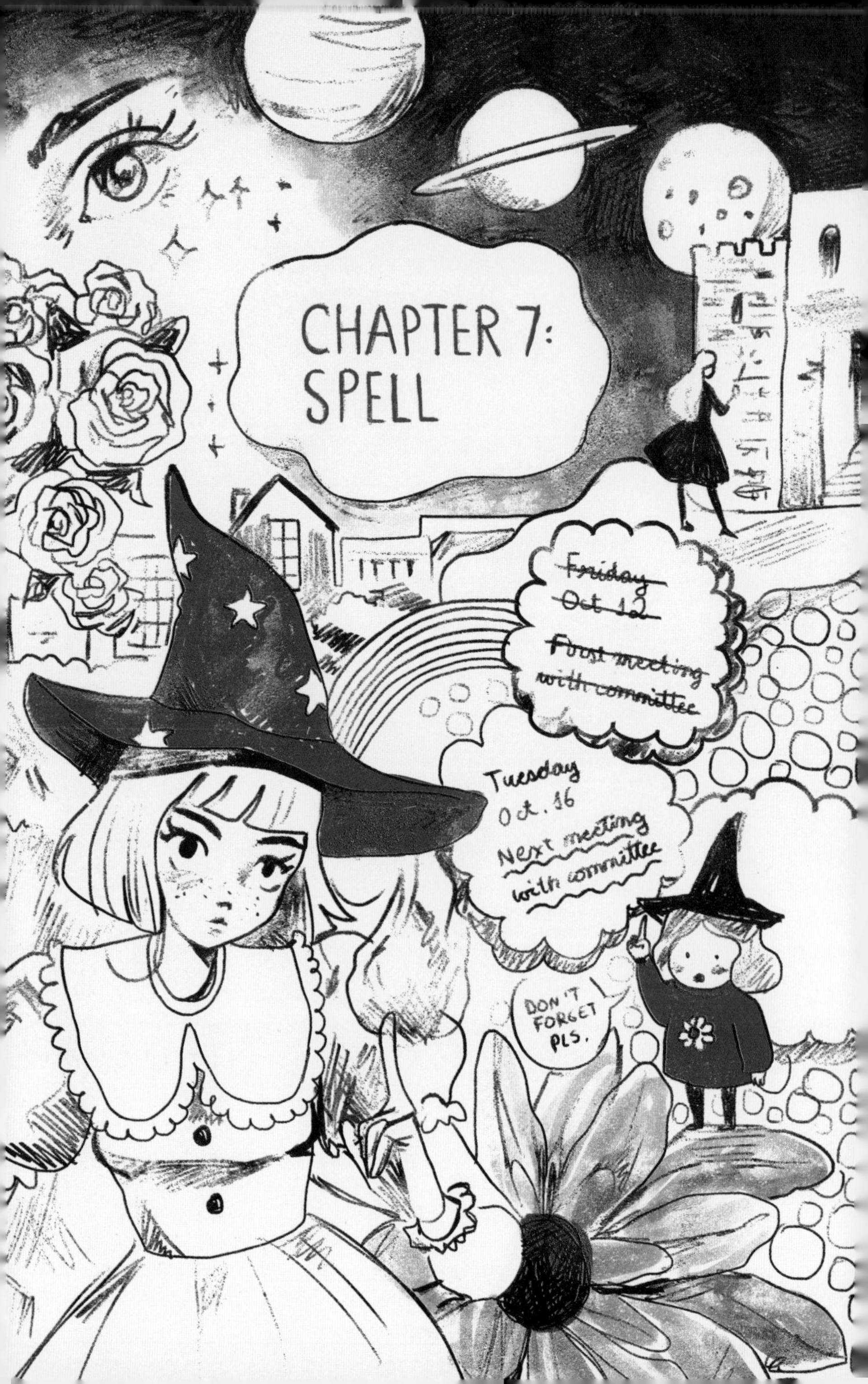

CHAPTER 7: SPELL
Friday Oct 12 First meeting with committee
Tuesday Oct. 16 Next meeting with committee
DON'T FORGET PLS.

WAS GOOD FIRST MEETING!

OUI! WAS FUN!

EEK!!! MY HAIR IS SUCH A MESS!

HEY!

LIA...?

BRAVO ſᴅᴡᴇᴛᴀᴇᴏ ᴏɴ ᴛɴᴀᴛᴄ ᴠᴇᴀᴅᴍ ᴏᴄᴇᴀᴀᴛᴇᴠ ᴜᴀᴄᴀ ᴀᴏᴜᴇᴄᴛᴇᴇʟ ɪᴘ ᴄᴀᴛᴇᴏɴ ᴀᴅᴄᴇᴛᴜɴ ᴀʟᴛᴀᴛ ᴢᴜᴋᴄ ᴀᴛᴘᴀ ᴘᴀᴛᴀᴍ ᴡᴜᴀᴛ ᴀʟᴡᴇᴛᴀ ᴀᴅ.

DÉSOLÉE! UH...CAN YOU NOT TALK, UH... FAST? I DON'T SPEAK GOOD FRENCH.

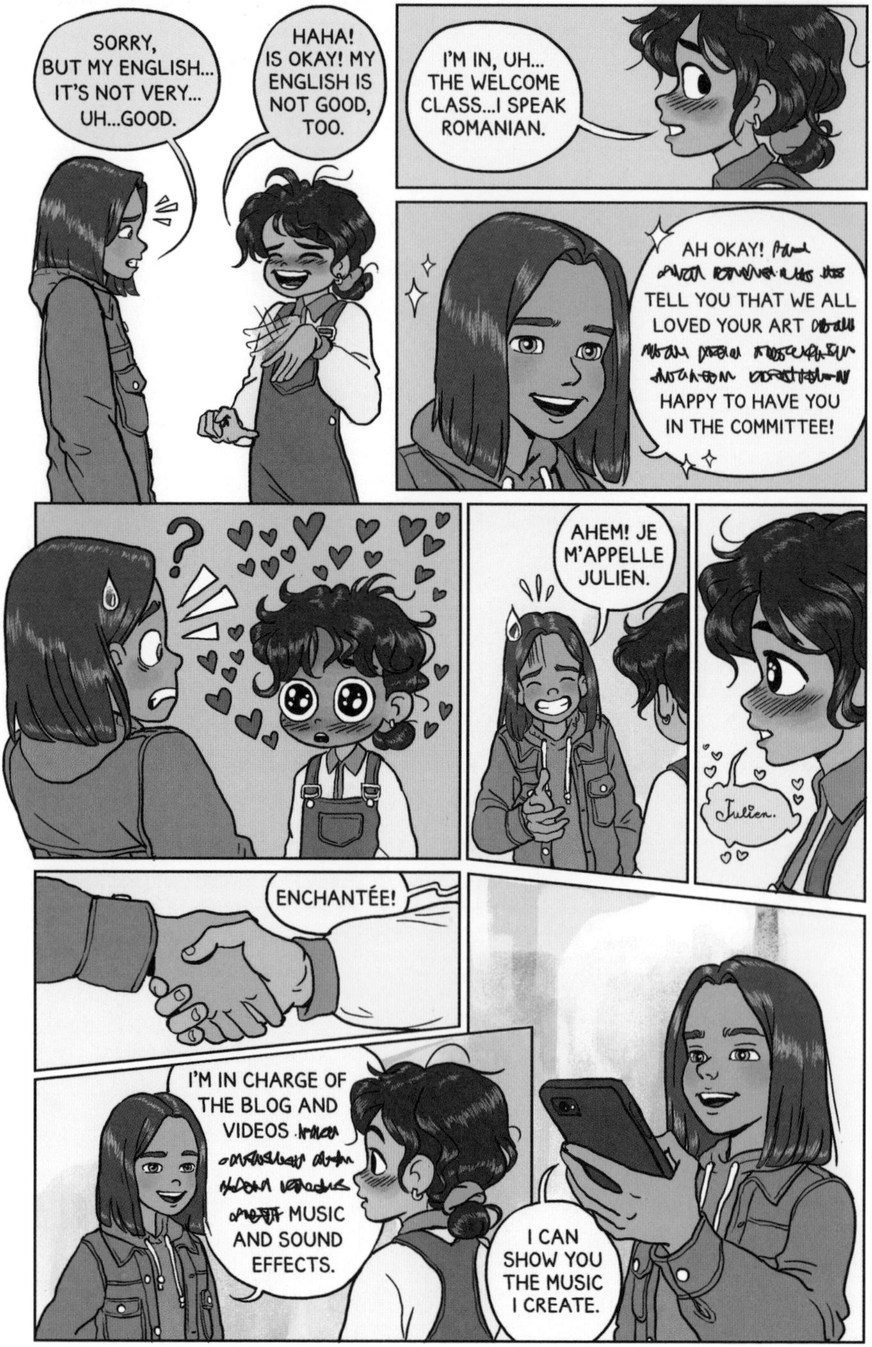
SORRY, BUT MY ENGLISH... IT'S NOT VERY... UH...GOOD.
HAHA! IS OKAY! MY ENGLISH IS NOT GOOD, TOO.
I'M IN, UH... THE WELCOME CLASS...I SPEAK ROMANIAN.
AH OKAY! TELL YOU THAT WE ALL LOVED YOUR ART HAPPY TO HAVE YOU IN THE COMMITTEE!
AHEM! JE M'APPELLE JULIEN.
Julien.
ENCHANTÉE!
I'M IN CHARGE OF THE BLOG AND VIDEOS MUSIC AND SOUND EFFECTS.
I CAN SHOW YOU THE MUSIC I CREATE.

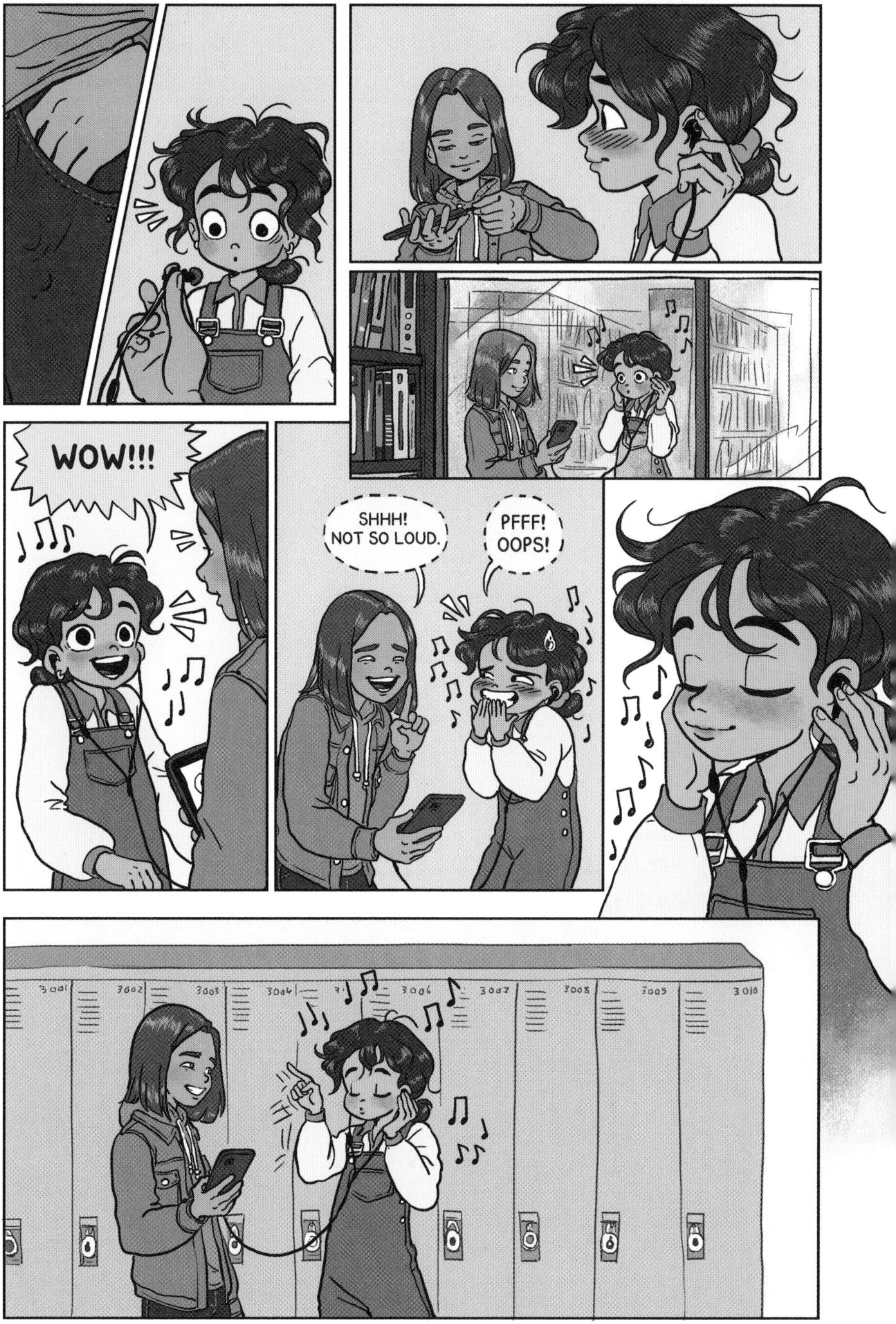
WOW!!!
SHHH! NOT SO LOUD.
PFFF! OOPS!

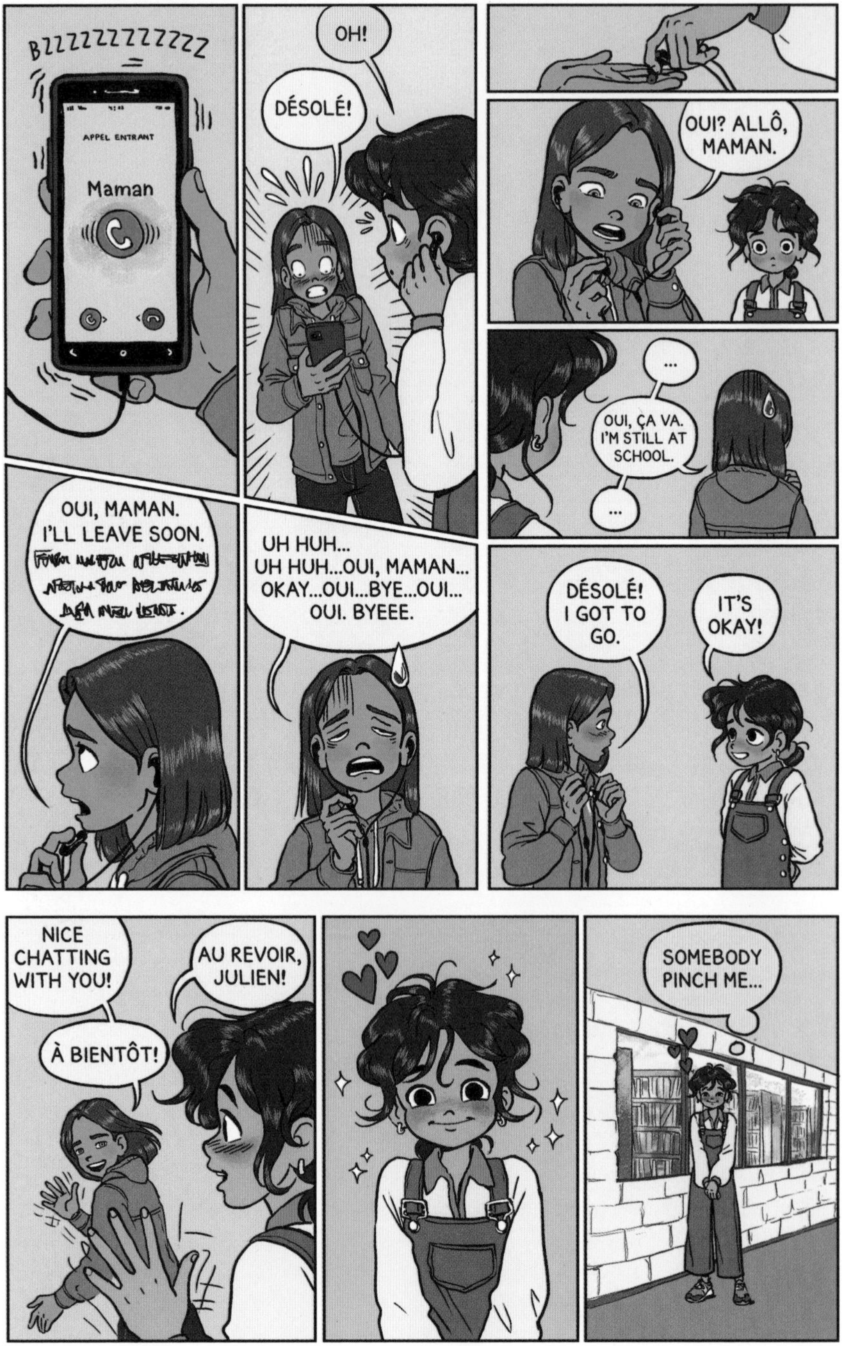
BZZZZZZZZZZZZ
APPEL ENTRANT
Maman
OH!
DÉSOLÉ!
OUI? ALLÔ, MAMAN.
...
OUI, ÇA VA. I'M STILL AT SCHOOL.
...
OUI, MAMAN. I'LL LEAVE SOON.
UH HUH... UH HUH...OUI, MAMAN... OKAY...OUI...BYE...OUI... OUI. BYEEE.
DÉSOLÉ! I GOT TO GO.
IT'S OKAY!
NICE CHATTING WITH YOU!
AU REVOIR, JULIEN!
À BIENTÔT!
SOMEBODY PINCH ME...

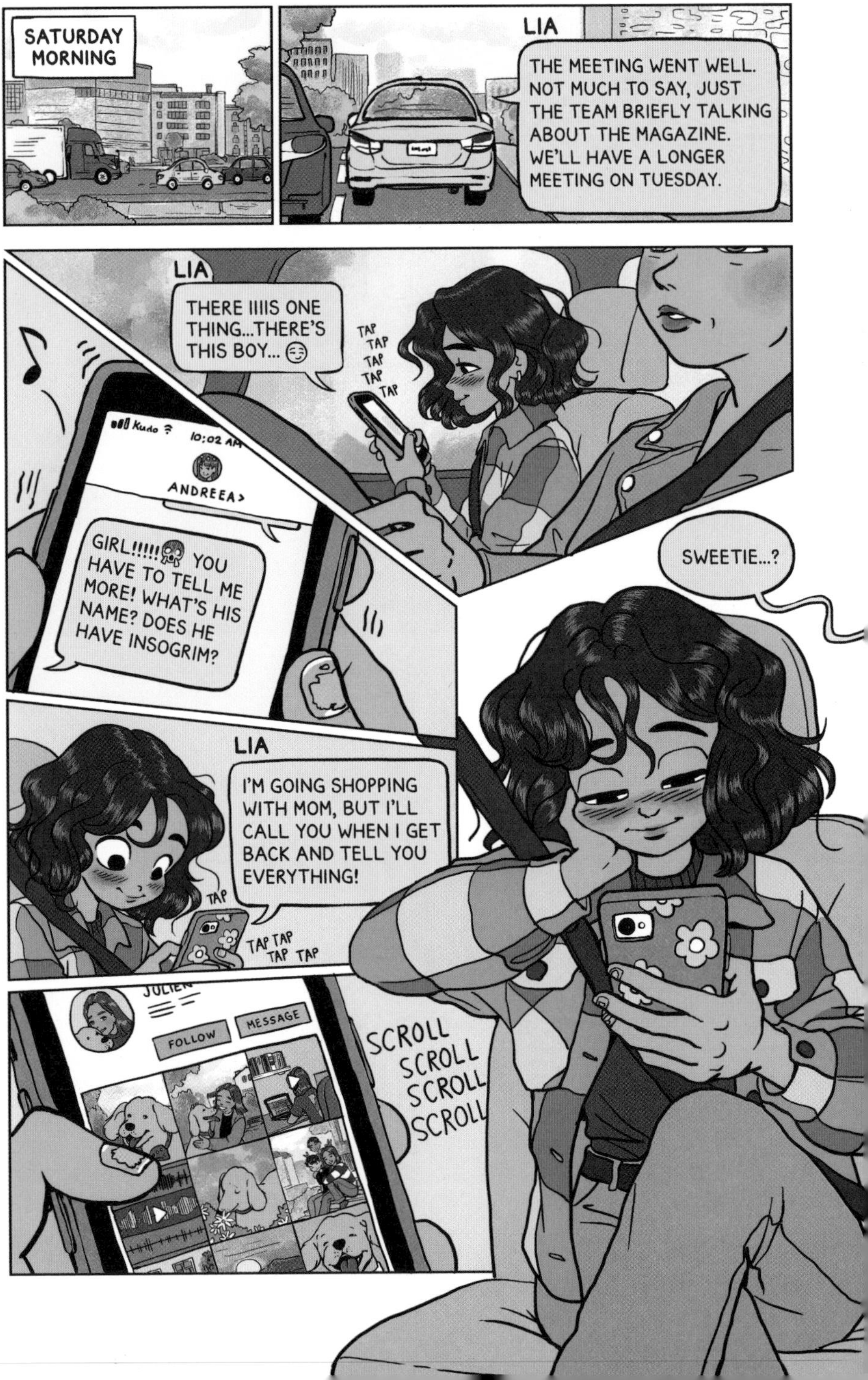
SATURDAY MORNING
LIA
THE MEETING WENT WELL. NOT MUCH TO SAY, JUST THE TEAM BRIEFLY TALKING ABOUT THE MAGAZINE. WE'LL HAVE A LONGER MEETING ON TUESDAY.
LIA
THERE IIIIS ONE THING...THERE'S THIS BOY...
TAP TAP TAP TAP TAP
10:02 AM
ANDREEA
GIRL!!!!! YOU HAVE TO TELL ME MORE! WHAT'S HIS NAME? DOES HE HAVE INSOGRIM?
SWEETIE...?
LIA
I'M GOING SHOPPING WITH MOM, BUT I'LL CALL YOU WHEN I GET BACK AND TELL YOU EVERYTHING!
TAP
TAP TAP TAP TAP
FOLLOW
MESSAGE
SCROLL SCROLL SCROLL SCROLL

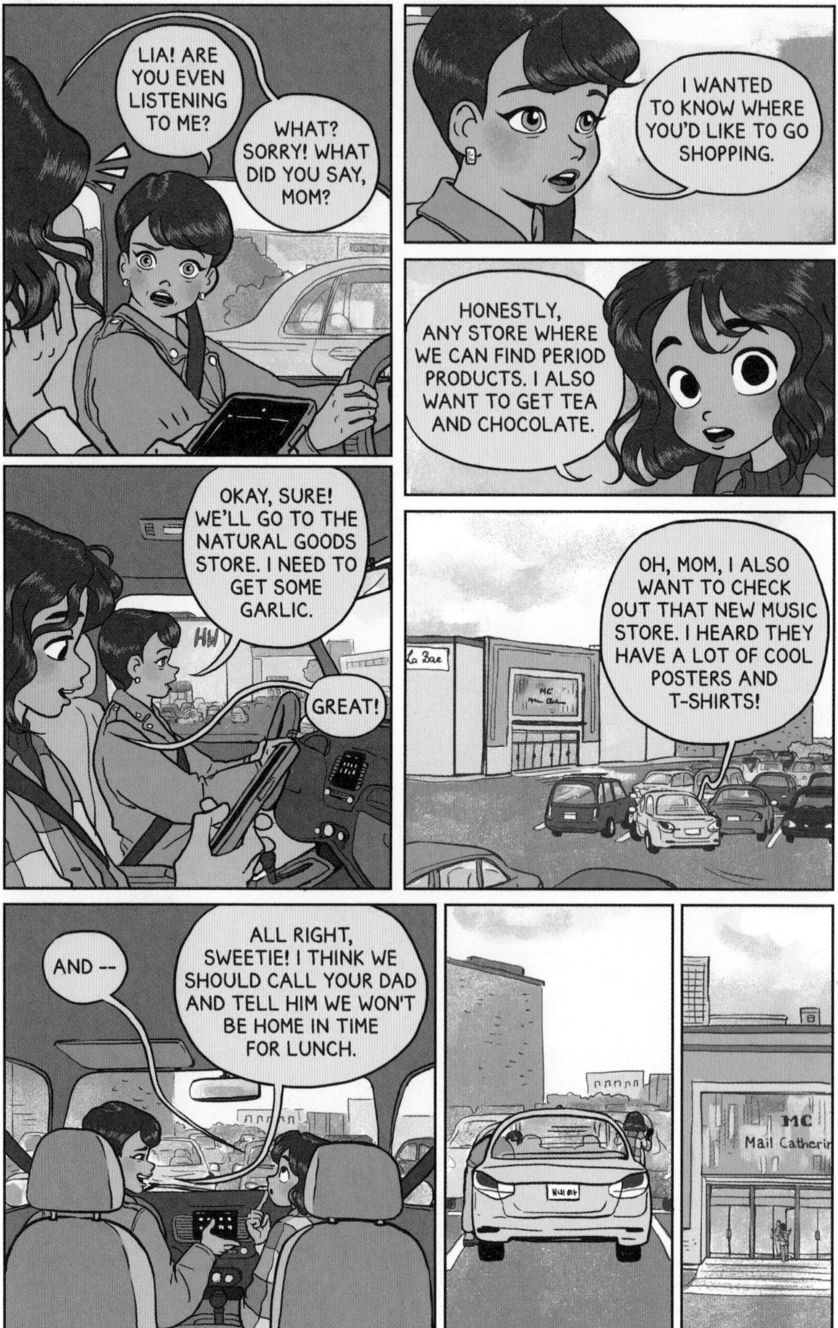

LIA! ARE YOU EVEN LISTENING TO ME?
WHAT? SORRY! WHAT DID YOU SAY, MOM?
I WANTED TO KNOW WHERE YOU'D LIKE TO GO SHOPPING.
HONESTLY, ANY STORE WHERE WE CAN FIND PERIOD PRODUCTS. I ALSO WANT TO GET TEA AND CHOCOLATE.
OKAY, SURE! WE'LL GO TO THE NATURAL GOODS STORE. I NEED TO GET SOME GARLIC.
GREAT!
La Baie
OH, MOM, I ALSO WANT TO CHECK OUT THAT NEW MUSIC STORE. I HEARD THEY HAVE A LOT OF COOL POSTERS AND T-SHIRTS!
AND --
ALL RIGHT, SWEETIE! I THINK WE SHOULD CALL YOUR DAD AND TELL HIM WE WON'T BE HOME IN TIME FOR LUNCH.
MC
Mail Catherin

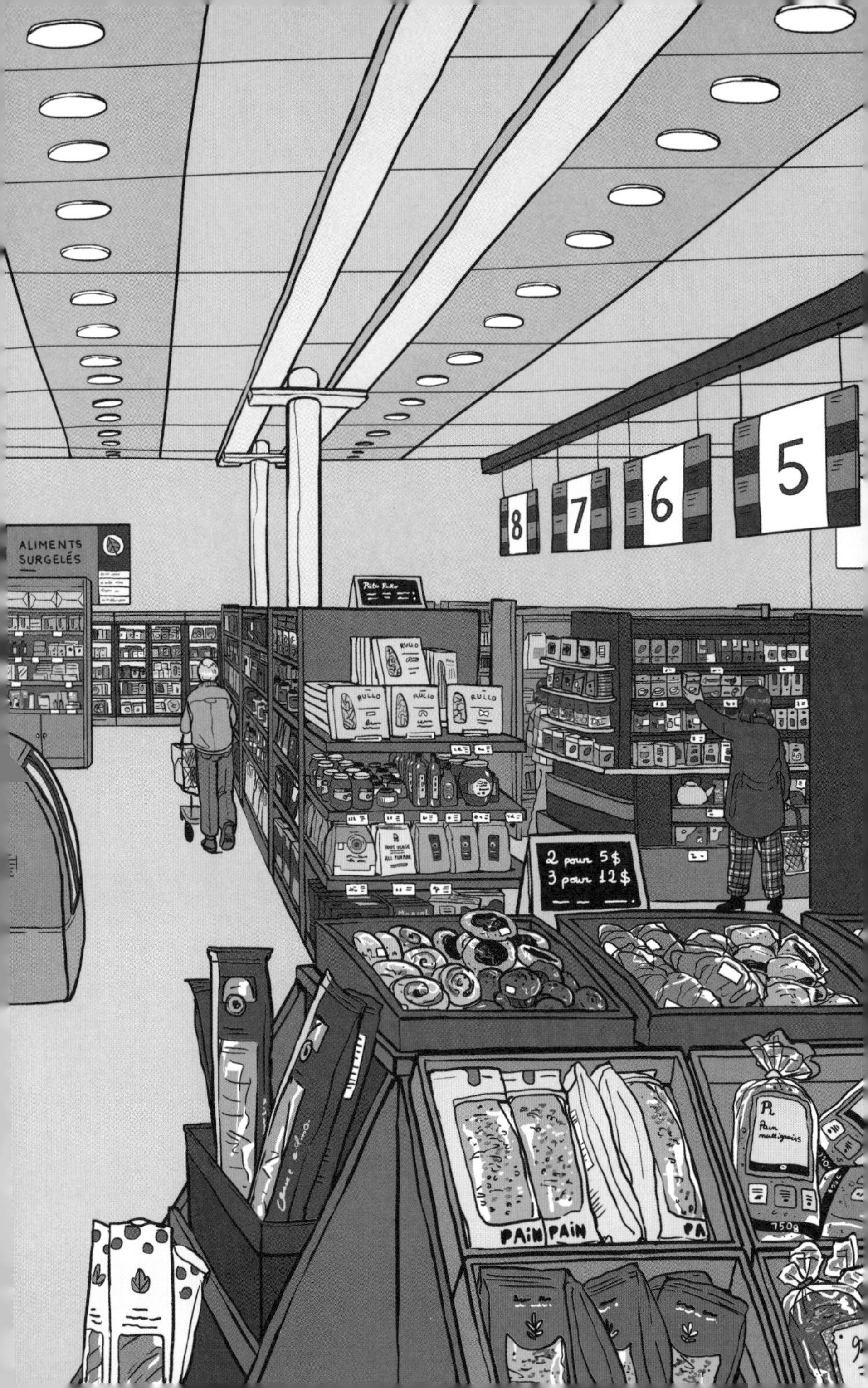
ALIMENTS SURGELÉS
8
7
6
5
RULLO
RULLO
RULLO
RULLO
TOUT USAGE
ALL PURPOSE
2 pour 5 $
3 pour 12 $
PAIN PAIN
Pain multigrains
750g

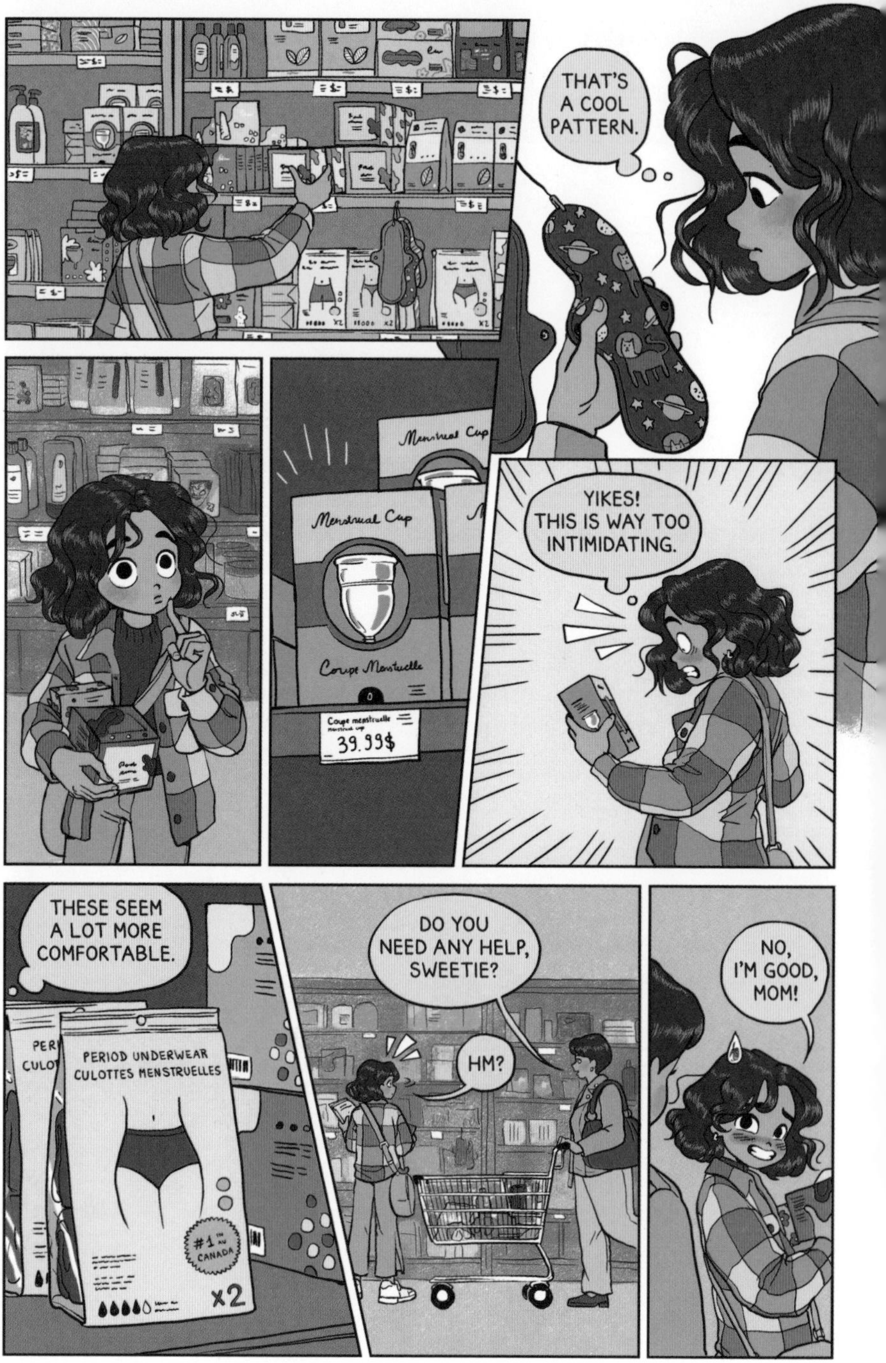
THAT'S A COOL PATTERN.
Menstrual Cup
Coupe Menstruelle
Coupe menstruelle
39.99$
YIKES! THIS IS WAY TOO INTIMIDATING.
THESE SEEM A LOT MORE COMFORTABLE.
PERIOD UNDERWEAR
CULOTTES MENSTRUELLES
#1 CANADA
x2
DO YOU NEED ANY HELP, SWEETIE?
HM?
NO, I'M GOOD, MOM!

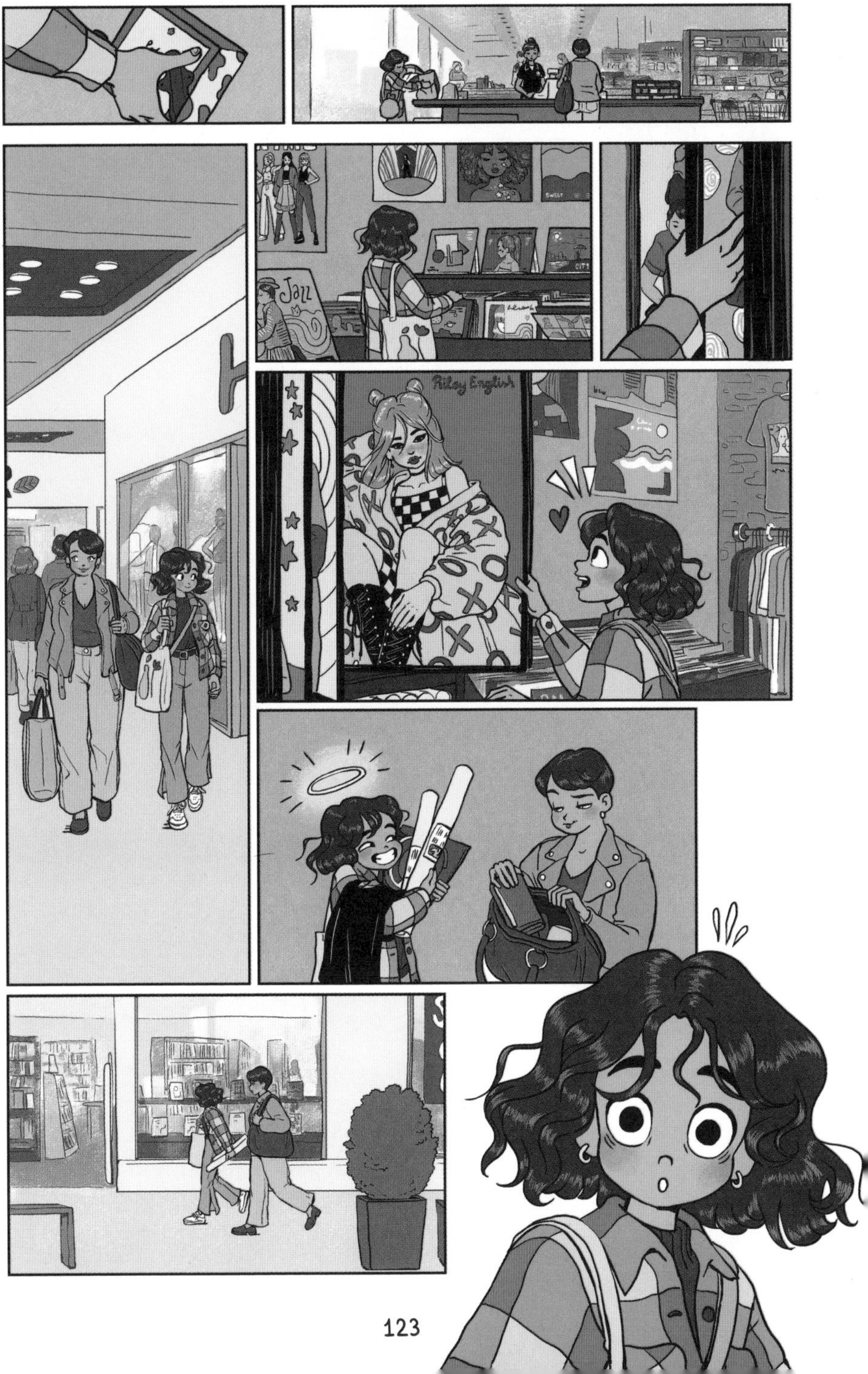
Jazz
Riley English

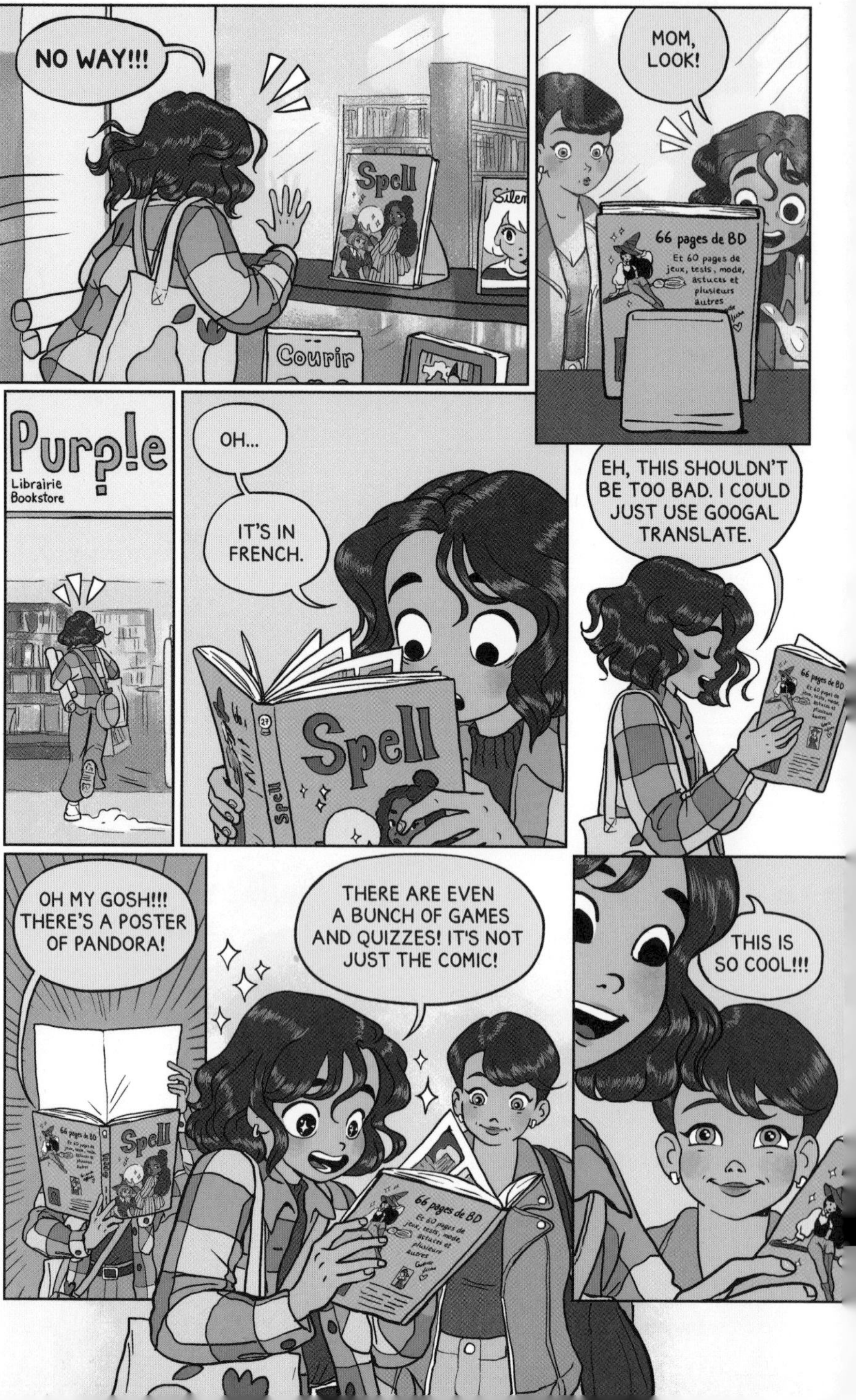
NO WAY!!!
Spell
Courir
MOM, LOOK!
66 pages de BD
Et 60 pages de jeux, tests, mode, astuces et plusieurs autres
Purple
Librairie
Bookstore
OH...
IT'S IN FRENCH.
Spell
EH, THIS SHOULDN'T BE TOO BAD. I COULD JUST USE GOOGAL TRANSLATE.
OH MY GOSH!!! THERE'S A POSTER OF PANDORA!
THERE ARE EVEN A BUNCH OF GAMES AND QUIZZES! IT'S NOT JUST THE COMIC!
THIS IS SO COOL!!!

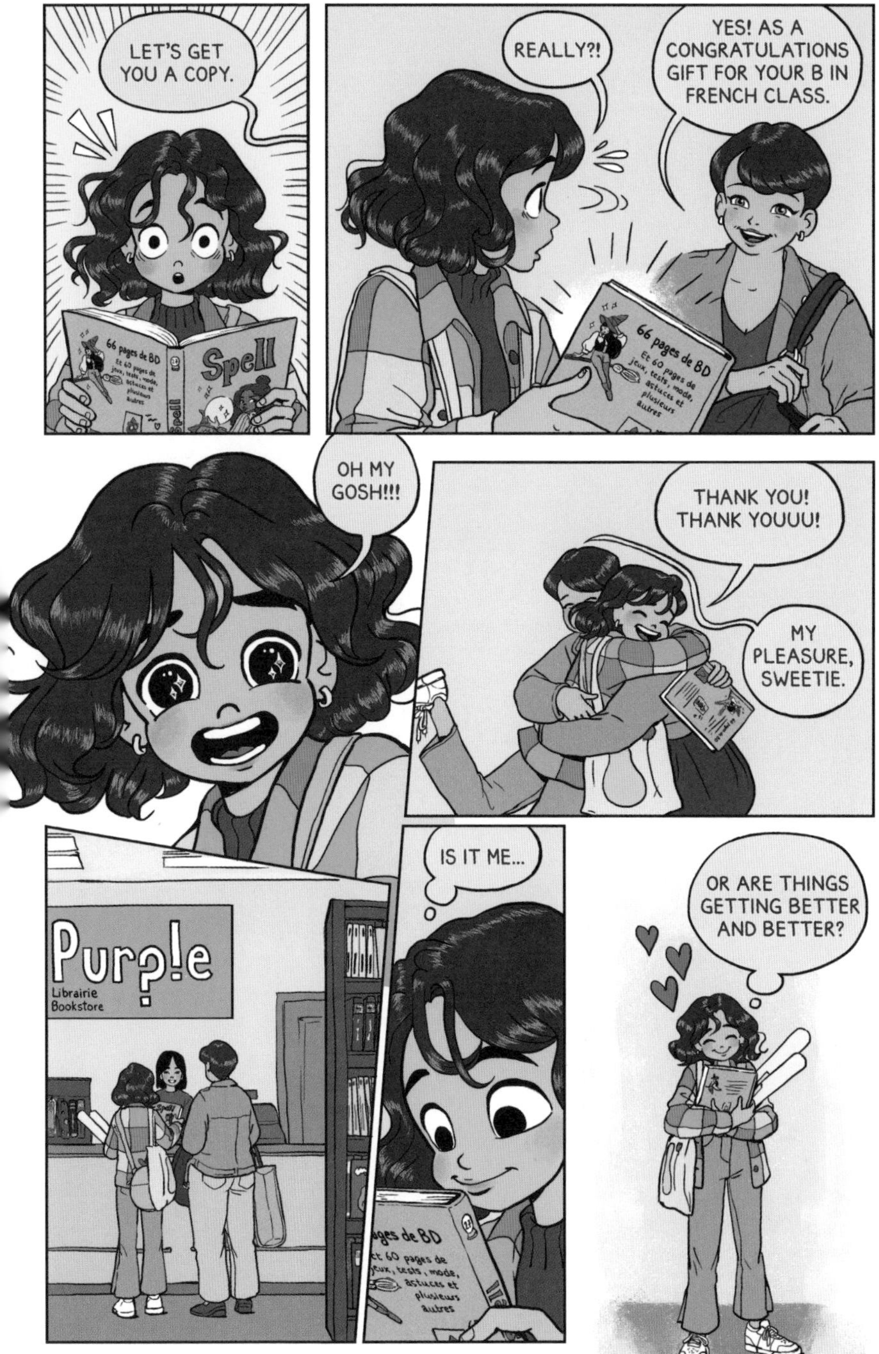
LET'S GET YOU A COPY.
66 pages de BD
Spell
REALLY?!
YES! AS A CONGRATULATIONS GIFT FOR YOUR B IN FRENCH CLASS.
66 pages de BD
Et 60 pages de jeux, tests, mode, astuces et plusieurs autres
OH MY GOSH!!!
THANK YOU! THANK YOUUU!
MY PLEASURE, SWEETIE.
Purp?!e
Librairie
Bookstore
IS IT ME...
OR ARE THINGS GETTING BETTER AND BETTER?

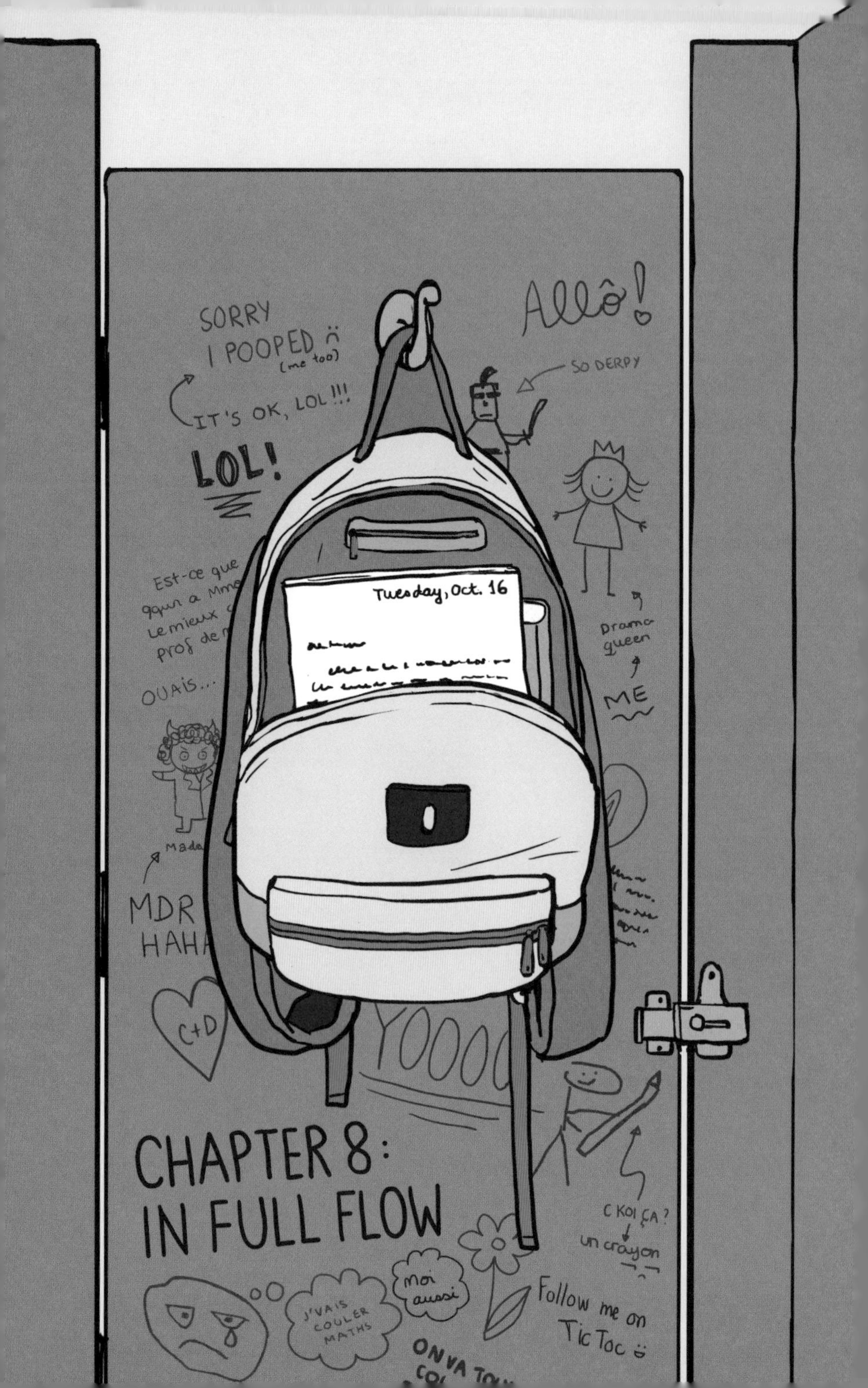

SORRY I POOPED
(me too)
IT'S OK, LOL!!!
LOL!
Allô!
SO DERPY
Tuesday, Oct. 16
Drama queen
ME
OUAIS...
MDR
C+D
CHAPTER 8:
IN FULL FLOW
C KOI ÇA ?
un crayon
J'VAIS COULER MATHS
moi aussi
Follow me on TicToc

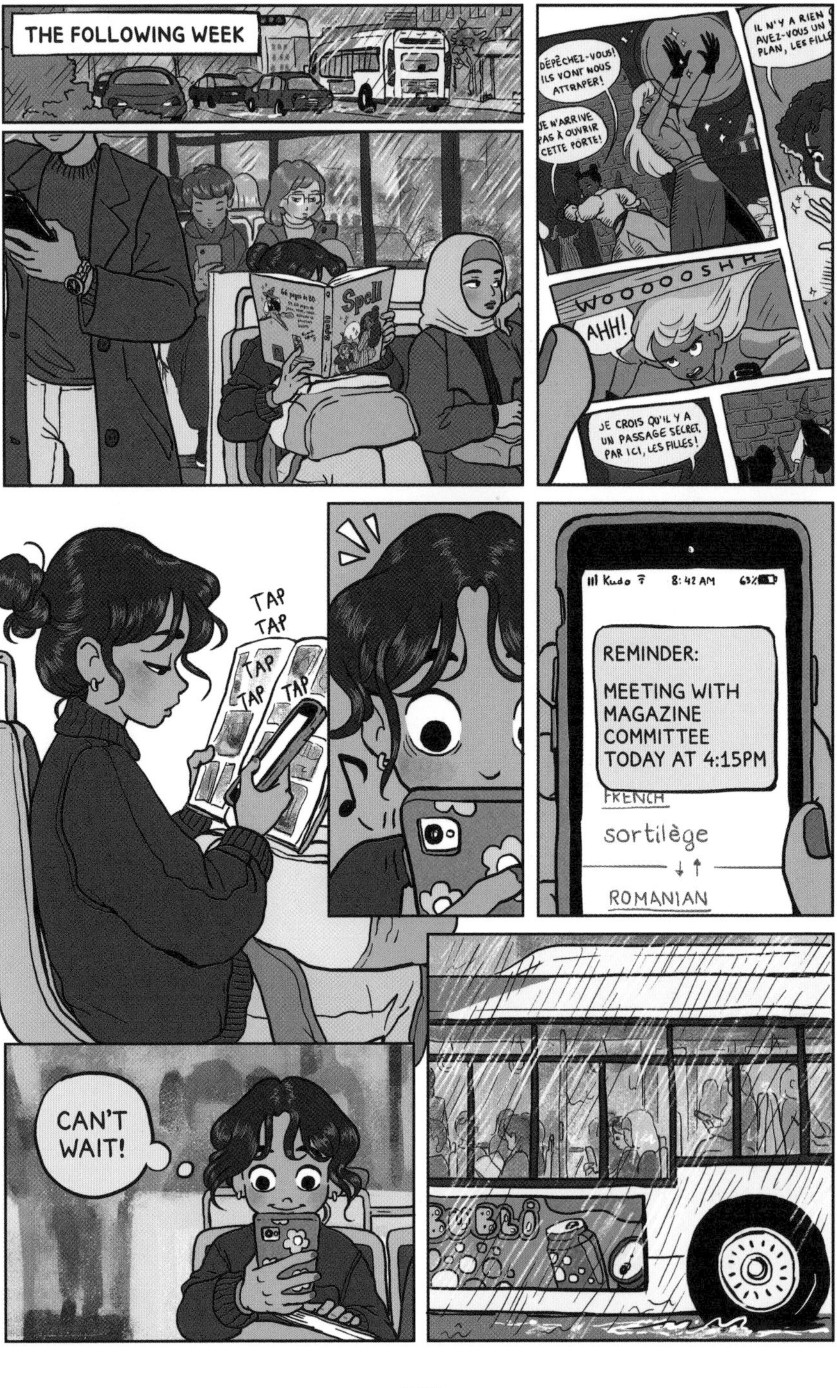
THE FOLLOWING WEEK
Spell
DÉPÊCHEZ-VOUS! ILS VONT NOUS ATTRAPER!
JE N'ARRIVE PAS À OUVRIR CETTE PORTE!
IL N'Y A RIEN
AVEZ-VOUS UN
PLAN, LES FILLE
WOOOOOOSHH
AHH!
JE CROIS QU'IL Y A UN PASSAGE SECRET, PAR ICI, LES FILLES!
TAP TAP
TAP TAP TAP
Kudo 8:42 AM 63%
REMINDER:
MEETING WITH MAGAZINE COMMITTEE TODAY AT 4:15PM
FRENCH
sortilège
ROMANIAN
CAN'T WAIT!
BUBLÍ

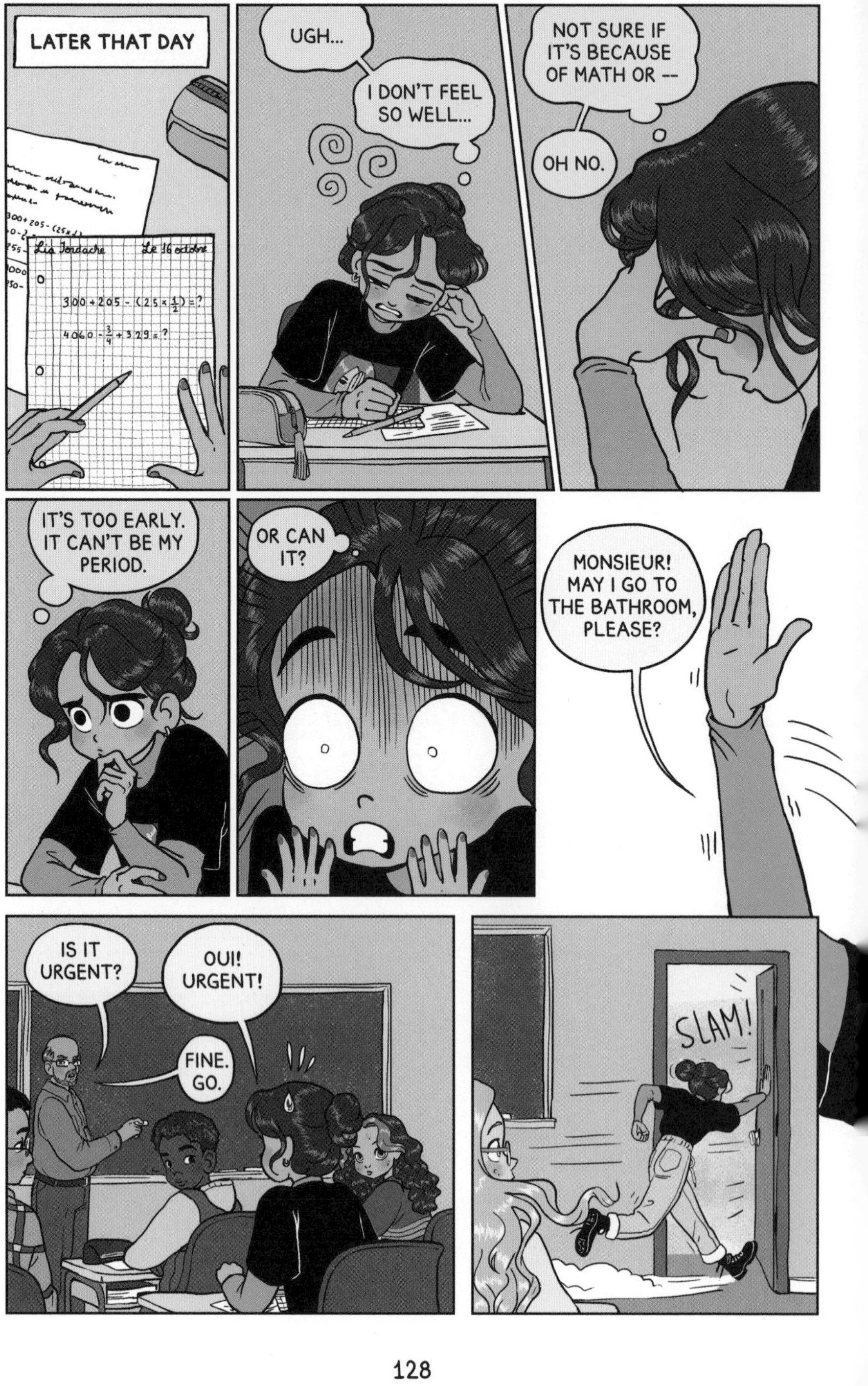
LATER THAT DAY
Lia Iordache
Le 16 octobre
300 + 205 - (25 × 1/2) = ?
4060 - 3/4 + 329 = ?
UGH...
I DON'T FEEL SO WELL...
NOT SURE IF IT'S BECAUSE OF MATH OR --
OH NO.
IT'S TOO EARLY. IT CAN'T BE MY PERIOD.
OR CAN IT?
MONSIEUR! MAY I GO TO THE BATHROOM, PLEASE?
IS IT URGENT?
OUI! URGENT!
FINE. GO.
SLAM!

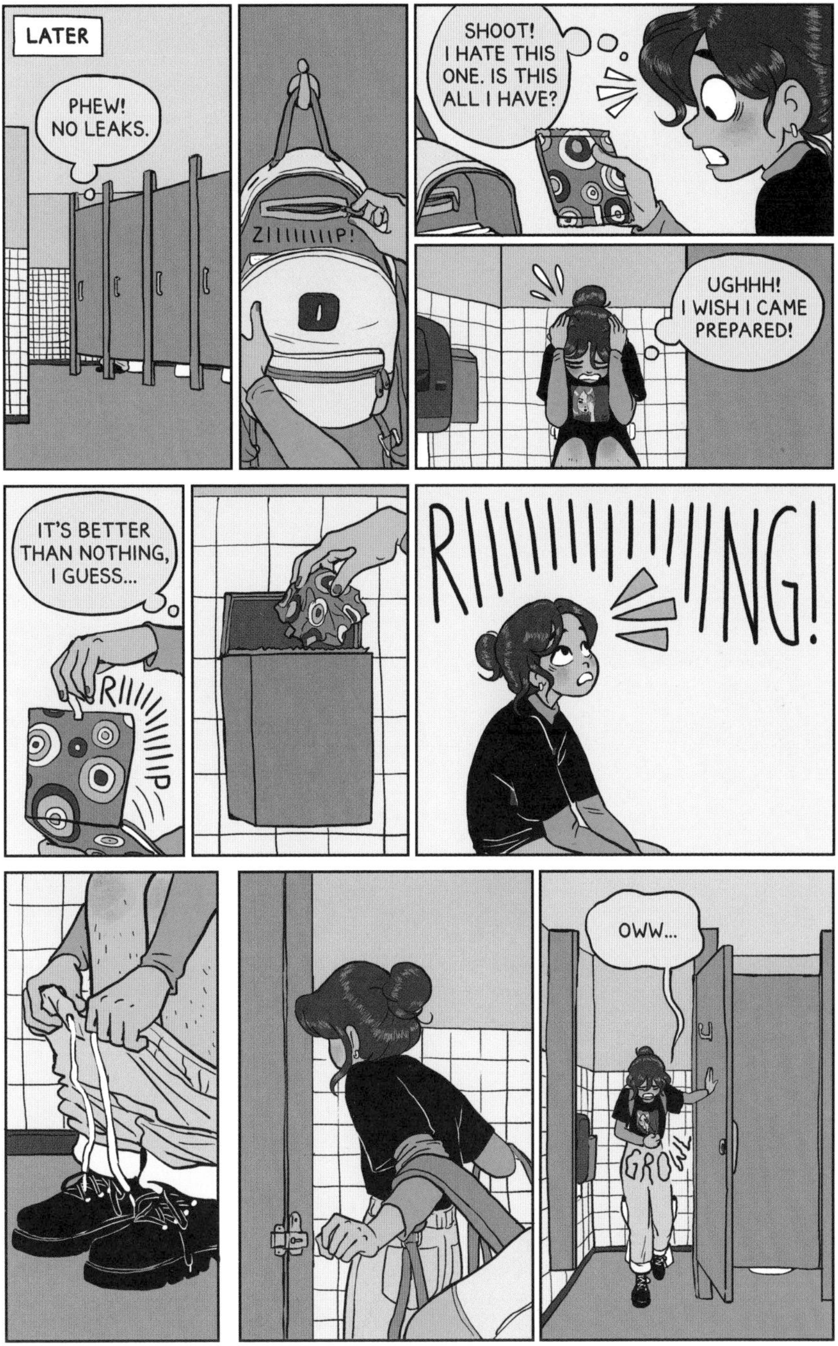
LATER
PHEW! NO LEAKS.
ZIIIIIIIP!
SHOOT! I HATE THIS ONE. IS THIS ALL I HAVE?
UGHHH! I WISH I CAME PREPARED!
IT'S BETTER THAN NOTHING, I GUESS...
RIIIIIIP
RIIIIIIIIIIIING!
OWW...
GROWL

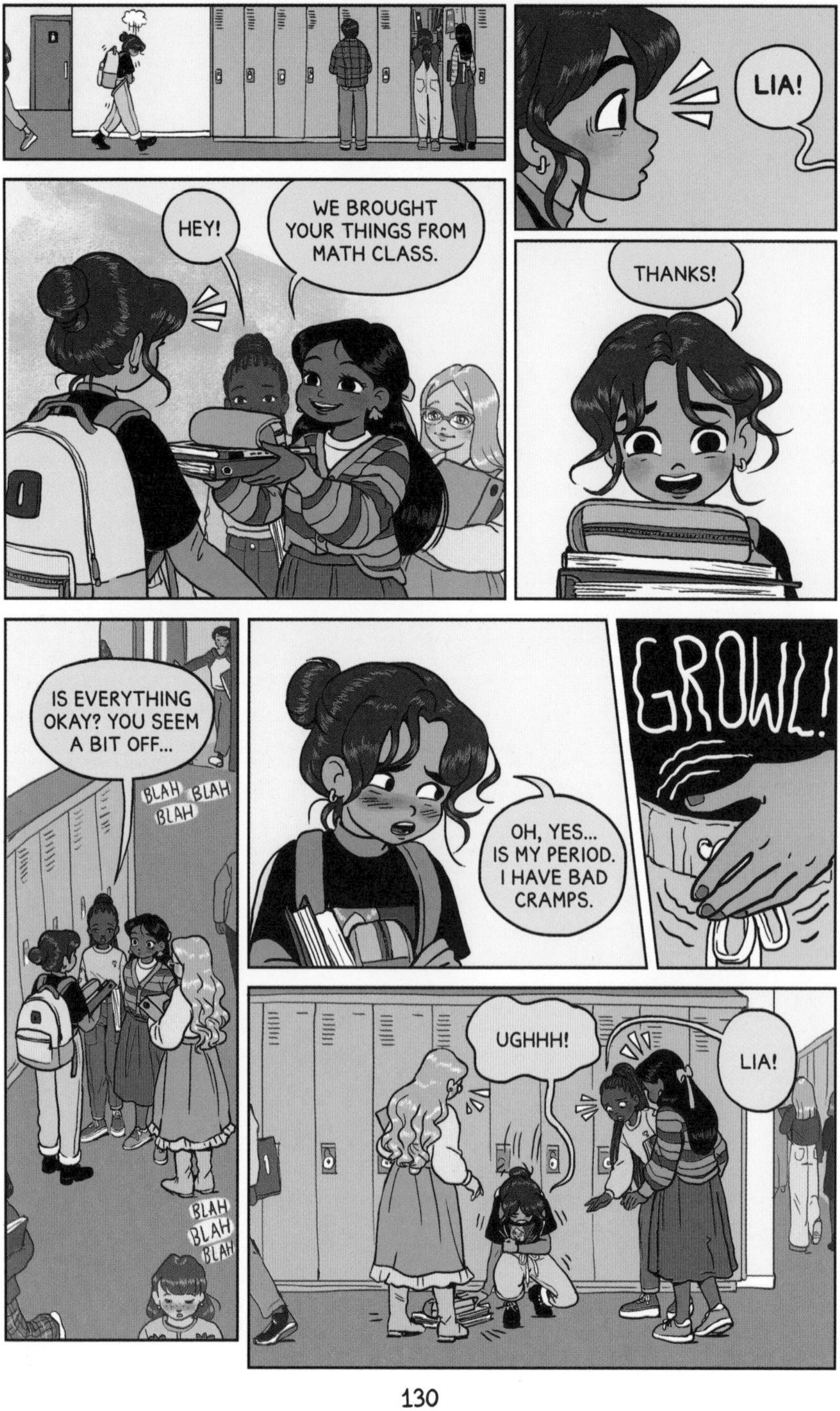
LIA!
HEY!
WE BROUGHT YOUR THINGS FROM MATH CLASS.
THANKS!
IS EVERYTHING OKAY? YOU SEEM A BIT OFF...
BLAH BLAH BLAH
BLAH BLAH BLAH
OH, YES... IS MY PERIOD. I HAVE BAD CRAMPS.
GROWL!
UGHHH!
LIA!

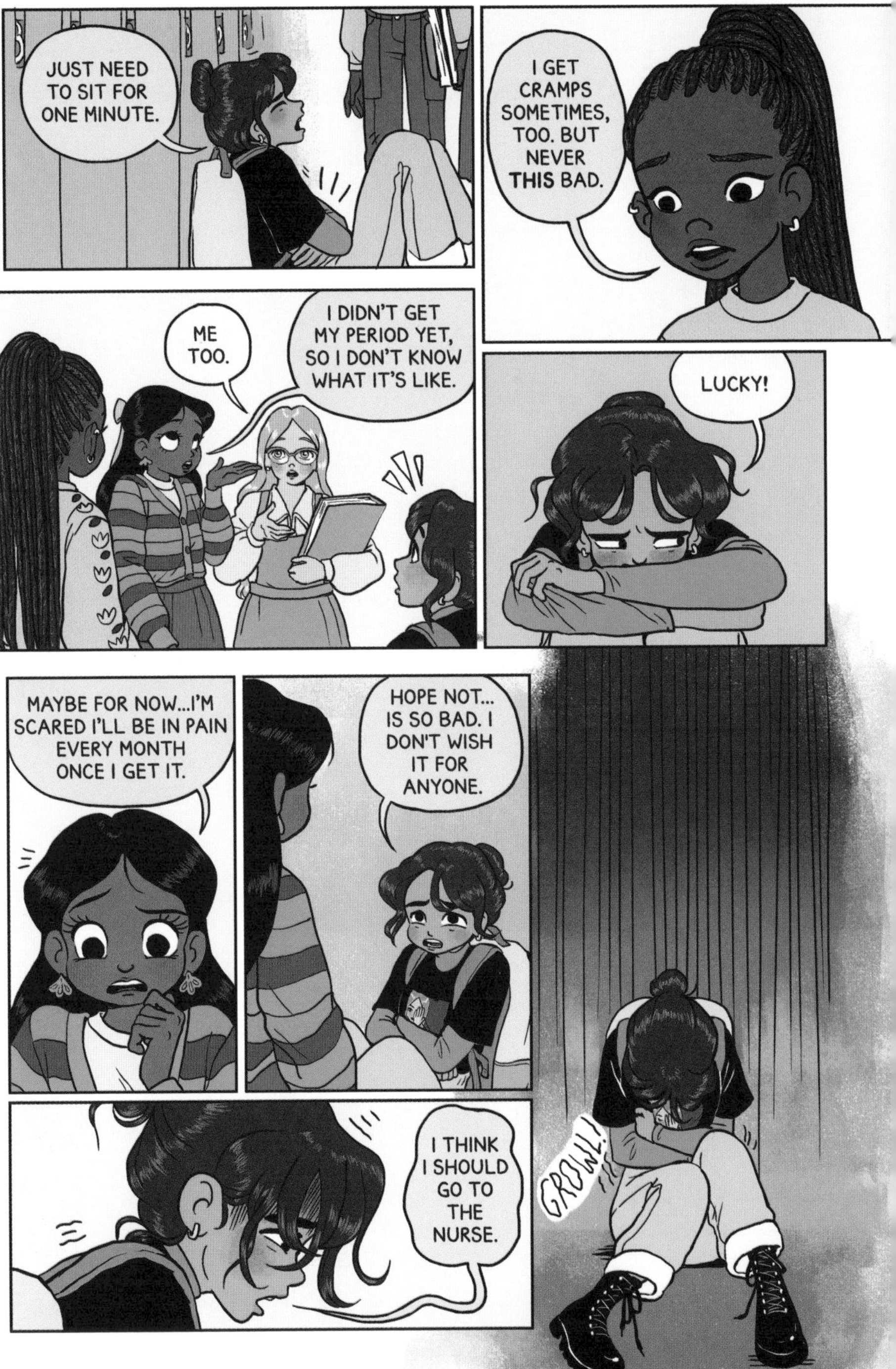
JUST NEED TO SIT FOR ONE MINUTE.
I GET CRAMPS SOMETIMES, TOO. BUT NEVER THIS BAD.
ME TOO.
I DIDN'T GET MY PERIOD YET, SO I DON'T KNOW WHAT IT'S LIKE.
LUCKY!
MAYBE FOR NOW...I'M SCARED I'LL BE IN PAIN EVERY MONTH ONCE I GET IT.
HOPE NOT... IS SO BAD. I DON'T WISH IT FOR ANYONE.
I THINK I SHOULD GO TO THE NURSE.
GROWL!

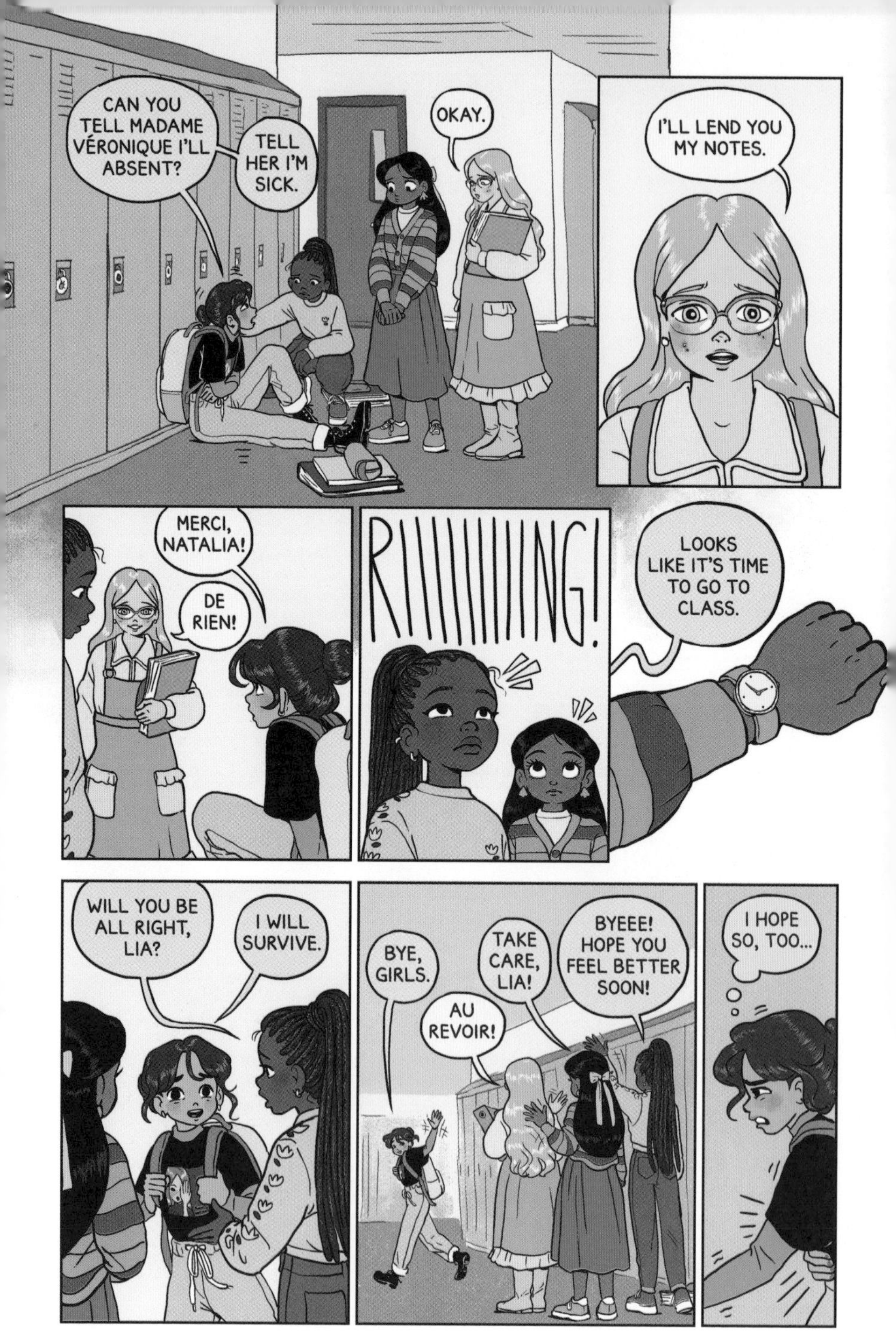
CAN YOU TELL MADAME VÉRONIQUE I'LL ABSENT?
TELL HER I'M SICK.
OKAY.
I'LL LEND YOU MY NOTES.
MERCI, NATALIA!
DE RIEN!
RIIIIIIIIING!
LOOKS LIKE IT'S TIME TO GO TO CLASS.
WILL YOU BE ALL RIGHT, LIA?
I WILL SURVIVE.
BYE, GIRLS.
AU REVOIR!
TAKE CARE, LIA!
BYEEE! HOPE YOU FEEL BETTER SOON!
I HOPE SO, TOO...

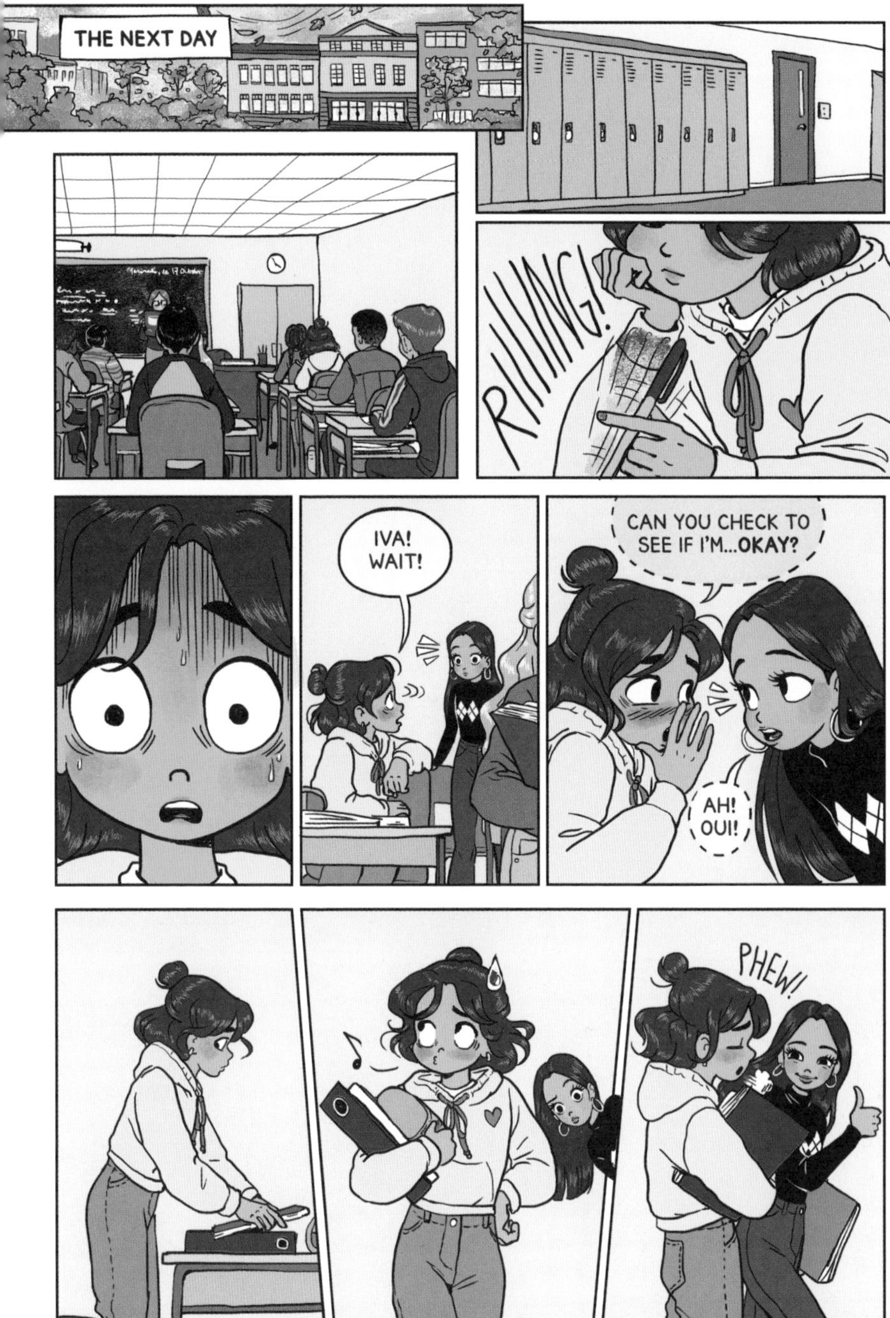
THE NEXT DAY
RIIING!
IVA! WAIT!
CAN YOU CHECK TO SEE IF I'M...OKAY?
AH! OUI!
PHEW!

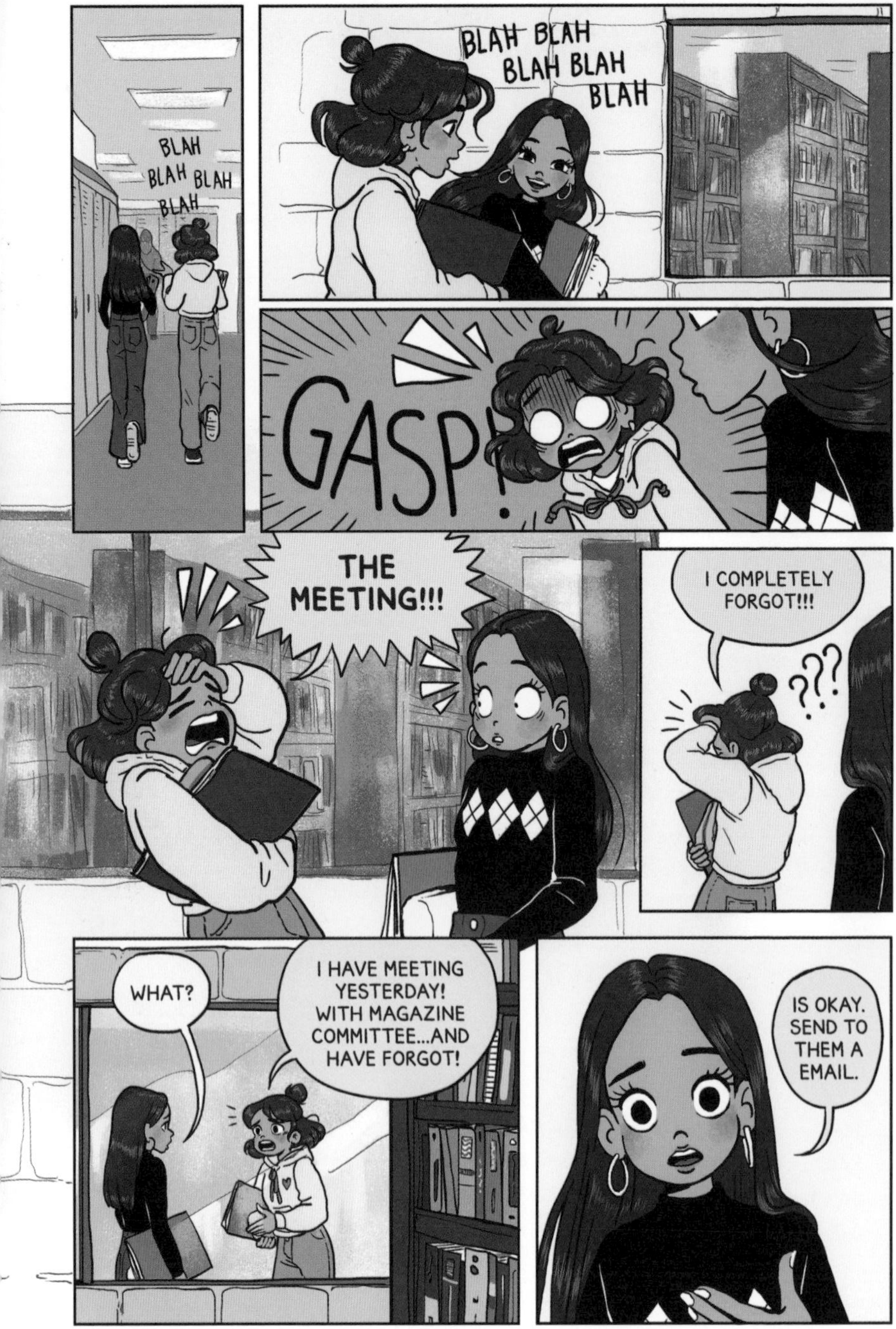
BLAH
BLAH BLAH
BLAH
BLAH BLAH
BLAH BLAH
BLAH
GASP!
THE MEETING!!!
I COMPLETELY FORGOT!!!
???
WHAT?
I HAVE MEETING YESTERDAY! WITH MAGAZINE COMMITTEE...AND HAVE FORGOT!
IS OKAY. SEND TO THEM A EMAIL.

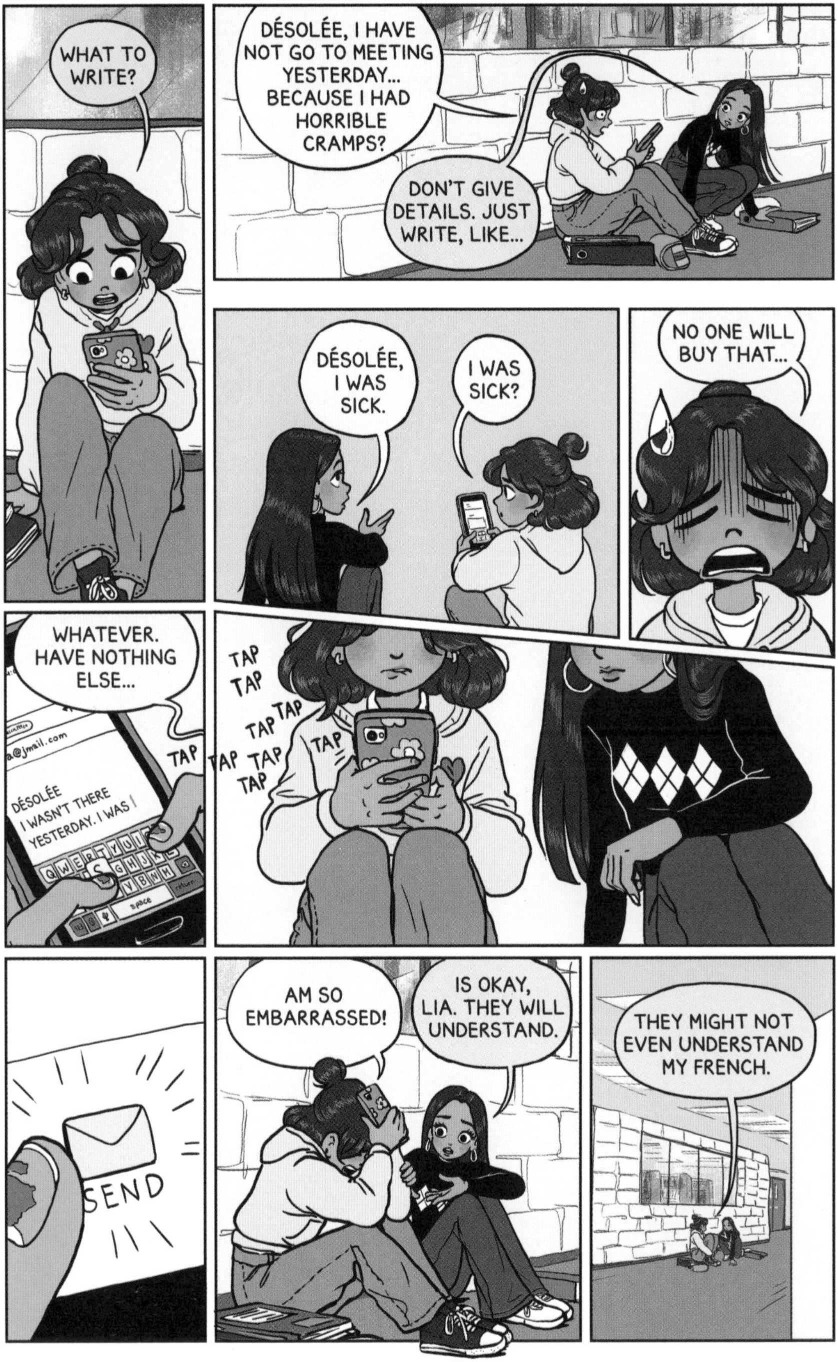
WHAT TO WRITE?
DÉSOLÉE, I HAVE NOT GO TO MEETING YESTERDAY... BECAUSE I HAD HORRIBLE CRAMPS?
DON'T GIVE DETAILS. JUST WRITE, LIKE...
DÉSOLÉE, I WAS SICK.
I WAS SICK?
NO ONE WILL BUY THAT...
WHATEVER. HAVE NOTHING ELSE...
a@jmail.com
DÉSOLÉE
I WASN'T THERE
YESTERDAY. I WAS
TAP
TAP TAP
TAP TAP
TAP TAP TAP
TAP TAP
TAP
SEND
AM SO EMBARRASSED!
IS OKAY, LIA. THEY WILL UNDERSTAND.
THEY MIGHT NOT EVEN UNDERSTAND MY FRENCH.

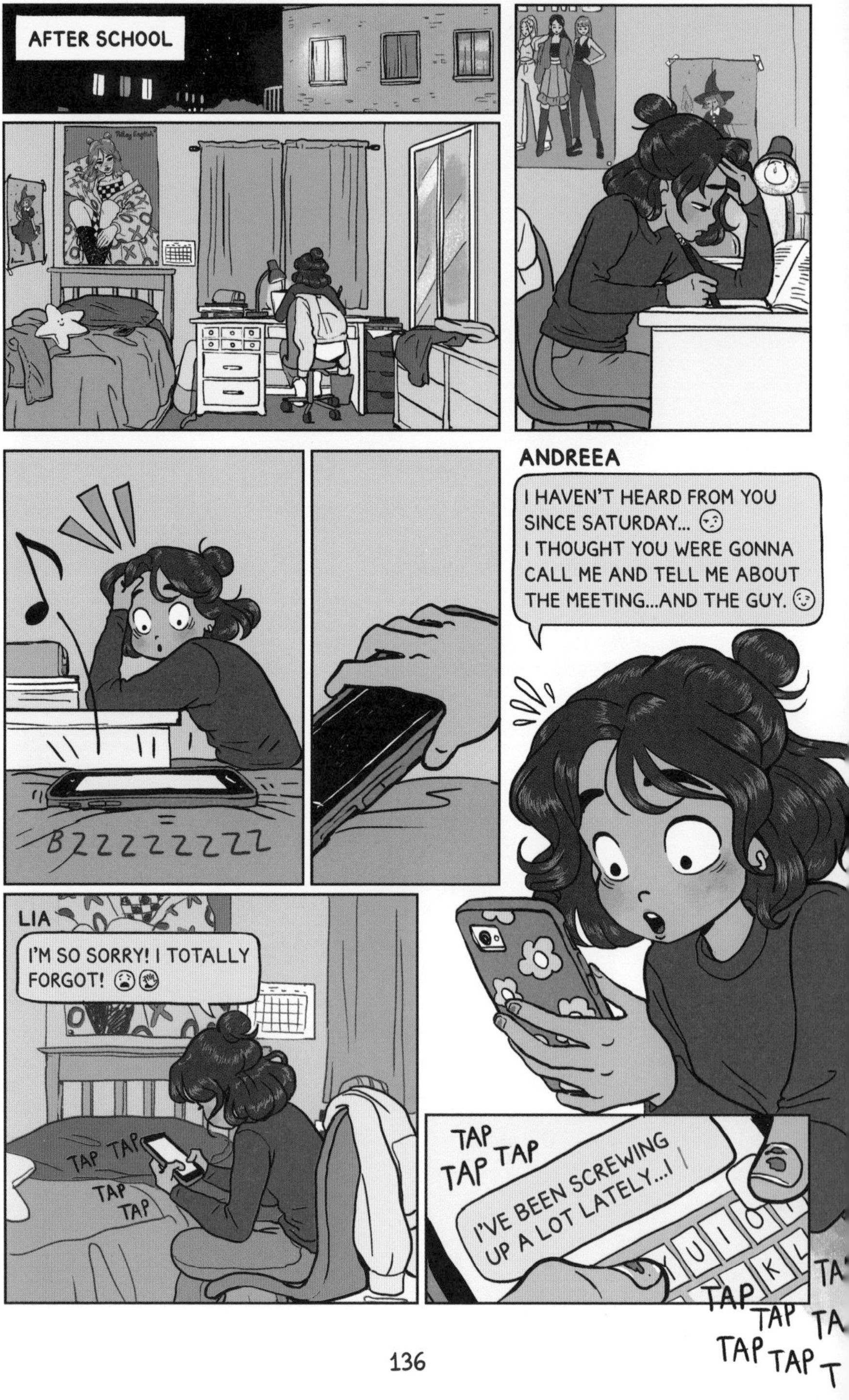
AFTER SCHOOL
BZZZZZZZZ
ANDREEA
I HAVEN'T HEARD FROM YOU SINCE SATURDAY... I THOUGHT YOU WERE GONNA CALL ME AND TELL ME ABOUT THE MEETING...AND THE GUY.
LIA
I'M SO SORRY! I TOTALLY FORGOT!
TAP TAP TAP TAP
TAP TAP TAP
I'VE BEEN SCREWING UP A LOT LATELY...I
TAP TAP TAP TAP

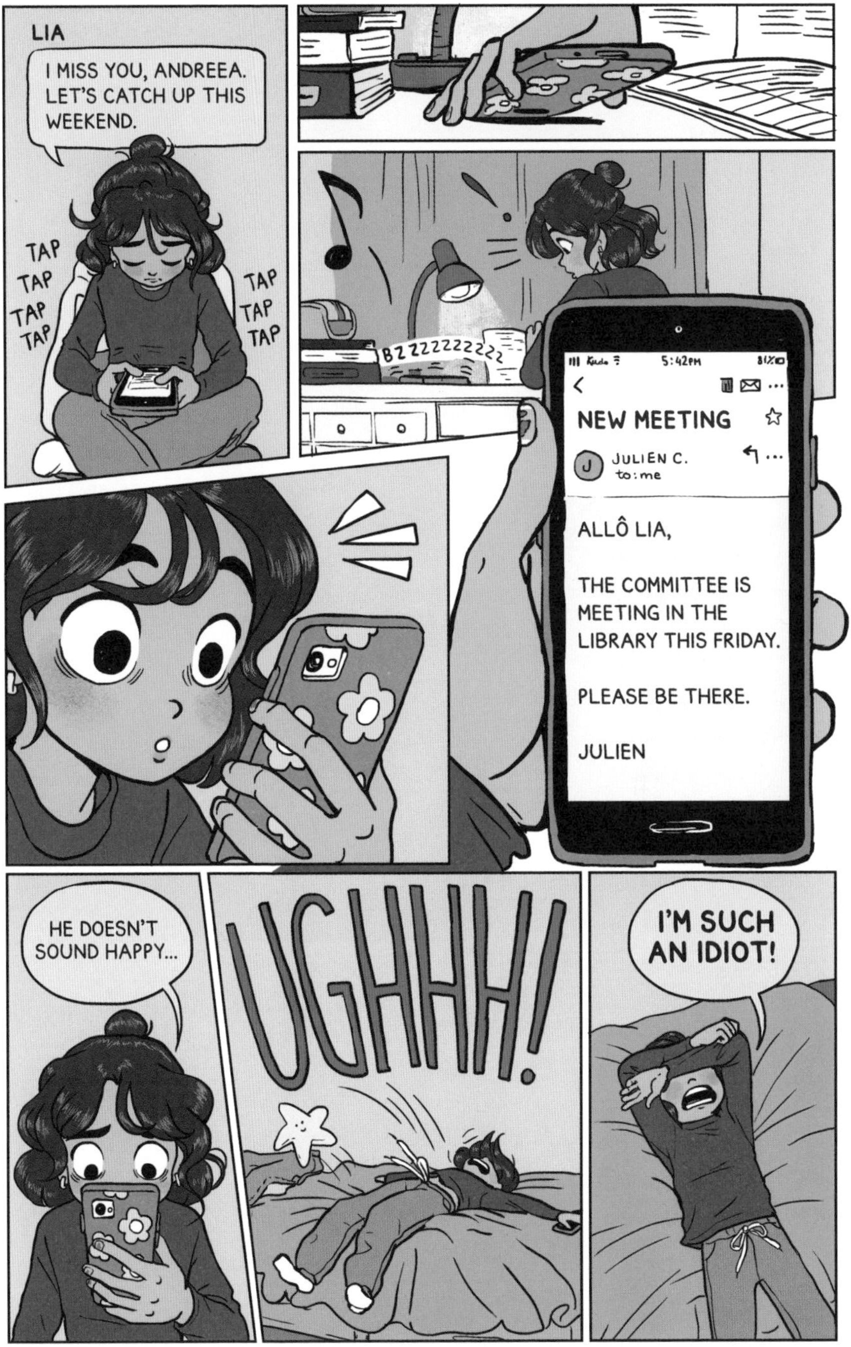
LIA
I MISS YOU, ANDREEA. LET'S CATCH UP THIS WEEKEND.
TAP TAP TAP TAP
TAP TAP TAP
BZZZZZZZZZZ
5:42PM
NEW MEETING
JULIEN C.
to: me
ALLÔ LIA,
THE COMMITTEE IS MEETING IN THE LIBRARY THIS FRIDAY.
PLEASE BE THERE.
JULIEN
HE DOESN'T SOUND HAPPY...
UGHHH!
I'M SUCH AN IDIOT!

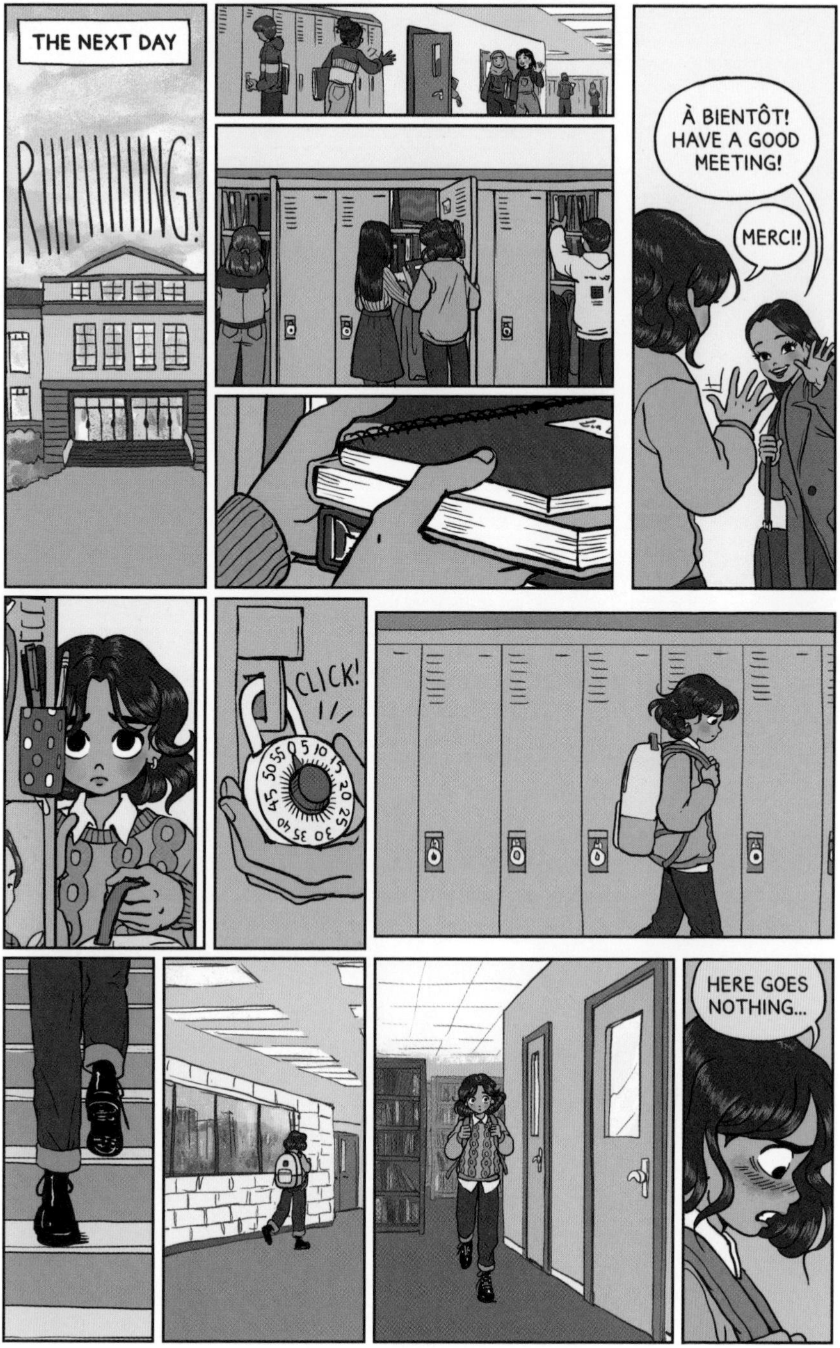
THE NEXT DAY
RIIIIIIIIING!
À BIENTÔT! HAVE A GOOD MEETING!
MERCI!
CLICK!
HERE GOES NOTHING...

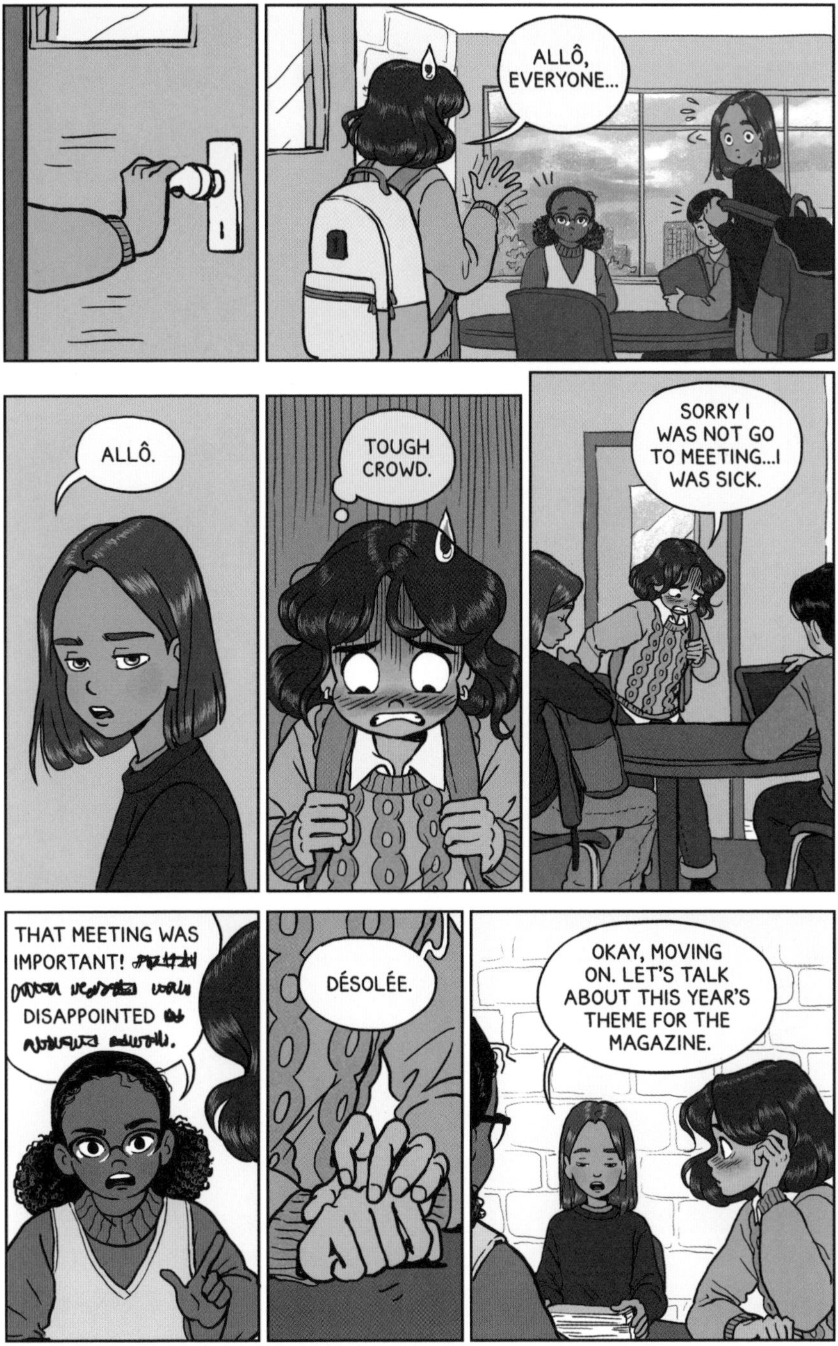
ALLÔ, EVERYONE...
ALLÔ.
TOUGH CROWD.
SORRY I WAS NOT GO TO MEETING...I WAS SICK.
THAT MEETING WAS IMPORTANT! DISAPPOINTED
DÉSOLÉE.
OKAY, MOVING ON. LET'S TALK ABOUT THIS YEAR'S THEME FOR THE MAGAZINE.

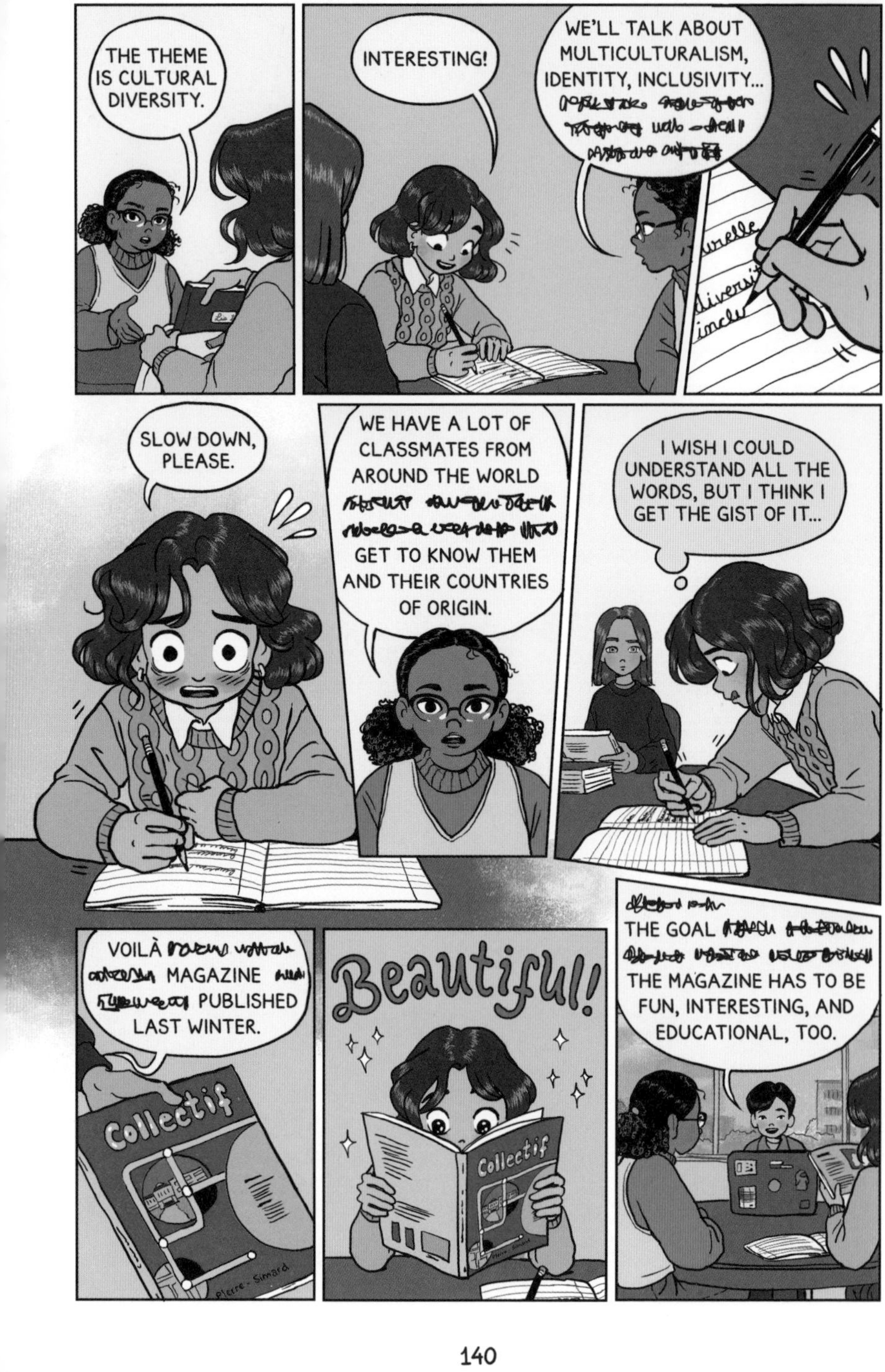
THE THEME IS CULTURAL DIVERSITY.
INTERESTING!
WE'LL TALK ABOUT MULTICULTURALISM, IDENTITY, INCLUSIVITY...
SLOW DOWN, PLEASE.
WE HAVE A LOT OF CLASSMATES FROM AROUND THE WORLD
GET TO KNOW THEM AND THEIR COUNTRIES OF ORIGIN.
I WISH I COULD UNDERSTAND ALL THE WORDS, BUT I THINK I GET THE GIST OF IT...
VOILÀ
MAGAZINE
PUBLISHED LAST WINTER.
Collectif
Beautiful!
Collectif
THE GOAL
THE MAGAZINE HAS TO BE FUN, INTERESTING, AND EDUCATIONAL, TOO.

WE WANT ~~text~~ A COUPLE OF ILLUSTRATIONS FOLLOWING THE THEME ~~text~~

AND ALSO ~~text~~ WRITE YOUR OWN ARTICLE. ~~text~~

I WRITE WHAT I WANT?

OUI.

BUT WE HAVE TO APPROVE IT FIRST.

OKAY!

~~text~~ THE NEXT MEETING ~~text~~

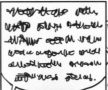

LIA?

HUH?

IF YOU HAVE ANY QUESTIONS, CONTACT JULIEN.

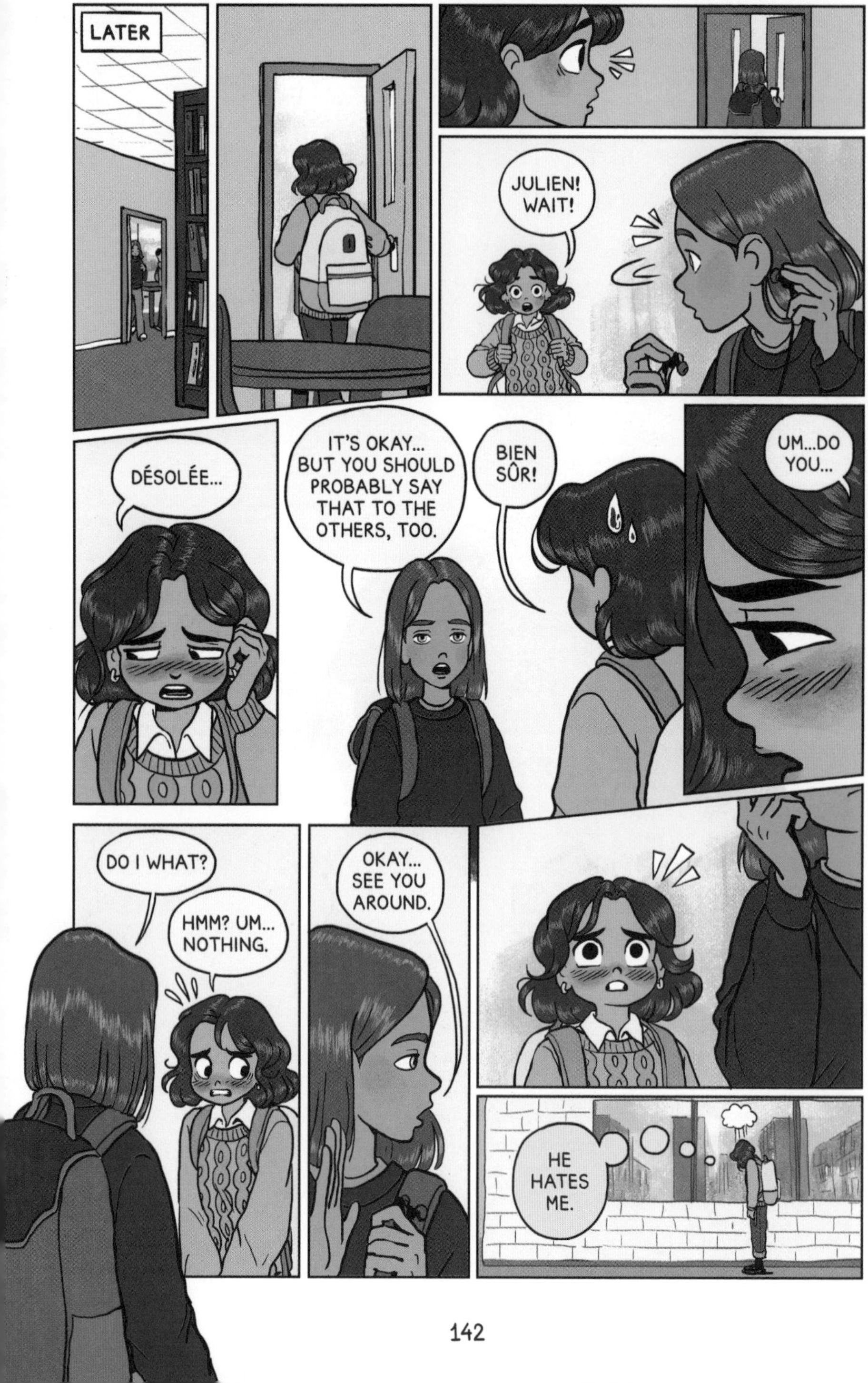
LATER
JULIEN! WAIT!
DÉSOLÉE...
IT'S OKAY... BUT YOU SHOULD PROBABLY SAY THAT TO THE OTHERS, TOO.
BIEN SÛR!
UM...DO YOU...
DO I WHAT?
HMM? UM... NOTHING.
OKAY... SEE YOU AROUND.
HE HATES ME.

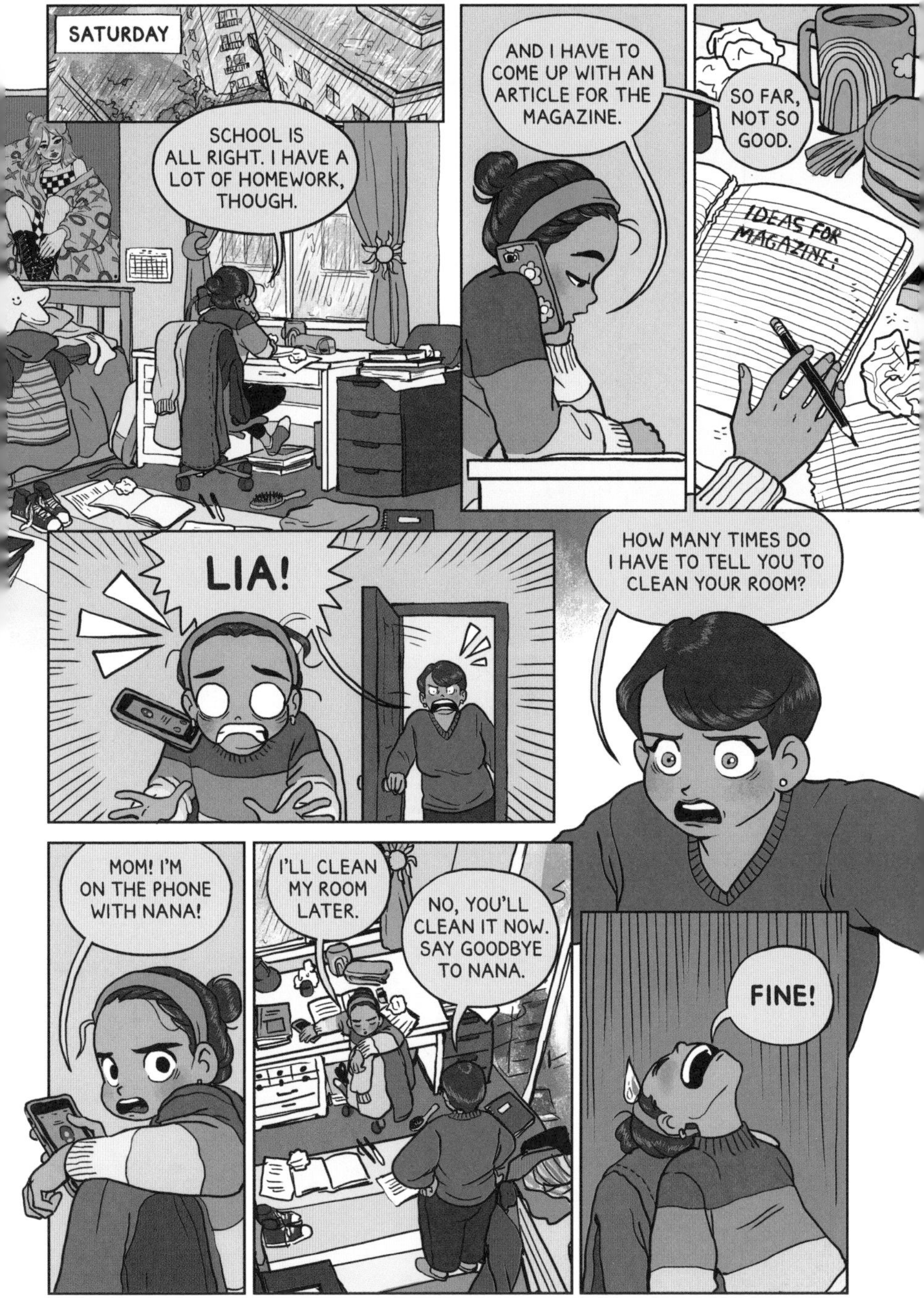
SATURDAY
SCHOOL IS ALL RIGHT. I HAVE A LOT OF HOMEWORK, THOUGH.
AND I HAVE TO COME UP WITH AN ARTICLE FOR THE MAGAZINE.
SO FAR, NOT SO GOOD.
IDEAS FOR MAGAZINE:
LIA!
HOW MANY TIMES DO I HAVE TO TELL YOU TO CLEAN YOUR ROOM?
MOM! I'M ON THE PHONE WITH NANA!
I'LL CLEAN MY ROOM LATER.
NO, YOU'LL CLEAN IT NOW. SAY GOODBYE TO NANA.
FINE!

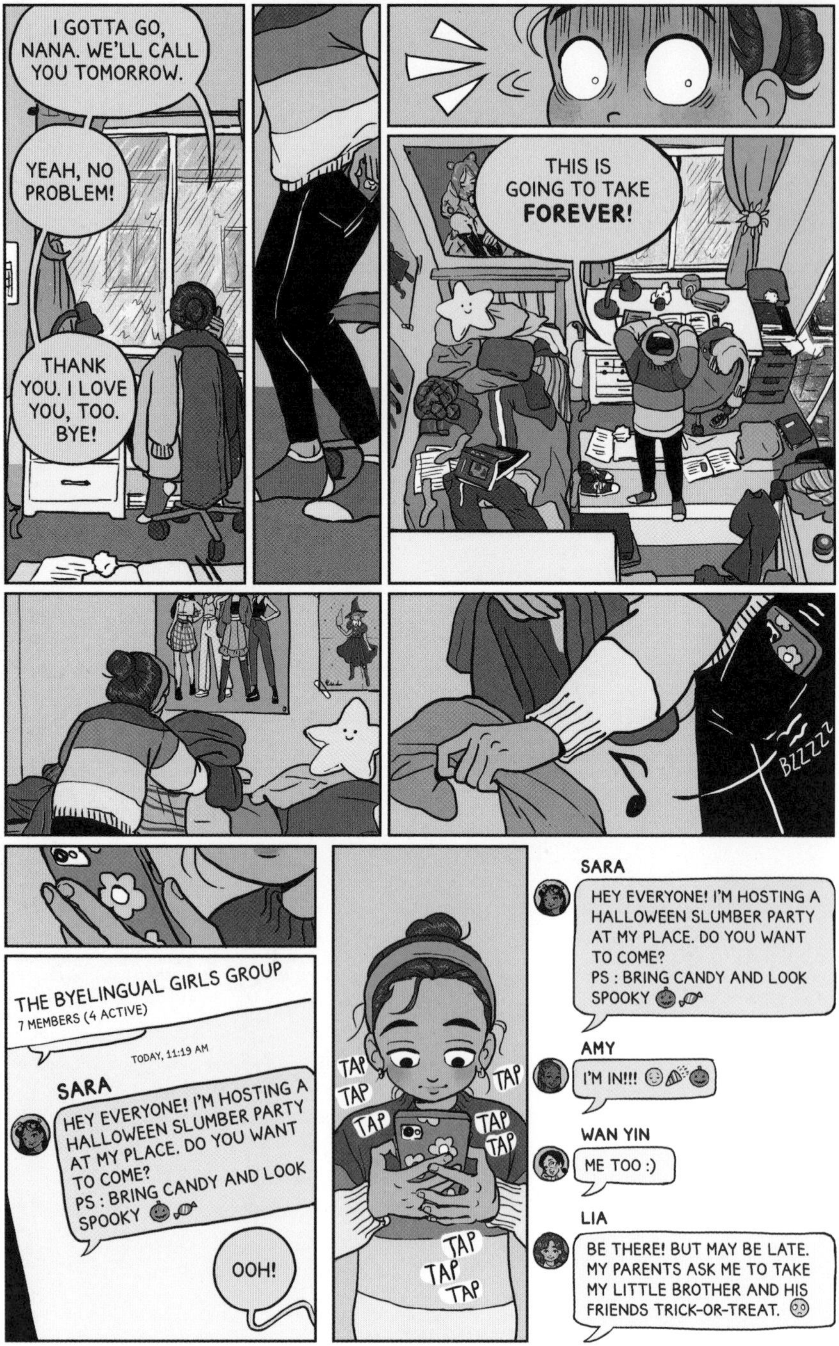
I GOTTA GO, NANA. WE'LL CALL YOU TOMORROW.
YEAH, NO PROBLEM!
THANK YOU. I LOVE YOU, TOO. BYE!
THIS IS GOING TO TAKE **FOREVER!**
BZZZZZ
THE BYELINGUAL GIRLS GROUP
7 MEMBERS (4 ACTIVE)
TODAY, 11:19 AM
SARA
HEY EVERYONE! I'M HOSTING A HALLOWEEN SLUMBER PARTY AT MY PLACE. DO YOU WANT TO COME?
PS : BRING CANDY AND LOOK SPOOKY
OOH!
TAP TAP TAP TAP TAP TAP
TAP TAP TAP
SARA
HEY EVERYONE! I'M HOSTING A HALLOWEEN SLUMBER PARTY AT MY PLACE. DO YOU WANT TO COME?
PS : BRING CANDY AND LOOK SPOOKY
AMY
I'M IN!!!
WAN YIN
ME TOO :)
LIA
BE THERE! BUT MAY BE LATE. MY PARENTS ASK ME TO TAKE MY LITTLE BROTHER AND HIS FRIENDS TRICK-OR-TREAT.

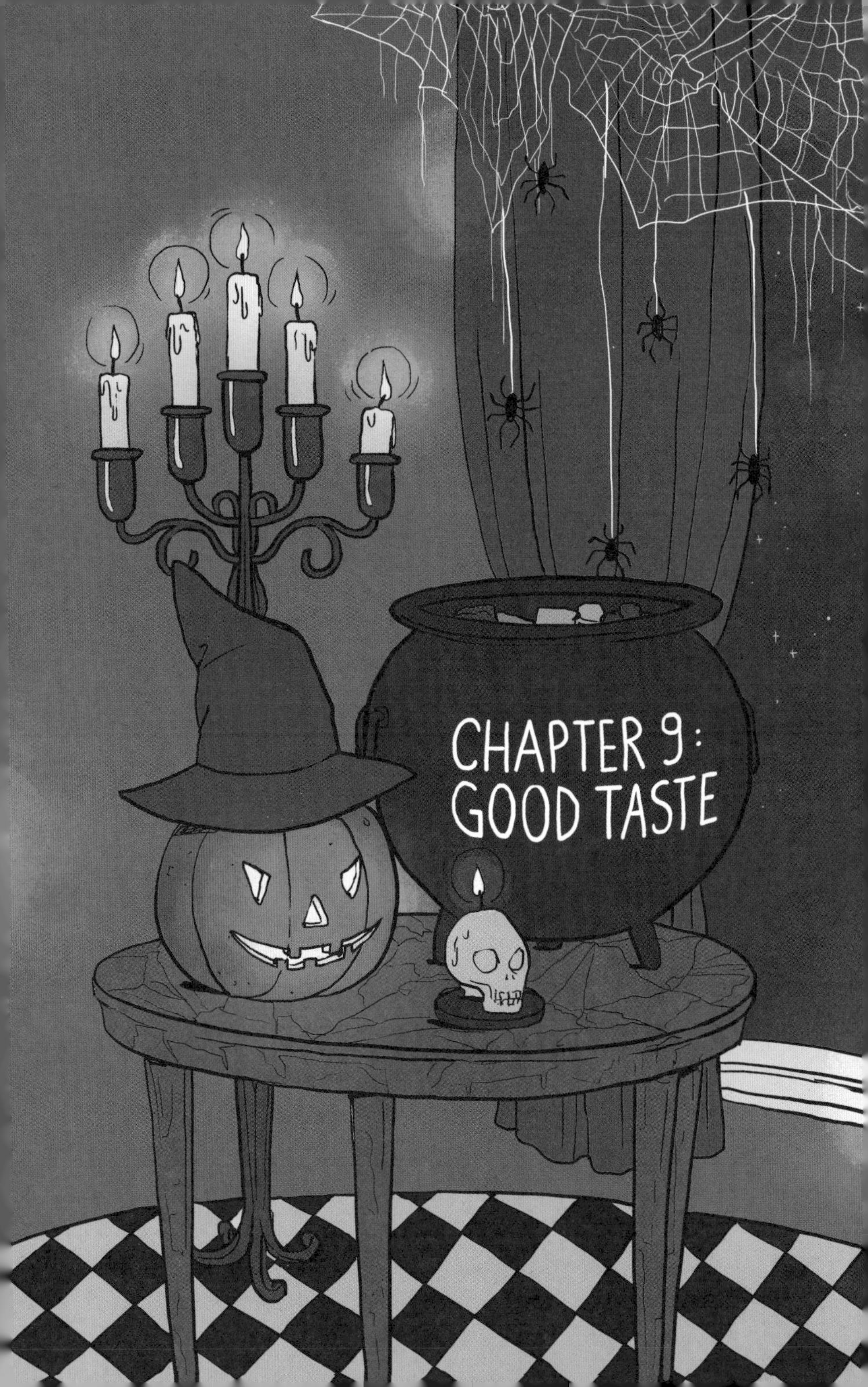
CHAPTER 9:
GOOD TASTE

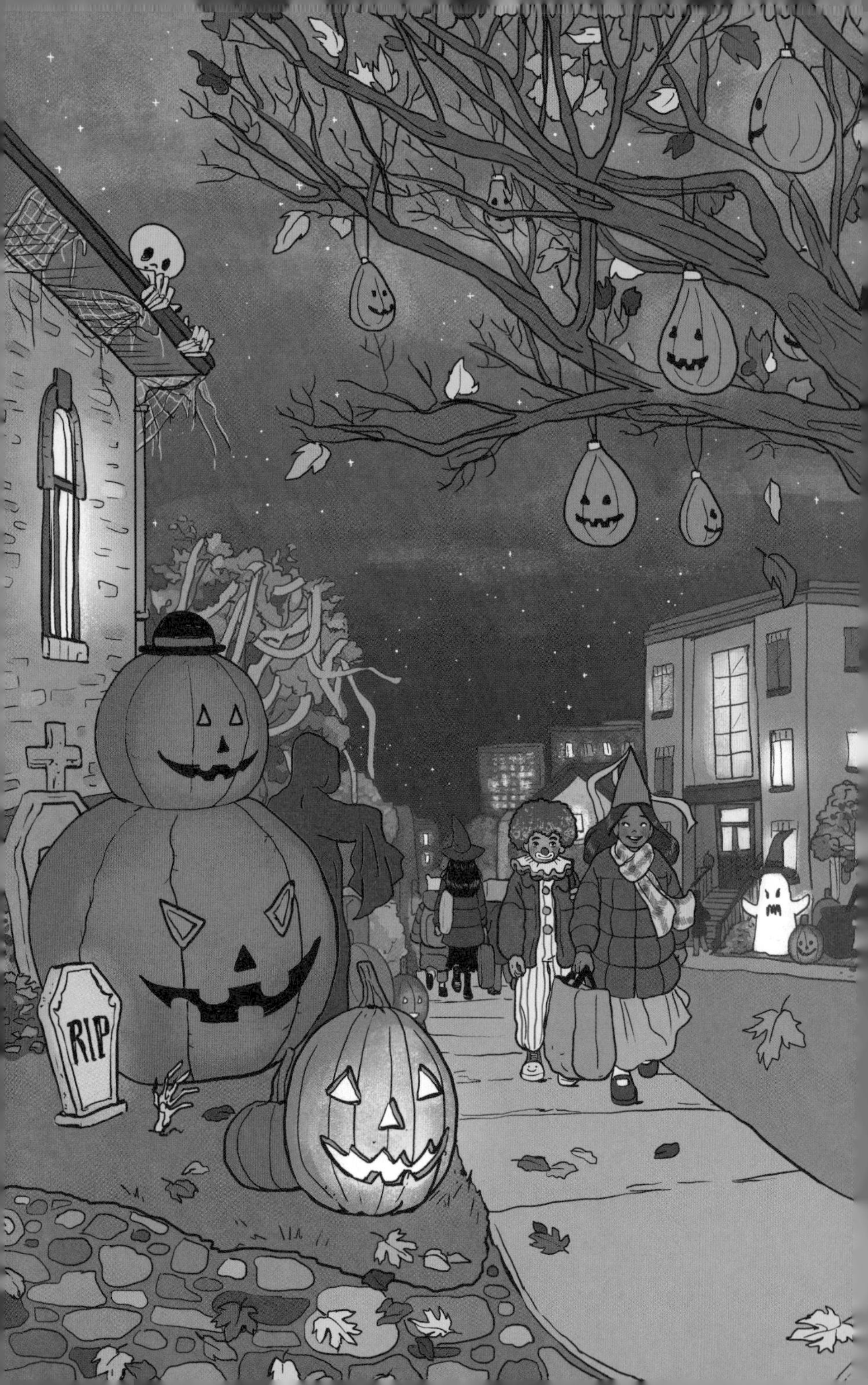
RIP

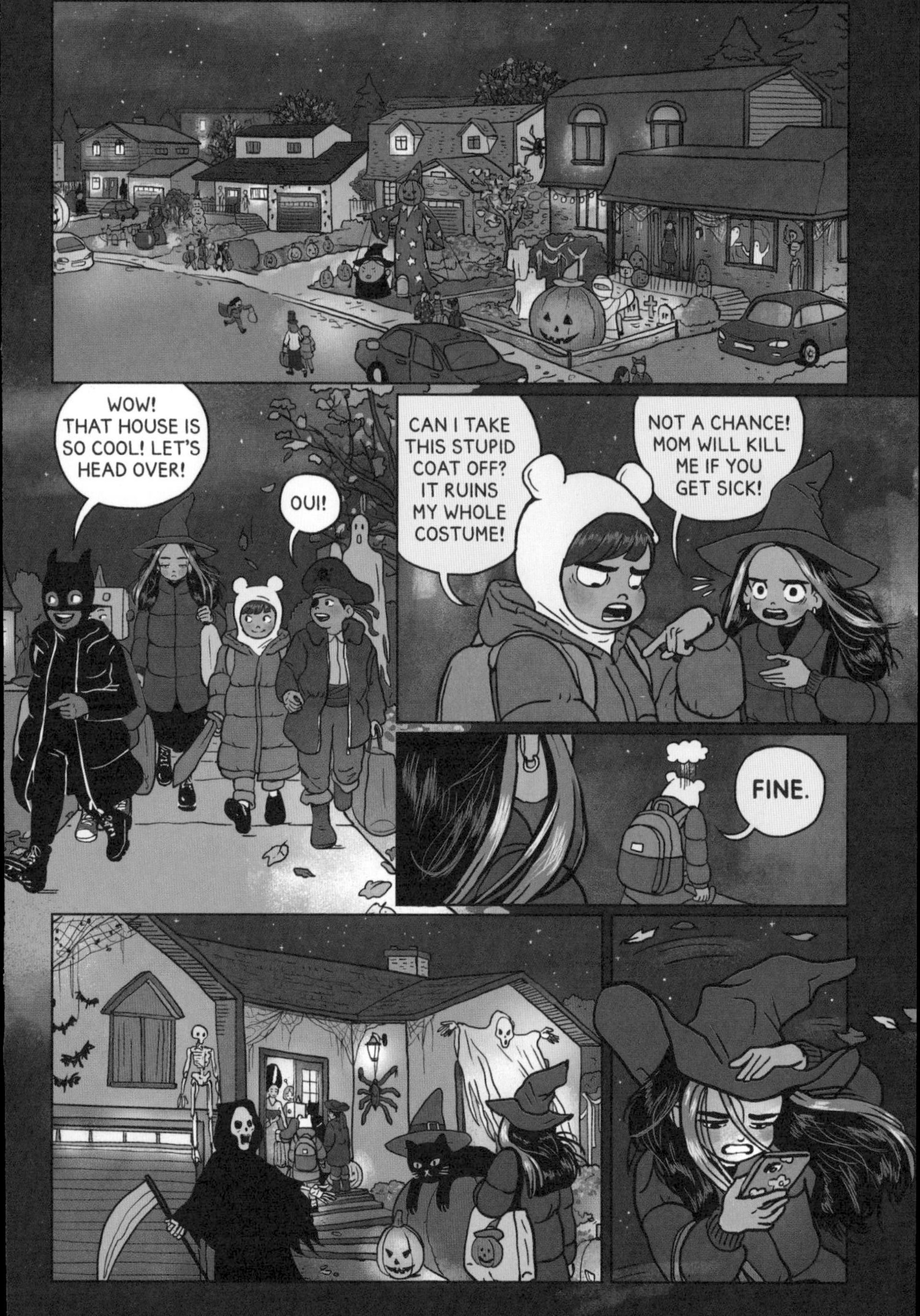
WOW! THAT HOUSE IS SO COOL! LET'S HEAD OVER!
OUI!
CAN I TAKE THIS STUPID COAT OFF? IT RUINS MY WHOLE COSTUME!
NOT A CHANCE! MOM WILL KILL ME IF YOU GET SICK!
FINE.

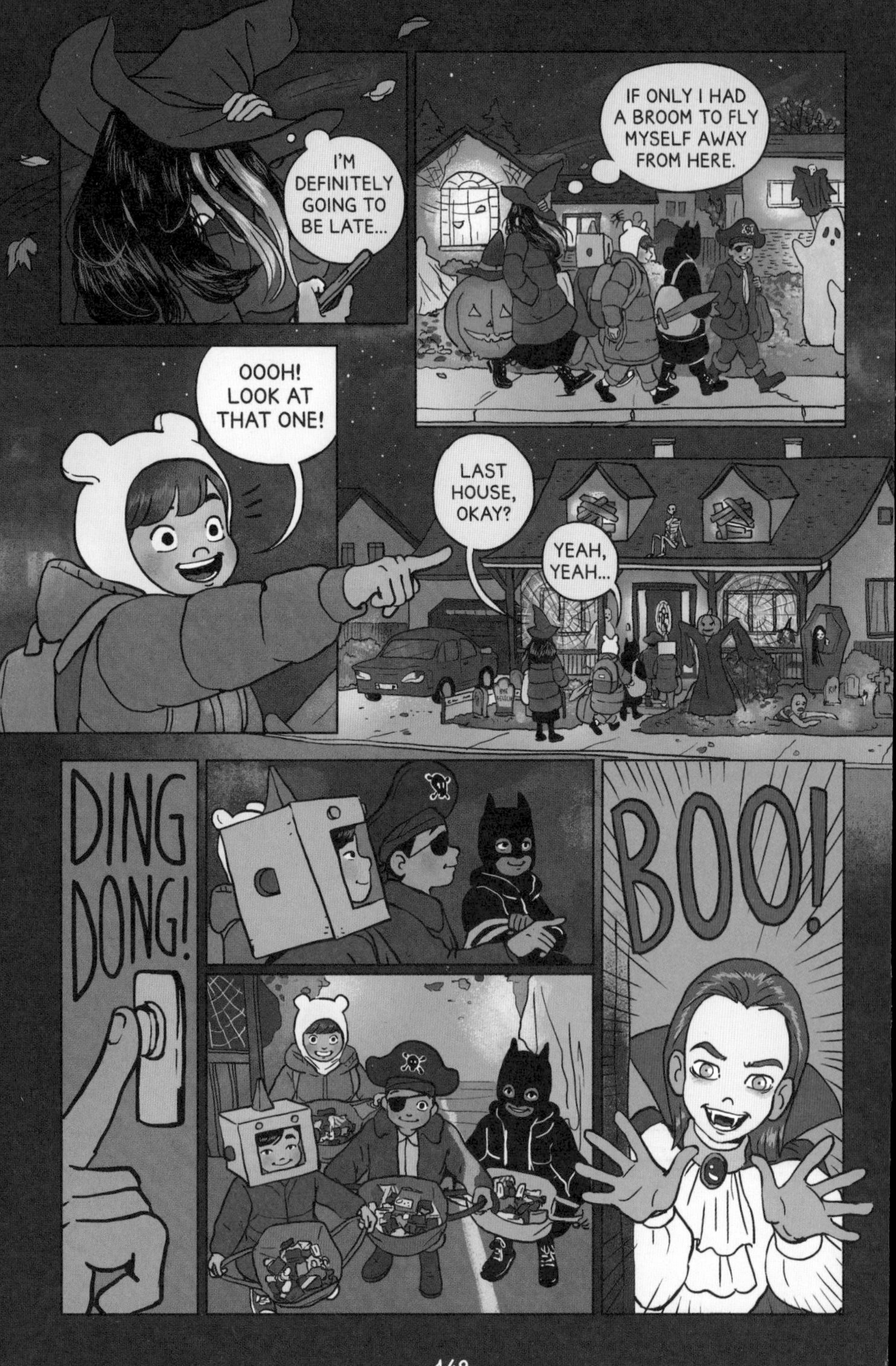
I'M DEFINITELY GOING TO BE LATE...
IF ONLY I HAD A BROOM TO FLY MYSELF AWAY FROM HERE.
OOOH! LOOK AT THAT ONE!
LAST HOUSE, OKAY?
YEAH, YEAH...
DING DONG!
BOO!

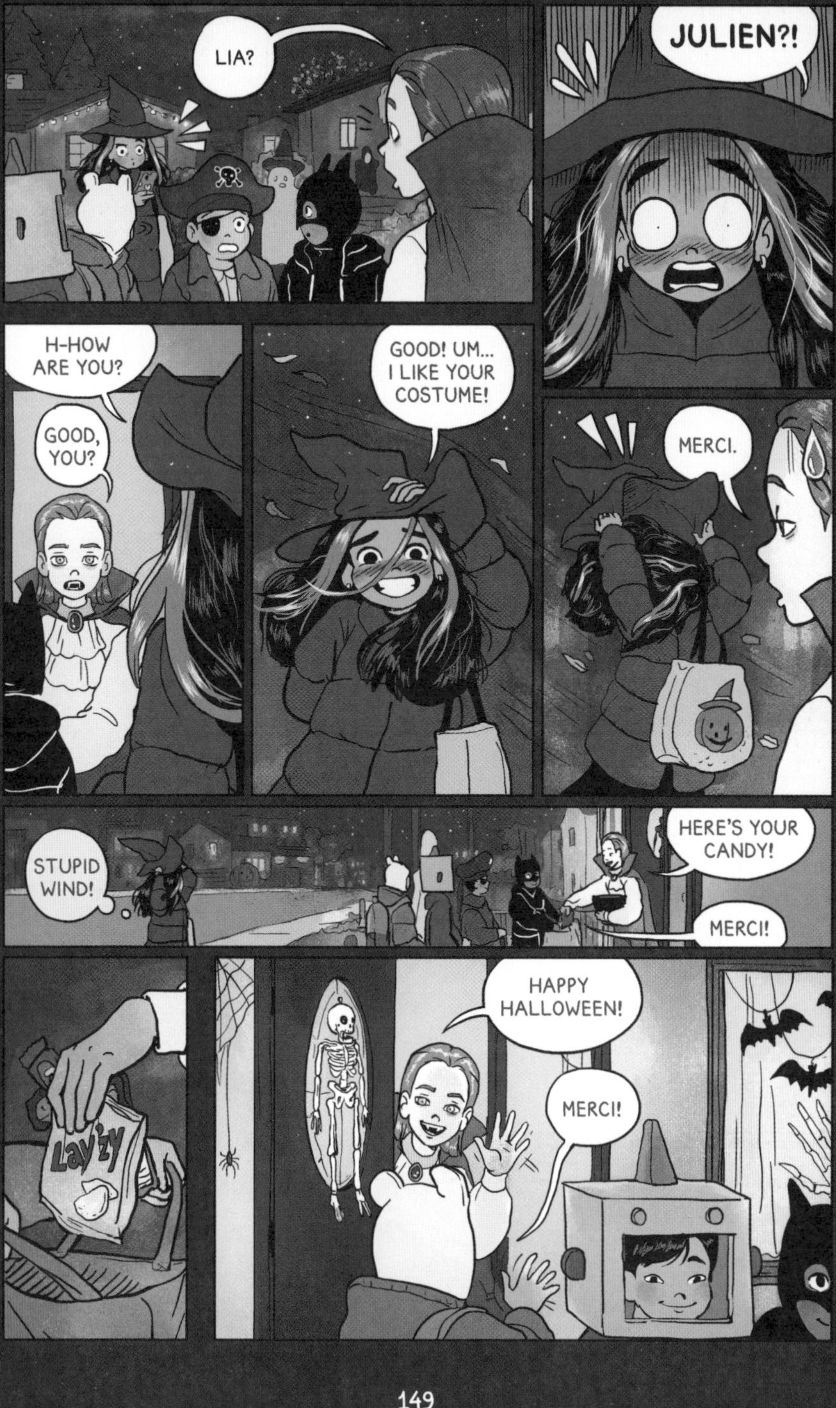
LIA?
JULIEN?!
H-HOW ARE YOU?
GOOD, YOU?
GOOD! UM... I LIKE YOUR COSTUME!
MERCI.
STUPID WIND!
HERE'S YOUR CANDY!
MERCI!
Lay'zy
HAPPY HALLOWEEN!
MERCI!

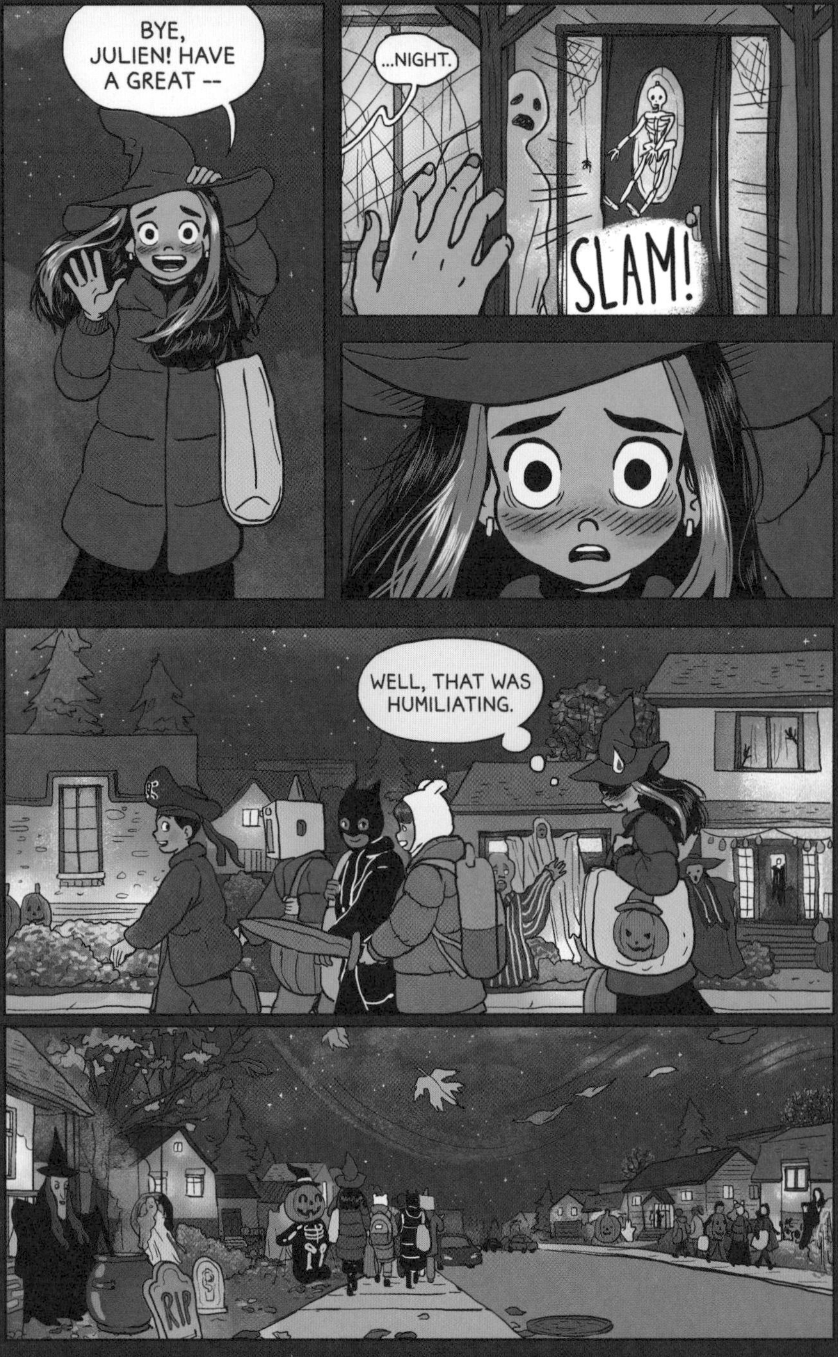
BYE, JULIEN! HAVE A GREAT --
...NIGHT.
SLAM!
WELL, THAT WAS HUMILIATING.
RIP

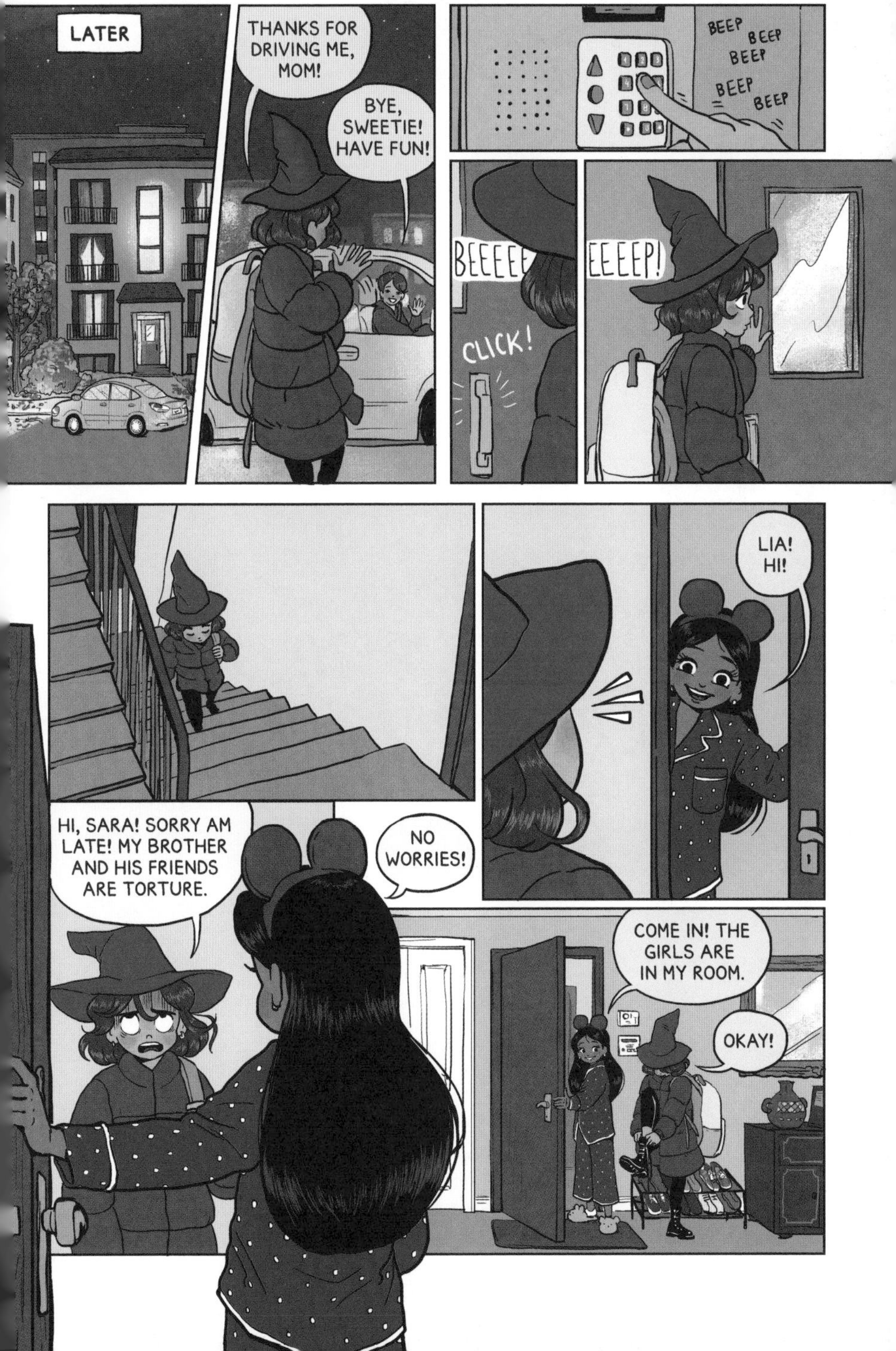
LATER
THANKS FOR DRIVING ME, MOM!
BYE, SWEETIE! HAVE FUN!
BEEP BEEP BEEP BEEP BEEP
BEEEEEEEEP!
CLICK!
LIA! HI!
HI, SARA! SORRY AM LATE! MY BROTHER AND HIS FRIENDS ARE TORTURE.
NO WORRIES!
COME IN! THE GIRLS ARE IN MY ROOM.
OKAY!

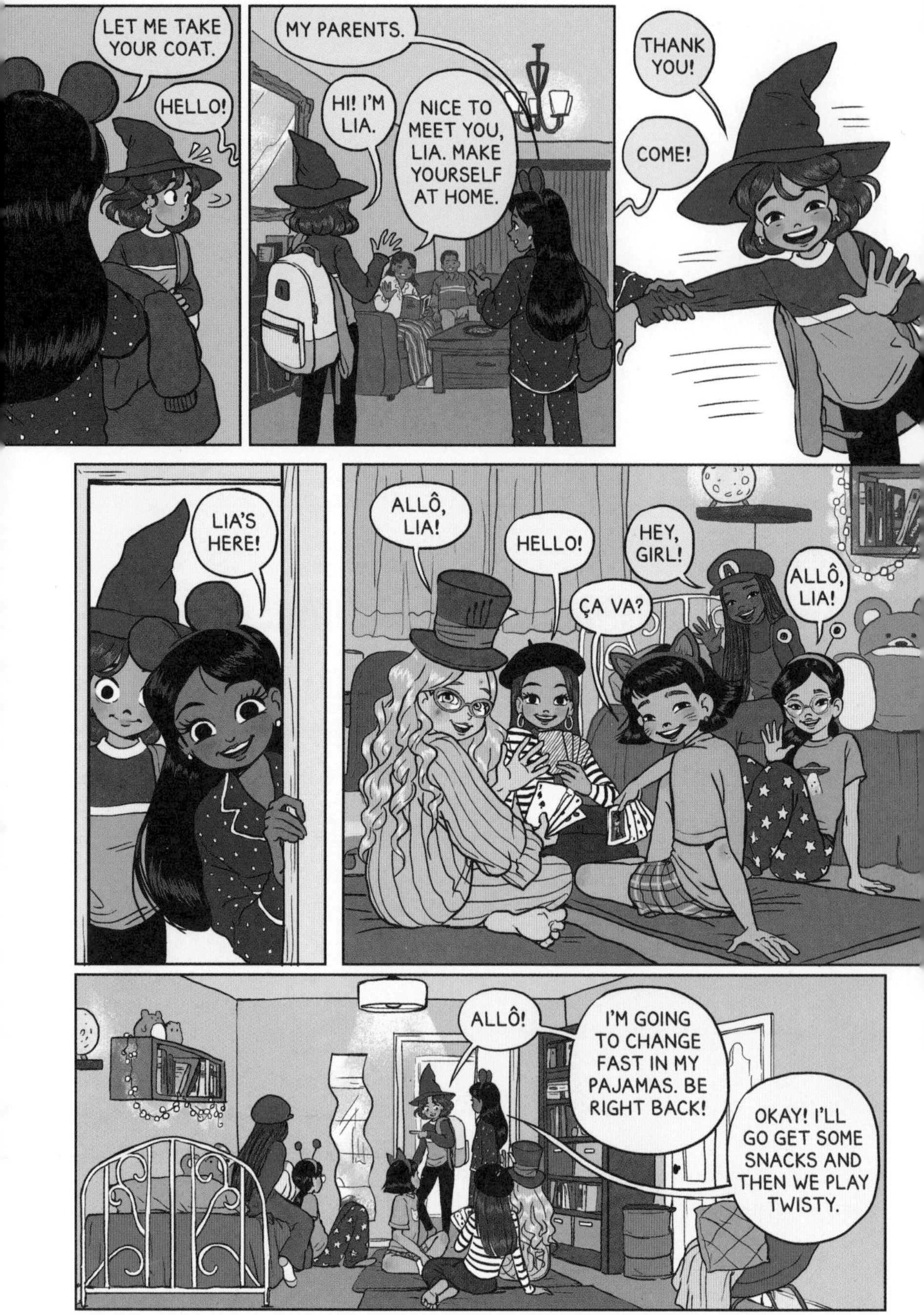
LET ME TAKE YOUR COAT.
HELLO!
MY PARENTS.
HI! I'M LIA.
NICE TO MEET YOU, LIA. MAKE YOURSELF AT HOME.
THANK YOU!
COME!
LIA'S HERE!
ALLÔ, LIA!
HELLO!
ÇA VA?
HEY, GIRL!
ALLÔ, LIA!
ALLÔ!
I'M GOING TO CHANGE FAST IN MY PAJAMAS. BE RIGHT BACK!
OKAY! I'LL GO GET SOME SNACKS AND THEN WE PLAY TWISTY.

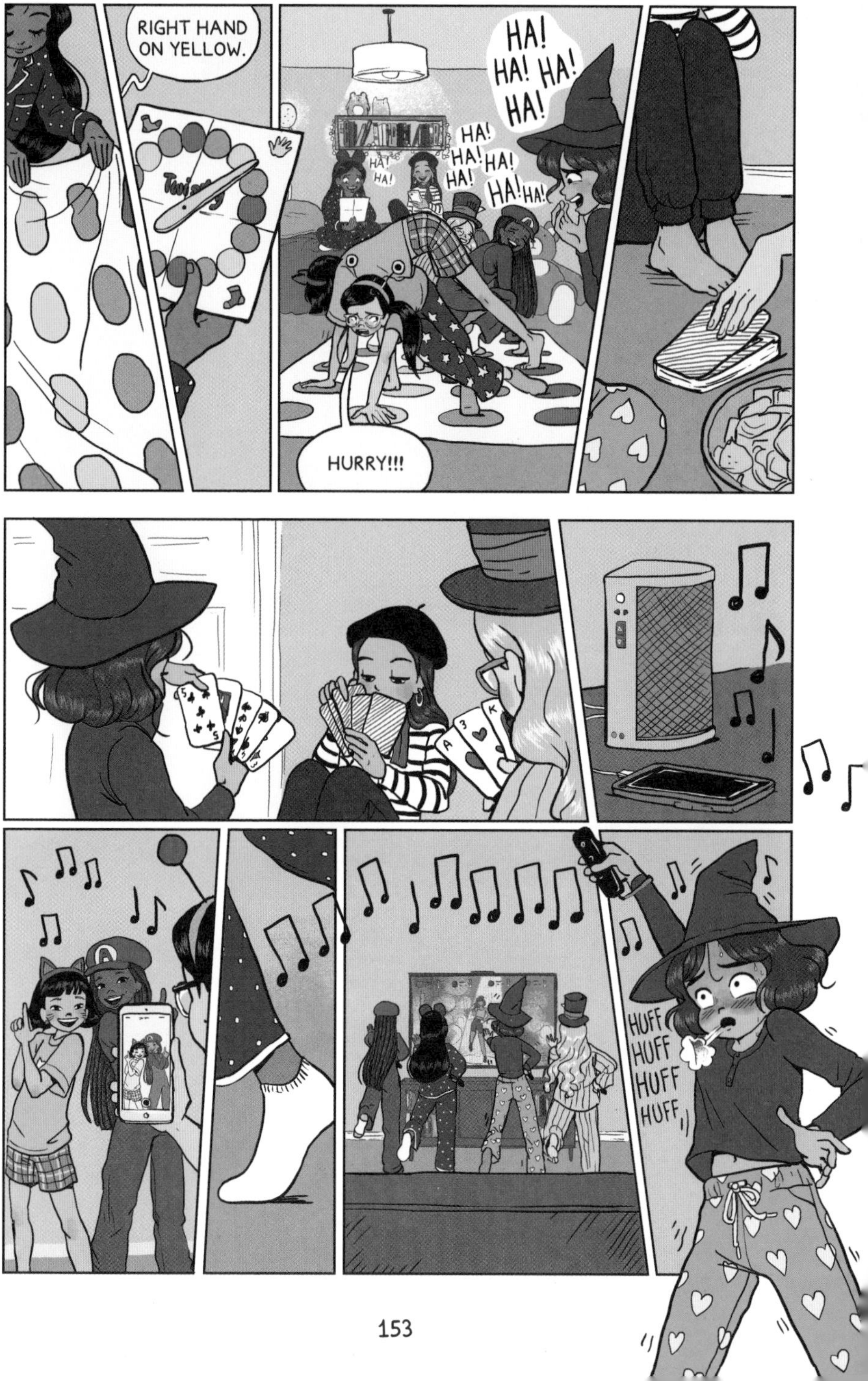

RIGHT HAND ON YELLOW.
HA! HA! HA! HA!
HA! HA! HA! HA! HA! HA!
HA! HA!
HURRY!!!
HUFF HUFF HUFF HUFF

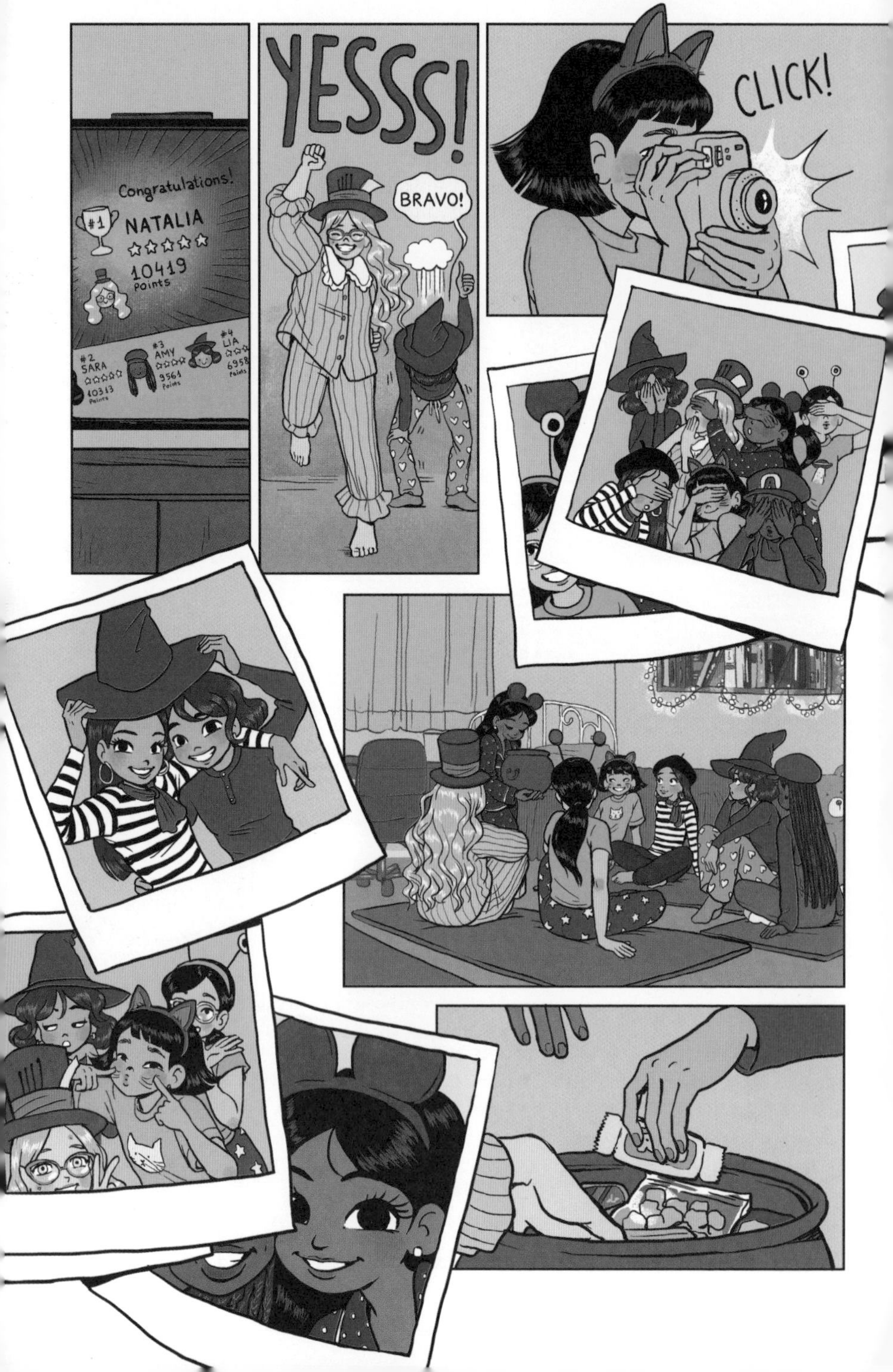

Congratulations!
#1
NATALIA
10419
Points
#2
SARA
10313
Points
#3
AMY
9561
Points
#4
LIA
6958
Points
YESSS!
BRAVO!
CLICK!

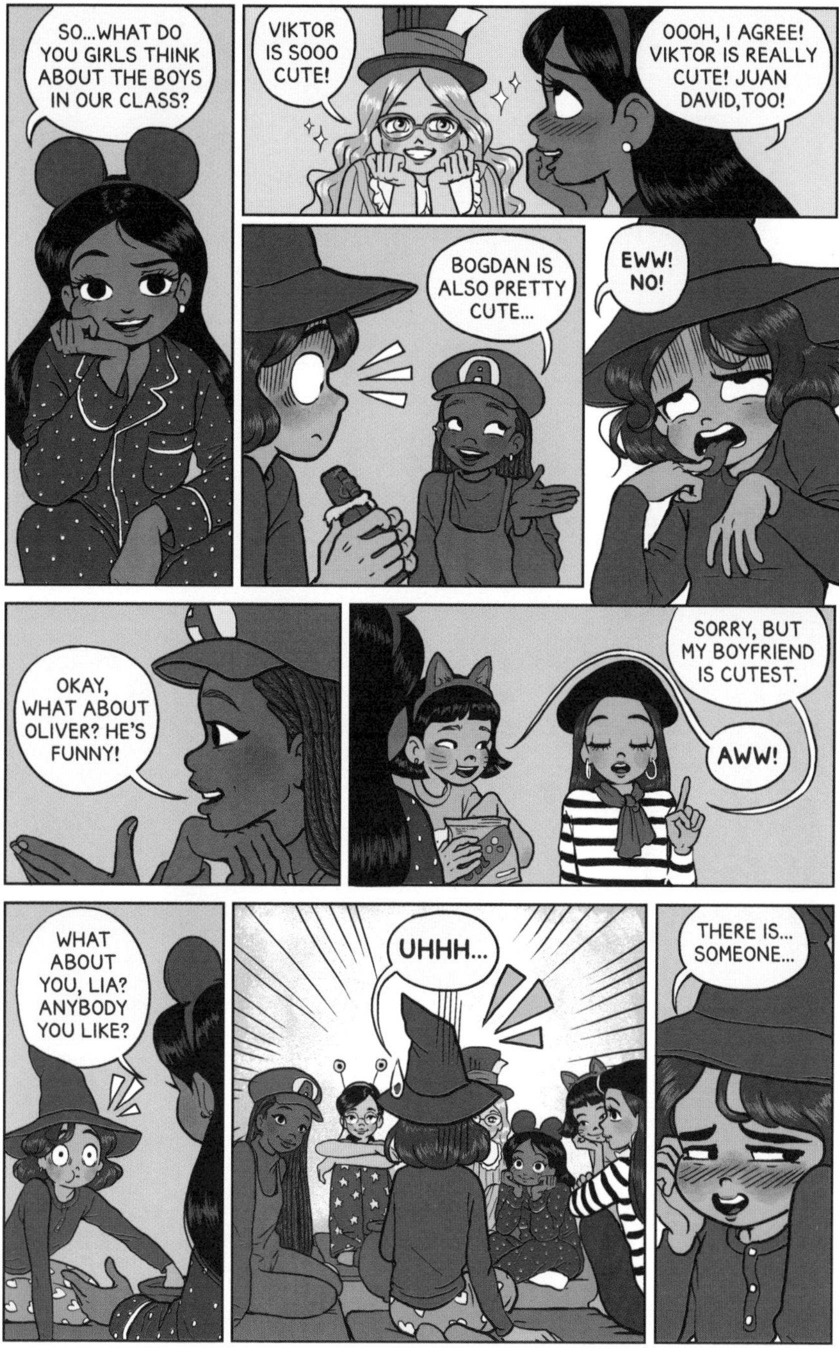
SO...WHAT DO YOU GIRLS THINK ABOUT THE BOYS IN OUR CLASS?
VIKTOR IS SOOO CUTE!
OOOH, I AGREE! VIKTOR IS REALLY CUTE! JUAN DAVID, TOO!
BOGDAN IS ALSO PRETTY CUTE...
EWW! NO!
OKAY, WHAT ABOUT OLIVER? HE'S FUNNY!
SORRY, BUT MY BOYFRIEND IS CUTEST.
AWW!
WHAT ABOUT YOU, LIA? ANYBODY YOU LIKE?
UHHH...
THERE IS... SOMEONE...

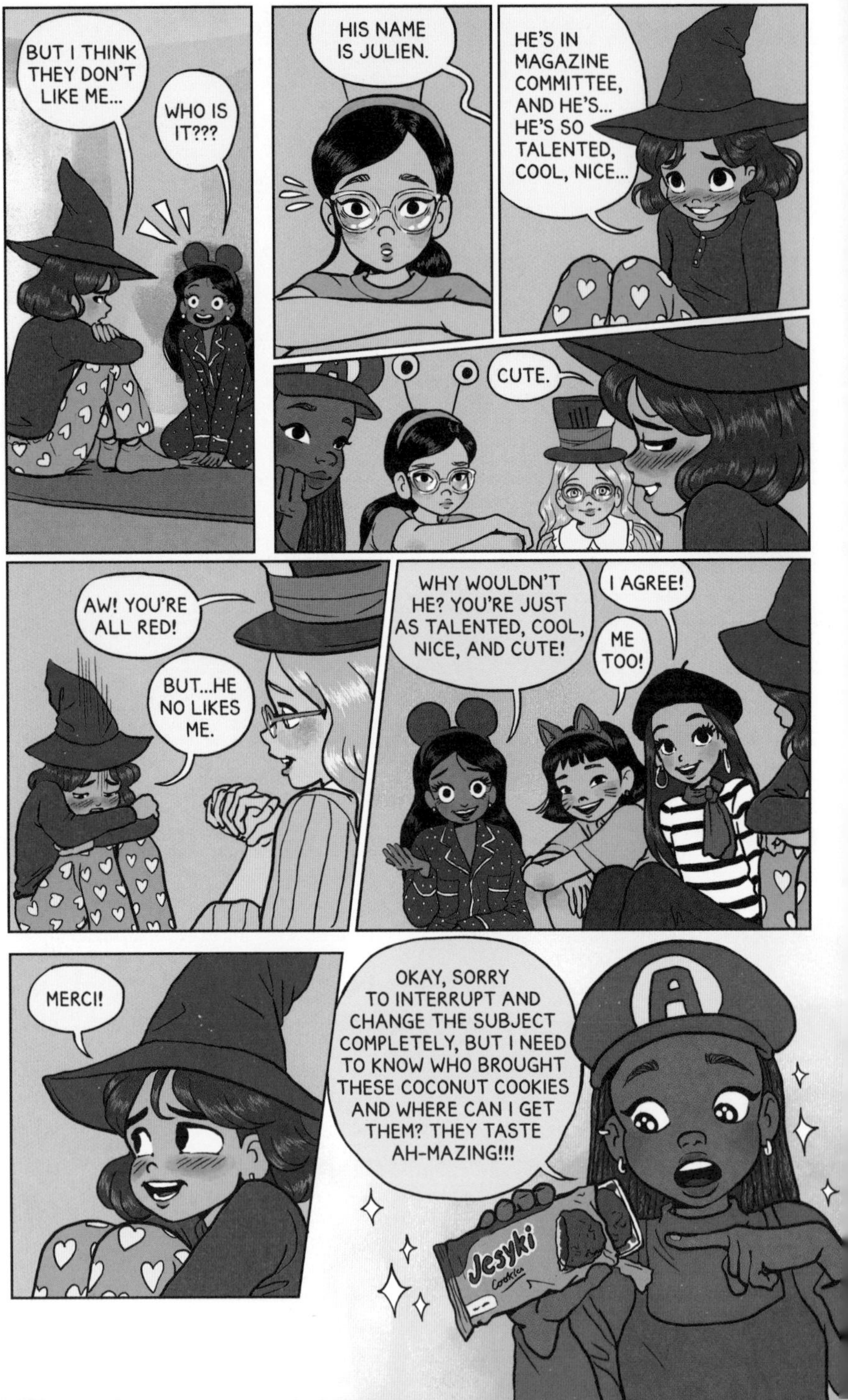
BUT I THINK THEY DON'T LIKE ME...
WHO IS IT???
HIS NAME IS JULIEN.
HE'S IN MAGAZINE COMMITTEE, AND HE'S... HE'S SO TALENTED, COOL, NICE...
CUTE.
AW! YOU'RE ALL RED!
BUT...HE NO LIKES ME.
WHY WOULDN'T HE? YOU'RE JUST AS TALENTED, COOL, NICE, AND CUTE!
I AGREE!
ME TOO!
MERCI!
OKAY, SORRY TO INTERRUPT AND CHANGE THE SUBJECT COMPLETELY, BUT I NEED TO KNOW WHO BROUGHT THESE COCONUT COOKIES AND WHERE CAN I GET THEM? THEY TASTE AH-MAZING!!!
Jesyki

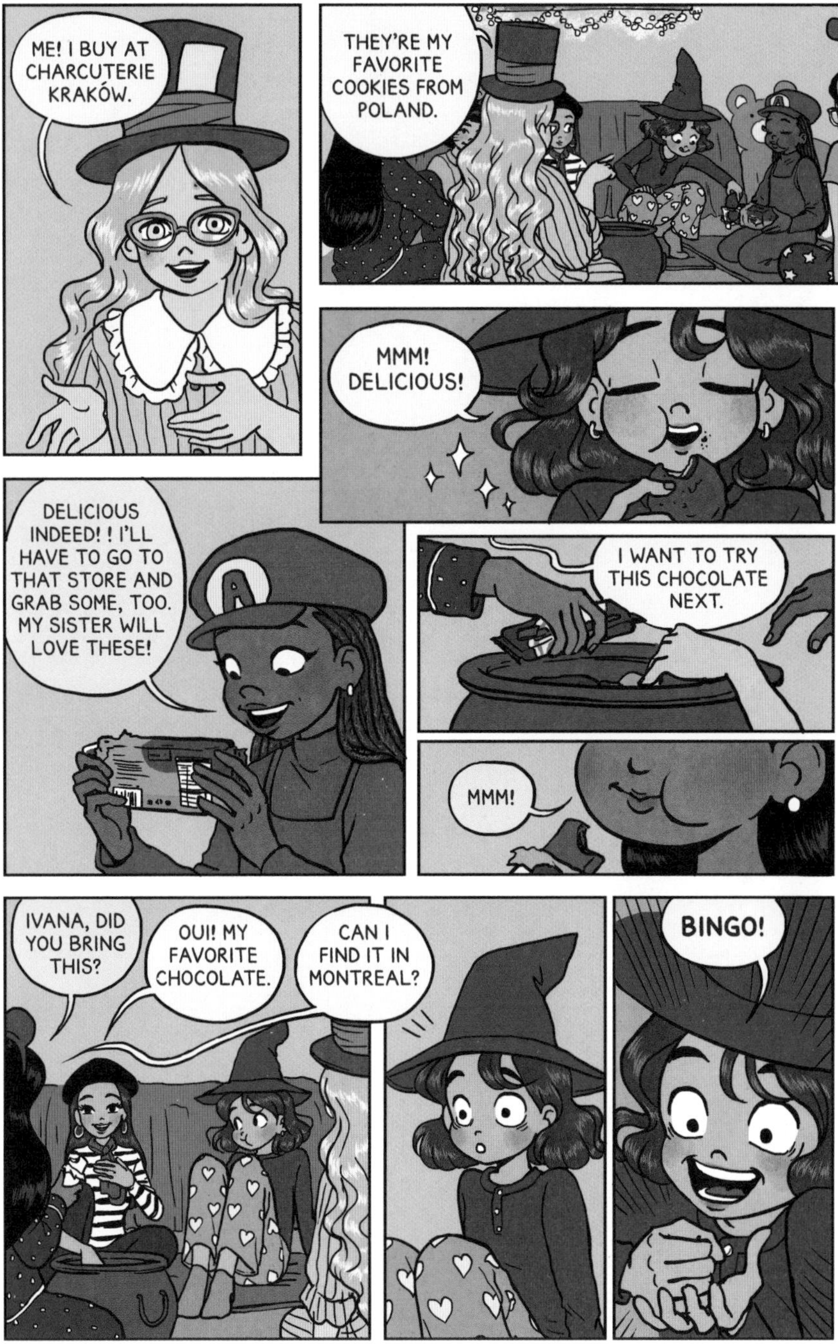
ME! I BUY AT CHARCUTERIE KRAKÓW.
THEY'RE MY FAVORITE COOKIES FROM POLAND.
MMM! DELICIOUS!
DELICIOUS INDEED! ! I'LL HAVE TO GO TO THAT STORE AND GRAB SOME, TOO. MY SISTER WILL LOVE THESE!
I WANT TO TRY THIS CHOCOLATE NEXT.
MMM!
IVANA, DID YOU BRING THIS?
OUI! MY FAVORITE CHOCOLATE.
CAN I FIND IT IN MONTREAL?
BINGO!

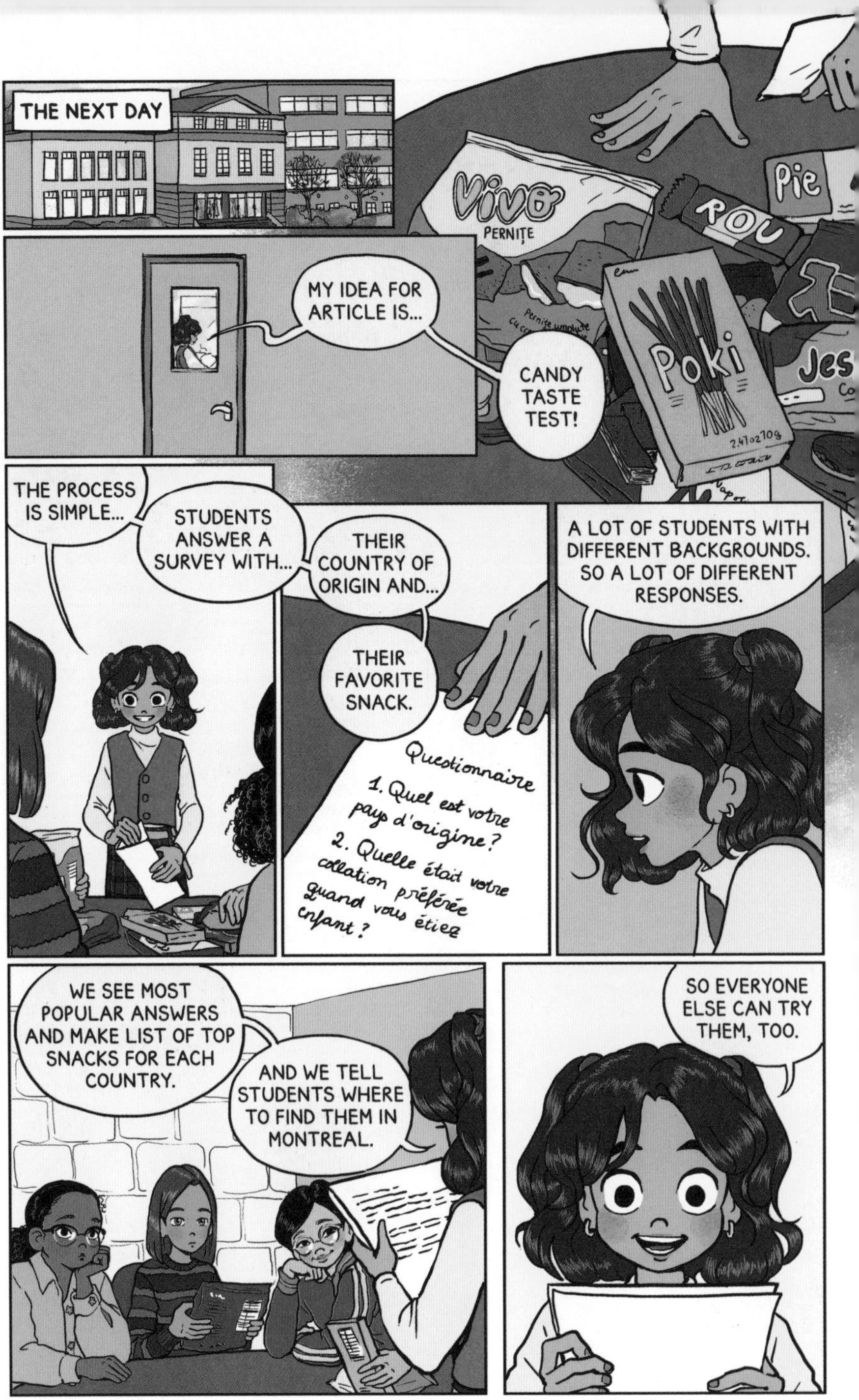
THE NEXT DAY
VIVO
PERNIȚE
Pie
ROU
MY IDEA FOR ARTICLE IS...
CANDY TASTE TEST!
Poki
THE PROCESS IS SIMPLE...
STUDENTS ANSWER A SURVEY WITH...
THEIR COUNTRY OF ORIGIN AND...
THEIR FAVORITE SNACK.
Questionnaire
1. Quel est votre pays d'origine?
2. Quelle était votre collation préférée quand vous étiez enfant?
A LOT OF STUDENTS WITH DIFFERENT BACKGROUNDS. SO A LOT OF DIFFERENT RESPONSES.
WE SEE MOST POPULAR ANSWERS AND MAKE LIST OF TOP SNACKS FOR EACH COUNTRY.
AND WE TELL STUDENTS WHERE TO FIND THEM IN MONTREAL.
SO EVERYONE ELSE CAN TRY THEM, TOO.

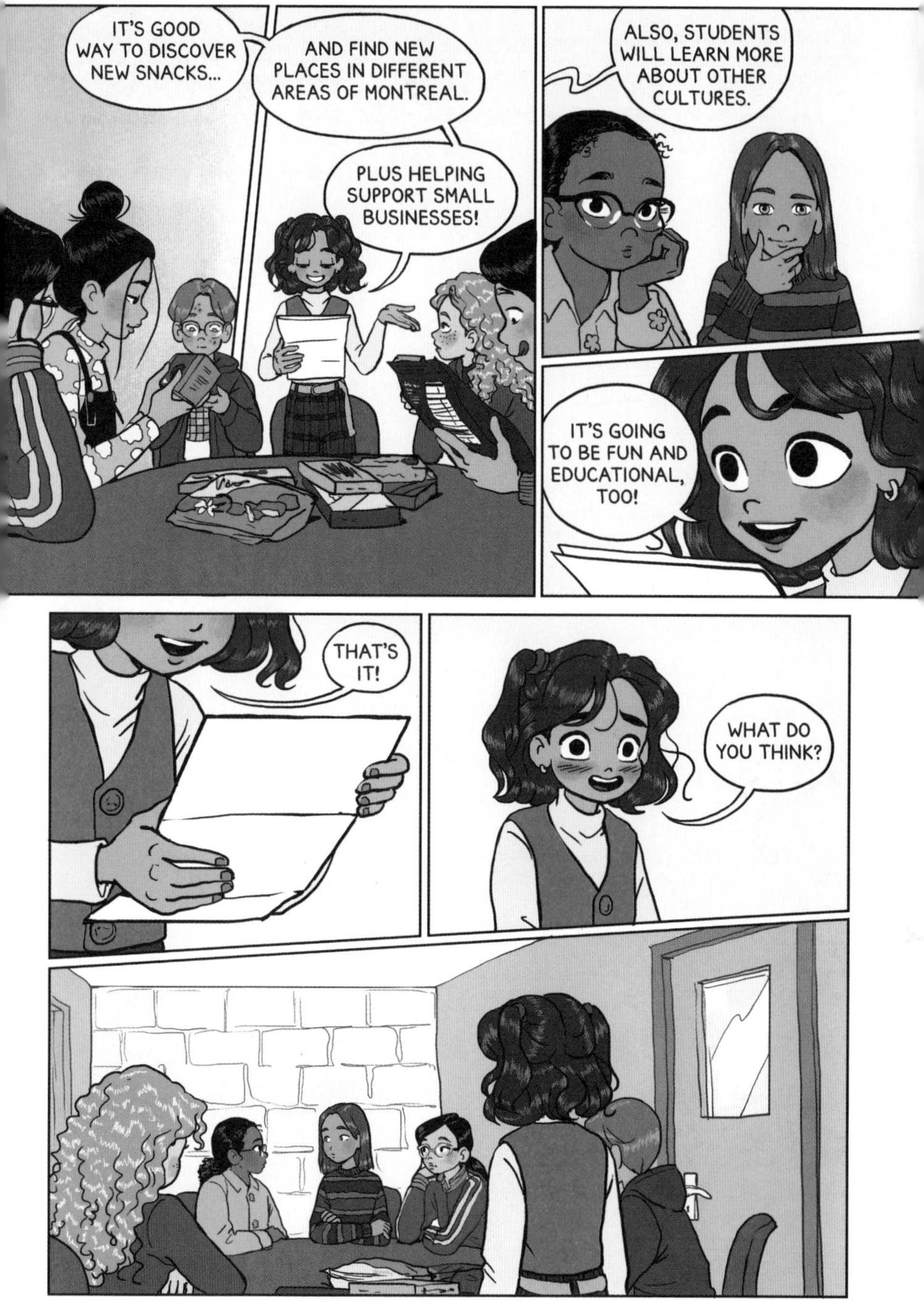
IT'S GOOD WAY TO DISCOVER NEW SNACKS...
AND FIND NEW PLACES IN DIFFERENT AREAS OF MONTREAL.
PLUS HELPING SUPPORT SMALL BUSINESSES!
ALSO, STUDENTS WILL LEARN MORE ABOUT OTHER CULTURES.
IT'S GOING TO BE FUN AND EDUCATIONAL, TOO!
THAT'S IT!
WHAT DO YOU THINK?

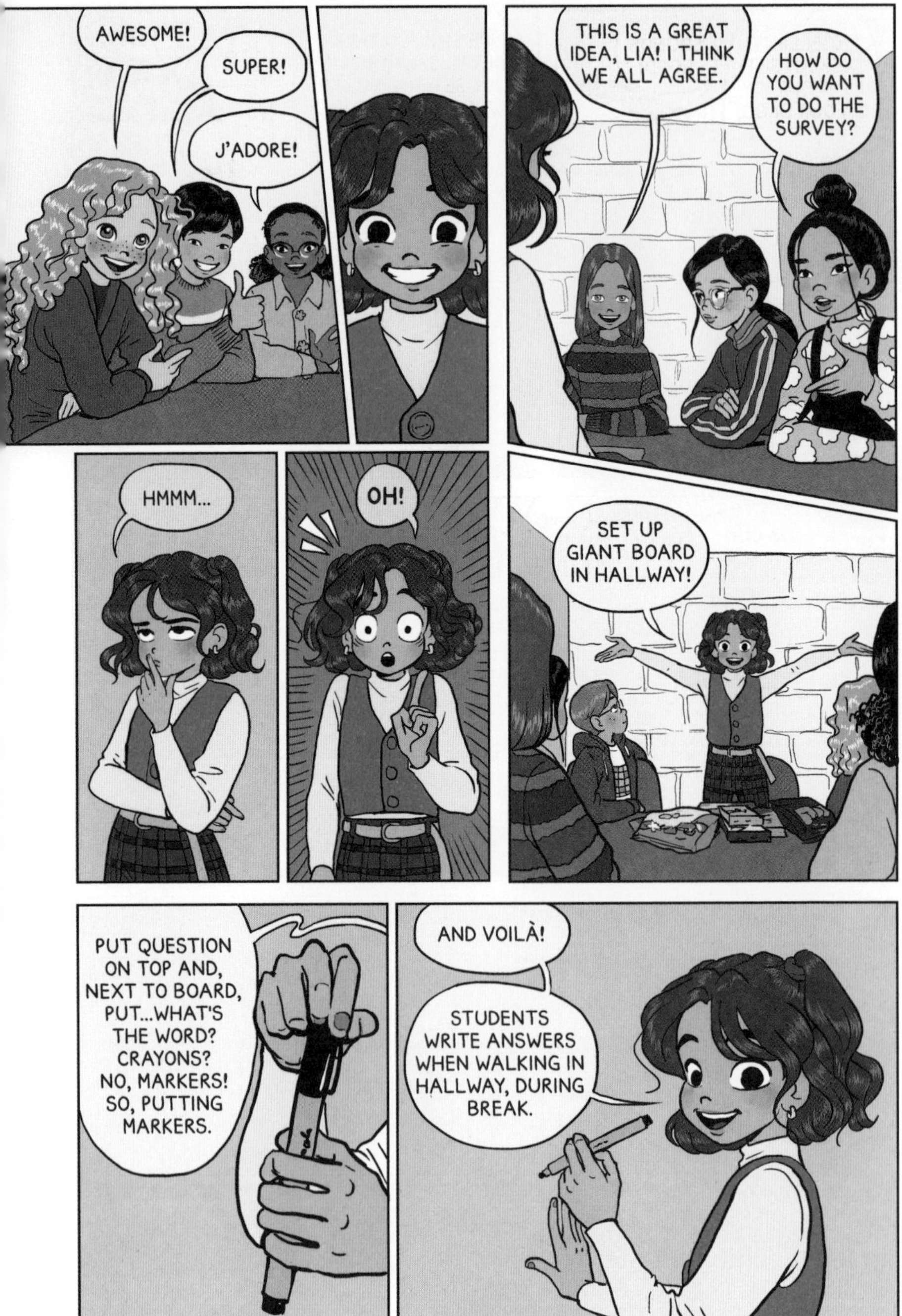
AWESOME!
SUPER!
J'ADORE!
THIS IS A GREAT IDEA, LIA! I THINK WE ALL AGREE.
HOW DO YOU WANT TO DO THE SURVEY?
HMMM...
OH!
SET UP GIANT BOARD IN HALLWAY!
PUT QUESTION ON TOP AND, NEXT TO BOARD, PUT...WHAT'S THE WORD? CRAYONS? NO, MARKERS! SO, PUTTING MARKERS.
AND VOILÀ!
STUDENTS WRITE ANSWERS WHEN WALKING IN HALLWAY, DURING BREAK.

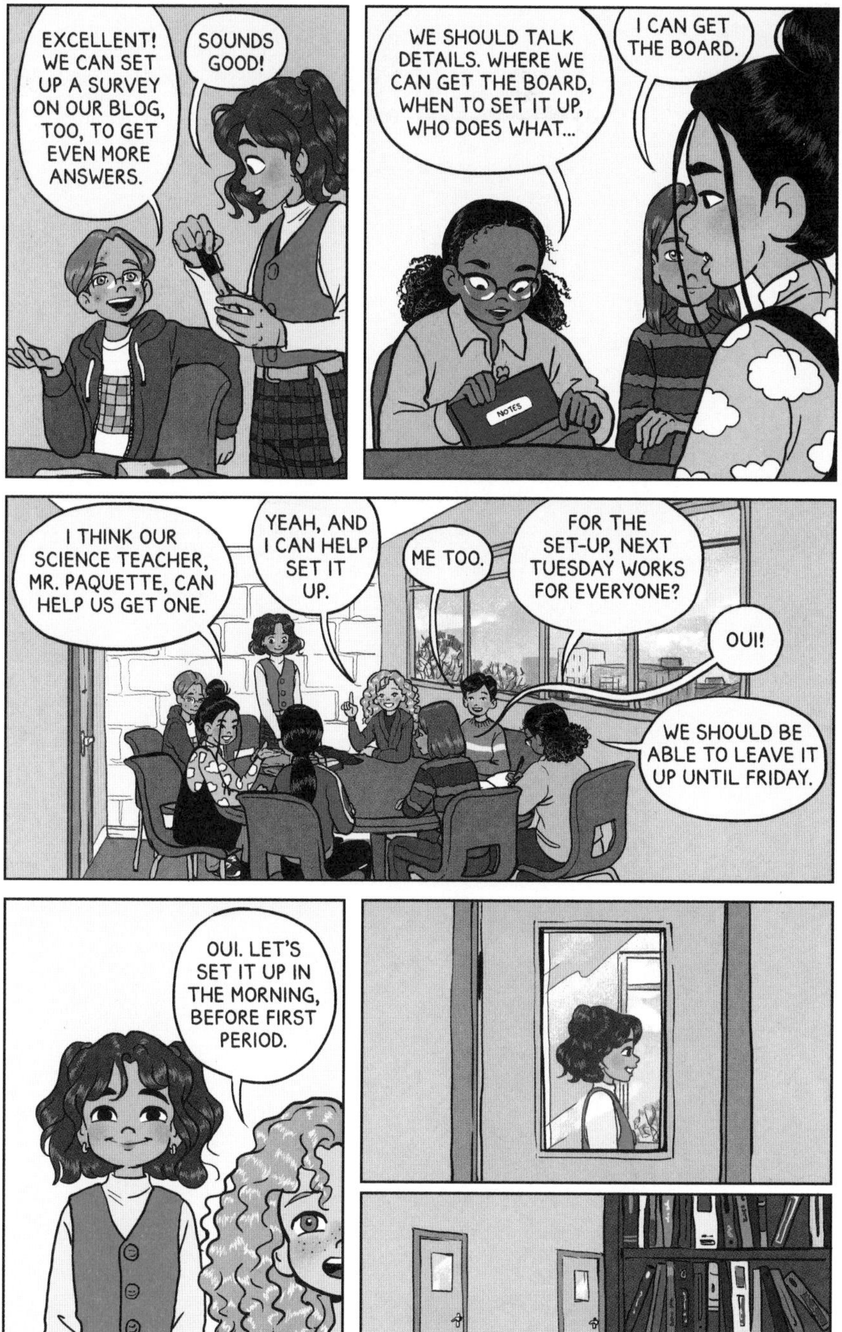
EXCELLENT! WE CAN SET UP A SURVEY ON OUR BLOG, TOO, TO GET EVEN MORE ANSWERS.
SOUNDS GOOD!
WE SHOULD TALK DETAILS. WHERE WE CAN GET THE BOARD, WHEN TO SET IT UP, WHO DOES WHAT...
I CAN GET THE BOARD.
NOTES
I THINK OUR SCIENCE TEACHER, MR. PAQUETTE, CAN HELP US GET ONE.
YEAH, AND I CAN HELP SET IT UP.
ME TOO.
FOR THE SET-UP, NEXT TUESDAY WORKS FOR EVERYONE?
OUI!
WE SHOULD BE ABLE TO LEAVE IT UP UNTIL FRIDAY.
OUI. LET'S SET IT UP IN THE MORNING, BEFORE FIRST PERIOD.

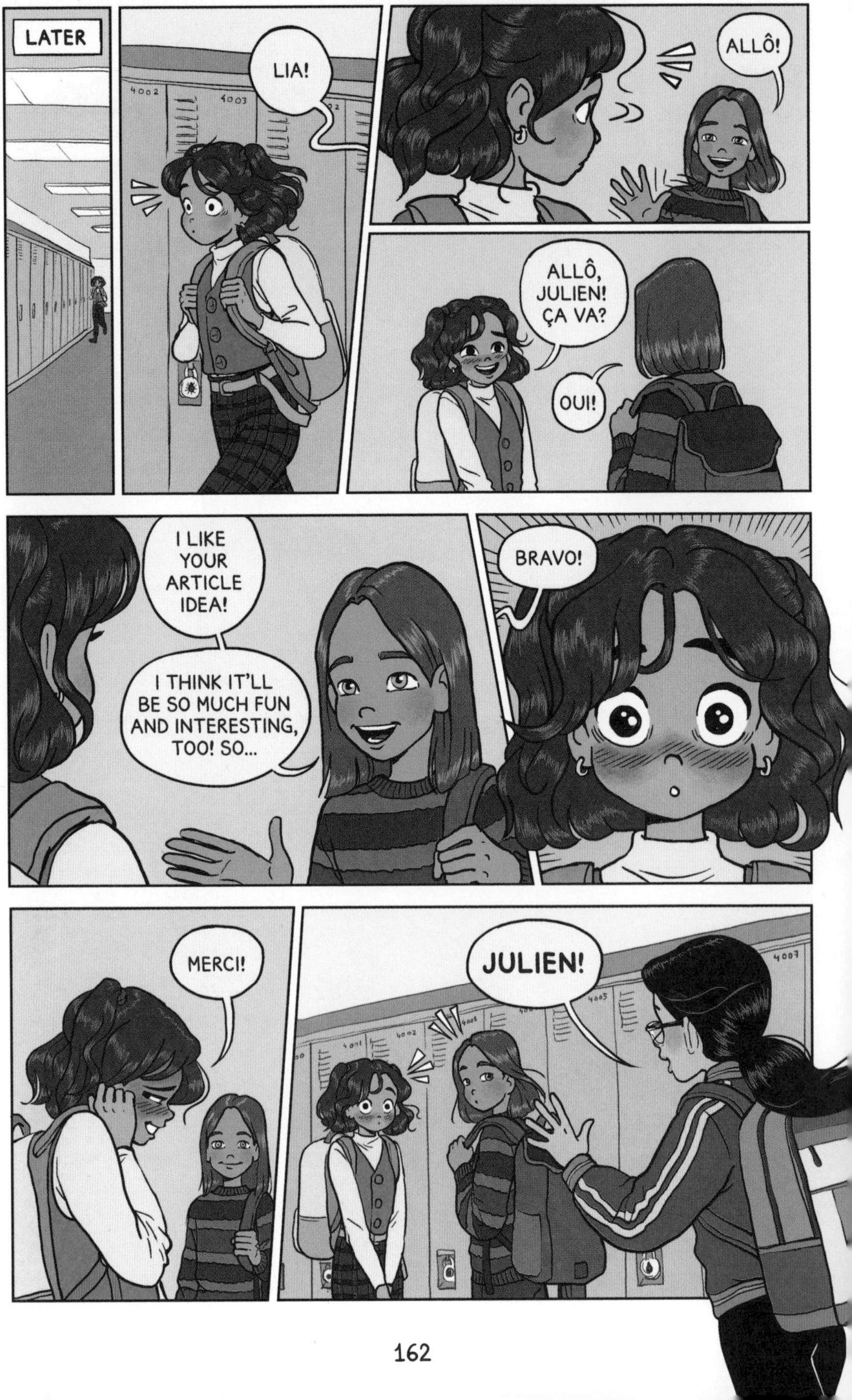
LATER
LIA!
ALLÔ!
ALLÔ, JULIEN! ÇA VA?
OUI!
I LIKE YOUR ARTICLE IDEA!
I THINK IT'LL BE SO MUCH FUN AND INTERESTING, TOO! SO...
BRAVO!
MERCI!
JULIEN!

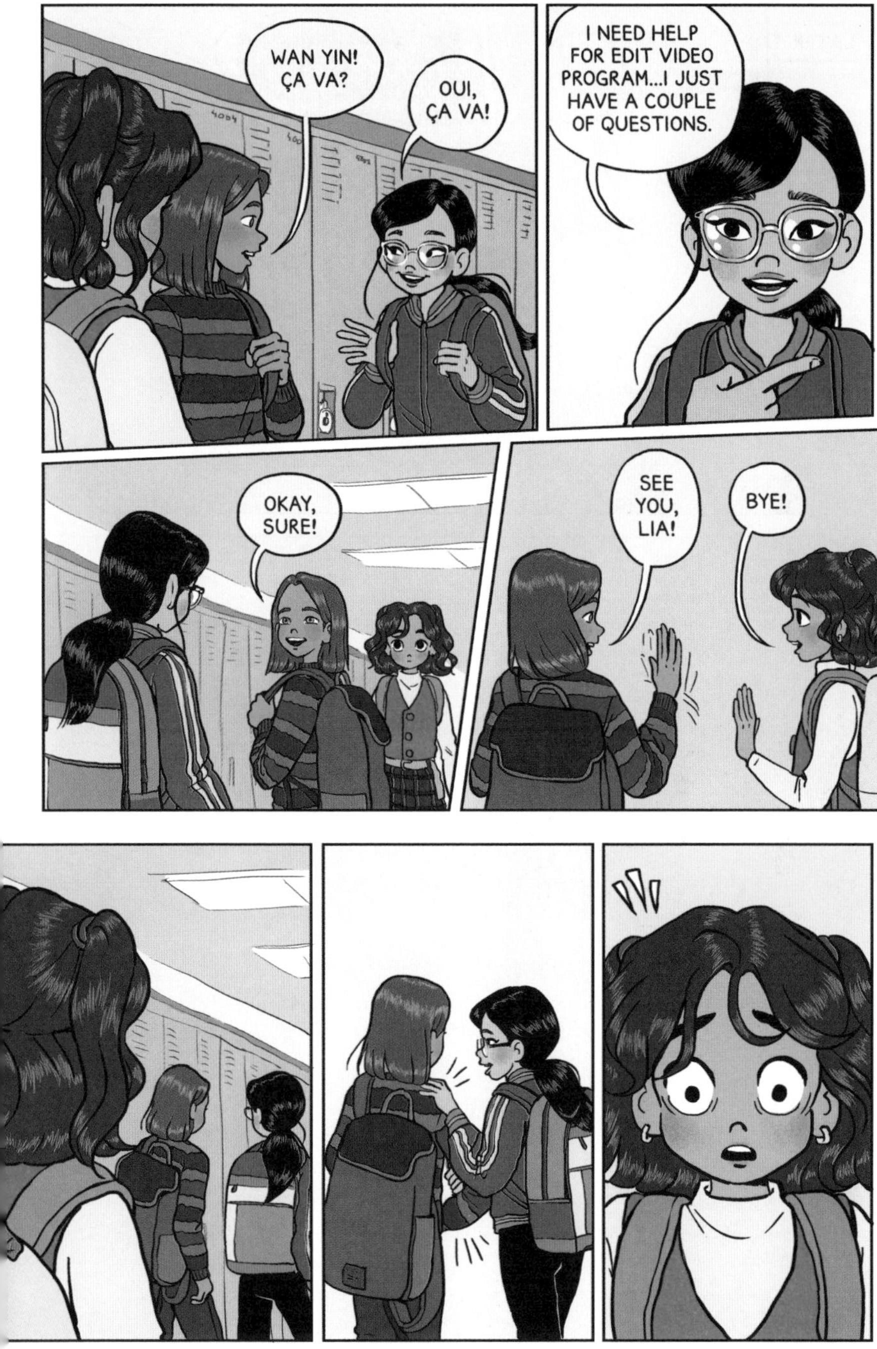
WAN YIN! ÇA VA?
OUI, ÇA VA!
I NEED HELP FOR EDIT VIDEO PROGRAM...I JUST HAVE A COUPLE OF QUESTIONS.
OKAY, SURE!
SEE YOU, LIA!
BYE!

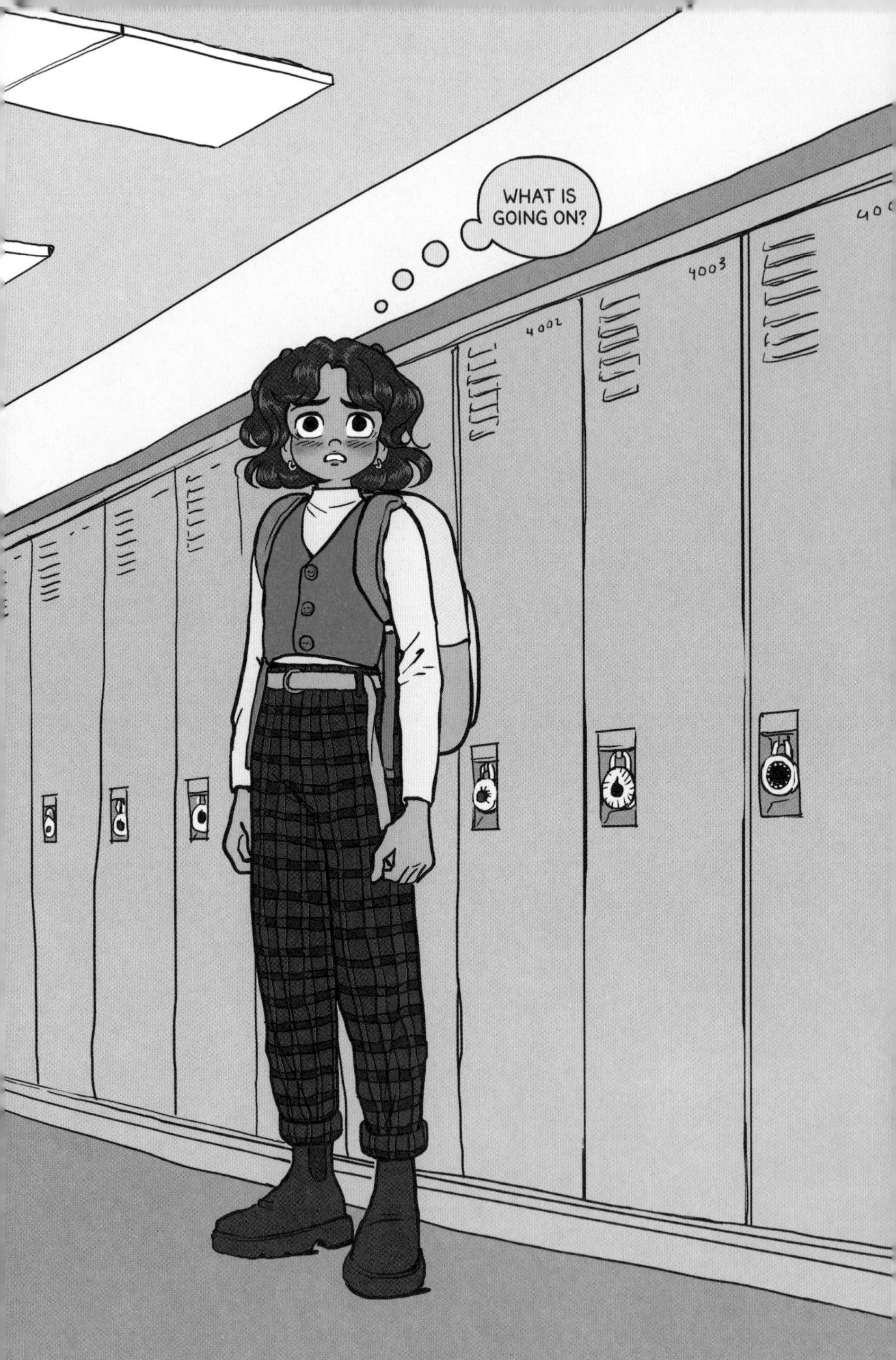
WHAT IS GOING ON?
4002
4003

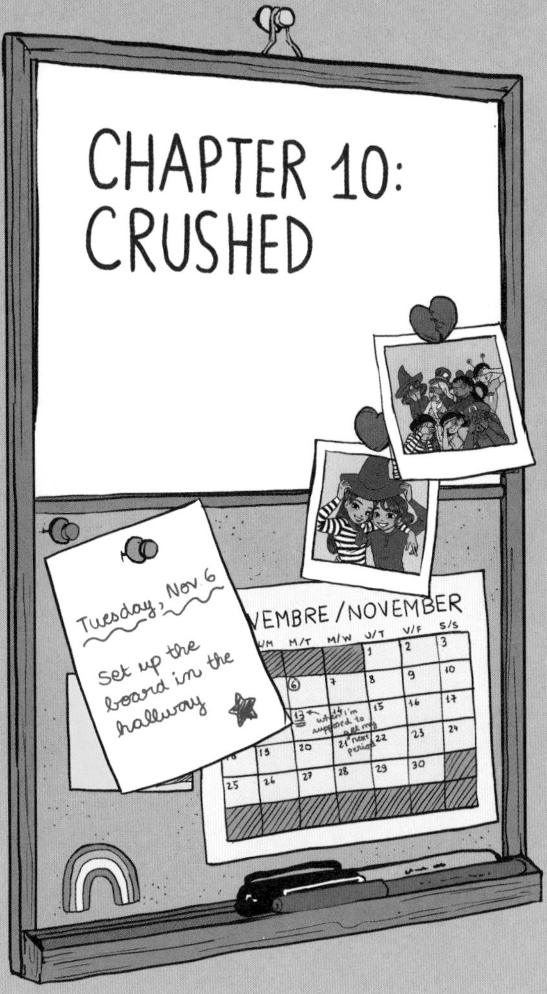
CHAPTER 10:
CRUSHED
Tuesday, Nov 6
Set up the board in the hallway
VEMBRE/NOVEMBER
when I'm supposed to get my next period

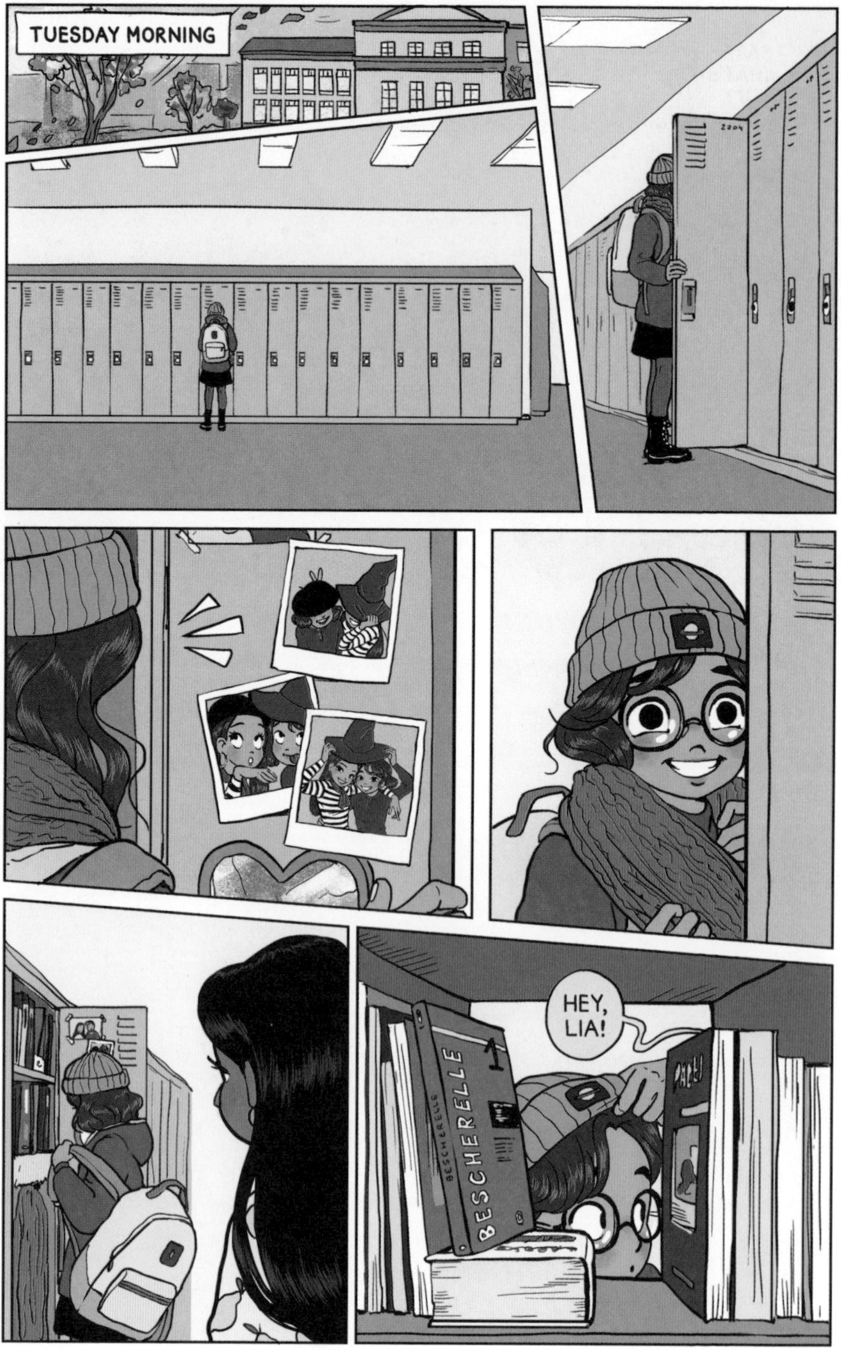
TUESDAY MORNING
2204
BESCHERELLE
BESCHERELLE
HEY, LIA!

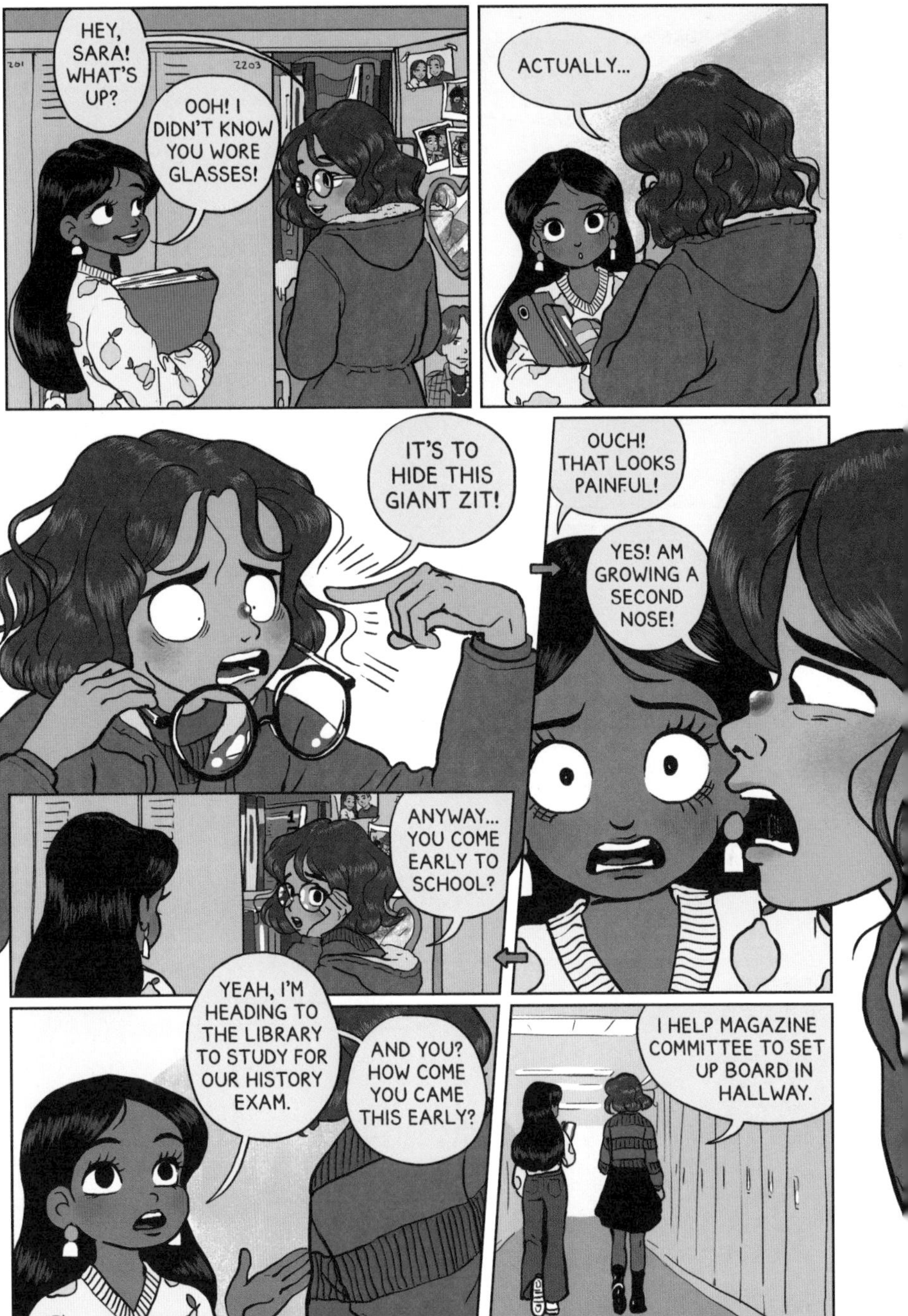
HEY, SARA! WHAT'S UP?
OOH! I DIDN'T KNOW YOU WORE GLASSES!
ACTUALLY...
IT'S TO HIDE THIS GIANT ZIT!
OUCH! THAT LOOKS PAINFUL!
YES! AM GROWING A SECOND NOSE!
ANYWAY... YOU COME EARLY TO SCHOOL?
YEAH, I'M HEADING TO THE LIBRARY TO STUDY FOR OUR HISTORY EXAM.
AND YOU? HOW COME YOU CAME THIS EARLY?
I HELP MAGAZINE COMMITTEE TO SET UP BOARD IN HALLWAY.

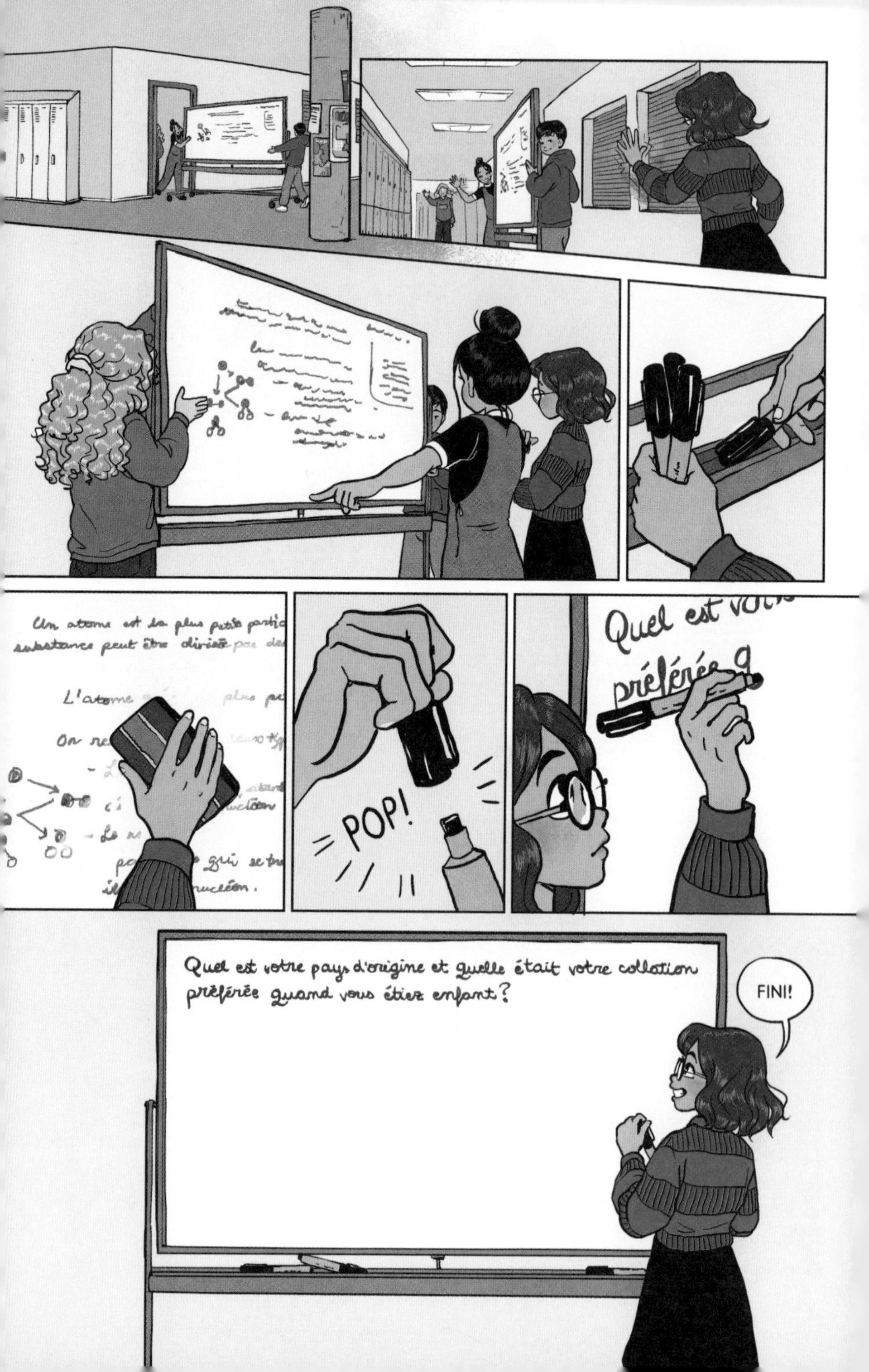
POP!
Quel est votre pays d'origine et quelle était votre collation préférée quand vous étiez enfant?
FINI!

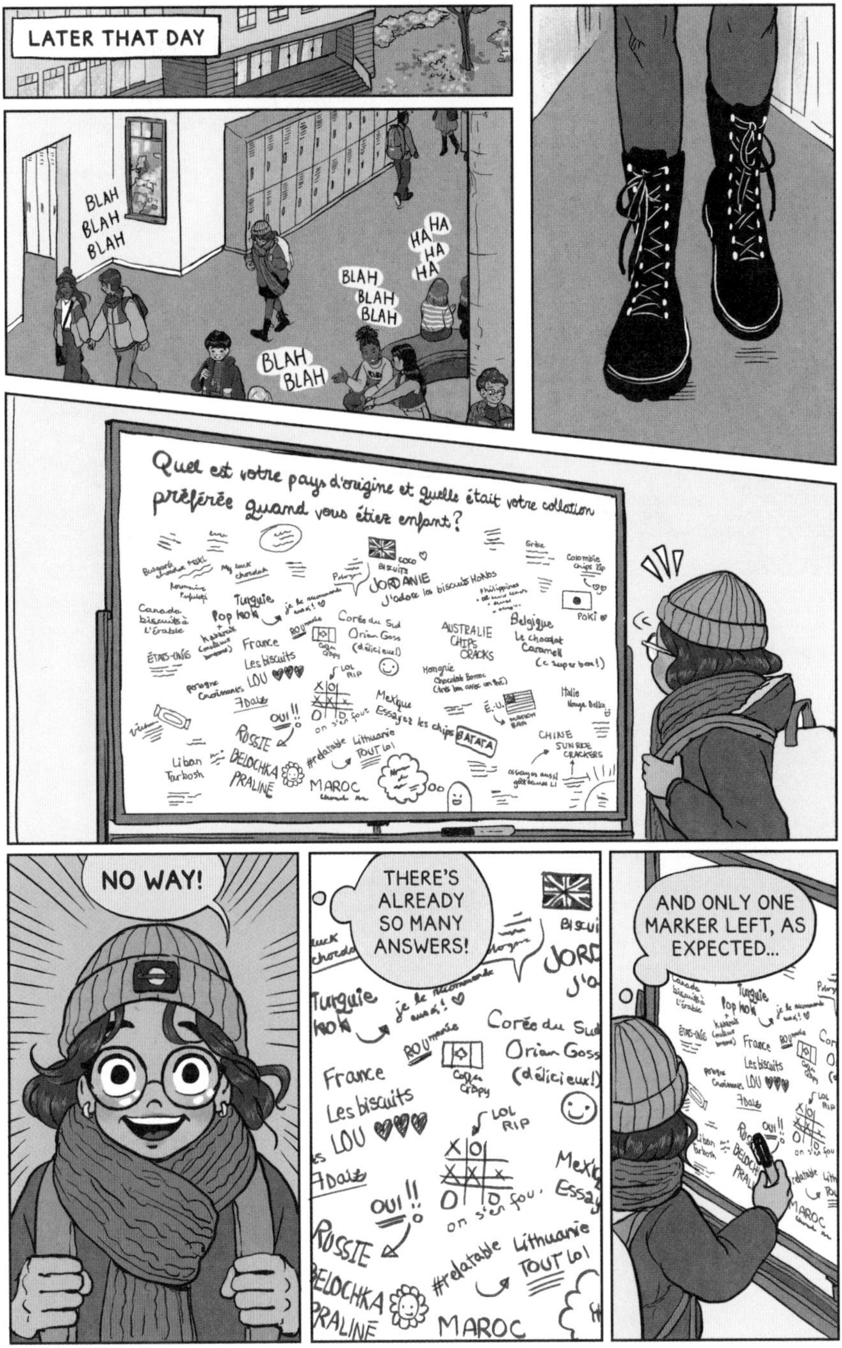
LATER THAT DAY
BLAH BLAH BLAH
HA HA HA HA
BLAH BLAH BLAH
BLAH BLAH
Quel est votre pays d'origine et quelle était votre collation préférée quand vous étiez enfant?
NO WAY!
THERE'S ALREADY SO MANY ANSWERS!
AND ONLY ONE MARKER LEFT, AS EXPECTED...

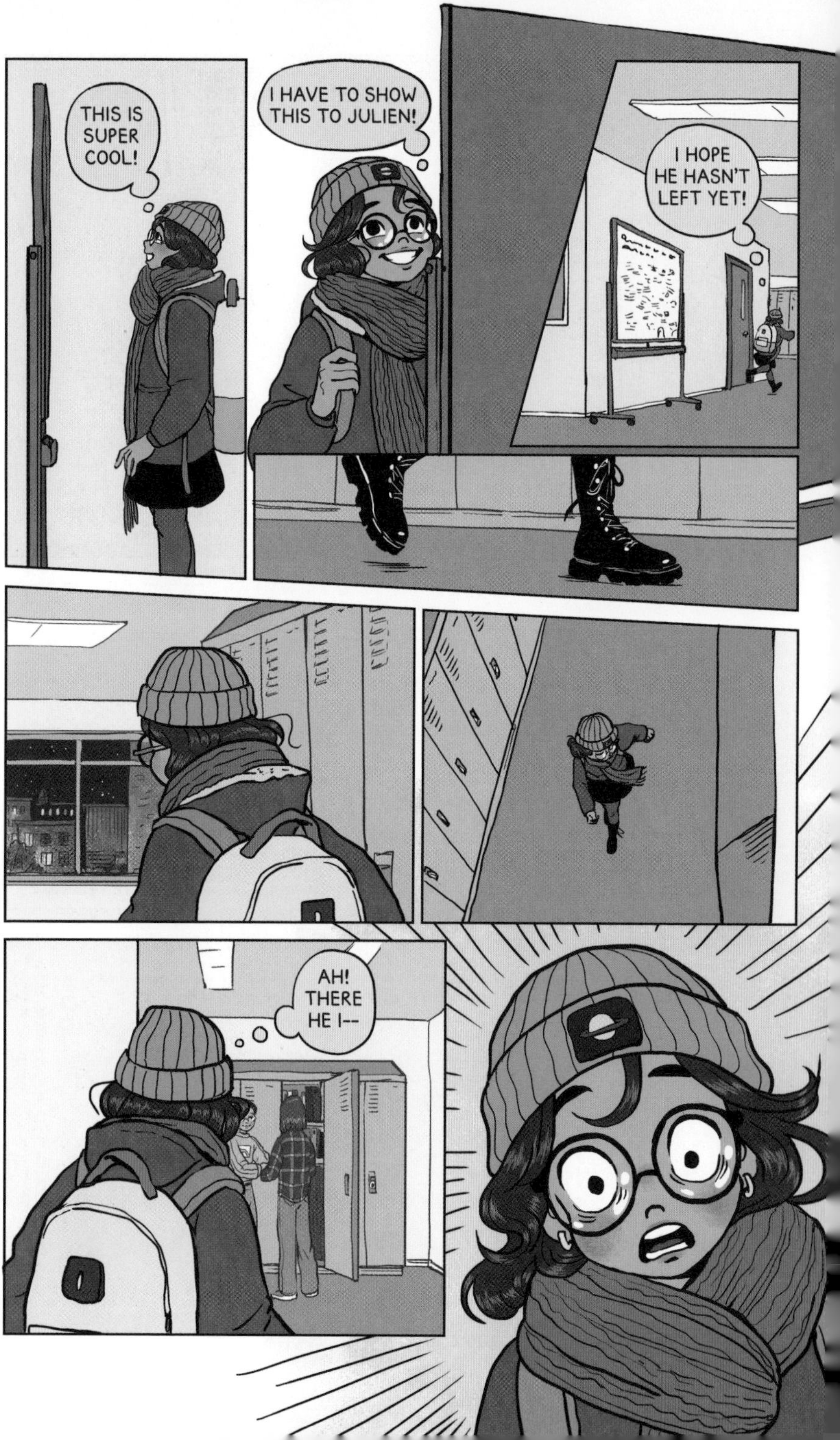
THIS IS SUPER COOL!
I HAVE TO SHOW THIS TO JULIEN!
I HOPE HE HASN'T LEFT YET!
AH! THERE HE I--

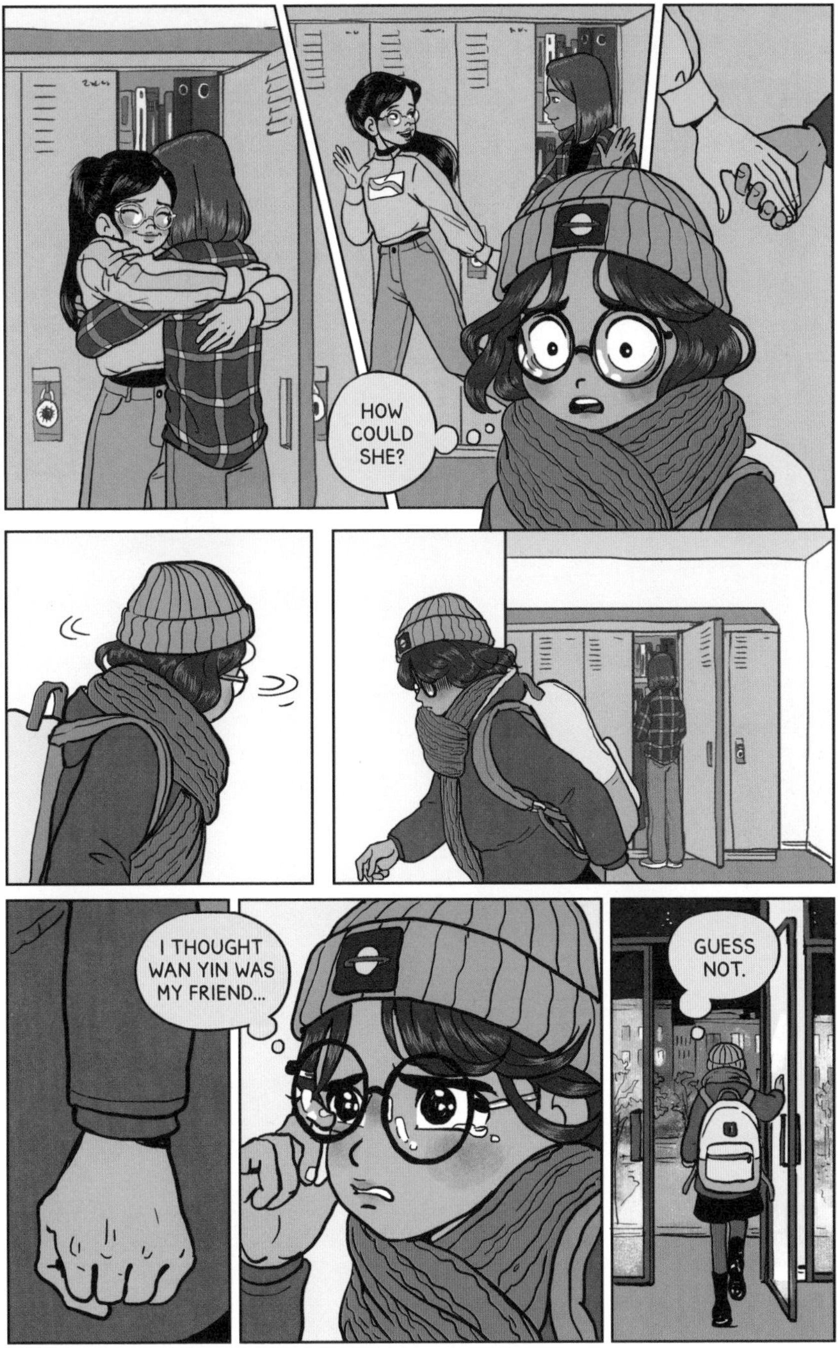
HOW COULD SHE?
I THOUGHT WAN YIN WAS MY FRIEND...
GUESS NOT.

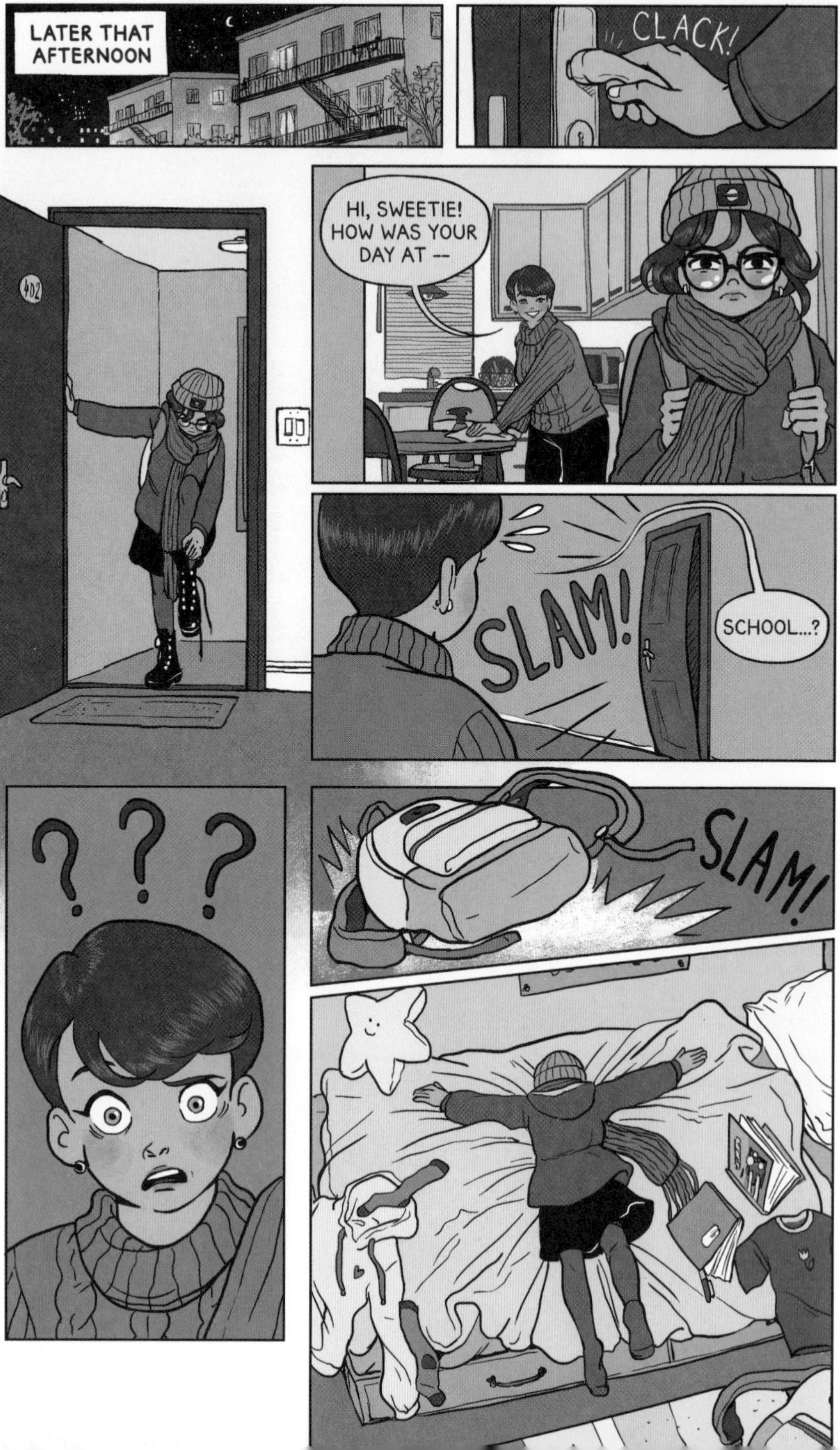
LATER THAT AFTERNOON
CLACK!
402
HI, SWEETIE! HOW WAS YOUR DAY AT --
SLAM!
SCHOOL...?
???
SLAM!

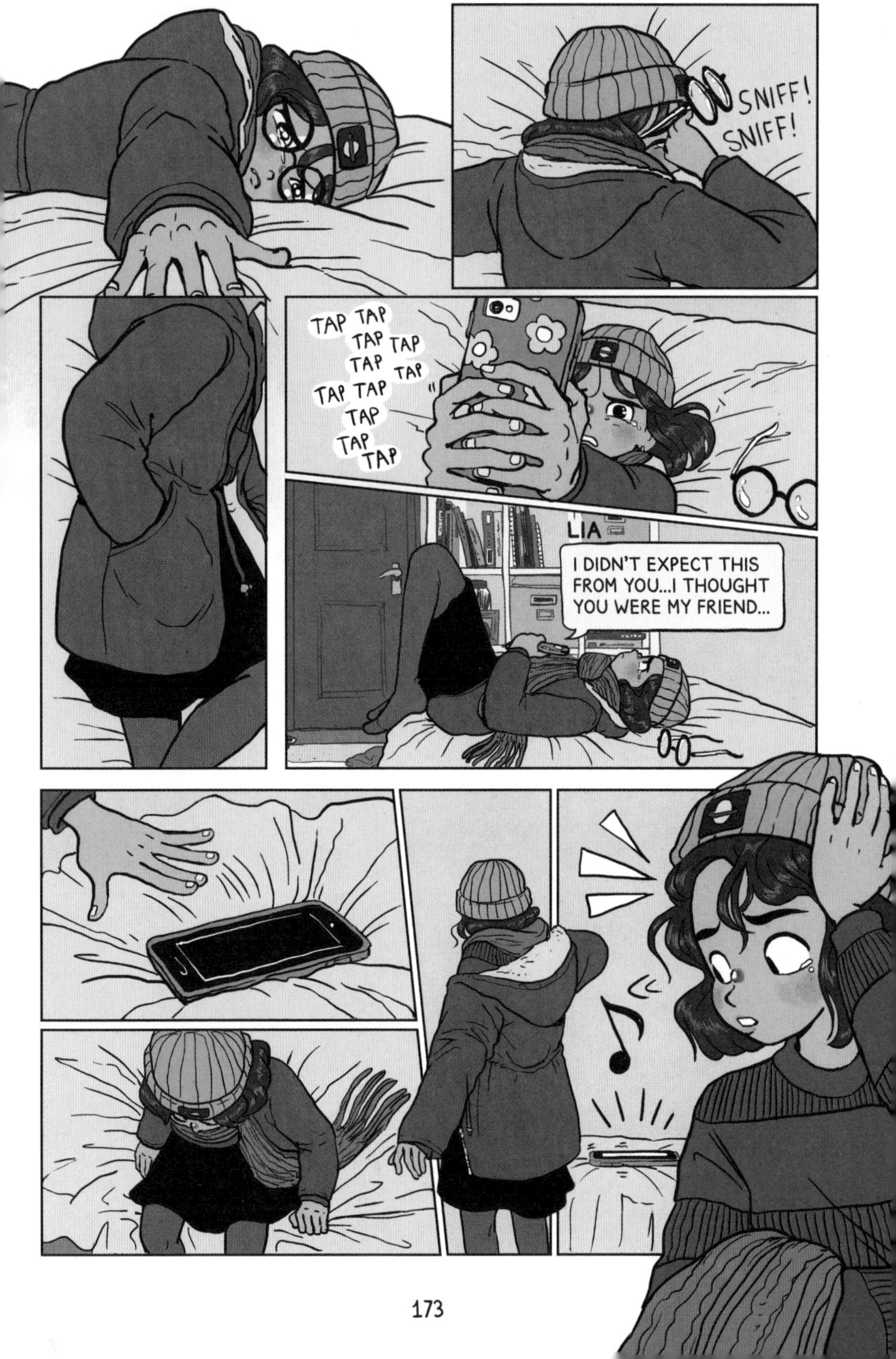
SNIFF! SNIFF!
TAP TAP TAP TAP TAP TAP TAP TAP TAP TAP TAP
LIA
I DIDN'T EXPECT THIS FROM YOU...I THOUGHT YOU WERE MY FRIEND...

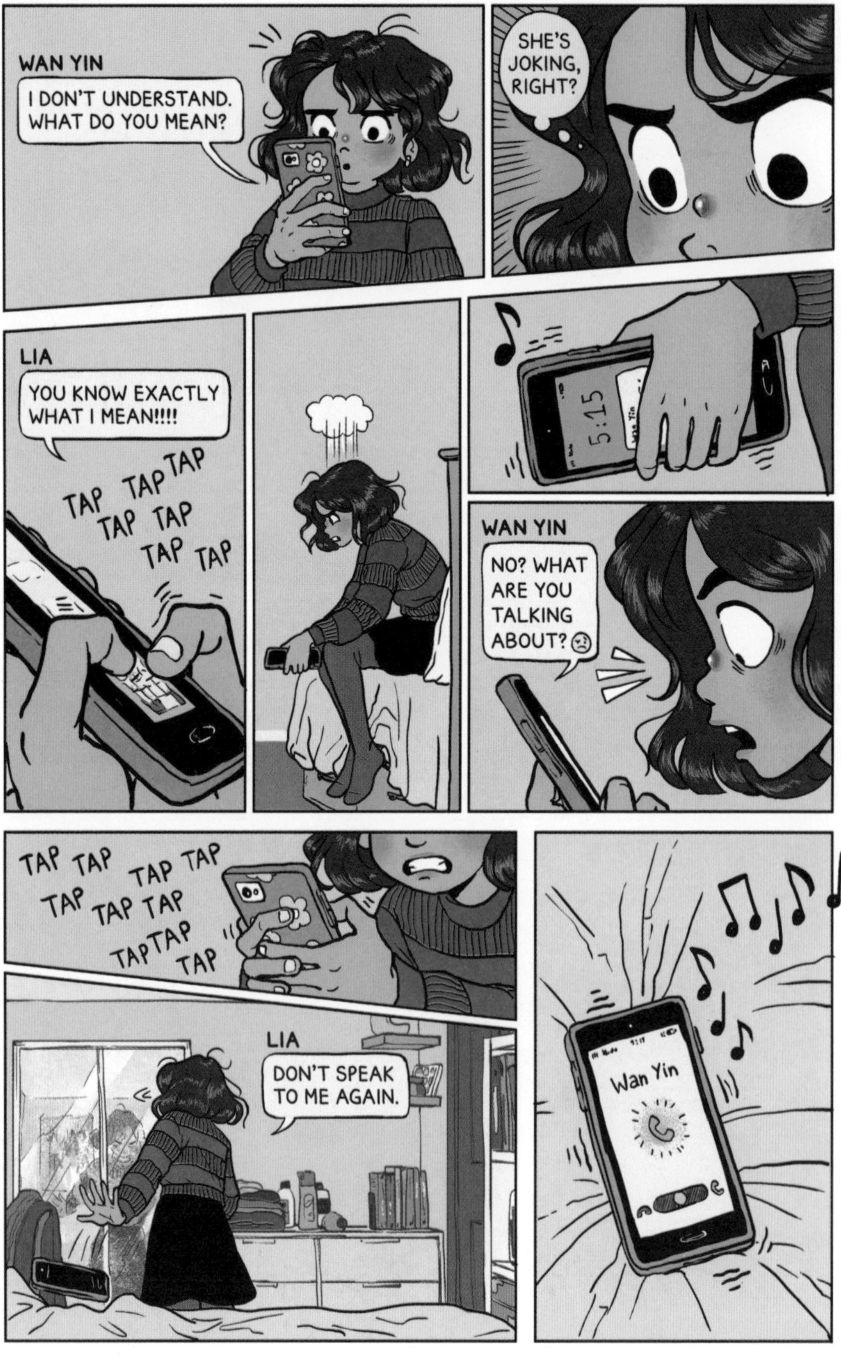
WAN YIN
I DON'T UNDERSTAND. WHAT DO YOU MEAN?
SHE'S JOKING, RIGHT?
LIA
YOU KNOW EXACTLY WHAT I MEAN!!!!
TAP TAP TAP TAP TAP TAP TAP
5:15
WAN YIN
NO? WHAT ARE YOU TALKING ABOUT?
TAP TAP TAP TAP TAP TAP TAP TAP TAP TAP
LIA
DON'T SPEAK TO ME AGAIN.
Wan Yin

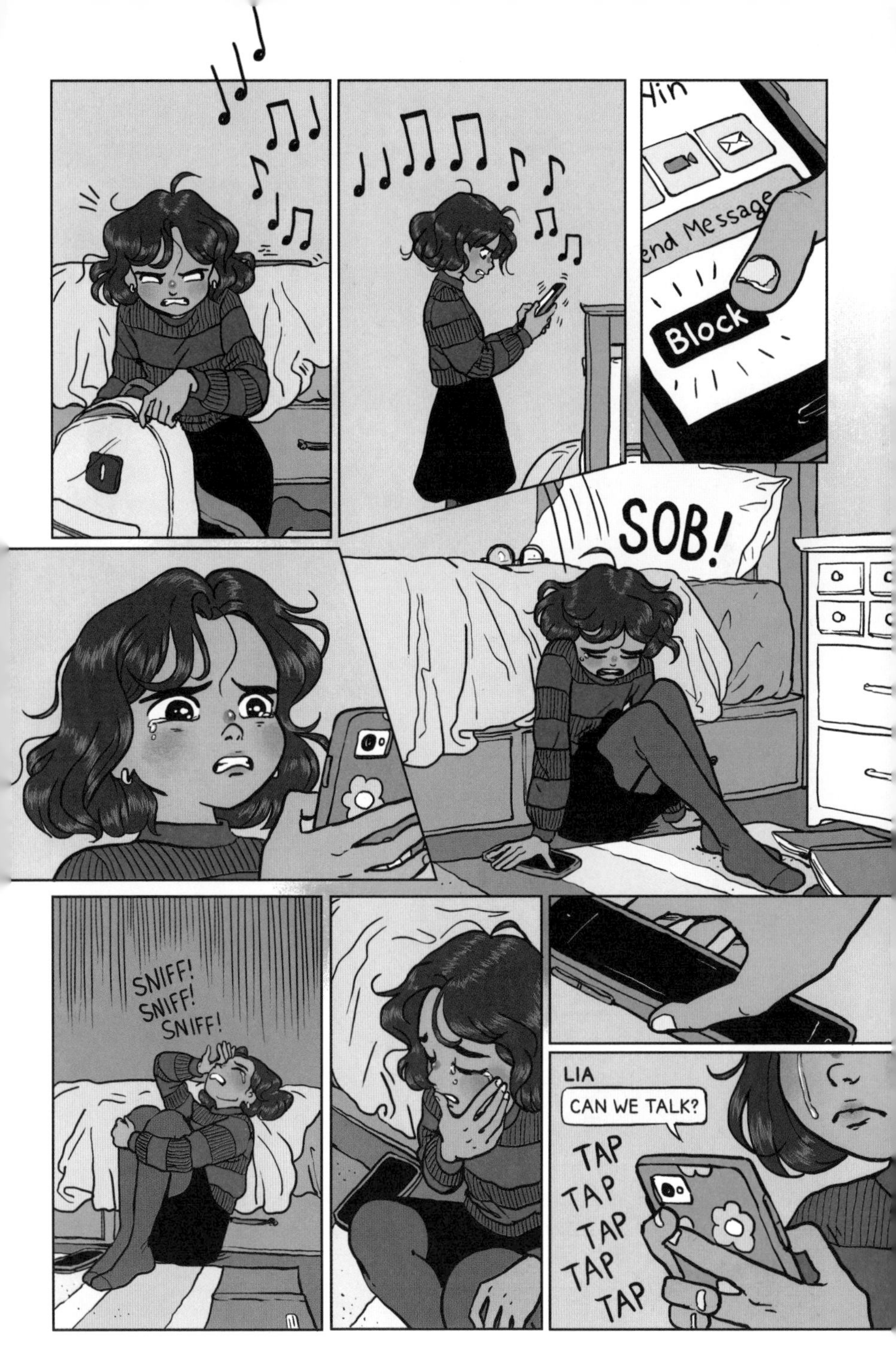
Hin
Send Message
Block
SOB!
SNIFF!
SNIFF!
SNIFF!
LIA
CAN WE TALK?
TAP
TAP
TAP
TAP
TAP

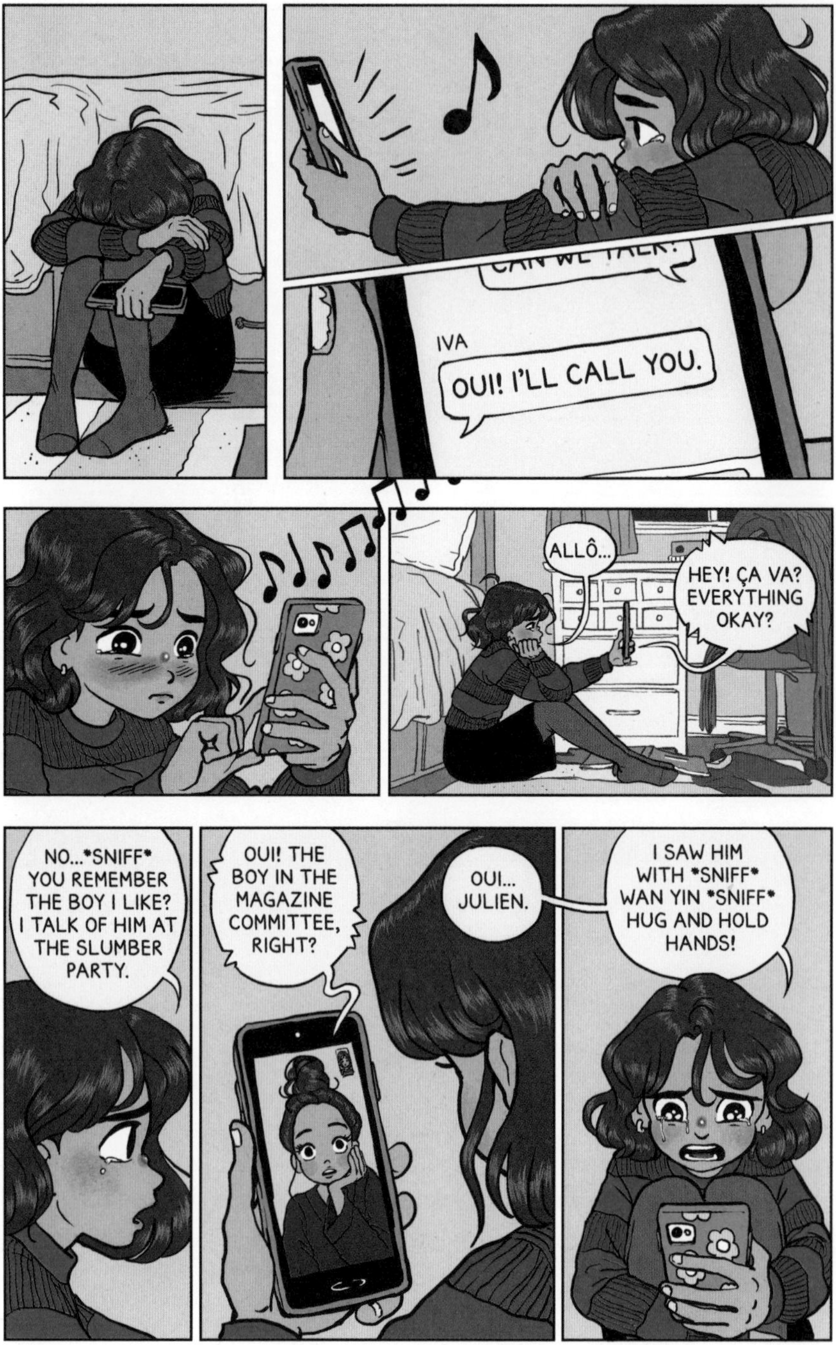
CAN WE TALK?
IVA
OUI! I'LL CALL YOU.
ALLÔ...
HEY! ÇA VA? EVERYTHING OKAY?
NO...*SNIFF* YOU REMEMBER THE BOY I LIKE? I TALK OF HIM AT THE SLUMBER PARTY.
OUI! THE BOY IN THE MAGAZINE COMMITTEE, RIGHT?
OUI... JULIEN.
I SAW HIM WITH *SNIFF* WAN YIN *SNIFF* HUG AND HOLD HANDS!

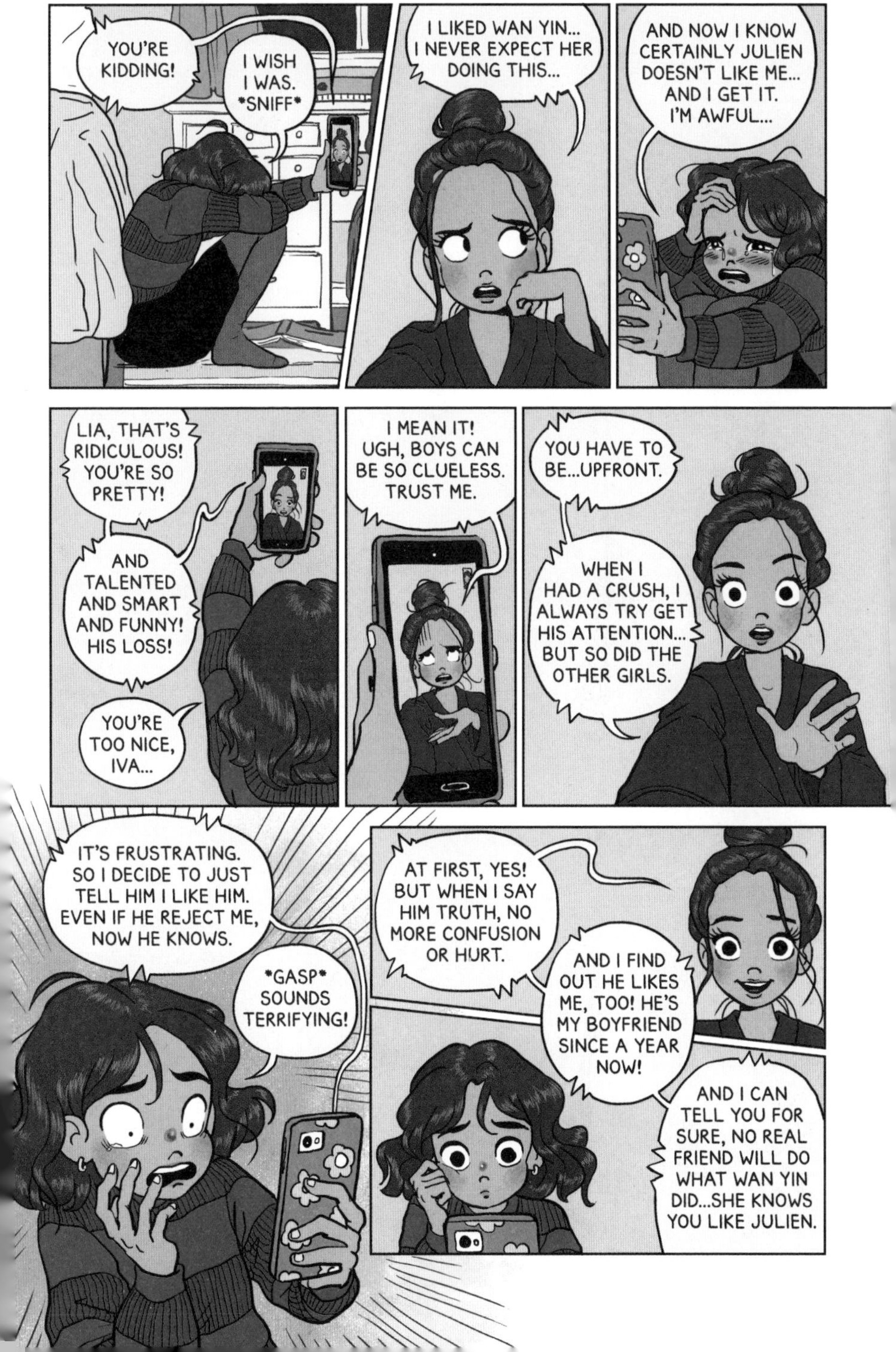
YOU'RE KIDDING!
I WISH I WAS. *SNIFF*
I LIKED WAN YIN... I NEVER EXPECT HER DOING THIS...
AND NOW I KNOW CERTAINLY JULIEN DOESN'T LIKE ME... AND I GET IT. I'M AWFUL...
LIA, THAT'S RIDICULOUS! YOU'RE SO PRETTY!
AND TALENTED AND SMART AND FUNNY! HIS LOSS!
YOU'RE TOO NICE, IVA...
I MEAN IT! UGH, BOYS CAN BE SO CLUELESS. TRUST ME.
YOU HAVE TO BE...UPFRONT.
WHEN I HAD A CRUSH, I ALWAYS TRY GET HIS ATTENTION... BUT SO DID THE OTHER GIRLS.
IT'S FRUSTRATING. SO I DECIDE TO JUST TELL HIM I LIKE HIM. EVEN IF HE REJECT ME, NOW HE KNOWS.
GASP SOUNDS TERRIFYING!
AT FIRST, YES! BUT WHEN I SAY HIM TRUTH, NO MORE CONFUSION OR HURT.
AND I FIND OUT HE LIKES ME, TOO! HE'S MY BOYFRIEND SINCE A YEAR NOW!
AND I CAN TELL YOU FOR SURE, NO REAL FRIEND WILL DO WHAT WAN YIN DID...SHE KNOWS YOU LIKE JULIEN.

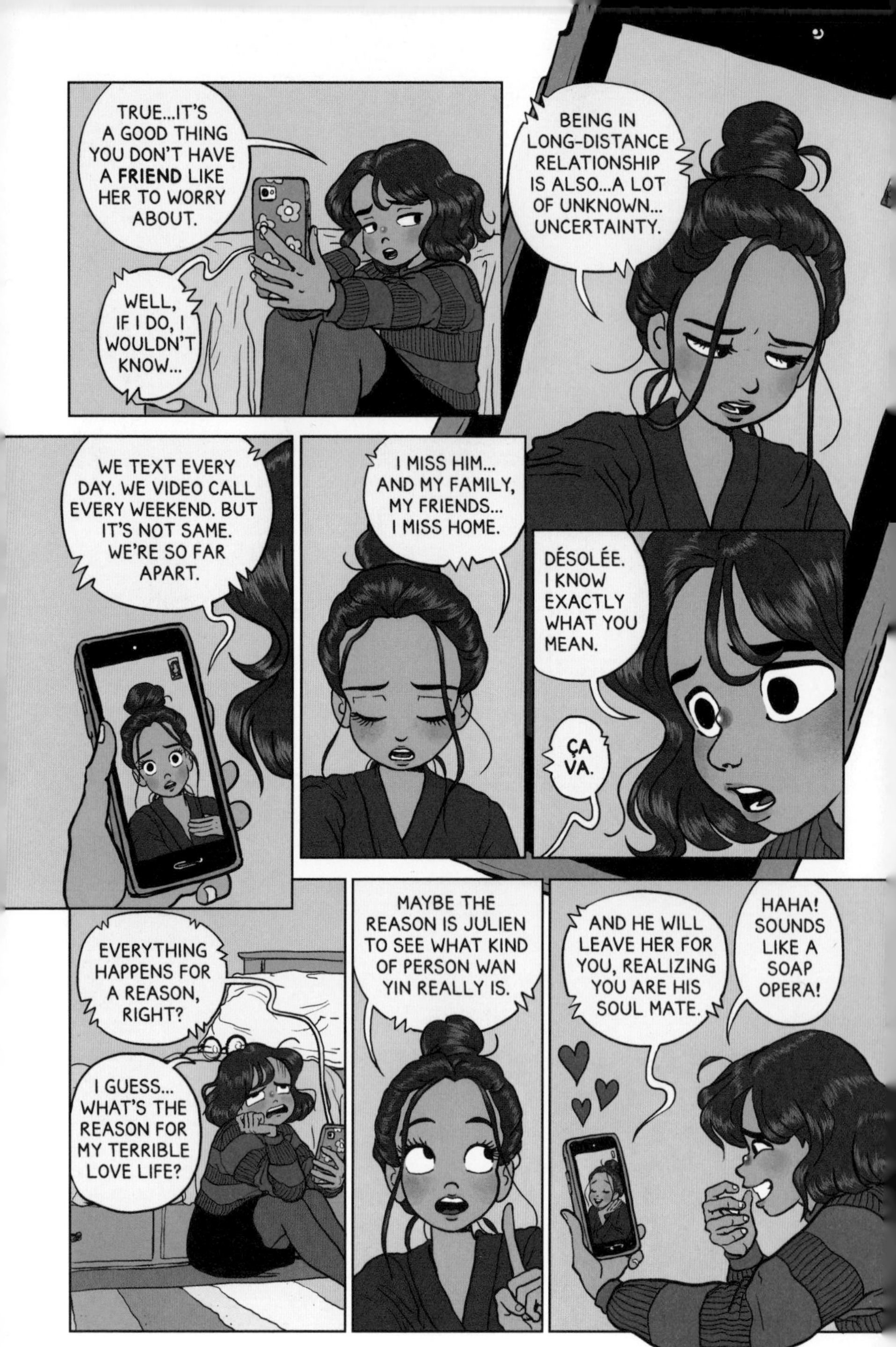
TRUE...IT'S A GOOD THING YOU DON'T HAVE A **FRIEND** LIKE HER TO WORRY ABOUT.
WELL, IF I DO, I WOULDN'T KNOW...
BEING IN LONG-DISTANCE RELATIONSHIP IS ALSO...A LOT OF UNKNOWN... UNCERTAINTY.
WE TEXT EVERY DAY. WE VIDEO CALL EVERY WEEKEND. BUT IT'S NOT SAME. WE'RE SO FAR APART.
I MISS HIM... AND MY FAMILY, MY FRIENDS... I MISS HOME.
DÉSOLÉE. I KNOW EXACTLY WHAT YOU MEAN.
ÇA VA.
EVERYTHING HAPPENS FOR A REASON, RIGHT?
I GUESS... WHAT'S THE REASON FOR MY TERRIBLE LOVE LIFE?
MAYBE THE REASON IS JULIEN TO SEE WHAT KIND OF PERSON WAN YIN REALLY IS.
AND HE WILL LEAVE HER FOR YOU, REALIZING YOU ARE HIS SOUL MATE.
HAHA! SOUNDS LIKE A SOAP OPERA!

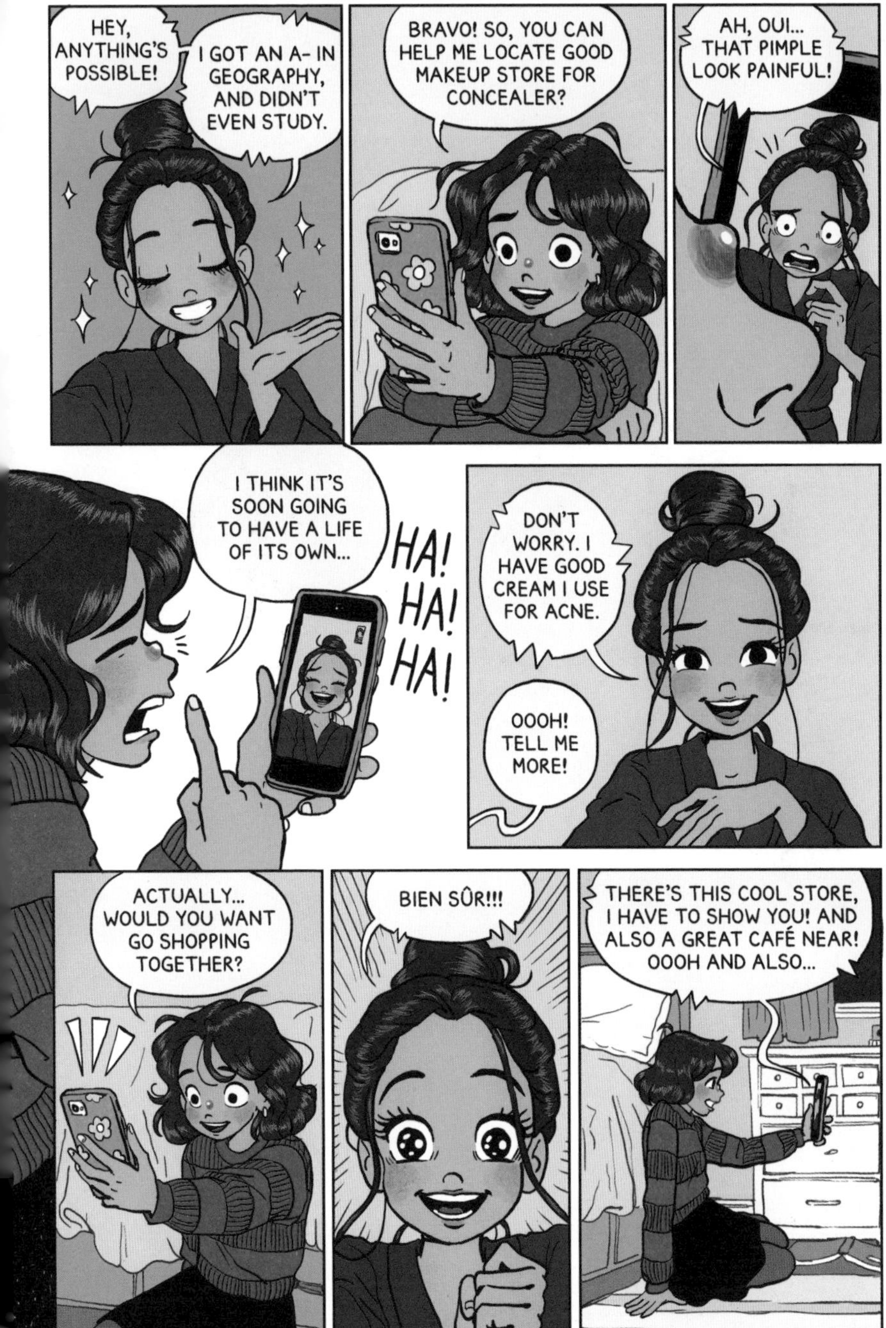
HEY, ANYTHING'S POSSIBLE!
I GOT AN A- IN GEOGRAPHY, AND DIDN'T EVEN STUDY.
BRAVO! SO, YOU CAN HELP ME LOCATE GOOD MAKEUP STORE FOR CONCEALER?
AH, OUI... THAT PIMPLE LOOK PAINFUL!
I THINK IT'S SOON GOING TO HAVE A LIFE OF ITS OWN...
HA! HA! HA!
DON'T WORRY. I HAVE GOOD CREAM I USE FOR ACNE.
OOOH! TELL ME MORE!
ACTUALLY... WOULD YOU WANT GO SHOPPING TOGETHER?
BIEN SÛR!!!
THERE'S THIS COOL STORE, I HAVE TO SHOW YOU! AND ALSO A GREAT CAFÉ NEAR! OOOH AND ALSO...

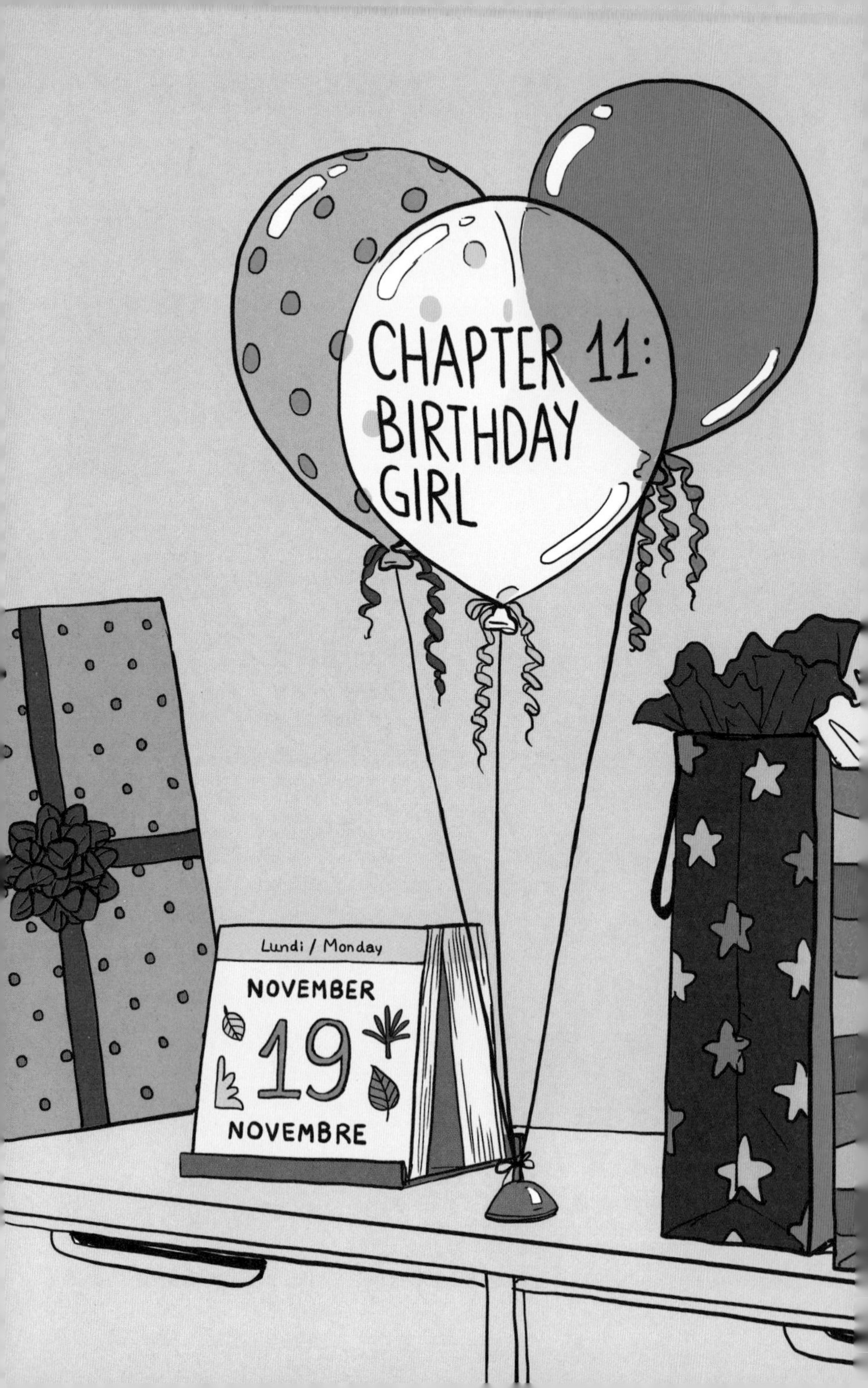
CHAPTER 11:
BIRTHDAY
GIRL
Lundi / Monday
NOVEMBER
19
NOVEMBRE

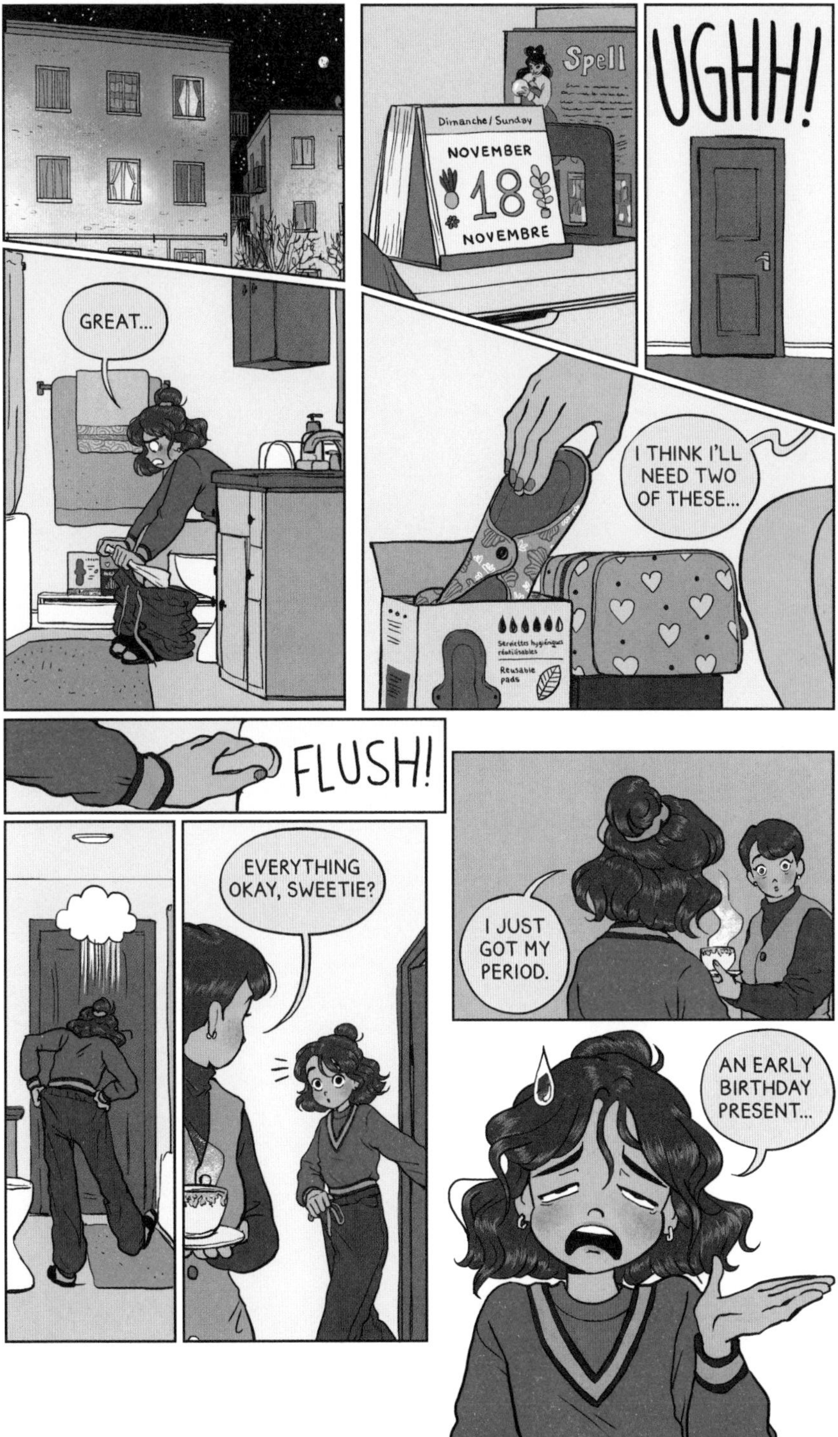

Spell
Dimanche / Sunday
NOVEMBER
18
NOVEMBRE
UGHH!
GREAT...
I THINK I'LL NEED TWO OF THESE...
Serviettes hygiéniques réutilisables
Reusable pads
FLUSH!
EVERYTHING OKAY, SWEETIE?
I JUST GOT MY PERIOD.
AN EARLY BIRTHDAY PRESENT...

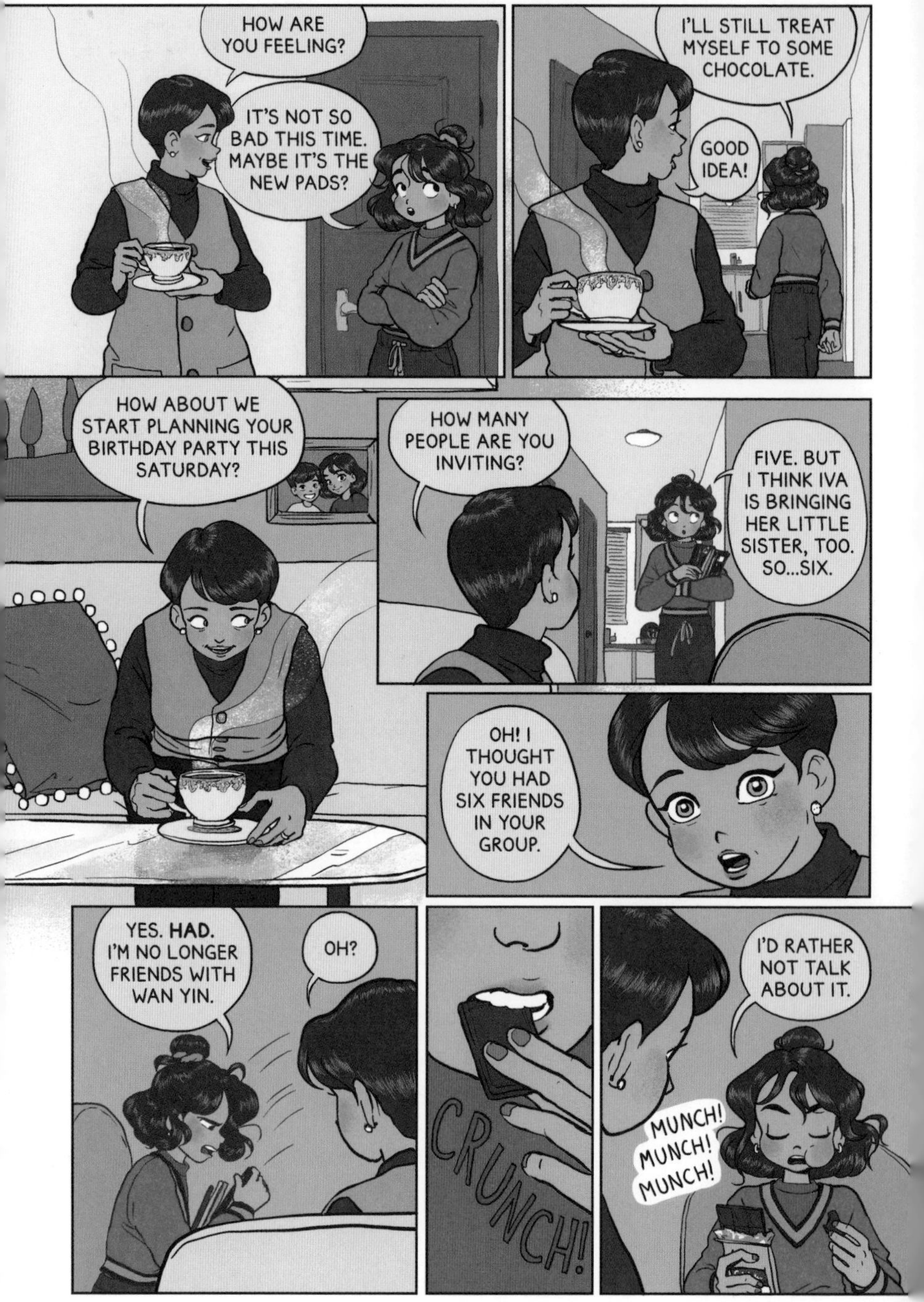
HOW ARE YOU FEELING?
IT'S NOT SO BAD THIS TIME. MAYBE IT'S THE NEW PADS?
I'LL STILL TREAT MYSELF TO SOME CHOCOLATE.
GOOD IDEA!
HOW ABOUT WE START PLANNING YOUR BIRTHDAY PARTY THIS SATURDAY?
HOW MANY PEOPLE ARE YOU INVITING?
FIVE. BUT I THINK IVA IS BRINGING HER LITTLE SISTER, TOO. SO...SIX.
OH! I THOUGHT YOU HAD SIX FRIENDS IN YOUR GROUP.
YES. **HAD.** I'M NO LONGER FRIENDS WITH WAN YIN.
OH?
CRUNCH!
I'D RATHER NOT TALK ABOUT IT.
MUNCH! MUNCH! MUNCH!

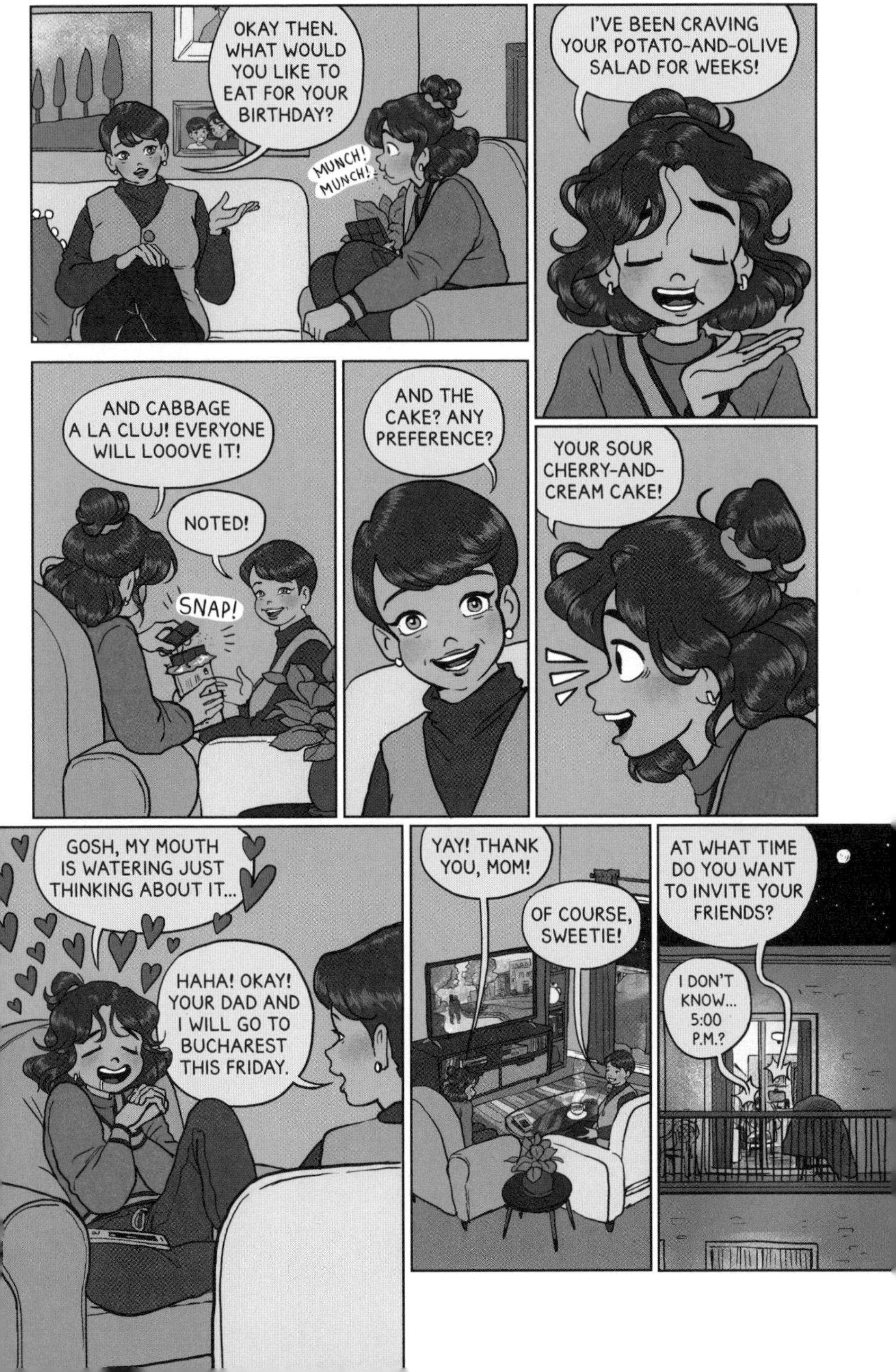
OKAY THEN. WHAT WOULD YOU LIKE TO EAT FOR YOUR BIRTHDAY?
MUNCH! MUNCH!
I'VE BEEN CRAVING YOUR POTATO-AND-OLIVE SALAD FOR WEEKS!
AND CABBAGE A LA CLUJ! EVERYONE WILL LOOOVE IT!
NOTED!
SNAP!
AND THE CAKE? ANY PREFERENCE?
YOUR SOUR CHERRY-AND-CREAM CAKE!
GOSH, MY MOUTH IS WATERING JUST THINKING ABOUT IT...
HAHA! OKAY! YOUR DAD AND I WILL GO TO BUCHAREST THIS FRIDAY.
YAY! THANK YOU, MOM!
OF COURSE, SWEETIE!
AT WHAT TIME DO YOU WANT TO INVITE YOUR FRIENDS?
I DON'T KNOW... 5:00 P.M.?

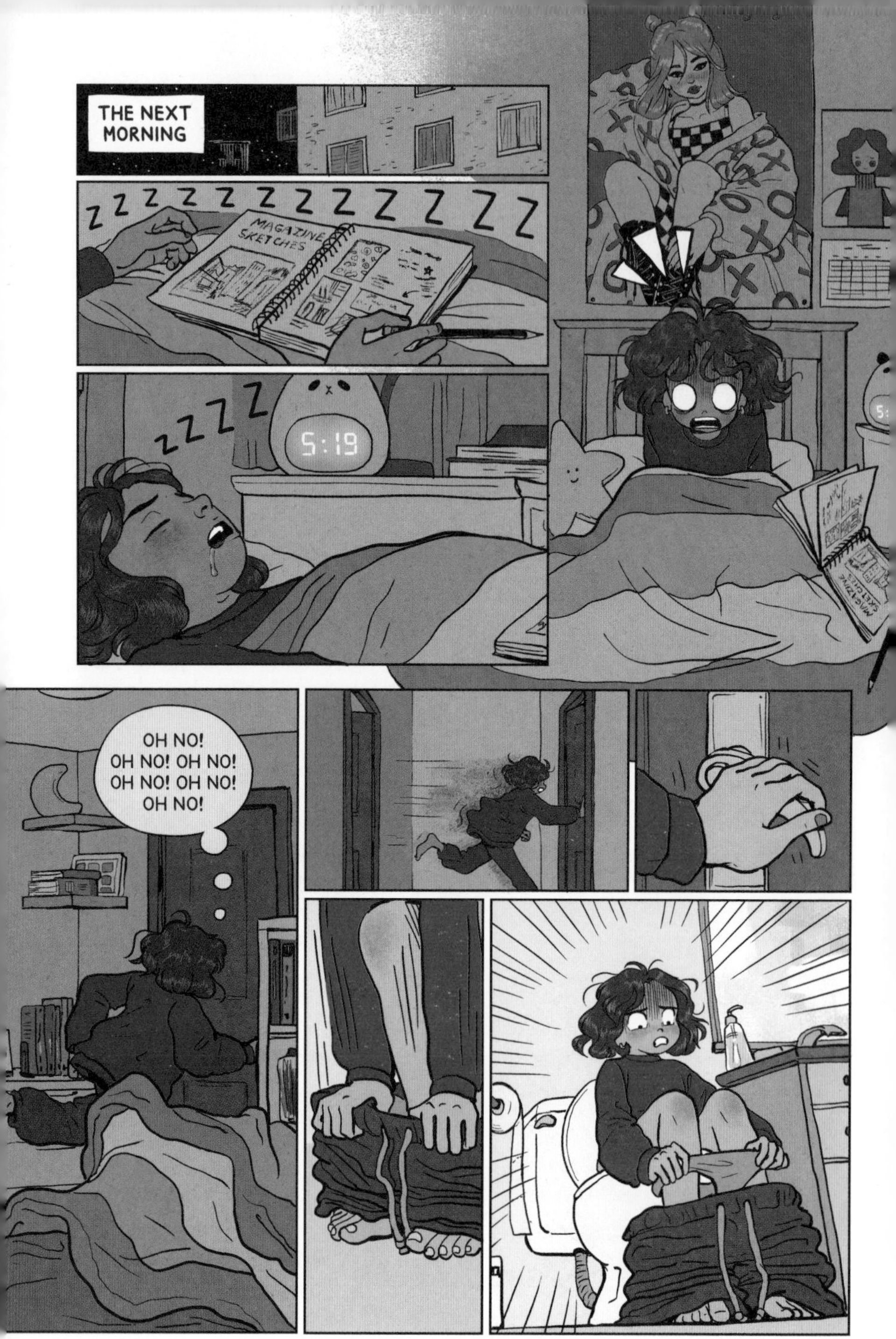
THE NEXT MORNING
Z Z Z Z Z Z Z Z Z Z Z Z Z
MAGAZINE SKETCHES
Z Z Z Z
5:19
OH NO! OH NO! OH NO! OH NO! OH NO! OH NO!

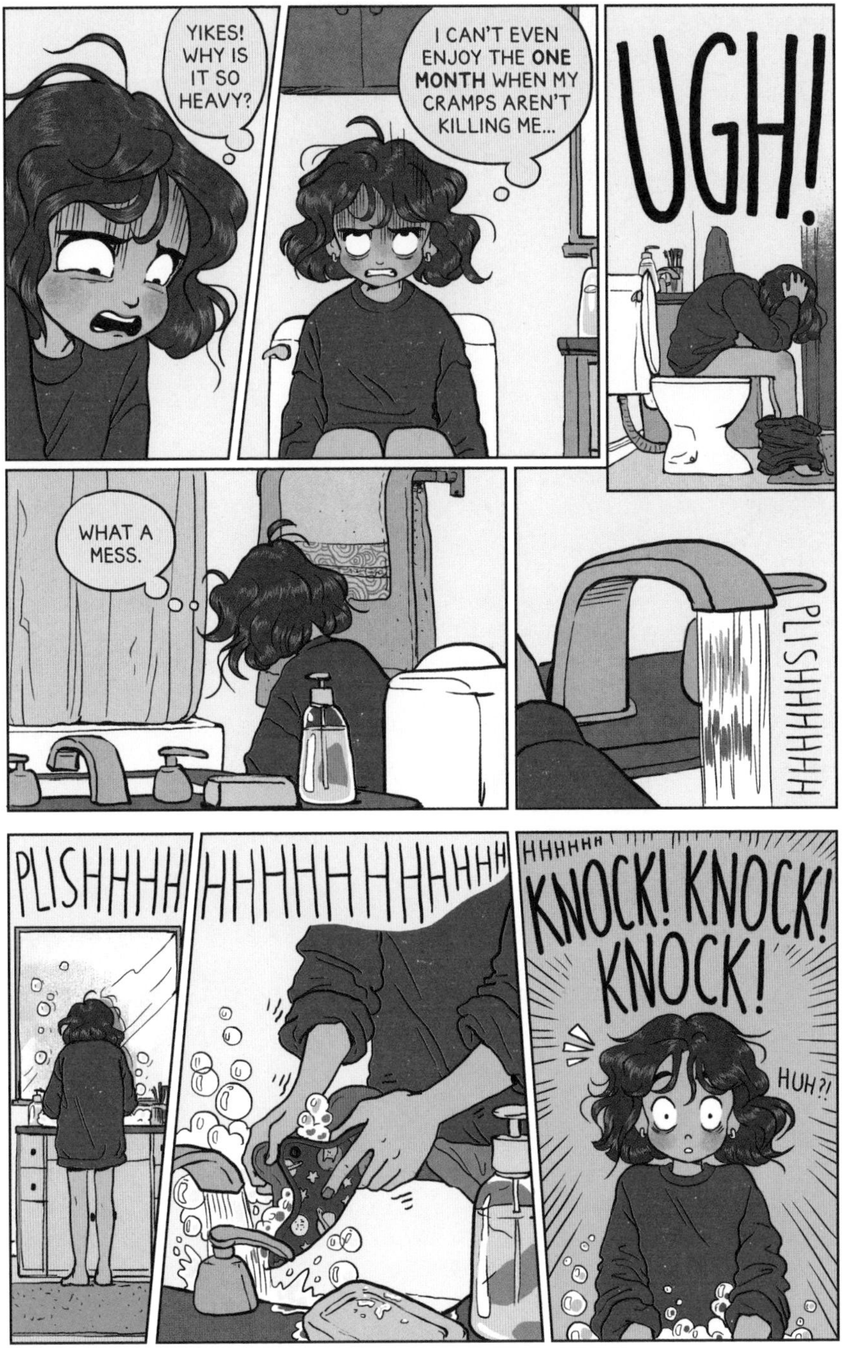
YIKES! WHY IS IT SO HEAVY?
I CAN'T EVEN ENJOY THE ONE MONTH WHEN MY CRAMPS AREN'T KILLING ME...
UGH!
WHAT A MESS.
PLISHHHHHHHH
PLISHHHHH
HHHHHHHHHHH
HHHHHH
KNOCK! KNOCK! KNOCK!
HUH?!

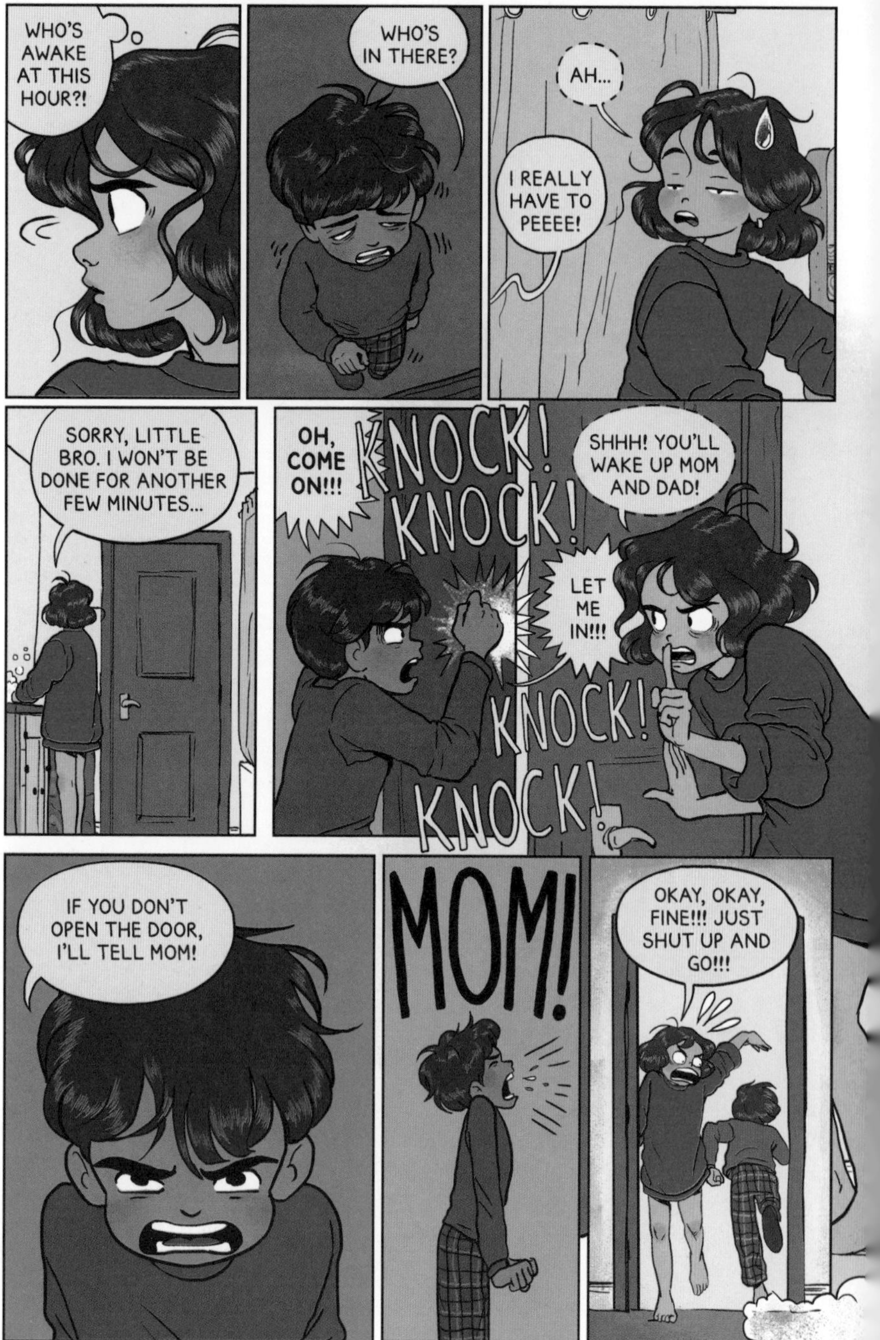
WHO'S AWAKE AT THIS HOUR?!
WHO'S IN THERE?
AH...
I REALLY HAVE TO PEEEE!
SORRY, LITTLE BRO. I WON'T BE DONE FOR ANOTHER FEW MINUTES...
OH, COME ON!!!
KNOCK! KNOCK!
SHHH! YOU'LL WAKE UP MOM AND DAD!
LET ME IN!!!
KNOCK! KNOCK!
IF YOU DON'T OPEN THE DOOR, I'LL TELL MOM!
MOM!
OKAY, OKAY, FINE!!! JUST SHUT UP AND GO!!!

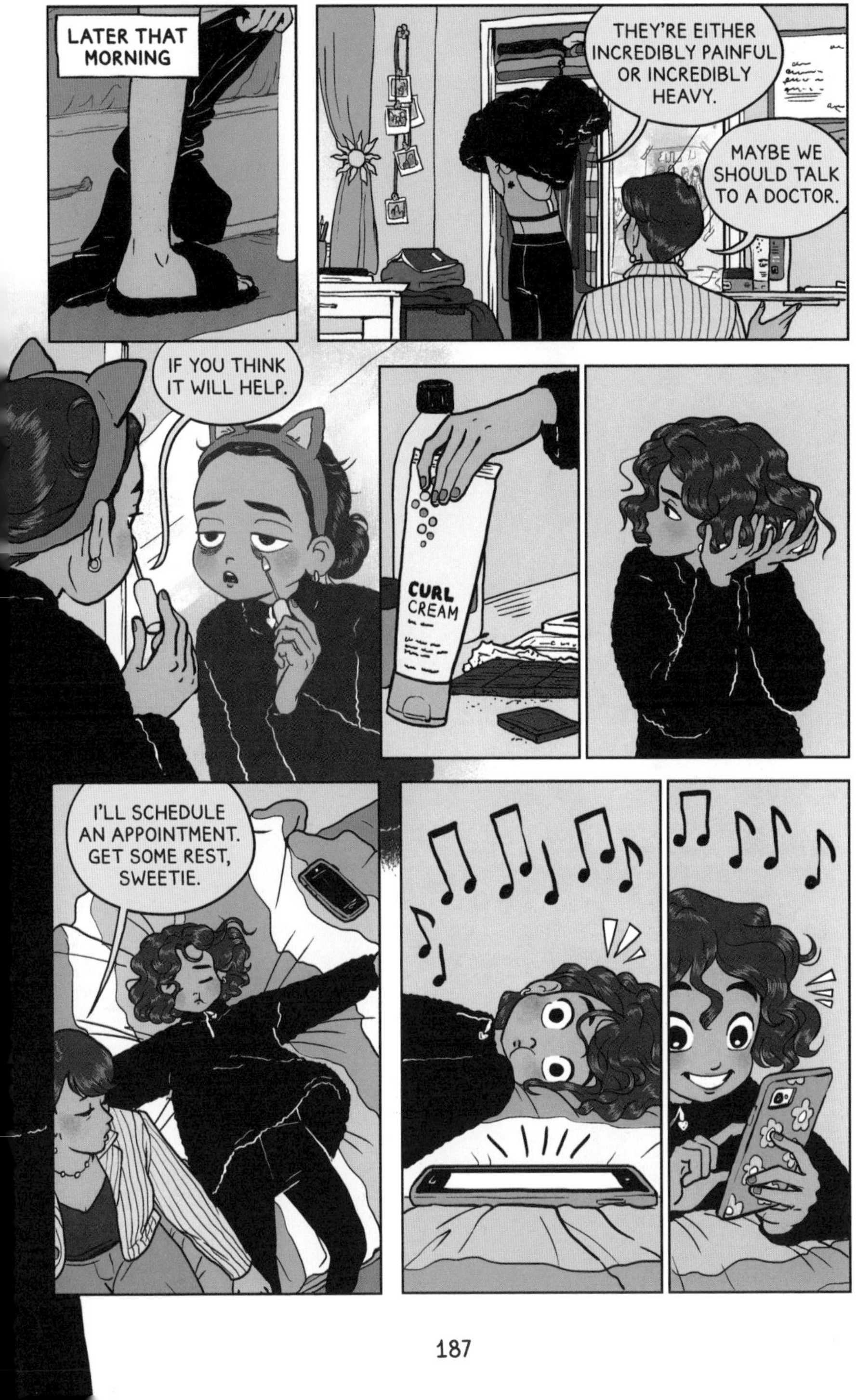
LATER THAT MORNING
THEY'RE EITHER INCREDIBLY PAINFUL OR INCREDIBLY HEAVY.
MAYBE WE SHOULD TALK TO A DOCTOR.
IF YOU THINK IT WILL HELP.
CURL CREAM
I'LL SCHEDULE AN APPOINTMENT. GET SOME REST, SWEETIE.

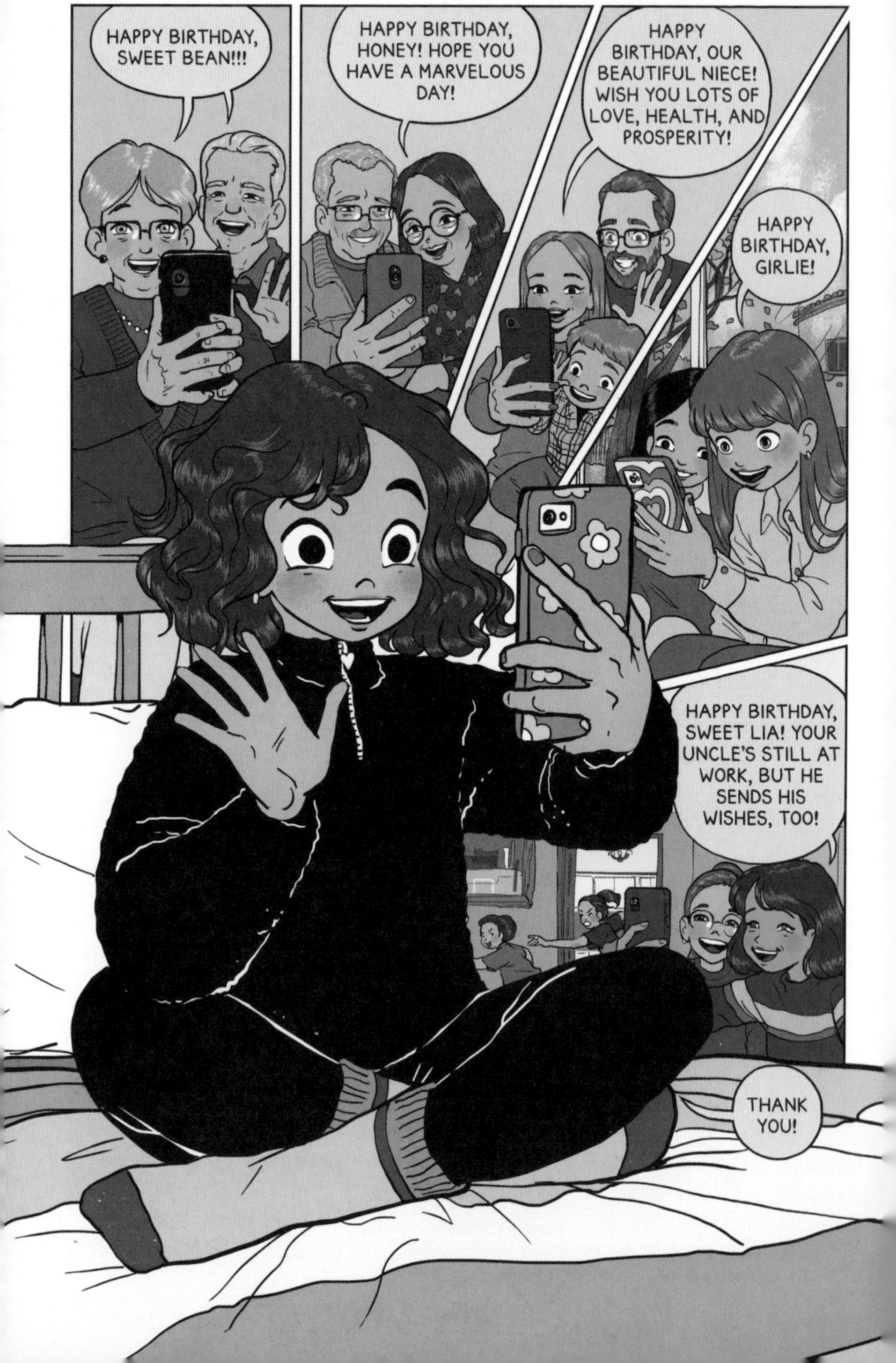
HAPPY BIRTHDAY, SWEET BEAN!!!
HAPPY BIRTHDAY, HONEY! HOPE YOU HAVE A MARVELOUS DAY!
HAPPY BIRTHDAY, OUR BEAUTIFUL NIECE! WISH YOU LOTS OF LOVE, HEALTH, AND PROSPERITY!
HAPPY BIRTHDAY, GIRLIE!
HAPPY BIRTHDAY, SWEET LIA! YOUR UNCLE'S STILL AT WORK, BUT HE SENDS HIS WISHES, TOO!
THANK YOU!

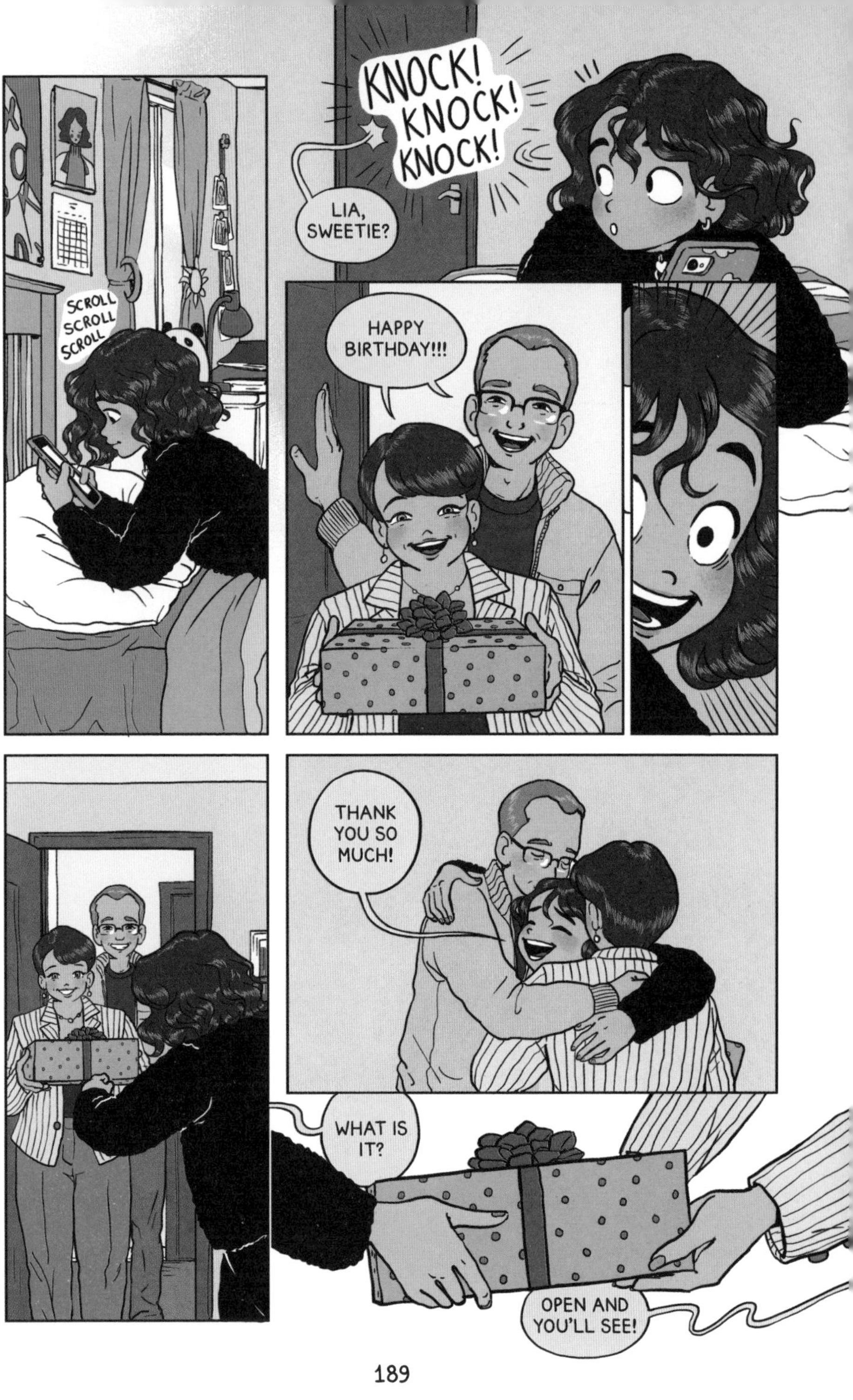
SCROLL
SCROLL
SCROLL
KNOCK! KNOCK! KNOCK!
LIA, SWEETIE?
HAPPY BIRTHDAY!!!
THANK YOU SO MUCH!
WHAT IS IT?
OPEN AND YOU'LL SEE!

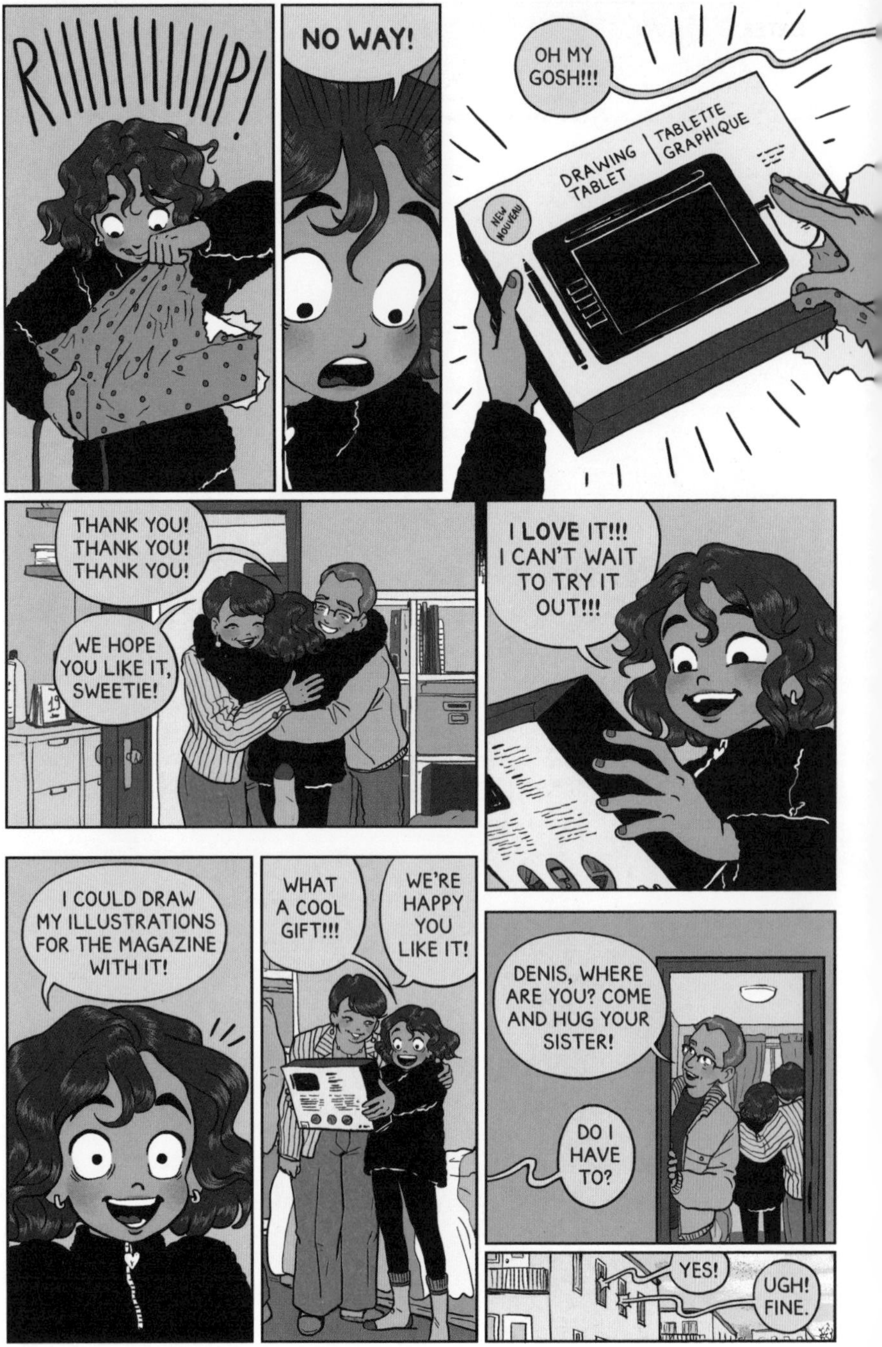
RIIIIIIIIIP!
NO WAY!
OH MY GOSH!!!
DRAWING TABLET
TABLETTE GRAPHIQUE
NEW NOUVEAU
THANK YOU! THANK YOU! THANK YOU!
WE HOPE YOU LIKE IT, SWEETIE!
I LOVE IT!!! I CAN'T WAIT TO TRY IT OUT!!!
I COULD DRAW MY ILLUSTRATIONS FOR THE MAGAZINE WITH IT!
WHAT A COOL GIFT!!!
WE'RE HAPPY YOU LIKE IT!
DENIS, WHERE ARE YOU? COME AND HUG YOUR SISTER!
DO I HAVE TO?
YES!
UGH! FINE.

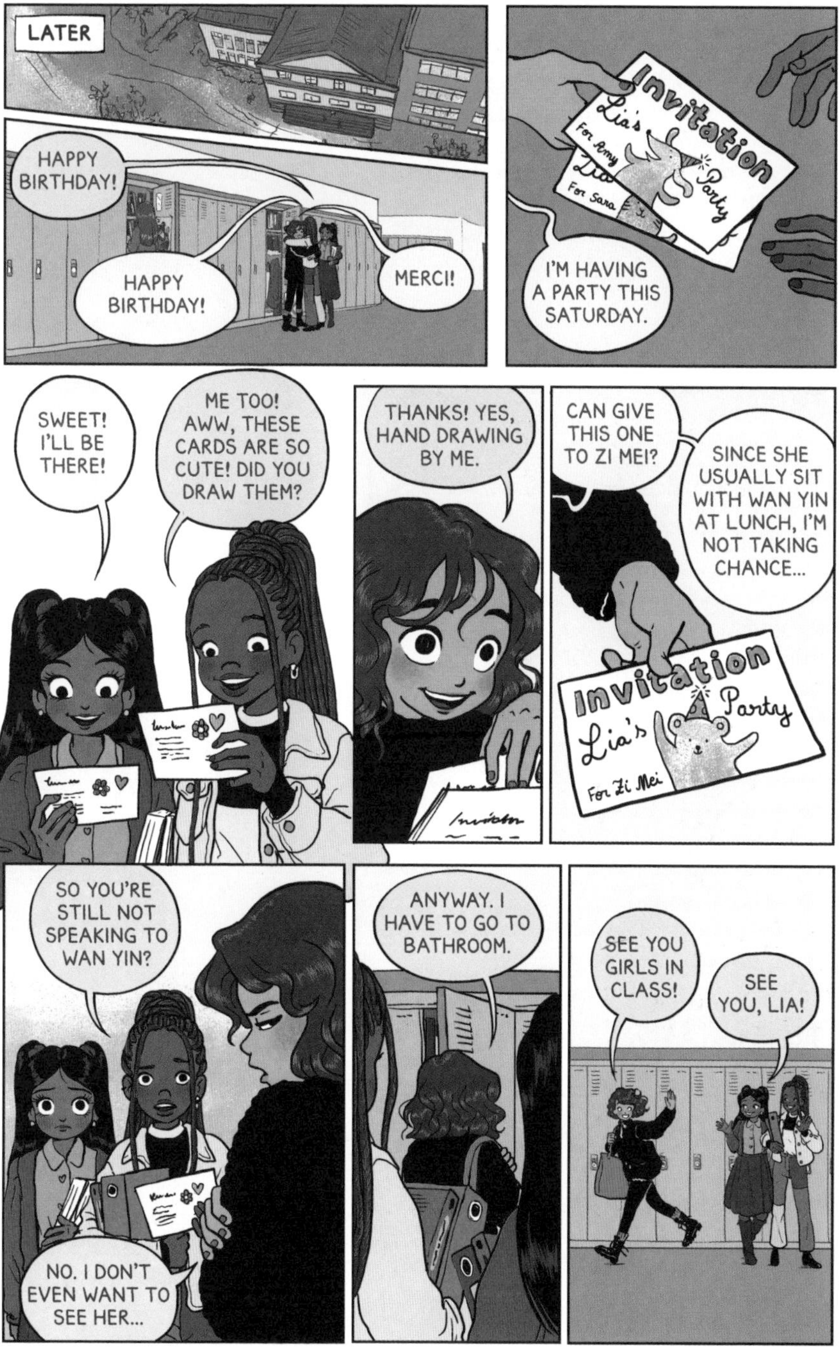
LATER
HAPPY BIRTHDAY!
HAPPY BIRTHDAY!
MERCI!
Invitation
Lia's Party
For Amy
For Sara
I'M HAVING A PARTY THIS SATURDAY.
SWEET! I'LL BE THERE!
ME TOO! AWW, THESE CARDS ARE SO CUTE! DID YOU DRAW THEM?
THANKS! YES, HAND DRAWING BY ME.
CAN GIVE THIS ONE TO ZI MEI?
SINCE SHE USUALLY SIT WITH WAN YIN AT LUNCH, I'M NOT TAKING CHANCE...
Invitation
Lia's Party
For Zi Mei
SO YOU'RE STILL NOT SPEAKING TO WAN YIN?
NO. I DON'T EVEN WANT TO SEE HER...
ANYWAY. I HAVE TO GO TO BATHROOM.
SEE YOU GIRLS IN CLASS!
SEE YOU, LIA!

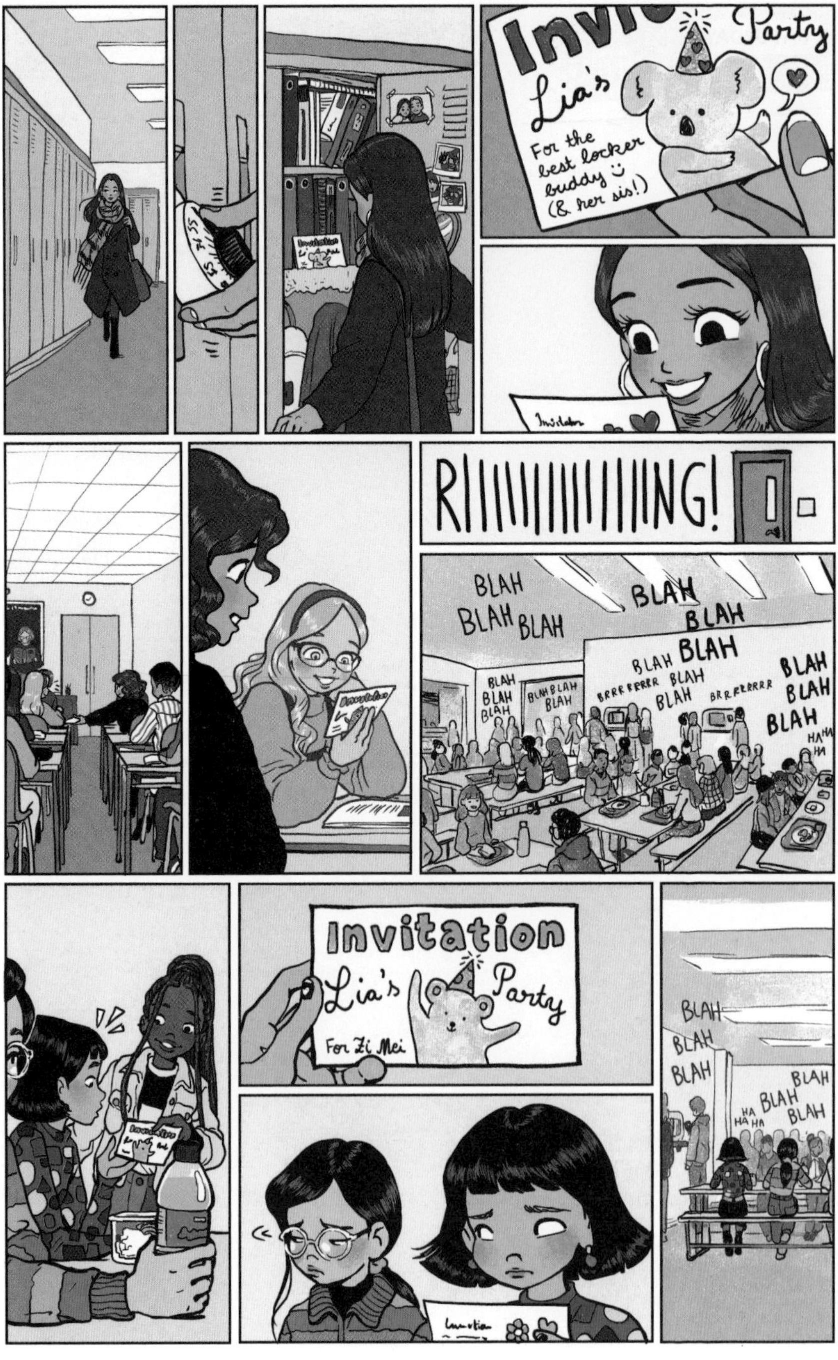
Invit
Party
Lia's
For the best locker buddy :)
(& her sis!)
RIIIIIIIIIIIIING!
BLAH
BLAH BLAH
BLAH
BLAH
BLAH
BLAH BLAH
BRRRRRRRR BLAH
BLAH
BRRRRRRRR
BLAH
BLAH
BLAH
Invitation
Lia's Party
For Zi Mei
BLAH
BLAH
BLAH
BLAH
HA HA HA BLAH
BLAH

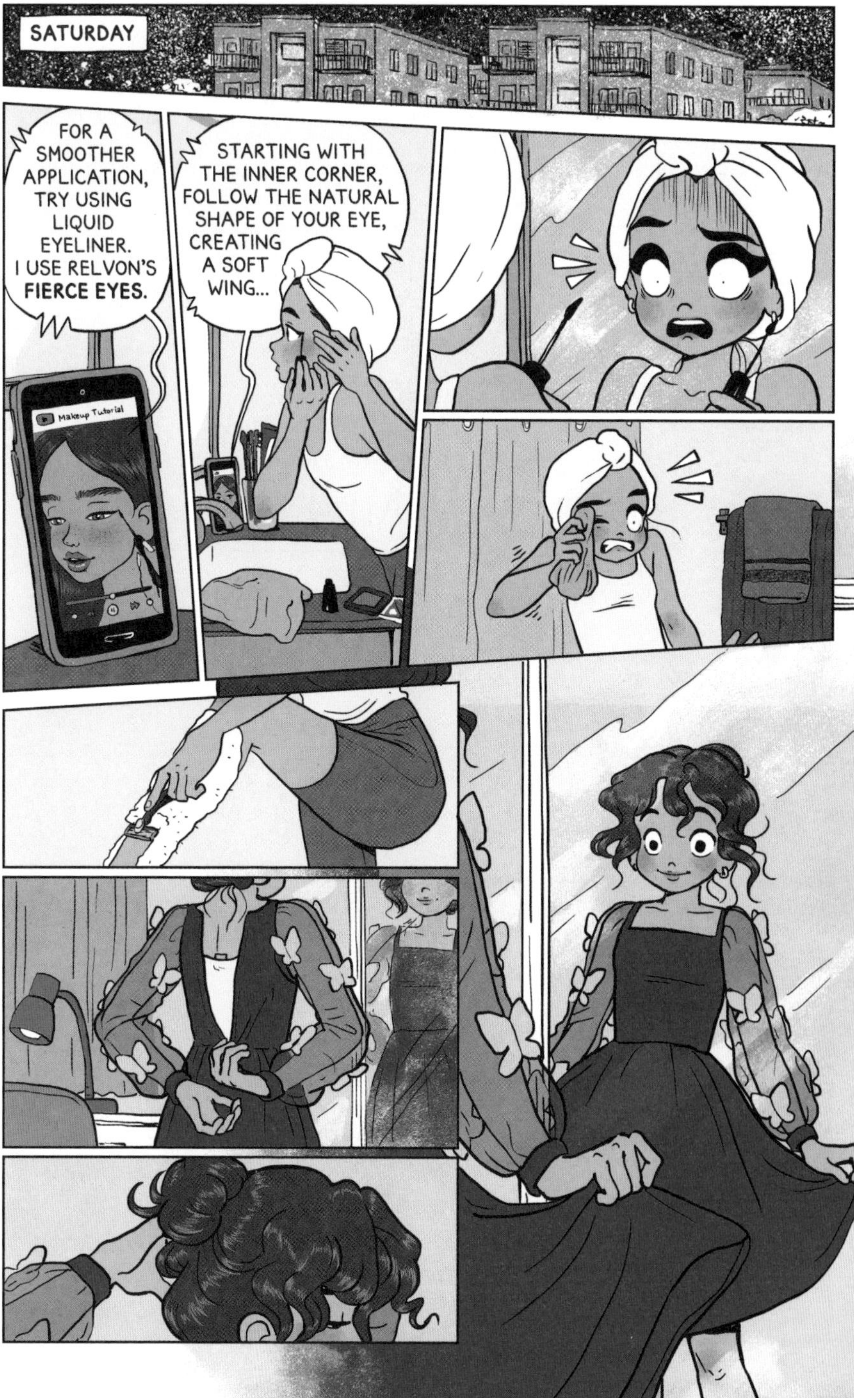
SATURDAY
FOR A SMOOTHER APPLICATION, TRY USING LIQUID EYELINER. I USE RELVON'S **FIERCE EYES.**
Makeup Tutorial
STARTING WITH THE INNER CORNER, FOLLOW THE NATURAL SHAPE OF YOUR EYE, CREATING A SOFT WING...

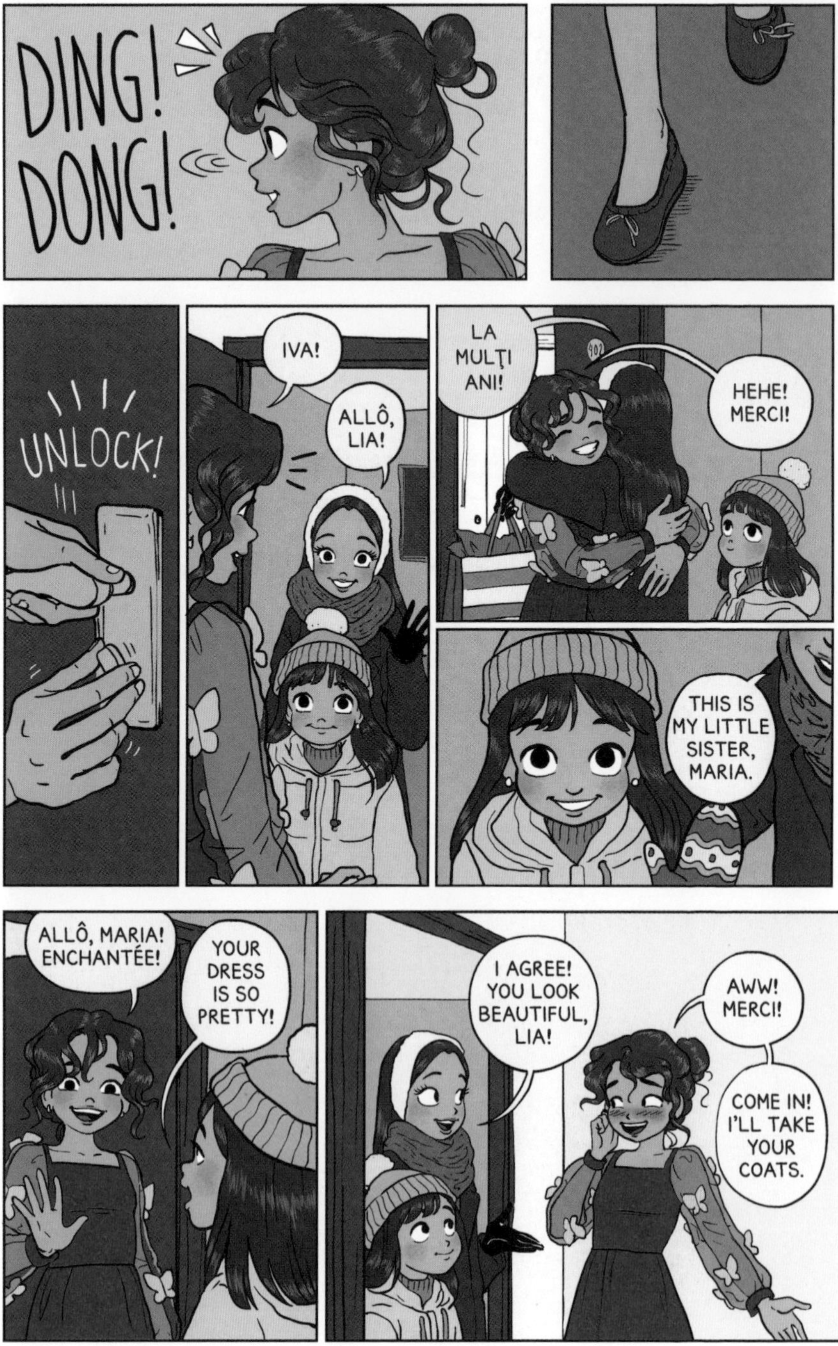
DING! DONG!
UNLOCK!
IVA!
ALLÔ, LIA!
LA MULŢI ANI!
HEHE! MERCI!
THIS IS MY LITTLE SISTER, MARIA.
ALLÔ, MARIA! ENCHANTÉE!
YOUR DRESS IS SO PRETTY!
I AGREE! YOU LOOK BEAUTIFUL, LIA!
AWW! MERCI!
COME IN! I'LL TAKE YOUR COATS.

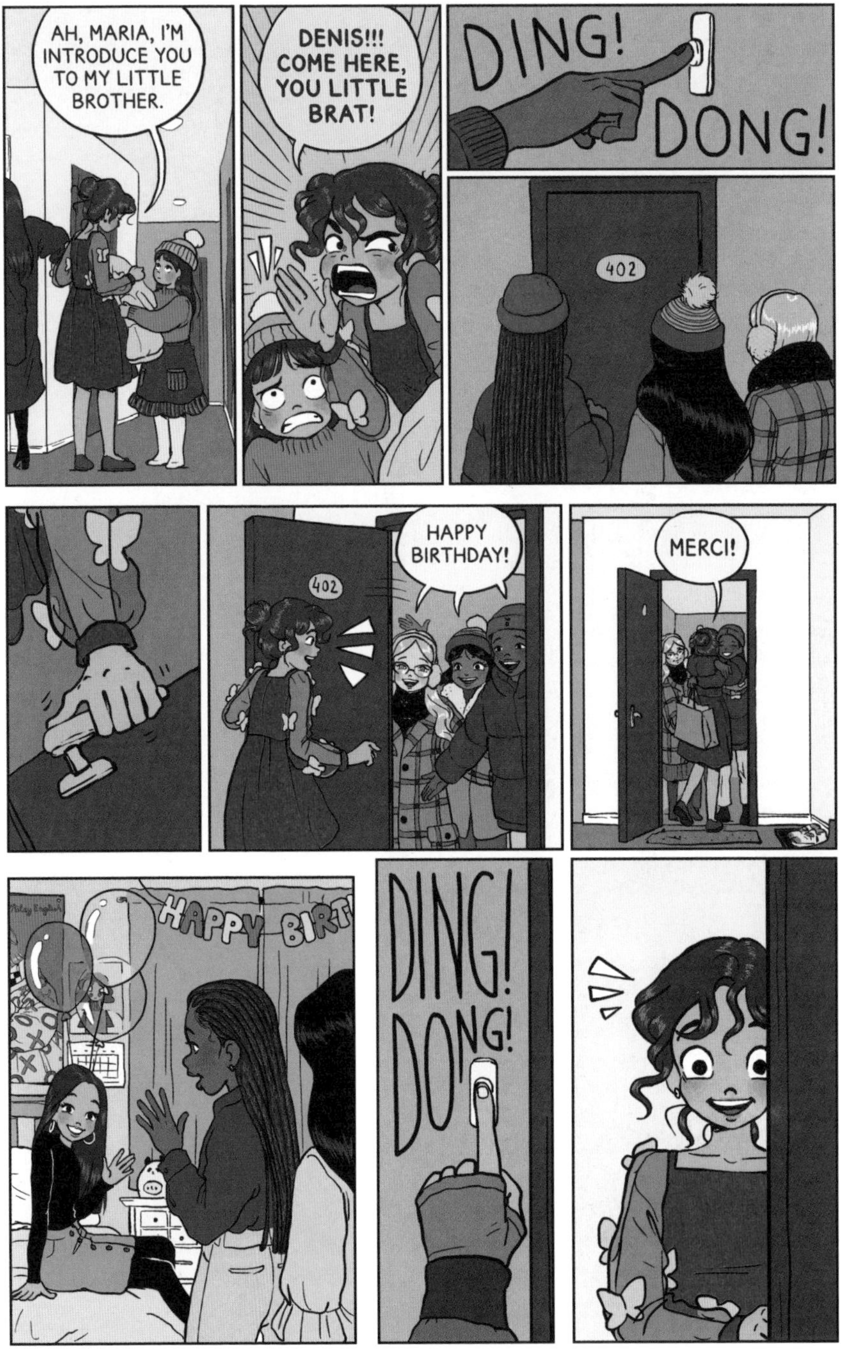
AH, MARIA, I'M INTRODUCE YOU TO MY LITTLE BROTHER.
DENIS!!! COME HERE, YOU LITTLE BRAT!
DING!
DONG!
402
402
HAPPY BIRTHDAY!
MERCI!
HAPPY BIRT
DING!
DONG!

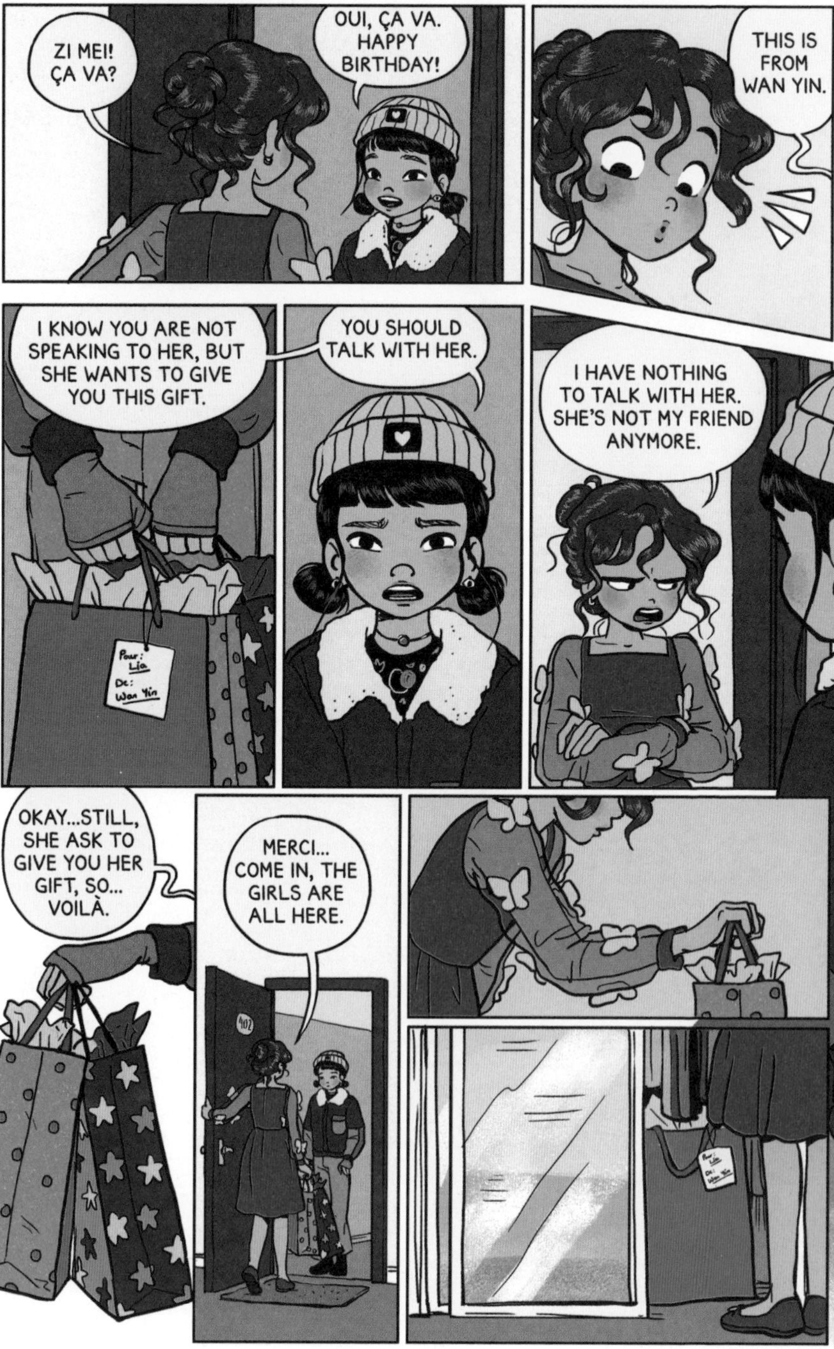
ZI MEI! ÇA VA?
OUI, ÇA VA. HAPPY BIRTHDAY!
THIS IS FROM WAN YIN.
I KNOW YOU ARE NOT SPEAKING TO HER, BUT SHE WANTS TO GIVE YOU THIS GIFT.
YOU SHOULD TALK WITH HER.
Pour: Lia
De: Wan Yin
I HAVE NOTHING TO TALK WITH HER. SHE'S NOT MY FRIEND ANYMORE.
OKAY...STILL, SHE ASK TO GIVE YOU HER GIFT, SO... VOILÀ.
MERCI... COME IN, THE GIRLS ARE ALL HERE.
402

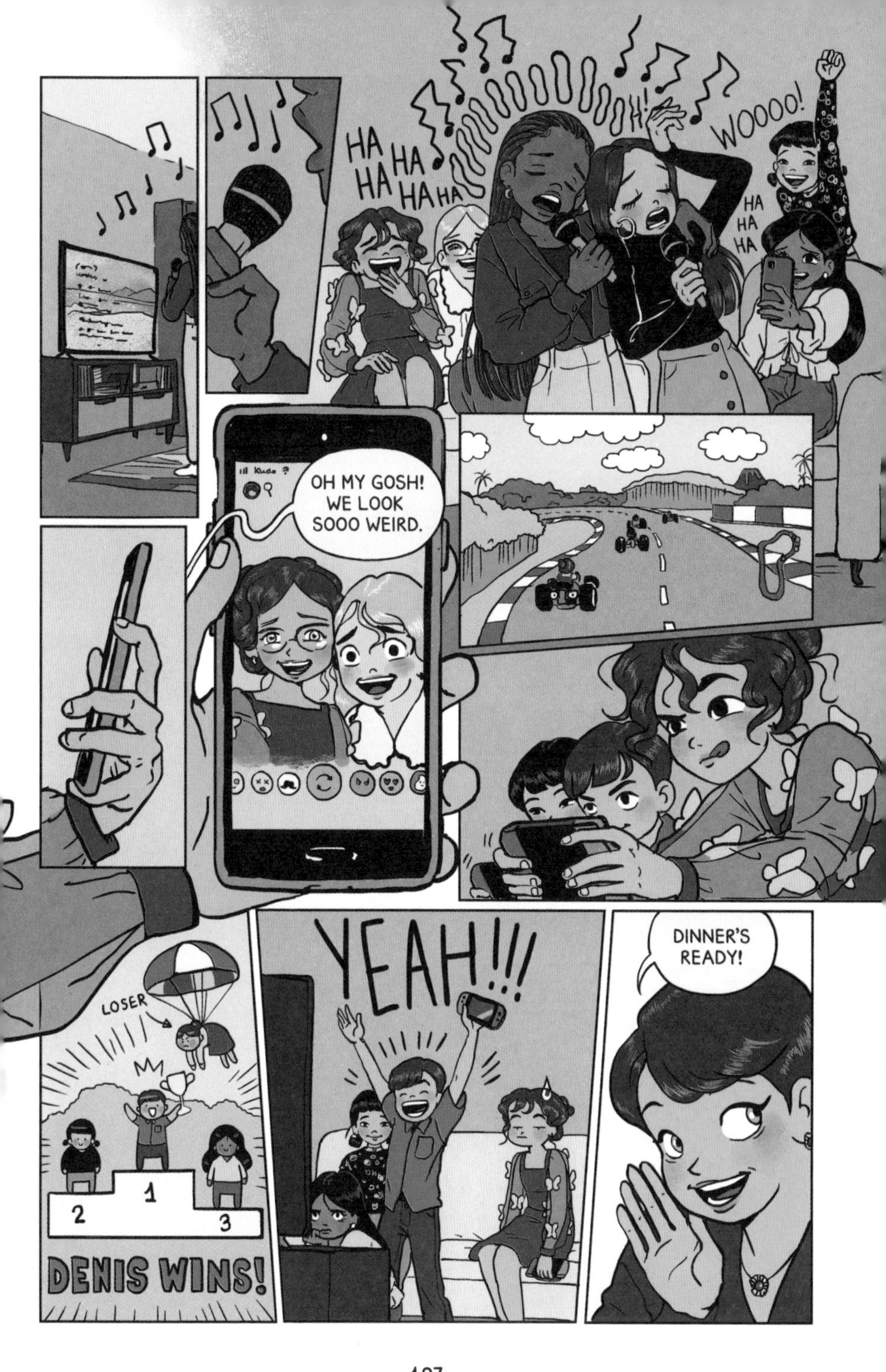
HA HA HA HA HA HA
OOOOOOOOOOOOH!
WOOOO!
HA HA HA
OH MY GOSH! WE LOOK SOOO WEIRD.
LOSER
1
2
3
DENIS WINS!
YEAH!!!
DINNER'S READY!

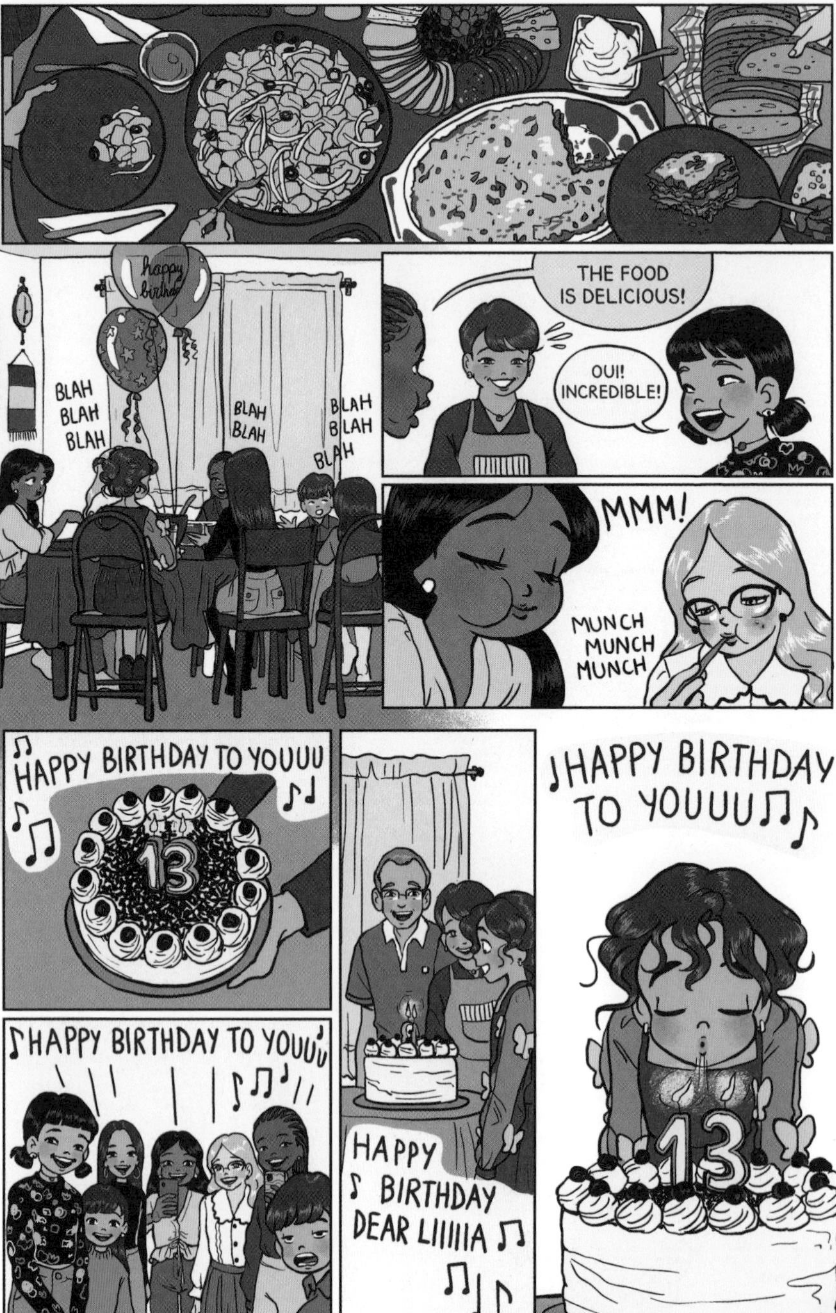
BLAH
BLAH
BLAH
BLAH
BLAH
BLAH
BLAH
BLAH
THE FOOD IS DELICIOUS!
OUI! INCREDIBLE!
MMM!
MUNCH
MUNCH
MUNCH
HAPPY BIRTHDAY TO YOUUU
HAPPY BIRTHDAY TO YOUUU
HAPPY BIRTHDAY DEAR LIIIIIA
HAPPY BIRTHDAY TO YOUUU

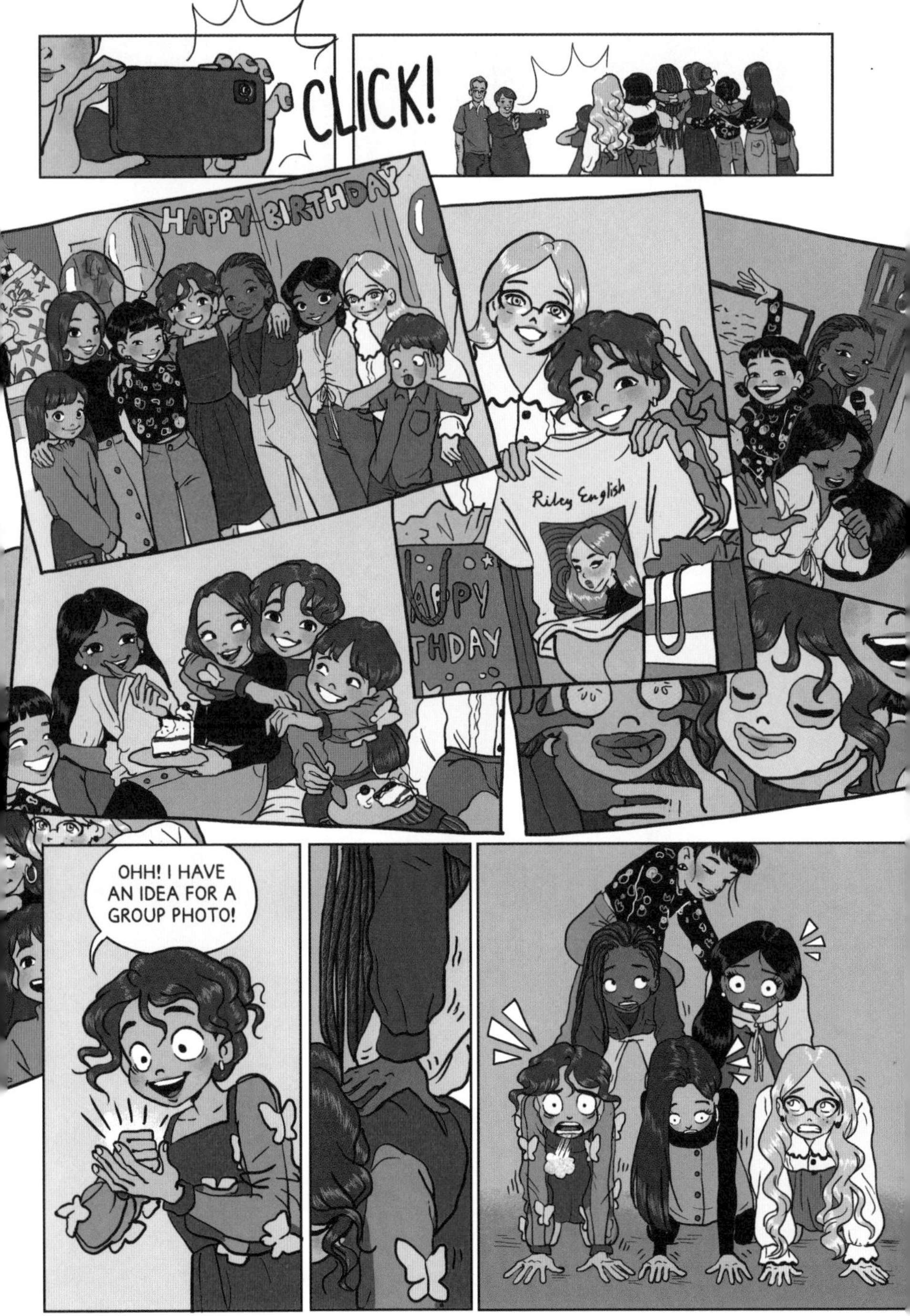
CLICK!
HAPPY BIRTHDAY
Riley English
HAPPY BIRTHDAY
OHH! I HAVE AN IDEA FOR A GROUP PHOTO!

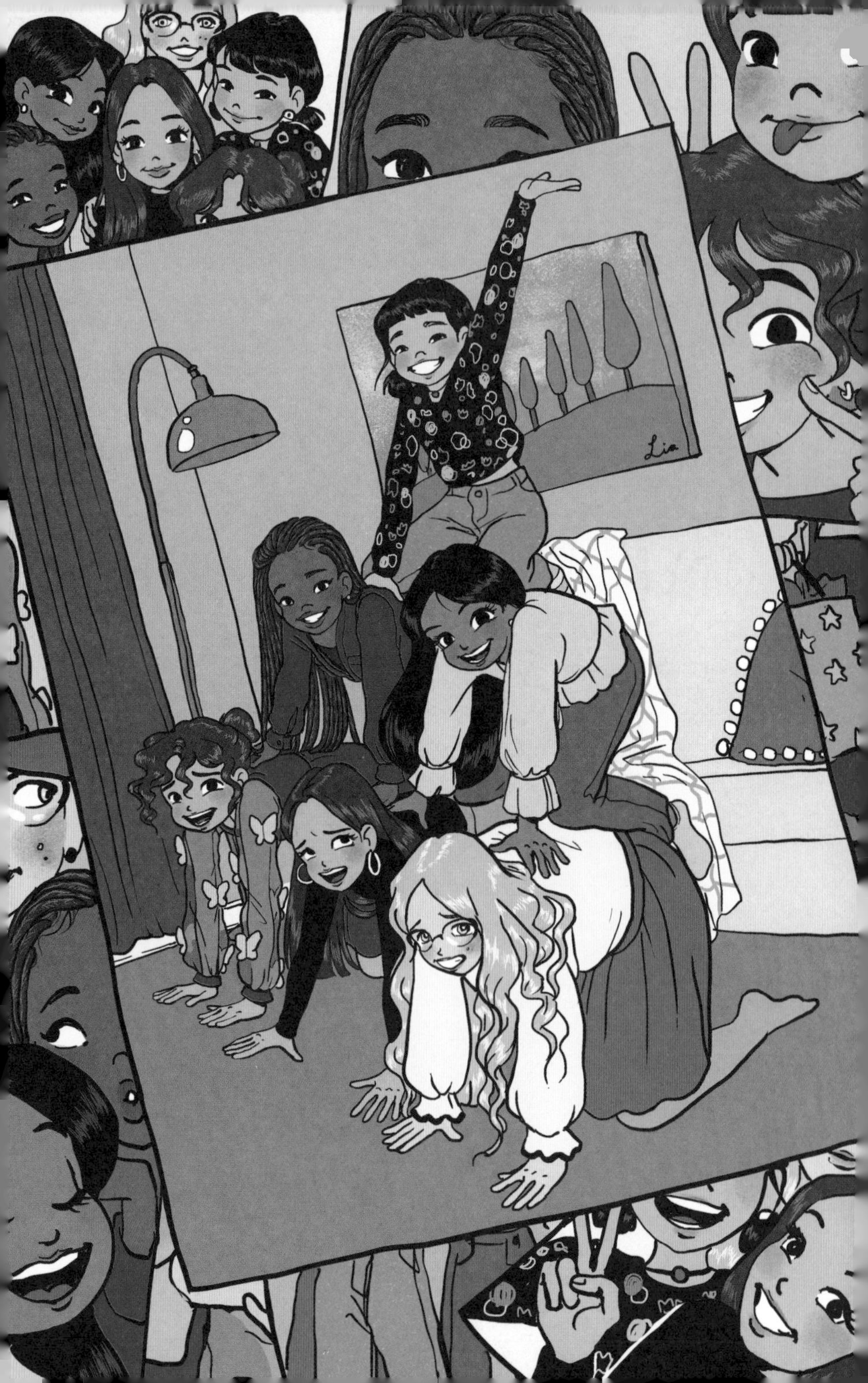
Lia

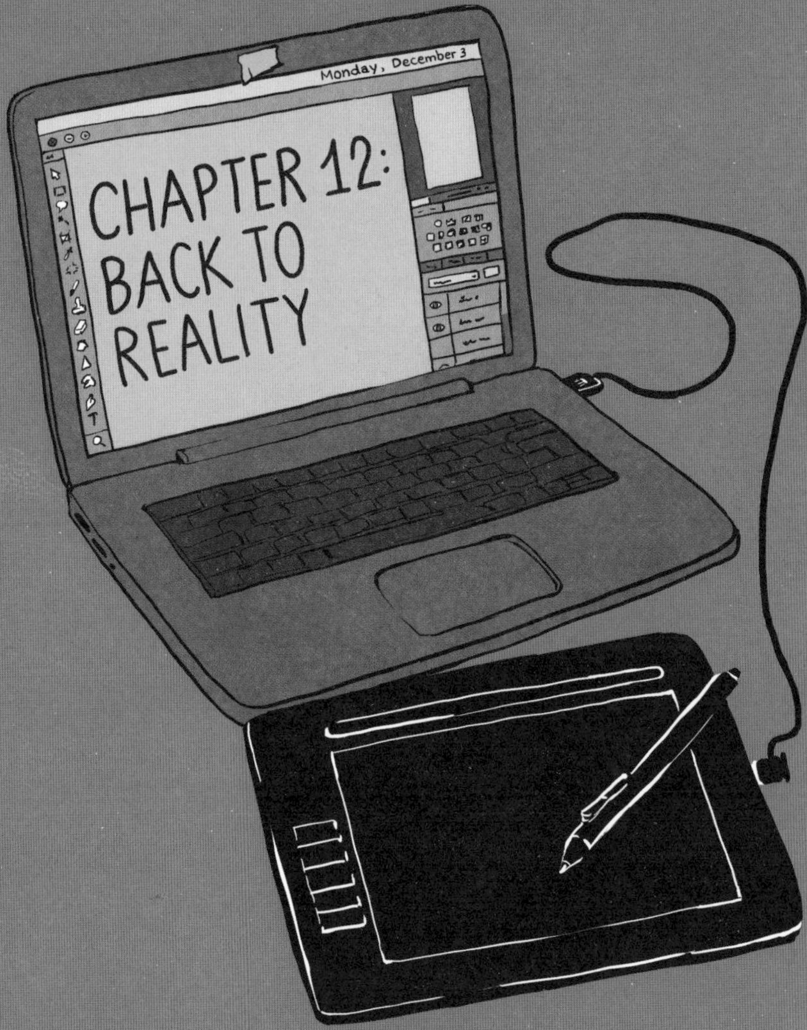
Monday, December 3
CHAPTER 12:
BACK TO
REALITY

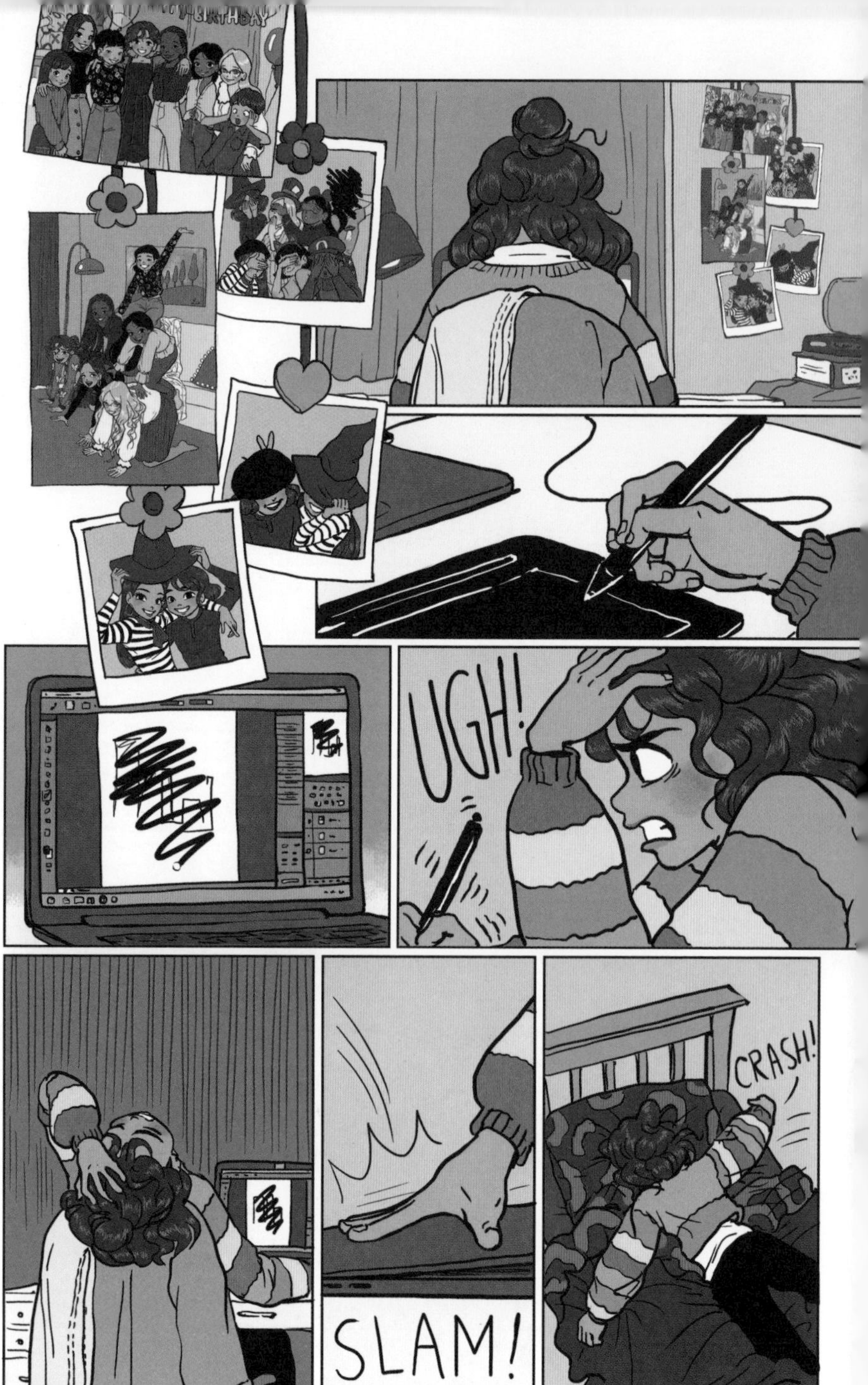
UGH!
SLAM!
CRASH!

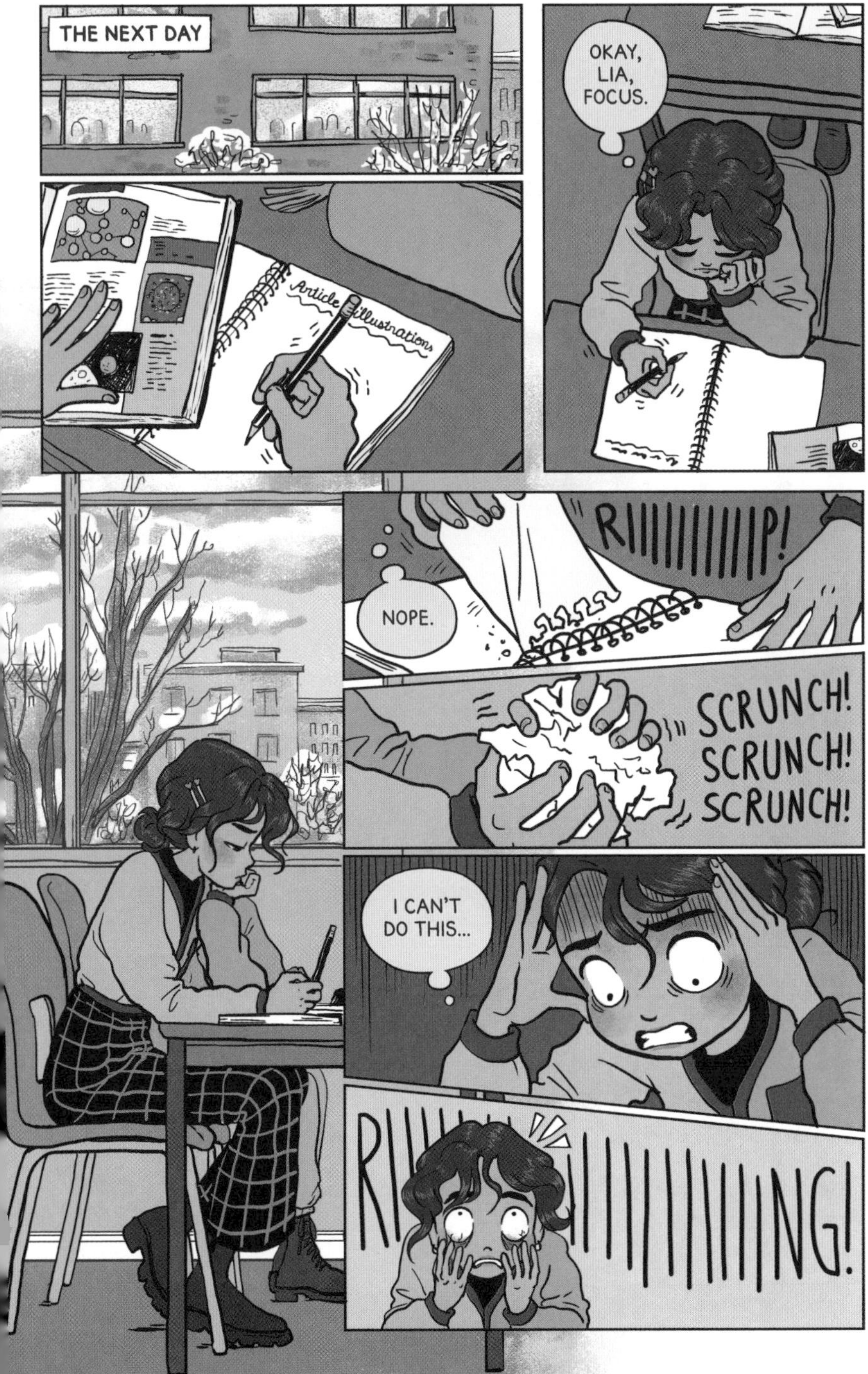
THE NEXT DAY
OKAY, LIA, FOCUS.
Article illustrations
RIIIIIIIIIIP!
NOPE.
SCRUNCH! SCRUNCH! SCRUNCH!
I CAN'T DO THIS...
RIIIIIIIIIIIIIIIIIIIING!

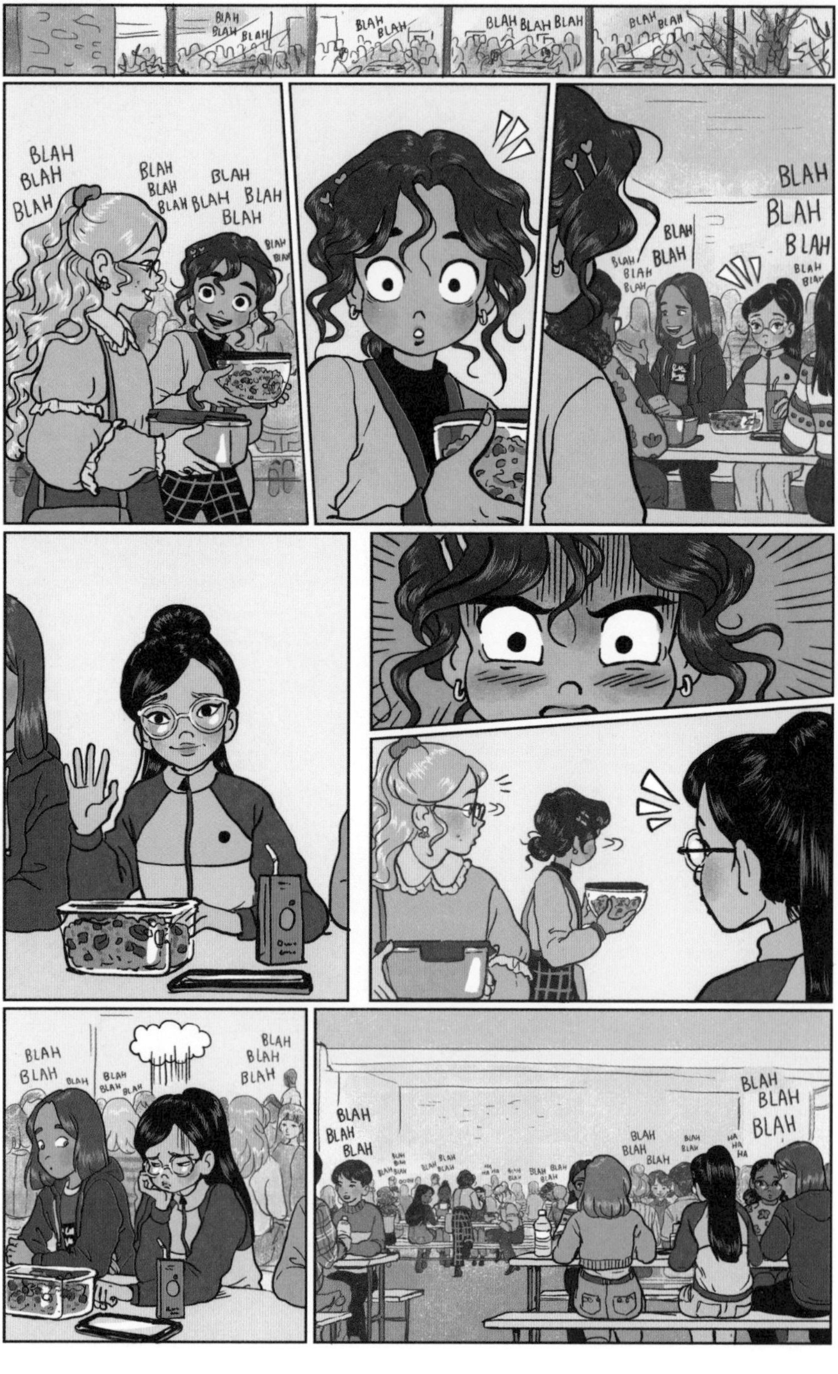
BLAH BLAH BLAH
BLAH BLAH
BLAH BLAH BLAH
BLAH BLAH
BLAH BLAH BLAH
BLAH BLAH BLAH
BLAH BLAH BLAH
BLAH BLAH BLAH
BLAH BLAH
BLAH BLAH
BLAH BLAH BLAH
BLAH BLAH
BLAH BLAH BLAH
BLAH BLAH BLAH
BLAH BLAH BLAH
BLAH BLAH BLAH
HA HA HA

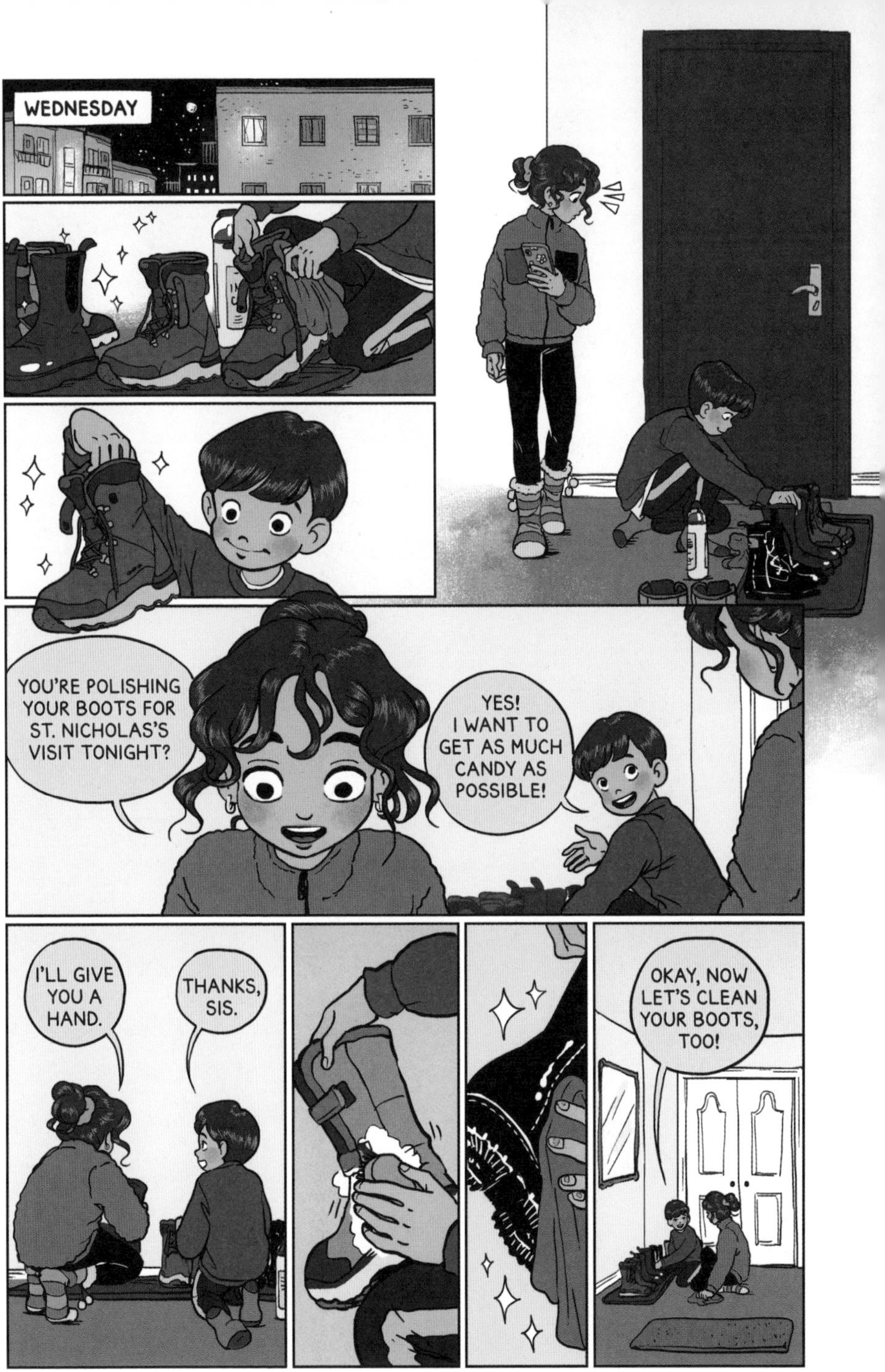
WEDNESDAY
YOU'RE POLISHING YOUR BOOTS FOR ST. NICHOLAS'S VISIT TONIGHT?
YES! I WANT TO GET AS MUCH CANDY AS POSSIBLE!
I'LL GIVE YOU A HAND.
THANKS, SIS.
OKAY, NOW LET'S CLEAN YOUR BOOTS, TOO!

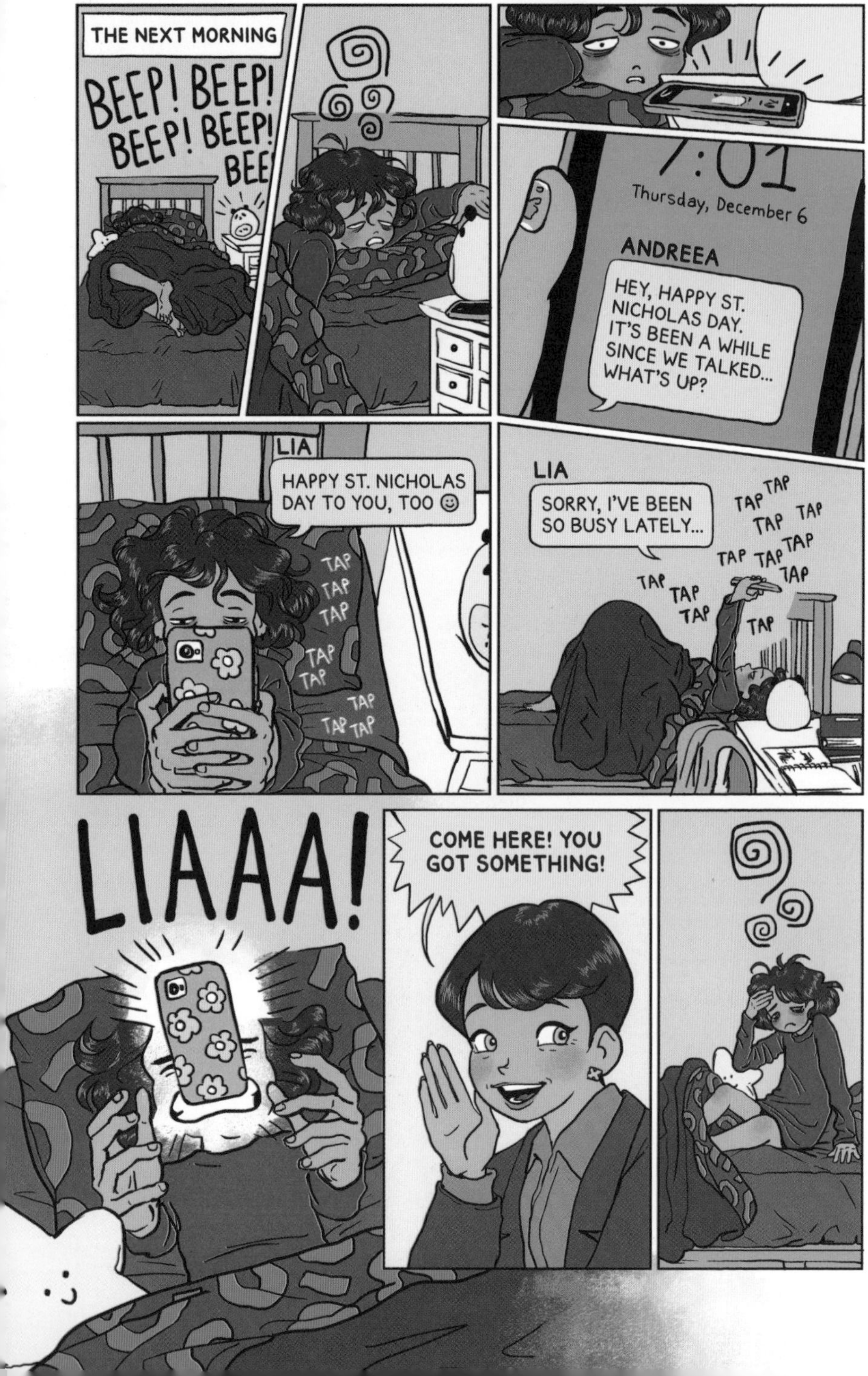
THE NEXT MORNING
BEEP! BEEP! BEEP! BEEP! BEE
7:01
Thursday, December 6
ANDREEA
HEY, HAPPY ST. NICHOLAS DAY. IT'S BEEN A WHILE SINCE WE TALKED... WHAT'S UP?
LIA
HAPPY ST. NICHOLAS DAY TO YOU, TOO ☺
TAP TAP TAP TAP TAP TAP TAP TAP
LIA
SORRY, I'VE BEEN SO BUSY LATELY...
TAP TAP TAP TAP TAP TAP TAP TAP TAP TAP TAP TAP
LIAAA!
COME HERE! YOU GOT SOMETHING!

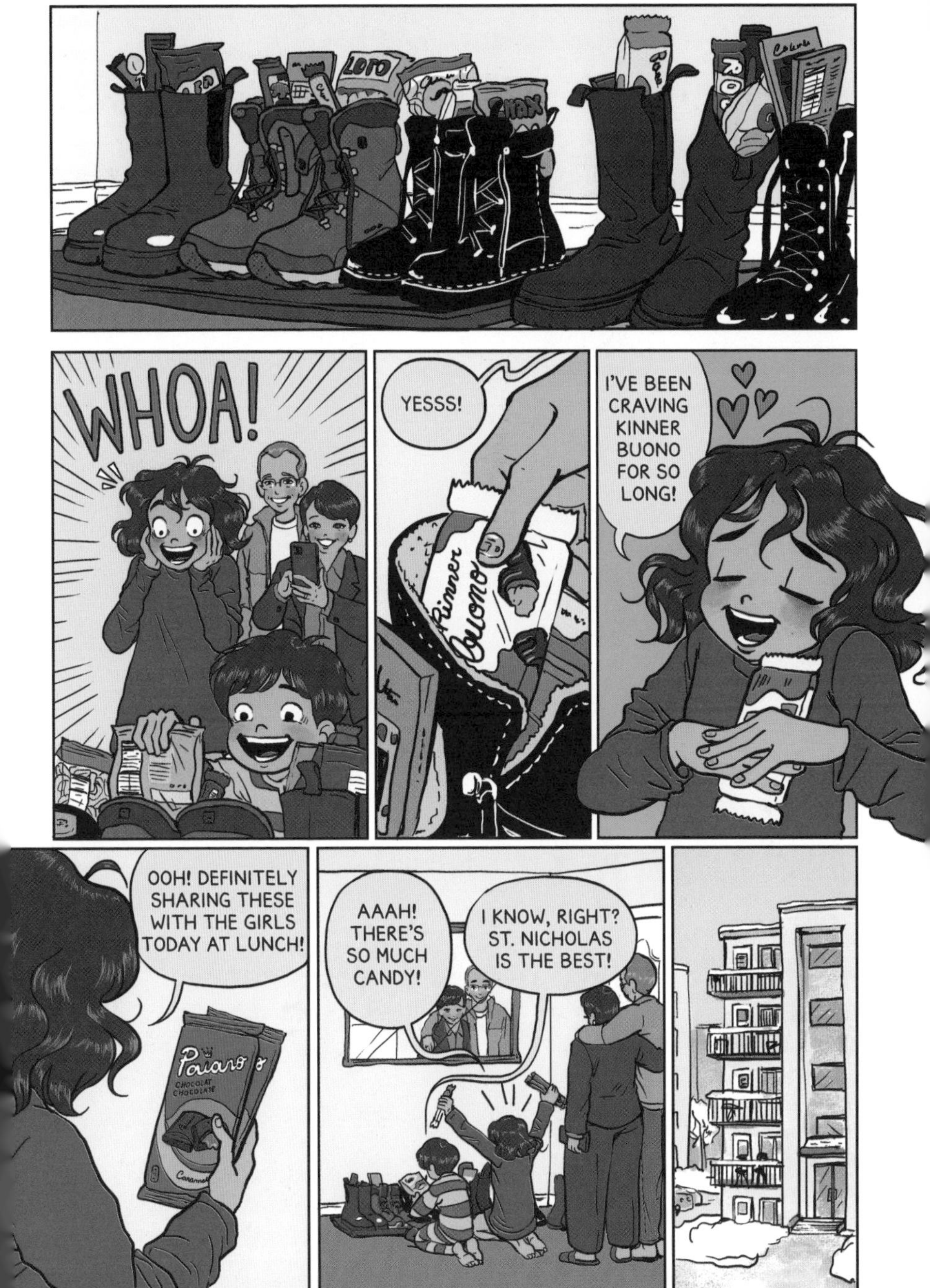
WHOA!
YESSS!
I'VE BEEN CRAVING KINNER BUONO FOR SO LONG!
OOH! DEFINITELY SHARING THESE WITH THE GIRLS TODAY AT LUNCH!
AAAH! THERE'S SO MUCH CANDY!
I KNOW, RIGHT? ST. NICHOLAS IS THE BEST!

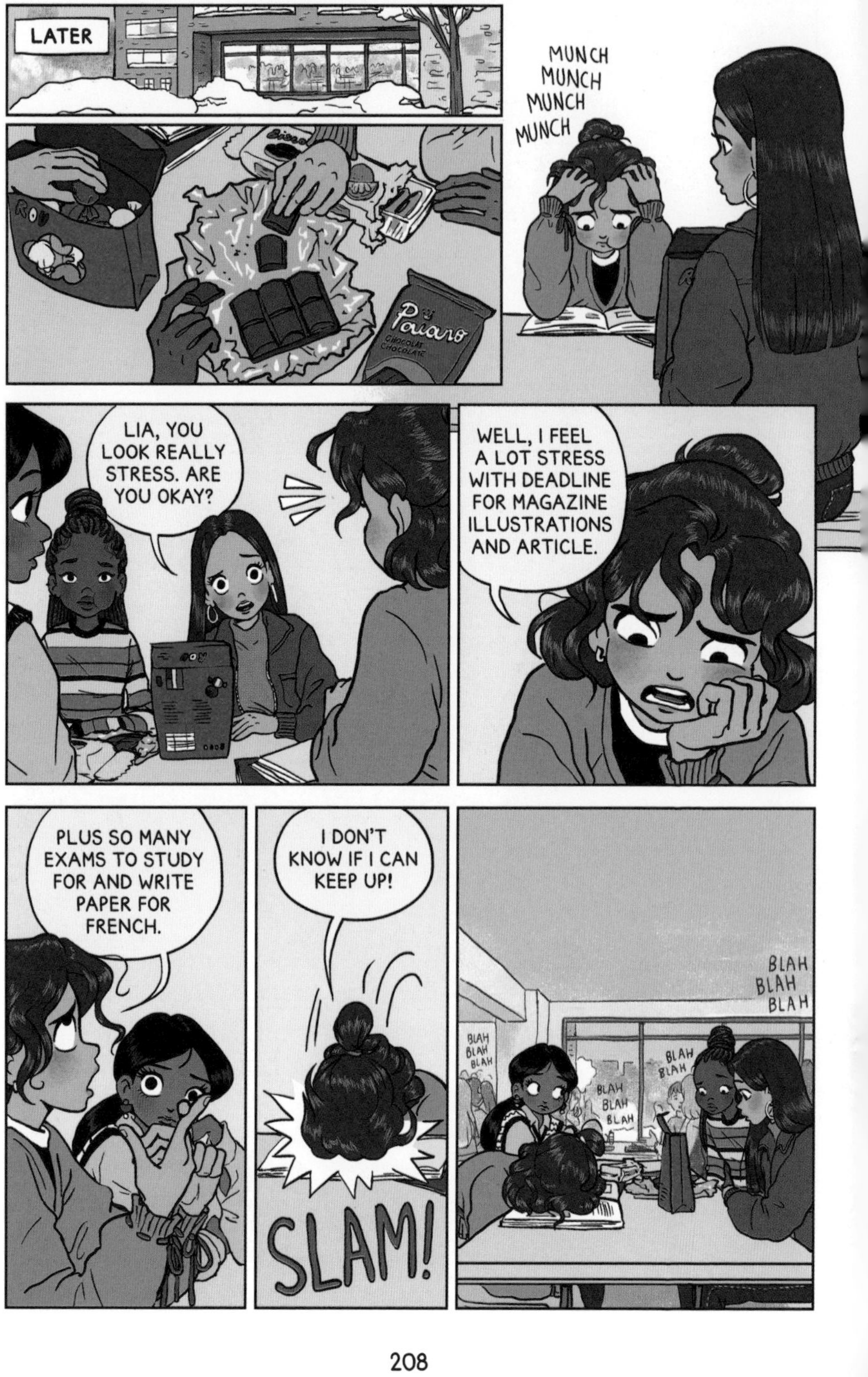
LATER
MUNCH
MUNCH
MUNCH
MUNCH
LIA, YOU LOOK REALLY STRESS. ARE YOU OKAY?
WELL, I FEEL A LOT STRESS WITH DEADLINE FOR MAGAZINE ILLUSTRATIONS AND ARTICLE.
PLUS SO MANY EXAMS TO STUDY FOR AND WRITE PAPER FOR FRENCH.
I DON'T KNOW IF I CAN KEEP UP!
SLAM!
BLAH BLAH BLAH
BLAH BLAH BLAH
BLAH BLAH
BLAH BLAH BLAH

LET'S DO A GROUP STUDY SESSION AT THE LIBRARY.

WE CAN HELP EACH OTHER OUT, QUIZ ONE ANOTHER...PLUS IT'LL BE NICE TO BE IN GOOD COMPANY.

GOOD IDEA!

NO, IS OKAY! THINK I CAN DO THIS.

BLAH BLAH BLAH

COME ON, LIA. WHAT DO YOU HAVE TO LOSE?

BLAH BLAH

I AGREE. I THINK STUDY TOGETHER WILL REALLY HELP.

BLAH BLAH BLAH BLAH BLAH BLAH BLAH BLAH

HMMM...

ALL RIGHT, BUT IT'LL BE JUST US, OUI? NO WAN YIN.

OUI.

BLAH BLAH BLAH

HA HA

BLAH BLAH BLAH

HA HA

BLAH BLAH BLAH

OKAY.

RIIIIIIIIIING!

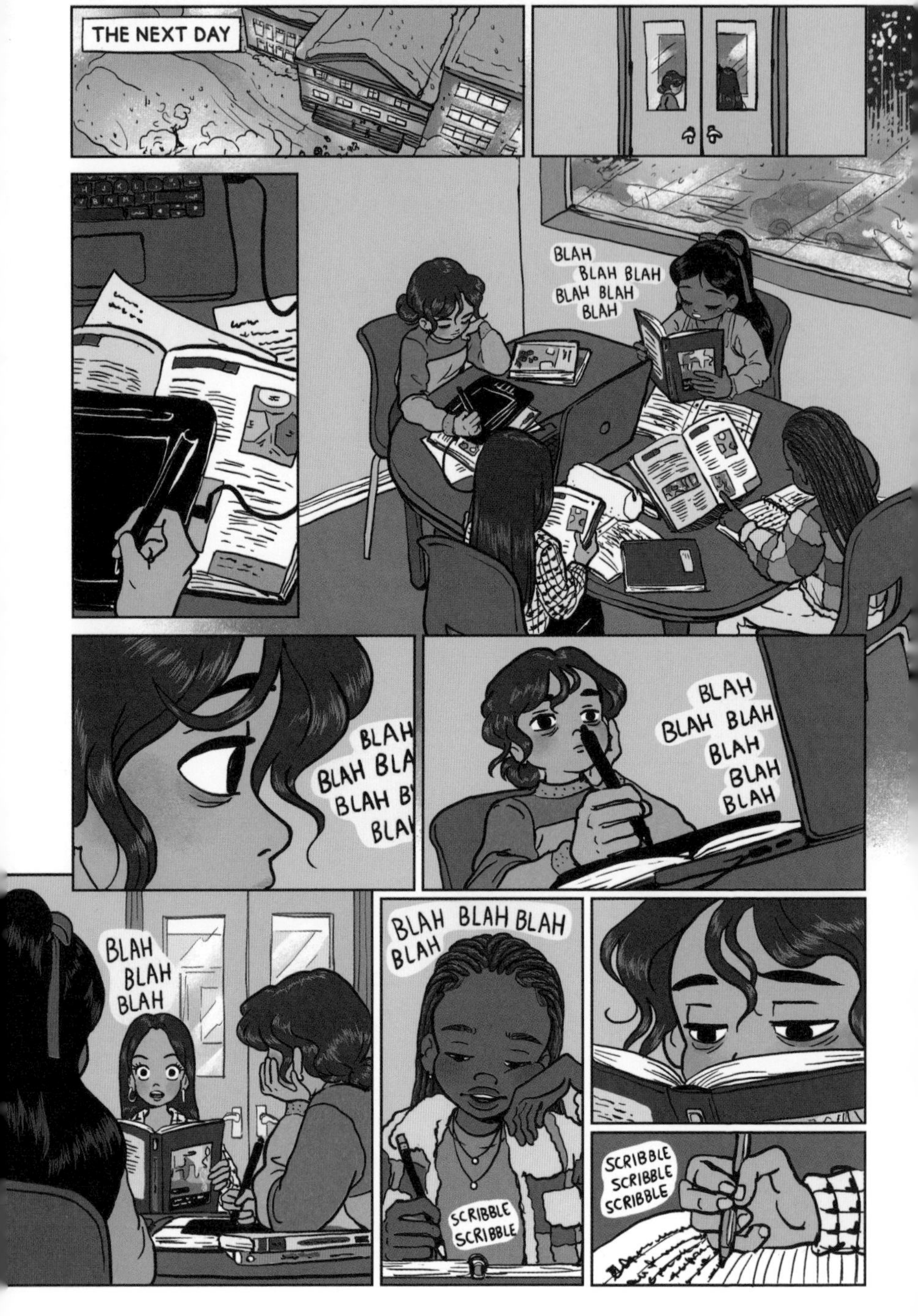
THE NEXT DAY
BLAH BLAH BLAH BLAH BLAH BLAH
BLAH BLAH BLA BLAH B BLA
BLAH BLAH BLAH BLAH BLAH BLAH
BLAH BLAH BLAH
BLAH BLAH BLAH BLAH
SCRIBBLE SCRIBBLE
SCRIBBLE SCRIBBLE SCRIBBLE

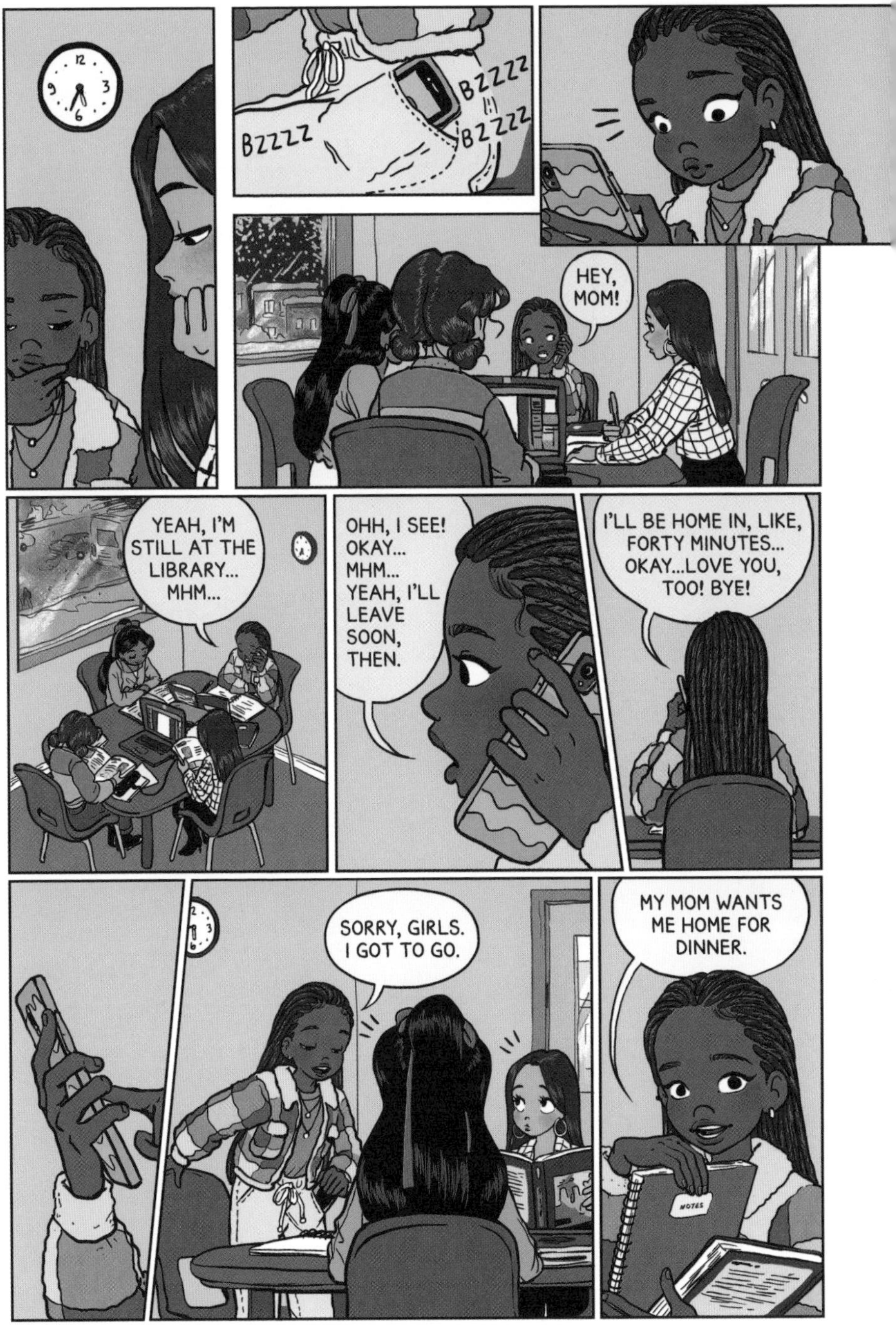

BZZZZ
BZZZZ
BZZZZ
HEY, MOM!
YEAH, I'M STILL AT THE LIBRARY... MHM...
OHH, I SEE! OKAY... MHM... YEAH, I'LL LEAVE SOON, THEN.
I'LL BE HOME IN, LIKE, FORTY MINUTES... OKAY...LOVE YOU, TOO! BYE!
SORRY, GIRLS. I GOT TO GO.
MY MOM WANTS ME HOME FOR DINNER.
NOTES

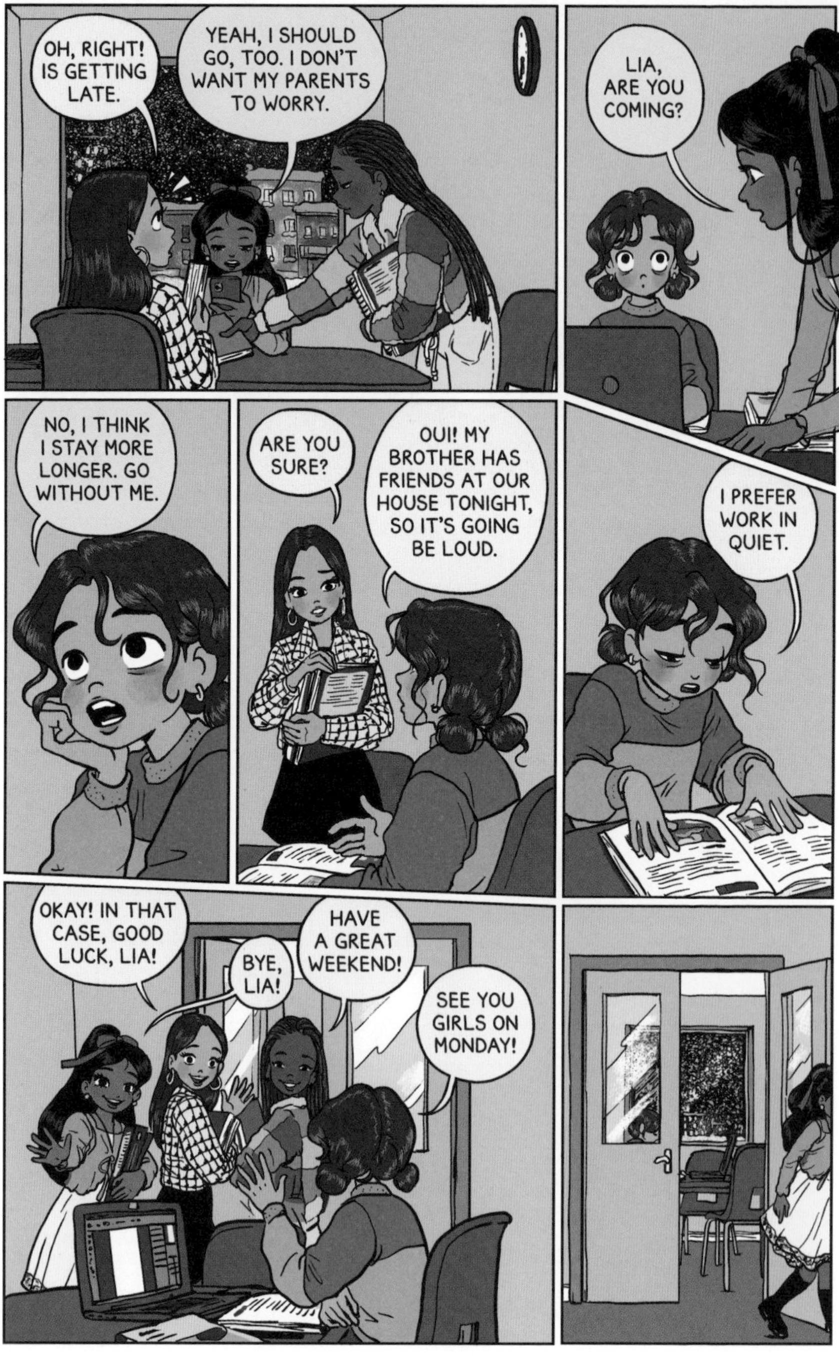

OH, RIGHT! IS GETTING LATE.
YEAH, I SHOULD GO, TOO. I DON'T WANT MY PARENTS TO WORRY.
LIA, ARE YOU COMING?
NO, I THINK I STAY MORE LONGER. GO WITHOUT ME.
ARE YOU SURE?
OUI! MY BROTHER HAS FRIENDS AT OUR HOUSE TONIGHT, SO IT'S GOING BE LOUD.
I PREFER WORK IN QUIET.
OKAY! IN THAT CASE, GOOD LUCK, LIA!
BYE, LIA!
HAVE A GREAT WEEKEND!
SEE YOU GIRLS ON MONDAY!

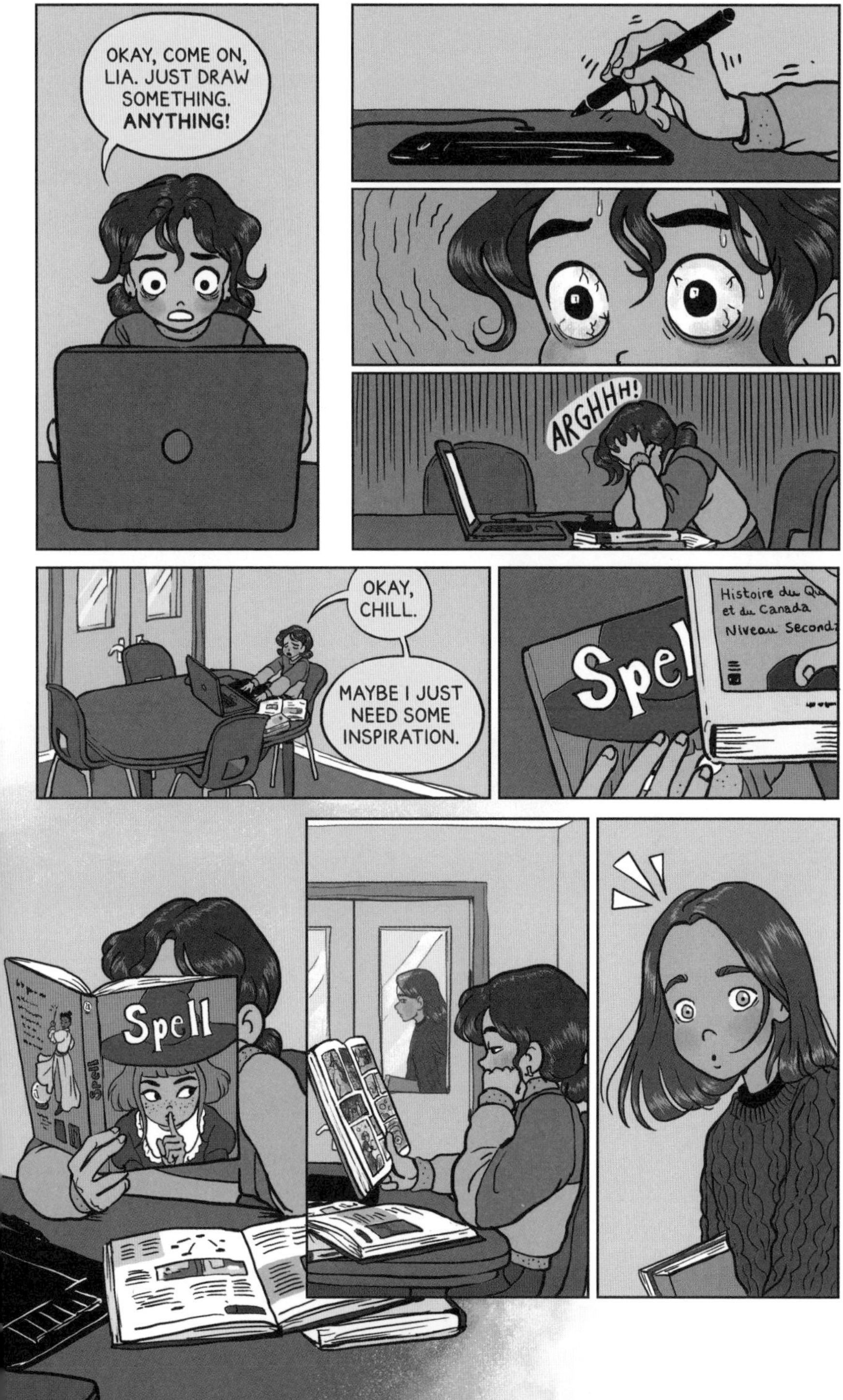
OKAY, COME ON, LIA. JUST DRAW SOMETHING. **ANYTHING!**
ARGHHH!
OKAY, CHILL.
MAYBE I JUST NEED SOME INSPIRATION.
Histoire du
et du Canada
Niveau
Spell
Spell

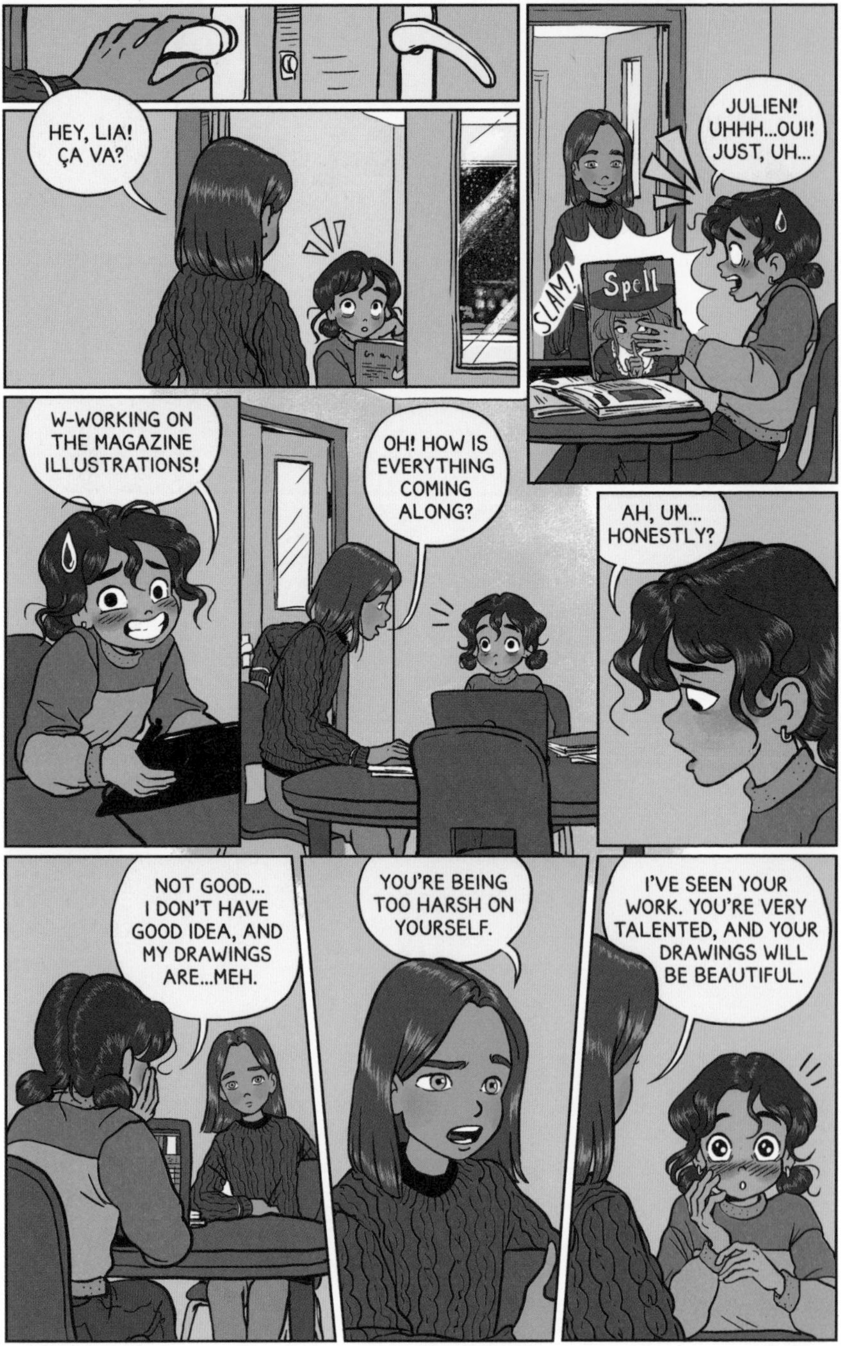
HEY, LIA! ÇA VA?
JULIEN! UHHH...OUI! JUST, UH...
SLAM!
Spell
W-WORKING ON THE MAGAZINE ILLUSTRATIONS!
OH! HOW IS EVERYTHING COMING ALONG?
AH, UM... HONESTLY?
NOT GOOD... I DON'T HAVE GOOD IDEA, AND MY DRAWINGS ARE...MEH.
YOU'RE BEING TOO HARSH ON YOURSELF.
I'VE SEEN YOUR WORK. YOU'RE VERY TALENTED, AND YOUR DRAWINGS WILL BE BEAUTIFUL.

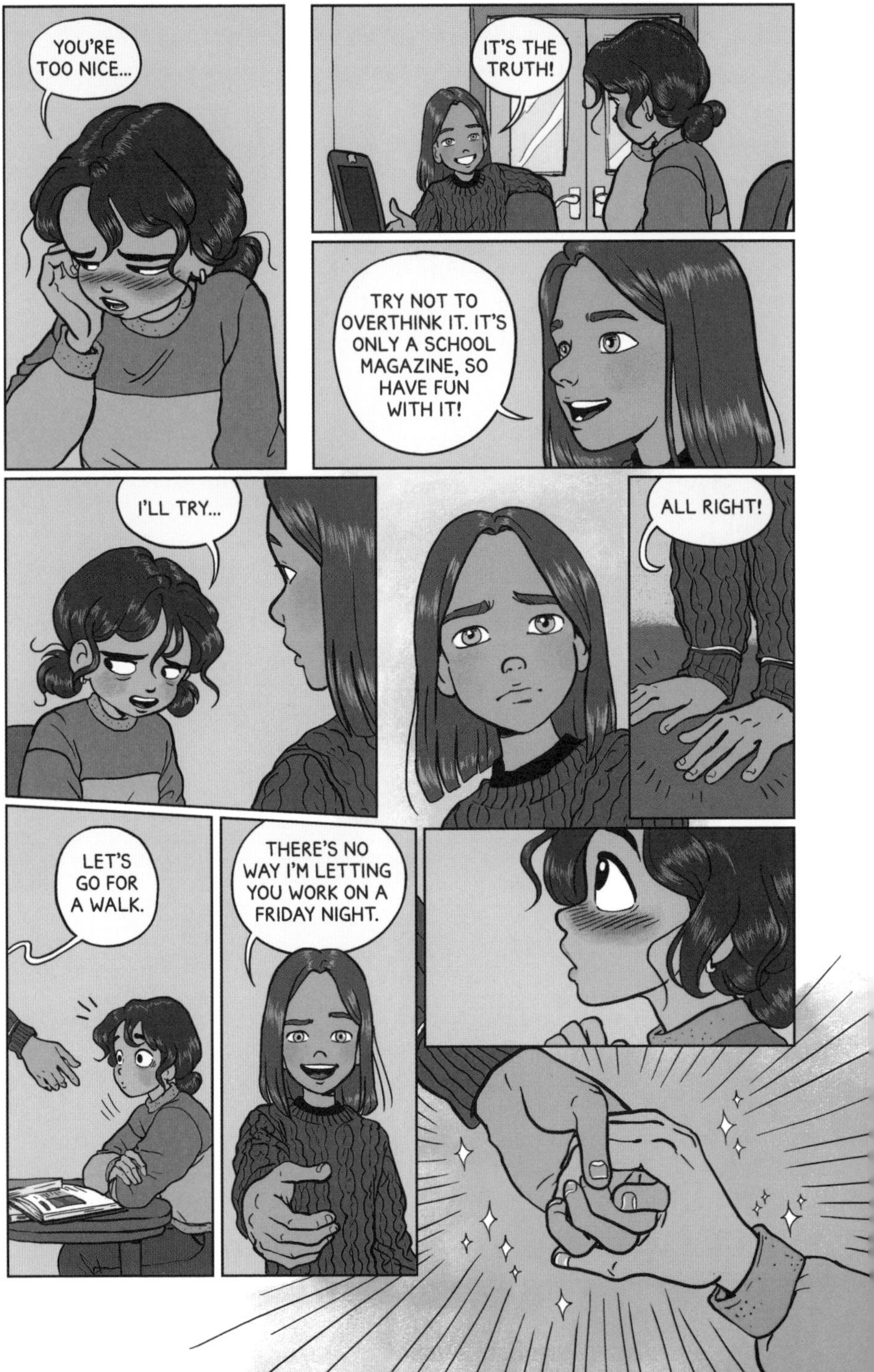
YOU'RE TOO NICE...
IT'S THE TRUTH!
TRY NOT TO OVERTHINK IT. IT'S ONLY A SCHOOL MAGAZINE, SO HAVE FUN WITH IT!
I'LL TRY...
ALL RIGHT!
LET'S GO FOR A WALK.
THERE'S NO WAY I'M LETTING YOU WORK ON A FRIDAY NIGHT.

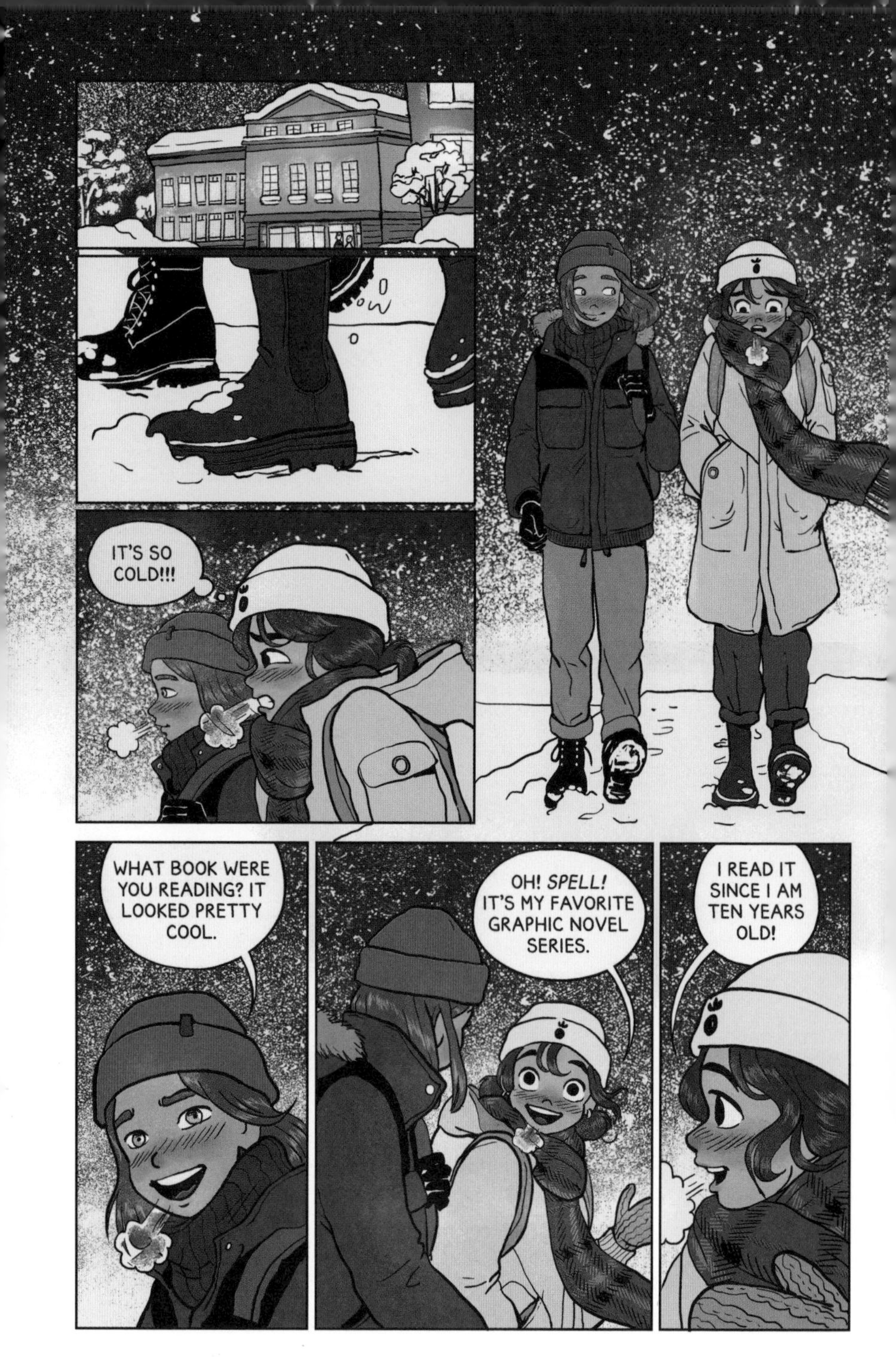
IT'S SO COLD!!!
WHAT BOOK WERE YOU READING? IT LOOKED PRETTY COOL.
OH! *SPELL!* IT'S MY FAVORITE GRAPHIC NOVEL SERIES.
I READ IT SINCE I AM TEN YEARS OLD!

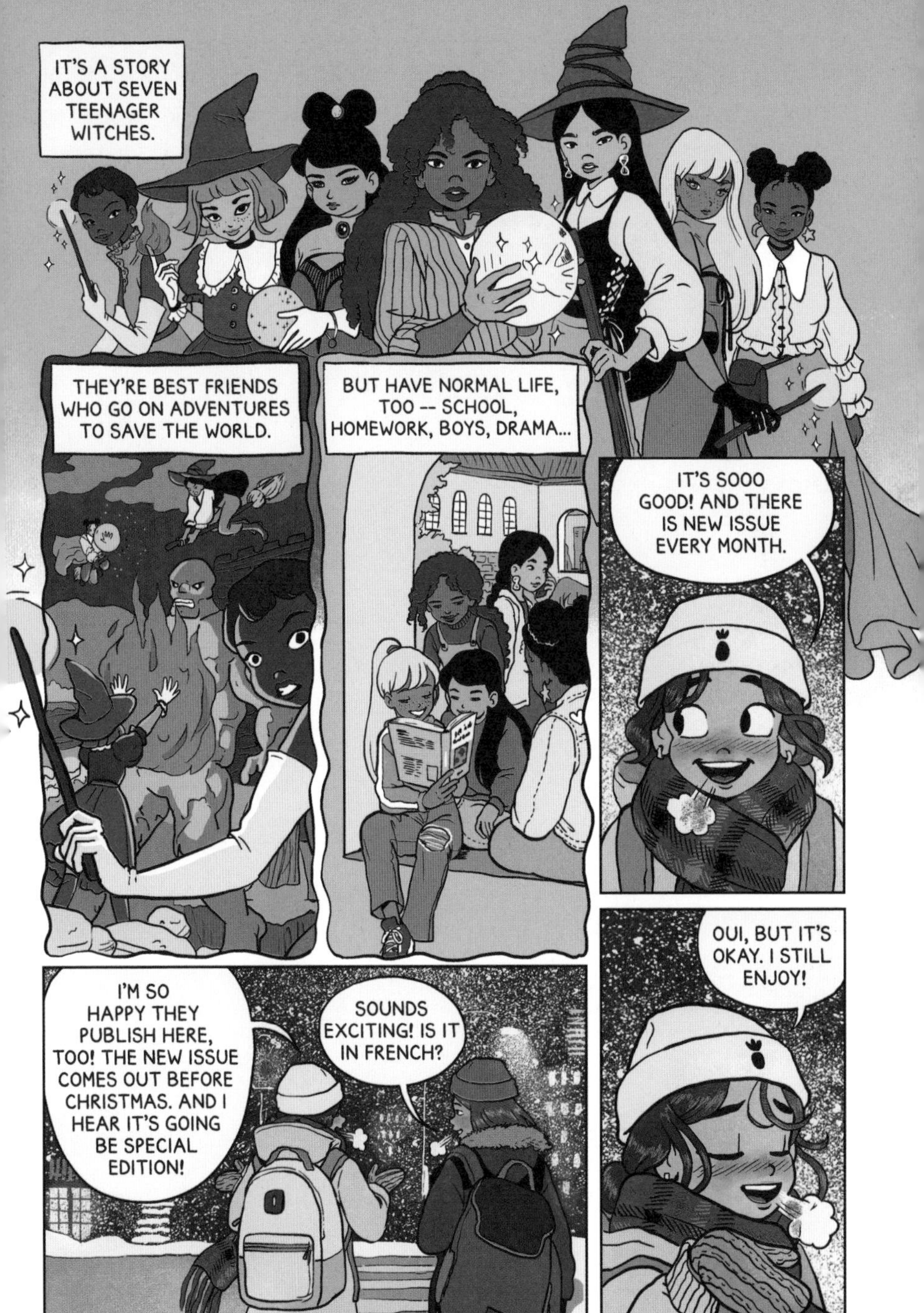
IT'S A STORY ABOUT SEVEN TEENAGER WITCHES.
THEY'RE BEST FRIENDS WHO GO ON ADVENTURES TO SAVE THE WORLD.
BUT HAVE NORMAL LIFE, TOO -- SCHOOL, HOMEWORK, BOYS, DRAMA...
IT'S SOOO GOOD! AND THERE IS NEW ISSUE EVERY MONTH.
OUI, BUT IT'S OKAY. I STILL ENJOY!
I'M SO HAPPY THEY PUBLISH HERE, TOO! THE NEW ISSUE COMES OUT BEFORE CHRISTMAS. AND I HEAR IT'S GOING BE SPECIAL EDITION!
SOUNDS EXCITING! IS IT IN FRENCH?

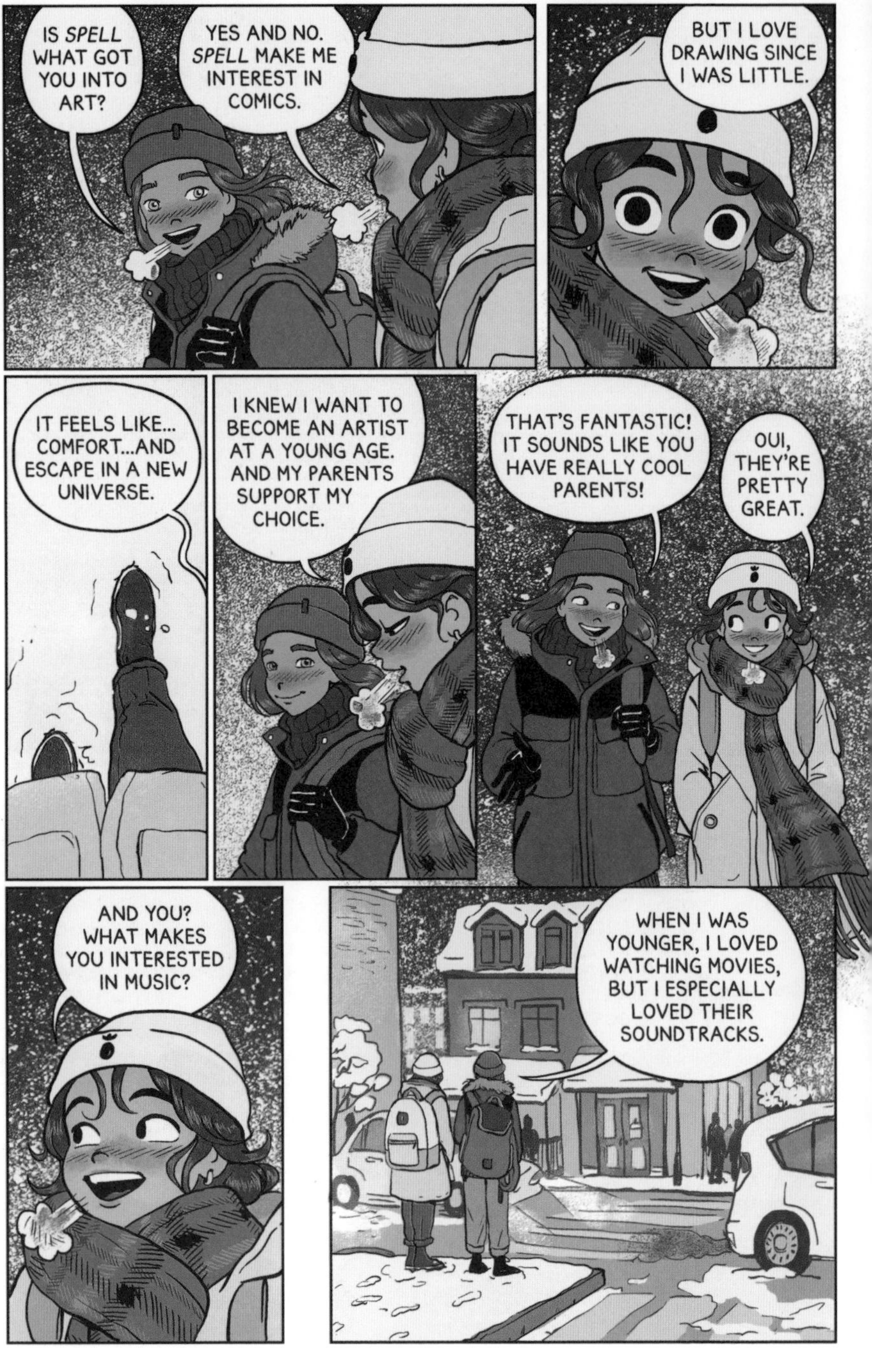
IS *SPELL* WHAT GOT YOU INTO ART?
YES AND NO. *SPELL* MAKE ME INTEREST IN COMICS.
BUT I LOVE DRAWING SINCE I WAS LITTLE.
IT FEELS LIKE... COMFORT...AND ESCAPE IN A NEW UNIVERSE.
I KNEW I WANT TO BECOME AN ARTIST AT A YOUNG AGE. AND MY PARENTS SUPPORT MY CHOICE.
THAT'S FANTASTIC! IT SOUNDS LIKE YOU HAVE REALLY COOL PARENTS!
OUI, THEY'RE PRETTY GREAT.
AND YOU? WHAT MAKES YOU INTERESTED IN MUSIC?
WHEN I WAS YOUNGER, I LOVED WATCHING MOVIES, BUT I ESPECIALLY LOVED THEIR SOUNDTRACKS.

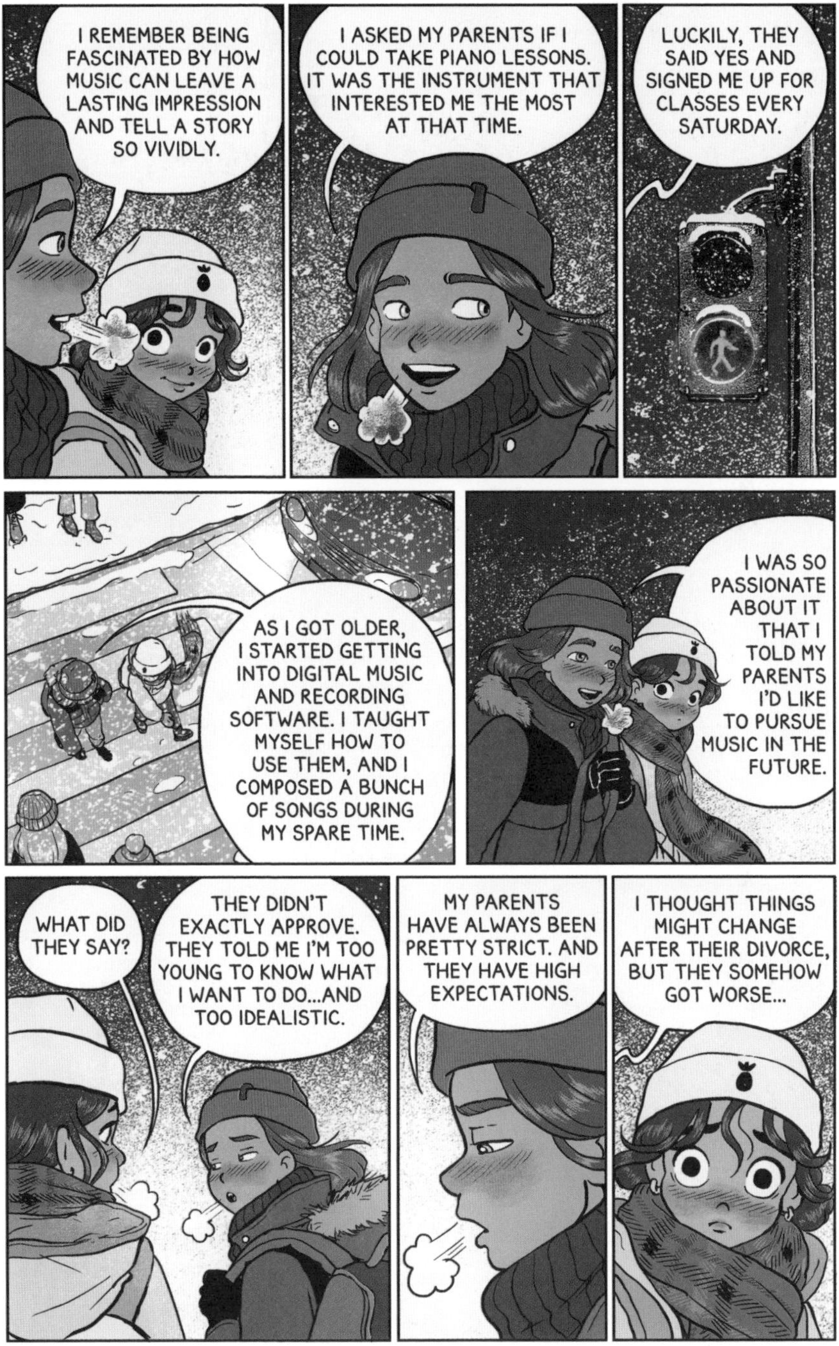
I REMEMBER BEING FASCINATED BY HOW MUSIC CAN LEAVE A LASTING IMPRESSION AND TELL A STORY SO VIVIDLY.
I ASKED MY PARENTS IF I COULD TAKE PIANO LESSONS. IT WAS THE INSTRUMENT THAT INTERESTED ME THE MOST AT THAT TIME.
LUCKILY, THEY SAID YES AND SIGNED ME UP FOR CLASSES EVERY SATURDAY.
AS I GOT OLDER, I STARTED GETTING INTO DIGITAL MUSIC AND RECORDING SOFTWARE. I TAUGHT MYSELF HOW TO USE THEM, AND I COMPOSED A BUNCH OF SONGS DURING MY SPARE TIME.
I WAS SO PASSIONATE ABOUT IT THAT I TOLD MY PARENTS I'D LIKE TO PURSUE MUSIC IN THE FUTURE.
WHAT DID THEY SAY?
THEY DIDN'T EXACTLY APPROVE. THEY TOLD ME I'M TOO YOUNG TO KNOW WHAT I WANT TO DO...AND TOO IDEALISTIC.
MY PARENTS HAVE ALWAYS BEEN PRETTY STRICT. AND THEY HAVE HIGH EXPECTATIONS.
I THOUGHT THINGS MIGHT CHANGE AFTER THEIR DIVORCE, BUT THEY SOMEHOW GOT WORSE...

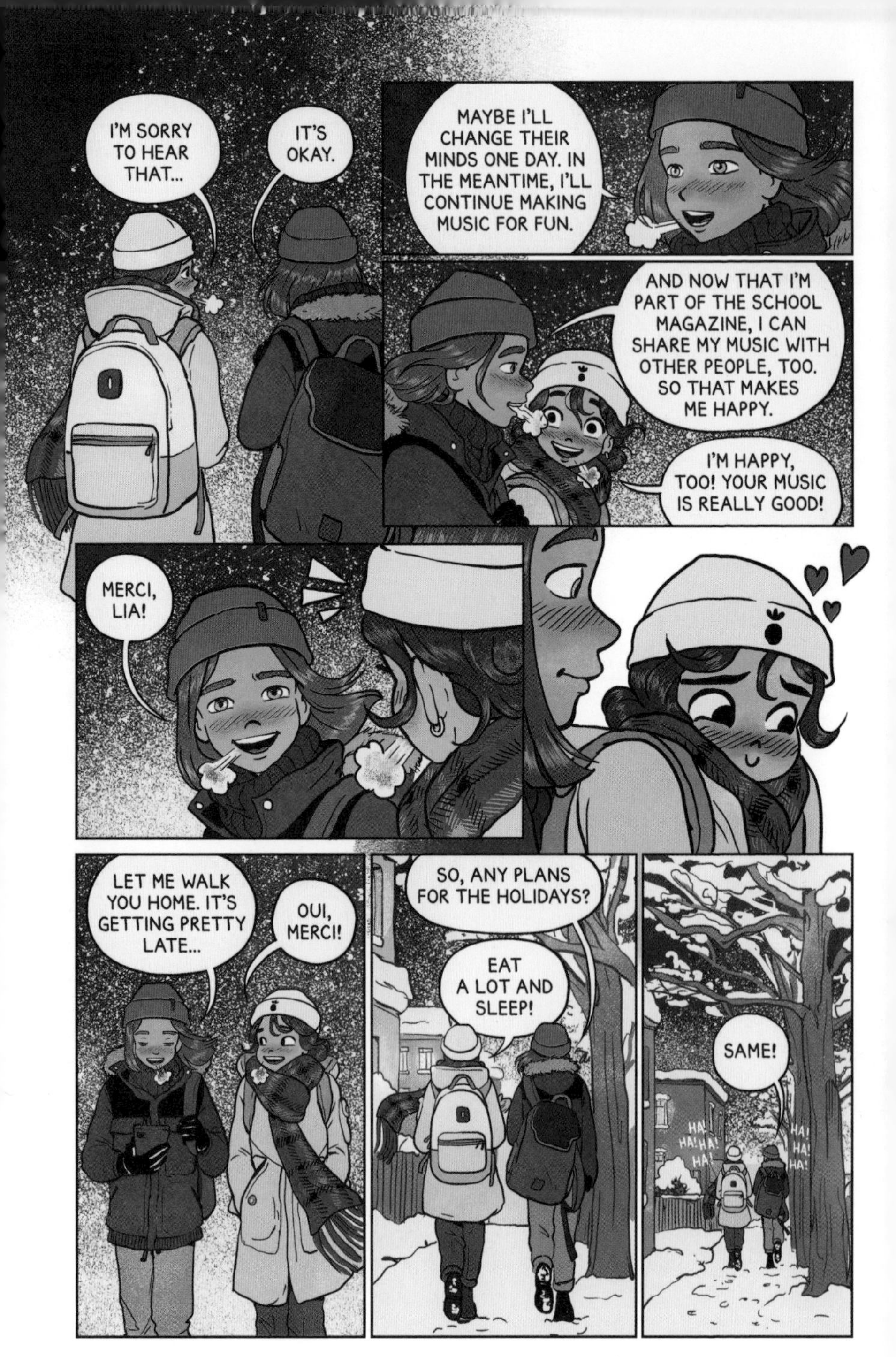
I'M SORRY TO HEAR THAT...
IT'S OKAY.
MAYBE I'LL CHANGE THEIR MINDS ONE DAY. IN THE MEANTIME, I'LL CONTINUE MAKING MUSIC FOR FUN.
AND NOW THAT I'M PART OF THE SCHOOL MAGAZINE, I CAN SHARE MY MUSIC WITH OTHER PEOPLE, TOO. SO THAT MAKES ME HAPPY.
I'M HAPPY, TOO! YOUR MUSIC IS REALLY GOOD!
MERCI, LIA!
LET ME WALK YOU HOME. IT'S GETTING PRETTY LATE...
OUI, MERCI!
SO, ANY PLANS FOR THE HOLIDAYS?
EAT A LOT AND SLEEP!
SAME!
HA! HA! HA! HA!
HA! HA! HA!

CHAPTER 13: COUNTING THE DAYS

Décembre / December
D/S L/M M/T M/W J/T V/F S/S
NOTES
Dec 16:
My next period (???)
Dec 21:
Last day of school
YAY!
CHRISTMAS
BREAK !!!

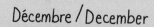

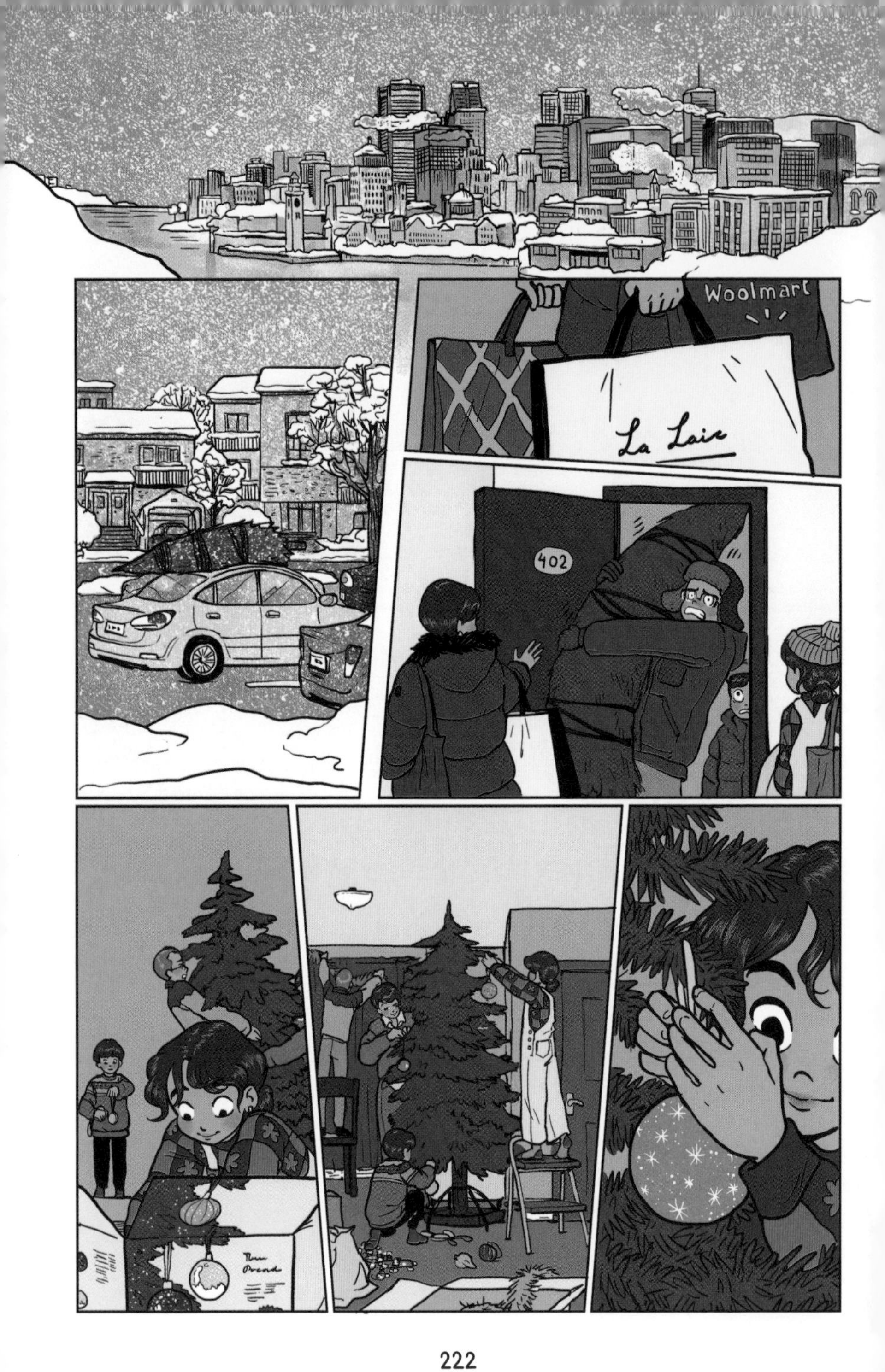
Woolmart
La Laie
402

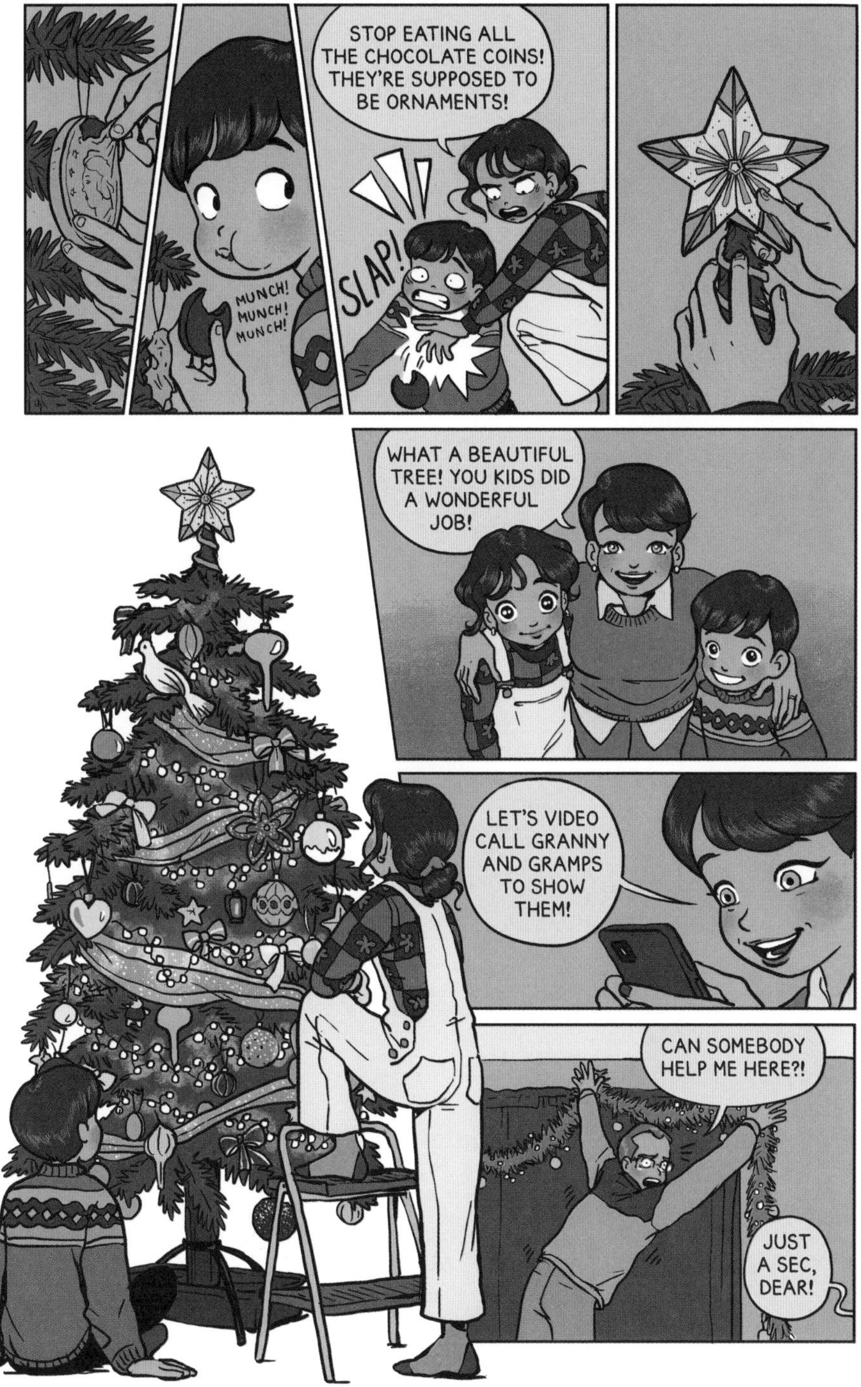
MUNCH! MUNCH! MUNCH!
STOP EATING ALL THE CHOCOLATE COINS! THEY'RE SUPPOSED TO BE ORNAMENTS!
SLAP!
WHAT A BEAUTIFUL TREE! YOU KIDS DID A WONDERFUL JOB!
LET'S VIDEO CALL GRANNY AND GRAMPS TO SHOW THEM!
CAN SOMEBODY HELP ME HERE?!
JUST A SEC, DEAR!

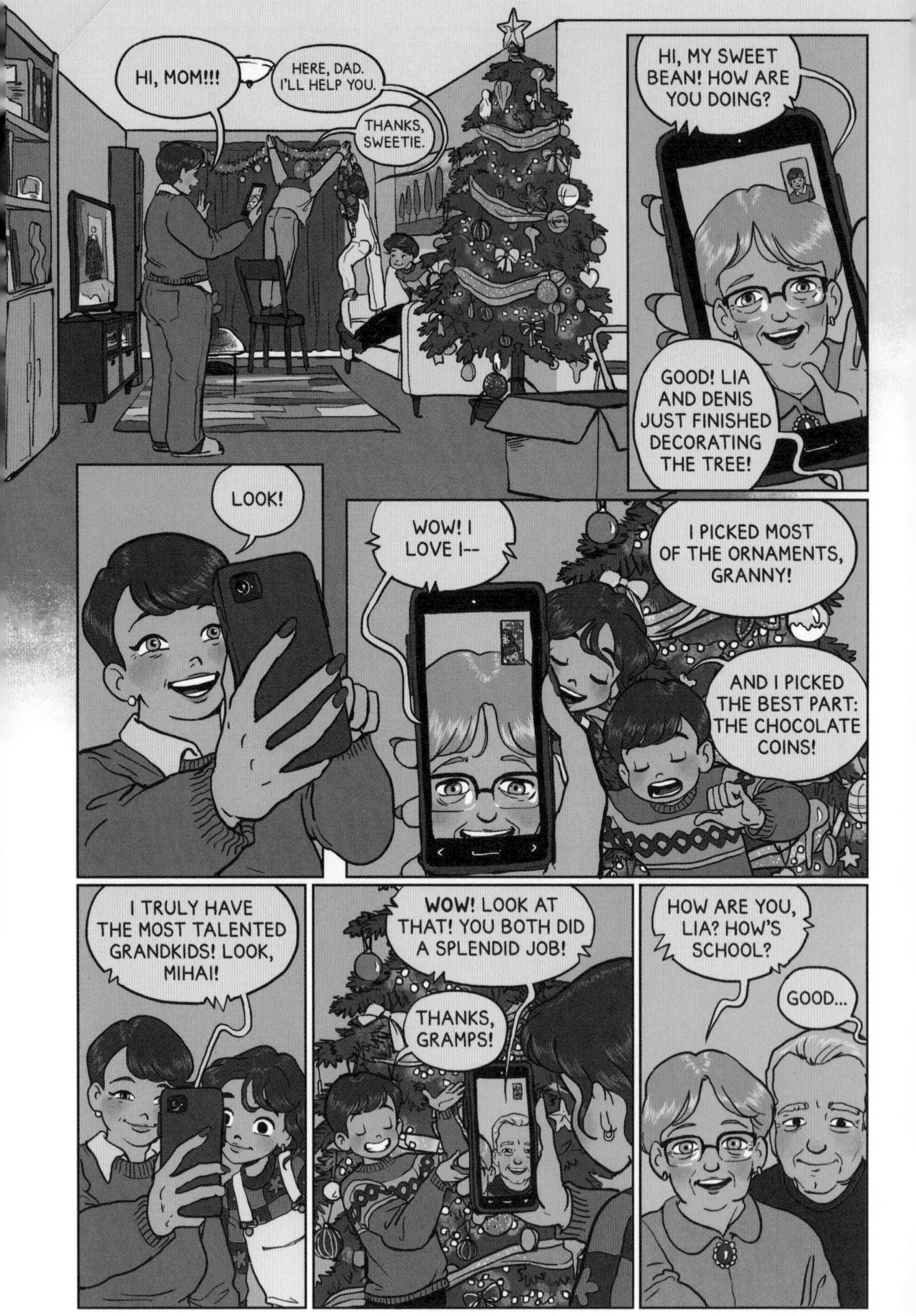

HI, MOM!!!
HERE, DAD. I'LL HELP YOU.
THANKS, SWEETIE.
HI, MY SWEET BEAN! HOW ARE YOU DOING?
GOOD! LIA AND DENIS JUST FINISHED DECORATING THE TREE!
LOOK!
WOW! I LOVE I--
I PICKED MOST OF THE ORNAMENTS, GRANNY!
AND I PICKED THE BEST PART: THE CHOCOLATE COINS!
I TRULY HAVE THE MOST TALENTED GRANDKIDS! LOOK, MIHAI!
WOW! LOOK AT THAT! YOU BOTH DID A SPLENDID JOB!
THANKS, GRAMPS!
HOW ARE YOU, LIA? HOW'S SCHOOL?
GOOD...

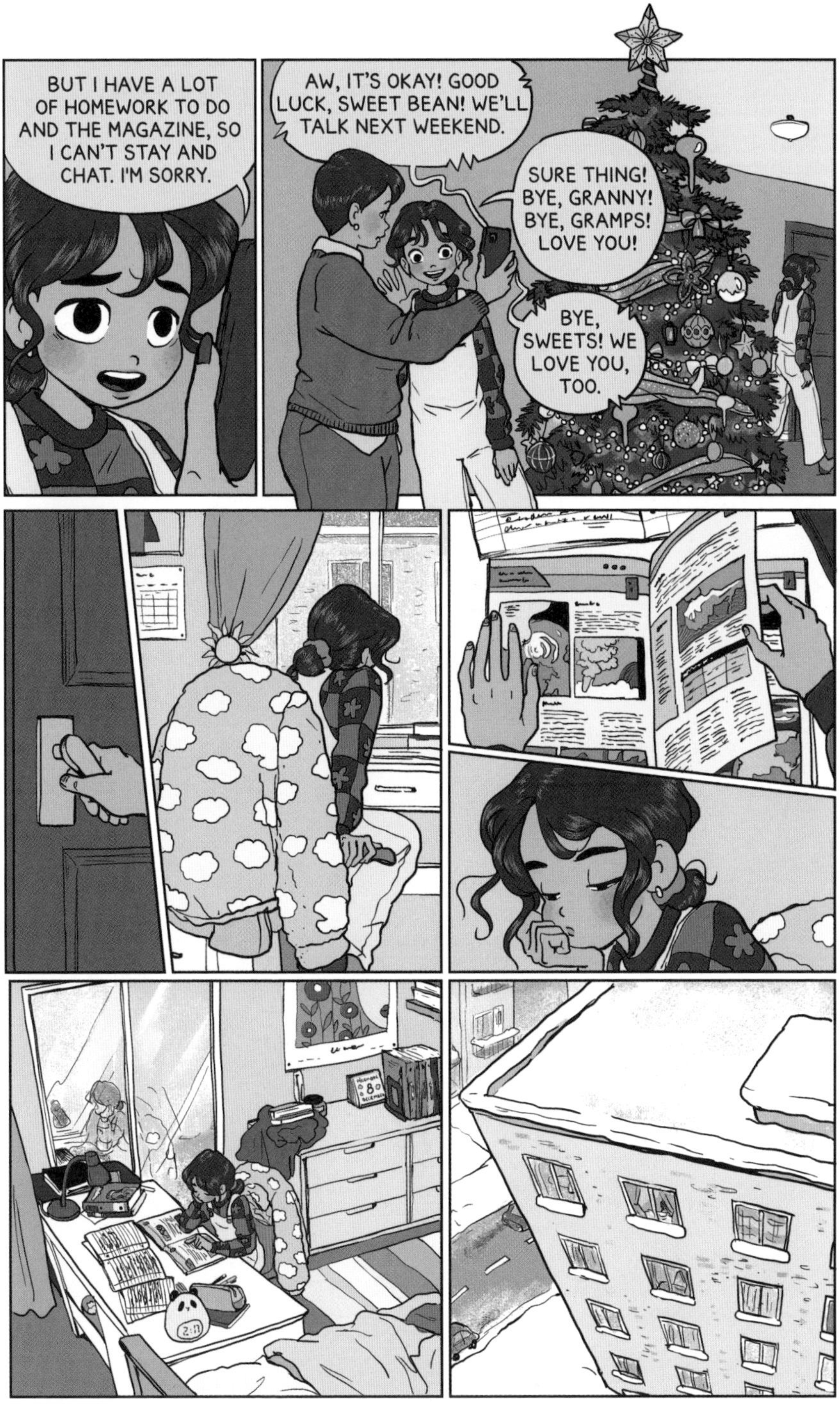
BUT I HAVE A LOT OF HOMEWORK TO DO AND THE MAGAZINE, SO I CAN'T STAY AND CHAT. I'M SORRY.
AW, IT'S OKAY! GOOD LUCK, SWEET BEAN! WE'LL TALK NEXT WEEKEND.
SURE THING! BYE, GRANNY! BYE, GRAMPS! LOVE YOU!
BYE, SWEETS! WE LOVE YOU, TOO.

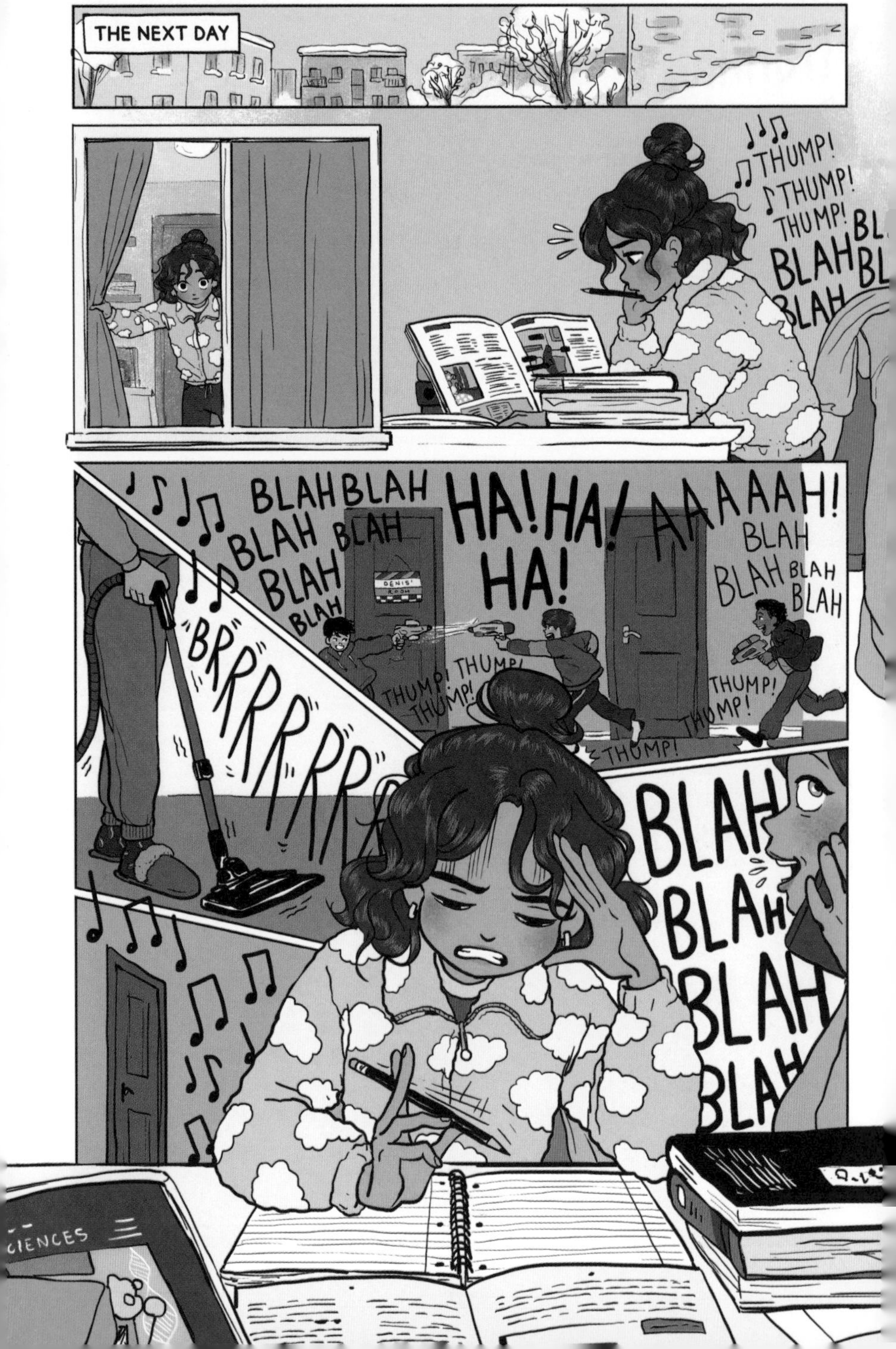
THE NEXT DAY
THUMP!
THUMP!
THUMP!
BLAH
BLAH
BLAH BLAH
BLAH BLAH
BLAH BLAH
BLAH
BLAH
DENIS' ROOM
HA! HA! HA!
AAAAAH!
BLAH BLAH BLAH BLAH
BRRRRRRRR
THUMP! THUMP! THUMP!
THUMP! THUMP!
THUMP!
BLAH BLAH BLAH BLAH
CIENCES

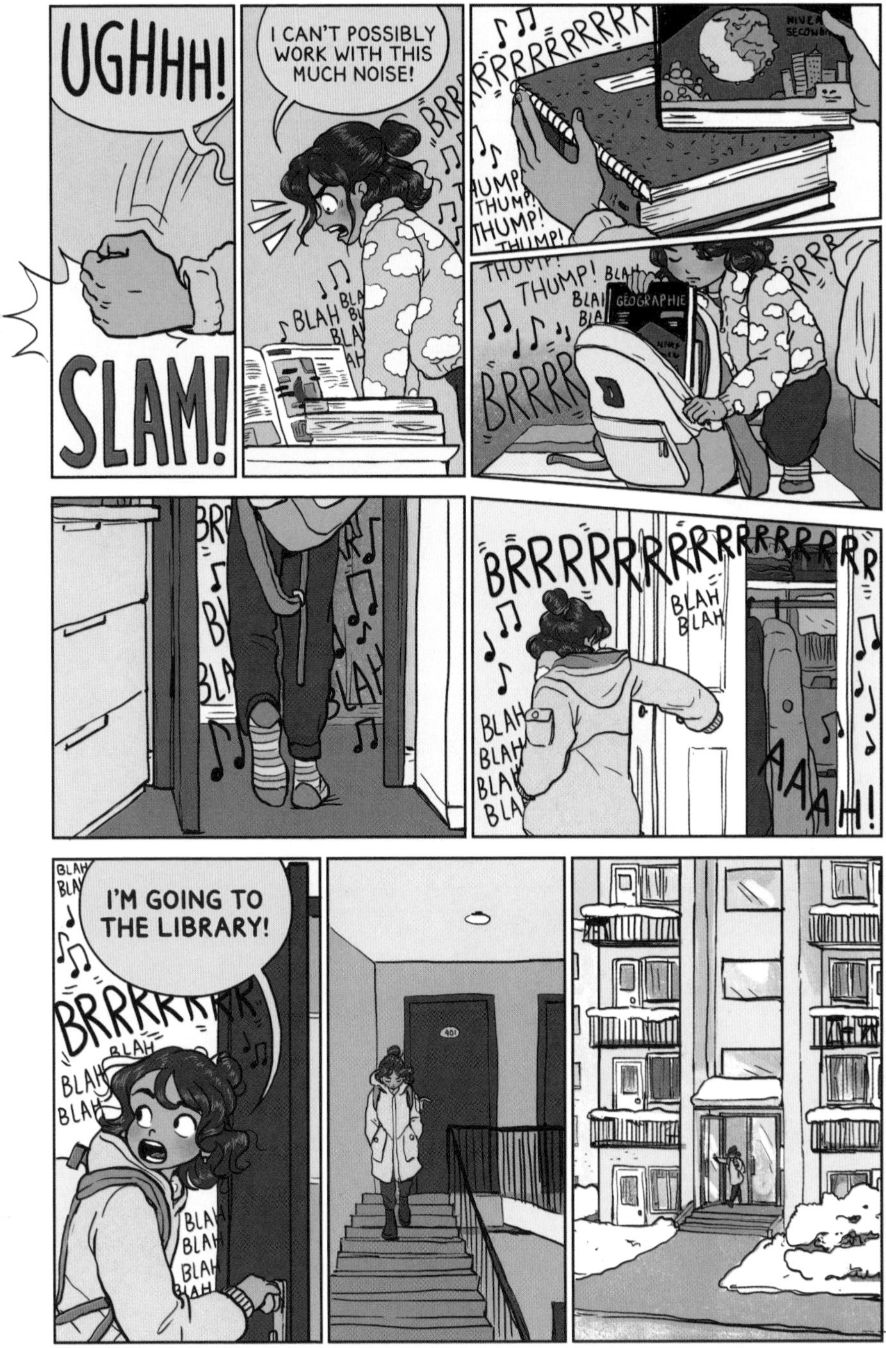
UGHHH!
SLAM!
I CAN'T POSSIBLY WORK WITH THIS MUCH NOISE!
BRRR
BLAH BLAH BLAH BLAH BLAH
RRRRRRRRRRR
THUMP! THUMP! THUMP! THUMP!
THUMP! THUMP!
BLAH BLAH BLAH
GEOGRAPHIE
BRRRR
BRRRR
BLAH
BRRRRRRRRRRRRRRR
BLAH BLAH
BLAH BLAH BLAH BLAH
AAAAH!
I'M GOING TO THE LIBRARY!
BRRRRRR
BLAH BLAH BLAH
BLAH BLAH BLAH
401

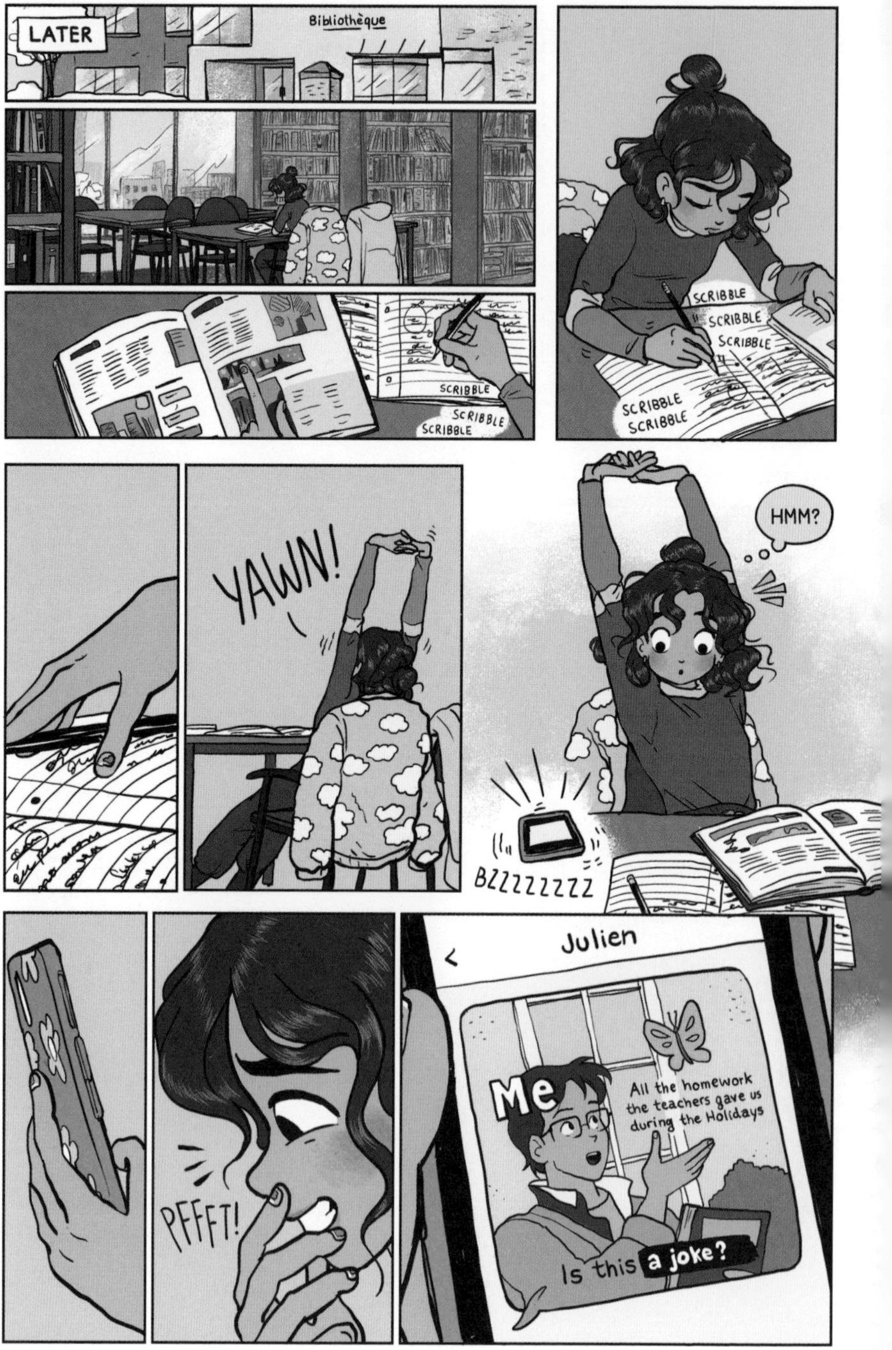
LATER
Bibliothèque
SCRIBBLE
SCRIBBLE
SCRIBBLE
SCRIBBLE
SCRIBBLE
SCRIBBLE
SCRIBBLE
SCRIBBLE
YAWN!
HMM?
BZZZZZZZZ
PFFFT!
Julien
Me
All the homework the teachers gave us during the Holidays
Is this a joke?

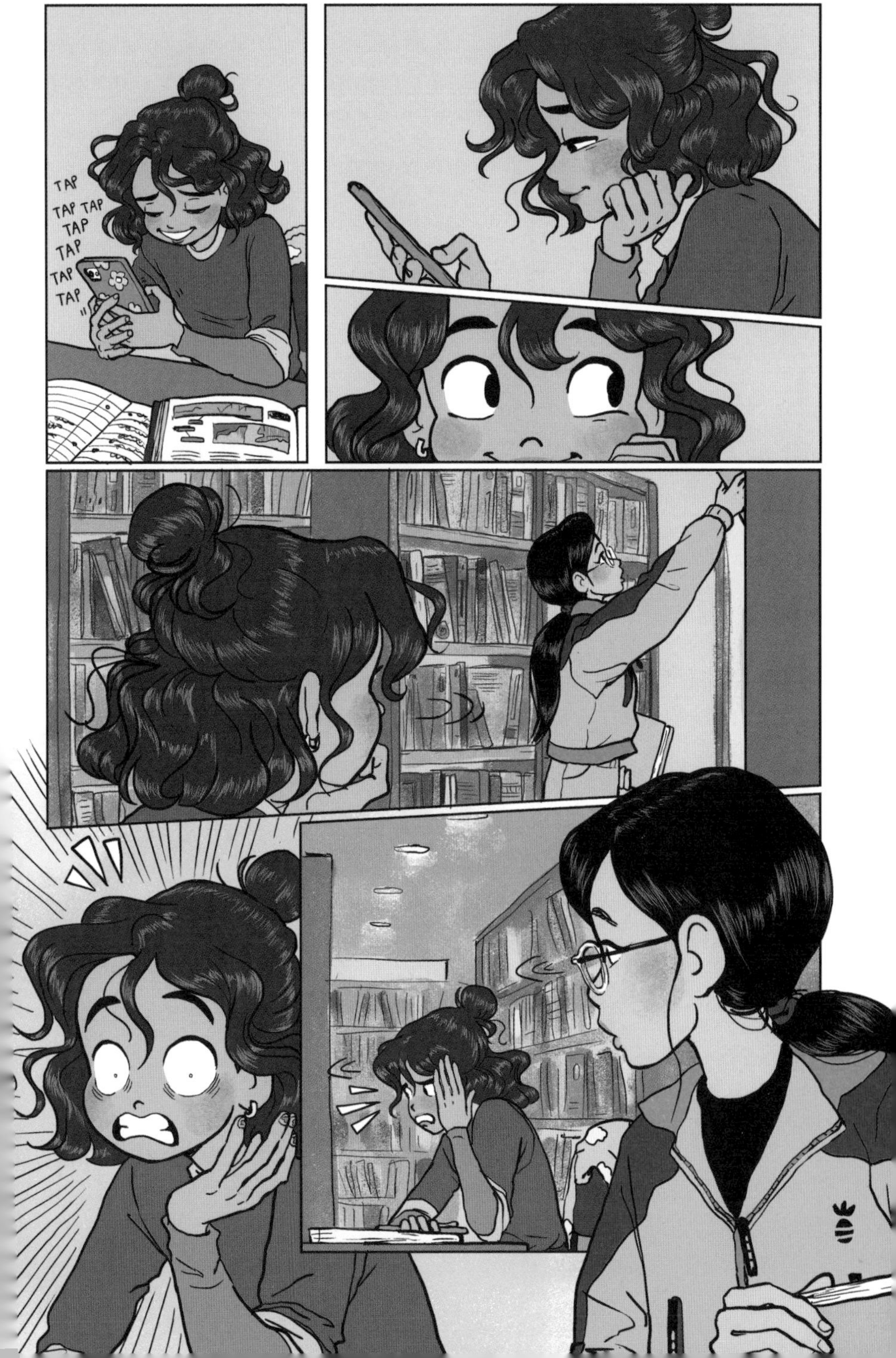
TAP
TAP TAP
TAP
TAP
TAP
TAP

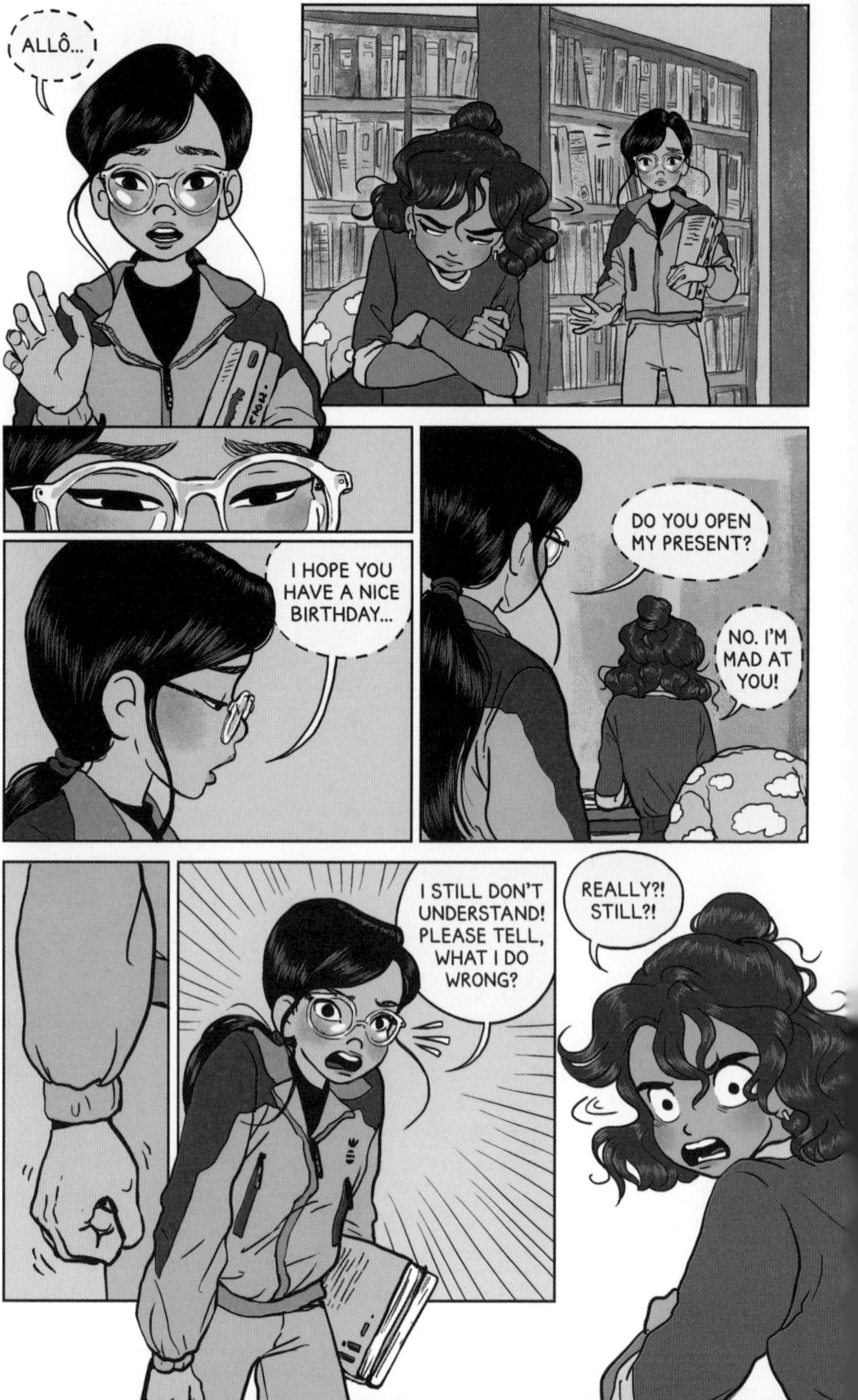
ALLÔ...
I HOPE YOU HAVE A NICE BIRTHDAY...
DO YOU OPEN MY PRESENT?
NO. I'M MAD AT YOU!
I STILL DON'T UNDERSTAND! PLEASE TELL, WHAT I DO WRONG?
REALLY?! STILL?!

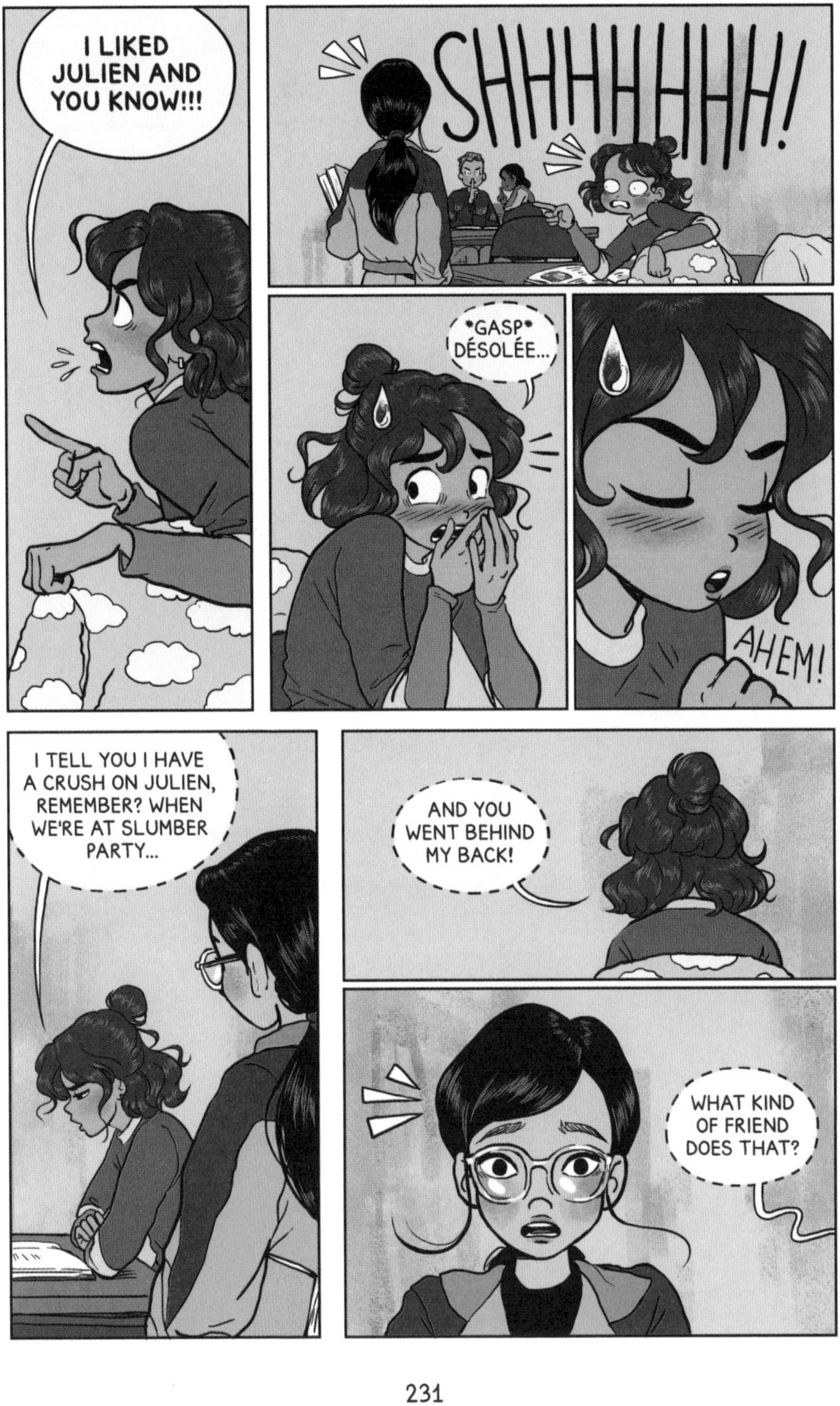
I LIKED JULIEN AND YOU KNOW!!!
SHHHHHHH!
GASP DÉSOLÉE...
AHEM!
I TELL YOU I HAVE A CRUSH ON JULIEN, REMEMBER? WHEN WE'RE AT SLUMBER PARTY...
AND YOU WENT BEHIND MY BACK!
WHAT KIND OF FRIEND DOES THAT?

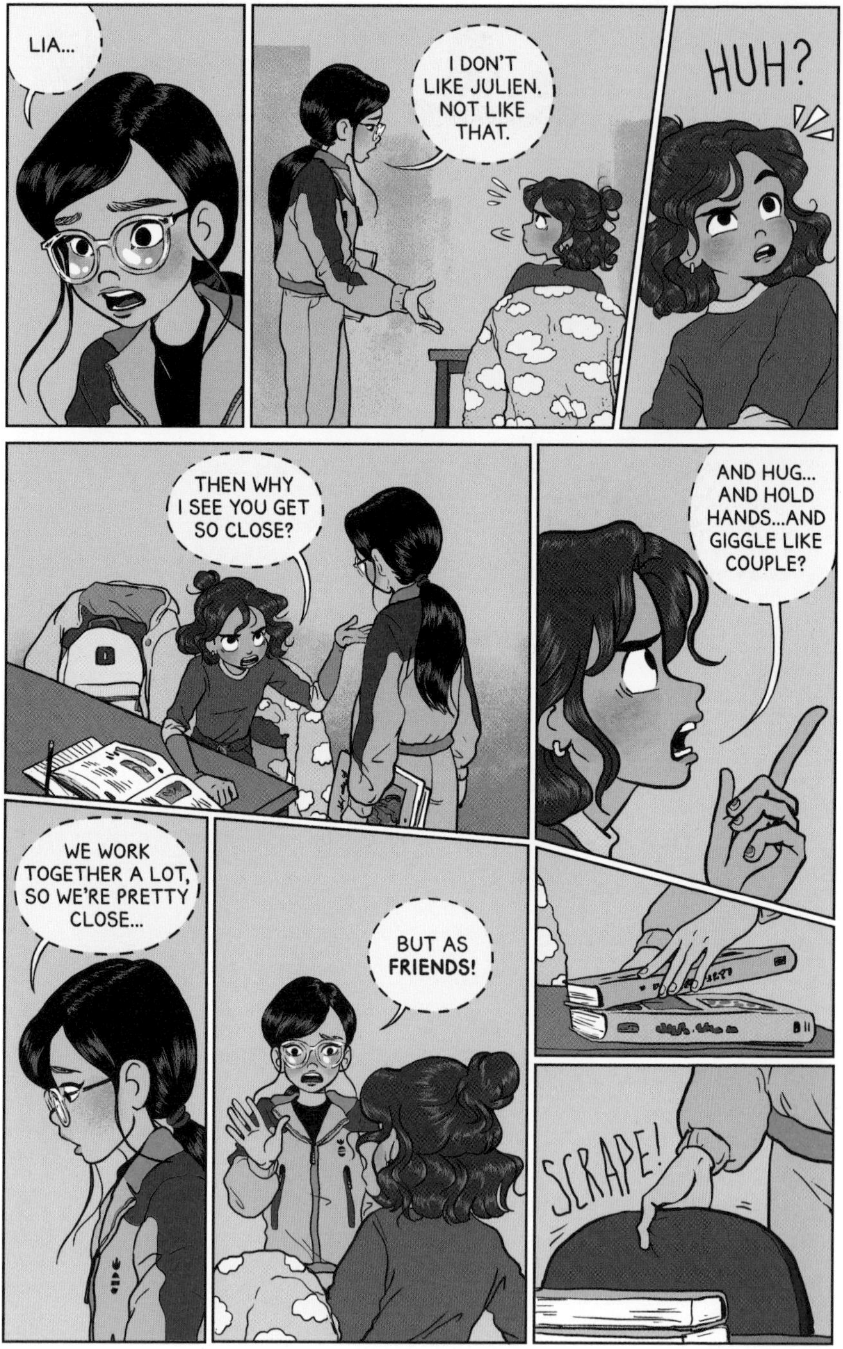
LIA...
I DON'T LIKE JULIEN. NOT LIKE THAT.
HUH?
THEN WHY I SEE YOU GET SO CLOSE?
AND HUG... AND HOLD HANDS...AND GIGGLE LIKE COUPLE?
WE WORK TOGETHER A LOT, SO WE'RE PRETTY CLOSE...
BUT AS **FRIENDS!**
SCRAPE!

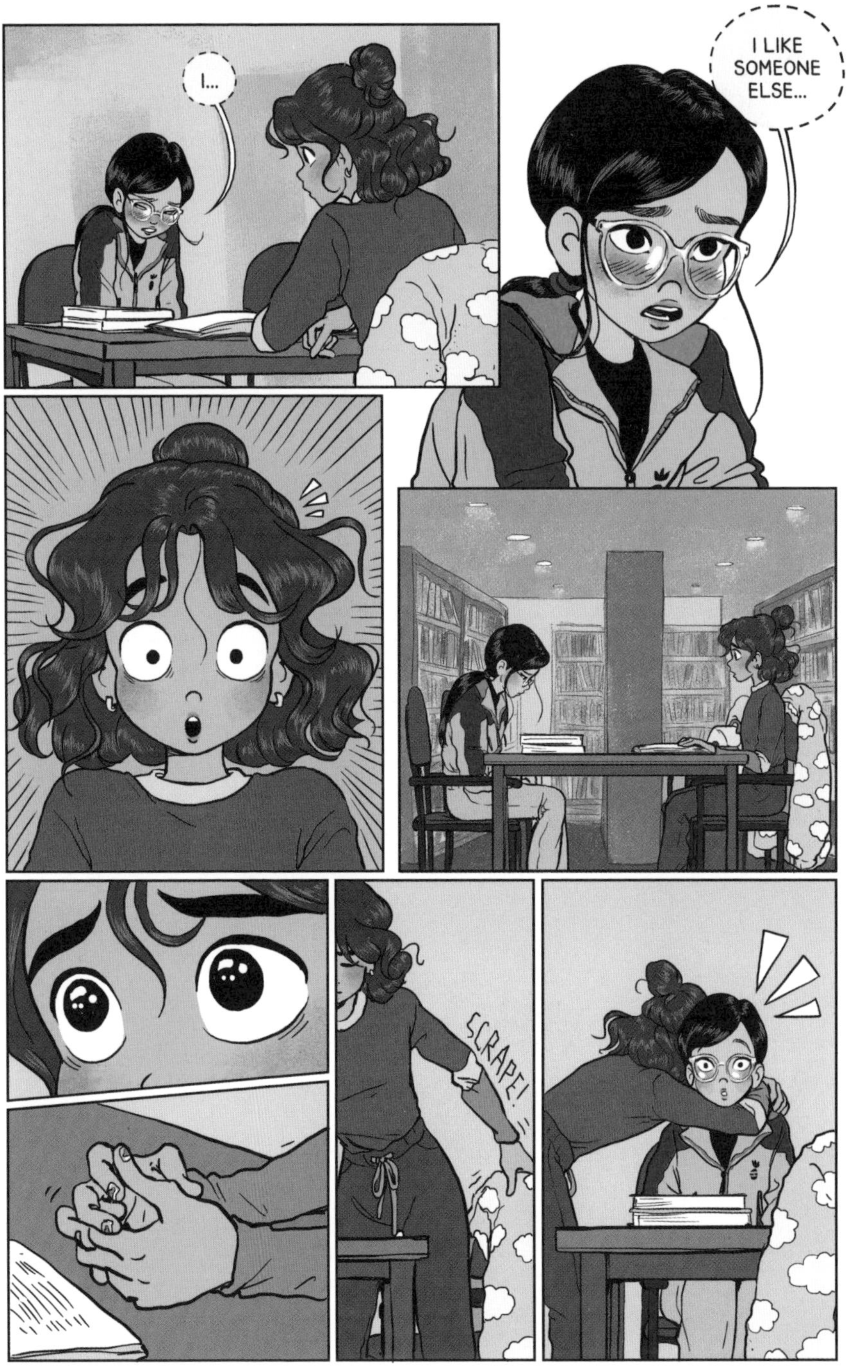
I...
I LIKE SOMEONE ELSE...
SCRAPE!

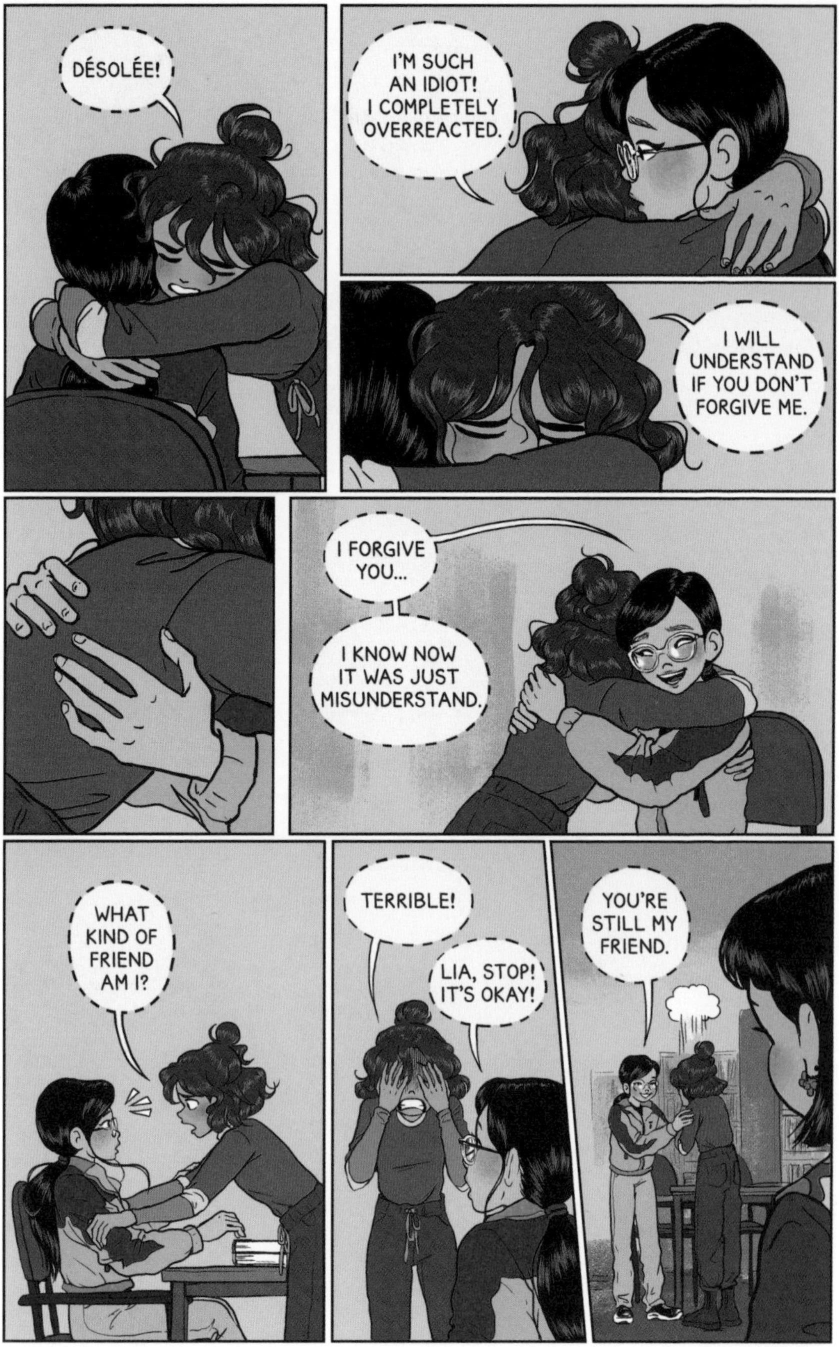
DÉSOLÉE!
I'M SUCH AN IDIOT! I COMPLETELY OVERREACTED.
I WILL UNDERSTAND IF YOU DON'T FORGIVE ME.
I FORGIVE YOU...
I KNOW NOW IT WAS JUST MISUNDERSTAND.
WHAT KIND OF FRIEND AM I?
TERRIBLE!
LIA, STOP! IT'S OKAY!
YOU'RE STILL MY FRIEND.

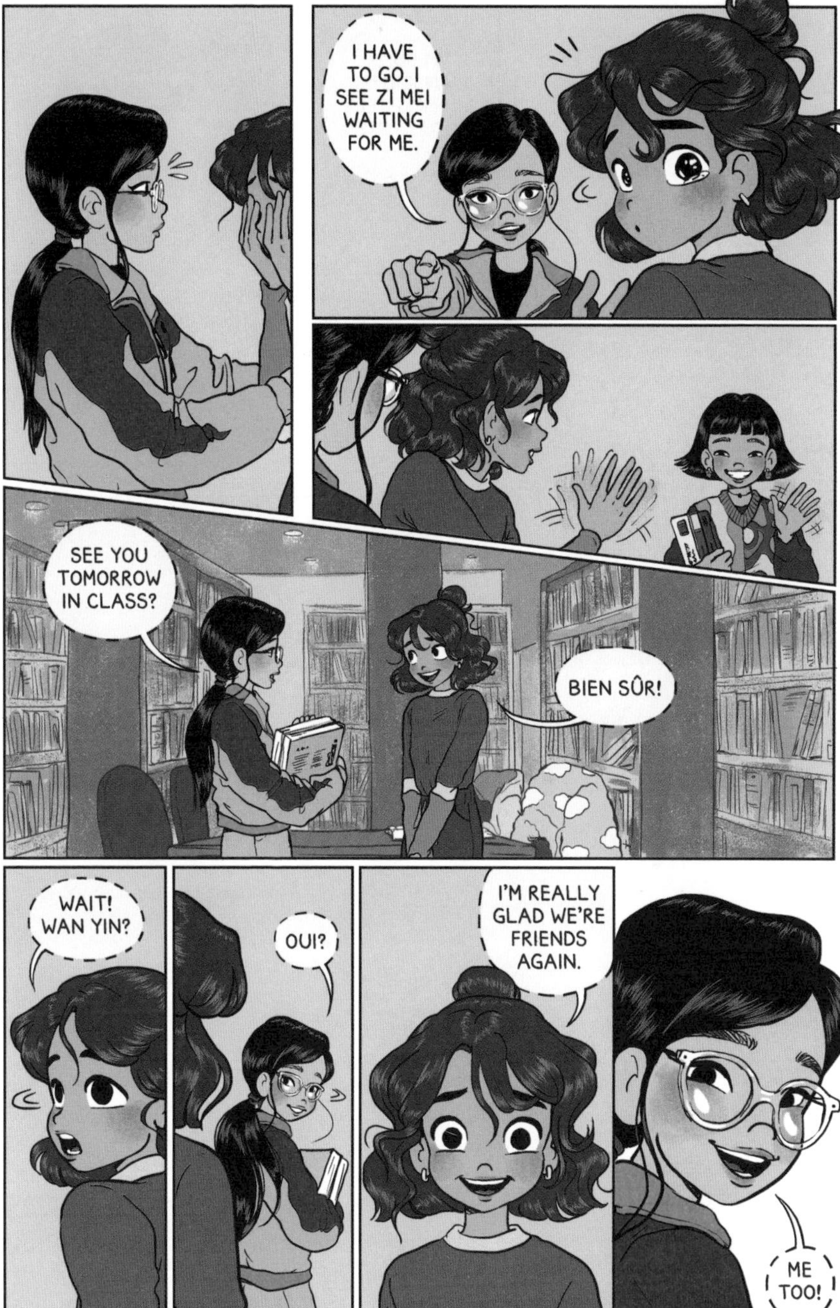
I HAVE TO GO. I SEE ZI MEI WAITING FOR ME.
SEE YOU TOMORROW IN CLASS?
BIEN SÛR!
WAIT! WAN YIN?
OUI?
I'M REALLY GLAD WE'RE FRIENDS AGAIN.
ME TOO!

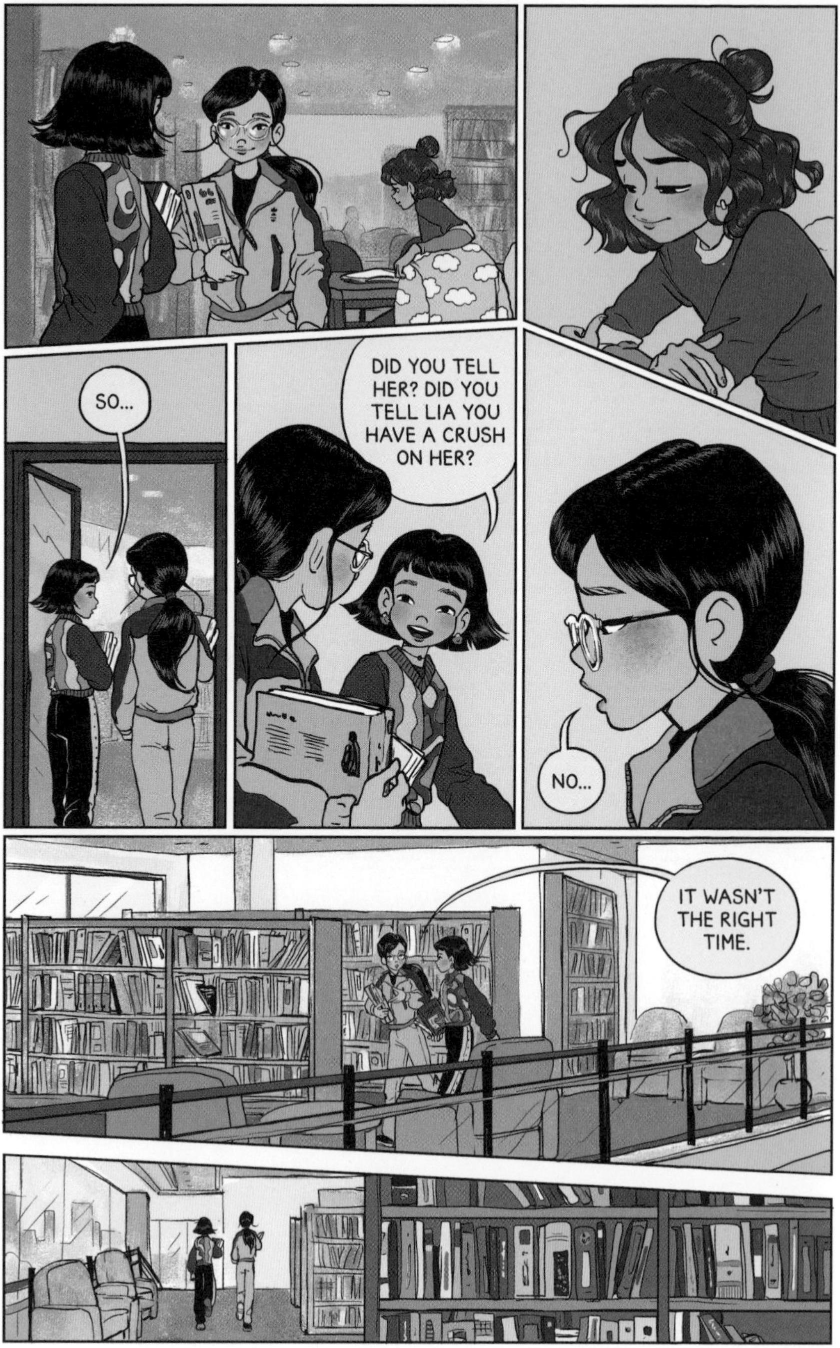
SO...
DID YOU TELL HER? DID YOU TELL LIA YOU HAVE A CRUSH ON HER?
NO...
IT WASN'T THE RIGHT TIME.

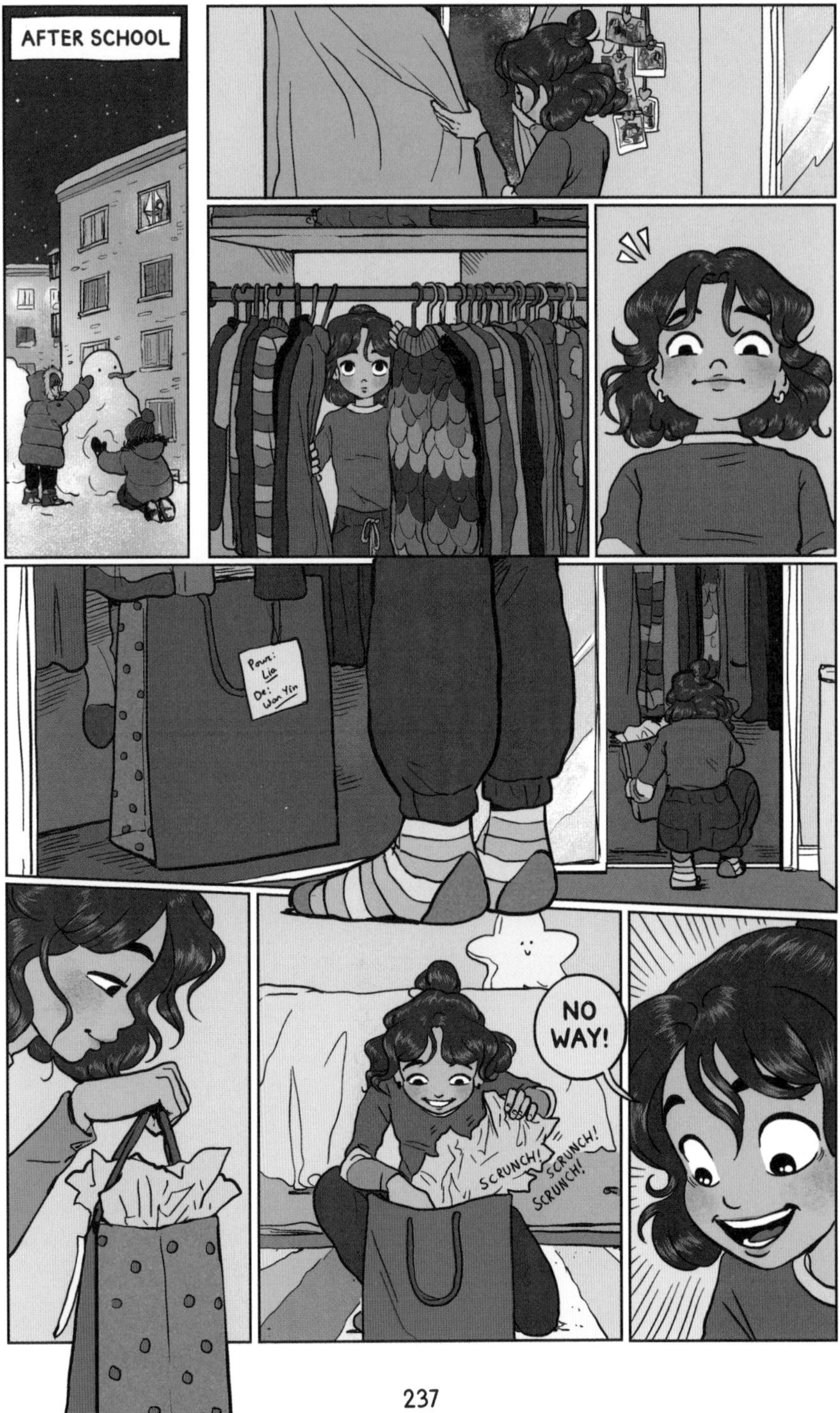
AFTER SCHOOL
Pour:
Lia
De:
Wan Yin
SCRUNCH! SCRUNCH! SCRUNCH!
NO WAY!

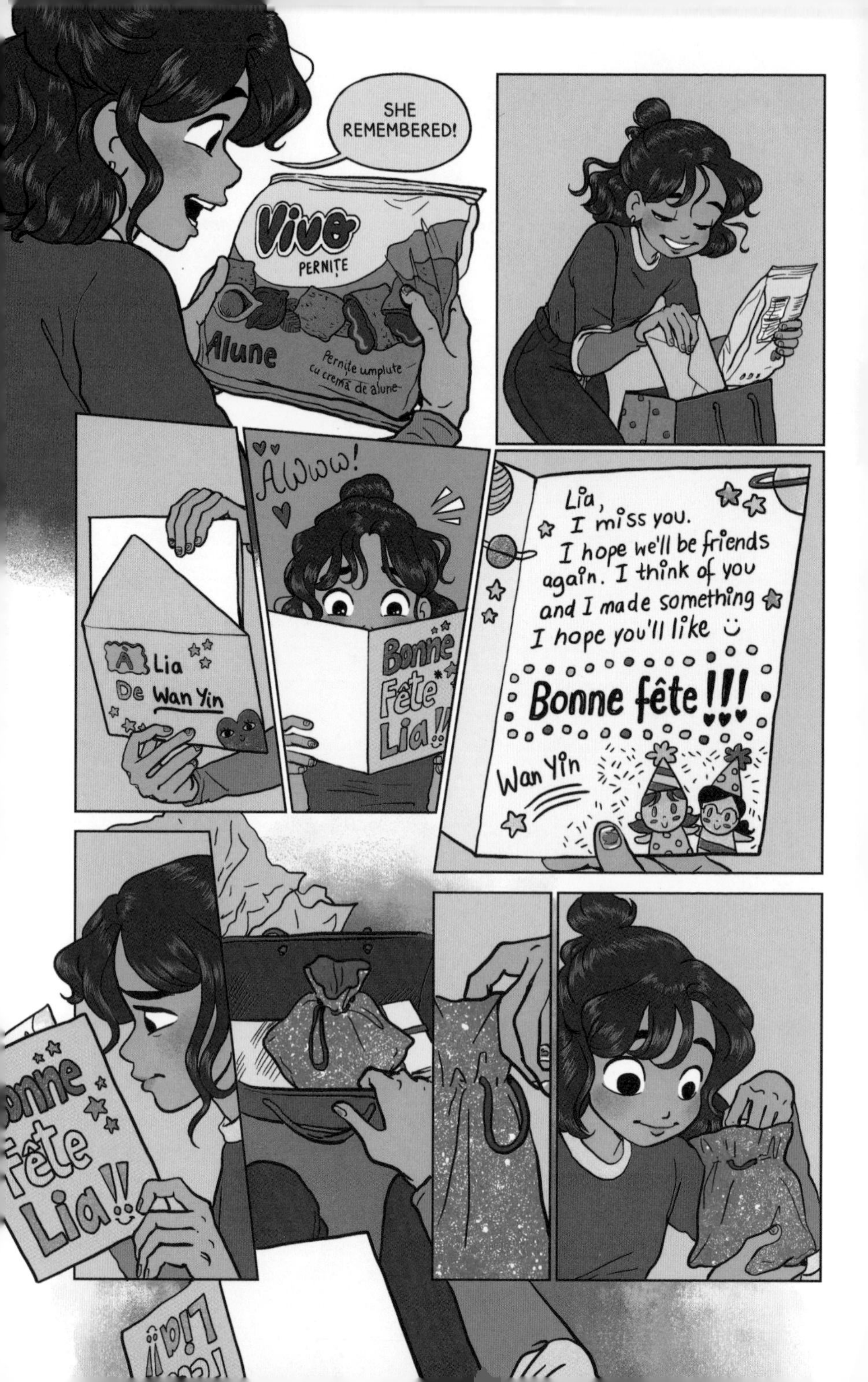
SHE REMEMBERED!
Vivo
PERNIȚE
Alune
Pernițe umplute cu cremă de alune
Awww!
À Lia
De Wan Yin
Bonne Fête Lia!!
Lia,
I miss you.
I hope we'll be friends again. I think of you and I made something I hope you'll like
Bonne fête!!!
Wan Yin
Bonne Fête Lia!!

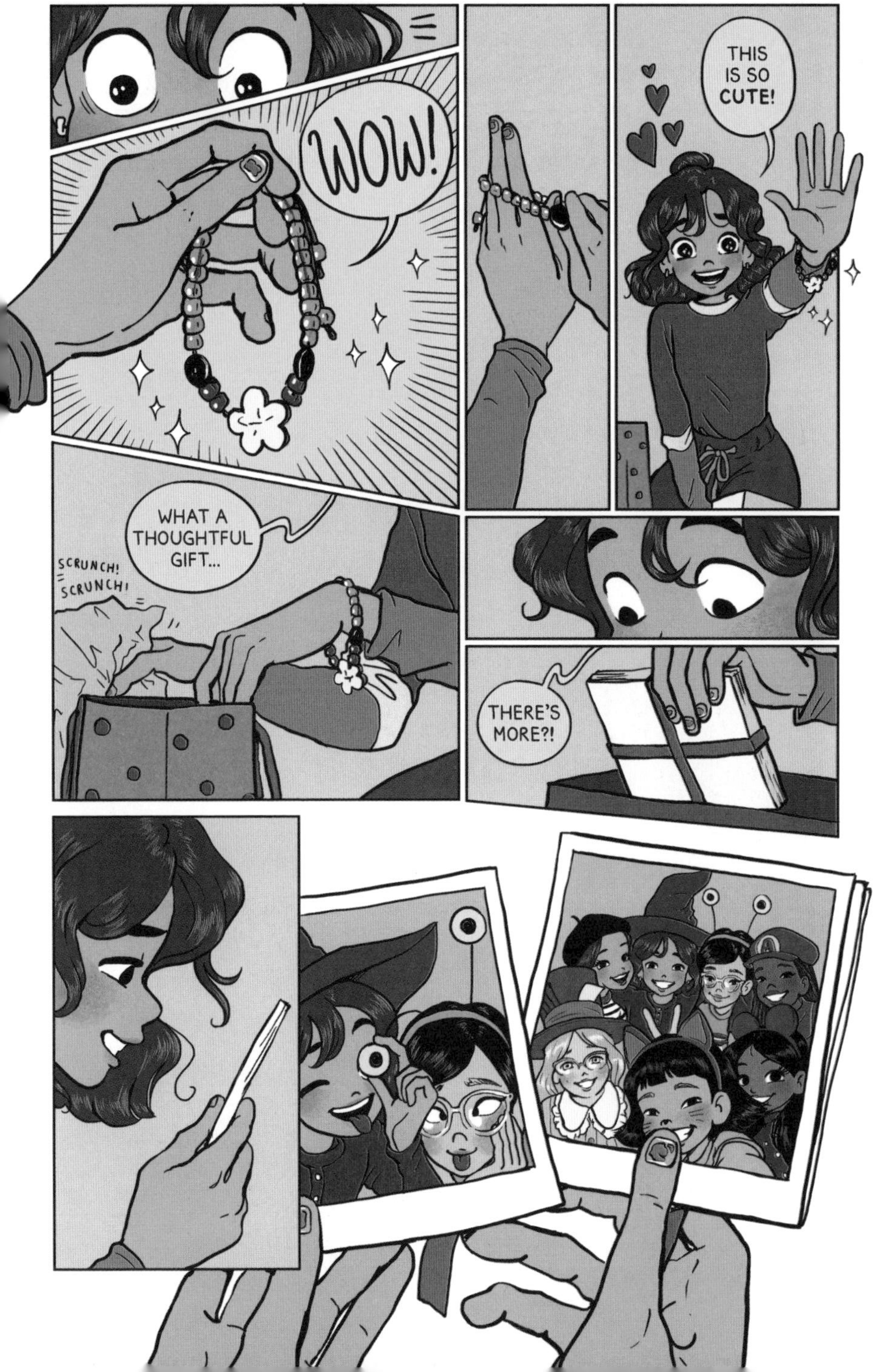
WOW!
THIS IS SO CUTE!
WHAT A THOUGHTFUL GIFT...
SCRUNCH! SCRUNCH!
THERE'S MORE?!

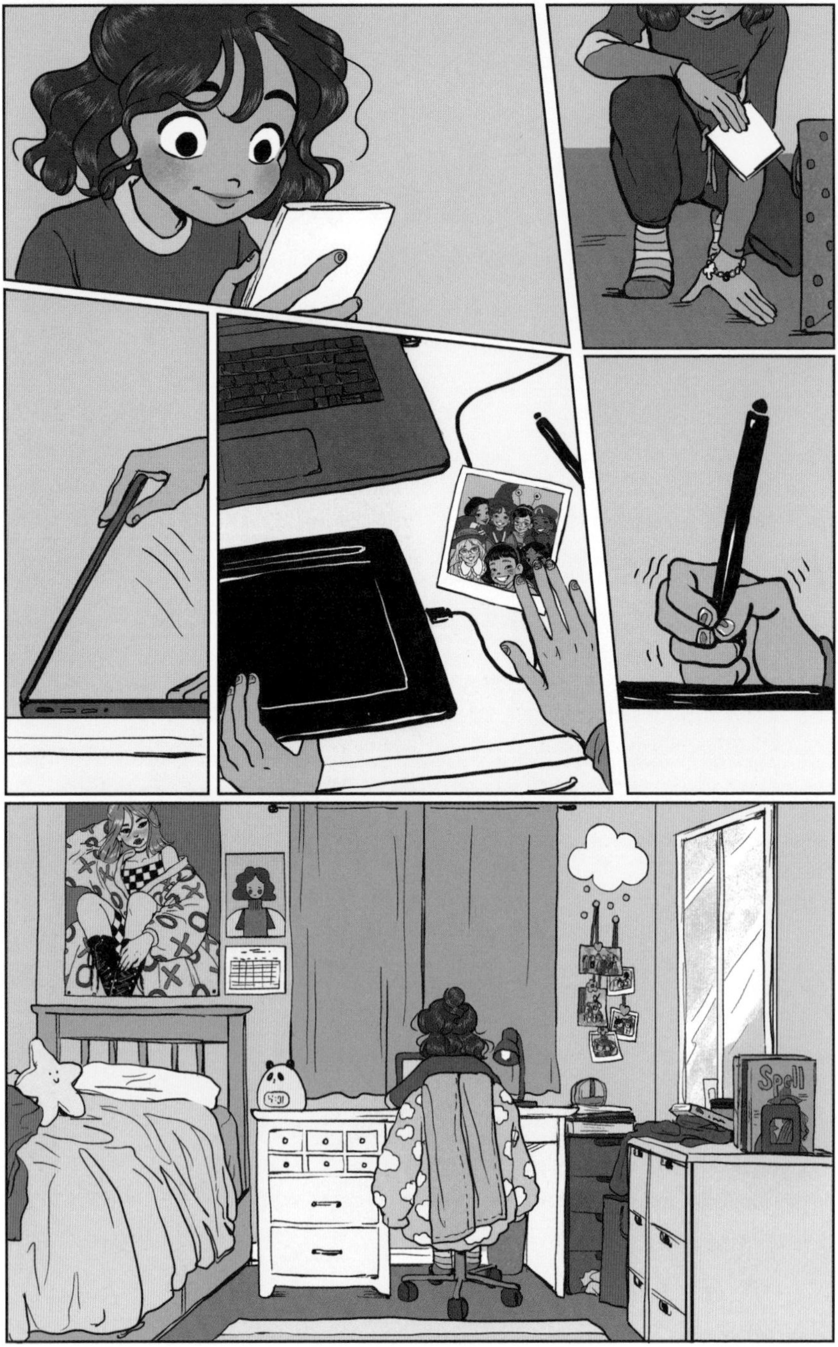
Spell

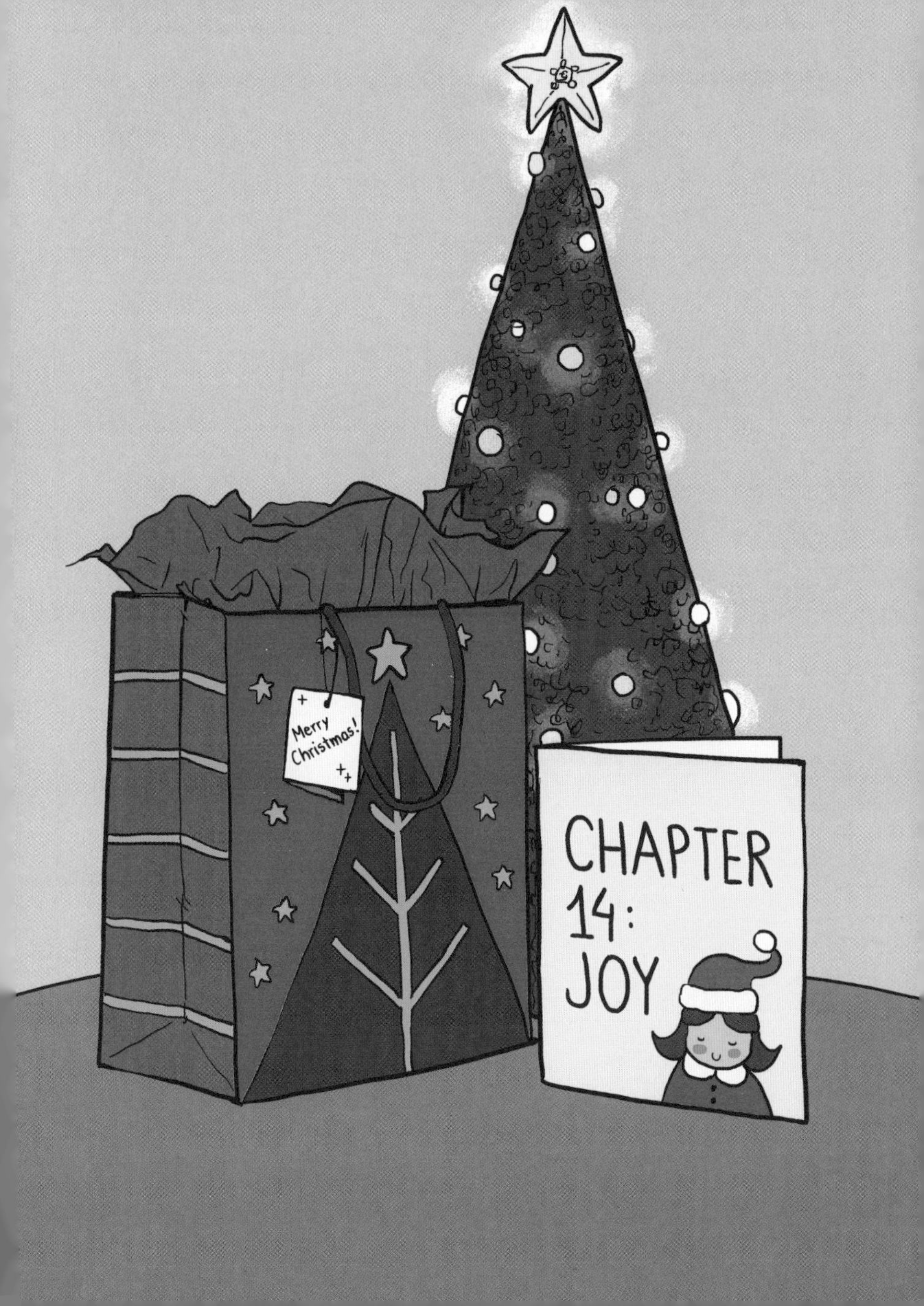
Merry Christmas!
CHAPTER 14: JOY

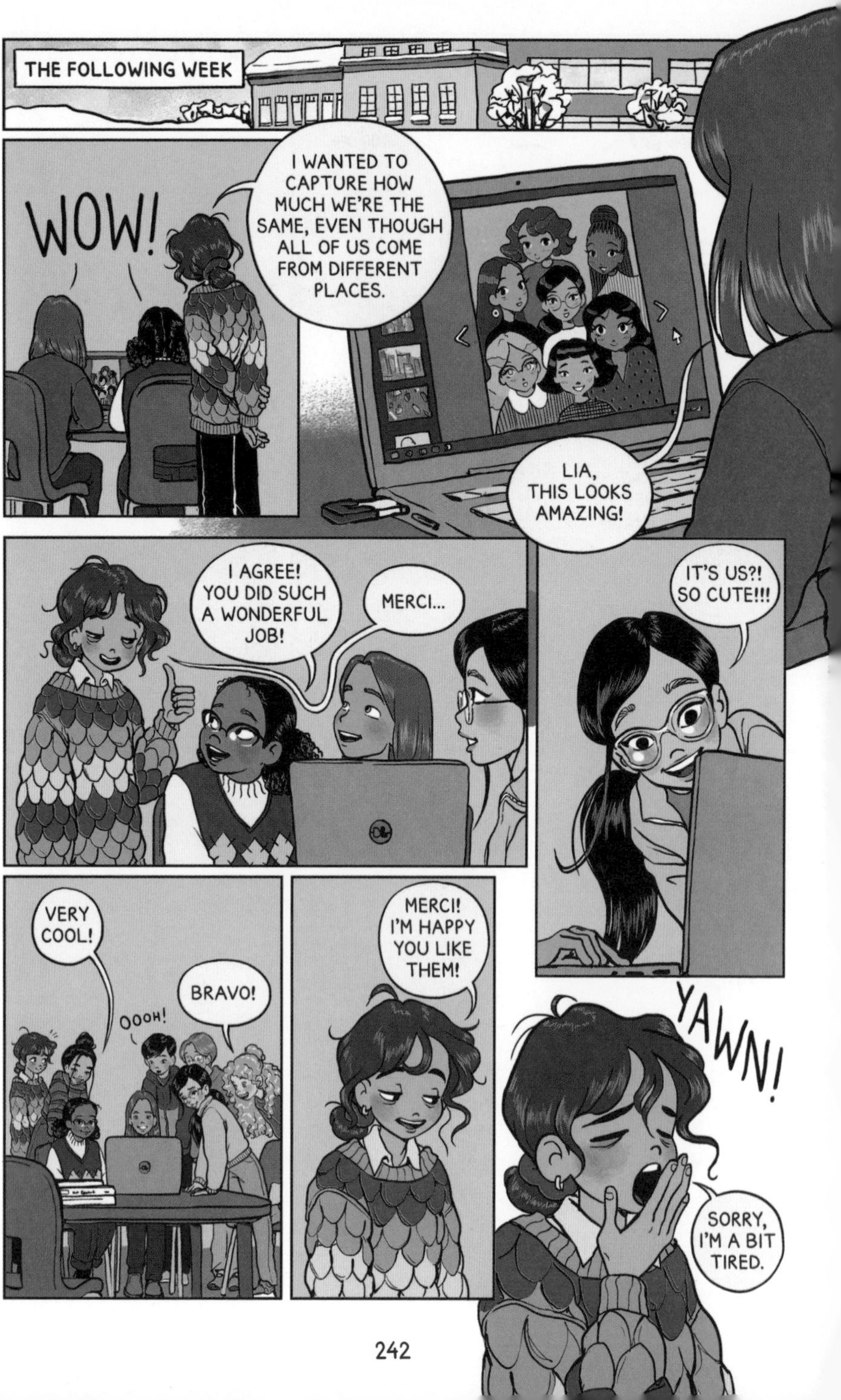
THE FOLLOWING WEEK
WOW!
I WANTED TO CAPTURE HOW MUCH WE'RE THE SAME, EVEN THOUGH ALL OF US COME FROM DIFFERENT PLACES.
LIA, THIS LOOKS AMAZING!
I AGREE! YOU DID SUCH A WONDERFUL JOB!
MERCI...
IT'S US?! SO CUTE!!!
VERY COOL!
OOOH!
BRAVO!
MERCI! I'M HAPPY YOU LIKE THEM!
YAWN!
SORRY, I'M A BIT TIRED.

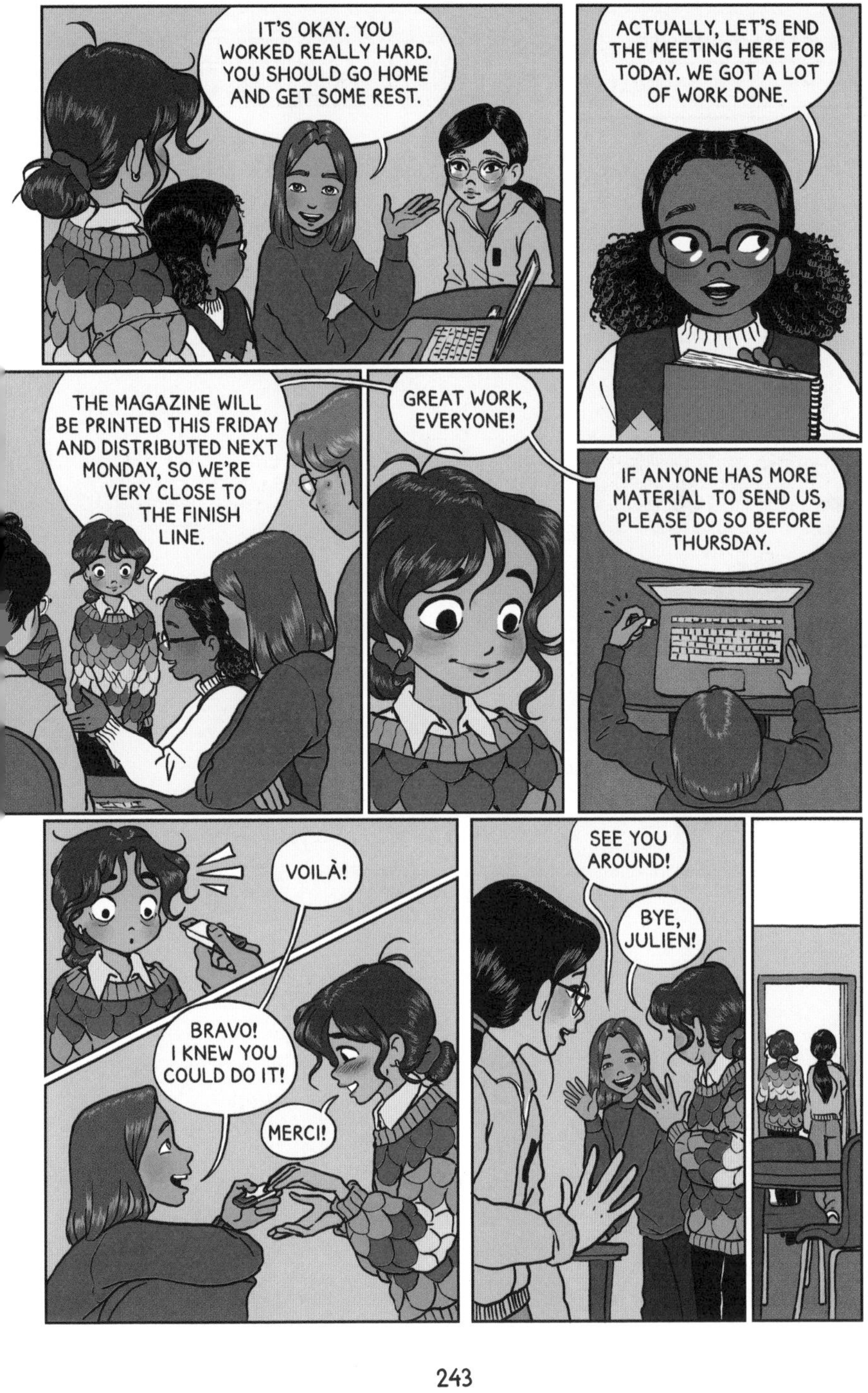
IT'S OKAY. YOU WORKED REALLY HARD. YOU SHOULD GO HOME AND GET SOME REST.
ACTUALLY, LET'S END THE MEETING HERE FOR TODAY. WE GOT A LOT OF WORK DONE.
THE MAGAZINE WILL BE PRINTED THIS FRIDAY AND DISTRIBUTED NEXT MONDAY, SO WE'RE VERY CLOSE TO THE FINISH LINE.
GREAT WORK, EVERYONE!
IF ANYONE HAS MORE MATERIAL TO SEND US, PLEASE DO SO BEFORE THURSDAY.
VOILÀ!
BRAVO! I KNEW YOU COULD DO IT!
MERCI!
SEE YOU AROUND!
BYE, JULIEN!

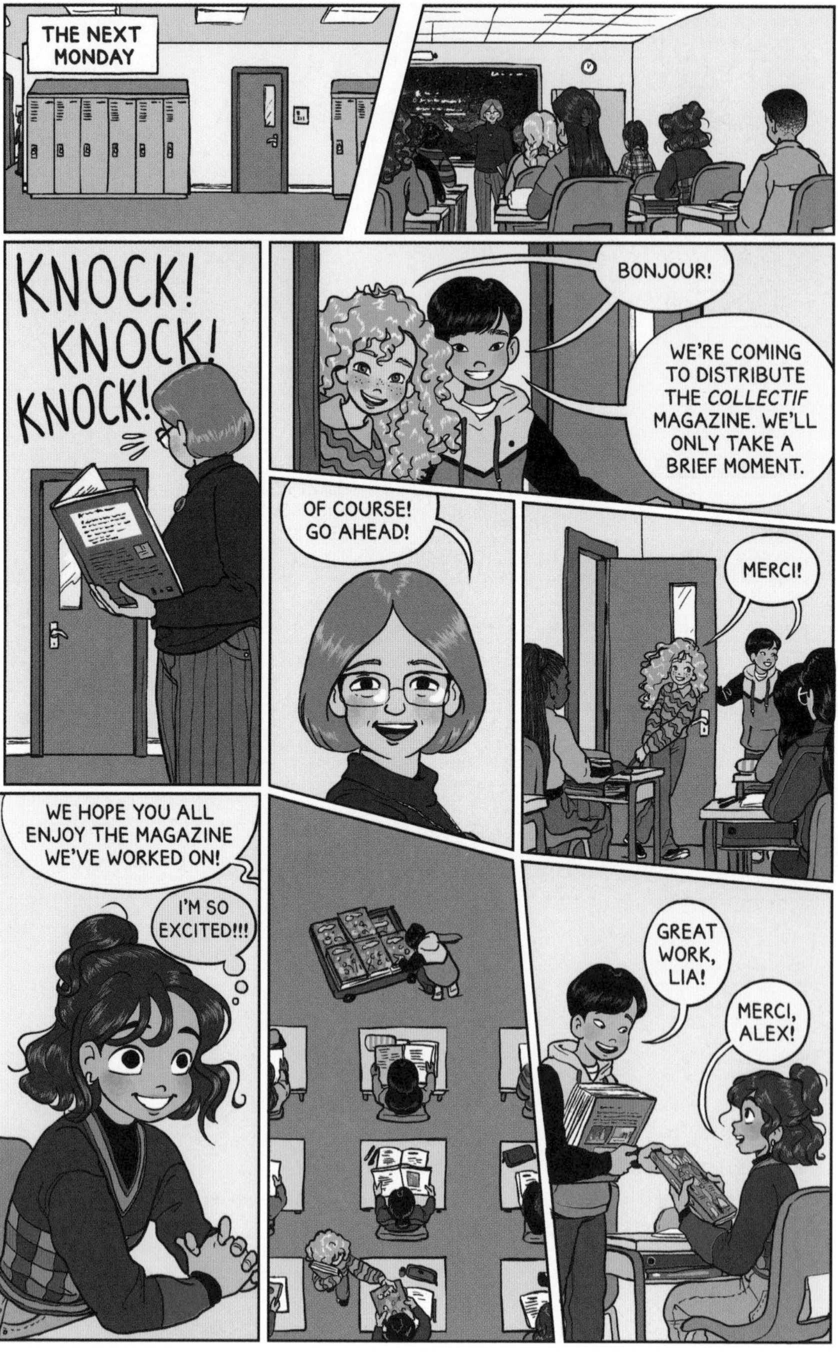
THE NEXT MONDAY
KNOCK! KNOCK! KNOCK!
BONJOUR!
WE'RE COMING TO DISTRIBUTE THE *COLLECTIF* MAGAZINE. WE'LL ONLY TAKE A BRIEF MOMENT.
OF COURSE! GO AHEAD!
MERCI!
WE HOPE YOU ALL ENJOY THE MAGAZINE WE'VE WORKED ON!
I'M SO EXCITED!!!
GREAT WORK, LIA!
MERCI, ALEX!

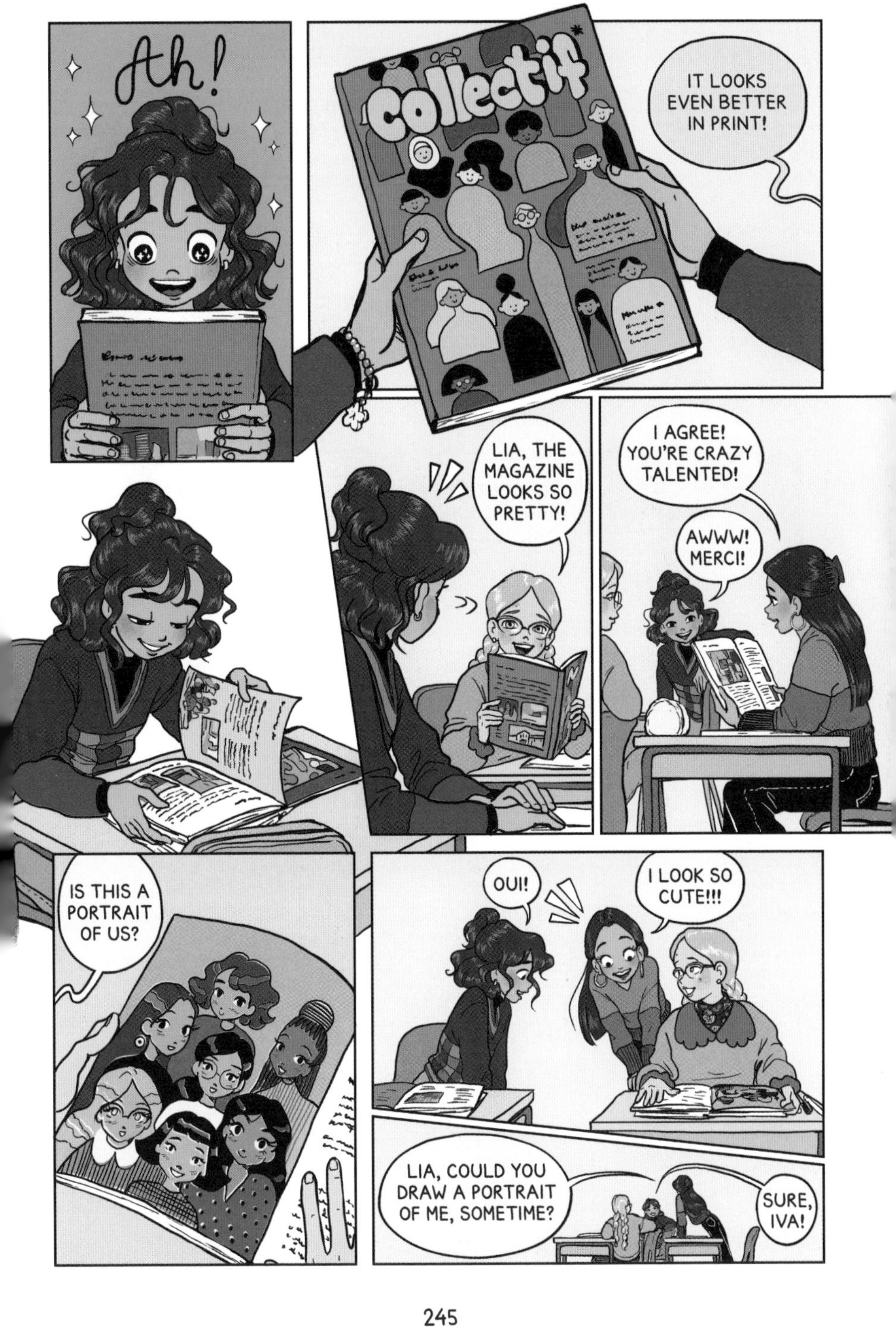
Ah!
Collectif
IT LOOKS EVEN BETTER IN PRINT!
LIA, THE MAGAZINE LOOKS SO PRETTY!
I AGREE! YOU'RE CRAZY TALENTED!
AWWW! MERCI!
IS THIS A PORTRAIT OF US?
OUI!
I LOOK SO CUTE!!!
LIA, COULD YOU DRAW A PORTRAIT OF ME, SOMETIME?
SURE, IVA!

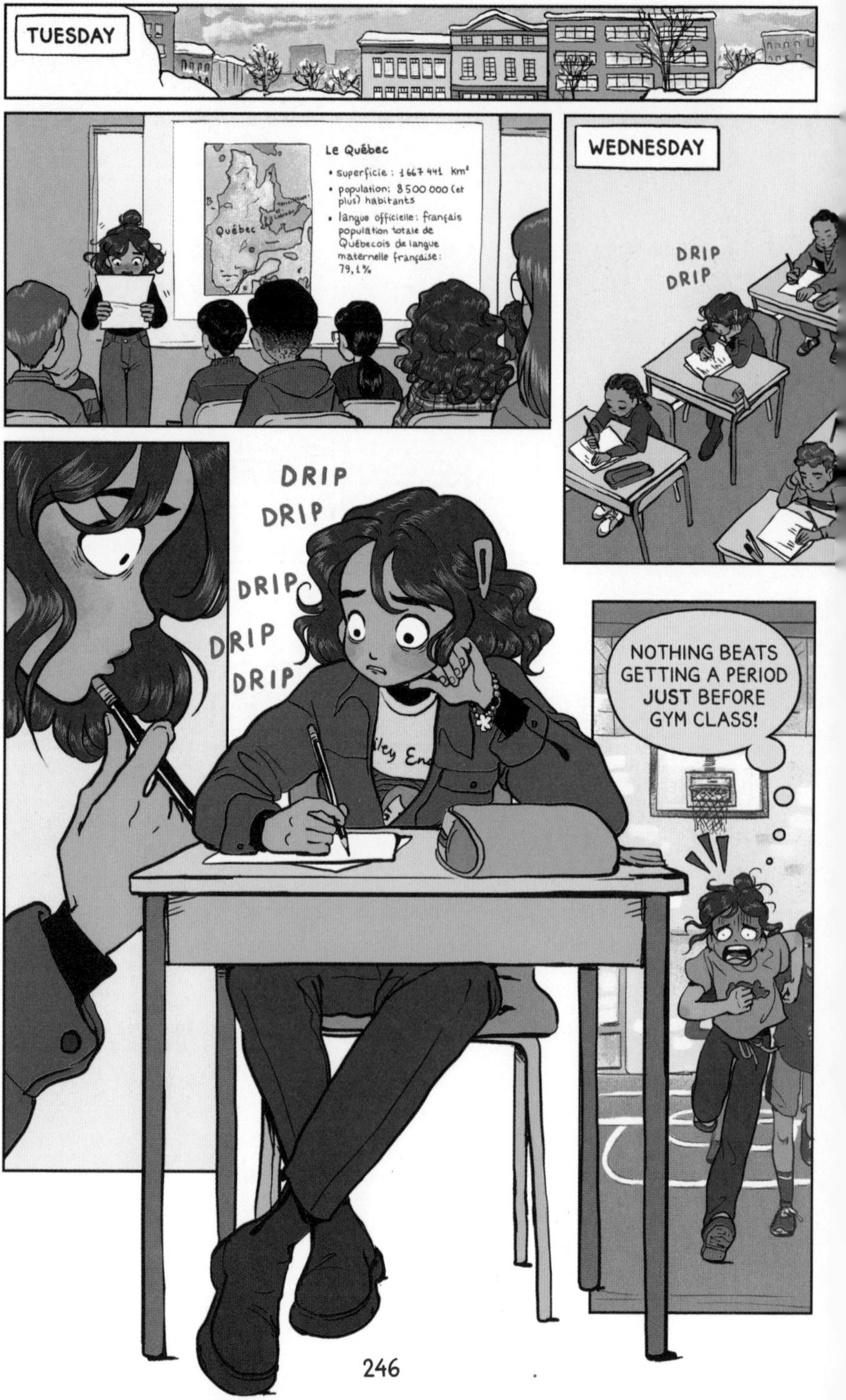
TUESDAY
Le Québec
• superficie : 1 667 441 km²
• population: 8 500 000 (et plus) habitants
• langue officielle: français
population totale de Québecois de langue maternelle française: 79,1 %
Québec
WEDNESDAY
DRIP
DRIP
DRIP
DRIP
DRIP
DRIP
DRIP
NOTHING BEATS GETTING A PERIOD JUST BEFORE GYM CLASS!

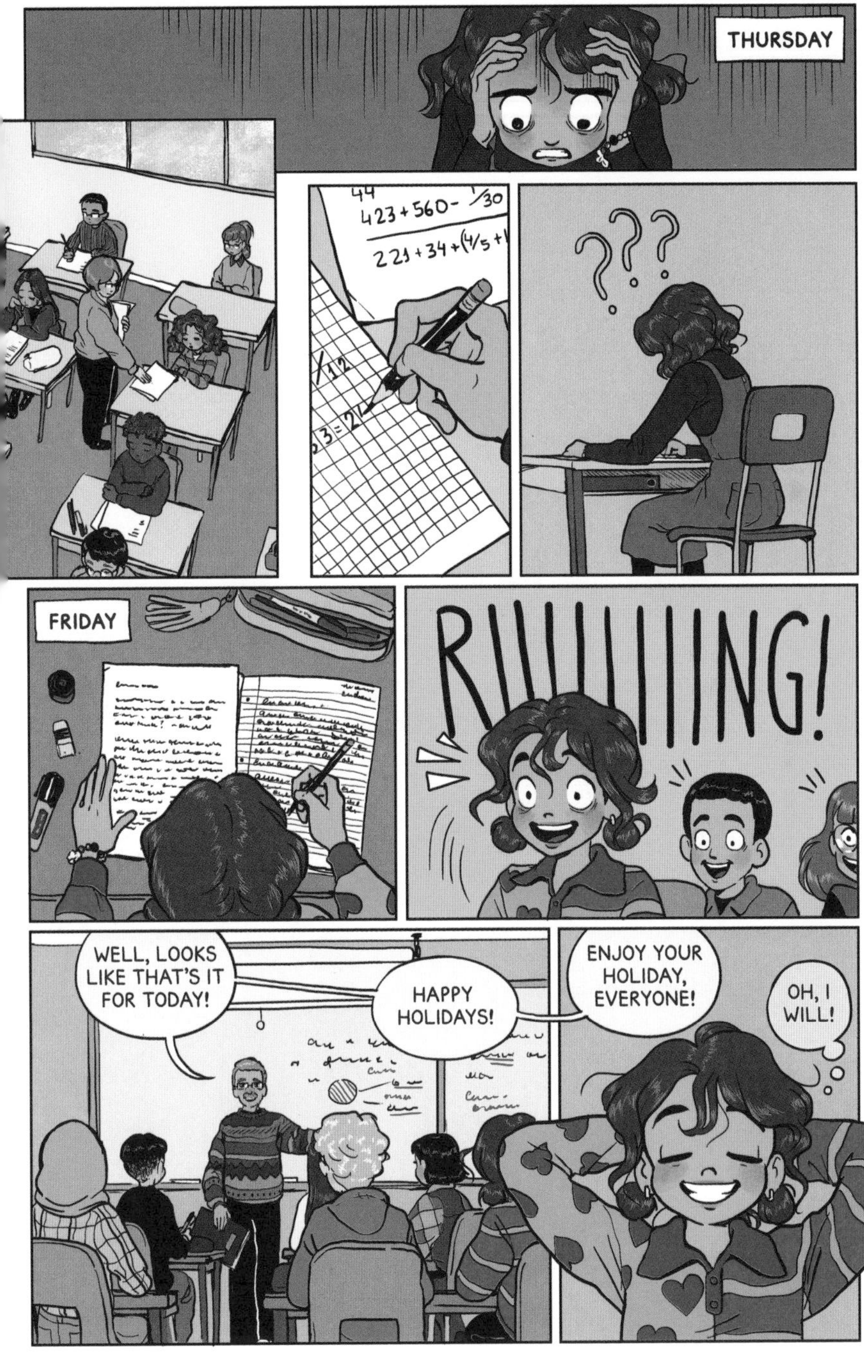
THURSDAY
44
423 + 560 - 1/30
221 + 34 + (4/5 +
FRIDAY
RIIIIIING!
WELL, LOOKS LIKE THAT'S IT FOR TODAY!
HAPPY HOLIDAYS!
ENJOY YOUR HOLIDAY, EVERYONE!
OH, I WILL!

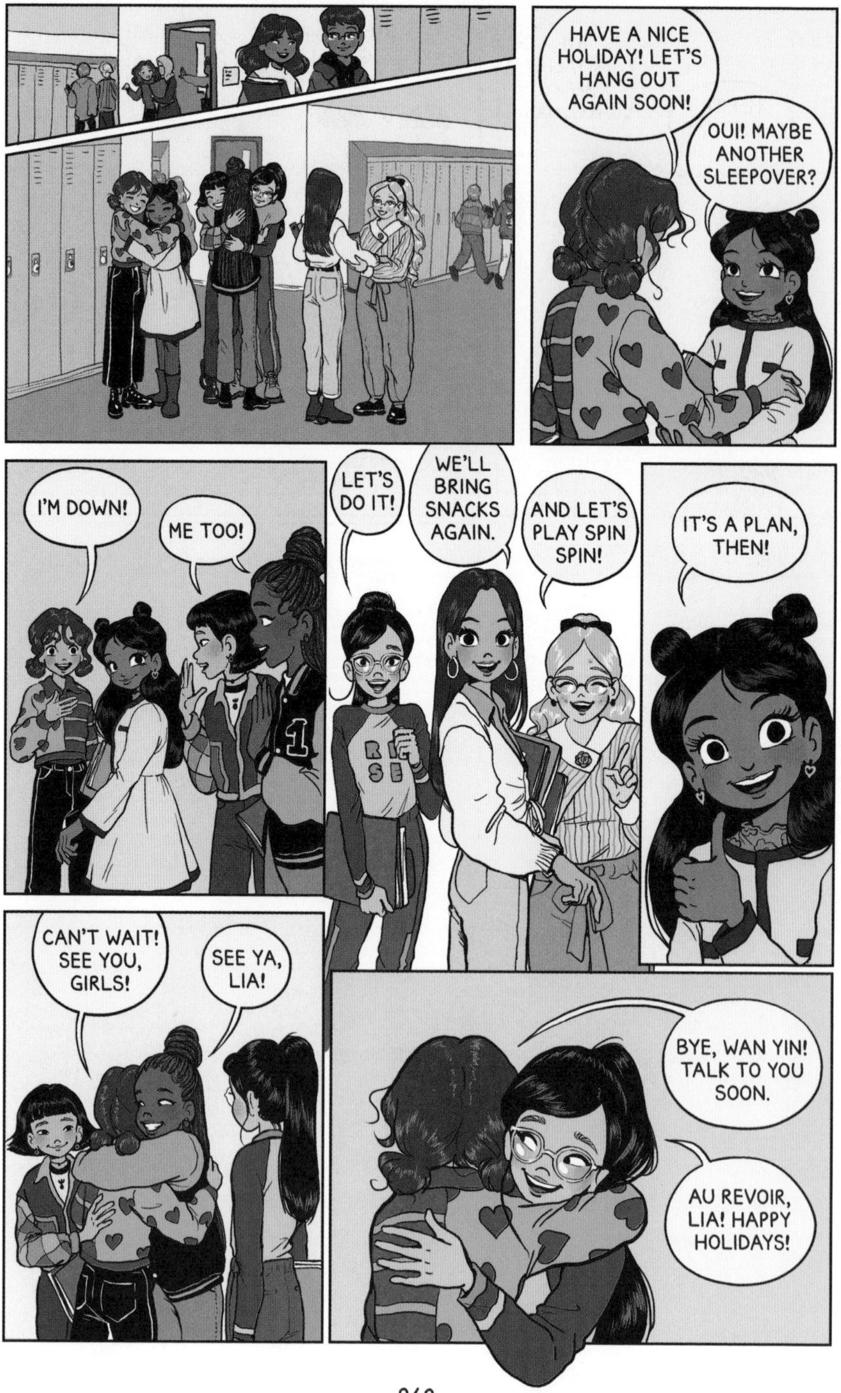
HAVE A NICE HOLIDAY! LET'S HANG OUT AGAIN SOON!
OUI! MAYBE ANOTHER SLEEPOVER?
I'M DOWN!
ME TOO!
LET'S DO IT!
WE'LL BRING SNACKS AGAIN.
AND LET'S PLAY SPIN SPIN!
IT'S A PLAN, THEN!
CAN'T WAIT! SEE YOU, GIRLS!
SEE YA, LIA!
BYE, WAN YIN! TALK TO YOU SOON.
AU REVOIR, LIA! HAPPY HOLIDAYS!

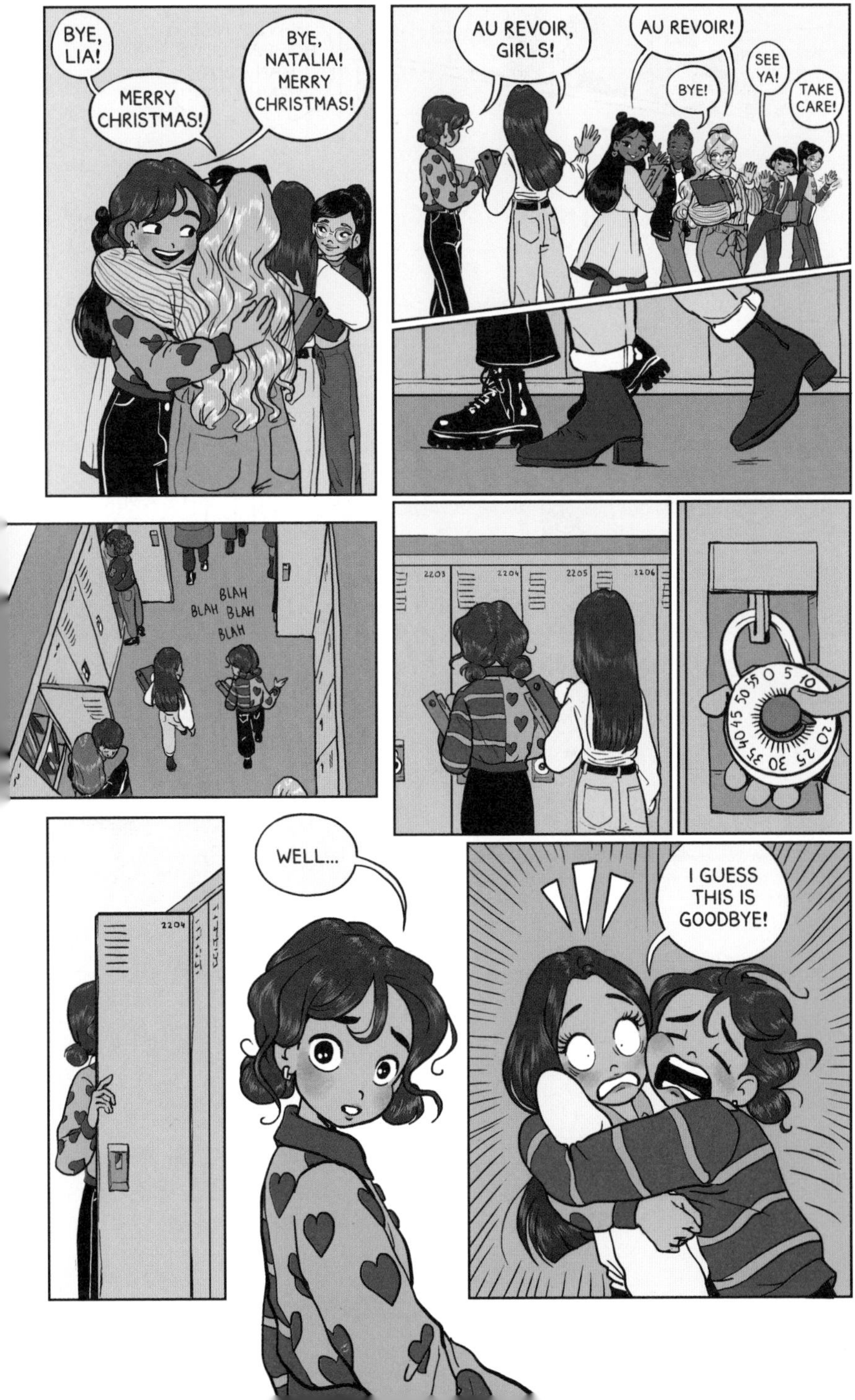
BYE, LIA!
MERRY CHRISTMAS!
BYE, NATALIA! MERRY CHRISTMAS!
AU REVOIR, GIRLS!
AU REVOIR!
BYE!
SEE YA!
TAKE CARE!
BLAH BLAH BLAH BLAH
2203
2204
2205
2206
2204
WELL...
I GUESS THIS IS GOODBYE!

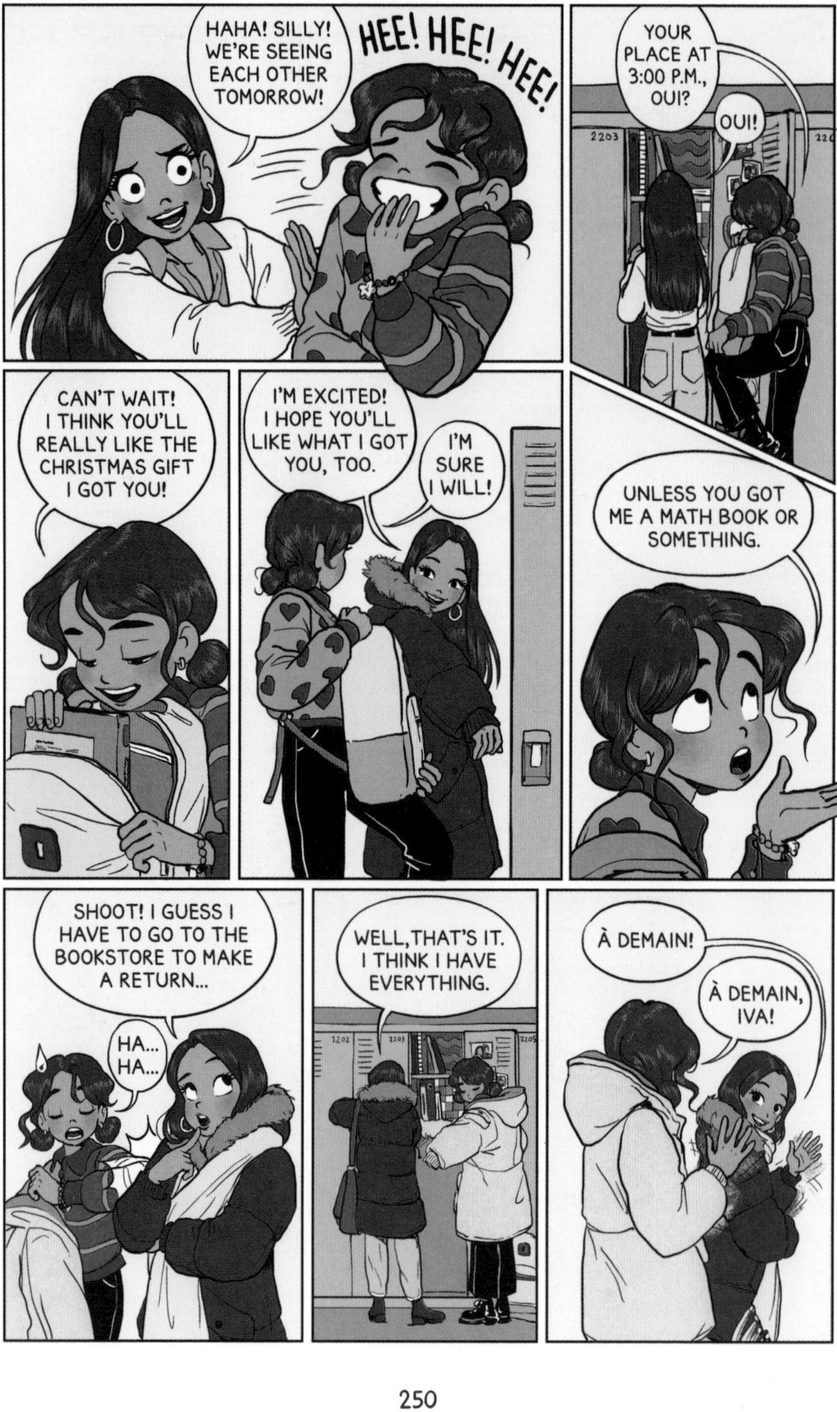
HAHA! SILLY! WE'RE SEEING EACH OTHER TOMORROW!
HEE! HEE! HEE!
YOUR PLACE AT 3:00 P.M., OUI?
OUI!
CAN'T WAIT! I THINK YOU'LL REALLY LIKE THE CHRISTMAS GIFT I GOT YOU!
I'M EXCITED! I HOPE YOU'LL LIKE WHAT I GOT YOU, TOO.
I'M SURE I WILL!
UNLESS YOU GOT ME A MATH BOOK OR SOMETHING.
SHOOT! I GUESS I HAVE TO GO TO THE BOOKSTORE TO MAKE A RETURN...
HA... HA...
WELL, THAT'S IT. I THINK I HAVE EVERYTHING.
À DEMAIN!
À DEMAIN, IVA!

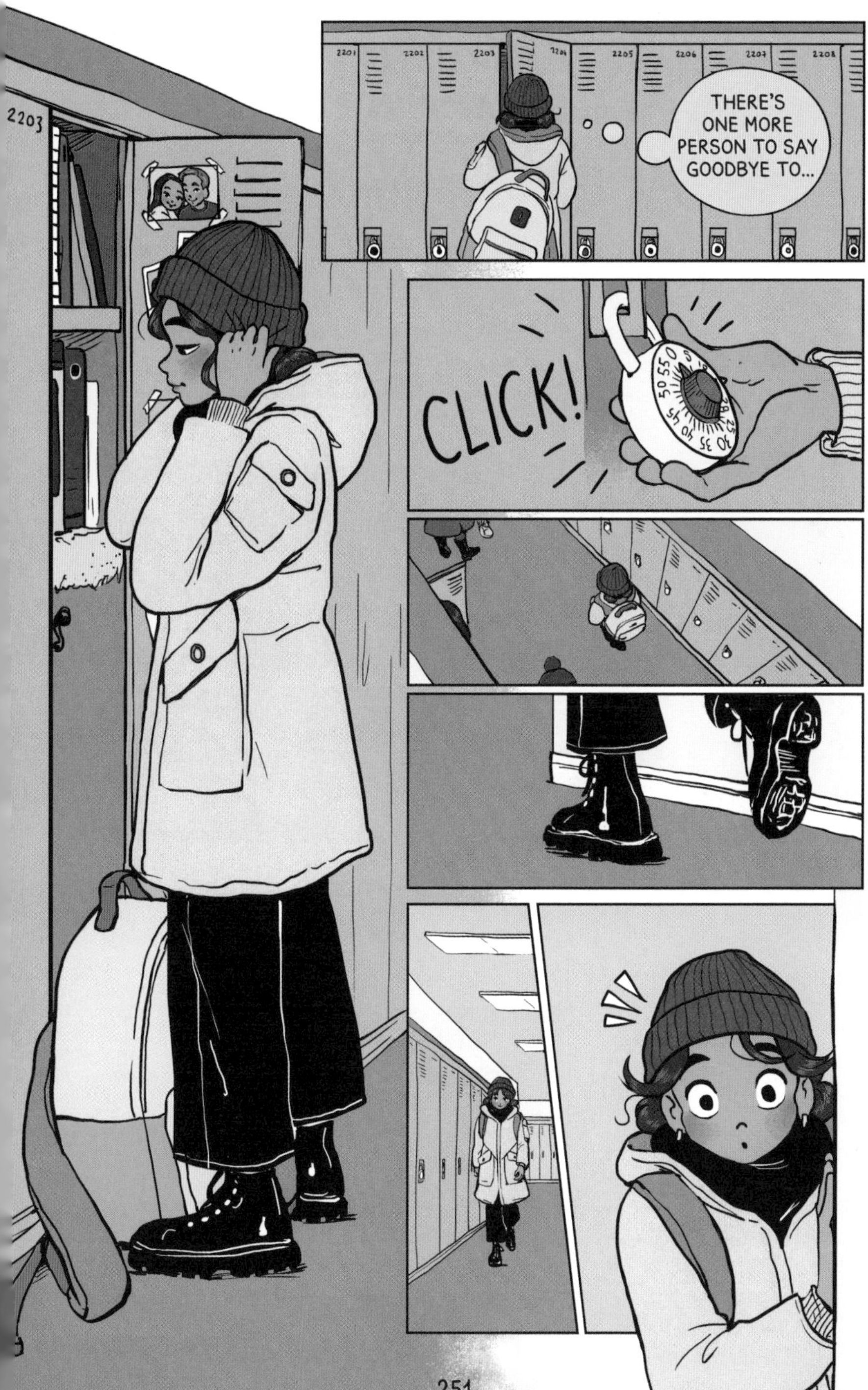
THERE'S ONE MORE PERSON TO SAY GOODBYE TO...
CLICK!

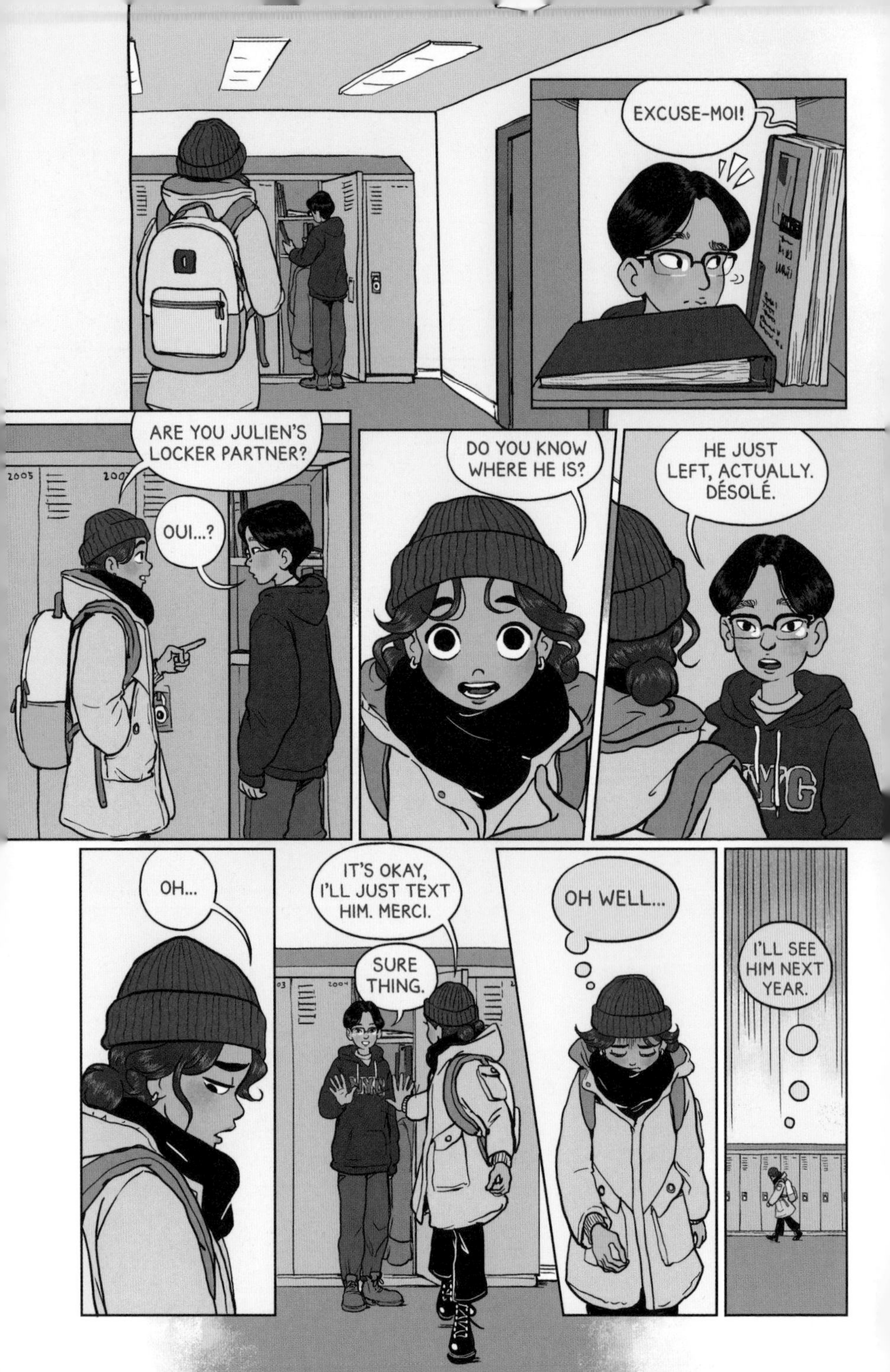
EXCUSE-MOI!
ARE YOU JULIEN'S LOCKER PARTNER?
OUI...?
DO YOU KNOW WHERE HE IS?
HE JUST LEFT, ACTUALLY. DÉSOLÉ.
OH...
IT'S OKAY, I'LL JUST TEXT HIM. MERCI.
SURE THING.
OH WELL...
I'LL SEE HIM NEXT YEAR.

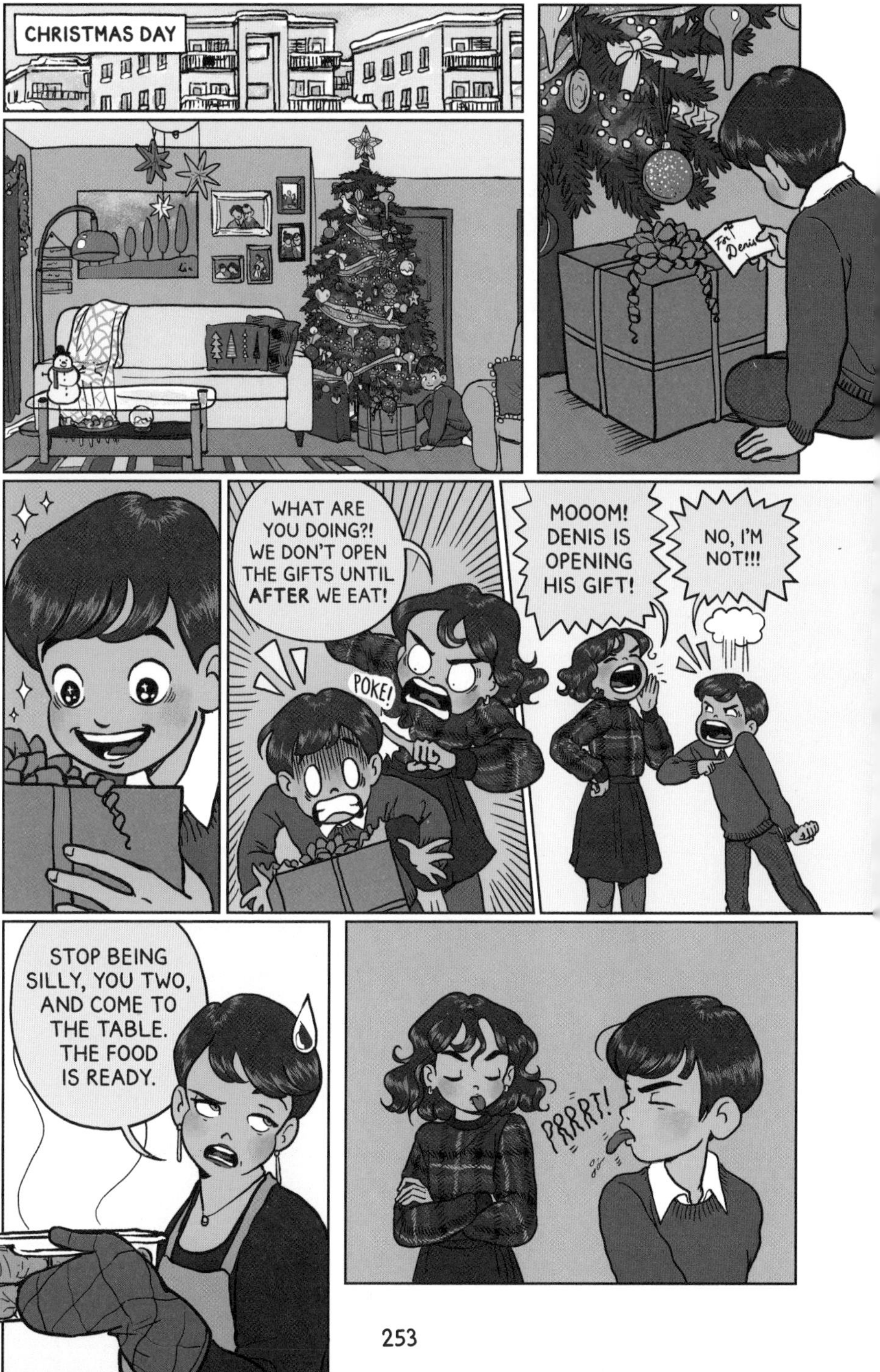
CHRISTMAS DAY
For Denis
WHAT ARE YOU DOING?! WE DON'T OPEN THE GIFTS UNTIL **AFTER** WE EAT!
POKE!
MOOOM! DENIS IS OPENING HIS GIFT!
NO, I'M NOT!!!
STOP BEING SILLY, YOU TWO, AND COME TO THE TABLE. THE FOOD IS READY.
PRRRT!

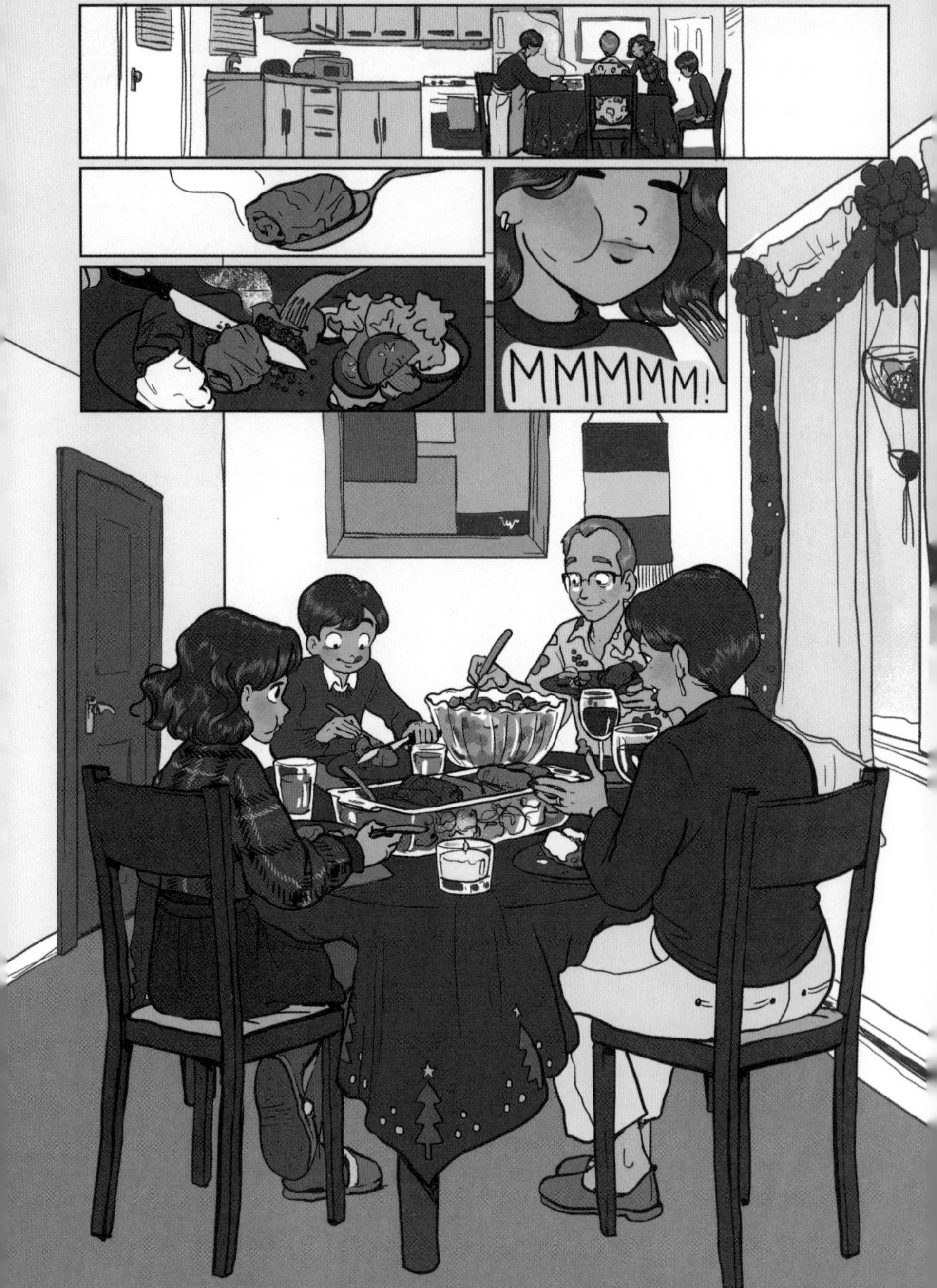
MMMMM!

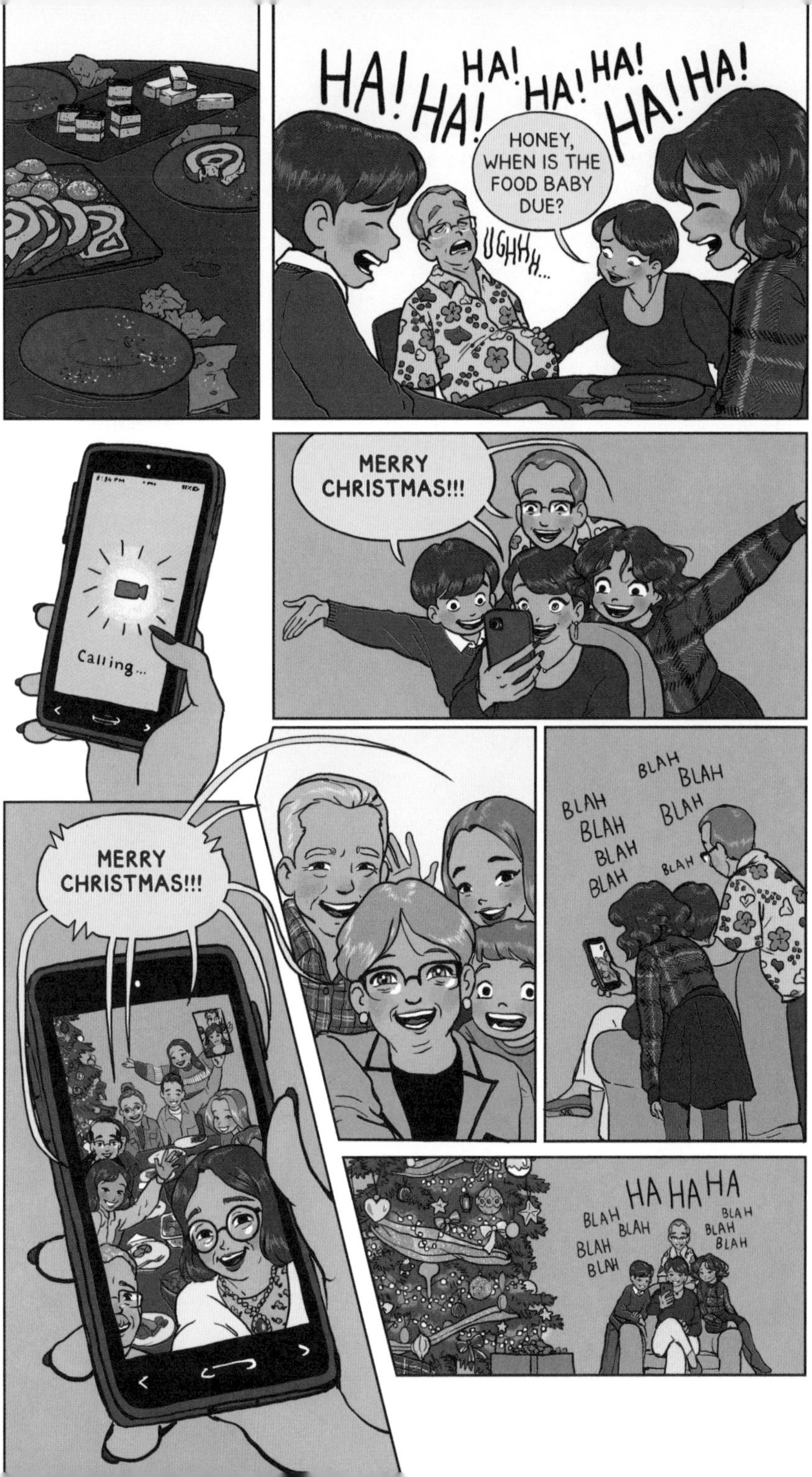
HA! HA! HA! HA! HA! HA! HA! HA!
HONEY, WHEN IS THE FOOD BABY DUE?
UGHHH...
Calling...
MERRY CHRISTMAS!!!
MERRY CHRISTMAS!!!
BLAH BLAH BLAH BLAH BLAH BLAH BLAH BLAH
HA HA HA
BLAH BLAH BLAH BLAH BLAH BLAH BLAH

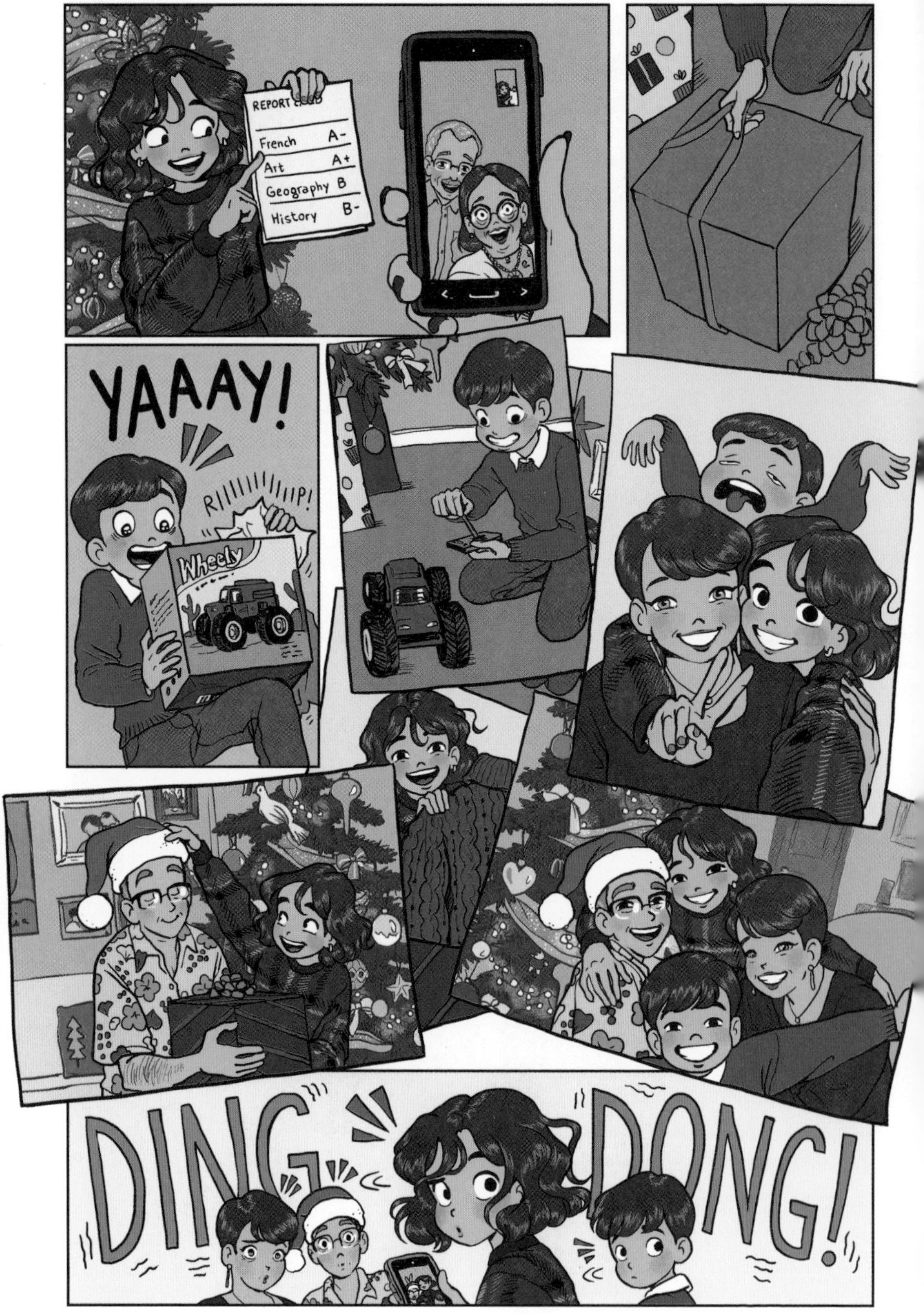
REPORT CARD
French A-
Art A+
Geography B
History B-
YAAAY!
RIIIIIIP!
Wheely
DING
DONG!

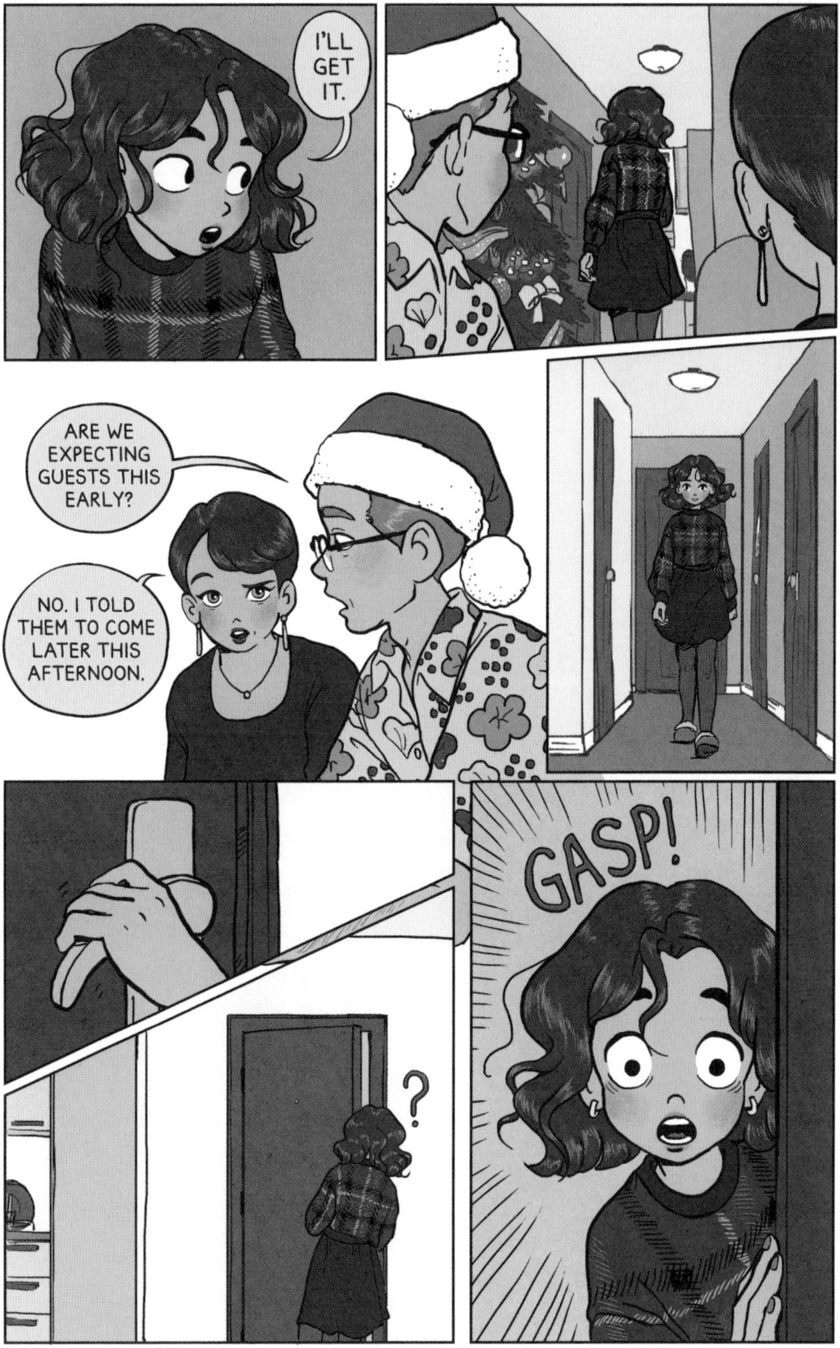
I'LL GET IT.
ARE WE EXPECTING GUESTS THIS EARLY?
NO. I TOLD THEM TO COME LATER THIS AFTERNOON.
?
GASP!

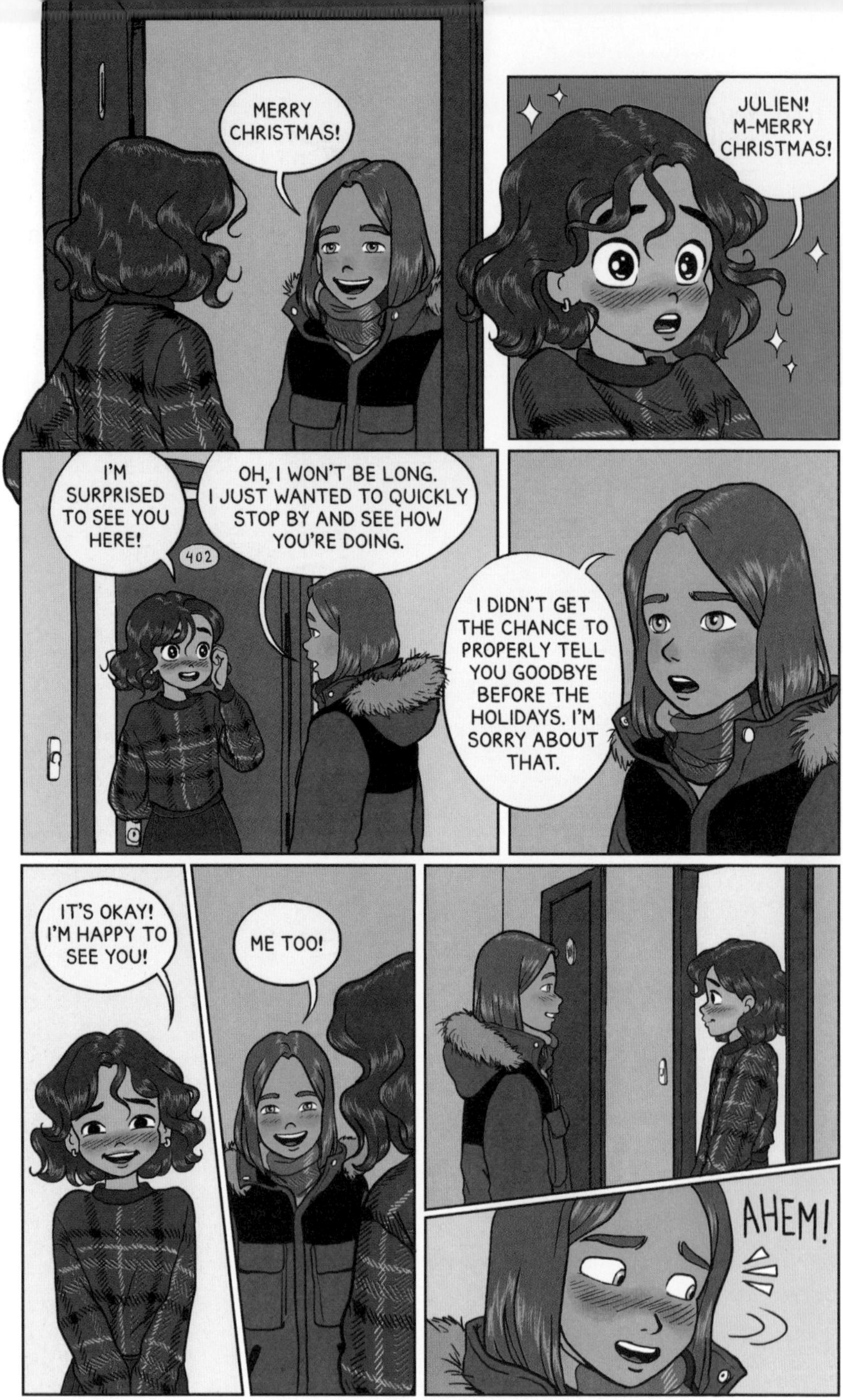
MERRY CHRISTMAS!
JULIEN! M-MERRY CHRISTMAS!
I'M SURPRISED TO SEE YOU HERE!
402
OH, I WON'T BE LONG. I JUST WANTED TO QUICKLY STOP BY AND SEE HOW YOU'RE DOING.
I DIDN'T GET THE CHANCE TO PROPERLY TELL YOU GOODBYE BEFORE THE HOLIDAYS. I'M SORRY ABOUT THAT.
IT'S OKAY! I'M HAPPY TO SEE YOU!
ME TOO!
AHEM!

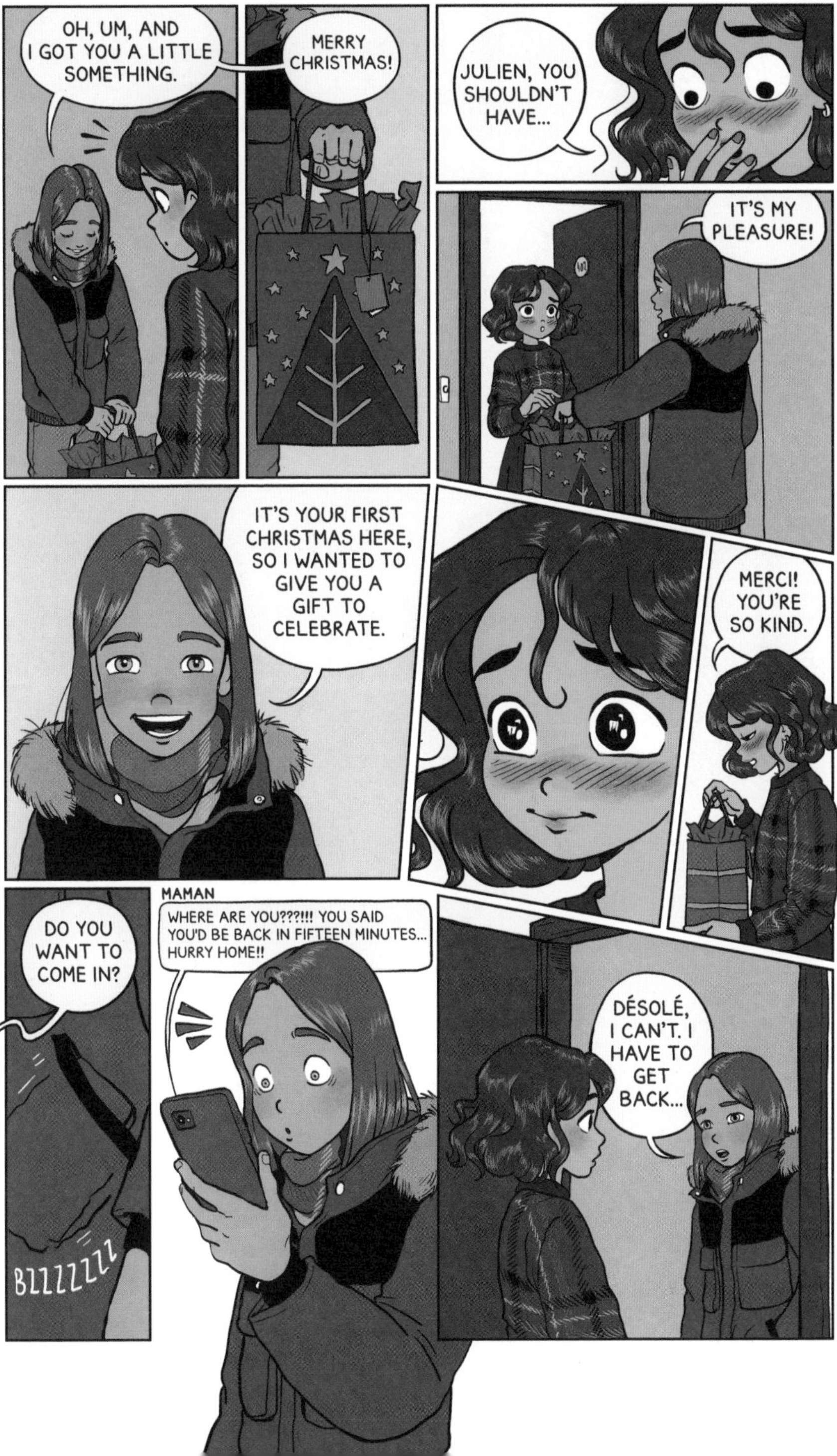
OH, UM, AND I GOT YOU A LITTLE SOMETHING.
MERRY CHRISTMAS!
JULIEN, YOU SHOULDN'T HAVE...
IT'S MY PLEASURE!
IT'S YOUR FIRST CHRISTMAS HERE, SO I WANTED TO GIVE YOU A GIFT TO CELEBRATE.
MERCI! YOU'RE SO KIND.
DO YOU WANT TO COME IN?
BZZZZZZZ
MAMAN
WHERE ARE YOU???!!! YOU SAID YOU'D BE BACK IN FIFTEEN MINUTES... HURRY HOME!!
DÉSOLÉ, I CAN'T. I HAVE TO GET BACK...

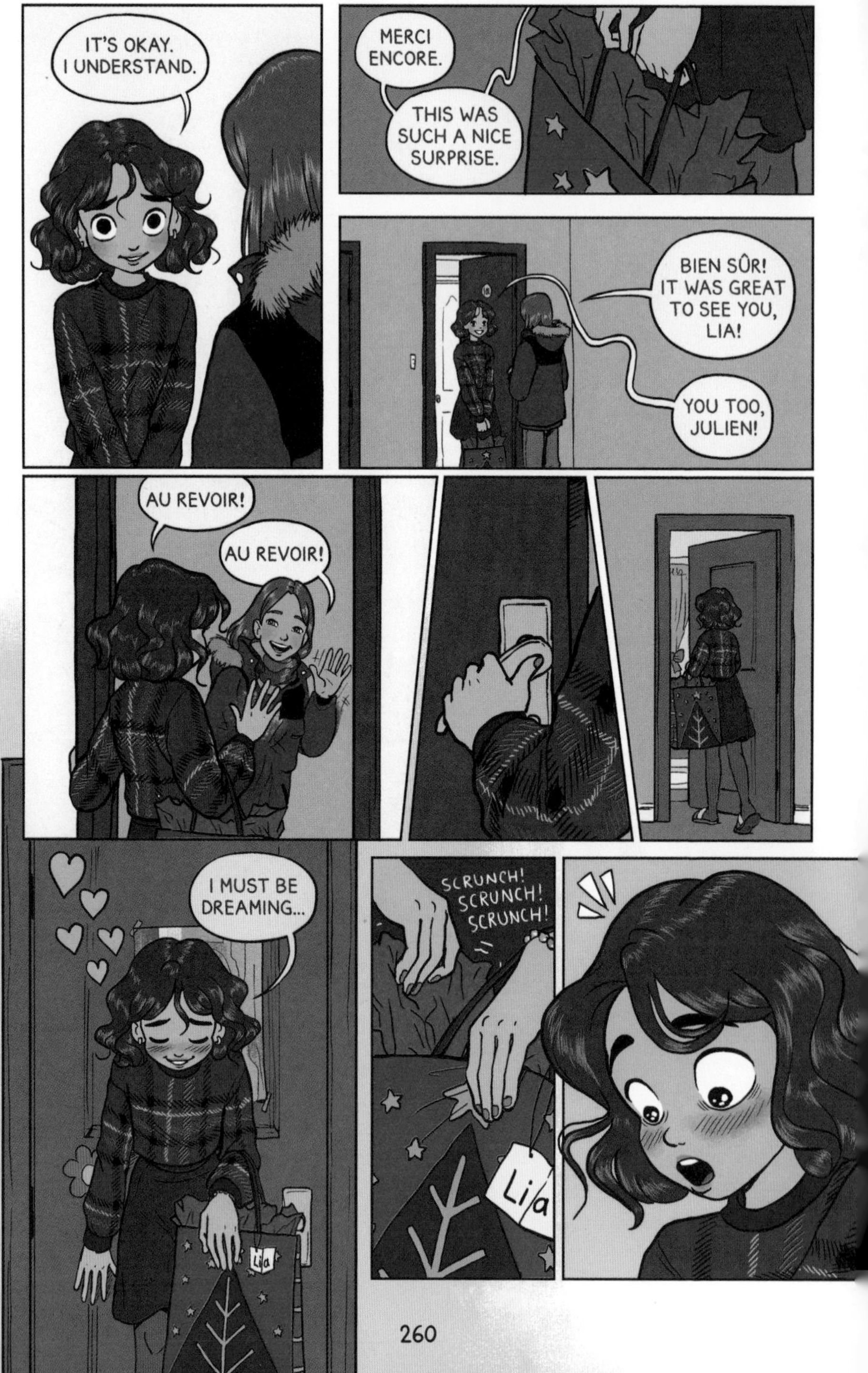
IT'S OKAY. I UNDERSTAND.
MERCI ENCORE.
THIS WAS SUCH A NICE SURPRISE.
BIEN SÛR! IT WAS GREAT TO SEE YOU, LIA!
YOU TOO, JULIEN!
AU REVOIR!
AU REVOIR!
I MUST BE DREAMING...
SCRUNCH! SCRUNCH! SCRUNCH!
Lia

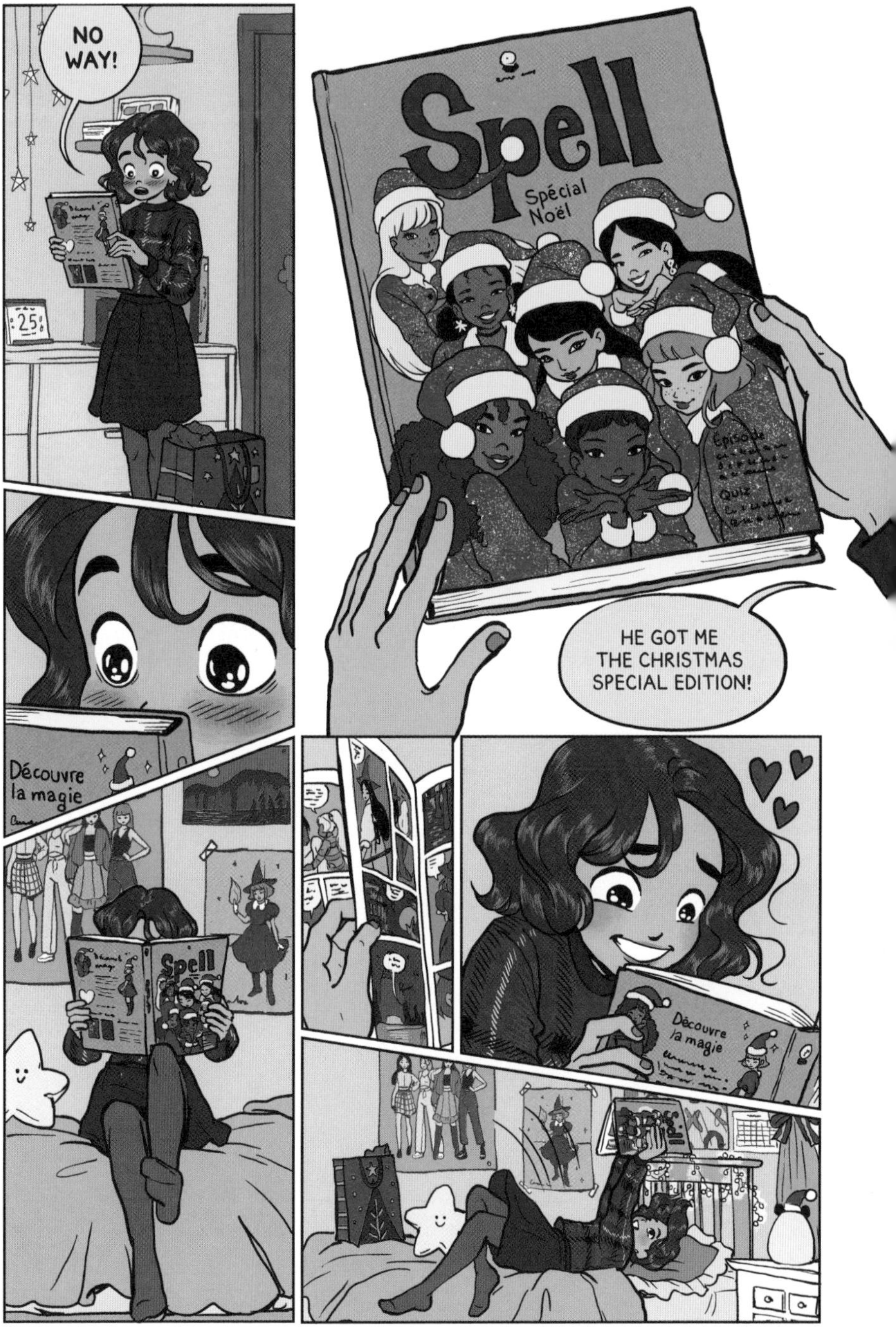
NO WAY!
Spell
Spécial Noël
HE GOT ME THE CHRISTMAS SPECIAL EDITION!
Découvre la magie
Spell
Découvre la magie

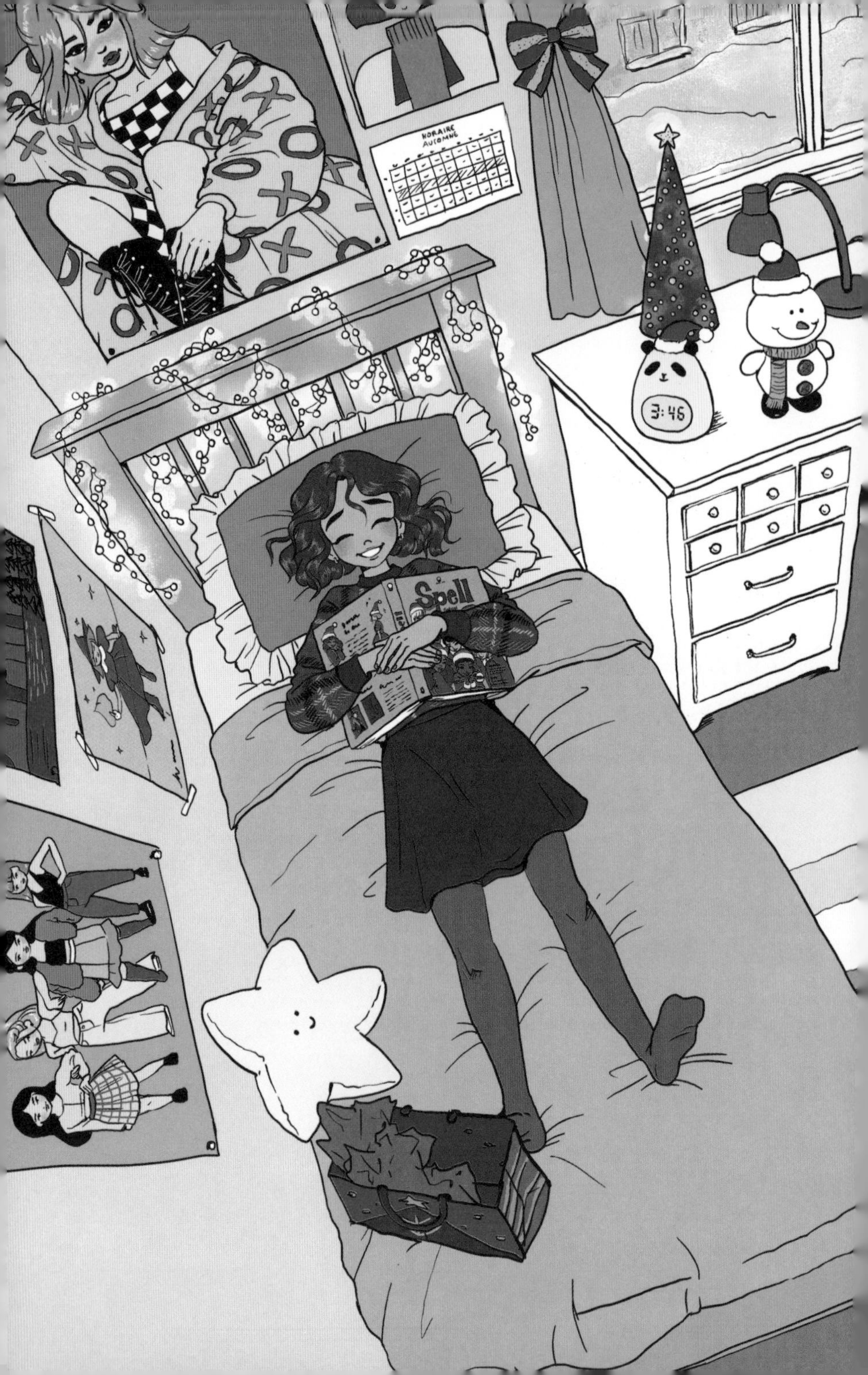

HORAIRE
AUTOMNE
3:46
Spell

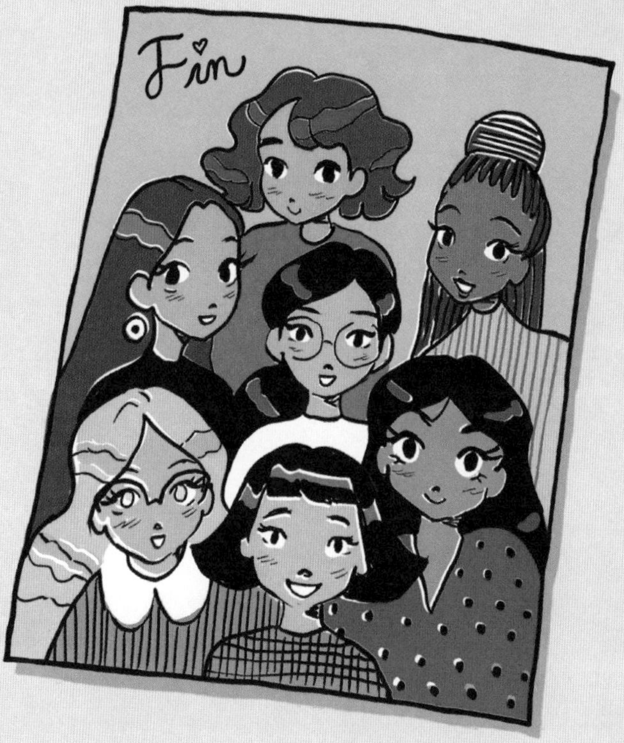
Fin

GLOSSARY

FRENCH

À BIENTÔT! — See you soon!

À DEMAIN! — See you tomorrow!

ALLÔ! — Hello!

AU REVOIR! — Bye!

BIEN SÛR! — Of course!

BONJOUR! — Hello! / Good day!

BONNE CHANCE! — Good luck!

BRAVO! — Well done!

ÇA VA? — How are you? / Are you okay?

ÇA VA! — I'm okay! / Everything is good!

DE RIEN! — You're welcome!

DÉSOLÉ(E)! — Sorry!

DEUX ANS — Two years old

ENCHANTÉ(E)! — Nice to meet you!

ENCORE — Again

EXCUSE-MOI! — Excuse me!

FIN! — The end!

FINI! — Done! / Finished!

J'ADORE! — I love it!

J'AI DOUZE ANS. — I'm twelve years old.

JE M'APPELLE... — My name is...

JOLI — Pretty / Nice / Lovely

MADAME — Mrs. / Ma'am

MAMAN — Mom

MERCI! — Thank you!

MOI — Me

MONSIEUR — Mister / sir

PARFAIT! — Perfect!

POUR TOI! — For you!

OUI! — Yes!

VOILÁ! — There! / Here it is!

ROMANIAN

CREION — Pencil

DICTARE — Dictation / Read out test

LA MULȚI ANI! — Happy birthday!

MICI — Romanian sausages made from a mixture of beef and pork, typically seasoned with garlic, paprika, black pepper, and thyme.

NU UITA: PENARUL, GHIOZDANUL, CĂRȚILE — Don't forget: the pencil case, the schoolbag, the books

PRIMA ZI DE ȘCOALĂ — First day of school

SIMPLIFIED CHINESE

你从哪里来? — Where are you from?

闻起来很香! 你在吃什么? — Smells good! What are you eating?

ACKNOWLEDGMENTS

To Mom and Dad, I don't think there will ever be enough words to express my gratitude. You're the reason I am able to tell this story to begin with. Twenty years ago, you made a very big decision, moving so far away and leaving behind your home, family, and jobs to give us a chance at a better life. And I simply can't thank you enough. Thank you for showing me the perfect example of fearlessness, selflessness, and love without limitations. Thank you for always being by my side and guiding me. Thank you for nurturing my passion for art throughout my entire life, for hanging all my paintings (and I really mean ALL), for believing in me, and for teaching me that no dream is too big. With all my heart, thank you for everything.

To my love, David, thank you for being my ray of sunshine, my source of strength, love, and support. While working on this book, you saw my ups and downs the most, but you always had faith in me and cheered me on. To this day, you're teaching me to be kinder to myself, to challenge those feelings of self-doubt, and to celebrate victories, no matter how small . . . Basically, you're giving me a great reason to treat myself to more pastries than I probably should. Seriously, though, you're the best.

To my family and close friends, I am very thankful for you, your words of encouragement, and your curiosity in every project I do. I was so touched by the enthusiasm you showed every time I talked about this book. Thank you for embarking on this journey with me and being so supportive every step of the way.

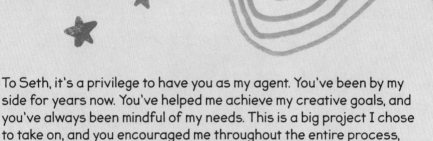

To Seth, it's a privilege to have you as my agent. You've been by my side for years now. You've helped me achieve my creative goals, and you've always been mindful of my needs. This is a big project I chose to take on, and you encouraged me throughout the entire process, while also making sure I took care of myself. Thank you for always having my back.

Many thanks to the Graphix team: David Saylor, Cassandra Pelham Fulton, Phil Falco, and Carina Taylor, all of whom I've had such a pleasure working with. And a very special thank-you to my editor, Megan Peace. Our teamwork is what shaped this book beyond my expectations, and I honestly couldn't have done this without you. I still remember when you first reached out to me a few years ago, and how excited you were for this project. You trusted my vision and my ideas, while also sharing your knowledge and insightful feedback in order to make this graphic novel as amazing as it could be. You've been so committed and professional, and also so kind and understanding. You taught me a lot, while also helping me build more confidence as a writer. I am really thankful that this project brought us together.

Last, but of course not least, I want to extend my appreciation to the readers and everyone who has supported me throughout my creative journey on the Internet. I see you, I read your heartfelt comments, I even met some of you, and I am very grateful. Whether you've followed my work since the very beginning or this book is your introduction to it, I want to say thank you for being here!

Merci!

C. Cassandra

CASSANDRA CALIN is a cartoonist and humorist best known for her semi-autobiographical webcomic series, Cassandra Comics, in which she talks about her life with curly hair, high expectations, and other daily problems. Originally from Romania, Cassandra immigrated to Canada when she was a child and later earned her BA in graphic design from L'Université du Québec à Montréal (UQAM). *The New Girl* is her long-form graphic novel debut.

Learn more about Cassandra and her comics at cassandracalin.com.